Case Studies in Contemporary Cri...

...EGE LIBR

CHARLES DICKENS

Great Expectations

Case Studies in Contemporary Criticism
SERIES EDITOR: Ross C Murfin

Case Studies in Contemporary Criticism

SERIES EDITOR: Ross C Murfin, *University of Miami*

CHARLES DICKENS
Great Expectations

Complete, Authoritative Text with
Biographical and Historical Contexts,
Critical History, and Essays from
Five Contemporary Critical Perspectives

EDITED BY
Janice Carlisle
Tulane University

Bedford/St. Martin's
BOSTON ♦ NEW YORK

For Bedford Books

President and Publisher: Charles H. Christensen
General Manager and Associate Publisher: Joan E. Feinberg
Managing Editor: Elizabeth M. Schaaf
Developmental Editor: Stephen A. Scipione
Editorial Assistant: Mark Reimold
Production Editor: Michelle McSweeney
Production Assistant: Karen S. Baart
Copyeditor: Nancy Bell Scott
Text Design: Sandra Rigney, The Book Department
Cover Design: Richard Emery Design, Inc.
Cover Photograph: Stock, Boston / Jeff Albertson

Library of Congress Catalog Card Number: 95–76721
Copyright © 1996 by BEDFORD BOOKS *of* St. Martin's Press

Manufactured in the United States of America.

5   4   3   2   1
i   h   g   f   e

For information, write: Bedford/St. Martin's.
75 Arlington Street, Boston, MA 02116 (617–399–4000)

ISBN: 0–312–08082–4 (paperback)
ISBN: 0–312–12797–9 (hardcover)

Published and distributed outside North America by:

MACMILLAN PRESS LTD.
Houndmills, Basingstoke, Hampshire RG21 2XS and London
Companies and representatives throughout the world.

ISBN: 0–333–65583–4

Acknowledgments

Acknowledgments and copyrights are at the back of the book on page 641, which constitutes an extension of the copyright page. It is a violation of the law to reproduce these selections by any means whatsoever without the written permission of the copyright holder.

About the Series

Volumes in the *Case Studies in Contemporary Criticism* series provide college students with an entrée into the current critical and theoretical ferment in literary studies. Each volume reprints the complete text of a classic literary work and presents critical essays that approach the work from different theoretical perspectives, together with the editors' introductions to both the literary work and the critics' theoretical perspectives.

The volume editor of each *Case Study* has selected and prepared an authoritative text of the classic work, written an introduction to the work's biographical and historical contexts, and surveyed the critical responses to the work since its initial publication. Thus situated biographically, historically, and critically, the work is examined in five critical essays, each representing a theoretical perspective of importance to contemporary literary studies. These essays, prepared especially for undergraduates, show theory in praxis; whether written by established scholars or exceptional young critics, they demonstrate how current theoretical approaches can generate compelling readings of great literature.

As series editor, I have prepared introductions, with bibliographies, to the theoretical perspectives represented in the five critical essays. Each introduction presents the principal concepts of a particular theory in their historical context and discusses the major figures and key works that have influenced their formulation. It is my hope that these introductions will reveal to students that good criticism is informed by a set of coherent assumptions, and will encourage them to recognize and examine their own assumptions about literature. Finally, I have compiled a glossary of key terms that recur in these volumes and in the discourse of contemporary theory and criticism. We hope that the *Case Studies in Contemporary Criticism* series will reaffirm the richness of its literary works, even as it introduces invigorating new ways to mine their apparently inexhaustible wealth.

Acknowledgment

I would especially like to thank Janice Carlisle, the editor of this particular volume. In the interest of persuading me to use *Great Expectations* to introduce gender criticism as a new critical category to the *Case Studies* series, she was willing to gather information and opinion on short notice. She even drafted whole paragraphs and has graciously allowed several to appear "on loan" in "What is Gender Criticism?" I'm indeed grateful for her quiet insistence on expanding the series into the area of gender studies—and for her informed efforts to make that expansion possible.

Ross C Murfin
Series Editor
University of Miami

About This Volume

Part One of this edition of *Great Expectations* reprints the text of the 1861 three-volume edition, which followed the novel's original publication in weekly parts in Dickens's magazine *All the Year Round* (December 1, 1860–August 3, 1861). Although four subsequent editions appeared in Dickens's lifetime, all of which he presumably corrected, most scholars agree that these editions introduced more errors than they amended. While essentially true to the 1861 version, including some of its minor irregularities ("up town" and "up-town," for instance), this text has been collated with the 1868 Charles Dickens Edition, resulting in a few substantive corrections. In addition, some variants from the manuscript, now available in Margaret Cardwell's scholarly edition of the novel (Oxford: Clarendon, 1993), have been adopted.

The chapters of *Great Expectations* are here numbered continuously rather than in the three separate series of numbers used in the three volumes of the 1861 edition. The points at which the first two volumes end, however, are still indicated by Dickens's references to the first and second "stages" of Pip's career (160, 302). The thirty-six weekly installments of the initial magazine publication are indicated by bracketed part numbers. In annotating the novel, I have consulted the work done by previous editors—Louis Crompton (1964), Angus Calder (1965), and Edward Guiliano and Philip Collins (1986)—as well as the notes to the novel published by T. W. Hill in the *Dicken-sian* (1957–60). A brief appendix reprints the novel's ending as it first appeared in proof and its subsequent variations. Introducing the text is an account of the personal and professional considerations that influenced its writing and the form in which it was originally published.

Part Two begins with a critical history of *Great Expectations,* examining the responses to it in terms of the institutions—education, publishing, and criticism—from which they emerged. I have briefly introduced each of the five critical essays included in this volume with a commentary that points out the relations between current categories in literary studies. The first of the essays is Peter Brooks's influential psychoanalytic interpretation. Two selections from the work of Edward W. Said identify the deconstructive principles inherent in the novel and demonstrate the extension of such principles to postcolonial issues. Hilary Schor offers a feminist reading that appears here for the first time, and William A. Cohen treats issues of gender and sexuality. Jay Clayton, whose essay is also printed here for the first time, uses *Great Expectations* to chart the contours of contemporary culture. All these essays are grounded in poststructuralist theory, illuminating not only the text in question, but also the state of contemporary literary criticism.

Acknowledgments

My thanks go to: Ross C Murfin for exploring the possibility of adding a Dickens novel to the *Case Studies* series and for his acute readings of the drafts of all the work printed here; those at Bedford Books who supported and worked on this project—Charles Christensen, Joan Feinberg, Stephen Scipione, Mark Reimold, and Donna Dennison—and Michelle McSweeney, whose work as production editor I particularly appreciated; Sandra Haro for word processing and keeping track of hundreds and hundreds of text pages; John Rouse for the timely gift of a coffee mug; Maaja Stewart for her characteristically insightful comments on the drafts of my introductions; Robyn Warhol for advice on the selected bibliography of feminist criticism; William A. Cohen for responses to a draft of the introduction to gender criticism; and Charles A. Ferguson and Barbara F. Ginsberg for their generous support of the Josephine G. Ferguson Lecture Series, which provided the occasion for the first presentation of Jay Clayton's work on *Great Expectations.* I am particularly indebted to Richard Rambuss for responding to numerous drafts of the material on gender studies; it was a great pleasure to discuss with him the questions raised by this emerging field. In considering plans and drafts, Joseph Roach gave freely of his time and advice, for both of which I am, as always, grateful.

Janice Carlisle
Tulane University

Contents

Case Studies in Contemporary Criticism

CHARLES DICKENS

Great Expectations

PART ONE

Great Expectations:
The Complete Text

Introduction:
Biographical and
Historical Contexts

On either side of a coffee mug recently given me by a colleague, there is a caricature of Charles Dickens. The top half of this depiction consists of the older Dickens, with a long, wild beard encircling his mature, even haggard, face. The bottom half of the drawing, out of all proportion to the top, is a cartoon of a small boy's bare legs and feet. What unites the two halves is a pair of hands holding out an empty bowl. This bifurcated image—meant, of course, to sell coffee mugs to those who recognize it—plays with one of the many myths or legends that so often constitute our understanding of Dickens, a man who was perhaps in his own day and who is now undoubtedly the best-known Victorian writer. The empty bowl refers to a famous moment in one of Dickens's early novels, when the parish-boy Oliver Twist asks for "more": kept on insufficient rations by his community's so-called charity, Oliver's fellow sufferers select him to present their petition for more food. The caricature on the coffee mug emphasizes the connection between Dickens's experience as a poor boy and his mature work as a writer—a connection that readers of *Great Expectations* need both to understand and to question.

By 1860, when Dickens was writing *Great Expectations*, he had reached the mature middle age of forty-eight years, and he could look back on a life filled with more than its share of pain, confusion, contradiction, and success. He had begun his career as a novelist thirty years earlier, and he had achieved wealth and security, despite his enormous expenses, by publishing in an inexpensive format all twelve of his previous novels. Two years before, he had begun giving public readings of his fiction for large and enthusiastic crowds willing to pay well for such performances. By Victorian standards, he was also an unusually substantial man of property. Although separated from Catherine Hogarth Dickens, his wife of over twenty years, he was the father of nine children, eight of whom were living with him. In many ways he seemed the epitome of the Victorian success story: self-made man, entrepreneur of the imagination, and paterfamilias all in one.

Dickens, of course, became a legend by creating characters and plots that quickly attained legendary status; and he drew upon his own success story in the writing of *Great Expectations*, which treats it as a nineteenth-century version of the foundling legend. According to this ancient plot, a child of royal birth is mistakenly or purposely set in circumstances below his or her station. In similar fashion, Pip, a boy raised by simple village folk and intended for a life as a blacksmith, tells

Largely Literary® COFFEE MUG

CHARLES DICKENS

the story of discovering that he has far finer prospects than he had dared to hope. Although Dickens gives this traditional tale a twist, it is a story evocative of his sense of his own past. Told in the first person and set in Kent—in the towns of Chatham and Rochester, where he passed his childhood—*Great Expectations* is an obviously, but not often directly, autobiographical novel.

Dickens pointed to the autobiographical impulse behind the novel in his historical location of its action. As the most recent and most detailed analysis of the chronology of *Great Expectations* shows, its main action spans the period between the beginning of 1812, when Pip is about seven years old, and late June 1829 (Meckier 164); it begins, therefore, in the year when Dickens was born and ends in the year when he was, at eighteen, deciding among a number of careers that he could have pursued. By making Pip seven years older than himself and by focusing repeatedly on the fact that Pip is presumably writing his story shortly before it was published in 1860–61, Dickens offers images of two distinct historical periods—the early, Regency decades of the century and the high Victorian period of the midcentury.

Although the images in *Great Expectations* of these two periods tend at times to become superimposed on each other, the basic distinction between them is fairly straightforward. During the first, Great Britain was engaged in wars against Napoleon and the United States; at home economic hardships augmented radical protest, which was put down by increasingly repressive legislation and, when necessary, armed force; and the Prince of Wales who ruled the country, first as Regent and then as George IV, commanded virtually no one's respect. By almost all accounts, the central years of the nineteenth century were, in contrast, times of relative prosperity, political calm, and rising expectations for even greater social order and more substantial economic gains. The most common historical cliché about this mid-Victorian period was that it saw the final consolidation of the social, political, and economic dominance of the middle classes. Despite whatever qualifications one must add to that formulation—the power of the landed gentry, for instance, remained significant, if not dominant, even into the twentieth century—the members of the middle classes were certainly self-conscious and self-congratulatory about their importance. Middle-class conceptions of morality extended to other classes, and the ethos of middle-class respectability was embodied in Queen Victoria and her consort, Prince Albert. There were, of course, setbacks and problems: the late 1850s saw a severe, although short-lived, economic crash; and there were serious strains in Britain's foreign relations and in its rule of its colonial empire, with the former resulting in the Crimean War (1854–56) and the latter in the Indian Rebellion (1857–58). In general, however, for many middle-class Victorians in the early 1860s, the worst of times seemed behind them and the best of times seemed to be ahead.

Between the periods evoked in *Great Expectations*, between the time of Pip's story and the time of its telling, were years of political unrest, social and legislative reform, repeated financial and agricultural crises, continuing industrialization, unprecedented population growth, and rapid urbanization—all the factors that turned the stagecoach world of Pip's youth into the technologically advanced, capitalist, and imperialist nation of the midcentury. Although critics disagree on which of the two periods evoked in *Great Expectations* actually determines the quality of the social life depicted in it (see Gilmour 123–24; House, qtd. in Cotsell 46; Morris 108; Lohman), Victorian readers would have had little difficulty recognizing that the novel tells a story of social progress and amelioration, however it may comment on that story. For most of Dickens's contemporaries, if not for Dickens himself, and for many historians since, Victorian Britain offers a success story enacted on a national scale; and from some perspectives Dickens's own life may be read as an individualized reflection of that success.

The circumstances of Dickens's early years certainly offered him disadvantages to be overcome, and they were epitomized by the famous episode of the blacking warehouse: when Dickens was twelve, he was sent to work as a manual laborer in Warren's Blacking, a shoe-polish warehouse. Throughout his life Dickens kept secret this story even from his wife and children, sharing it only with his closest friend, John Forster, who told it publicly for the first time in his posthumous biography of the novelist (1871–73). The labor involved at Warren's was certainly not hard labor—Dickens and several other boys put paper on the blacking jars, tied them with string, and attached labels—but when Dickens did tell this story to Forster in the late 1840s, he presented it as a version of Paradise Lost. The Eden from which he was exiled was the provincial, middle-class security of his younger years and the future gentility that his early experience had seemed to promise; the wilderness in which he found himself wandering at twelve was the close, crowded, dirty urban world of the London working classes. Nearly a quarter of a century later, Dickens began an autobiography that he found too painful to complete, but in which he described his response to this exile:

> No words can express the secret agony of my soul as I sunk into this companionship; compared these everyday associates with those of my happier childhood; and felt my early hopes of growing up to be a learned and distinguished man crushed in my breast. . . . My whole nature was so penetrated with the grief and humiliation of such considerations, that even now, famous and caressed and happy, I often forget in my dreams that I have a dear wife and children; even that I am a man; and wander desolately back to that time of my life. (Forster 1: 23–24)

The episode of the blacking warehouse, so unspeakably painful to the adult who remembered it, constituted a fall from grace that attained mythic proportions in Dickens's sense of his childhood. Since his family moved fourteen times in the first fourteen years of his life (Allen 10), his early experience cannot be called either settled or secure, but his backward view saw the time before Warren's Blacking as an ideal existence. As Fred Kaplan, one of Dickens's most recent biographers, explains, "Like all paradises, Kent was retrospective" (23).

During Dickens's earlier childhood, it had seemed as if his family was enacting their own version of a fable of progress. As the contemporary writer Walter Bagehot explained, the Victorian system of class was based on the principle of "removable inequalities" (qtd. in Best 233), differences in status that could be removed when the individual rose socially through, as the Victorians saw it, great effort and strength of character. Dickens's father, John Dickens, had already accomplished such a rise in status when he secured work as a clerk in the Navy Pay Office in various ports on the coast of England. John Dickens's parents had been servants—servants of a superior sort, since his father was a butler and his mother rose to the position of housekeeper, but servants nonetheless. Charles Dickens's mother, Elizabeth, was the daughter of a relatively important official at the Navy Pay Office in London, so John Dickens's marriage in 1809 to the woman who was virtually the boss's daughter consolidated the social advance that the nature of his work had already proclaimed.

When Charles Dickens was born in 1812, the second child and first son of the family, his birth was listed in the local paper: "BIRTHS— On Friday, at Mile-end Terrace, the Lady of John Dickens, Esq. a son." As Michael Allen, the scholar who has done painstaking archival research into Dickens's childhood, argues, "The aspirations of the father shine through this small announcement: note that telling phrase 'the Lady of John Dickens, Esq.'" (19). Both *lady* and *esquire* were terms then reserved for the gentry, not in 1812 for a minor clerk in the government's employ. When Charles Dickens was five, the family moved to Chatham in Kent, and for the next seven years, the small, sensitive, often sickly child enjoyed the status and security of middle-class life. As Michael Allen describes this "most secure period in Dickens' childhood":

> At Chatham the genteel way of life in an otherwise violent and bawdy town formed Charles' view of his family's position in the community and his own expectations from life: here John Dickens enjoyed his best ever income, the family employed two servants and Charles thrived on success and encouragement at school, visits to the theatre, books to read, parties to go to, friends to play with. No doubt John Dickens' plans for his eldest son were expansive, and known to be so. . . . (9)

As the obviously gifted and precocious first son of the family, Charles Dickens had every reason to believe that this was the kind of life he both deserved and required.

Yet even before moving the family to Chatham, John Dickens had begun to experience the financial difficulties that would soon exile his son from what he would later view as paradise: too large a family (up to six surviving children at one point), too small an income, too many expenses, and too many debts. When his father was transferred to the London headquarters of the Navy Pay Office when Charles was ten, the financial difficulties became financial disaster. John Dickens's pay was reduced because he no longer deserved the stipend allotted clerks who served at British ports, and the cost of living in London was significantly higher than that in Chatham. The financial crisis worsened with every attempt to alleviate it, the most spectacularly costly being Mrs. Dickens's plans to open a school for genteel scholars, who never came to enroll. Throughout this period Charles Dickens was left at home to find ways of making himself useful by polishing his father's boots and tending the younger children. Later, he remembered his "descent into the poor little drudge" that he became in London as simply incomprehensible: "It is wonderful to me how I could have been so easily cast away at such an age" (Forster 1: 21). A relation of the family finally suggested that Charles could earn a small wage, perhaps six or seven shillings a week, by working at Warren's Blacking. If earlier he had thought longingly of "all I had lost in losing Chatham," he now had positive suffering and humiliation to take the place of the school and friends he had left behind him: "I worked, from morning to night, with common men and boys, a shabby child" (Forster 1: 12, 25).

Entering his new employ near his twelfth birthday, Charles Dickens stayed there, according to Michael Allen's estimate, for twelve or even thirteen months (81, 103), although earlier accounts have set the length of his service at approximately six months. Initially, he went back and forth to work from his home, where his parents were fending off the effects of their mounting debt by selling off their belongings, among which was a modest collection of eighteenth-century fiction that their bookish son particularly prized. But greater troubles soon followed. Shortly after Charles's entry into Warren's, John Dickens was arrested for debt and sent, as was then the practice, to Marshalsea Prison, where his wife and the younger siblings joined him. As the oldest son and the only one capable of earning money, Charles was lodged first with an old family friend and later in a back attic room closer to the prison. For every working day of the week, from Monday through Saturday, he was on his own. Now a child laborer, like so many working-class children, Dickens might have become, he later thought, "for any care that was taken of me, a little robber or a little vagabond." Yet he also remembered that even in the midst of his suffering, he did not entirely lose all the status that he had earlier enjoyed. As he explained, "my conduct and manners were different enough from [the other boys'] to place a space between us." That "space" was marked as a class distinction by the nickname Dickens carried at Warren's: he was called "the young gentleman," and a particularly kind boy, Bob Fagin, "settled" another boy who "rebelled against the 'young-gentleman' usage" (Forster 1: 25–26).

Whether his time in Warren's Blacking lasted six months or thirteen, Dickens seems to have experienced it and he certainly remembered it as a potentially permanent abandonment. Even when John Dickens was released from prison by the end of May in 1824 and Charles returned to live with his family, no one suggested that he cease working at Warren's. Indeed, his humiliation increased when the establishment moved to Covent Garden and he found himself working at a front window, where small crowds would gather to watch the dexterity with which he papered and tied up the blacking pots. Finally, a quarrel between his father and the relative who had suggested that Charles work at Warren's released him from this servitude. Yet here too was cause for dismay and hurt: his mother wanted to patch up the quarrel and return her son to his position performing his hated working-class status for the audiences at the window of Warren's. In his autobiographical fragment, he looked back on her wishes, upon which his father did not act, with bitter anger: "I never afterwards forgot, I never shall forget, I never can forget, that my mother was warm for my being sent back" (Forster 1: 32).

Not surprisingly, virtually all of Dickens's biographers have viewed his time at Warren's as the chief formative experience of his early life, and its impress is evident throughout his fiction. Bob Fagin's concern for the "young gentleman" was repaid, but not in kind, when Dickens named the archvillain of *Oliver Twist* after him, and the autobiographical fragment provided the basis for the stint of manual labor endured by the hero of *David Copperfield* (1849–50). Critics argue repeatedly for the more general relevance of this episode to the later fiction by pointing to the long list of abandoned, poverty-stricken, or misused children in Dickens's novels and to the equally long list of negligent, selfish, and even childish parents. Although Pip is certainly not a self-portrait of his creator, *Great Expectations* repeats the emotional pattern of Dickens's early years: Pip's older sister, Mrs. Joe Gargery, plays the role of the cruel mother, and his brother-in-law, Joe, is cast in the part of the kindly but ineffectual father (Kaplan 434). Warren's even comes up unaccountably in *Great Expectations*, for instance, when Joe Gargery mentions "the Blacking Ware'us" as the first tourist attraction that he sets out to see in London. More important, *Great Expectations* tells another version of the story of Paradise Lost, but it reverses the order in which Dickens viewed himself as living that story. His family had been comfortably, if not securely, middle class at Chatham, and he had fallen into a working-class existence in London. Pip, however, starts out in the position of "a common labouring-boy," as Estella calls him. Pip is living the plot of his creator's youth, but in reverse: he is acting out the shame that his creator still felt over his earlier fall from an elevation that Pip as a child has not yet experienced and can only imagine.

The years in Chatham contained another formative experience that suggests the extent to which Dickens enacted the Victorian success story. While living in Kent between the ages of five and ten, Charles Dickens often accompanied his father on walks past a large, imposing house set above the road to the cathedral town of Rochester. The house, called Gad's Hill Place, associated with legends of Shakespeare and Falstaff, became for the young child the embodiment of his ambitions. In "Travelling Abroad," an essay written in the spring of the year in which he began writing *Great Expectations,* Dickens retold the story of his early longing for the house by quoting what his father had told him about Gad's Hill: "If you were to be very persevering and were to work hard, you might some day come to live in it" (*Uncommercial* 62). By the time he wrote this essay, Dickens had already proved that such an unlikely dream of proprietorship could become a reality: he had purchased Gad's Hill Place in 1856, almost forty years after he had learned to long for it.

The story is distinctly Dickensian in its oddity and intensity. Most early-nineteenth-century children longed for a pony or a particularly ornate toy, but, urged on by his father, Dickens wanted a big house, and not just any big house, but Gad's Hill, exactly the one that he first admired in his childhood. The unusual nature of this desire is highlighted by the fact that only a small fraction of Victorian families lived in houses that they owned; most middle-class families held long- or short-term, renewable leases on their homes (Thompson 168). Although Dickens originally planned to buy Gad's Hill as an investment to be rented out to others, just before he began writing *Great Expectations* he decided to sell the lease on his London house and move back to the country of his childhood by establishing his main residence at Gad's Hill Place.

The novel and the house seem to have been intricately connected in Dickens's mind. In the same sentence in one of his letters from the fall of 1860, he relates the two to each other: alterations to Gad's Hill, the house "I was extraordinarily fond of when a child," are proceeding on the "restless eve" of a "new big book" (*Letters* 3: 170, 178). In fact, the original owner of the house was himself a kind of Dick Whittington, source of the medieval legend about the orphan who became the Lord Mayor of London: the builder of Gad's Hill, a nearly illiterate man, began life as an ostler and ended as the mayor of Rochester after having succeeded in business as a brewer (Forster 2: 209), the trade that is the source of Miss Havisham's wealth. Gad's Hill may have been on Dickens's mind, therefore, in his depiction of Satis House, the building in which Pip first recognizes his ambitions. Whether that fact helps one evaluate Estella's dismissive comments on the meaning of the name of the house—whether owning it is really "enough" (*satis* in Latin) to fulfill one's ambitions—is a more complicated speculation.

How Dickens progressed from Warren's Blacking to the big house on the hill may be explained in at least two different fashions. One way in which to tell this story is to point to the speed with which he turned his inadequate schooling, his self-tutoring as a court stenographer, and his early work as a journalist into a career as a novelist. This version of the story would emphasize what a contemporary called "the great intellectual mystery of Dickens's fertile genius" (Collins, *Dickens: The Critical Heritage* 519), most obviously evidenced by the series of twelve novels that began with *Pickwick Papers* in 1836 and 1837. Unlike earlier novelists such as Sir Walter Scott or Jane Austen, who had other sources of income or support, Dickens set the pattern for his Victorian contemporaries by demonstrating that one could live—and live very well—as the result of great popular success. From this perspective Dickens's most striking characteristics were his extraordinary, even compulsive, drive and industry. In the 1830s and 1840s, he added to the writing of fiction one enterprise after another, attacking all challenges with what Forster calls "fixed and eager determination, . . . restless and resistless energy" (1: 34). Dickens was, in many ways, the proverbial self-made man.

A different way to tell this story, however, is to emphasize the propitious conjunction between Dickens's gifts and his circumstances: he was the right man in the right place at the right time. He knew how to take advantage of a popular novelist's opportunities to profit from the labors of imagination in an emerging consumer economy. In fact, by the early 1860s Dickens seemed to have understood exactly where publishing was heading in an increasingly capitalist system: for his own works and those of other writers, he controlled the processes of production and distribution and, in the case of his own novels, he provided the imaginative labor—an arrangement in the annals of Victorian publishing that is even more unusual than his ownership of his own home. This unique situation came about, as I will explain, through a combination of Dickens's personal unhappiness, characteristically willful self-indulgence, and shrewd business sense, but it created the pressing occasion and perfectly appropriate format for *Great Expectations.*

At the beginning of his career, Dickens had defied the advice of friends worried about the young writer's respectability by becoming involved in and then dominating a scheme to publish fiction serially in relatively cheap monthly installments. The result was *Pickwick Papers* and a nationwide craze for everything Pickwick—from hats, canes, cups, and fabrics to parodies, sequels, and theatrical renditions. As one of Dickens's biographers noted, Pickwick and his servant, Sam Weller, "had become more than national figures—they had become a mania" (Johnson 1: 156)—a mania that was clearly a forerunner of the kind of concerted merchandising extravaganzas that we now expect from popular entertainments like cartoons and movies. Throughout the 1840s and 1850s, Dickens had published what he called his "big" novels in the same monthly-number format in which he presented *Pickwick*: twenty illustrated installments with thirty-two pages of text at a cost of one shilling each.

This approach to a large readership, which did indeed run the risk of being seen as "cheap" or "low," was not original with Dickens, but he was the one who saw its potential in a system of publication that had previously relied on selling relatively expensive novels published in three volumes to lending libraries as well as to those individuals able to afford them. As soon as Dickens demonstrated the financial advantages of serial publication, other novelists, such as Thackeray, followed suit. Yet Dickens also experimented with other ways of reaching a large audience: in the 1840s he began a series of tales published yearly as "Christmas books," the first of which, *A Christmas Carol*, has remained the most successful; in the 1850s he originated and edited *Household Words*, a weekly magazine, priced at two pence, in which he published essays, Christmas stories, and the weekly installments of the novel *Hard Times* (1854).

None of these activities, however, could be insulated from the results of the domestic crisis that Dickens faced in 1858. After twenty-two years of marriage and ten children, Dickens and his wife Catherine separated—she to live in London on an allowance with their eldest son, and he to live at Gad's Hill with the rest of the children and with Catherine's unmarried sister Georgina as substitute mother and housekeeper. This separation was, for the times, a highly unusual move—unhappy couples in this period of difficult and expensive divorces usually went to different parts of the house, not different parts of the country. Dickens attributed the separation to basic incompatibility, but at least some of his acquaintances located its cause in an affair he was rumored to be having with a young actress named Ellen Ternan or in what would have been then thought of as an incestuous relation with his sister-in-law, Georgina. Since Dickens was, if anything, a highly visible public figure whose fiction championed domesticity, the ugly and hurtful rumors surrounding this domestic breakdown had the potential to diminish greatly the sales of his novels and magazine and, therefore, his income.

Dickens responded willfully to this danger by adding more fuel to the flames: he published in *Household Words* a personal statement in which he claimed that all parties involved were guiltless of any wrongdoing. When Bradbury and Evans, the publishers of *Household Words*, refused to reprint the statement in their comic magazine *Punch* —a publicizing of personal woes that would have been even more unaccountable and unseemly than its appearance in the magazine that Dickens edited—he severed relations with the firm, discontinued publication of *Household Words*, and arranged to buy the firm's share of the copyright and stock so that he could start his own magazine, *All the Year Round*. In the economic context of the period, when publishers were increasing their control over authors (Feltes), Dickens's desire for autonomy was striking and strikingly effective. As he told a friend, "I have made up my mind to work what I do with my own capital, and to have no publisher at all except as a paid agent and instrument" (qtd. in Kaplan 401).

The drive for control, apparent throughout Dickens's career, now became both unyielding and literal in its emphasis on ownership. To this drive was also added, almost perversely, a need for increased publicity or, as Dickens himself put it, a need to strengthen "that particular relation (personally affectionate and like no other man's) which subsists between me and the public" (Forster 2: 205). In the 1850s, Dickens had contributed to a variety of charitable causes by giving, for their benefit, public readings from his novels and Christmas books. In 1857 he began suggesting that he should give a series of such readings for his own profit. Since he put that plan into action just weeks before he announced the decision to separate from Catherine, it seems clear that he wanted to provide a new way of demonstrating his power over an audience that might be offended by the imminent change in his personal circumstances. More than could have been expected, the readings did elicit the wildly affectionate adoration of his readers: young ladies literally lay at his feet so that they could hear him perform his works.[1]

Since Dickens first mentioned the possibility of undertaking these readings as a way of paying for Gad's Hill, he was also clearly looking forward to immediate and substantial financial rewards from this marketing of his presence. Certainly, his increasingly complicated domestic arrangements required that he earn more and more money. In addi-

[1]The first three series of readings in 1858–59 took place before the writing of *Great Expectations*, and its composition was interrupted by another, shorter series in 1861 (Collins, *Readings* xxiii–xxiv). This timing may explain the renewed vitality and increased intimacy of the voice that he created in the novel: like Dickens reading to a crowded hall of eager audience members, Pip writes his story almost as if he were speaking to a listener in the room with him.

tion to the separate homes Dickens was supporting for Catherine and himself, he also financed the household sheltering his aging mother, the widow of one of his brothers, and her five children. By 1860 he had probably added to the list yet another household—the one comprising Ellen Ternan and, at various times, her mother and her two sisters.

There has been much speculation about Ellen Ternan's unconscious role as a model for the cold and taunting Estella of *Great Expectations*, although at least one commentator, Michael Slater, has argued against that identification by finding the model for Estella in Maria Beadnell, a young lady with whom Dickens was hopelessly and desperately in love in the early 1830s (73–75). Less speculative and perhaps just as significant is the role that Ellen Ternan played as a financial demand on Dickens's resources, yet another reason for him to choose the format and publishing venue in which he presented *Great Expectations*. In 1859 she had withdrawn from the stage, presumably accepting full support from Dickens. A year earlier he had sent her eldest sister, Fanny, chaperoned by their mother, to study music in Florence. By 1860, when Ellen Ternan was twenty-one and had known Dickens for three years, she became the legal owner of the long-term lease of the house in which she lived with her mother and sisters, a lease for which Dickens seems to have paid (Kaplan 409). Whether his attraction to her was a cause of the breakdown of his marriage or simply a symptom of its inevitable dissolution, when and if she became his mistress, are all matters of debate. It is indisputable, however, that Ellen Ternan was an expensive and potentially very costly companion for a man who based his living on the public's regard for him. If, as Dickens said of his sons, "their father's name is their best possession" (qtd. in Kaplan 399), the same could be said of Ellen Ternan: from 1859 Dickens's name became her livelihood.

The financial pressures that impelled Dickens to begin his reading tours—the continued physical and emotional strains of which contributed to his early death in 1870—also included his concern for his many sons, who were reaching maturity without demonstrating much sense of how to make their way in the world. Throughout the earlier years of his marriage, Dickens had commented continually on his growing and increasingly burdensome family without ever recognizing that any behavior on his part had had anything to do with his wife's frequent pregnancies. Now that his sons needed to be either trained for professions or set up in business, he commented often and cruelly on their manifest incapacities for independence, and he never seemed to recognize or sympathize with the fact that their being raised in the shadow of a national phenomenon might not provide the best basis for successful adulthood.

Just as Dickens began *Great Expectations*, his youngest son, Edward, was being tutored at home, Henry was still in school, Sydney was a naval cadet in training for a career as a naval officer, Alfred was studying engineering to prepare for a career in the army, Frank was supposedly "in business" in London, Walter was in the army in India, and Charley, at twenty-three the eldest, was in the Far East buying tea to learn the import business before setting up on his own (Page 106). This list of activities, however, does not reveal the reasons for Dickens's disappointment in his sons: a number of them seemed beset by the lethargy that characterized their mother, and a number of the others, by the propensity to debt typical of their paternal grandfather and their father's brothers; none of them, except perhaps Henry, had a fraction of their father's energy or determination. No wonder, as one of Dickens's recent biographers suggests, Dickens "should begin [a] novel which shows the folly of spendthrift youth" (Ackroyd 880). There is, of course, another autobiographical transposition at work here: Dickens wrote *Great Expectations* in the company of his sons, boys and young men who seemed to be, like Pip through much of his story, simply waiting to see how their great expectations would become reality.[2]

All these factors—the houses, the sons, the women in his life—may have been on Dickens's mind in the fall of 1860 when he decided how and where to publish, and therefore how to write, *Great Expectations.* In September he told Forster that he had written a "little piece," an essay for publication in *All the Year Round*, but it contained such a "very fine, new, and grotesque idea" that he thought it would provide the basis for a new serial novel. The serial, as he told another correspondent, was to be a "new big book," issued in twenty monthly numbers as *David Copperfield* had been. Until that fall the new

---

[2]If writing a plot in which Pip achieves modest success was Dickens's hopeful prophecy for his sons, it did not, except in the case of Henry, prove true. Several of them tried, like Pip, to capitalize on the opportunities provided by empire, but they largely failed: before Dickens's death, one of his sons died in debt in India, where another tried unsuccessfully to make his fortune; two were sent off to become sheep farmers in Australia; two others were constantly in debt, Charley having to declare bankruptcy before he joined the staff of his father's magazine. Their stories, perhaps more obviously poignant than those of many of their middle-class contemporaries, do convey the difficulty of "getting on" for Victorian young men in the 1850s and '60s (see Lohman).

magazine, *All the Year Round*, had been doing well. Its first issue had carried the first installment of *A Tale of Two Cities*, and the popular success of the magazine had been consolidated by the appearance of the next novel serialized there, Wilkie Collins's *The Woman in White*. To follow Collins's novel, Dickens had tried to engage the services of other successful novelists, the well-established Elizabeth Gaskell and the recent new success George Eliot, but both declined, scared off by the difficulties of writing novels in short weekly installments. Finally, Dickens settled on Charles Lever, whose novel *A Day's Ride* drove down the sales of the magazine "rapidly and continuously," as Dickens tactlessly told the author himself. After a "council of war" with the staff of *All the Year Round*, Dickens decided to "sacrifice" the idea of a "new big book" by writing *Great Expectations* as a weekly serial to be run, along with the rest of Lever's serial, in the magazine starting in December of 1860. The financial motivation for this decision was clear: as Dickens told Forster, the "property of *All the Year Round* is far too valuable, in every way, to be much endangered" (*Letters* 3: 182–83). The healthy sales of the magazine once *Great Expectations* began its run there proved yet again that Dickens had made the right move.

To a great extent, Dickens's decision to publish the novel in *All the Year Round* determined the form ultimately taken by what he called its "grotesque tragi-comic conception" (*Letters* 3: 186). Since a weekly serial by Dickens was less than half the length of a twenty-number, monthly serial, this decision largely accounts for the unity and concision that readers have praised in *Great Expectations*. The autobiographical form of the story may also have been the result of its placement in the magazine. As a modern scholar of Dickens's publishing practices in *All the Year Round* explains, autobiographical narratives were the preferred mode for weekly serialization because they "waste no time in making an impact on the reader," and, in fact, four of the first six novels serialized in the magazine took that form (Sutherland 173). Dickens may indeed have decided that the story was to "be written in the first person throughout" (*Letters* 3: 186) only after he decided to write it for publication in *All the Year Round*.

The odd fate of the novel's original ending also resulted from Dickens's association with the magazine. When he finished the manuscript in June 1861—the novel was scheduled to run in *All the Year Round* until August 1861—he had already engaged for the next serial the services of Edward Bulwer-Lytton, an older popular novelist and aristocrat with peculiar interests in the occult. Throughout 1861, as

Bulwer-Lytton was writing his aptly named novel, *A Strange Story*, and as Dickens completed the writing of *Great Expectations*, they developed a reciprocal relation as each other's reader and adviser. When Bulwer-Lytton saw in proof the ending of Dickens's novel, he objected to it; and Dickens, who had already advised him on the ending of his novel, decided to recast the conclusion of his own (see The Endings of *Great Expectations*, pp. 440–41). The revision of the novel's ending is sometimes presented as an unaccountable yielding on Dickens's part to the inappropriate pressure exerted by Bulwer-Lytton. It was, in fact, very much the result of their working relation (Sutherland 185); and that relation, if not perhaps the content of the ending actually published in 1861, resulted, like the length and form of the novel itself, from the importance to Dickens of *All the Year Round* as his "property."

FROM WHOM WE HAVE
GREAT EXPECTATIONS

Great Expectations was widely advertised in booksellers' windows with a placard showing Dickens at his writing desk as the author "FROM WHOM WE HAVE GREAT EXPECTATIONS." The caricature, like the popular understanding of Dickens and Dickens's understanding of himself, is an exaggerated and disproportionate portrait of its subject. The drawing embarrassed and amused Dickens; as he told a friend,

> I hope you may have seen a large-headed photograph with little legs, representing the undersigned, pen in hand, tapping his forehead to knock an idea out. It has just sprung up so abundantly in all the shops, that I am ashamed to go about town looking in at the picture-windows, which is my delight. It seems to me extraordinarily ludicrous, and much more like than the grave portrait done in earnest. It made me laugh when I first came upon it, until I shook again, in open sunlighted Piccadilly. (*Letters* 3: 228)

Dickens may have responded with so much pleasure because the caricature, admittedly charming, also depicts a man who looks considerably younger than he did in 1861. Although not yet fifty years old, he had, over the course of more than thirty years, carried on multiple, frenetic careers as novelist, public reader, impresario, editor, and proprietor. Along with his professional obligations, the personal burdens of a failed marriage, single parenthood, and a demanding clandestine romance had more than obviously taken their toll.

In the years that followed the publication of *Great Expectations*—the success of which I will consider in the critical history that follows the text in this edition—Dickens continued to live out the life that had already made him a legend, "one of the foremost Englishmen of the age," as the London *Times* said in his obituary (Collins, *Dickens: The Critical Heritage* 508). Before his death, Dickens published one more novel, *Our Mutual Friend* (1864–65), once again a "big book" in monthly numbers. He continued to refurbish Gad's Hill Place until within a week of his death. He engaged in several series of public readings until ordered by his doctor to discontinue them—the one in America was especially lucrative and especially taxing—and he continued his liaison, whatever its terms, with Ellen Ternan. Dickens also watched in his last decade as his sons tried to make their way in the world, until he exclaimed in despair, "Why was I ever a father! Why was *my* father ever a father!" (qtd. in Kaplan 531). Yet if the calm, unwrinkled, almost youthful face on the contemporary advertisement for *Great Expectations* is less accurate as a depiction of the mature Dickens than the marked and darkened visage on my coffee mug, its caption remains quite pertinent: Dickens's fiction has made him the novelist FROM WHOM WE still HAVE GREAT EXPECTATIONS.

Janice Carlisle

WORKS CITED

Ackroyd, Peter. *Dickens.* New York: HarperCollins, 1990.

Allen, Michael. *Charles Dickens' Childhood.* London: Macmillan, 1988.

Best, Geoffrey. *Mid-Victorian Britain 1851–1875.* New York: Schocken, 1972.

Collins, Philip, ed. *Charles Dickens: The Public Readings.* Oxford: Clarendon, 1975.

———, ed. *Dickens: The Critical Heritage.* New York: Barnes and Noble, 1971.

Cotsell, Michael, ed. *Critical Essays on Charles Dickens's* Great Expectations. Boston: G. K. Hall, 1990.

Dickens, Charles. *The Letters of Charles Dickens.* Ed. Walter Dexter. Nonesuch Dickens. 3 vols. Bloomsbury: Nonesuch, 1938.

———. *The Uncommercial Traveller and Reprinted Pieces.* Intro. Leslie C. Staples. London: Oxford, 1968.

Feltes, N. N. *Modes of Production of Victorian Novels.* Chicago: U of Chicago P, 1986.

Forster, John. *The Life of Charles Dickens.* 1871–73. 2 vols. London: Dent, 1966.

Gilmour, Robin. *The Idea of the Gentleman in the Victorian Novel.* London: Allen, 1981.

Johnson, Edgar. *Charles Dickens: His Tragedy and Triumph.* 2 vols. New York: Simon, 1952.

Kaplan, Fred. *Dickens: A Biography.* New York: Morrow, 1988.

Lohman, W. J., Jr. "The Economic Background of *Great Expectations.*" *Victorians Institute Journal* 14 (1986): 53–66.

Meckier, Jerome. "Dating the Action in *Great Expectations:* A New Chronology." *Dickens Studies Annual* 21 (1992): 157–94.

Morris, Pam. *Dickens's Class Consciousness: A Marginal View.* New York: St. Martin's, 1991.

Page, Norman. *A Dickens Chronology.* Boston: G. K. Hall, 1988.

Slater, Michael. *Dickens and Women.* Stanford: Stanford UP, 1983.

Sutherland, J. A. *Victorian Novelists and Publishers.* Chicago: U of Chicago, 1976.

Thompson, F. M. L. *The Rise of Respectable Society: A Social History of Victorian Britain 1830–1900.* Cambridge: Harvard UP, 1988.

Great Expectations

[PART 1]

Chapter 1

My father's family name being Pirrip, and my christian name Philip, my infant tongue could make of both names nothing longer or more explicit than Pip. So, I called myself Pip, and came to be called Pip.

I give Pirrip as my father's family name, on the authority of his tombstone and my sister—Mrs. Joe Gargery, who married the blacksmith. As I never saw my father or my mother, and never saw any likeness of either of them (for their days were long before the days of photographs°), my first fancies regarding what they were like, were unreasonably derived from their tombstones. The shape of the letters on my father's, gave me an odd idea that he was a square, stout, dark man, with curly black hair. From the character and turn of the inscription, "*Also Georgiana Wife of the Above*," I drew a childish conclusion that my mother was freckled and sickly. To five little stone lozenges, each about a foot and a half long, which were arranged in a neat row

before . . . photographs: Before the widespread use of photography in the 1840s and 1850s.

beside their grave, and were sacred to the memory of five little brothers of mine—who gave up trying to get a living, exceedingly early in that universal struggle—I am indebted for a belief I religiously entertained that they had all been born on their backs with their hands in their trousers-pockets, and had never taken them out in this state of existence.

Ours was the marsh country, down by the river, within, as the river wound, twenty miles of the sea.° My first most vivid and broad impression of the identity of things, seems to me to have been gained on a memorable raw afternoon towards evening. At such a time I found out for certain, that this bleak place overgrown with nettles was the churchyard; and that Philip Pirrip, late of this parish, and also Georgiana wife of the above, were dead and buried; and that Alexander, Bartholomew, Abraham, Tobias, and Roger, infant children of the aforesaid, were also dead and buried; and that the dark flat wilderness beyond the churchyard, intersected with dykes and mounds and gates, with scattered cattle feeding on it, was the marshes; and that the low leaden line beyond, was the river; and that the distant savage lair from which the wind was rushing, was the sea; and that the small bundle of shivers growing afraid of it all and beginning to cry, was Pip.

"Hold your noise!" cried a terrible voice, as a man started up from among the graves at the side of the church porch. "Keep still, you little devil, or I'll cut your throat!"

A fearful man, all in coarse grey, with a great iron on his leg. A man with no hat, and with broken shoes, and with an old rag tied round his head. A man who had been soaked in water, and smothered in mud, and lamed by stones, and cut by flints, and stung by nettles, and torn by briars; who limped, and shivered, and glared and growled; and whose teeth chattered in his head as he seized me by the chin.

"O! Don't cut my throat, sir," I pleaded in terror. "Pray don't do it, sir."

"Tell us your name!" said the man. "Quick!"

"Pip, sir."

"Once more," said the man, staring at me. "Give it mouth!"

"Pip. Pip, sir."

"Show us where you live," said the man. "Pint out the place!"

I pointed to where our village lay, on the flat in-shore among the alder-trees and pollards, a mile or more from the church.

marsh . . . sea: The area south of the Thames near its mouth.

The man, after looking at me for a moment, turned me upside-down, and emptied my pockets. There was nothing in them but a piece of bread. When the church came to itself—for he was so sudden and strong that he made it go head over heels before me, and I saw the steeple under my feet—when the church came to itself, I say, I was seated on a high tombstone, trembling, while he ate the bread ravenously.

"You young dog," said the man, licking his lips, "what fat cheeks you ha' got."

I believe they were fat, though I was at that time undersized for my years, and not strong.

"Darn Me if I couldn't eat 'em," said the man with a threatening shake of his head, "and if I han't half a mind to't!"

I earnestly expressed my hope that he wouldn't, and held tighter to the tombstone on which he had put me; partly, to keep myself upon it; partly, to keep myself from crying.

"Now then, lookee here!" said the man. "Where's your mother?"

"There, sir!" said I.

He started, made a short run, and stopped and looked over his shoulder.

"There, sir!" I timidly explained. "Also Georgiana. That's my mother."

"Oh!" said he, coming back. "And is that your father alonger your mother?"

"Yes, sir," said I; "him too; late of this parish."

"Ha!" he muttered then, considering. "Who d'ye live with—supposin' you're kindly let to live, which I han't made up my mind about?"

"My sister, sir—Mrs. Joe Gargery—wife of Joe Gargery, the blacksmith, sir."

"Blacksmith, eh?" said he. And looked down at his leg.

After darkly looking at his leg and at me several times, he came closer to my tombstone, took me by both arms, and tilted me back as far as he could hold me; so that his eyes looked most powerfully down into mine, and mine looked most helplessly up into his.

"Now lookee here," he said, "the question being whether you're to be let to live. You know what a file is."

"Yes, sir."

"And you know what wittles°·is."

wittles: Victuals, food.

"Yes, sir."

After each question he tilted me over a little more, so as to give me a greater sense of helplessness and danger.

"You get me a file." He tilted me again. "And you get me wittles." He tilted me again. "You bring 'em both to me." He tilted me again. "Or I'll have your heart and liver out." He tilted me again.

I was dreadfully frightened, and so giddy that I clung to him with both hands, and said, "If you would kindly please to let me keep upright, sir, perhaps I shouldn't be sick, and perhaps I could attend more."

He gave me a most tremendous dip and roll, so that the church jumped over its own weather-cock. Then, he held me by the arms, in an upright position on the top of the stone, and went on in these fearful terms:

"You bring me, to-morrow morning early, that file and them wittles. You bring the lot to me, at that old Battery° over yonder. You do it, and you never dare to say a word or dare to make a sign concerning your having seen such a person as me, or any person sumever, and you shall be let to live. You fail, or you go from my words in any partickler, no matter how small it is, and your heart and your liver shall be tore out, roasted and ate. Now, I ain't alone, as you may think I am. There's a young man hid with me, in comparison with which young man I am a Angel. That young man hears the words I speak. That young man has a secret way pecooliar to himself, of getting at a boy, and at his heart, and at his liver. It is in wain for a boy to attempt to hide himself from that young man. A boy may lock his door, may be warm in bed, may tuck himself up, may draw the clothes over his head, may think himself comfortable and safe, but that young man will softly creep and creep his way to him and tear him open. I am a keeping that young man from harming of you at the present moment, with great difficulty. I find it wery hard to hold that young man off of your inside. Now, what do you say?"

I said that I would get him the file, and I would get him what broken bits of food I could, and I would come to him at the Battery, early in the morning.

"Say Lord strike you dead if you don't!" said the man.

I said so, and he took me down.

"Now," he pursued, "you remember what you've undertook, and you remember that young man, and you get home!"

Battery: Ruined fortifications.

"Goo-good night, sir," I faltered.

"Much of that!" said he, glancing about him over the cold wet flat. "I wish I was a frog. Or a eel!"

At the same time, he hugged his shuddering body in both his arms—clasping himself, as if to hold himself together—and limped towards the low church wall. As I saw him go, picking his way among the nettles, and among the brambles that bound the green mounds, he looked in my young eyes as if he were eluding the hands of the dead people, stretching up cautiously out of their graves, to get a twist upon his ankle and pull him in.

When he came to the low church wall, he got over it, like a man whose legs were numbed and stiff, and then turned round to look for me. When I saw him turning, I set my face towards home, and made the best use of my legs. But presently I looked over my shoulder, and saw him going on again towards the river, still hugging himself in both arms, and picking his way with his sore feet among the great stones dropped into the marshes here and there, for stepping-places when the rains were heavy, or the tide was in.

The marshes were just a long black horizontal line then, as I stopped to look after him; and the river was just another horizontal line, not nearly so broad nor yet so black; and the sky was just a row of long angry red lines and dense black lines intermixed. On the edge of the river I could faintly make out the only two black things in all the prospect that seemed to be standing upright; one of these was the beacon by which the sailors steered—like an unhooped cask upon a pole—an ugly thing when you were near it; the other, a gibbet° with some chains hanging to it which had once held a pirate. The man was limping on towards this latter, as if he were the pirate come to life, and come down, and going back to hook himself up again. It gave me a terrible turn when I thought so; and as I saw the cattle lifting their heads to gaze after him, I wondered whether they thought so too. I looked all round for the horrible young man, and could see no signs of him. But, now I was frightened again, and ran home without stopping.

Chapter 2

My sister, Mrs. Joe Gargery, was more than twenty years older than I, and had established a great reputation with herself and the neighbours because she had brought me up "by hand."° Having at

gibbet: Gallows from which, until 1832, criminals were left hanging after execution.
"by hand": Bottle-feeding rather than breast-feeding an infant.

that time to find out for myself what the expression meant, and knowing her to have a hard and heavy hand, and to be much in the habit of laying it upon her husband as well as upon me, I supposed that Joe Gargery and I were both brought up by hand.

She was not a good-looking woman, my sister; and I had a general impression that she must have made Joe Gargery marry her by hand. Joe was a fair man, with curls of flaxen hair on each side of his smooth face, and with eyes of such a very undecided blue that they seemed to have somehow got mixed with their own whites. He was a mild, good-natured, sweet-tempered, easygoing, foolish, dear fellow—a sort of Hercules in strength, and also in weakness.

My sister, Mrs. Joe, with black hair and eyes, had such a prevailing redness of skin that I sometimes used to wonder whether it was possible she washed herself with a nutmeg-grater instead of soap. She was tall and bony, and almost always wore a coarse apron, fastened over her figure behind with two loops, and having a square impregnable bib in front, that was stuck full of pins and needles. She made it a powerful merit in herself, and a strong reproach against Joe, that she wore this apron so much. Though I really see no reason why she should have worn it at all: or why, if she did wear it at all, she should not have taken it off, every day of her life.

Joe's forge adjoined our house, which was a wooden house, as many of the dwellings in our country were—most of them, at that time. When I ran home from the churchyard, the forge was shut up, and Joe was sitting alone in the kitchen. Joe and I being fellow-sufferers, and having confidences as such, Joe imparted a confidence to me, the moment I raised the latch of the door and peeped in at him opposite to it, sitting in the chimney corner.

"Mrs. Joe has been out a dozen times, looking for you, Pip. And she's out now, making it a baker's dozen."

"Is she?"

"Yes, Pip," said Joe, "and what's worse, she's got Tickler with her."

At this dismal intelligence, I twisted the only button on my waistcoat round and round, and looked in great depression at the fire. Tickler was a wax-ended piece of cane, worn smooth by collision with my tickled frame.

"She sot down," said Joe, "and she got up, and she made a grab at Tickler, and she Ram-paged out. That's what she did," said Joe, slowly clearing the fire between the lower bars with the poker, and looking at it: "she Ram-paged out, Pip."

"Has she been gone long, Joe?" I always treated him as a larger species of child, and as no more than my equal.

"Well," said Joe, glancing up at the Dutch clock,° "she's been on the Ram-page, this last spell, about five minutes, Pip. She's a coming! Get behind the door, old chap, and have the jack-towel° betwixt you."

I took the advice. My sister, Mrs. Joe, throwing the door wide open, and finding an obstruction behind it, immediately divined the cause, and applied Tickler to its further investigation. She concluded by throwing me—I often served her as a connubial missile—at Joe, who, glad to get hold of me on any terms, passed me on into the chimney and quietly fenced me up there with his great leg.

"Where have you been, you young monkey?" said Mrs. Joe, stamping her foot. "Tell me directly what you've been doing to wear me away with fret and fright and worrit, or I'd have you out of that corner if you was fifty Pips, and he was five hundred Gargerys."

"I have only been to the churchyard," said I, from my stool, crying and rubbing myself.

"Churchyard!" repeated my sister. "If it warn't for me you'd have been to the churchyard long ago, and stayed there. Who brought you up by hand?"

"You did," said I.

"And why did I do it, I should like to know!" exclaimed my sister.

I whimpered, "I don't know."

"*I* don't!" said my sister. "I'd never do it again! I know that. I may truly say I've never had this apron of mine off, since born you were. It's bad enough to be a blacksmith's wife (and him a Gargery) without being your mother."

My thoughts strayed from that question as I looked disconsolately at the fire. For, the fugitive out on the marshes with the ironed leg, the mysterious young man, the file, the food, and the dreadful pledge I was under to commit a larceny on those sheltering premises, rose before me in the avenging coals.

"Hah!" said Mrs. Joe, restoring Tickler to his station. "Churchyard, indeed! You may well say churchyard, you two." One of us, by-the-by, had not said it at all. "You'll drive *me* to the churchyard betwixt you, one of these days, and oh, a pr-r-recious pair you'd be without me!"

As she applied herself to set the tea-things, Joe peeped down at me over his leg, as if he were mentally casting me and himself up, and

---

Dutch clock: Inexpensive, wooden German clock.   **jack-towel:** Towel on a roller.

calculating what kind of pair we practically should make, under the grievous circumstances foreshadowed. After that, he sat feeling his right-side flaxen curls and whisker, and following Mrs. Joe about with his blue eyes, as his manner always was at squally times.

My sister had a trenchant way of cutting our bread-and-butter for us, that never varied. First, with her left hand she jammed the loaf hard and fast against her bib—where it sometimes got a pin into it, and sometimes a needle, which we afterwards got into our mouths. Then she took some butter (not too much) on a knife and spread it on the loaf, in an apothecary kind of way as if she were making a plaister°— using both sides of the knife with a slapping dexterity, and trimming and moulding the butter off round the crust. Then, she gave the knife a final smart wipe on the edge of the plaister, and then sawed a very thick round off the loaf: which she finally, before separating from the loaf, hewed into two halves, of which Joe got one, and I the other.

On the present occasion, though I was hungry, I dared not eat my slice. I felt that I must have something in reserve for my dreadful acquaintance, and his ally the still more dreadful young man. I knew Mrs. Joe's housekeeping to be of the strictest kind, and that my larcenous researches might find nothing available in the safe. Therefore I resolved to put my hunk of bread-and-butter down the leg of my trousers.

The effort of resolution necessary to the achievement of this purpose, I found to be quite awful. It was as if I had to make up my mind to leap from the top of a high house, or plunge into a great depth of water. And it was made the more difficult by the unconscious Joe. In our already-mentioned freemasonry as fellow-sufferers, and in his good-natured companionship with me, it was our evening habit to compare the way we bit through our slices, by silently holding them up to each other's admiration now and then—which stimulated us to new exertions. To-night, Joe several times invited me, by the display of his fast-diminishing slice, to enter upon our usual friendly competition; but he found me, each time, with my yellow mug of tea on one knee, and my untouched bread-and-butter on the other. At last, I desperately considered that the thing I contemplated must be done, and that it had best be done in the least improbable manner consistent with the circumstances. I took advantage of a moment when Joe had just looked at me, and got my bread-and-butter down my leg.

Joe was evidently made uncomfortable by what he supposed to be my loss of appetite, and took a thoughtful bite out of his slice, which

plaister: Bandage spread with ointment.

he didn't seem to enjoy. He turned it about in his mouth much longer than usual, pondering over it a good deal, and after all gulped it down like a pill. He was about to take another bite, and had just got his head on one side for a good purchase on it, when his eye fell on me, and he saw that my bread-and-butter was gone.

The wonder and consternation with which Joe stopped on the threshold of his bite and stared at me, were too evident to escape my sister's observation.

"What's the matter now?" said she, smartly, as she put down her cup.

"I say, you know!" muttered Joe, shaking his head at me in very serious remonstrance. "Pip, old chap! You'll do yourself a mischief. It'll stick somewhere. You can't have chawed it, Pip."

"What's the matter *now?*" repeated my sister, more sharply than before.

"If you can cough any trifle on it up, Pip, I'd recommend you to do it," said Joe, all aghast. "Manners is manners, but still your elth's your elth."

By this time, my sister was quite desperate, so she pounced on Joe, and, taking him by the two whiskers, knocked his head for a little while against the wall behind him: while I sat in the corner, looking guiltily on.

"Now, perhaps you'll mention what's the matter," said my sister, out of breath, "you staring great stuck pig."

Joe looked at her in a helpless way; then took a helpless bite, and looked at me again.

"You know, Pip," said Joe, solemnly, with his last bite in his cheek, and speaking in a confidential voice, as if we two were quite alone, "you and me is always friends, and I'd be the last to tell upon you, any time. But such a"—he moved his chair and looked about the floor between us, and then again at me—"such a most oncommon Bolt as that!"

"Been bolting his food, has he?" cried my sister.

"You know, old chap," said Joe, looking at me, and not at Mrs. Joe, with his bite still in his cheek, "I Bolted, myself, when I was your age—frequent—and as a boy I've been among a many Bolters; but I never see your Bolting equal yet, Pip, and it's a mercy you ain't Bolted dead."

My sister made a dive at me, and fished me up by the hair: saying nothing more than the awful words, "You come along and be dosed."

Some medical beast had revived Tar-water° in those days as a fine medicine, and Mrs. Joe always kept a supply of it in the cupboard; having a belief in its virtues correspondent to its nastiness. At the best of times, so much of this elixir was administered to me as a choice restorative, that I was conscious of going about, smelling like a new fence. On this particular evening the urgency of my case demanded a pint of this mixture, which was poured down my throat, for my greater comfort, while Mrs. Joe held my head under her arm, as a boot would be held in a boot-jack. Joe got off with half a pint; but was made to swallow that (much to his disturbance, as he sat slowly munching and meditating before the fire), "because he had had a turn." Judging from myself, I should say he certainly had a turn afterwards, if he had had none before.

Conscience is a dreadful thing when it accuses man or boy; but when, in the case of a boy, that secret burden co-operates with another secret burden down the leg of his trousers, it is (as I can testify) a great punishment. The guilty knowledge that I was going to rob Mrs. Joe — I never thought I was going to rob Joe, for I never thought of any of the housekeeping property as his — united to the necessity of always keeping one hand on my bread-and-butter as I sat, or when I was ordered about the kitchen on any small errand, almost drove me out of my mind. Then, as the marsh winds made the fire glow and flare, I thought I heard the voice outside, of the man with the iron on his leg who had sworn me to secrecy, declaring that he couldn't and wouldn't starve until to-morrow, but must be fed now. At other times, I thought, What if the young man who was with so much difficulty restrained from imbruing his hands in me, should yield to a constitutional impatience, or should mistake the time, and should think himself accredited to my heart and liver to-night, instead of to-morrow! If ever anybody's hair stood on end with terror, mine must have done so then. But, perhaps, nobody's ever did?

It was Christmas Eve, and I had to stir the pudding for next day, with a copper-stick, from seven to eight by the Dutch clock. I tried it with the load upon my leg (and that made me think afresh of the man with the load on *his* leg), and found the tendency of exercise to bring the bread-and-butter out at my ankle, quite unmanageable. Happily, I slipped away, and deposited that part of my conscience in my garret bedroom.

Tar-water: A mixture of cold water and wood-tar, mistakenly thought to cure stomach-aches and more serious illnesses.

"Hark!" said I, when I had done my stirring, and was taking a final warm in the chimney corner before being sent up to bed; "was that great guns, Joe?"

"Ah!" said Joe. "There's another conwict off."

"What does that mean, Joe?" said I.

Mrs. Joe, who always took explanations upon herself, said, snappishly, "Escaped. Escaped." Administering the definition like Tarwater.

While Mrs. Joe sat with her head bending over her needlework, I put my mouth into the forms of saying to Joe, "What's a convict?" Joe put *his* mouth into the forms of returning such a highly elaborate answer, that I could make out nothing of it but the single word "Pip."

"There was a conwict off last night," said Joe, aloud, "after sunsetgun. And they fired warning of him. And now, it appears they're firing warning of another."

"*Who's* firing?" said I.

"Drat that boy," interposed my sister, frowning at me over her work, "what a questioner he is. Ask no questions, and you'll be told no lies."

It was not very polite to herself, I thought, to imply that I should be told lies by her, even if I did ask questions. But she never was polite, unless there was company.

At this point, Joe greatly augmented my curiosity by taking the utmost pains to open his mouth very wide, and to put it into the form of a word that looked to me like "sulks." Therefore, I naturally pointed to Mrs. Joe, and put my mouth into the form of saying, "her?" But Joe wouldn't hear of that, at all, and again opened his mouth very wide, and shook the form of a most emphatic word out of it. But I could make nothing of the word.

"Mrs. Joe," said I, as a last resource, "I should like to know—if you wouldn't much mind—where the firing comes from?"

"Lord bless the boy!" exclaimed my sister, as if she didn't quite mean that, but rather the contrary. "From the Hulks."

"Oh-h!" said I, looking at Joe. "Hulks!"

Joe gave a reproachful cough, as much as to say, "Well, I told you so."

"And please what's Hulks?" said I.

"That's the way with this boy!" exclaimed my sister, pointing me out with her needle and thread, and shaking her head at me. "Answer him one question, and he'll ask you a dozen directly. Hulks are prison-ships,° right 'cross th' meshes." We always used that name for marshes, in our country.

"I wonder who's put into prison-ships, and why they're put there?" said I, in a general way, and with quiet desperation.

It was too much for Mrs. Joe, who immediately rose. "I tell you what, young fellow," said she, "I didn't bring you up by hand to badger people's lives out. It would be blame to me, and not praise, if I had. People are put in the Hulks because they murder, and because they rob, and forge, and do all sorts of bad; and they always begin by asking questions. Now, you get along to bed!"

I was never allowed a candle to light me to bed, and, as I went upstairs in the dark, with my head tingling—from Mrs. Joe's thimble, having played the tambourine upon it, to accompany her last words— I felt fearfully sensible of the great convenience that the Hulks were handy for me. I was clearly on my way there. I had begun by asking questions, and I was going to rob Mrs. Joe.

Since that time, which is far enough away now, I have often thought that few people know what secrecy there is in the young, under terror. No matter how unreasonable the terror, so that it be terror. I was in mortal terror of the young man who wanted my heart and liver; I was in mortal terror of my interlocutor with the ironed leg; I was in mortal terror of myself, from whom an awful promise had been extracted; I had no hope of deliverance through my all-powerful sister, who repulsed me at every turn; I am afraid to think of what I might have done, on requirement, in the secrecy of my terror.

If I slept at all that night, it was only to imagine myself drifting down the river on a strong spring tide, to the Hulks; a ghostly pirate calling out to me through a speaking-trumpet, as I passed the gibbet-station, that I had better come ashore and be hanged there at once, and not put it off. I was afraid to sleep, even if I had been inclined, for I knew that at the first faint dawn of morning I must rob the pantry. There was no doing it in the night, for there was no getting a light by easy friction then; to have got one, I must have struck it out of flint and steel, and have made a noise like the very pirate himself rattling his chains.

As soon as the great black velvet pall outside my little window was shot with grey, I got up and went down stairs; every board upon the way, and every crack in every board, calling after me, "Stop thief!" and

prison-ships: Old, mastless ships that were moored and used as prisons, particularly to hold convicts awaiting transportation to serve their sentences in the penal colonies. The Hulks were abolished in 1858; transportation was being phased out in the 1840s and 1850s and finally ended in 1868.

"Get up, Mrs. Joe!" In the pantry, which was far more abundantly supplied than usual, owing to the season, I was very much alarmed, by a hare hanging up by the heels, whom I rather thought I caught, when my back was half turned, winking. I had no time for verification, no time for selection, no time for anything, for I had no time to spare. I stole some bread, some rind of cheese, about half a jar of mincemeat (which I tied up in my pocket-handkerchief with my last night's slice), some brandy from a stone bottle (which I decanted into a glass bottle I had secretly used for making that intoxicating fluid, Spanish-liquorice-water, up in my room: diluting the stone bottle from a jug in the kitchen cupboard), a meat bone with very little on it, and a beautiful round compact pork pie. I was nearly going away without the pie, but I was tempted to mount upon a shelf, to look what it was that was put away so carefully in a covered earthenware dish in a corner, and I found it was the pie, and I took it, in the hope that it was not intended for early use, and would not be missed for some time.

There was a door in the kitchen, communicating with the forge; I unlocked and unbolted that door, and got a file from among Joe's tools. Then, I put the fastenings as I had found them, opened the door at which I had entered when I ran home last night, shut it, and ran for the misty marshes.

[PART 2]

Chapter 3

It was a rimy morning, and very damp. I had seen the damp lying on the outside of my little window, as if some goblin had been crying there all night, and using the window for a pocket-handkerchief. Now, I saw the damp lying on the bare hedges and spare grass, like a coarser sort of spiders' webs; hanging itself from twig to twig and blade to blade. On every rail and gate, wet lay clammy; and the marsh-mist was so thick, that the wooden finger on the post directing people to our village—a direction which they never accepted, for they never came there—was invisible to me until I was quite close under it. Then, as I looked up at it, while it dripped, it seemed to my oppressed conscience like a phantom devoting me to the Hulks.

The mist was heavier yet when I got out upon the marshes, so that instead of my running at everything, everything seemed to run at me. This was very disagreeable to a guilty mind. The gates and dykes and banks came bursting at me through the mist, as if they cried as plainly as could be, "A boy with Somebody-else's pork pie! Stop him!" The cattle came upon me with like suddenness, staring out of their eyes, and steaming out of their nostrils, "Holloa, young thief!" One black ox, with a white cravat on—who even had to my awakened conscience something of a clerical air°—fixed me so obstinately with his eyes, and moved his blunt head round in such an accusatory manner as I moved round, that I blubbered out to him, "I couldn't help it, sir! It wasn't for myself I took it!" Upon which he put down his head, blew a cloud of smoke out of his nose, and vanished with a kick-up of his hind-legs and a flourish of his tail.

All this time, I was getting on towards the river; but however fast I went, I couldn't warm my feet, to which the damp cold seemed riveted, as the iron was riveted to the leg of the man I was running to meet. I knew my way to the Battery, pretty straight, for I had been down there on a Sunday with Joe, and Joe, sitting on an old gun, had told me that when I was 'prentice to him regularly bound, we would have such Larks there! However, in the confusion of the mist, I found myself at last too far to the right, and consequently had to try back along the river-side, on the bank of loose stones above the mud and the stakes that staked the tide out. Making my way along here with all despatch, I had just crossed a ditch which I knew to be very near the Battery, and had just scrambled up the mound beyond the ditch, when I saw the man sitting before me. His back was towards me, and he had his arms folded, and was nodding forward, heavy with sleep.

I thought he would be more glad if I came upon him with his breakfast, in that unexpected manner, so I went forward softly and touched him on the shoulder. He instantly jumped up, and it was not the same man, but another man!

And yet this man was dressed in coarse grey, too, and had a great iron on his leg, and was lame, and hoarse, and cold, and was everything that the other man was; except that he had not the same face, and had a flat broad-brimmed low-crowned felt hat on. All this, I saw in a moment, for I had only a moment to see it in: he swore an oath at me, made a hit at me—it was a round weak blow that missed me and almost knocked himself down, for it made him stumble—and then he ran into the mist, stumbling twice as he went, and I lost him.

"It's the young man!" I thought, feeling my heart shoot as I identified him. I dare say I should have felt a pain in my liver, too, if I had known where it was.

clerical air: Looking like a clergyman.

I was soon at the Battery, after that, and there was the right man—hugging himself and limping to and fro, as if he had never all night left off hugging and limping—waiting for me. He was awfully cold, to be sure. I half expected to see him drop down before my face and die of deadly cold. His eyes looked so awfully hungry, too, that when I handed him the file and he laid it down on the grass, it occurred to me he would have tried to eat it, if he had not seen my bundle. He did not turn me upside down, this time, to get at what I had, but left me right side upwards while I opened the bundle and emptied my pockets.

"What's in the bottle, boy?" said he.

"Brandy," said I.

He was already handing mincemeat down his throat in the most curious manner—more like a man who was putting it away somewhere in a violent hurry, than a man who was eating it—but he left off to take some of the liquor. He shivered all the while, so violently, that it was quite as much as he could do to keep the neck of the bottle between his teeth, without biting it off.

"I think you have got the ague,"° said I.

"I'm much of your opinion, boy," said he.

"It's bad about here," I told him. "You've been lying out on the meshes, and they're dreadful aguish. Rheumatic, too."

"I'll eat my breakfast afore they're the death of me," said he. "I'd do that, if I was going to be strung up to that there gallows as there is over there, directly arterwards. I'll beat the shivers so far, *I'll* bet you."

He was gobbling mincemeat, meat-bone, bread, cheese, and pork pie, all at once: staring distrustfully while he did so at the mist all round us, and often stopping—even stopping his jaws—to listen. Some real or fancied sound, some clink upon the river or breathing of beast upon the marsh, now gave him a start, and he said, suddenly:

"You're not a deceiving imp? You brought no one with you?"

"No, sir! No!"

"Nor giv' no one the office° to follow you?"

"No!"

"Well," said he, "I believe you. You'd be but a fierce young hound indeed, if at your time of life you could help to hunt a wretched warmint, hunted as near death and dunghill as this poor wretched warmint is!"

Something clicked in his throat, as if he had works in him like a clock, and was going to strike. And he smeared his ragged rough sleeve over his eyes.

ague: Fever, chills.   **office:** Information.

Pitying his desolation, and watching him as he gradually settled down upon the pie, I made bold to say, "I am glad you enjoy it."

"Did you speak?"

"I said I was glad you enjoyed it."

"Thankee, my boy. I do."

I had often watched a large dog of ours eating his food; and I now noticed a decided similarity between the dog's way of eating, and the man's. The man took strong sharp sudden bites, just like the dog. He swallowed, or rather snapped up, every mouthful, too soon and too fast; and he looked sideways here and there while he ate, as if he thought there was danger in every direction, of somebody's coming to take the pie away. He was altogether too unsettled in his mind over it, to appreciate it comfortably, I thought, or to have anybody to dine with him, without making a chop with his jaws at the visitor. In all of which particulars he was very like the dog.

"I am afraid you won't leave any of it for him," said I, timidly; after a silence during which I had hesitated as to the politeness of making the remark. "There's no more to be got where that came from." It was the certainty of this fact that impelled me to offer the hint.

"Leave any for him? Who's him?" said my friend, stopping in his crunching of pie-crust.

"The young man. That you spoke of. That was hid with you."

"Oh ah!" he returned, with something like a gruff laugh. "Him? Yes, yes! *He* don't want no wittles."

"I thought he looked as if he did," said I.

The man stopped eating, and regarded me with the keenest scrutiny and the greatest surprise.

"Looked? When?"

"Just now."

"Where?"

"Yonder," said I, pointing; "over there, where I found him nodding asleep, and thought it was you."

He held me by the collar and stared at me so, that I began to think his first idea about cutting my throat had revived.

"Dressed like you, you know, only with a hat," I explained, trembling; "and—and"—I was very anxious to put this delicately—"and with—the same reason for wanting to borrow a file. Didn't you hear the cannon last night?"

"Then, there *was* firing!" he said to himself.

"I wonder you shouldn't have been sure of that," I returned, "for we heard it up at home, and that's further away, and we were shut in besides."

"Why, see now!" said he. "When a man's alone on these flats, with a light head and a light stomach, perishing of cold and want, he hears nothin' all night, but guns firing, and voices calling. Hears? He sees the soldiers, with their red coats lighted up by the torches carried afore, closing in round him. Hears his number called, hears himself challenged, hears the rattle of the muskets, hears the orders 'Make ready! Present! Cover him steady, men!' and is laid hands on—and there's nothin'! Why, if I see one pursuing party last night—coming up in order, Damn 'em, with their tramp, tramp—I see a hundred. And as to firing! Why, I see the mist shake with the cannon, arter it was broad day.—But this man;" he had said all the rest, as if he had forgotten my being there; "did you notice anything in him?"

"He had a badly bruised face," said I, recalling what I hardly knew I knew.

"Not here?" exclaimed the man, striking his left cheek mercilessly, with the flat of his hand.

"Yes, there!"

"Where is he?" He crammed what little food was left, into the breast of his grey jacket. "Show me the way he went. I'll pull him down, like a bloodhound. Curse this iron on my sore leg! Give us hold of the file, boy."

I indicated in what direction the mist had shrouded the other man, and he looked up at it for an instant. But he was down on the rank wet grass, filing at his iron like a madman, and not minding me or minding his own leg, which had an old chafe upon it and was bloody, but which he handled as roughly as if it had no more feeling in it than the file. I was very much afraid of him again, now that he had worked himself into this fierce hurry, and I was likewise very much afraid of keeping away from home any longer. I told him I must go, but he took no notice, so I thought the best thing I could do was to slip off. The last I saw of him, his head was bent over his knee and he was working hard at his fetter, muttering impatient imprecations at it and at his leg. The last I heard of him, I stopped in the mist to listen, and the file was still going.

Chapter 4

I fully expected to find a Constable in the kitchen, waiting to take me up. But not only was there no Constable there, but no discovery had yet been made of the robbery. Mrs. Joe was prodigiously busy in getting the house ready for the festivities of the day, and Joe had been put upon the kitchen door-step to keep him out of the dustpan—an article into which his destiny always led him sooner or later, when my sister was vigorously reaping the floors of her establishment.

"And where the deuce ha' *you* been?" was Mrs. Joe's Christmas salutation, when I and my conscience showed ourselves.

I said I had been down to hear the Carols. "Ah! well!" observed Mrs. Joe. "You might ha' done worse." Not a doubt of that, I thought.

"Perhaps if I warn't a blacksmith's wife, and (what's the same thing) a slave with her apron never off, *I* should have been to hear the Carols," said Mrs. Joe. "I'm rather partial to Carols, myself, and that's the best of reasons for my never hearing any."

Joe, who had ventured into the kitchen after me as the dustpan had retired before us, drew the back of his hand across his nose with a conciliatory air when Mrs. Joe darted a look at him, and, when her eyes were withdrawn, secretly crossed his two forefingers, and exhibited them to me, as our token that Mrs. Joe was in a cross temper. This was so much her normal state, that Joe and I would often, for weeks together, be, as to our fingers, like monumental Crusaders as to their legs.°

We were to have a superb dinner, consisting of a leg of pickled pork and greens, and a pair of roast stuffed fowls. A handsome mince-pie had been made yesterday morning (which accounted for the mincemeat not being missed), and the pudding was already on the boil. These extensive arrangements occasioned us to be cut off unceremoniously in respect of breakfast; "for I an't," said Mrs. Joe, "I an't a going to have no formal cramming and busting and washing up now, with what I've got before me, I promise you!"

So, we had our slices served out, as if we were two thousand troops on a forced march instead of a man and boy at home; and we took gulps of milk and water, with apologetic countenances, from a jug on the dresser. In the mean time, Mrs. Joe put clean white curtains up, and tacked a new flowered-flounce across the wide chimney to replace the old one, and uncovered the little state parlour across the passage, which was never uncovered at any other time, but passed the rest of the year in a cool haze of silver paper, which even extended to the four little white crockery poodles on the mantelshelf, each with a black nose and a basket of flowers in his mouth, and each the counterpart of

monumental . . . legs: It was believed that knights who died in the Crusades were represented on their tombs as figures with crossed legs.

the other. Mrs. Joe was a very clean housekeeper, but had an exquisite art of making her cleanliness more uncomfortable and unacceptable than dirt itself. Cleanliness is next to Godliness, and some people do the same by their religion.

My sister having so much to do, was going to church vicariously; that is to say, Joe and I were going. In his working clothes, Joe was a well-knit characteristic-looking blacksmith; in his holiday clothes, he was more like a scarecrow in good circumstances, than anything else. Nothing that he wore then, fitted him or seemed to belong to him; and everything that he wore then, grazed him. On the present festive occasion he emerged from his room, when the blithe bells were going, the picture of misery, in a full suit of Sunday penitentials. As to me, I think my sister must have had some general idea that I was a young offender whom an Accoucheur Policeman° had taken up (on my birthday) and delivered over to her, to be dealt with according to the outraged majesty of the law. I was always treated as if I had insisted on being born, in opposition to the dictates of reason, religion, and morality, and against the dissuading arguments of my best friends. Even when I was taken to have a new suit of clothes, the tailor had orders to make them like a kind of Reformatory, and on no account to let me have the free use of my limbs.

Joe and I going to church, therefore, must have been a moving spectacle for compassionate minds. Yet, what I suffered outside, was nothing to what I underwent within. The terrors that had assailed me whenever Mrs. Joe had gone near the pantry, or out of the room, were only to be equalled by the remorse with which my mind dwelt on what my hands had done. Under the weight of my wicked secret, I pondered whether the Church would be powerful enough to shield me from the vengeance of the terrible young man, if I divulged to that establishment. I conceived the idea that the time when the banns were read and when the clergyman said, "Ye are now to declare it!" would be the time for me to rise and propose a private conference in the vestry. I am far from being sure that I might not have astonished our small congregation by resorting to this extreme measure, but for its being Christmas Day and no Sunday.°

Mr. Wopsle, the clerk at church, was to dine with us; and Mr. Hubble the wheelwright and Mrs. Hubble; and Uncle Pumblechook (Joe's uncle, but Mrs. Joe appropriated him), who was a well-to-do

---

Accoucheur Policeman: Policeman serving as a midwife.   **Christmas . . . Sunday:** Announcements of intended marriages, to which members of the congregation might object, are not read on Christmas day.

corn-chandler° in the nearest town, and drove his own chaise-cart. The dinner hour was half-past one. When Joe and I got home, we found the table laid, and Mrs. Joe dressed, and the dinner dressing, and the front door unlocked (it never was, at any other time) for the company to enter by, and everything most splendid. And still, not a word of the robbery.

The time came, without bringing with it any relief to my feelings, and the company came. Mr. Wopsle, united to a Roman nose and a large shining bald forehead, had a deep voice which he was uncommonly proud of; indeed it was understood among his acquaintance that if you could only give him his head, he would read the clergyman into fits; he himself confessed that if the Church was "thrown open," meaning to competition, he would not despair of making his mark in it. The Church not being "thrown open," he was, as I have said, our clerk. But he punished the Amens tremendously; and when he gave out the psalm—always giving the whole verse—he looked all round the congregation first, as much as to say, "You have heard my friend overhead;° oblige me with your opinion of this style!"

I opened the door to the company—making believe that it was a habit of ours to open that door—and I opened it first to Mr. Wopsle, next to Mr. and Mrs. Hubble, and last of all to Uncle Pumblechook. N.B. *I* was not allowed to call him uncle, under the severest penalties.

"Mrs. Joe," said Uncle Pumblechook: a large hard-breathing middle-aged slow man, with a mouth like a fish, dull staring eyes, and sandy hair standing upright on his head, so that he looked as if he had just been all but choked, and had that moment come to; "I have brought you, as the compliments of the season—I have brought you, Mum, a bottle of sherry wine—and I have brought you, Mum, a bottle of port wine."

Every Christmas Day he presented himself, as a profound novelty, with exactly the same words, and carrying the two bottles like dumbbells. Every Christmas Day, Mrs. Joe replied, as she now replied, "Oh, Un—cle Pum—ble—chook! This is kind!" Every Christmas Day, he retorted, as he now retorted, "It's no more than your merits. And now are you all bobbish,° and how's Sixpennorth of halfpence?" meaning me.

We dined on these occasions in the kitchen, and adjourned, for the nuts and oranges and apples, to the parlour; which was a change very

---

corn-chandler: Grain merchant.   **my friend overhead:** The clergyman is seated in the pulpit above the clerk.   **bobbish:** Well, in good spirits.

like Joe's change from his working clothes to his Sunday dress. My sister was uncommonly lively on the present occasion, and indeed was generally more gracious in the society of Mrs. Hubble than in any other company. I remember Mrs. Hubble as a little curly sharp-edged person in sky-blue, who held a conventionally juvenile position, because she had married Mr. Hubble—I don't know at what remote period—when she was much younger than he. I remember Mr. Hubble as a tough high-shouldered stooping old man, of a sawdusty fragrance, with his legs extraordinarily wide apart: so that in my short days I always saw some miles of open country between them when I met him coming up the lane.

Among this good company I should have felt myself, even if I hadn't robbed the pantry, in a false position. Not because I was squeezed in at an acute angle of the tablecloth, with the table in my chest, and the Pumblechookian elbow in my eye, nor because I was not allowed to speak (I didn't want to speak), nor because I was regaled with the scaly tips of the drumsticks of the fowls, and with those obscure corners of pork of which the pig, when living, had had the least reason to be vain. No; I should not have minded that, if they would only have left me alone. But they wouldn't leave me alone. They seemed to think the opportunity lost, if they failed to point the conversation at me, every now and then, and stick the point into me. I might have been an unfortunate little bull in a Spanish arena, I got so smartingly touched up by these moral goads.

It began the moment we sat down to dinner. Mr. Wopsle said grace with theatrical declamation—as it now appears to me, something like a religious cross of the Ghost in Hamlet with Richard the Third—and ended with the very proper aspiration that we might be truly grateful. Upon which my sister fixed me with her eye, and said, in a low reproachful voice, "Do you hear that? Be grateful."

"Especially," said Mr. Pumblechook, "be grateful, boy, to them which brought you up by hand."

Mrs. Hubble shook her head, and contemplating me with a mournful presentiment that I should come to no good, asked, "Why is it that the young are never grateful?" This moral mystery seemed too much for the company until Mr. Hubble tersely solved it by saying, "Naterally wicious." Everybody then murmured "True!" and looked at me in a particularly unpleasant and personal manner.

Joe's station and influence were something feebler (if possible) when there was company, than when there was none. But he always aided and comforted me when he could, in some way of his own, and he always did so at dinner-time by giving me gravy, if there were any. There being plenty of gravy to-day, Joe spooned into my plate, at this point, about half a pint.

A little later on in the dinner, Mr. Wopsle reviewed the sermon with some severity, and intimated—in the usual hypothetical case of the Church being "thrown open"—what kind of sermon *he* would have given them. After favouring them with some heads of that discourse, he remarked that he considered the subject of the day's homily, ill chosen; which was the less excusable, he added, when there were so many subjects "going about."

"True again," said Uncle Pumblechook. "You've hit it, sir! Plenty of subjects going about, for them that know how to put salt upon their tails.° That's what's wanted. A man needn't go far to find a subject, if he's ready with his salt-box." Mr. Pumblechook added, after a short interval of reflection, "Look at Pork alone. There's a subject! If you want a subject, look at Pork!"

"True, sir. Many a moral for the young," returned Mr. Wopsle; and I knew he was going to lug me in, before he said it; "might be deduced from that text."

("You listen to this," said my sister to me, in a severe parenthesis.)

Joe gave me some more gravy.

"Swine," pursued Mr. Wopsle, in his deepest voice, and pointing his fork at my blushes, as if he were mentioning my christian name; "Swine were the companions of the prodigal. The gluttony of Swine is put before us, as an example to the young." (I thought this pretty well in him who had been praising up the pork for being so plump and juicy.) "What is detestable in a pig, is more detestable in a boy."

"Or girl," suggested Mr. Hubble.

"Of course, or girl, Mr. Hubble," assented Mr. Wopsle, rather irritably, "but there is no girl present."

"Besides," said Mr. Pumblechook, turning sharp on me, "think what you've got to be grateful for. If you'd been born a Squeaker——"

"He *was*, if ever a child was," said my sister, most emphatically.

Joe gave me some more gravy.

"Well, but I mean a four-footed Squeaker," said Mr. Pumblechook. "If you had been born such, would you have been here now? Not you——"

---

put salt upon their tails: To catch, as children are proverbially advised to catch birds by putting salt on their tails.

"Unless in that form," said Mr. Wopsle, nodding towards the dish.

"But I don't mean in that form, sir," returned Mr. Pumblechook, who had an objection to being interrupted; "I mean, enjoying himself with his elders and betters, and improving himself with their conversation, and rolling in the lap of luxury. Would he have been doing that? No, he wouldn't. And what would have been your destination?" turning on me again. "You would have been disposed of for so many shillings according to the market price of the article, and Dunstable the butcher would have come up to you as you lay in your straw, and he would have whipped you under his left arm, and with his right he would have tucked up his frock to get a pen-knife from out of his waistcoat-pocket, and he would have shed your blood and had your life. No bringing up by hand then. Not a bit of it!"

Joe offered me more gravy, which I was afraid to take.

"He was a world of trouble to you, ma'am," said Mrs. Hubble, commiserating my sister.

"Trouble?" echoed my sister; "trouble?" And then entered on a fearful catalogue of all the illnesses I had been guilty of, and all the acts of sleeplessness I had committed, and all the high places I had tumbled from, and all the low places I had tumbled into, and all the injuries I had done myself, and all the times she had wished me in my grave, and I had contumaciously refused to go there.

I think the Romans must have aggravated one another very much, with their noses. Perhaps, they became the restless people they were, in consequence. Anyhow, Mr. Wopsle's Roman nose so aggravated me, during the recital of my misdemeanours, that I should have liked to pull it until he howled. But, all I had endured up to this time, was nothing in comparison with the awful feelings that took possession of me when the pause was broken which ensued upon my sister's recital, and in which pause everybody had looked at me (as I felt painfully conscious) with indignation and abhorrence.

"Yet," said Mr. Pumblechook, leading the company gently back to the theme from which they had strayed, "Pork—regarded as biled—is rich, too; ain't it?"

"Have a little brandy, uncle," said my sister.

O Heavens, it had come at last! He would find it was weak, he would say it was weak, and I was lost! I held tight to the leg of the table under the cloth, with both hands, and awaited my fate.

My sister went for the stone bottle, came back with the stone bottle, and poured his brandy out: no one else taking any. The wretched man trifled with his glass—took it up, looked at it through the light, put it down—prolonged my misery. All this time, Mrs. Joe and Joe were briskly clearing the table for the pie and pudding.

I couldn't keep my eyes off him. Always holding tight by the leg of the table with my hands and feet, I saw the miserable creature finger his glass playfully, take it up, smile, throw his head back, and drink the brandy off. Instantly afterwards, the company were seized with unspeakable consternation, owing to his springing to his feet, turning round several times in an appalling spasmodic whooping-cough dance, and rushing out at the door; he then became visible through the window, violently plunging and expectorating, making the most hideous faces, and apparently out of his mind

I held on tight, while Mrs. Joe and Joe ran to him. I didn't know how I had done it, but I had no doubt I had murdered him somehow. In my dreadful situation, it was a relief when he was brought back, and, surveying the company all round as if *they* had disagreed with him, sank down into his chair with the one significant gasp, "Tar!"

I had filled up the bottle from the tar-water jug. I knew he would be worse by-and-by. I moved the table, like a Medium of the present day,° by the vigour of my unseen hold upon it.

"Tar!" cried my sister, in amazement. "Why, how ever could Tar come there?"

But, Uncle Pumblechook, who was omnipotent in that kitchen, wouldn't hear the word, wouldn't hear of the subject, imperiously waved it all away with his hand, and asked for hot gin-and-water. My sister, who had begun to be alarmingly meditative, had to employ herself actively in getting the gin, the hot water, the sugar, and the lemon-peel, and mixing them. For the time at least, I was saved. I still held on the leg of the table, but clutched it now with the fervour of gratitude.

By degrees, I became calm enough to release my grasp and partake of pudding. Mr. Pumblechook partook of pudding. All partook of pudding. The course terminated, and Mr. Pumblechook had begun to beam under the genial influence of gin-and-water. I began to think I should get over the day, when my sister said to Joe, "Clean plates—cold."

I clutched the leg of the table again immediately, and pressed it to my bosom as if it had been the companion of my youth and friend of my soul. I foresaw what was coming, and I felt that this time I really was gone.

Medium . . . day: Spiritualists, who claimed to be able to move objects telepathically, were a fad during the 1850s and 1860s.

"You must taste," said my sister, addressing the guests with her best grace, "you must taste, to finish with, such a delightful and delicious present of Uncle Pumblechook's!"

Must they! Let them not hope to taste it!

"You must know," said my sister, rising, "it's a pie; a savoury pork pie."

The company murmured their compliments. Uncle Pumblechook, sensible of having deserved well of his fellow-creatures, said—quite vivaciously, all things considered—"Well, Mrs. Joe, we'll do our best endeavours; let us have a cut at this same pie."

My sister went out to get it. I heard her steps proceed to the pantry. I saw Mr. Pumblechook balance his knife. I saw reawakening appetite in the Roman nostrils of Mr. Wopsle. I heard Mr. Hubble remark that "a bit of savoury pork pie would lay atop of anything you could mention, and do no harm," and I heard Joe say, "You shall have some, Pip." I have never been absolutely certain whether I uttered a shrill yell of terror, merely in spirit, or in the bodily hearing of the company. I felt that I could bear no more, and that I must run away. I released the leg of the table, and ran for my life.

But, I ran no further than the house door, for there I ran head foremost into a party of soldiers with their muskets: one of whom held out a pair of handcuffs to me, saying, "Here you are, look sharp, come on!"

[PART 3]

Chapter 5

The apparition of a file of soldiers ringing down the butt-ends of their loaded muskets on our door-step, caused the dinner-party to rise from table in confusion, and caused Mrs. Joe re-entering the kitchen empty-handed, to stop short and stare, in her wondering lament of "Gracious goodness gracious me, what's gone—with the—pie!"

The sergeant and I were in the kitchen when Mrs. Joe stood staring; at which crisis I partially recovered the use of my senses. It was the sergeant who had spoken to me, and he was now looking round at the company, with his handcuffs invitingly extended towards them in his right hand, and his left on my shoulder.

"Excuse me, ladies and gentlemen," said the sergeant, "but as I have mentioned at the door to this smart young shaver" (which he hadn't), "I am on a chase in the name of the King, and I want the blacksmith."

"And pray what might you want with *him?*" retorted my sister, quick to resent his being wanted at all.

"Missis," returned the gallant sergeant, "speaking for myself, I should reply, the honour and pleasure of his fine wife's acquaintance; speaking for the King, I answer, a little job done."

This was received as rather neat in the sergeant; insomuch that Mr. Pumblechook cried audibly, "Good again!"

"You see, blacksmith," said the sergeant, who had by this time picked out Joe with his eye, "we have had an accident with these, and I find the lock of one of 'em goes wrong, and the coupling don't act pretty. As they are wanted for immediate service, will you throw your eye over them?"

Joe threw his eye over them, and pronounced that the job would necessitate the lighting of his forge fire, and would take nearer two hours than one. "Will it? Then will you set about it at once, black-smith," said the off-hand sergeant, "as it's on his Majesty's service. And if my men can bear a hand anywhere, they'll make themselves useful." With that, he called to his men, who came trooping into the kitchen one after another, and piled their arms in a corner. And then they stood about, as soldiers do; now, with their hands loosely clasped before them; now, resting a knee or a shoulder; now, easing a belt or a pouch; now, opening the door to spit stiffly over their high stocks, out into the yard.

All these things I saw without then knowing that I saw them, for I was in an agony of apprehension. But, beginning to perceive that the handcuffs were not for me, and that the military had so far got the bet-ter of the pie as to put it in the background, I collected a little more of my scattered wits.

"Would you give me the Time?" said the sergeant, addressing himself to Mr. Pumblechook, as to a man whose appreciative powers justified the inference that he was equal to the time.

"It's just gone half-past two."

"That's not so bad," said the sergeant, reflecting; "even if I was forced to halt here nigh two hours, that'll do. How far might you call yourselves from the marshes, hereabouts? Not above a mile, I reckon?"

"Just a mile," said Mrs. Joe.

"That'll do. We begin to close in upon 'em about dusk. A little be-fore dusk, my orders are. That'll do."

"Convicts, sergeant?" asked Mr. Wopsle, in a matter-of-course way.

"Ay!" returned the sergeant, "two. They're pretty well known to be out on the marshes still, and they won't try to get clear of 'em before dusk. Anybody here seen anything of any such game?"

Everybody, myself excepted, said no, with confidence. Nobody thought of me.

"Well!" said the sergeant, "they'll find themselves trapped in a circle, I expect, sooner than they count on. Now, blacksmith! If you're ready, His Majesty the King is."

Joe had got his coat and waistcoat and cravat off, and his leather apron on, and passed into the forge. One of the soldiers opened its wooden windows, another lighted the fire, another turned to at the bellows, the rest stood round the blaze, which was soon roaring. Then Joe began to hammer and clink, hammer and clink, and we all looked on.

The interest of the impending pursuit not only absorbed the general attention, but even made my sister liberal. She drew a pitcher of beer from the cask, for the soldiers, and invited the sergeant to take a glass of brandy. But Mr. Pumblechook said, sharply, "Give him wine, Mum. I'll engage there's no Tar in that:" so, the sergeant thanked him and said that as he preferred his drink without tar, he would take wine, if it was equally convenient. When it was given him, he drank his Majesty's health and Compliments of the Season, and took it all at a mouthful and smacked his lips.

"Good stuff, eh, sergeant?" said Mr. Pumblechook.

"I'll tell you something," returned the sergeant; "I suspect that stuff's of *your* providing."

Mr. Pumblechook, with a fat sort of laugh, said, "Ay, ay? Why?"

"Because," returned the sergeant, clapping him on the shoulder, "you're a man that knows what's what."

"D'ye think so?" said Mr. Pumblechook, with his former laugh. "Have another glass!"

"With you. Hob and nob," returned the sergeant. "The top of mine to the foot of yours—the foot of yours to the top of mine°— Ring once, ring twice—the best tune on the Musical Glasses! Your health. May you live a thousand years, and never be a worse judge of the right sort than you are at the present moment of your life!"

The . . . mine: A saying used when two people drink a toast to each other while touching glasses.

The sergeant tossed off his glass again and seemed quite ready for another glass. I noticed that Mr. Pumblechook in his hospitality appeared to forget that he had made a present of the wine, but took the bottle from Mrs. Joe and had all the credit of handing it about in a gush of joviality. Even I got some. And he was so very free of the wine that he even called for the other bottle and handed that about with the same liberality, when the first was gone.

As I watched them while they all stood clustering about the forge, enjoying themselves so much, I thought what terrible good sauce for a dinner my fugitive friend on the marshes was. They had not enjoyed themselves a quarter so much, before the entertainment was brightened with the excitement he furnished. And now, when they were all in lively anticipation of "the two villains" being taken, and when the bellows seemed to roar for the fugitives, the fire to flare for them, the smoke to hurry away in pursuit of them, Joe to hammer and clink for them, and all the murky shadows on the wall to shake at them in menace as the blaze rose and sank and the red-hot sparks dropped and died, the pale afternoon outside, almost seemed in my pitying young fancy to have turned pale on their account, poor wretches.

At last, Joe's job was done, and the ringing and roaring stopped. As Joe got on his coat, he mustered courage to propose that some of us should go down with the soldiers and see what came of the hunt. Mr. Pumblechook and Mr. Hubble declined, on the plea of a pipe and ladies' society; but Mr. Wopsle said he would go, if Joe would. Joe said he was agreeable, and would take me, if Mrs. Joe approved. We never should have got leave to go, I am sure, but for Mrs. Joe's curiosity to know all about it and how it ended. As it was, she merely stipulated, "If you bring the boy back with his head blown to bits by a musket, don't look to me to put it together again."

The sergeant took a polite leave of the ladies, and parted from Mr. Pumblechook as from a comrade; though I doubt if he were quite as fully sensible of that gentleman's merits under arid conditions, as when something moist was going. His men resumed their muskets and fell in. Mr. Wopsle, Joe, and I, received strict charge to keep in the rear, and to speak no word after we reached the marshes. When we were all out in the raw air and were steadily moving towards our business, I treasonably whispered to Joe, "I hope, Joe, we shan't find them." And Joe whispered to me, "I'd give a shilling if they had cut and run, Pip."

We were joined by no stragglers from the village, for the weather was cold and threatening, the way dreary, the footing bad, darkness coming on, and the people had good fires in-doors and were keeping the day. A few faces hurried to glowing windows and looked after us, but none came out. We passed the finger-post, and held straight on to the churchyard. There, we were stopped a few minutes by a signal from the sergeant's hand, while two or three of his men dispersed themselves among the graves, and also examined the porch. They came in again without finding anything, and then we struck out on the open marshes, through the gate at the side of the churchyard. A bitter sleet came rattling against us here on the east wind, and Joe took me on his back.

Now that we were out upon the dismal wilderness where they little thought I had been within eight or nine hours and had seen both men hiding, I considered for the first time, with great dread, if we should come upon them, would my particular convict suppose that it was I who had brought the soldiers there? He had asked me if I was a deceiving imp, and he had said I should be a fierce young hound if I joined the hunt against him. Would he believe that I was both imp and hound in treacherous earnest, and had betrayed him?

It was of no use asking myself this question now. There I was, on Joe's back, and there was Joe beneath me, charging at the ditches like a hunter, and stimulating Mr. Wopsle not to tumble on his Roman nose, and to keep up with us. The soldiers were in front of us, extended into a pretty wide line with an interval between man and man. We were taking the course I had begun with, and from which I had diverged in the mist. Either the mist was not out again yet, or the wind had dispelled it. Under the low red glare of sunset, the beacon, and the gibbet, and the mound of the Battery, and the opposite shore of the river, were plain, though all of a watery lead colour.

With my heart thumping like a blacksmith at Joe's broad shoulder, I looked all about for any sign of the convicts. I could see none, I could hear none. Mr. Wopsle had greatly alarmed me more than once, by his blowing and hard breathing; but I knew the sounds by this time, and could dissociate them from the object of pursuit. I got a dreadful start, when I thought I heard the file still going; but it was only a sheep bell. The sheep stopped in their eating and looked timidly at us; and the cattle, their heads turned from the wind and sleet, stared angrily as if they held us responsible for both annoyances; but, except these things, and the shudder of the dying day in every blade of grass, there was no break in the bleak stillness of the marshes.

The soldiers were moving on in the direction of the old Battery, and we were moving on a little way behind them, when, all of a sud-

den, we all stopped. For, there had reached us on the wings of the
wind and rain, a long shout. It was repeated. It was at a distance towards the east, but it was long and loud. Nay, there seemed to be two
or more shouts raised together—if one might judge from a confusion
in the sound.

To this effect the sergeant and the nearest men were speaking
under their breath, when Joe and I came up. After another moment's
listening, Joe (who was a good judge) agreed, and Mr. Wopsle (who
was a bad judge) agreed. The sergeant, a decisive man, ordered that
the sound should not be answered, but that the course should be
changed, and that his men should make towards it "at the double." So
we slanted to the right (where the East was), and Joe pounded away so
wonderfully, that I had to hold on tight to keep my seat.

It was a run indeed now, and what Joe called, in the only two
words he spoke all the time, "a Winder." Down banks and up banks,
and over gates, and splashing into dykes, and breaking among coarse
rushes: no man cared where he went. As we came nearer to the shout-
ing, it became more and more apparent that it was made by more than
one voice. Sometimes, it seemed to stop altogether, and then the soldiers stopped. When it broke out again, the soldiers made for it at a
greater rate than ever, and we after them. After a while, we had so run
it down, that we could hear one voice calling "Murder!" and another
voice, "Convicts! Runaways! Guard! This way for the runaway convicts!" Then both voices would seem to be stifled in a struggle, and
then would break out again. And when it had come to this, the soldiers ran like deer, and Joe too.

The sergeant ran in first, when we had run the noise quite down,
and two of his men ran in close upon him. Their pieces were cocked
and levelled when we all ran in.

"Here are both men!" panted the sergeant, struggling at the bottom of a ditch. "Surrender, you two! and confound you for two wild
beasts! Come asunder!"

Water was splashing, and mud was flying, and oaths were being
sworn, and blows were being struck, when some more men went
down into the ditch to help the sergeant, and dragged out, separately,
my convict and the other one. Both were bleeding and panting and
execrating and struggling; but of course I knew them both directly.

"Mind!" said my convict, wiping blood from his face with his
ragged sleeves, and shaking torn hair from his fingers; "*I* took him! *I*
give him up to you! Mind that!"

"It's not much to be particular about," said the sergeant; "it'll do you small good, my man, being in the same plight yourself. Handcuffs there!"

"I don't expect it to do me any good. I don't want it to do me more good than it does now," said my convict, with a greedy laugh. "I took him. He knows it. That's enough for me."

The other convict was livid to look at, and, in addition to the old bruised left side of his face, seemed to be bruised and torn all over. He could not so much as get his breath to speak, until they were both separately handcuffed, but leaned upon a soldier to keep himself from falling.

"Take notice, guard—he tried to murder me," were his first words.

"Tried to murder him?" said my convict, disdainfully. "Try, and not do it? I took him, and giv' him up; that's what I done. I not only prevented him getting off the marshes, but I dragged him here— dragged him this far on his way back. He's a gentleman, if you please, this villain. Now, the Hulks has got its gentleman again, through me. Murder him? Worth my while, too, to murder him, when I could do worse and drag him back!"

The other one still gasped, "He tried—he tried—to—murder me. Bear—bear witness."

"Lookee here!" said my convict to the sergeant. "Single-handed I got clear of the prison-ship; I made a dash and I done it. I could ha' got clear of these death-cold flats likewise—look at my leg: you won't find much iron on it—if I hadn't made discovery that *he* was here. Let *him* go free? Let *him* profit by the means as I found out? Let *him* make a tool of me afresh and again? Once more? No, no, no. If I had died at the bottom there;" and he made an emphatic swing at the ditch with his manacled hands; "I'd have held to him with that grip, that you should have been safe to find him in my hold."

The other fugitive, who was evidently in extreme horror of his companion, repeated, "He tried to murder me. I should have been a dead man if you had not come up."

"He lies!" said my convict, with fierce energy. "He's a liar born, and he'll die a liar. Look at his face; ain't it written there? Let him turn those eyes of his on me. I defy him to do it."

The other, with an effort at a scornful smile—which could not, however, collect the nervous working of his mouth into any set expression—looked at the soldiers, and looked about at the marshes and at the sky, but certainly did not look at the speaker.

"Do you see him?" pursued my convict. "Do you see what a villain he is? Do you see those grovelling and wandering eyes? That's how he looked when we were tried together. He never looked at me."

The other, always working and working his dry lips and turning his eyes restlessly about him far and near, did at last turn them for a moment on the speaker, with the words, "You are not much to look at," and with a half-taunting glance at the bound hands. At that point, my convict became so frantically exasperated, that he would have rushed upon him but for the interposition of the soldiers. "Didn't I tell you," said the other convict then, "that he would murder me, if he could?" And any one could see that he shook with fear, and that there broke out upon his lips, curious white flakes, like thin snow.

"Enough of this parley," said the sergeant. "Light those torches."

As one of the soldiers, who carried a basket in lieu of a gun, went down on his knee to open it, my convict looked round him for the first time, and saw me. I had alighted from Joe's back on the brink of the ditch when we came up, and had not moved since. I looked at him eagerly when he looked at me, and slightly moved my hands and shook my head. I had been waiting for him to see me, that I might try to assure him of my innocence. It was not at all expressed to me that he even comprehended my intention, for he gave me a look that I did not understand, and it all passed in a moment. But if he had looked at me for an hour or for a day, I could not have remembered his face ever afterwards, as having been more attentive.

The soldier with the basket soon got a light, and lighted three or four torches, and took one himself and distributed the others. It had been almost dark before, but now it seemed quite dark, and soon afterwards very dark. Before we departed from that spot, four soldiers standing in a ring, fired twice into the air. Presently we saw other torches kindled at some distance behind us, and others on the marshes on the opposite bank of the river. "All right," said the sergeant. "March."

We had not gone far when three cannon were fired ahead of us with a sound that seemed to burst something inside my ear. "You are expected on board," said the sergeant to my convict; "they know you are coming. Don't straggle, my man. Close up here."

The two were kept apart, and each walked surrounded by a separate guard. I had hold of Joe's hand now, and Joe carried one of the torches. Mr. Wopsle had been for going back, but Joe was resolved to see it out, so we went on with the party. There was a reasonably good path now, mostly on the edge of the river, with a divergence here and there where a dyke came, with a miniature windmill on it and a muddy sluice-gate. When I looked round, I could see the other lights coming in after us. The torches we carried, dropped great blotches of fire upon the track, and I could see those, too, lying smoking and flaring. I could see nothing else but black darkness. Our lights warmed the air about us with their pitchy blaze, and the two prisoners seemed rather to like that, as they limped along in the midst of the muskets. We could not go fast, because of their lameness; and they were so spent, that two or three times we had to halt while they rested.

After an hour or so of this travelling, we came to a rough wooden hut and a landing-place. There was a guard in the hut, and they challenged, and the sergeant answered. Then, we went into the hut where there was a smell of tobacco and whitewash, and a bright fire, and a lamp, and a stand of muskets, and a drum, and a low wooden bedstead, like an overgrown mangle without the machinery,° capable of holding about a dozen soldiers all at once. Three or four soldiers who lay upon it in their great-coats, were not much interested in us, but just lifted their heads and took a sleepy stare, and then lay down again. The sergeant made some kind of report, and some entry in a book, and then the convict whom I call the other convict was drafted off with his guard, to go on board first.

My convict never looked at me, except that once. While we stood in the hut, he stood before the fire looking thoughtfully at it, or putting up his feet by turns upon the hob, and looking thoughtfully at them as if he pitied them for their recent adventures. Suddenly, he turned to the sergeant, and remarked:

"I wish to say something respecting this escape. It may prevent some persons laying under suspicion alonger me."

"You can say what you like," returned the sergeant, standing coolly looking at him with his arms folded, "but you have no call to say it here. You'll have opportunity enough to say about it, and hear about it, before it's done with, you know."

"I know, but this is another pint, a separate matter. A man can't starve; at least *I* can't. I took some wittles, up at the willage over yonder—where the church stands a'most out on the marshes."

"You mean stole," said the sergeant.

"And I'll tell you where from. From the blacksmith's."

"Halloa!" said the sergeant, staring at Joe.

mangle without the machinery: A clothes wringer without its roller.

"Halloa, Pip!" said Joe, staring at me.

"It was some broken wittles—that's what it was—and a dram of liquor, and a pie."

"Have you happened to miss such an article as a pie, blacksmith?" asked the sergeant, confidentially.

"My wife did, at the very moment when you came in. Don't you know, Pip?"

"So," said my convict, turning his eyes on Joe in a moody manner, and without the least glance at me; "so you're the blacksmith, are you? Then I'm sorry to say, I've eat your pie."

"God knows you're welcome to it—so far as it was ever mine," returned Joe, with a saving remembrance of Mrs. Joe. "We don't know what you have done, but we wouldn't have you starved to death for it, poor miserable fellow-creatur.—Would us, Pip?"

The something that I had noticed before, clicked in the man's throat again, and he turned his back. The boat had returned, and his guard were ready, so we followed him to the landing-place made of rough stakes and stones, and saw him put into the boat, which was rowed by a crew of convicts like himself. No one seemed surprised to see him, or interested in seeing him, or glad to see him, or sorry to see him, or spoke a word, except that somebody in the boat growled as if to dogs, "Give way, you!" which was the signal for the dip of the oars. By the light of the torches, we saw the black Hulk lying out a little way from the mud of the shore, like a wicked Noah's ark. Cribbed and barred and moored by massive rusty chains, the prison-ship seemed in my young eyes to be ironed like the prisoners. We saw the boat go alongside, and we saw him taken up the side and disappear. Then, the ends of the torches were flung hissing into the water, and went out, as if it were all over with him.

[PART 4]

Chapter 6

My state of mind regarding the pilfering from which I had been so unexpectedly exonerated, did not impel me to frank disclosure; but I hope it had some dregs of good at the bottom of it.

I do not recal that I felt any tenderness of conscience in reference to Mrs. Joe, when the fear of being found out was lifted off me. But I loved Joe—perhaps for no better reason in those early days than because the dear fellow let me love him—and, as to him, my inner self was not so easily composed. It was much upon my mind (particularly when I first saw him looking about for his file) that I ought to tell Joe the whole truth. Yet I did not, and for the reason that I mistrusted that if I did, he would think me worse than I was. The fear of losing Joe's confidence, and of thenceforth sitting in the chimney corner at night staring drearily at my for ever lost companion and friend, tied up my tongue. I morbidly represented to myself that if Joe knew it, I never afterwards could see him at the fireside feeling his fair whisker, without thinking that he was meditating on it. That, if Joe knew it, I never afterwards could see him glance, however casually, at yesterday's meat or pudding when it came on to-day's table, without thinking that he was debating whether I had been in the pantry. That, if Joe knew it, and at any subsequent period of our joint domestic life re-marked that his beer was flat or thick, the conviction that he suspected Tar in it, would bring a rush of blood to my face. In a word, I was too cowardly to do what I knew to be right, as I had been too cowardly to avoid doing what I knew to be wrong. I had had no intercourse with the world at that time, and I imitated none of its many inhabitants who act in this manner. Quite an untaught genius, I made the discov-ery of the line of action for myself.

As I was sleepy before we were far away from the prison-ship, Joe took me on his back again and carried me home. He must have had a tiresome journey of it, for Mr. Wopsle, being knocked up, was in such a very bad temper that if the Church had been thrown open, he would probably have excommunicated the whole expedition, beginning with Joe and myself. In his lay capacity, he persisted in sitting down in the damp to such an insane extent, that when his coat was taken off to be dried at the kitchen fire, the circumstantial evidence on his trousers would have hanged him if it had been a capital offence.

By that time, I was staggering on the kitchen floor like a little drunkard, through having been newly set upon my feet, and through having been fast asleep, and through waking in the heat and lights and noise of tongues. As I came to myself (with the aid of a heavy thump between the shoulders, and the restorative exclamation "Yah! Was there ever such a boy as this!" from my sister), I found Joe telling them about the convict's confession, and all the visitors suggesting different ways by which he had got into the pantry. Mr. Pumblechook made out, after carefully surveying the premises, that he had first got upon the roof of the forge, and had then got upon the roof of the house, and had then let himself down the kitchen chimney by a rope made of his bedding cut into strips; and as Mr. Pumblechook was very positive and drove his own chaise-cart—over everybody—it was agreed that it must be so. Mr. Wopsle, indeed, wildly cried out "No!" with the feeble malice of a tired man; but, as he had no theory, and no coat on, he was unanimously set at naught—not to mention his smoking hard behind, as he stood with his back to the kitchen fire to draw the damp out: which was not calculated to inspire confidence.

This was all I heard that night before my sister clutched me, as a slumberous offence to the company's eyesight, and assisted me up to bed with such a strong hand that I seemed to have fifty boots on, and to be dangling them all against the edges of the stairs. My state of mind, as I have described it, began before I was up in the morning, and lasted long after the subject had died out, and had ceased to be mentioned saving on exceptional occasions.

Chapter 7

At the time when I stood in the churchyard, reading the family tombstones, I had just enough learning to be able to spell them out. My construction even of their simple meaning was not very correct, for I read "wife of the Above" as a complimentary reference to my father's exaltation to a better world; and if any one of my deceased relations had been referred to as "Below," I have no doubt I should have formed the worst opinions of that member of the family. Neither, were my notions of the theological positions to which my Catechism bound me, at all accurate; for, I have a lively remembrance that I supposed my declaration that I was to "walk in the same all the days of my life," laid me under an obligation always to go through the village from our house in one particular direction, and never to vary it by turning down by the wheelwright's or up by the mill.

When I was old enough, I was to be apprenticed to Joe, and until I could assume that dignity I was not to be what Mrs. Joe called "Pompeyed," or (as I render it) pampered. Therefore, I was not only odd-boy about the forge, but if any neighbour happened to want an extra boy to frighten birds, or pick up stones, or do any such job, I was favoured with the employment. In order, however, that our superior position might not be compromised thereby, a money-box was kept on the kitchen mantelshelf, into which it was publicly made known that all my earnings were dropped. I have an impression that they were to be contributed eventually towards the liquidation of the National

Debt, but I know I had no hope of any personal participation in the treasure.

Mr. Wopsle's great-aunt kept an evening school° in the village; that is to say, she was a ridiculous old woman of limited means and unlimited infirmity, who used to go to sleep from six to seven every evening, in the society of youth who paid twopence per week each, for the improving opportunity of seeing her do it. She rented a small cottage, and Mr. Wopsle had the room up-stairs, where we students used to overhear him reading aloud in a most dignified and terrific manner, and occasionally bumping on the ceiling. There was a fiction that Mr. Wopsle "examined" the scholars, once a quarter. What he did on those occasions, was to turn up his cuffs, stick up his hair, and give us Mark Antony's oration over the body of Cæsar. This was always followed by Collins's Ode on the Passions,° wherein I particularly venerated Mr. Wopsle as Revenge, throwing his blood-stain'd sword in thunder down, and taking the War denouncing trumpet with a withering look. It was not with me then, as it was in later life, when I fell into the society of the Passions, and compared them with Collins and Wopsle, rather to the disadvantage of both gentlemen.

Mr. Wopsle's great-aunt, besides keeping this Educational Institution, kept—in the same room—a little general shop. She had no idea what stock she had, or what the price of anything in it was; but there was a little greasy memorandum-book kept in a drawer, which served as a Catalogue of Prices, and by this oracle Biddy arranged all the shop transactions. Biddy was Mr. Wopsle's great-aunt's granddaughter; I confess myself quite unequal to the working-out of the problem, what relation she was to Mr. Wopsle. She was an orphan like myself; like me, too, had been brought up by hand. She was most noticeable, I thought, in respect of her extremities; for, her hair always wanted brushing, her hands always wanted washing, and her shoes always wanted mending and pulling up at heel. This description must be received with a week-day limitation. On Sundays, she went to church elaborated.

Much of my unassisted self, and more by the help of Biddy than of Mr. Wopsle's great-aunt, I struggled through the alphabet as if it had been a bramble-bush; getting considerably worried and scratched by every letter. After that, I fell among those thieves, the nine figures, who seemed every evening to do something new to disguise

---

evening school: An elementary school or dame-school, often run by a poorly educated woman.   **Mark . . . Passions:** Passages from Shakespeare's *Julius Caesar* and from an ode by William Collins (1721–1759).

themselves and baffle recognition. But, at last I began, in a purblind groping way, to read, write, and cipher, on the very smallest scale.

One night, I was sitting in the chimney corner with my slate, expending great efforts on the production of a letter to Joe. I think it must have been a full year after our hunt upon the marshes, for it was a long time after, and it was winter and a hard frost. With an alphabet on the hearth at my feet for reference, I contrived in an hour or two to print and smear this epistle:

"mI deEr JO i opE U r krWitE wEll i opE i shAl soN B haBelL 4 2 teeDge U JO aN theN wE shOrl b sO glOdd aN wEn i M preNgtD 2 u JO woT larX an blEvE ME inF xn PiP."

There was no indispensable necessity for my communicating with Joe by letter, inasmuch as he sat beside me and we were alone. But, I delivered this written communication (slate and all) with my own hand, and Joe received it as a miracle of erudition.

"I say, Pip, old chap!" cried Joe, opening his blue eyes wide, "what a scholar you are! An't you?"

"I should like to be," said I, glancing at the slate as he held it: with a misgiving that the writing was rather hilly.

"Why, here's a J," said Joe, "and a O equal to anythink! Here's a J and a O, Pip, and a J-O, Joe."

I had never heard Joe read aloud to any greater extent than this monosyllable, and I had observed at church last Sunday when I accidentally held our Prayer-Book upside down, that it seemed to suit his convenience quite as well as if it had been all right. Wishing to embrace the present occasion of finding out whether in teaching Joe, I should have to begin quite at the beginning, I said, "Ah! But read the rest, Joe."

"The rest, eh, Pip?" said Joe, looking at it with a slowly searching eye, "One, two, three. Why, here's three Js, and three Os, and three J-O, Joes in it, Pip!"

I leaned over Joe, and, with the aid of my forefinger, read him the whole letter.

"Astonishing!" said Joe, when I had finished. "You ARE a scholar."

"How do you spell Gargery, Joe?" I asked him, with a modest patronage.

"I don't spell it at all," said Joe.

"But supposing you did?"

"It *can't* be supposed," said Joe. "Tho' I'm oncommon fond of reading, too."

"Are you, Joe?"

"On-common. Give me," said Joe, "a good book, or a good news-paper, and sit me down afore a good fire, and I ask no better. Lord!" he continued, after rubbing his knees a little, "when you *do* come to a J and a O, and says you, 'Here, at last, is a J-O, Joe,' how interesting reading is!"

I derived from this, that Joe's education, like Steam, was yet in its infancy. Pursuing the subject, I inquired:

"Didn't you ever go to school, Joe, when you were as little as me?"

"No, Pip."

"Why didn't you ever go to school, Joe, when you were as little as me?"

"Well, Pip," said Joe, taking up the poker, and settling himself to his usual occupation when he was thoughtful, of slowly raking the fire between the lower bars: "I'll tell you. My father, Pip, he were given to drink, and when he were overtook with drink, he hammered away at my mother, most onmerciful. It were a'most the only hammering he did, indeed, 'xcepting at myself. And he hammered at me with a wigour only to be equalled by the wigour with which he didn't ham-mer at his anwil.—You're a listening and understanding, Pip?"

"Yes, Joe."

" 'Consequence, my mother and me we ran away from my father, several times; and then my mother she'd go out to work, and she'd say, 'Joe,' she'd say, 'now, please God, you shall have some schooling, child,' and she'd put me to school. But my father were that good in his hart that he couldn't abear to be without us. So, he'd come with a most tremenjous crowd and make such a row at the doors of the houses where we was, that they used to be obligated to have no more to do with us and to give us up to him. And then he took us home and hammered us. Which, you see, Pip," said Joe, pausing in his medita-tive raking of the fire, and looking at me, "were a drawback on my learning."

"Certainly, poor Joe!"

"Though mind you, Pip," said Joe, with a judicial touch or two of the poker on the top bar, "rendering unto all their doo, and maintain-ing equal justice betwixt man and man, my father were that good in his hart, don't you see?"

I didn't see; but I didn't say so.

"Well!" Joe pursued, "somebody must keep the pot a biling, Pip, or the pot won't bile, don't you know?"

I saw that, and said so.

" 'Consequence, my father didn't make objections to my going to work; so I went to work at my present calling, which were his too, if he would have followed it, and I worked tolerable hard, I assure *you*, Pip. In time I were able to keep him, and I kep him till he went off in a purple leptic° fit. And it were my intentions to have had put upon his tombstone that Whatsume'er the failings on his part, Remember reader he were that good in his hart."

Joe recited this couplet with such manifest pride and careful perspicuity, that I asked him if he had made it himself?

"I made it," said Joe, "my own self. I made it in a moment. It was like striking out a horseshoe complete, in a single blow. I never was so much surprised in all my life—couldn't credit my own ed—to tell you the truth, hardly believed it *were* my own ed. As I was saying, Pip, it were my intentions to have had it cut over him; but poetry costs money, cut it how you will, small or large, and it were not done. Not to mention bearers, all the money that could be spared were wanted for my mother. She were in poor elth, and quite broke. She weren't long of following, poor soul, and her share of peace come round at last."

Joe's blue eyes turned a little watery; he rubbed, first one of them, and then the other, in a most uncongenial and uncomfortable manner, with the round knob on the top of the poker.

"It were but lonesome then," said Joe, "living here alone, and I got acquainted with your sister. Now, Pip;" Joe looked firmly at me, as if he knew I was not going to agree with him; "your sister is a fine figure of a woman."

I could not help looking at the fire, in an obvious state of doubt.

"Whatever family opinions, or whatever the world's opinions, on that subject may be, Pip, your sister is," Joe tapped the top bar with the poker after every word following, "a—fine—figure—of—a—woman!"

I could think of nothing better to say than "I am glad you think so, Joe."

"So am I," returned Joe, catching me up. "*I* am glad I think so, Pip. A little redness, or a little matter of Bone, here or there, what does it signify to Me?"

I sagaciously observed, if it didn't signify to him, to whom did it signify?

a purple leptic: Apoplectic: seizure, stroke.

"Certainly!" assented Joe. "That's it. You're right, old chap! When I got acquainted with your sister, it were the talk how she was bringing you up by hand. Very kind of her too, all the folks said, and I said, along with all the folks. As to you," Joe pursued, with a countenance expressive of seeing something very nasty indeed: "if you could have been aware how small and flabby and mean you was, dear me, you'd have formed the most contemptible opinions of yourself!"

Not exactly relishing this, I said, "Never mind me, Joe."

"But I did mind you, Pip," he returned, with tender simplicity. "When I offered to your sister to keep company, and to be asked in church at such times as she was willing and ready to come to the forge, I said to her, 'And bring the poor little child. God bless the poor little child,' I said to your sister, 'there's room for *him* at the forge!' "

I broke out crying and begging pardon, and hugged Joe round the neck: who dropped the poker to hug me, and to say, "Ever the best of friends; an't us, Pip? Don't cry, old chap!"

When this little interruption was over, Joe resumed:

"Well, you see, Pip, and here we are! That's about where it lights; here we are! Now, when you take me in hand in my learning, Pip (and I tell you beforehand I am awful dull, most awful dull), Mrs. Joe mustn't see too much of what we're up to. It must be done, as I may say, on the sly. And why on the sly? I'll tell you why, Pip."

He had taken up the poker again; without which, I doubt if he could have proceeded in his demonstration.

"Your sister is given to government."

"Given to government, Joe?" I was startled, for I had some shadowy idea (and I am afraid I must add, hope) that Joe had divorced her in favour of the Lords of the Admiralty, or Treasury.

"Given to government," said Joe. "Which I meantersay the government of you and myself."

"Oh!"

"And she an't over partial to having scholars on the premises," Joe continued, "and in partickler would not be over partial to my being a scholar, for fear as I might rise. Like a sort of rebel, don't you see?"

I was going to retort with an inquiry, and had got as far as "Why——" when Joe stopped me.

"Stay a bit. I know what you're a going to say, Pip; stay a bit! I don't deny that your sister comes the Mo-gul over us, now and again. I don't deny that she do throw us back-falls,° and that she do drop

back-falls: Throws in wrestling.

down upon us heavy. At such times as when your sister is on the Rampage, Pip," Joe sank his voice to a whisper and glanced at the door, "candour compels fur to admit that she is a Buster."

Joe pronounced this word, as if it began with at least twelve capital Bs.

"Why don't I rise? That were your observation when I broke it off, Pip?"

"Yes, Joe."

"Well," said Joe, passing the poker into his left hand, that he might feel his whisker; and I had no hope of him whenever he took to that placid occupation; "your sister's a master-mind. A master-mind."

"What's that?" I asked, in some hope of bringing him to a stand. But, Joe was readier with his definition than I had expected, and completely stopped me by arguing circularly, and answering with a fixed look, "Her."

"And I an't a master-mind," Joe resumed, when had unfixed his look, and got back to his whisker. "And last of all, Pip—and this I want to say very serous to you, old chap—I see so much in my poor mother, of a woman drudging and slaving and breaking her honest hart and never getting no peace in her mortal days, that I'm dead afeerd of going wrong in the way of not doing what's right by a woman, and I'd fur rather of the two go wrong the t'other way, and be a little ill-conwenienced myself. I wish it was only me that got put out, Pip; I wish there warn't no Tickler for you, old chap; I wish I could take it all on myself; but this is the up-and-down-and-straight on it, Pip, and I hope you'll overlook shortcomings."

Young as I was, I believe that I dated a new admiration of Joe from that night. We were equals afterwards, as we had been before; but, afterwards at quiet times when I sat looking at Joe and thinking about him, I had a new sensation of feeling conscious that I was looking up to Joe in my heart.

"However," said Joe, rising to replenish the fire; "here's the Dutch-clock a working himself up to being equal to strike Eight of 'em, and she's not come home yet! I hope Uncle Pumblechook's mare mayn't have set a fore-foot on a piece o' ice, and gone down."

Mrs. Joe made occasional trips with Uncle Pumblechook on market-days, to assist him in buying such household stuffs and goods as required a woman's judgment; Uncle Pumblechook being a bachelor and reposing no confidences in his domestic servant. This was market-day, and Mrs. Joe was out on one of these expeditions.

Joe made the fire and swept the hearth, and then we went to the door to listen for the chaise-cart. It was a dry cold night, and the wind blew keenly, and the frost was white and hard. A man would die tonight of lying out on the marshes, I thought. And then I looked at the stars, and considered how awful it would be for a man to turn his face up to them as he froze to death, and see no help or pity in all the glittering multitude.

"Here comes the mare," said Joe, "ringing like a peal of bells!"

The sound of her iron shoes upon the hard road was quite musical, as she came along at a much brisker trot than usual. We got a chair out, ready for Mrs. Joe's alighting, and stirred up the fire that they might see a bright window, and took a final survey of the kitchen that nothing might be out of its place. When we had completed these preparations, they drove up, wrapped to the eyes. Mrs. Joe was soon landed, and Uncle Pumblechook was soon down too, covering the mare with a cloth, and we were soon all in the kitchen, carrying so much cold air in with us that it seemed to drive all the heat out of the fire.

"Now," said Mrs. Joe, unwrapping herself with haste and excitement, and throwing her bonnet back on her shoulders where it hung by the strings: "if this boy an't grateful this night, he never will be!"

I looked as grateful as any boy possibly could, who was wholly uninformed why he ought to assume that expression.

"It's only to be hoped," said my sister, "that he won't be Pompeyed. But I have my fears."

"She an't in that line, Mum," said Mr. Pumblechook. "She knows better."

She? I looked at Joe, making the motion with my lips and eyebrows, "She?" Joe looked at me, making the motion with *his* lips and eyebrows, "She?" My sister catching him in the act, he drew the back of his hand across his nose with his usual conciliatory air on such occasions, and looked at her.

"Well?" said my sister, in her snappish way. "What are you staring at? Is the house a-fire?"

"—Which some individual," Joe politely hinted, "mentioned—she."

"And she is a she, I suppose?" said my sister. "Unless you call Miss Havisham a he. And I doubt if even you'll go so far as that."

"Miss Havisham, up town?" said Joe.

"Is there any Miss Havisham down town?" returned my sister. "She wants this boy to go and play there. And of course he's going. And he had better play there," said my sister, shaking her head at me as an encouragement to be extremely light and sportive, "or I'll work him."

I had heard of Miss Havisham up town—everybody for miles round, had heard of Miss Havisham up town—as an immensely rich and grim lady who lived in a large and dismal house barricaded against robbers, and who led a life of seclusion.

"Well to be sure!" said Joe, astounded. "I wonder how she come to know Pip!"

"Noodle!" cried my sister. "Who said she knew him?"

"—Which some individual," Joe again politely hinted, "mentioned that she wanted him to go and play there."

"And couldn't she ask Uncle Pumblechook if he knew of a boy to go and play there? Isn't it just barely possible that Uncle Pumblechook may be a tenant of hers, and that he may sometimes—we won't say quarterly or half yearly, for that would be requiring too much of you—but sometimes—go there to pay his rent? And couldn't she then ask Uncle Pumblechook if he knew of a boy to go and play there? And couldn't Uncle Pumblechook, being always considerate and thoughtful for us—though you may not think it, Joseph," in a tone of the deepest reproach, as if he were the most callous of nephews, "then mention this boy, standing Prancing here"—which I solemnly declare I was not doing—"that I have for ever been a willing slave to?"

"Good again!" cried Uncle Pumblechook. "Well put! Prettily pointed! Good indeed! Now Joseph, you know the case."

"No, Joseph," said my sister, still in a reproachful manner, while Joe apologetically drew the back of his hand across and across his nose, "you do not yet—though you may not think it—know the case. You may consider that you do, but you do *not*, Joseph. For you do not know that Uncle Pumblechook, being sensible that for anything we can tell, this boy's fortune may be made by his going to Miss Havisham's, has offered to take him into town to-night in his own chaise-cart, and to keep him to-night, and to take him with his own hands to Miss Havisham's to-morrow morning. And Lor-a-mussy me!" cried my sister, casting off her bonnet in sudden desperation, "here I stand talking to mere Mooncalfs, with Uncle Pumblechook waiting, and the mare catching cold at the door, and the boy grimed with crock and dirt from the hair of his head to the sole of his foot!"

With that, she pounced upon me, like an eagle on a lamb, and my face was squeezed into wooden bowls in sinks, and my head was put under taps of water-butts, and I was soaped, and kneaded, and towelled, and thumped, and harrowed, and rasped, until I really was quite beside myself. (I may here remark that I suppose myself to be better acquainted than any living authority, with the ridgy effect of a wedding-ring, passing unsympathetically over the human countenance.)

When my ablutions were completed, I was put into clean linen of the stiffest character, like a young penitent into sackcloth, and was trussed up in my tightest and fearfullest suit. I was then delivered over to Mr. Pumblechook, who formally received me as if he were the Sheriff, and who let off upon me the speech that I knew he had been dying to make all along: "Boy, be for ever grateful to all friends, but especially unto them which brought you up by hand!"

"Good-by, Joe!"

"God bless you, Pip, old chap!"

I had never parted from him before, and what with my feelings and what with soapsuds, I could at first see no stars from the chaise-cart. But they twinkled out one by one, without throwing any light on the questions why on earth I was going to play at Miss Havisham's, and what on earth I was expected to play at.

[PART 5]

Chapter 8

Mr. Pumblechook's premises in the High-street of the market town, were of a pepper-corny and farinaceous character, as the premises of a corn-chandler and seedsman should be. It appeared to me that he must be a very happy man indeed, to have so many little drawers in his shop; and I wondered when I peeped into one or two on the lower tiers, and saw the tied-up brown paper packets inside, whether the flower-seeds and bulbs ever wanted of a fine day to break out of those jails, and bloom.

It was in the early morning after my arrival that I entertained this speculation. On the previous night, I had been sent straight to bed in an attic with a sloping roof, which was so low in the corner where the bedstead was, that I calculated the tiles as being within a foot of my eyebrows. In the same early morning, I discovered a singular affinity between seeds and corduroys. Mr. Pumblechook wore corduroys, and so did his shopman; and somehow, there was a general air and flavour about the corduroys, so much in the nature of seeds, and a general air and flavour about the seeds, so much in the nature of corduroys, that I hardly knew which was which. The same opportunity served me for noticing that Mr. Pumblechook appeared to conduct his business by looking across the street at the saddler, who appeared to transact *his* business by keeping his eye on the coachmaker, who appeared to get on in life by putting his hands in his pockets and contemplating the baker, who in his turn folded his arms and stared at the grocer, who stood at his door and yawned at the chemist. The watchmaker, always poring over a little desk with a magnifying glass at his eye, and always inspected by a group in smock-frocks poring over him through the glass of his shop-window, seemed to be about the only person in the High-street whose trade engaged his attention.

Mr. Pumblechook and I breakfasted at eight o'clock in the parlour behind the shop, while the shopman took his mug of tea and hunch of bread-and-butter on a sack of peas in the front premises. I considered Mr. Pumblechook wretched company. Besides being possessed by my sister's idea that a mortifying and penitential character ought to be imparted to my diet—besides giving me as much crumb as possible in combination with as little butter, and putting such a quantity of warm water into my milk that it would have been more candid to have left the milk out altogether—his conversation consisted of nothing but arithmetic. On my politely bidding him Good morning, he said, pompously, "Seven times nine, boy!" And how should *I* be able to answer, dodged in that way, in a strange place, on an empty stomach! I was hungry, but before I had swallowed a morsel, he began a running sum that lasted all through the breakfast. "Seven?" "And four?" "And eight?" "And six?" "And two?" "And ten?" And so on. And after each figure was disposed of, it was as much as I could do to get a bite or a sup, before the next came; while he sat at his ease guessing nothing, and eating bacon and hot roll, in (if I may be allowed the expression) a gorging and gormandising manner.

For such reasons, I was very glad when ten o'clock came and we started for Miss Havisham's; though I was not at all at my ease regarding the manner in which I should acquit myself under that lady's roof. Within a quarter of an hour we came to Miss Havisham's house, which was of old brick, and dismal, and had a great many iron bars to it. Some of the windows had been walled up; of those that remained, all the lower were rustily barred. There was a court-yard in front, and that was barred; so, we had to wait, after ringing the bell, until some one should come to open it. While we waited at the gate, I peeped in (even then Mr. Pumblechook said, "And fourteen?" but I pretended not to hear him), and saw that at the side of the house there was a large brewery. No brewing was going on in it, and none seemed to have gone on for a long long time.

A window was raised, and a clear voice demanded "What name?" To which my conductor replied, "Pumblechook." The voice returned, "Quite right," and the window was shut again, and a young lady came across the court-yard, with keys in her hand.

"This," said Mr. Pumblechook, "is Pip."

"This is Pip, is it?" returned the young lady, who was very pretty and seemed very proud; "come in, Pip."

Mr. Pumblechook was coming in also, when she stopped him with the gate.

"Oh!" she said. "Did you wish to see Miss Havisham?"

"If Miss Havisham wished to see me," returned Mr. Pumblechook, discomfited.

"Ah!" said the girl; "but you see she don't."

She said it so finally, and in such an undiscussible way, that Mr. Pumblechook, though in a condition of ruffled dignity, could not protest. But he eyed me severely—as if *I* had done anything to him!—and departed with the words reproachfully delivered: "Boy! Let your behaviour here be a credit unto them which brought you up by hand!" I was not free from apprehension that he would come back to propound through the gate, "And sixteen?" But he didn't.

My young conductress locked the gate, and we went across the court-yard. It was paved and clean, but grass was growing in every crevice. The brewery buildings had a little lane of communication with it; and the wooden gates of that lane stood open, and all the brewery beyond, stood open, away to the high enclosing wall; and all was empty and disused. The cold wind seemed to blow colder there, than outside the gate; and it made a shrill noise in howling in and out at the open sides of the brewery, like the noise of wind in the rigging of a ship at sea.

She saw me looking at it, and she said, "You could drink without hurt all the strong beer that's brewed there now, boy."

"I should think I could, miss," said I, in a shy way.

"Better not try to brew beer there now, or it would turn out sour, boy; don't you think so?"

"It looks like it, miss."

"Not that anybody means to try," she added, "for that's all done with, and the place will stand as idle as it is, till it falls. As to strong beer, there's enough of it in the cellars already, to drown the Manor House."

"Is that the name of this house, miss?"

"One of its names, boy."

"It has more than one, then, miss?"

"One more. Its other name was Satis; which is Greek, or Latin, or Hebrew, or all three—or all one to me—for enough."

"Enough House," said I; "that's a curious name, miss."

"Yes," she replied; "but it meant more than it said. It meant, when it was given, that whoever had this house, could want nothing else. They must have been easily satisfied in those days, I should think. But don't loiter, boy."

Though she called me "boy" so often, and with a carelessness that was far from complimentary, she was of about my own age. She seemed much older than I, of course, being a girl, and beautiful and self-possessed; and she was as scornful of me as if she had been one-and-twenty, and a queen.

We went into the house by a side door—the great front entrance had two chains across it outside—and the first thing I noticed was, that the passages were all dark, and that she had left a candle burning there. She took it up, and we went through more passages and up a staircase, and still it was all dark, and only the candle lighted us.

At last we came to the door of a room, and she said, "Go in."

I answered more in shyness than politeness, "After you, miss."

To this, she returned: "Don't be ridiculous, boy; I am not going in." And scornfully walked away, and—what was worse—took the candle with her.

This was very uncomfortable, and I was half afraid. However, the only thing to be done being to knock at the door, I knocked, and was told from within to enter. I entered, therefore, and found myself in a pretty large room, well lighted with wax candles. No glimpse of day-light was to be seen in it. It was a dressing-room, as I supposed from the furniture, though much of it was of forms and uses then quite un-known to me. But prominent in it was a draped table with a gilded looking-glass, and that I made out at first sight to be a fine lady's dressing-table.

Whether I should have made out this object so soon, if there had been no fine lady sitting at it, I cannot say. In an arm-chair, with an elbow resting on the table and her head leaning on that hand, sat the strangest lady I have ever seen, or shall ever see.

She was dressed in rich materials—satins, and lace, and silks—all of white. Her shoes were white. And she had a long white veil depen-dent from her hair, and she had bridal flowers in her hair, but her hair was white. Some bright jewels sparkled on her neck and on her hands, and some other jewels lay sparkling on the table. Dresses, less splendid than the dress she wore, and half-packed trunks, were scattered about. She had not quite finished dressing, for she had but one shoe on — the other was on the table near her hand — her veil was but half arranged, her watch and chain were not put on, and some lace for her bosom lay with those trinkets, and with her handkerchief, and gloves, and some flowers, and a prayer-book, all confusedly heaped about the looking-glass.

It was not in the first moments that I saw all these things, though I saw more of them in the first moments than might be supposed. But, I saw that everything within my view which ought to be white, had been white long ago, and had lost its lustre, and was faded and yellow. I saw that the bride within the bridal dress had withered like the dress, and like the flowers, and had no brightness left but the brightness of her sunken eyes. I saw that the dress had been put upon the rounded figure of a young woman, and that the figure upon which it now hung loose, had shrunk to skin and bone. Once, I had been taken to see some ghastly wax-work at the Fair, representing I know not what impossible personage lying in state. Once, I had been taken to one of our old marsh churches to see a skeleton in the ashes of a rich dress, that had been dug out of a vault under the church pavement. Now, wax-work and skeleton seemed to have dark eyes that moved and looked at me. I should have cried out, if I could.

"Who is it?" said the lady at the table.

"Pip, ma'am."

"Pip?"

"Mr. Pumblechook's boy, ma'am. Come — to play."

"Come nearer; let me look at you. Come close."

It was when I stood before her, avoiding her eyes, that I took note of the surrounding objects in detail, and saw that her watch had stopped at twenty minutes to nine, and that a clock in the room had stopped at twenty minutes to nine.

"Look at me," said Miss Havisham. "You are not afraid of a woman who has never seen the sun since you were born?"

I regret to state that I was not afraid of telling the enormous lie comprehended in the answer "No."

"Do you know what I touch here?" she said, laying her hands, one upon the other, on her left side.

"Yes, ma'am." (It made me think of the young man.)

"What do I touch?"

"Your heart."

"Broken!"

She uttered the word with an eager look, and with strong emphasis, and with a weird smile that had a kind of boast in it. Afterwards, she kept her hands there for a little while, and slowly took them away as if they were heavy.

"I am tired," said Miss Havisham. "I want diversion, and I have done with men and women. Play."

I think it will be conceded by my most disputatious reader, that she could hardly have directed an unfortunate boy to do anything in the wide world more difficult to be done under the circumstances.

"I sometimes have sick fancies," she went on, "and I have a sick fancy that I want to see some play. There, there!" with an impatient movement of the fingers of her right hand; "play, play, play!"

For a moment, with the fear of my sister's working me before my eyes, I had a desperate idea of starting round the room in the assumed character of Mr. Pumblechook's chaise-cart. But, I felt myself so unequal to the performance that I gave it up, and stood looking at Miss Havisham in what I suppose she took for a dogged manner, inasmuch as she said, when we had taken a good look at each other:

"Are you sullen and obstinate?"

"No, ma'am, I am very sorry for you, and very sorry I can't play just now. If you complain of me I shall get into trouble with my sister, so I would do it if I could; but it's so new here, and so strange, and so fine—and melancholy——" I stopped, fearing I might say too much, or had already said it, and we took another look at each other.

Before she spoke again, she turned her eyes from me, and looked at the dress she wore, and at the dressing-table, and finally at herself in the looking-glass.

"So new to him," she muttered, "so old to me; so strange to him, so familiar to me; so melancholy to both of us! Call Estella."

As she was still looking at the reflexion of herself, I thought she was still talking to herself, and kept quiet.

"Call Estella," she repeated, flashing a look at me. "You can do that. Call Estella. At the door."

To stand in the dark in a mysterious passage of an unknown house, bawling Estella to a scornful young lady neither visible nor responsive, and feeling it a dreadful liberty so to roar out her name, was almost as bad as playing to order. But, she answered at last, and her light came along the long dark passage like a star.

Miss Havisham beckoned her to come close, and took up a jewel from the table, and tried its effect upon her fair young bosom and against her pretty brown hair. "Your own, one day, my dear, and you will use it well. Let me see you play cards with this boy."

"With this boy! Why, he is a common labouring-boy!"

I thought I overheard Miss Havisham answer—only it seemed so unlikely—"Well? You can break his heart."

"What do you play, boy?" asked Estella of myself, with the greatest disdain.

"Nothing but beggar my neighbour, miss."

"Beggar him," said Miss Havisham to Estella. So we sat down to cards.

It was then I began to understand that everything in the room had stopped, like the watch and the clock, a long time ago. I noticed that Miss Havisham put down the jewel exactly on the spot from which she had taken it up. As Estella dealt the cards, I glanced at the dressing-table again, and saw that the shoe upon it, once white, now yellow, had never been worn. I glanced down at the foot from which the shoe was absent, and saw that the silk stocking on it, once white, now yellow, had been trodden ragged. Without this arrest of everything, this standing still of all the pale decayed objects, not even the withered bridal dress on the collapsed form could have looked so like grave-clothes, or the long veil so like a shroud.

So she sat, corpse-like, as we played at cards; the frillings and trimmings on her bridal dress, looking like earthy paper. I knew nothing then, of the discoveries that are occasionally made of bodies buried in ancient times, which fall to powder in the moment of being distinctly seen; but, I have often thought since, that she must have looked as if the admission of the natural light of day would have struck her to dust.

"He calls the knaves, Jacks,° this boy!" said Estella with disdain, before our first game was out. "And what coarse hands he has. And what thick boots!"

I had never thought of being ashamed of my hands before; but I began to consider them a very indifferent pair. Her contempt was so strong, that it became infectious, and I caught it.

She won the game, and I dealt. I misdealt, as was only natural, when I knew she was lying in wait for me to do wrong; and she denounced me for a stupid, clumsy labouring-boy.

Jacks: A lower-class term for servants or laborers.

"You say nothing of her," remarked Miss Havisham to me, as she looked on. "She says many hard things of you, but you say nothing of her. What do you think of her?"

"I don't like to say," I stammered.

"Tell me in my ear," said Miss Havisham, bending down.

"I think she is very proud," I replied, in a whisper.

"Anything else?"

"I think she is very pretty."

"Anything else?"

"I think she is very insulting." (She was looking at me then, with a look of supreme aversion.)

"Anything else?"

"I think I should like to go home."

"And never see her again, though she is so pretty?"

"I am not sure that I shouldn't like to see her again, but I should like to go home now."

"You shall go soon," said Miss Havisham, aloud. "Play the game out."

Saving for the one weird smile at first, I should have felt almost sure that Miss Havisham's face could not smile. It had dropped into a watchful and brooding expression—most likely when all the things about her had become transfixed—and it looked as if nothing could ever lift it up again. Her chest had dropped, so that she stooped; and her voice had dropped, so that she spoke low, and with a dead lull upon her; altogether, she had the appearance of having dropped, body and soul, within and without, under the weight of a crushing blow.

I played the game to an end with Estella, and she beggared me. She threw the cards down on the table when she had won them all, as if she despised them for having been won of me.

"When shall I have you here again?" said Miss Havisham. "Let me think."

I was beginning to remind her that to-day was Wednesday, when she checked me with her former impatient movement of the fingers of her right hand.

"There, there! I know nothing of days of the week; I know nothing of weeks of the year. Come again after six days. You hear?"

"Yes, ma'am."

"Estella, take him down. Let him have something to eat, and let him roam and look about him while he eats. Go, Pip."

I followed the candle down, as I had followed the candle up, and she stood it in the place where we had found it. Until she opened the side entrance, I had fancied, without thinking about it, that it must necessarily be night-time. The rush of the daylight quite confounded me, and made me feel as if I had been in the candlelight of the strange room many hours.

"You are to wait here, you boy," said Estella; and disappeared and closed the door.

I took the opportunity of being alone in the court-yard, to look at my coarse hands and my common boots. My opinion of those accessories was not favourable. They had never troubled me before, but they troubled me now, as vulgar appendages. I determined to ask Joe why he had ever taught me to call those picture-cards, Jacks, which ought to be called knaves. I wished Joe had been rather more genteelly brought up, and then I should have been so too.

She came back, with some bread and meat and a little mug of beer. She put the mug down on the stones of the yard, and gave me the bread and meat without looking at me, as insolently as if I were a dog in disgrace. I was so humiliated, hurt, spurned, offended, angry, sorry—I cannot hit upon the right name for the smart—God knows what its name was—that tears started to my eyes. The moment they sprang there, the girl looked at me with a quick delight in having been the cause of them. This gave me power to keep them back and to look at her: so, she gave a contemptuous toss—but with a sense, I thought, of having made too sure that I was so wounded—and left me.

But, when she was gone, I looked about me for a place to hide my face in, and got behind one of the gates in the brewery-lane, and leaned my sleeve against the wall there, and leaned my forehead on it and cried. As I cried, I kicked the wall, and took a hard twist at my hair; so bitter were my feelings, and so sharp was the smart without a name, that needed counteraction.

My sister's bringing up had made me sensitive. In the little world in which children have their existence whosoever brings them up, there is nothing so finely perceived and so finely felt, as injustice. It may be only small injustice that the child can be exposed to; but the child is small, and its world is small, and its rocking-horse stands as many hands high, according to scale, as a big-boned Irish hunter.° Within myself, I had sustained, from my babyhood, a perpetual con-

---

big-boned Irish hunter: A large horse bred for hunting.

flict with injustice. I had known, from the time when I could speak,
that my sister, in her capricious and violent coercion, was unjust to
me. I had cherished a profound conviction that her bringing me up by
hand, gave her no right to bring me up by jerks. Through all my punishments, disgraces, fasts and vigils, and other penitential performances, I had nursed this assurance; and to my communing so much
with it, in a solitary and unprotected way, I in great part refer the fact
that I was morally timid and very sensitive.

I got rid of my injured feelings for the time, by kicking them into
the brewery wall, and twisting them out of my hair, and then I
smoothed my face with my sleeve, and came from behind the gate.
The bread and meat were acceptable, and the beer was warming and
tingling, and I was soon in spirits to look about me.

To be sure, it was a deserted place, down to the pigeon-house in
the brewery-yard, which had been blown crooked on its pole by some
high wind, and would have made the pigeons think themselves at sea,
if there had been any pigeons there to be rocked by it. But, there were
no pigeons in the dovecot, no horses in the stable, no pigs in the sty,
no malt in the storehouse, no smells of grains and beer in the copper
or the vat. All the uses and scents of the brewery might have evaporated with its last reek of smoke. In a by-yard, there was a wilderness of
empty casks, which had a certain sour remembrance of better days lingering about them; but it was too sour to be accepted as a sample of
the beer that was gone — and in this respect I remember those recluses
as being like most others.

Behind the furthest end of the brewery, was a rank garden with an
old wall: not so high but that I could struggle up and hold on long
enough to look over it, and see that the rank garden was the garden of
the house, and that it was overgrown with tangled weeds, but that
there was a track upon the green and yellow paths, as if some one
sometimes walked there, and that Estella was walking away from me
even then. But she seemed to be everywhere. For, when I yielded to
the temptation presented by the casks, and began to walk on them, I
saw *her* walking on them at the end of the yard of casks. She had her
back towards me, and held her pretty brown hair spread out in her two
hands, and never looked round, and passed out of my view directly.
So, in the brewery itself—by which I mean the large paved lofty place
in which they used to make the beer, and where the brewing utensils
still were. When I first went into it, and, rather oppressed by its
gloom, stood near the door looking about me, I saw her pass among

the extinguished fires, and ascend some light iron stairs, and go out by a gallery high overhead, as if she were going out into the sky.

It was in this place, and at this moment, that a strange thing happened to my fancy. I thought it a strange thing then, and I thought it a stranger thing long afterwards. I turned my eyes—a little dimmed by looking up at the frosty light—towards a great wooden beam in a low nook of the building near me on my right hand, and I saw a figure hanging there by the neck. A figure all in yellow white, with but one shoe to the feet; and it hung so, that I could see that the faded trimmings of the dress were like earthy paper, and that the face was Miss Havisham's, with a movement going over the whole countenance as if she were trying to call to me. In the terror of seeing the figure, and in the terror of being certain that it had not been there a moment before, I at first ran from it, and then ran towards it. And my terror was greatest of all, when I found no figure there.

Nothing less than the frosty light of the cheerful sky, the sight of people passing beyond the bars of the court-yard gate, and the reviving influence of the rest of the bread and meat and beer, would have brought me round. Even with those aids, I might not have come to myself as soon as I did, but that I saw Estella approaching with the keys, to let me out. She would have some fair reason for looking down upon me, I thought, if she saw me frightened; and she should have no fair reason.

She gave me a triumphant glance in passing me, as if she rejoiced that my hands were so coarse and my boots were so thick, and she opened the gate, and stood holding it. I was passing out without looking at her, when she touched me with a taunting hand.

"Why don't you cry?"

"Because I don't want to."

"You do," said she. "You have been crying till you are half blind, and you are near crying again now."

She laughed contemptuously, pushed me out, and locked the gate upon me. I went straight to Mr. Pumblechook's, and was immensely relieved to find him not at home. So, leaving word with the shopman on what day I was wanted at Miss Havisham's again, I set off on the four-mile walk to our forge; pondering, as I went along, on all I had seen, and deeply revolving that I was a common labouring-boy; that my hands were coarse, that my boots were thick; that I had fallen into a despicable habit of calling knaves Jacks; that I was much more ignorant than I had considered myself last night, and generally that I was in a low-lived bad way.

[PART 6]

Chapter 9

When I reached home, my sister was very curious to know all about Miss Havisham's, and asked a number of questions. And I soon found myself getting heavily bumped from behind in the nape of the neck and the small of the back, and having my face ignominiously shoved against the kitchen wall, because I did not answer those questions at sufficient length.

If a dread of not being understood be hidden in the breasts of other young people to anything like the extent to which it used to be hidden in mine—which I consider probable, as I have no particular reason to suspect myself of having been a monstrosity—it is the key to many reservations. I felt convinced that if I described Miss Havisham's as my eyes had seen it, I should not be understood. Not only that, but I felt convinced that Miss Havisham too would not be understood; and although she was perfectly incomprehensible to me, I entertained an impression that there would be something coarse and treacherous in my dragging her as she really was (to say nothing of Miss Estella) before the contemplation of Mrs. Joe. Consequently, I said as little as I could, and had my face shoved against the kitchen wall.

The worst of it was that that bullying old Pumblechook, preyed upon by a devouring curiosity to be informed of all I had seen and heard, came gaping over in his chaise-cart at tea-time, to have the details divulged to him. And the mere sight of the torment, with his fishy eyes and mouth open, his sandy hair inquisitively on end, and his waistcoat heaving with windy arithmetic, made me vicious in my reticence.

"Well, boy," Uncle Pumblechook began, as soon as he was seated in the chair of honour by the fire. "How did you get on up town?"

I answered, "Pretty well, sir," and my sister shook her fist at me.

"Pretty well?" Mr. Pumblechook repeated. "Pretty well is no answer. Tell us what you mean by pretty well, boy?"

Whitewash on the forehead hardens the brain into a state of obstinacy perhaps. Anyhow, with whitewash from the wall on my forehead, my obstinacy was adamantine. I reflected for some time, and then answered as if I had discovered a new idea, "I mean pretty well."

My sister with an exclamation of impatience was going to fly at me —I had no shadow of defence, for Joe was busy in the forge—when Mr. Pumblechook interposed with "No! Don't lose your temper.

Leave this lad to me, ma'am; leave this lad to me." Mr. Pumblechook then turned me towards him, as if he were going to cut my hair, and said:

"First (to get our thoughts in order): Forty-three pence?"

I calculated the consequences of replying "Four Hundred Pound," and finding them against me, went as near the answer as I could — which was somewhere about eight-pence off. Mr. Pumblechook then put me through my pence-table from "twelve pence making one shilling," up to "forty pence make three and fourpence," and then triumphantly demanded, as if he had done for me, "*Now!* How much is forty-three pence?" To which I replied, after a long interval of reflection, "I don't know." And I was so aggravated that I almost doubt if I did know.

Mr. Pumblechook worked his head like a screw to screw it out of me, and said, "Is forty-three pence seven and sixpence three fardens, for instance?"

"Yes!" said I. And although my sister instantly boxed my ears, it was highly gratifying to me to see that the answer spoilt his joke, and brought him to a dead stop.

"Boy! What like is Miss Havisham?" Mr. Pumblechook began again when he had recovered; folding his arms tight on his chest and applying the screw.

"Very tall and dark," I told him.

"Is she, uncle?" asked my sister.

Mr. Pumblechook winked assent; from which I at once inferred that he had never seen Miss Havisham, for she was nothing of the kind.

"Good!" said Mr. Pumblechook, conceitedly. ("This is the way to have him! We are beginning to hold our own, I think, Mum?")

"I am sure, uncle," returned Mrs. Joe, "I wish you had him always: you know so well how to deal with him."

"Now, boy! What was she a doing of, when you went in to-day?" asked Mr. Pumblechook.

"She was sitting," I answered, "in a black velvet coach."

Mr. Pumblechook and Mrs. Joe stared at one another — as they well might — and both repeated, "In a black velvet coach?"

"Yes," said I. "And Miss Estella — that's her niece, I think — handed her in cake and wine at the coach-window, on a gold plate. And we all had cake and wine on gold plates. And I got up behind the coach to eat mine, because she told me to."

"Was anybody else there?" asked Mr. Pumblechook.

"Four dogs," said I.

"Large or small?"

"Immense," said I. "And they fought for veal-cutlets out of a silver basket."

Mr. Pumblechook and Mrs. Joe stared at one another again, in utter amazement. I was perfectly frantic—a reckless witness under the torture—and would have told them anything.

"Where *was* this coach, in the name of gracious?" asked my sister.

"In Miss Havisham's room." They stared again. "But there weren't any horses to it." I added this saving clause, in the moment of rejecting four richly caparisoned coursers which I had had wild thoughts of harnessing.

"Can this be possible, uncle?" asked Mrs. Joe. "What can the boy mean?"

"I'll tell you, Mum," said Mr. Pumblechook. "My opinion is, it's a sedan-chair. She's flighty, you know—very flighty—quite flighty enough to pass her days in a sedan-chair."

"Did you ever see her in it, uncle?" asked Mrs. Joe.

"How could I?" he returned, forced to the admission, "when I never see her in my life? Never clapped eyes upon her!"

"Goodness, uncle! And yet you have spoken to her?"

"Why, don't you know," said Mr. Pumblechook, testily, "that when I have been there, I have been took up to the outside of her door, and the door has stood ajar, and she has spoke to me that way. Don't say you don't know *that*, Mum. Howsever, the boy went there to play. What did you play at, boy?"

"We played with flags," I said. (I beg to observe that I think of myself with amazement, when I recal the lies I told on this occasion.)

"Flags!" echoed my sister.

"Yes," said I. "Estella waved a blue flag, and I waved a red one, and Miss Havisham waved one sprinkled all over with little gold stars, out at the coach-window. And then we all waved our swords and hurrahed."

"Swords!" repeated my sister. "Where did you get swords from?"

"Out of a cupboard," said I. "And I saw pistols in it—and jam— and pills. And there was no daylight in the room, but it was all lighted up with candles."

"That's true, Mum," said Mr. Pumblechook, with a grave nod. "That's the state of the case, for that much I've seen myself." And then they both stared at me, and I, with an obtrusive show of artlessness on my countenance, stared at them, and plaited the right leg of my trousers with my right hand.

If they had asked me any more questions I should undoubtedly have betrayed myself, for I was even then on the point of mentioning that there was a balloon in the yard, and should have hazarded the statement but for my invention being divided between that phenomenon and a bear in the brewery. They were so much occupied, however, in discussing the marvels I had already presented for their consideration, that I escaped. The subject still held them when Joe came in from his work to have a cup of tea. To whom my sister, more for the relief of her own mind than for the gratification of his, related my pretended experiences.

Now, when I saw Joe open his blue eyes and roll them all round the kitchen in helpless amazement, I was overtaken by penitence; but only as regarded him—not in the least as regarded the other two. Towards Joe, and Joe only, I considered myself a young monster, while they sat debating what results would come to me from Miss Havisham's acquaintance and favour. They had no doubt that Miss Havisham would "do something" for me; their doubts related to the form that something would take. My sister stood out for "property." Mr. Pumblechook was in favour of a handsome premium for binding me apprentice to some genteel trade—say, the corn and seed trade, for instance. Joe fell into the deepest disgrace with both, for offering the bright suggestion that I might only be presented with one of the dogs who had fought for the veal-cutlets. "If a fool's head can't express better opinions than that," said my sister, "and you have got any work to do, you had better go and do it." So he went.

After Mr. Pumblechook had driven off, and when my sister was washing up, I stole into the forge to Joe, and remained by him until he had done for the night. Then I said, "Before the fire goes out, Joe, I should like to tell you something."

"Should you, Pip?" said Joe, drawing his shoeing-stool near the forge. "Then tell us. What is it, Pip?"

"Joe," said I, taking hold of his rolled-up shirt sleeve, and twisting it between my finger and thumb, "you remember all that about Miss Havisham's?"

"Remember?" said Joe. "I believe you! Wonderful!"

"It's a terrible thing, Joe; it ain't true."

"What are you telling of, Pip?" cried Joe, falling back in the greatest amazement. "You don't mean to say it's——"

"Yes I do; it's lies, Joe."

"But not all of it? Why sure you don't mean to say, Pip, that there was no black welwet co——eh?" For, I stood shaking my head. "But at least there was dogs, Pip. Come, Pip," said Joe, persuasively, "if there warn't no weal-cutlets, at least there was dogs?"

"No, Joe."

"*A* dog?" said Joe. "A puppy? Come?"

"No, Joe, there was nothing at all of the kind."

As I fixed my eyes hopelessly on Joe, Joe contemplated me in dismay. "Pip, old chap! This won't do, old fellow! I say! Where do you expect to go to?"

"It's terrible, Joe; an't it?"

"Terrible?" cried Joe. "Awful! What possessed you?"

"I don't know what possessed me, Joe," I replied, letting his shirt sleeve go, and sitting down in the ashes at his feet, hanging my head; "but I wish you hadn't taught me to call Knaves at cards, Jacks; and I wish my boots weren't so thick nor my hands so coarse."

And then I told Joe that I felt very miserable, and that I hadn't been able to explain myself to Mrs. Joe and Pumblechook who were so rude to me, and that there had been a beautiful young lady at Miss Havisham's who was dreadfully proud, and that she had said I was common, and that I knew I was common, and that I wished I was not common, and that the lies had come of it somehow, though I didn't know how.

This was a case of metaphysics, at least as difficult for Joe to deal with, as for me. But Joe took the case altogether out of the region of metaphysics, and by that means vanquished it.

"There's one thing you may be sure of, Pip," said Joe, after some rumination, "namely, that lies is lies. Howsever they come, they didn't ought to come, and they come from the father of lies, and work round to the same. Don't you tell no more of 'em, Pip. *That* ain't the way to get out of being common, old chap. And as to being common, I don't make it out at all clear. You are oncommon in some things. You're oncommon small. Likewise you're a oncommon scholar."

"No, I am ignorant and backward, Joe."

"Why, see what a letter you wrote last night. Wrote in print even! I've seen letters—Ah! and from gentlefolks!—that I'll swear weren't wrote in print," said Joe.

"I have learnt next to nothing, Joe. You think much of me. It's only that."

"Well, Pip," said Joe, "be it so or be it son't, you must be a common scholar afore you can be a oncommon one, I should hope! The king upon his throne, with his crown upon his ed, can't sit and write his acts of Parliament in print, without having begun, when he were a unpromoted Prince, with the alphabet—Ah!" added Joe, with a shake of the head that was full of meaning, "and begun at A too, and worked his way to Z. And *I* know what that is to do, though I can't say I've exactly done it."

There was some hope in this piece of wisdom, and it rather encouraged me.

"Whether common ones as to callings and earnings," pursued Joe, reflectively, "mightn't be the better of continuing for to keep company with common ones, instead of going out to play with oncommon ones—which reminds me to hope that there were a flag, perhaps?"

"No, Joe."

"(I'm sorry there weren't a flag, Pip.) Whether that might be or mightn't be, is a thing as can't be looked into now, without putting your sister on the Rampage; and that's a thing not to be thought of, as being done intentional. Lookee here, Pip, at what is said to you by a true friend. Which this to you the true friend say. If you can't get to be oncommon through going straight, you'll never get to do it through going crooked. So don't tell no more on 'em, Pip, and live well and die happy."

"You are not angry with me, Joe?"

"No, old chap. But bearing in mind that them were which I meantersay of a stunning and outdacious sort—alluding to them which bordered on weal-cutlets and dog-fighting—a sincere well-wisher would adwise, Pip, their being dropped into your meditations, when you go up-stairs to bed. That's all, old chap, and don't never do it no more."

When I got up to my little room and said my prayers, I did not forget Joe's recommendation, and yet my young mind was in that disturbed and unthankful state, that I thought long after I laid me down, how common Estella would consider Joe, a mere blacksmith: how thick his boots, and how coarse his hands. I thought how Joe and my sister were then sitting in the kitchen, and how I had come up to bed from the kitchen, and how Miss Havisham and Estella never sat in a kitchen, but were far above the level of such common doings. I fell asleep recalling what I "used to do" when I was at Miss Havisham's; as though I had been there weeks or months, instead of hours; and as though it were quite an old subject of remembrance, instead of one that had arisen only that day.

That was a memorable day to me, for it made great changes in me. But, it is the same with any life. Imagine one selected day struck out of it, and think how different its course would have been. Pause you who read this, and think for a moment of the long chain of iron or gold, of thorns or flowers, that would never have bound you, but for the formation of the first link on one memorable day.

Chapter 10

The felicitous idea occurred to me a morning or two later when I woke, that the best step I could take towards making myself uncommon was to get out of Biddy everything she knew. In pursuance of this luminous conception I mentioned to Biddy when I went to Mr. Wopsle's great-aunt's at night, that I had a particular reason for wishing to get on in life, and that I should feel very much obliged to her if she would impart all her learning to me. Biddy, who was the most obliging of girls, immediately said she would, and indeed began to carry out her promise within five minutes.

The Educational scheme or Course established by Mr. Wopsle's great-aunt may be resolved into the following synopsis. The pupils ate apples and put straws up one another's backs, until Mr. Wopsle's great-aunt collected her energies, and made an indiscriminate totter at them with a birch-rod. After receiving the charge with every mark of derision, the pupils formed in line and buzzingly passed a ragged book from hand to hand. The book had an alphabet in it, some figures and tables, and a little spelling—that is to say, it had had once. As soon as this volume began to circulate, Mr. Wopsle's great-aunt fell into a state of coma; arising either from sleep or a rheumatic paroxysm. The pupils then entered among themselves upon a competitive examination on the subject of Boots, with the view of ascertaining who could tread the hardest upon whose toes. This mental exercise lasted until Biddy made a rush at them and distributed three defaced Bibles (shaped as if they had been unskilfully cut off the chump-end of something), more illegibly printed at the best than any curiosities of literature I have since met with, speckled all over with ironmould, and having various specimens of the insect world smashed between their leaves. This part of the Course was usually lightened by several single combats between Biddy and refractory students. When the fights were over, Biddy gave out the number of a page, and then we all read aloud what we could—or what we couldn't—in a frightful chorus; Biddy leading with a high shrill monotonous voice, and none of us having the least notion of, or reverence for, what we were reading about. When this horrible din had lasted a certain time, it mechanically awoke Mr. Wopsle's great-aunt, who staggered at a boy fortuitously, and pulled his ears. This was understood to terminate the Course for the evening, and we emerged into the air with shrieks of intellectual victory. It is fair to remark that there was no prohibition against any pupil's entertaining himself with a slate or even with the ink (when there was any), but that it was not easy to pursue that branch of study in the winter season, on account of the little general shop in which the classes were holden—and which was also Mr. Wopsle's great-aunt's sitting-room and bed-chamber—being but faintly illuminated through the agency of one low-spirited dip-candle and no snuffers.

It appeared to me that it would take time, to become uncommon under these circumstances: nevertheless, I resolved to try it, and that very evening Biddy entered on our special agreement, by imparting some information from her little catalogue of Prices, under the head of moist sugar, and lending me, to copy at home, a large old English D which she had imitated from the heading of some newspaper, and which I supposed, until she told me what it was, to be a design for a buckle.

Of course there was a public-house in the village, and of course Joe liked sometimes to smoke his pipe there. I had received strict orders from my sister to call for him at the Three Jolly Bargemen, that evening, on my way from school, and bring him home at my peril. To the Three Jolly Bargemen, therefore, I directed my steps.

There was a bar at the Jolly Bargemen, with some alarmingly long chalk scores° in it on the wall at the side of the door, which seemed to me to be never paid off. They had been there ever since I could remember, and had grown more than I had. But there was a quantity of chalk about our country, and perhaps the people neglected no opportunity of turning it to account.

It being Saturday night, I found the landlord looking rather grimly at these records, but as my business was with Joe and not with him, I merely wished him good evening, and passed into the common room at the end of the passage, where there was a bright large kitchen fire, and where Joe was smoking his pipe in company with Mr. Wopsle and a stranger. Joe greeted me as usual with "Halloa, Pip, old chap!" and

chalk scores: Accounts of debts owed by the pub's customers.

the moment he said that, the stranger turned his head and looked at me.

He was a secret-looking man whom I had never seen before. His head was all on one side, and one of his eyes was half shut up, as if he were taking aim at something with an invisible gun. He had a pipe in his mouth, and he took it out, and, after slowly blowing all his smoke away and looking hard at me all the time, nodded. So, I nodded, and then he nodded again, and made room on the settle beside him that I might sit down there.

But, as I was used to sit beside Joe whenever I entered that place of resort, I said "No, thank you, sir," and fell into the space Joe made for me on the opposite settle. The strange man, after glancing at Joe, and seeing that his attention was otherwise engaged, nodded to me again when I had taken my seat, and then rubbed his leg—in a very odd way, as it struck me.

"You was saying," said the strange man, turning to Joe, "that you was a blacksmith."

"Yes. I said it, you know," said Joe.

"What'll you drink, Mr.——? You didn't mention your name, by-the-by."

Joe mentioned it now, and the strange man called him by it. "What'll you drink, Mr. Gargery? At my expense? To top up with?"

"Well," said Joe, "to tell you the truth, I ain't much in the habit of drinking at anybody's expense but my own."

"Habit? No," returned the stranger, "but once and away, and on a Saturday night too. Come! Put a name to it, Mr. Gargery."

"I wouldn't wish to be stiff company," said Joe. "Rum."

"Rum," repeated the stranger. "And will the other gentleman originate a sentiment?"

"Rum," said Mr. Wopsle.

"Three Rums!" cried the stranger, calling to the landlord. "Glasses round!"

"This other gentleman," observed Joe, by way of introducing Mr. Wopsle, "is a gentleman that you would like to hear give it out. Our clerk at church."

"Aha!" said the stranger, quickly, and cocking his eye at me. "The lonely church, right out on the marshes, with the graves round it!"

"That's it," said Joe.

The stranger, with a comfortable kind of grunt over his pipe, put his legs up on the settle that he had to himself. He wore a flapping broad-brimmed traveller's hat, and under it a handkerchief tied over his head in the manner of a cap: so that he showed no hair. As he looked at the fire, I thought I saw a cunning expression, followed by a half laugh, come into his face.

"I am not acquainted with this country, gentlemen, but it seems a solitary country towards the river."

"Most marshes is solitary," said Joe.

"No doubt, no doubt. Do you find any gipsies, now, or tramps, or vagrants of any sort, out there?"

"No," said Joe; "none but a runaway convict now and then. And we don't find *them*, easy. Eh, Mr. Wopsle?"

Mr. Wopsle, with a majestic remembrance of old discomfiture, assented; but not warmly.

"Seems you have been out after such?" asked the stranger.

"Once," returned Joe. "Not that we wanted to take them, you understand; we went out as lookers on; me, and Mr. Wopsle, and Pip. Didn't us, Pip?"

"Yes, Joe."

The stranger looked at me again—still cocking his eye, as if he were expressly taking aim at me with his invisible gun—and said, "He's a likely young parcel of bones that. What is it you call him?"

"Pip," said Joe.

"Christened Pip?"

"No, not christened Pip."

"Surname Pip?"

"No," said Joe, "it's a kind of a family name what he gave himself when a infant, and is called by."

"Son of yours?"

"Well," said Joe, meditatively—not, of course, that it could be in any wise necessary to consider about it, but because it was the way at the Jolly Bargemen to seem to consider deeply about everything that was discussed over pipes; "well—no. No, he ain't."

"Nevvy?" said the strange man.

"Well," said Joe, with the same appearance of profound cogitation, "he is not—no, not to deceive you, he is *not*—my nevvy."

"What the Blue Blazes is he?" asked the stranger. Which appeared to me to be an inquiry of unnecessary strength.

Mr. Wopsle struck in upon that; as one who knew all about relationships, having professional occasion to bear in mind what female relations a man might not marry;° and expounded the ties between me and Joe. Having his hand in, Mr. Wopsle finished off with a most terrifically snarling passage from Richard the Third, and seemed to think he had done quite enough to account for it when he added, "—as the poet says."

And here I may remark that when Mr. Wopsle referred to me, he considered it a necessary part of such reference to rumple my hair and poke it into my eyes. I cannot conceive why everybody of his standing who visited at our house should always have put me through the same inflammatory process under similar circumstances. Yet I do not call to mind that I was ever in my earlier youth the subject of remark in our social family circle, but some large-handed person took some such ophthalmic steps to patronise me.

All this while, the strange man looked at nobody but me, and looked at me as if he were determined to have a shot at me at last, and bring me down. But he said nothing after offering his Blue Blazes observation, until the glasses of rum-and-water were brought; and then he made his shot, and a most extraordinary shot it was.

It was not a verbal remark, but a proceeding in dumb-show, and was pointedly addressed to me. He stirred his rum-and-water pointedly at me, and he tasted his rum-and-water pointedly at me. And he stirred it and he tasted it: not with a spoon that was brought to him, but *with a file.*

He did this so that nobody but I saw the file; and when he had done it he wiped the file and put it in a breast-pocket. I knew it to be Joe's file, and I knew that he knew my convict, the moment I saw the instrument. I sat gazing at him, spell-bound. But he now reclined on his settle, taking very little notice of me, and talking principally about turnips.

There was a delicious sense of cleaning-up and making a quiet pause before going on in life afresh, in our village on Saturday nights, which stimulated Joe to dare to stay out half an hour longer on Saturdays than at other times. The half-hour and the rum-and-water running out together, Joe got up to go, and took me by the hand.

"Stop half a moment, Mr. Gargery," said the strange man. "I think I've got a bright new shilling somewhere in my pocket, and if I have, the boy shall have it."

He looked it out from a handful of small change, folded it in some crumpled paper, and gave it to me. "Yours!" said he. "Mind! Your own."

what . . . marry: These are listed in *The Book of Common Prayer.*

I thanked him, staring at him far beyond the bounds of good manners, and holding tight to Joe. He gave Joe good-night, and he gave Mr. Wopsle good-night (who went out with us), and he gave me only a look with his aiming eye—no, not a look, for he shut it up, but wonders may be done with an eye by hiding it.

On the way home, if I had been in a humour for talking, the talk must have been all on my side, for Mr. Wopsle parted from us at the door of the Jolly Bargemen, and Joe went all the way home with his mouth wide open, to rinse the rum out with as much air as possible. But I was in a manner stupified by this turning up of my old misdeed and old acquaintance, and could think of nothing else.

My sister was not in a very bad temper when we presented ourselves in the kitchen, and Joe was encouraged by that unusual circumstance to tell her about the bright shilling. "A bad un, I'll be bound," said Mrs. Joe, triumphantly, "or he wouldn't have given it to the boy! Let's look at it."

I took it out of the paper, and it proved to be a good one. "But what's this?" said Mrs. Joe, throwing down the shilling and catching up the paper. "Two One-Pound notes?"

Nothing less than two fat sweltering one-pound notes that seemed to have been on terms of the warmest intimacy with all the cattle markets in the county. Joe caught up his hat again, and ran with them to the Jolly Bargemen to restore them to their owner. While he was gone, I sat down on my usual stool and looked vacantly at my sister, feeling pretty sure that the man would not be there.

Presently, Joe came back, saying that the man was gone, but that he, Joe, had left word at the Three Jolly Bargemen concerning the notes. Then my sister sealed them up in a piece of paper, and put them under some dried rose-leaves in an ornamental teapot on the top of a press in the state parlour. There they remained, a nightmare to me, many and many a night and day.

I had sadly broken sleep when I got to bed, through thinking of the strange man taking aim at me with his invisible gun, and of the guiltily coarse and common thing it was, to be on secret terms of conspiracy with convicts—a feature in my low career that I had previously forgotten. I was haunted by the file too. A dread possessed me that when I least expected it, the file would reappear. I coaxed myself to sleep by thinking of Miss Havisham's, next Wednesday; and in my sleep I saw the file coming at me out of a door, without seeing who held it, and I screamed myself awake.

[PART 7]

Chapter 11

At the appointed time I returned to Miss Havisham's, and my hesitating ring at the gate brought out Estella. She locked it after admitting me, as she had done before, and again preceded me into the dark passage where her candle stood. She took no notice of me until she had the candle in her hand, when she looked over her shoulder, superciliously saying, "You are to come this way to-day," and took me to quite another part of the house.

The passage was a long one, and seemed to pervade the whole square basement of the Manor House. We traversed but one side of the square, however, and at the end of it she stopped, and put her candle down and opened a door. Here, the daylight reappeared, and I found myself in a small paved court-yard, the opposite side of which was formed by a detached dwelling-house, that looked as if it had once belonged to the manager or head clerk of the extinct brewery. There was a clock in the outer wall of this house. Like the clock in Miss Havisham's room, and like Miss Havisham's watch, it had stopped at twenty minutes to nine.

We went in at the door, which stood open, and into a gloomy room with a low ceiling, on the ground floor at the back. There was some company in the room, and Estella said to me as she joined it, "You are to go and stand there, boy, till you are wanted." "There," being the window, I crossed to it, and stood "there," in a very uncomfortable state of mind, looking out.

It opened to the ground, and looked into a most miserable corner of the neglected garden, upon a rank ruin of cabbage-stalks, and one box-tree that had been clipped round long ago, like a pudding, and had a new growth at the top of it, out of shape and of a different colour, as if that part of the pudding had stuck to the saucepan and got burnt. This was my homely thought, as I contemplated the box-tree. There had been some light snow, over-night, and it lay nowhere else to my knowledge; but, it had not quite melted from the cold shadow of this bit of garden, and the wind caught it up in little eddies and threw it at the window, as if it pelted me for coming there.

I divined that my coming had stopped conversation in the room, and that its other occupants were looking at me. I could see nothing of the room except the shining of the fire in the window-glass, but I stiffened in all my joints with the consciousness that I was under close inspection.

There were three ladies in the room and one gentleman. Before I had been standing at the window five minutes, they somehow conveyed to me that they were all toadies and humbugs, but that each of them pretended not to know that the others were toadies and humbugs: because the admission that he or she did know it, would have made him or her out to be a toady and humbug.

They all had a listless and dreary air of waiting somebody's pleasure, and the most talkative of the ladies had to speak quite rigidly to repress a yawn. This lady, whose name was Camilla, very much reminded me of my sister, with the difference that she was older, and (as I found when I caught sight of her) of a blunter cast of features. Indeed, when I knew her better I began to think it was a Mercy she had any features at all, so very blank and high was the dead wall of her face.

"Poor dear soul!" said this lady, with an abruptness of manner quite my sister's. "Nobody's enemy but his own!"

"It would be much more commendable to be somebody else's enemy," said the gentleman; "far more natural."

"Cousin Raymond," observed another lady, "we are to love our neighbour."

"Sarah Pocket," returned Cousin Raymond, "if a man is not his own neighbour, who is?"

Miss Pocket laughed, and Camilla laughed and said (checking a yawn), "The idea!" But I thought they seemed to think it rather a good idea too. The other lady, who had not spoken yet, said gravely and emphatically, "*Very* true!"

"Poor soul!" Camilla presently went on (I knew they had all been looking at me in the mean time), "he is so very strange! Would any one believe that when Tom's wife died, he actually could not be induced to see the importance of the children's having the deepest of trimmings to their mourning? 'Good Lord!' says he, 'Camilla, what can it signify so long as the poor bereaved little things are in black?' So like Matthew! The idea!"

"Good points in him, good points in him," said Cousin Raymond; "Heaven forbid I should deny good points in him; but he never had, and he never will have, any sense of the proprieties."

"You know I was obliged," said Camilla, "I was obliged to be firm. I said, 'It WILL NOT DO, for the credit of the family.' I told him that, without deep trimmings, the family was disgraced. I cried about it from breakfast till dinner. I injured my digestion. And at last he flung out in his violent way, and said with a D, 'Then do as you like.' Thank Goodness it will always be a consolation to me to know that I instantly went out in a pouring rain and bought the things."

"*He* paid for them, did he not?" asked Estella.

"It's not the question, my dear child, who paid for them," returned Camilla, "*I* bought them. And I shall often think of that with peace, when I wake up in the night."

The ringing of a distant bell, combined with the echoing of some cry or call along the passage by which I had come, interrupted the conversation and caused Estella to say to me, "Now, boy!" On my turning round, they all looked at me with the utmost contempt, and, as I went out, I heard Sarah Pocket say, "Well I am sure! What next!" and Camilla add, with indignation, "Was there ever such a fancy! The i-de-a!"

As we were going with our candle along the dark passage, Estella stopped all of a sudden, and, facing round, said in her taunting manner with her face quite close to mine:

"Well?"

"Well, miss?" I answered, almost falling over her and checking myself.

She stood looking at me, and, of course, I stood looking at her.

"Am I pretty?"

"Yes; I think you are very pretty."

"Am I insulting?"

"Not so much so as you were last time," said I.

"Not so much so?"

"No."

She fired when she asked the last question, and she slapped my face with such force as she had, when I answered it.

"Now?" said she. "You little coarse monster, what do you think of me now?"

"I shall not tell you."

"Because you are going to tell, up-stairs. Is that it?"

"No," said I, "that's not it."

"Why don't you cry again, you little wretch?"

"Because I'll never cry for you again," said I. Which was, I suppose, as false a declaration as ever was made; for I was inwardly crying for her then, and I know what I know of the pain she cost me afterwards.

We went on our way up-stairs after this episode; and, as we were going up, we met a gentleman groping his way down.

"Whom have we here?" asked the gentleman, stopping and looking at me.

"A boy," said Estella.

He was a burly man of an exceedingly dark complexion, with an exceedingly large head and a correspondingly large hand. He took my chin in his large hand and turned up my face to have a look at me by the light of the candle. He was prematurely bald on the top of his head, and had bushy black eyebrows that wouldn't lie down but stood up bristling. His eyes were set very deep in his head, and were disagreeably sharp and suspicious. He had a large watch-chain, and strong black dots where his beard and whiskers would have been if he had let them. He was nothing to me, and I could have had no foresight then, that he ever would be anything to me, but it happened that I had this opportunity of observing him well.

"Boy of the neighbourhood? Hey?" said he.

"Yes, sir," said I.

"How do *you* come here?"

"Miss Havisham sent for me, sir," I explained.

"Well! Behave yourself. I have a pretty large experience of boys, and you're a bad set of fellows. Now mind!" said he, biting the side of his great forefinger as he frowned at me, "you behave yourself!"

With those words, he released me—which I was glad of, for his hand smelt of scented soap—and went his way down stairs. I wondered whether he could be a doctor; but no, I thought; he couldn't be a doctor, or he would have a quieter and more persuasive manner. There was not much time to consider the subject, for we were soon in Miss Havisham's room, where she and everything else were just as I had left them. Estella left me standing near the door, and I stood there until Miss Havisham cast her eyes upon me from the dressing-table.

"So!" she said, without being startled or surprised; "the days have worn away, have they?"

"Yes, ma'am. To-day is——"

"There, there, there!" with the impatient movement of her fingers. "I don't want to know. Are you ready to play?"

I was obliged to answer in some confusion, "I don't think I am, ma'am."

"Not at cards again?" she demanded, with a searching look.

"Yes, ma'am; I could do that, if I was wanted."

"Since this house strikes you old and grave, boy," said Miss Havisham, impatiently, "and you are unwilling to play, are you willing to work?"

I could answer this inquiry with a better heart than I had been able to find for the other question, and I said I was quite willing.

"Then go into that opposite room," said she, pointing at the door behind me with her withered hand, "and wait there till I come."

I crossed the staircase landing, and entered the room she indicated. From that room, too, the daylight was completely excluded, and it had an airless smell that was oppressive. A fire had been lately kindled in the damp old-fashioned grate, and it was more disposed to go out than to burn up, and the reluctant smoke which hung in the room seemed colder than the clearer air—like our own marsh mist. Certain wintry branches of candles on the high chimney-piece faintly lighted the chamber: or, it would be more expressive to say, faintly troubled its darkness. It was spacious, and I dare say had once been handsome, but every discernible thing in it was covered with dust and mould, and dropping to pieces. The most prominent object was a long table with a tablecloth spread on it, as if a feast had been in preparation when the house and the clocks all stopped together. An epergne or centre-piece of some kind was in the middle of this cloth; it was so heavily overhung with cobwebs that its form was quite undistinguishable; and, as I looked along the yellow expanse out of which I remember its seeming to grow, like a black fungus, I saw speckled-legged spiders with blotchy bodies running home to it, and running out from it, as if some circumstance of the greatest public importance had just transpired in the spider community.

I heard the mice too, rattling behind the panels, as if the same occurrence were important to their interests. But, the black-beetles took no notice of the agitation, and groped about the hearth in a ponderous elderly way, as if they were short-sighted and hard of hearing, and not on terms with one another.

These crawling things had fascinated my attention and I was watching them from a distance, when Miss Havisham laid a hand upon my shoulder. In her other hand she had a crutch-headed stick on which she leaned, and she looked like the Witch of the place.

"This," said she, pointing to the long table with her stick, "is where I will be laid when I am dead. They shall come and look at me here."

With some vague misgiving that she might get upon the table then and there and die at once, the complete realisation of the ghastly waxwork at the Fair, I shrank under her touch.

"What do you think that is?" she asked me, again pointing with her stick; "that, where those cobwebs are?"

"I can't guess what it is, ma'am."

"It's a great cake. A bride-cake. Mine!"

She looked all round the room in a glaring manner, and then said, leaning on me while her hand twitched my shoulder, "Come, come, come! Walk me, walk me!"

I made out from this, that the work I had to do, was to walk Miss Havisham round and round the room. Accordingly, I started at once, and she leaned upon my shoulder, and we went away at a pace that might have been an imitation (founded on my first impulse under that roof) of Mr. Pumblechook's chaise-cart.

She was not physically strong, and after a little time said, "Slower!" Still, we went at an impatient fitful speed, and as we went, she twitched the hand upon my shoulder, and worked her mouth, and led me to believe that we were going fast because her thoughts went fast. After a while she said, "Call Estella!" so I went out on the landing and roared that name as I had done on the previous occasion. When her light appeared, I returned to Miss Havisham, and we started away again round and round the room.

If only Estella had come to be a spectator of our proceedings, I should have felt sufficiently disconcerted; but, as she brought with her the three ladies and the gentleman whom I had seen below, I didn't know what to do. In my politeness, I would have stopped; but, Miss Havisham twitched my shoulder, and we posted on—with a shame-faced consciousness on my part that they would think it was all my doing.

"Dear Miss Havisham," said Miss Sarah Pocket. "How well you look!"

"I do not," returned Miss Havisham. "I am yellow skin and bone."

Camilla brightened when Miss Pocket met with this rebuff; and she murmured, as she plaintively contemplated Miss Havisham, "Poor dear soul! Certainly not to be expected to look well, poor thing. The idea!"

"And how are *you?*" said Miss Havisham to Camilla. As we were close to Camilla then, I would have stopped as a matter of course, only Miss Havisham wouldn't stop. We swept on, and I felt that I was highly obnoxious to Camilla.

"Thank you, Miss Havisham," she returned, "I am as well as can be expected."

"Why, what's the matter with you?" asked Miss Havisham, with exceeding sharpness.

"Nothing worth mentioning," replied Camilla. "I don't wish to make a display of my feelings, but I have habitually thought of you more in the night than I am quite equal to."

"Then don't think of me," retorted Miss Havisham.

"Very easily said!" remarked Camilla, amiably repressing a sob, while a hitch came into her upper lip, and her tears overflowed. "Raymond is a witness what ginger and sal volatile I am obliged to take in the night. Raymond is a witness what nervous jerkings I have in my legs. Chokings and nervous jerkings, however, are nothing new to me when I think with anxiety of those I love. If I could be less affectionate and sensitive, I should have a better digestion and an iron set of nerves. I am sure I wish it could be so. But as to not thinking of you in the night—The idea!" Here, a burst of tears.

The Raymond referred to, I understood to be the gentleman present, and him I understood to be Mr. Camilla. He came to the rescue at this point, and said in a consolatory and complimentary voice, "Camilla, my dear, it is well known that your family feelings are gradually undermining you to the extent of making one of your legs shorter than the other."

"I am not aware," observed the grave lady whose voice I had heard but once, "that to think of any person is to make a great claim upon that person, my dear."

Miss Sarah Pocket, whom I now saw to be a little dry brown corrugated old woman, with a small face that might have been made of walnut-shells, and a large mouth like a cat's without the whiskers, supported this position by saying, "No, indeed, my dear. Hem!"

"Thinking is easy enough," said the grave lady.

"What is easier, you know?" assented Miss Sarah Pocket.

"Oh yes, yes!" cried Camilla, whose fermenting feelings appeared to rise from her legs to her bosom. "It's all very true! It's a weakness to be so affectionate, but I can't help it. No doubt my health would be much better if it was otherwise, still I wouldn't change my disposition if I could. It's the cause of much suffering, but it's a consolation to know I possess it, when I wake up in the night." Here another burst of feeling.

Miss Havisham and I had never stopped all this time, but kept going round and round the room: now, brushing against the skirts of the visitors: now, giving them the whole length of the dismal chamber.

"There's Matthew!" said Camilla. "Never mixing with any natural ties, never coming here to see how Miss Havisham is! I have taken to the sofa with my staylace cut, and have lain there hours, insensible, with my head over the side, and my hair all down, and my feet I don't know where——"

("Much higher than your head, my love," said Mr. Camilla.)

"I have gone off into that state, hours and hours, on account of Matthew's strange and inexplicable conduct, and nobody has thanked me."

"Really I must say I should think not!" interposed the grave lady.

"You see, my dear," added Miss Sarah Pocket (a blandly vicious personage), "the question to put to yourself is, who did you expect to thank you, my love?"

"Without expecting any thanks, or anything of the sort," resumed Camilla, "I have remained in that state, hours and hours, and Raymond is a witness of the extent to which I have choked, and what the total inefficacy of ginger has been, and I have been heard at the pianoforte-tuner's across the street, where the poor mistaken children have even supposed it to be pigeons cooing at a distance—and now to be told——" Here Camilla put her hand to her throat, and began to be quite chemical as to the formation of new combinations there.

When this same Matthew was mentioned, Miss Havisham stopped me and herself, and stood looking at the speaker. This change had a great influence in bringing Camilla's chemistry to a sudden end.

"Matthew will come and see me at last," said Miss Havisham, sternly, "when I am laid on that table. That will be his place—there," striking the table with her stick, "at my head! And yours will be there! And your husband's there! And Sarah Pocket's there! And Georgiana's there! Now you all know where to take your stations when you come to feast upon me. And now go!"

At the mention of each name, she had struck the table with her stick in a new place. She now said, "Walk me, walk me!" and we went on again.

"I suppose there's nothing to be done," exclaimed Camilla, "but comply and depart. It's something to have seen the object of one's love and duty, for even so short a time. I shall think of it with a melancholy satisfaction when I wake up in the night. I wish Matthew could have that comfort, but he sets it at defiance. I am determined not to make a display of my feelings, but it's very hard to be told one wants to feast on one's relations—as if one was a Giant—and to be told to go. The bare idea!"

Mr. Camilla interposing, as Mrs. Camilla laid her hand upon her heaving bosom, that lady assumed an unnatural fortitude of manner which I supposed to be expressive of an intention to drop and choke when out of view, and kissing her hand to Miss Havisham, was escorted forth. Sarah Pocket and Georgiana contended who should remain last; but, Sarah was too knowing to be outdone, and ambled round Georgiana with that artful slipperiness, that the latter was obliged to take precedence. Sarah Pocket then made her separate effect of departing with "Bless you, Miss Havisham dear!" and with a smile of forgiving pity on her walnut-shell countenance for the weaknesses of the rest.

While Estella was away lighting them down, Miss Havisham still walked with her hand on my shoulder, but more and more slowly. At last she stopped before the fire, and said, after muttering and looking at it some seconds:

"This is my birthday, Pip."

I was going to wish her many happy returns, when she lifted her stick.

"I don't suffer it to be spoken of. I don't suffer those who were here just now, or any one, to speak of it. They come here on the day, but they dare not refer to it."

Of course I made no further effort to refer to it.

"On this day of the year, long before you were born, this heap of decay," stabbing with her crutched stick at the pile of cobwebs on the table but not touching it, "was brought here. It and I have worn away together. The mice have gnawed at it, and sharper teeth than teeth of mice have gnawed at me."

She held the head of her stick against her heart as she stood looking at the table; she in her once white dress, all yellow and withered; the once white cloth all yellow and withered; everything around, in a state to crumble under a touch.

"When the ruin is complete," said she, with a ghastly look, "and when they lay me dead, in my bride's dress on the bride's table — which shall be done, and which will be the finished curse upon him — so much the better if it is done on this day!"

She stood looking at the table as if she stood looking at her own figure lying there. I remained quiet. Estella returned, and she too remained quiet. It seemed to me that we continued thus for a long time. In the heavy air of the room, and the heavy darkness that brooded in its remoter corners, I even had an alarming fancy that Estella and I might presently begin to decay.

At length, not coming out of her distraught state by degrees, but in an instant, Miss Havisham said, "Let me see you two play cards; why have you not begun?" With that, we returned to her room, and sat down as before; I was beggared, as before; and again, as before, Miss Havisham watched us all the time, directed my attention to Estella's beauty, and made me notice it the more by trying her jewels on Estella's breast and hair.

Estella, for her part, likewise treated me as before; except that she did not condescend to speak. When we had played some half-dozen games, a day was appointed for my return, and I was taken down into the yard to be fed in the former dog-like manner. There, too, I was again left to wander about as I liked.

It is not much to the purpose whether a gate in that garden wall which I had scrambled up to peep over on the last occasion was, on that last occasion, open or shut. Enough that I saw no gate then, and that I saw one now. As it stood open, and as I knew that Estella had let the visitors out—for, she had returned with the keys in her hand—I strolled into the garden and strolled all over it. It was quite a wilderness, and there were old melon-frames and cucumber-frames in it, which seemed in their decline to have produced a spontaneous growth of weak attempts at pieces of old hats and boots, with now and then a weedy offshoot into the likeness of a battered saucepan.

When I had exhausted the garden, and a greenhouse with nothing in it but a fallen-down grape-vine and some bottles, I found myself in the dismal corner upon which I had looked out of window. Never questioning for a moment that the house was now empty, I looked in at another window, and found myself, to my great surprise, exchanging a broad stare with a pale young gentleman with red eyelids and light hair.

This pale young gentleman quickly disappeared, and reappeared beside me. He had been at his books when I had found myself staring at him, and I now saw that he was inky.

"Halloa!" said he, "young fellow!"

Halloa being a general observation which I have usually observed to be best answered by itself, *I* said "Halloa!" politely omitting young fellow.

"Who let *you* in?" said he.

"Miss Estella."

"Who gave you leave to prowl about?"

"Miss Estella."

"Come and fight," said the pale young gentleman.

What could I do but follow him? I have often asked myself the question since: but, what else could I do? His manner was so final and I was so astonished, that I followed where he led, as if I had been under a spell.

"Stop a minute, though," he said, wheeling round before we had gone many paces. "I ought to give you a reason for fighting, too. There it is!" In a most irritating manner he instantly slapped his hands against one another, daintily flung one of his legs up behind him, pulled my hair, slapped his hands again, dipped his head, and butted it into my stomach.

The bull-like proceeding last mentioned, besides that it was unquestionably to be regarded in the light of a liberty, was particularly disagreeable just after bread and meat. I therefore hit out at him and was going to hit out again, when he said, "Aha! Would you?" and began dancing backwards and forwards in a manner quite unparalleled within my limited experience.

"Laws of the game!" said he. Here, he skipped from his left leg on to his right. "Regular rules!" Here, he skipped from his right leg on to his left. "Come to the ground, and go through the preliminaries!" Here, he dodged backwards and forwards, and did all sorts of things while I looked helplessly at him.

I was secretly afraid of him when I saw him so dexterous; but, I felt morally and physically convinced that his light head of hair could have had no business in the pit of my stomach, and that I had a right to consider it irrelevant when so obtruded on my attention. Therefore, I followed him without a word, to a retired nook of the garden, formed by the junction of two walls and screened by some rubbish. On his asking me if I was satisfied with the ground, and on my replying Yes, he begged my leave to absent himself for a moment, and quickly returned with a bottle of water and a sponge dipped in vinegar. "Available for both," he said, placing these against the wall. And then fell to pulling off, not only his jacket and waistcoat, but his shirt too, in a manner at once light-hearted, business-like, and bloodthirsty.

Although he did not look very healthy—having pimples on his face, and a breaking out at his mouth—these dreadful preparations quite appalled me. I judged him to be about my own age, but he was much taller, and he had a way of spinning himself about that was full of appearance. For the rest, he was a young gentleman in a grey suit (when not denuded for battle), with his elbows, knees, wrists, and heels, considerably in advance of the rest of him as to development.

My heart failed me when I saw him squaring at me with every demonstration of mechanical nicety, and eyeing my anatomy as if he were minutely choosing his bone. I never have been so surprised in my life, as I was when I let out the first blow, and saw him lying on his back, looking up at me with a bloody nose and his face exceedingly foreshortened.

But, he was on his feet directly, and after sponging himself with a great show of dexterity began squaring again. The second greatest surprise I have ever had in my life was seeing him on his back again, looking up at me out of a black eye.

His spirit inspired me with great respect. He seemed to have no strength, and he never once hit me hard, and he was always knocked down; but, he would be up again in a moment, sponging himself or drinking out of the water-bottle, with the greatest satisfaction in seconding himself according to form, and then came at me with an air and a show that made me believe he really was going to do for me at last. He got heavily bruised, for I am sorry to record that the more I hit him, the harder I hit him; but, he came up again and again and again, until at last he got a bad fall with the back of his head against the wall. Even after that crisis in our affairs, he got up and turned round and round confusedly a few times, not knowing where I was; but finally went on his knees to his sponge and threw it up: at the same time panting out, "That means you have won."

He seemed so brave and innocent, that although I had not proposed the contest I felt but a gloomy satisfaction in my victory. Indeed, I go so far as to hope that I regarded myself while dressing, as a species of savage young wolf, or other wild beast. However, I got dressed, darkly wiping my sanguinary face at intervals, and I said, "Can I help you?" and he said "No thankee," and I said "Good afternoon," and *he* said "Same to you."

When I got into the court-yard, I found Estella waiting with the keys. But, she neither asked me where I had been, nor why I had kept her waiting; and there was a bright flush upon her face, as though something had happened to delight her. Instead of going straight to the gate, too, she stepped back into the passage, and beckoned me.

"Come here! You may kiss me, if you like."

I kissed her cheek as she turned it to me. I think I would have gone through a great deal to kiss her cheek. But, I felt that the kiss was given to the coarse common boy as a piece of money might have been, and that it was worth nothing.

What with the birthday visitors, and what with the cards, and what with the fight, my stay had lasted so long, that when I neared home the light on the spit of sand off the point on the marshes was gleaming against a black night-sky, and Joe's furnace was flinging a path of fire across the road.

[PART 8]

Chapter 12

My mind grew very uneasy on the subject of the pale young gentleman. The more I thought of the fight, and recalled the pale young gentleman on his back in various stages of puffy and incrimsoned countenance, the more certain it appeared that something would be done to me. I felt that the pale young gentleman's blood was on my head, and that the Law would avenge it. Without having any definite idea of the penalties I had incurred, it was clear to me that village boys could not go stalking about the country, ravaging the houses of gentlefolks and pitching into the studious youth of England, without laying themselves open to severe punishment. For some days, I even kept close at home, and looked out at the kitchen door with the greatest caution and trepidation before going on an errand, lest the officers of the County Jail should pounce upon me. The pale young gentleman's nose had stained my trousers, and I tried to wash out that evidence of my guilt in the dead of night. I had cut my knuckles against the pale young gentleman's teeth, and I twisted my imagination into a thousand tangles, as I devised incredible ways of accounting for that damnatory circumstance when I should be haled before the Judges.

When the day came round for my return to the scene of the deed of violence, my terrors reached their height. Whether myrmidons of Justice, specially sent down from London, would be lying in ambush behind the gate? Whether Miss Havisham, preferring to take personal vengeance for an outrage done to her house, might rise in those graveclothes of hers, draw a pistol, and shoot me dead? Whether suborned boys—a numerous band of mercenaries—might be engaged to fall upon me in the brewery, and cuff me until I was no more? It was high testimony to my confidence in the spirit of the pale young gentleman, that I never imagined *him* accessary to these retaliations; they always came into my mind as the acts of injudicious relatives of his, goaded on by the state of his visage and an indignant sympathy with the family features.

However, go to Miss Havisham's I must, and go I did. And behold! nothing came of the late struggle. It was not alluded to in any way, and no pale young gentleman was to be discovered on the premises. I found the same gate open, and I explored the garden, and even looked in at the windows of the detached house; but, my view was suddenly stopped by the closed shutters within, and all was lifeless. Only in the corner where the combat had taken place, could I detect any evidence of the young gentleman's existence. There were traces of his gore in that spot, and I covered them with garden-mould from the eye of man.

On the broad landing between Miss Havisham's own room and that other room in which the long table was laid out, I saw a garden-chair—a light chair on wheels, that you pushed from behind. It had been placed there since my last visit, and I entered, that same day, on a regular occupation of pushing Miss Havisham in this chair (when she was tired of walking with her hand upon my shoulder) round her own room, and across the landing, and round the other room. Over and over and over again, we would make these journeys, and sometimes they would last as long as three hours at a stretch. I insensibly fall into a general mention of these journeys as numerous, because it was at once settled that I should return every alternate day at noon for these purposes, and because I am now going to sum up a period of at least eight or ten months.

As we began to be more used to one another, Miss Havisham talked more to me, and asked me such questions as what had I learnt and what was I going to be? I told her I was going to be apprenticed to Joe, I believed; and I enlarged upon my knowing nothing and wanting to know everything, in the hope that she might offer some help towards that desirable end. But, she did not; on the contrary, she seemed to prefer my being ignorant. Neither did she ever give me any money—or anything but my daily dinner—nor ever stipulate that I should be paid for my services.

Estella was always about, and always let me in and out, but never told me I might kiss her again. Sometimes, she would coldly tolerate me; sometimes, she would condescend to me; sometimes, she would be quite familiar with me; sometimes, she would tell me energetically that she hated me. Miss Havisham would often ask me in a whisper, or when we were alone, "Does she grow prettier and prettier, Pip?" And when I said yes (for indeed she did), would seem to enjoy it greedily. Also, when we played at cards Miss Havisham would look on, with a miserly relish of Estella's moods, whatever they were. And sometimes, when her moods were so many and so contradictory of one another that I was puzzled what to say or do, Miss Havisham would embrace her with lavish fondness, murmuring something in her ear that sounded like "Break their hearts my pride and hope, break their hearts and have no mercy!"

There was a song Joe used to hum fragments of at the forge, of which the burden was Old Clem.° This was not a very ceremonious way of rendering homage to a patron saint; but, I believe Old Clem stood in that relation towards smiths. It was a song that imitated the measure of beating upon iron, and was a mere lyrical excuse for the introduction of Old Clem's respected name. Thus, you were to hammer boys round—Old Clem! With a thump and a sound—Old Clem! Beat it out, beat it out—Old Clem! With a clink for the stout—Old Clem! Blow the fire, blow the fire—Old Clem! Roaring dryer, soaring higher—Old Clem! One day soon after the appearance of the chair, Miss Havisham suddenly saying to me, with the impatient movement of her fingers, "There, there, there! Sing!" I was surprised into crooning this ditty as I pushed her over the floor. It happened so to catch her fancy that, she took it up in a low brooding voice as if she were singing in her sleep. After that, it became customary with us to have it as we moved about, and Estella would often join in; though the whole strain was so subdued, even when there were three of us, that it made less noise in the grim old house than the lightest breath of wind.

What could I become with these surroundings? How could my character fail to be influenced by them? Is it to be wondered at if my thoughts were dazed, as my eyes were, when I came out into the natural light from the misty yellow rooms?

Perhaps, I might have told Joe about the pale young gentleman, if I had not previously been betrayed into those enormous inventions to which I had confessed. Under the circumstances, I felt that Joe could hardly fail to discern in the pale young gentleman, an appropriate passenger to be put into the black velvet coach; therefore, I said nothing of him. Besides: that shrinking from having Miss Havisham and Estella discussed, which had come upon me in the beginning, grew much more potent as time went on. I reposed complete confidence in no one but Biddy; but, I told poor Biddy everything. Why it came natural to me to do so, and why Biddy had a deep concern in everything I told her, I did not know then, though I think I know now.

Meanwhile, councils went on in the kitchen at home, fraught with almost insupportable aggravation to my exasperated spirit. That ass, Pumblechook, used often to come over of a night for the purpose of discussing my prospects with my sister; and I really do believe (to this hour with less penitence than I ought to feel), that if these hands could have taken a linchpin out of his chaise-cart, they would have done it. The mis-

Old Clem: Saint Clement, the patron saint of blacksmiths.

erable man was a man of that confined stolidity of mind, that he could not discuss my prospects without having me before him—as it were, to operate upon—and he would drag me up from my stool (usually by the collar) where I was quiet in a corner, and, putting me before the fire as if I were going to be cooked, would begin by saying, "Now, Mum, here is this boy! Here is this boy which you brought up by hand. Hold up your head, boy, and be for ever grateful unto them which so did do. Now, Mum, with respections to this boy!" And then he would rumple my hair the wrong way—which from my earliest remembrance, as already hinted, I have in my soul denied the right of any fellow-creature to do—and would hold me before him by the sleeve: a spectacle of imbecility only to be equalled by himself.

Then, he and my sister would pair off in such nonsensical speculations about Miss Havisham, and about what she would do with me and for me, that I used to want—quite painfully—to burst into spiteful tears, fly at Pumblechook, and pummel him all over. In these dialogues, my sister spoke of me as if she were morally wrenching one of my teeth out at every reference; while Pumblechook himself, self-constituted my patron, would sit supervising me with a depreciatory eye, like the architect of my fortunes who thought himself engaged on a very unremunerative job.

In these discussions, Joe bore no part. But he was often talked at, while they were in progress, by reason of Mrs. Joe's perceiving that he was not favourable to my being taken from the forge. I was fully old enough now, to be apprenticed to Joe; and when Joe sat with the poker on his knees thoughtfully raking out the ashes between the lower bars, my sister would so distinctly construe that innocent action into opposition on his part, that she would dive at him, take the poker out of his hands, shake him, and put it away. There was a most irritating end to every one of these debates. All in a moment, with nothing to lead up to it, my sister would stop herself in a yawn, and catching sight of me as it were incidentally, would swoop upon me with, "Come! There's enough of *you!* *You* get along to bed; *you*'ve given trouble enough for one night, I hope!" As if I had besought them as a favour to bother my life out.

We went on in this way for a long time, and it seemed likely that we should continue to go on in this way for a long time, when, one day Miss Havisham stopped short as she and I were walking, she leaning on my shoulder; and said with some displeasure:

"You are growing tall, Pip!"

I thought it best to hint, through the medium of a meditative look, that this might be occasioned by circumstances over which I had no control.

She said no more at the time; but, she presently stopped and looked at me again; and presently again; and after that, looked frowning and moody. On the next day of my attendance when our usual exercise was over, and I had landed her at her dressing-table, she stayed me with a movement of her impatient fingers:

"Tell me the name again of that blacksmith of yours."

"Joe Gargery, ma'am."

"Meaning the master you were to be apprenticed to?"

"Yes, Miss Havisham."

"You had better be apprenticed at once. Would Gargery come here with you, and bring your indentures,° do you think?"

I signified that I had no doubt he would take it as an honour to be asked.

"Then let him come."

"At any particular time, Miss Havisham?"

"There, there! I know nothing about times. Let him come soon, and come alone with you."

When I got home at night, and delivered this message for Joe, my sister "went on the Rampage," in a more alarming degree than at any previous period. She asked me and Joe whether we supposed she was doormats under our feet, and how we dared to use her so, and what company we graciously thought she *was* fit for? When she had exhausted a torrent of such inquiries, she threw a candlestick at Joe, burst into a loud sobbing, got out the dustpan—which was always a very bad sign—put on her coarse apron, and began cleaning up to a terrible extent. Not satisfied with a dry cleaning, she took to a pail and scrubbing-brush, and cleaned us out of house and home, so that we stood shivering in the back yard. It was ten o'clock at night before we ventured to creep in again, and then she asked Joe why he hadn't married a Negress Slave at once? Joe offered no answer, poor fellow, but stood feeling his whisker and looking dejectedly at me, as if he thought it really might have been a better speculation.

Chapter 13

It was a trial to my feelings, on the next day but one, to see Joe arraying himself in his Sunday clothes to accompany me to Miss Hav-

---

indentures: The contract stipulating the terms of one's apprenticeship, which typically lasted seven years beginning at the age of fourteen.

isham's. However, as he thought his court-suit necessary to the occasion, it was not for me to tell him that he looked far better in his working dress; the rather, because I knew he made himself so dreadfully uncomfortable, entirely on my account, and that it was for me he pulled up his shirt-collar so very high behind, that it made the hair on the crown of his head stand up like a tuft of feathers.

At breakfast-time my sister declared her intention of going to town with us, and being left at Uncle Pumblechook's, and called for "when we had done with our fine ladies"—a way of putting the case, from which Joe appeared inclined to augur the worst. The forge was shut up for the day, and Joe inscribed in chalk upon the door (as it was his custom to do on the very rare occasions when he was not at work) the monosyllable HOUT, accompanied by a sketch of an arrow supposed to be flying in the direction he had taken.

We walked to town, my sister leading the way in a very large beaver bonnet, and carrying a basket like the Great Seal of England in plaited straw, a pair of pattens, a spare shawl, and an umbrella, though it was a fine bright day. I am not quite clear whether these articles were carried penitentially or ostentatiously; but, I rather think they were displayed as articles of property—much as Cleopatra or any other sovereign lady on the Rampage might exhibit her wealth in a pageant or procession.

When we came to Pumblechook's, my sister bounced in and left us. As it was almost noon, Joe and I held straight on to Miss Havisham's house. Estella opened the gate as usual, and, the moment she appeared, Joe took his hat off and stood weighing it by the brim in both his hands: as if he had some urgent reason in his mind for being particular to half a quarter of an ounce.

Estella took no notice of either of us, but led us the way that I knew so well. I followed next to her, and Joe came last. When I looked back at Joe in the long passage, he was still weighing his hat with the greatest care, and was coming after us in long strides on the tips of his toes.

Estella told me we were both to go in, so I took Joe by the coat-cuff and conducted him into Miss Havisham's presence. She was seated at her dressing-table, and looked round at us immediately.

"Oh!" said she to Joe. "You are the husband of the sister of this boy?"

I could hardly have imagined dear old Joe looking so unlike himself or so like some extraordinary bird; standing, as he did, speechless, with his tuft of feathers ruffled, and his mouth open, as if he wanted a worm.

"You are the husband," repeated Miss Havisham, "of the sister of this boy?"

It was very aggravating; but, throughout the interview Joe persisted in addressing Me instead of Miss Havisham.

"Which I meantersay, Pip," Joe now observed in a manner that was at once expressive of forcible argumentation, strict confidence, and great politeness, "as I hup and married your sister, and I were at the time what you might call (if you was anyways inclined) a single man."

"Well!" said Miss Havisham. "And you have reared the boy, with the intention of taking him for your apprentice; is that so, Mr. Gargery?"

"You know, Pip," replied Joe, "as you and me were ever friends, and it were look'd for'ard to betwixt us, as being calc'lated to lead to larks. Not, but what, Pip, if you had ever made objections to the business—such as its being open to black and sut, or such-like—not but what they would have been attended to, don't you see?"

"Has the boy," said Miss Havisham, "ever made any objection? Does he like the trade?"

"Which it is well beknown to yourself, Pip," returned Joe, strengthening his former mixture of argumentation, confidence, and politeness, "that it were the wish of your own hart." (I saw the idea suddenly break upon him that he would adapt his epitaph to the occasion, before he went on to say) "And there weren't no objection on your part, and Pip it were the great wish of your hart!"

It was quite in vain for me to endeavour to make him sensible that he ought to speak to Miss Havisham. The more I made faces and gestures to him to do it, the more confidential, argumentative, and polite, he persisted in being to Me.

"Have you brought his indentures with you?" asked Miss Havisham.

"Well, Pip, you know," replied Joe, as if that were a little unreasonable, "you yourself see me put 'em in my 'at, and therefore you know as they are here." With which he took them out, and gave them, not to Miss Havisham, but to me. I am afraid I was ashamed of the dear good fellow—I *know* I was ashamed of him—when I saw that Estella stood at the back of Miss Havisham's chair, and that her eyes laughed mischievously. I took the indentures out of his hand and gave them to Miss Havisham.

"You expected," said Miss Havisham, as she looked them over, "no premium with the boy?"°

---

premium with the boy: The master craftsman was customarily paid a fee when the apprentice was "bound" to him.

"Joe!" I remonstrated; for he made no reply at all. "Why don't you answer——"

"Pip," returned Joe, cutting me short as if he were hurt, "which I meantersay that were not a question requiring a answer betwixt yourself and me, and which you know the answer to be full well No. You know it to be No, Pip, and wherefore should I say it?"

Miss Havisham glanced at him as if she understood what he really was, better than I had thought possible, seeing what he was there; and took up a little bag from the table beside her.

"Pip has earned a premium here," she said, "and here it is. There are five-and-twenty guineas in this bag. Give it to your master, Pip."

As if he were absolutely out of his mind with the wonder awakened in him by her strange figure and the strange room, Joe, even at this pass, persisted in addressing me.

"This is wery liberal on your part, Pip," said Joe, "and it is as such received and grateful welcome, though never looked for, far nor near nor nowheres. And now, old chap," said Joe, conveying to me a sensation, first of burning and then of freezing, for I felt as if that familiar expression were applied to Miss Havisham; "and now, old chap, may we do our duty! May you and me do our duty, both on us by one and another, and by them which your liberal present—have—conweyed —to be—for the satisfaction of mind—of—them as never——" here Joe showed that he felt he had fallen into frightful difficulties, until he triumphantly rescued himself with the words, "and from myself far be it!" These words had such a round and convincing sound for him that he said them twice.

"Good-by, Pip!" said Miss Havisham. "Let them out, Estella."

"Am I to come again, Miss Havisham?" I asked.

"No. Gargery is your master now. Gargery! One word!"

Thus calling him back as I went out of the door, I heard her say to Joe, in a distinct emphatic voice, "The boy has been a good boy here, and that is his reward. Of course, as an honest man, you will expect no other and no more."

How Joe got out of the room, I have never been able to determine; but, I know that when he did get out he was steadily proceeding up-stairs instead of coming down, and was deaf to all remonstrances until I went after him and laid hold of him. In another minute we were outside the gate, and it was locked, and Estella was gone.

When we stood in the daylight alone again, Joe backed up against a wall, and said to me, "Astonishing!" And there he remained so long, saying "Astonishing!" at intervals, so often, that I began to think his senses were never coming back. At length he prolonged his remark into "Pip, I do assure *you* this is as-TON-ishing!" and so, by degrees, became conversational and able to walk away.

I have reason to think that Joe's intellects were brightened by the encounter they had passed through, and that on our way to Pumble-chook's he invented a subtle and deep design. My reason is to be found in what took place in Mr. Pumblechook's parlour: where, on our presenting ourselves, my sister sat in conference with that detested seedsman.

"Well?" cried my sister, addressing us both at once. "And what's happened to *you*? I wonder you condescend to come back to such poor society as this, I am sure I do!"

"Miss Havisham," said Joe, with a fixed look at me, like an effort of remembrance, "made it wery partick'ler that we should give her— were it compliments or respects, Pip?"

"Compliments," I said.

"Which that were my own belief," answered Joe—"her compli-ments to Mrs. J. Gargery——"

"Much good they'll do me!" observed my sister; but rather grati-fied too.

"And wishing," pursued Joe, with another fixed look at me, like another effort of remembrance, "that the state of Miss Havisham's elth were sitch as would have—allowed, were it, Pip?"

"Of her having the pleasure," I added.

"Of ladies' company," said Joe. And drew a long breath.

"Well!" cried my sister, with a mollified glance at Mr. Pumble-chook. "She might have had the politeness to send that message at first, but it's better late than never. And what did she give young Rantipole° here?"

"She giv' him," said Joe, "nothing."

Mrs. Joe was going to break out, but Joe went on.

"What she giv'," said Joe, "she giv' to his friends. 'And by his friends,' were her explanation, 'I mean into the hands of his sister Mrs. J. Gargery.' Them were her words; 'Mrs. J. Gargery.' She mayn't have know'd," added Joe, with an appearance of reflection, "whether it were Joe, or Jorge."

Rantipole: A wild or reckless person; a mid-nineteenth-century nickname for Napoleon III.

My sister looked at Pumblechook: who smoothed the elbows of his wooden arm-chair, and nodded at her and at the fire, as if he had known all about it beforehand.

"And how much have you got?" asked my sister, laughing. Positively, laughing!

"What would present company say to ten pound?" demanded Joe.

"They'd say," returned my sister, curtly, "pretty well. Not too much, but pretty well."

"It's more than that, then," said Joe.

That fearful Impostor, Pumblechook, immediately nodded, and said, as he rubbed the arms of his chair: "It's more than that, Mum."

"Why you don't mean to say——" began my sister.

"Yes I do, Mum," said Pumblechook; "but wait a bit. Go on, Joseph. Good in you! Go on!"

"What would present company say," proceeded Joe, "to twenty pound?"

"Handsome would be the word," returned my sister.

"Well, then," said Joe, "it's more than twenty pound."

That abject hypocrite, Pumblechook, nodded again, and said, with a patronising laugh, "It's more than that, Mum. Good again! Follow her up, Joseph!"

"Then to make an end of it," said Joe, delightedly handing the bag to my sister; "it's five-and-twenty pound."

"It's five-and-twenty pound, Mum," echoed that basest of swindlers, Pumblechook, rising to shake hands with her; "and it's no more than your merits (as I said when my opinion was asked), and I wish you joy of the money!"

If the villain had stopped here, his case would have been sufficiently awful, but he blackened his guilt by proceeding to take me into custody, with the right of patronage that left all his former criminality far behind.

"Now you see, Joseph and wife," said Pumblechook, as he took me by the arm above the elbow, "I am one of them that always go right through with what they've begun. This boy must be bound, out of hand. That's *my* way. Bound out of hand."

"Goodness knows, Uncle Pumblechook," said my sister (grasping the money), "we're deeply beholden to you."

"Never mind me, Mum," returned that diabolical corn-chandler. "A pleasure's a pleasure, all the world over. But this boy, you know;

we must have him bound. I said I'd see to it—to tell you the truth."

The Justices were sitting in the Town Hall near at hand, and we at once went over to have me bound apprentice to Joe in the Magisterial presence. I say, we went over, but I was pushed over by Pumblechook, exactly as if I had that moment picked a pocket or fired a rick; indeed, it was the general impression in Court that I had been taken red-handed, for, as Pumblechook shoved me before him through the crowd, I heard some people say, "What's he done?" and others, "He's a young 'un, too, but looks bad, don't he?" One person of mild and benevolent aspect even gave me a tract ornamented with a woodcut of a malevolent young man fitted up with a perfect sausage-shop of fet-ters, and entitled TO BE READ IN MY CELL.

The Hall was a queer place, I thought, with higher pews in it than a church—and with people hanging over the pews looking on—and with mighty Justices (one with a powdered head) leaning back in chairs, with folded arms, or taking snuff, or going to sleep, or writing, or reading the newspapers—and with some shining black portraits on the walls, which my unartistic eye regarded as a composition of hard-bake° and sticking-plaister. Here, in a corner, my indentures were duly signed and attested, and I was "bound;" Mr. Pumblechook holding me all the while as if we had looked in on our way to the scaffold, to have those little preliminaries disposed of.

When we had come out again, and had got rid of the boys who had been put into great spirits by the expectation of seeing me publicly tortured, and who were much disappointed to find that my friends were merely rallying round me, we went back to Pumblechook's. And there my sister became so excited by the twenty-five guineas, that nothing would serve her but we must have a dinner out of that wind-fall, at the Blue Boar, and that Pumblechook must go over in his chaise-cart, and bring the Hubbles and Mr. Wopsle.

It was agreed to be done; and a most melancholy day I passed. For, it inscrutably appeared to stand to reason, in the minds of the whole company, that I was an excrescence on the entertainment. And to make it worse, they all asked me from time to time—in short, whenever they had nothing else to do—why I didn't enjoy myself. And what could I possibly do then, but say I *was* enjoying myself—when I wasn't?

However, they were grown up and had their own way, and they

---

hardbake: Almond toffee.

made the most of it. That swindling Pumblechook, exalted into the beneficent contriver of the whole occasion, actually took the top of the table; and, when he addressed them on the subject of my being bound, and had fiendishly congratulated them on my being liable to imprisonment if I played at cards, drank strong liquors, kept late hours or bad company, or indulged in other vagaries which the form of my indentures appeared to contemplate as next to inevitable, he placed me standing on a chair beside him, to illustrate his remarks.

My only other remembrances of the great festival are, That they wouldn't let me go to sleep, but whenever they saw me dropping off, woke me up and told me to enjoy myself. That, rather late in the evening Mr. Wopsle gave us Collins's ode, and threw his blood-stain'd sword in thunder down, with such effect, that a waiter came in and said, "The Commercials° underneath sent up their compliments, and it wasn't the Tumbler's Arms."° That, they were all in excellent spirits on the road home, and sang O Lady Fair!° Mr. Wopsle taking the bass, and asserting with a tremendously strong voice (in reply to the inquisitive bore who leads that piece of music in a most impertinent manner, by wanting to know all about everybody's private affairs) that *he* was the man with his white locks flowing, and that he was upon the whole the weakest pilgrim going.

Finally, I remember that when I got into my little bedroom I was truly wretched, and had a strong conviction on me that I should never like Joe's trade. I had liked it once, but once was not now.

[PART 9]

Chapter 14

It is a most miserable thing to feel ashamed of home. There may be black ingratitude in the thing, and the punishment may be retributive and well deserved; but, that it is a miserable thing, I can testify.

Home had never been a very pleasant place to me, because of my sister's temper. But, Joe had sanctified it, and I had believed in it. I had believed in the best parlour as a most elegant saloon; I had believed in the front door, as a mysterious portal of the Temple of State

Commercials: Traveling salesmen.   **sent up their compliments . . . Tumbler's Arms:** Complained about the noise upstairs by pointing out that the inn was not a lodging for acrobats.   **O Lady Fair:** A ballad by Thomas Moore (1779–1852).

whose solemn opening was attended with a sacrifice of roast fowls; I had believed in the kitchen as a chaste though not magnificent apartment; I had believed in the forge as the glowing road to manhood and independence. Within a single year, all this was changed. Now, it was all coarse and common, and I would not have had Miss Havisham and Estella see it on any account.

How much of my ungracious condition of mind may have been my own fault, how much Miss Havisham's, how much my sister's, is now of no moment to me or to any one. The change was made in me; the thing was done. Well or ill done, excusably or inexcusably, it was done.

Once, it had seemed to me that when I should at last roll up my shirt-sleeves and go into the forge, Joe's 'prentice, I should be distinguished and happy. Now the reality was in my hold, I only felt that I was dusty with the dust of small-coal, and that I had a weight upon my daily remembrance to which the anvil was a feather. There have been occasions in my later life (I suppose as in most lives) when I have felt for a time as if a thick curtain had fallen on all its interest and romance, to shut me out from anything save dull endurance any more. Never has that curtain dropped so heavy and blank, as when my way in life lay stretched out straight before me through the newly-entered road of apprenticeship to Joe.

I remember that at a later period of my "time," I used to stand about the churchyard on Sunday evenings when night was falling, comparing my own perspective with the windy marsh view, and making out some likeness between them by thinking how flat and low both were, and how on both there came an unknown way and a dark mist and then the sea. I was quite as dejected on the first working-day of my apprenticeship as in that after-time; but I am glad to know that I never breathed a murmur to Joe while my indentures lasted. It is about the only thing I *am* glad to know of myself in that connexion.

For, though it includes what I proceed to add, all the merit of what I proceed to add was Joe's. It was not because I was faithful, but because Joe was faithful, that I never ran away and went for a soldier or a sailor. It was not because I had a strong sense of the virtue of industry, but because Joe had a strong sense of the virtue of industry, that I worked with tolerable zeal against the grain. It is not possible to know how far the influence of any amiable honest-hearted duty-doing man flies out into the world; but it is very possible to know how it has touched one's self in going by, and I know right well, that any good that intermixed itself with my apprenticeship came of plain contented Joe, and not of restlessly aspiring discontented me.

What I wanted, who can say? How can *I* say, when I never knew? What I dreaded was, that in some unlucky hour I, being at my grimiest and commonest, should lift up my eyes and see Estella looking in at one of the wooden windows of the forge. I was haunted by the fear that she would, sooner or later, find me out, with a black face and hands, doing the coarsest part of my work, and would exult over me and despise me. Often after dark, when I was pulling the bellows for Joe, and we were singing Old Clem, and when the thought how we used to sing it at Miss Havisham's would seem to show me Estella's face in the fire, with her pretty hair fluttering in the wind and her eyes scorning me,—often at such a time I would look towards those panels of black night in the wall which the wooden windows then were, and would fancy that I saw her just drawing her face away, and would believe that she had come at last.

After that, when we went in to supper, the place and the meal would have a more homely look than ever, and I would feel more ashamed of home than ever, in my own ungracious breast.

Chapter 15

As I was getting too big for Mr. Wopsle's great-aunt's room, my education under that preposterous female terminated. Not, however, until Biddy had imparted to me everything she knew, from the little catalogue of prices, to a comic song she had once bought for a halfpenny. Although the only coherent part of the latter piece of literature were the opening lines,

When I went to Lunnon town sirs,
          Too rul loo rul
          Too rul loo rul
Wasn't I done very brown sirs,
          Too rul loo rul
          Too rul loo rul

—still, in my desire to be wiser, I got this composition by heart with the utmost gravity; nor do I recollect that I questioned its merit, except that I thought (as I still do) the amount of Too rul somewhat in excess of the poetry. In my hunger for information, I made proposals to Mr. Wopsle to bestow some intellectual crumbs upon me: with which he kindly complied. As it turned out, however, that he only wanted me for a dramatic lay-figure, to be contradicted and embraced and wept over and bullied and clutched and stabbed and knocked about in a variety of ways, I soon declined that course of instruction; though not until Mr. Wopsle in his poetic fury had severely mauled me.

Whatever I acquired, I tried to impart to Joe. This statement sounds so well, that I cannot in my conscience let it pass unexplained. I wanted to make Joe less ignorant and common, that he might be worthier of my society and less open to Estella's reproach.

The old Battery out on the marshes was our place of study, and a broken slate and a short piece of slate pencil were our educational implements: to which Joe always added a pipe of tobacco. I never knew Joe to remember anything from one Sunday to another, or to acquire, under my tuition, any piece of information whatever. Yet he would smoke his pipe at the Battery with a far more sagacious air than anywhere else—even with a learned air—as if he considered himself to be advancing immensely. Dear fellow, I hope he did.

It was pleasant and quiet, out there with the sails on the river passing beyond the earthwork, and sometimes, when the tide was low, looking as if they belonged to sunken ships that were still sailing on at the bottom of the water. Whenever I watched the vessels standing out to sea with their white sails spread, I somehow thought of Miss Havisham and Estella; and whenever the light struck aslant, afar off, upon a cloud or sail or green hill-side or water-line, it was just the same.— Miss Havisham and Estella and the strange house and the strange life appeared to have something to do with everything that was picturesque.

One Sunday when Joe, greatly enjoying his pipe, had so plumed himself on being "most awful dull," that I had given him up for the day, I lay on the earthwork for some time with my chin on my hand, descrying traces of Miss Havisham and Estella all over the prospect, in the sky and in the water, until at last I resolved to mention a thought concerning them that had been much in my head.

"Joe," said I; "don't you think I ought to make Miss Havisham a visit?"

"Well, Pip," returned Joe, slowly considering. "What for?"

"What for, Joe? What is any visit made for?"

"There is some wisits p'r'aps," said Joe, "as for ever remains open to the question, Pip. But in regard of wisiting Miss Havisham. She might think you wanted something—expected something of her."

"Don't you think I might say that I did not, Joe?"

"You might, old chap," said Joe. "And she might credit it. Similarly she mightn't."

Joe felt, as I did, that he had made a point there, and he pulled hard at his pipe to keep himself from weakening it by repetition.

"You see, Pip," Joe pursued, as soon as he was past that danger, "Miss Havisham done the handsome thing by you. When Miss Havisham done the handsome thing by you, she called me back to say to me as that were all."

"Yes, Joe. I heard her."

"ALL," Joe repeated, very emphatically.

"Yes, Joe. I tell you, I heard her."

"Which I meantersay, Pip, it might be that her meaning were—Make a end on it!—As you was!—Me to the North, and you to the South!—Keep in sunders!"

I had thought of that too, and it was very far from comforting to me to find that he had thought of it; for it seemed to render it more probable.

"But, Joe."

"Yes, old chap."

"Here am I, getting on in the first year of my time, and, since the day of my being bound, I have never thanked Miss Havisham, or asked after her, or shown that I remember her."

"That's true, Pip; and unless you was to turn her out a set of shoes all four round—and which I meantersay as even a set of shoes all four round might not act acceptable as a present, in a total wacancy of hoofs——"

"I don't mean that sort of remembrance, Joe; I don't mean a present."

But Joe had got the idea of a present in his head and must harp upon it. "Or even," said he, "if you was helped to knocking her up a new chain for the front door—or say a gross or two of shark-headed screws for general use—or some light fancy article, such as a toasting-fork when she took her muffins—or a gridiron when she took a sprat or such like——"

"I don't mean any present at all, Joe," I interposed.

"Well," said Joe, still harping on it as though I had particularly pressed it, "if I was yourself, Pip, I wouldn't. No, I would *not*. For what's a door-chain when she's got one always up? And shark-headers is open to misrepresentations. And if it was a toasting-fork, you'd go into brass and do yourself no credit. And the oncommonest workman

can't show himself oncommon in a gridiron—for a gridiron IS a gridiron," said Joe, steadfastly impressing it upon me, as if he were endeavouring to rouse me from a fixed delusion, "and you may haim at what
you like, but a gridiron it will come out, either by your leave or again
your leave, and you can't help yourself——"

"My dear Joe," I cried, in desperation, taking hold of his coat,
"don't go on in that way. I never thought of making Miss Havisham
any present."

"No, Pip," Joe assented, as if he had been contending for that, all
along; "and what I say to you is, you are right, Pip."

"Yes, Joe; but what I wanted to say, was, that as we are rather slack
just now, if you would give me a half-holiday to-morrow, I think I
would go up-town and make a call on Miss Est—Havisham."

"Which her name," said Joe, gravely, "ain't Estavisham, Pip, unless
she have been rechris'ened."

"I know, Joe, I know. It was a slip of mine. What do you think of
it, Joe?"

In brief, Joe thought that if I thought well of it, he thought well of
it. But, he was particular in stipulating that if I were not received with
cordiality, or if I were not encouraged to repeat my visit as a visit
which had no ulterior object but was simply one of gratitude for a
favour received, then this experimental trip should have no successor.
By these conditions I promised to abide.

Now, Joe kept a journeyman at weekly wages whose name was Orlick. He pretended that his christian name was Dolge—a clear impossibility—but he was a fellow of that obstinate disposition that I believe
him to have been the prey of no delusion in this particular, but wilfully
to have imposed that name upon the village as an affront to its understanding. He was a broad-shouldered loose-limbed swarthy fellow of
great strength, never in a hurry, and always slouching. He never even
seemed to come to his work on purpose, but would slouch in as if by
mere accident; and when he went to the Jolly Bargemen to eat his dinner, or went away at night, he would slouch out, like Cain or the Wandering Jew, as if he had no idea where he was going and no intention
of ever coming back. He lodged at a sluice-keeper's out on the
marshes, and on working days would come slouching from his her-
mitage, with his hands in his pockets and his dinner loosely tied in a
bundle round his neck and dangling on his back. On Sundays he
mostly lay all day on sluice-gates, or stood against ricks and barns. He
always slouched, locomotively, with his eyes on the ground; and, when

accosted or otherwise required to raise them, he looked up in a half re-
sentful, half puzzled way, as though the only thought he ever had,
was, that it was rather an odd and injurious fact that he should never
be thinking.

This morose journeyman had no liking for me. When I was very
small and timid, he gave me to understand that the Devil lived in a
black corner of the forge, and that he knew the fiend very well: also
that it was necessary to make up the fire, once in seven years, with a
live boy, and that I might consider myself fuel. When I became Joe's
'prentice, Orlick was perhaps confirmed in some suspicion that I
should displace him; howbeit, he liked me still less. Not that he ever
said anything, or did anything, openly importing hostility; I only noticed that he always beat his sparks in my direction, and that whenever
I sang Old Clem, he came in out of time.

Dolge Orlick was at work and present, next day, when I reminded
Joe of my half-holiday. He said nothing at the moment, for he and Joe
had just got a piece of hot iron between them, and I was at the bellows; but by-and-by he said, leaning on his hammer:

"Now, master! Sure you're not a going to favour only one of us. If
Young Pip has a half-holiday, do as much for Old Orlick." I suppose
he was about five-and-twenty, but he usually spoke of himself as an ancient person.

"Why, what'll you do with a half-holiday, if you get it?" said Joe.

"What'll *I* do with it! What'll *he* do with it? I'll do as much with it
as *him*," said Orlick.

"As to Pip, he's going up-town," said Joe.

"Well then, as to Old Orlick, *he's* a going up-town," retorted that
worthy. "Two can go up-town. Tan't only one wot can go up-town."

"Don't lose your temper," said Joe.

"Shall if I like," growled Orlick. "Some and their up-towning!
Now, master! Come. No favouring in this shop. Be a man!"

The master refusing to entertain the subject until the journeyman
was in a better temper, Orlick plunged at the furnace, drew out a red-
hot bar, made at me with it as if he were going to run it through my
body, whisked it round my head, laid it on the anvil, hammered it
out—as if it were I, I thought, and the sparks were my spirting
blood—and finally said, when he had hammered himself hot and the
iron cold, and he again leaned on his hammer:

"Now, master!"

"Are you all right now?" demanded Joe.

"Ah! I am all right," said gruff Old Orlick.

"Then, as in general you stick to your work as well as most men," said Joe, "let it be a half-holiday for all."

My sister had been standing silent in the yard, within hearing— she was a most unscrupulous spy and listener—and she instantly looked in at one of the windows.

"Like you, you fool!" said she to Joe, "giving holidays to great idle hulkers like that. You are a rich man, upon my life, to waste wages in that way. I wish *I* was his master!"

"You'd be everybody's master, if you durst," retorted Orlick, with an ill-favoured grin.

("Let her alone," said Joe.)

"I'd be a match for all noodles and all rogues," returned my sister, beginning to work herself into a mighty rage. "And I couldn't be a match for the noodles, without being a match for your master, who's the dunder-headed king of the noodles. And I couldn't be a match for the rogues, without being a match for you, who are the blackest-looking and the worst rogue between this and France. Now!"

"You're a foul shrew, Mother Gargery," growled the journeyman. "If that makes a judge of rogues, you ought to be a good'un."

("Let her alone, will you?" said Joe.)

"What did you say?" cried my sister, beginning to scream. "What did you say? What did that fellow Orlick say to me, Pip? What did he call me, with my husband standing by? O! O! O!" Each of these exclamations was a shriek; and I must remark of my sister, what is equally true of all the violent women I have ever seen, that passion was no excuse for her, because it is undeniable that instead of lapsing into passion, she consciously and deliberately took extraordinary pains to force herself into it, and became blindly furious by regular stages; "what was the name he gave me before the base man who swore to defend me? O! Hold me! O!"

"Ah-h-h!" growled the journeyman, between his teeth, "I'd hold you, if you was my wife. I'd hold you under the pump, and choke it out of you."

("I tell you, let her alone," said Joe.)

"Oh! To hear him!" cried my sister, with a clap of her hands and a scream together—which was her next stage. "To hear the names he's giving me! That Orlick! In my own house! Me, a married woman! With my husband standing by! O! O!" Here my sister, after a fit of clappings and screamings, beat her hands upon her bosom and upon her knees, and threw her cap off, and pulled her hair down—which were the last stages on her road to frenzy. Being by this time a perfect Fury and a complete success, she made a dash at the door, which I had fortunately locked.

What could the wretched Joe do now, after his disregarded paren-thetical interruptions, but stand up to his journeyman, and ask him what he meant by interfering betwixt himself and Mrs. Joe; and fur-ther whether he was man enough to come on? Old Orlick felt that the situation admitted of nothing less than coming on, and was on his de-fence straightway; so, without so much as pulling off their singed and burnt aprons, they went at one another, like two giants. But, if any man in that neighbourhood could stand up long against Joe, I never saw the man. Orlick, as if he had been of no more account than the pale young gentleman, was very soon among the coal-dust, and in no hurry to come out of it. Then, Joe unlocked the door and picked up my sister, who had dropped insensible at the window (but who had seen the fight first, I think), and who was carried into the house and laid down, and who was recommended to revive, and would do noth-ing but struggle and clench her hands in Joe's hair. Then, came that singular calm and silence which succeed all uproars; and then, with the vague sensation which I have always connected with such a lull—namely, that it was Sunday, and somebody was dead—I went up-stairs to dress myself.

When I came down again, I found Joe and Orlick sweeping up, without any other traces of discomposure than a slit in one of Orlick's nostrils, which was neither expressive nor ornamental. A pot of beer had appeared from the Jolly Bargemen, and they were sharing it by turns in a peaceable manner. The lull had a sedative and philosophical influence on Joe, who followed me out into the road to say, as a part-ing observation that might do me good, "On the Rampage, Pip, and off the Rampage, Pip—such is Life!"

With what absurd emotions (for, we think the feelings that are very serious in a man quite comical in a boy) I found myself again going to Miss Havisham's, matters little here. Nor, how I passed and repassed the gate many times before I could make up my mind to ring. Nor, how I debated whether I should go away without ringing; nor, how I should undoubtedly have gone, if my time had been my own, to come back.

Miss Sarah Pocket came to the gate. No Estella.

"How, then? You here again?" said Miss Pocket. "What do you want?"

When I said that I only came to see how Miss Havisham was,

Sarah evidently deliberated whether or no she should send me about my business. But, unwilling to hazard the responsibility, she let me in, and presently brought the sharp message that I was to "come up."

Everything was unchanged, and Miss Havisham was alone. "Well?" said she, fixing her eyes upon me. "I hope you want nothing? You'll get nothing."

"No indeed, Miss Havisham. I only wanted you to know that I am doing very well in my apprenticeship, and am always much obliged to you."

"There, there!" with the old restless fingers. "Come now and then; come on your birthday.—Ay!" she cried suddenly, turning herself and her chair towards me, "you are looking round for Estella? Hey?"

I had been looking round—in fact, for Estella—and I stammered that I hoped she was well.

"Abroad," said Miss Havisham; "educating for a lady; far out of reach; prettier than ever; admired by all who see her. Do you feel that you have lost her?"

There was such a malignant enjoyment in her utterance of the last words, and she broke into such a disagreeable laugh, that I was at a loss what to say. She spared me the trouble of considering, by dismissing me. When the gate was closed upon me by Sarah of the walnut-shell countenance, I felt more than ever dissatisfied with my home and with my trade and with everything; and that was all I took by *that* motion.

As I was loitering along the High-street, looking in disconsolately at the shop-windows, and thinking what I would buy if I were a gentleman, who should come out of the bookshop but Mr. Wopsle. Mr. Wopsle had in his hand the affecting tragedy of George Barnwell,° in which he had that moment invested sixpence, with the view of heaping every word of it on the head of Pumblechook, with whom he was going to drink tea. No sooner did he see me, than he appeared to consider that a special Providence had put a 'prentice in his way to be read at; and he laid hold of me, and insisted on my accompanying him to the Pumblechookian parlour. As I knew it would be miserable at home, and as the nights were dark and the way was dreary, and almost any companionship on the road was better than none, I made no great

tragedy of George Barnwell: *The London Merchant, or The History of George Barnwell* (1731), a play by George Lillo, in which the apprentice Barnwell murders his uncle at the instigation of the prostitute Sarah Millwood; both are hanged at Newgate for the crime.

resistance; consequently, we turned into Pumblechook's just as the street and the shops were lighting up.

As I never assisted at any other representation of George Barnwell, I don't know how long it may usually take; but I know very well that it took until half-past nine o'clock that night, and that when Mr. Wopsle got into Newgate, I thought he never would go to the scaffold, he became so much slower than at any former period of his disgraceful career. I thought it a little too much that he should complain of being cut short in his flower after all, as if he had not been running to seed, leaf after leaf, ever since his course began. This, however, was a mere question of length and wearisomeness. What stung me, was the identification of the whole affair with my unoffending self. When Barnwell began to go wrong, I declare that I felt positively apologetic, Pumblechook's indignant stare so taxed me with it. Wopsle, too, took pains to present me in the worst light. At once ferocious and maudlin, I was made to murder my uncle with no extenuating circumstances whatever; Millwood put me down in argument, on every occasion; it became sheer monomania in my master's daughter to care a button for me; and all I can say for my gasping and procrastinating conduct on the fatal morning, is, that it was worthy of the general feebleness of my character. Even after I was happily hanged and Wopsle had closed the book, Pumblechook sat staring at me, and shaking his head, and saying, "Take warning, boy, take warning!" as if it were a well-known fact that I contemplated murdering a near relation, provided I could only induce one to have the weakness to become my benefactor.

It was a very dark night when it was all over, and when I set out with Mr. Wopsle on the walk home. Beyond town, we found a heavy mist out, and it fell wet and thick. The turnpike lamp was a blur, quite out of the lamp's usual place apparently, and its rays looked solid substance on the fog. We were noticing this, and saying how that the mist rose with a change of wind from a certain quarter of our marshes, when we came upon a man, slouching under the lee of the turnpike house.

"Halloa!" we said, stopping. "Orlick, there?"

"Ah!" he answered, slouching out. "I was standing by, a minute, on the chance of company."

"You are late," I remarked.

Orlick not unnaturally answered, "Well? And *you*'re late."

"We have been," said Mr. Wopsle, exalted with his late performance, "we have been indulging, Mr. Orlick, in an intellectual evening."

Old Orlick growled, as if he had nothing to say about that, and we all went on together. I asked him presently whether he had been spending his half-holiday up and down town?

"Yes," said he, "all of it. I come in behind yourself. I didn't see you, but I must have been pretty close behind you. By-the-by, the guns is going again."

"At the Hulks?" said I.

"Ay! There's some of the birds flown from the cages. The guns have been going since dark, about. You'll hear one presently."

In effect, we had not walked many yards further, when the well-remembered boom came towards us, deadened by the mist, and heavily rolled away along the low grounds by the river, as if it were pursuing and threatening the fugitives.

"A good night for cutting off in," said Orlick. "We'd be puzzled how to bring down a jail-bird on the wing, to-night."

The subject was a suggestive one to me, and I thought about it in silence. Mr. Wopsle, as the ill-requited uncle of the evening's tragedy, fell to meditating aloud in his garden at Camberwell. Orlick, with his hands in his pockets, slouched heavily at my side. It was very dark, very wet, very muddy, and so we splashed along. Now and then, the sound of the signal cannon broke upon us again, and again rolled sulkily along the course of the river. I kept myself to myself and my thoughts. Mr. Wopsle died amiably at Camberwell, and exceedingly game on Bosworth Field, and in the greatest agonies at Glastonbury.° Orlick sometimes growled, "Beat it out, beat it out—old Clem! With a clink for the stout—old Clem!" I thought he had been drinking, but he was not drunk.

Thus, we came to the village. The way by which we approached it, took us past the Three Jolly Bargemen, which we were surprised to find—it being eleven o'clock—in a state of commotion, with the door wide open, and unwonted lights that had been hastily caught up and put down, scattered about. Mr. Wopsle dropped in to ask what was the matter (surmising that a convict had been taken), but came running out in a great hurry.

"There's something wrong," said he, without stopping, "up at your place, Pip. Run all!"

"What is it?" I asked, keeping up with him. So did Orlick, at my side.

Camberwell . . . Glastonbury: Camberwell is the town south of London where Barnwell murders his uncle; the second and third locations are probably meant to recall settings in Shakespeare's history plays.

"I can't quite understand. The house seems to have been violently entered when Joe Gargery was out. Supposed by convicts. Somebody has been attacked and hurt."

We were running too fast to admit of more being said, and we made no stop until we got into our kitchen. It was full of people; the whole village was there, or in the yard; and there was a surgeon, and there was Joe, and there were a group of women, all on the floor in the midst of the kitchen. The unemployed bystanders drew back when they saw me, and so I became aware of my sister—lying without sense or movement on the bare boards where she had been knocked down by a tremendous blow on the back of the head, dealt by some un-known hand when her face was turned towards the fire—destined never to be on the Rampage again, while she was wife of Joe.

[PART 10]

Chapter 16

With my head full of George Barnwell, I was at first disposed to believe that *I* must have had some hand in the attack upon my sister, or at all events that as her near relation, popularly known to be under obligations to her, I was a more legitimate object of suspicion than any one else. But when, in the clearer light of next morning, I began to re-consider the matter and to hear it discussed around me on all sides, I took another view of the case, which was more reasonable.

Joe had been at the Three Jolly Bargemen, smoking his pipe, from a quarter after eight o'clock to a quarter before ten. While he was there, my sister had been seen standing at the kitchen door, and had exchanged Good Night with a farm-labourer going home. The man could not be more particular as to the time at which he saw her (he got into dense confusion when he tried to be), than that it must have been before nine. When Joe went home at five minutes before ten, he found her struck down on the floor, and promptly called in assistance. The fire had not then burnt unusually low, nor was the snuff of the candle very long; the candle, however, had been blown out.

Nothing had been taken away from any part of the house. Neither, beyond the blowing out of the candle—which stood on a table be-tween the door and my sister, and was behind her when she stood fac-ing the fire and was struck—was there any disarrangement of the kitchen, excepting such as she herself had made, in falling and bleeding. But, there was one remarkable piece of evidence on the spot. She had been struck with something blunt and heavy, on the head and spine; after the blows were dealt, something heavy had been thrown down at her with considerable violence, as she lay on her face. And on the ground beside her, when Joe picked her up, was a convict's leg-iron which had been filed asunder.

Now, Joe, examining this iron with a smith's eye, declared it to have been filed asunder some time ago. The hue and cry going off to the Hulks, and people coming thence to examine the iron, Joe's opinion was corroborated. They did not undertake to say when it had left the prison-ships to which it undoubtedly had once belonged; but they claimed to know for certain that that particular manacle had not been worn by either of two convicts who had escaped last night. Further, one of those two was already retaken, and had not freed himself of his iron.

Knowing what I knew, I set up an inference of my own here. I believed the iron to be my convict's iron—the iron I had seen and heard him filing at, on the marshes— but my mind did not accuse him of having put it to its latest use. For, I believed one of two other persons to have become possessed of it, and to have turned it to this cruel account. Either Orlick, or the strange man who had shown me the file.

Now, as to Orlick; he had gone to town exactly as he told us when we picked him up at the turnpike, he had been seen about town all the evening, he had been in divers companies in several public-houses, and he had come back with myself and Mr. Wopsle. There was nothing against him, save the quarrel; and my sister had quarrelled with him, and with everybody else about her, ten thousand times. As to the strange man; if he had come back for his two bank-notes there could have been no dispute about them, because my sister was fully prepared to restore them. Besides, there had been no altercation; the assailant had come in so silently and suddenly, that she had been felled before she could look round.

It was horrible to think that I had provided the weapon, however undesignedly, but I could hardly think otherwise. I suffered unspeakable trouble while I considered and reconsidered whether I should at last dissolve that spell of my childhood, and tell Joe all the story. For months afterwards, I every day settled the question finally in the negative, and reopened and reargued it next morning. The contention came, after all, to this;—the secret was such an old one now, had so grown into me and become a part of myself, that I could not tear it away. In addition to the dread that, having led up to so much mischief, it would be now more likely than ever to alienate Joe from me if he believed it, I had the further restraining dread that he would not believe it, but would assort it with the fabulous dogs and veal-cutlets as a monstrous invention. However, I temporised with myself, of course—for, was I not wavering between right and wrong, when the thing is always done?—and resolved to make a full disclosure if I should see any such new occasion as a new chance of helping in the discovery of the assailant.

The Constables, and the Bow-street men° from London—for, this happened in the days of the extinct red waistcoated police—were about the house for a week or two, and did pretty much what I have heard and read of like authorities doing in other such cases. They took up several obviously wrong people, and they ran their heads very hard against wrong ideas, and persisted in trying to fit the circumstances to the ideas, instead of trying to extract ideas from the circumstances. Also, they stood about the door of the Jolly Bargemen, with knowing and reserved looks that filled the whole neighbourhood with admiration; and they had a mysterious manner of taking their drink, that was almost as good as taking the culprit. But not quite, for they never did it.

Long after these constitutional powers had dispersed, my sister lay very ill in bed. Her sight was disturbed, so that she saw objects multiplied, and grasped at visionary teacups and wine-glasses instead of the realities; her hearing was greatly impaired; her memory also; and her speech was unintelligible. When, at last, she came round so far as to be helped down stairs, it was still necessary to keep my slate always by her, that she might indicate in writing what she could not indicate in speech. As she was (very bad handwriting apart) a more than indifferent speller, and as Joe was a more than indifferent reader, extraordinary complications arose between them, which I was always called in to solve. The administration of mutton instead of medicine, the substitution of Tea for Joe, and the baker for bacon, were among the mildest of my own mistakes.

However, her temper was greatly improved, and she was patient. A tremulous uncertainty of the action of all her limbs soon became a part of her regular state, and afterwards, at intervals of two or three months, she would often put her hands to her head, and would then remain for about a week at a time in some gloomy aberration of mind.

Bow-street men: A detective force, the Bow-Street Runners were superseded by the Metropolitan Police in 1829.

We were at a loss to find a suitable attendant for her, until a circumstance happened conveniently to relieve us. Mr. Wopsle's great-aunt conquered a confirmed habit of living into which she had fallen, and Biddy became a part of our establishment.

It may have been about a month after my sister's reappearance in the kitchen, when Biddy came to us with a small speckled box containing the whole of her worldly effects, and became a blessing to the household. Above all, she was a blessing to Joe, for the dear old fellow was sadly cut up by the constant contemplation of the wreck of his wife, and had been accustomed, while attending on her of an evening, to turn to me every now and then and say, with his blue eyes moistened, "Such a fine figure of a woman as she once were, Pip!" Biddy instantly taking the cleverest charge of her as though she had studied her from infancy, Joe became able in some sort to appreciate the greater quiet of his life, and to get down to the Jolly Bargemen now and then for a change that did him good. It was characteristic of the police people that they had all more or less suspected poor Joe (though he never knew it), and that they had to a man concurred in regarding him as one of the deepest spirits they had ever encountered.

Biddy's first triumph in her new office, was to solve a difficulty that had completely vanquished me. I had tried hard at it, but had made nothing of it. Thus it was:

Again and again and again, my sister had traced upon the slate, a character that looked like a curious T, and then with the utmost eagerness had called our attention to it as something she particularly wanted. I had in vain tried everything producible that began with a T, from tar to toast and tub. At length it had come into my head that the sign looked like a hammer, and on my lustily calling that word in my sister's ear, she had begun to hammer on the table and had expressed a qualified assent. Thereupon, I had brought in all our hammers, one after another, but without avail. Then I bethought me of a crutch, the shape being much the same, and I borrowed one in the village, and displayed it to my sister with considerable confidence. But she shook her head to that extent when she was shown it, that we were terrified lest in her weak and shattered state she should dislocate her neck.

When my sister found that Biddy was very quick to understand her, this mysterious sign reappeared on the slate. Biddy looked thoughtfully at it, heard my explanation, looked thoughtfully at my sister, looked thoughtfully at Joe (who was always represented on the slate by his initial letter), and ran into the forge, followed by Joe and me.

"Why, of course!" cried Biddy, with an exultant face. "Don't you see? It's *him!*"

Orlick, without a doubt! She had lost his name, and could only signify him by his hammer. We told him why we wanted him to come into the kitchen, and he slowly laid down his hammer, wiped his brow with his arm, took another wipe at it with his apron, and came slouching out, with a curious loose vagabond bend in the knees that strongly distinguished him.

I confess that I expected to see my sister denounce him, and that I was disappointed by the different result. She manifested the greatest anxiety to be on good terms with him, was evidently much pleased by his being at length produced, and motioned that she would have him given something to drink. She watched his countenance as if she were particularly wishful to be assured that he took kindly to his reception, she showed every possible desire to conciliate him, and there was an air of humble propitiation in all she did, such as I have seen pervade the bearing of a child towards a hard master. After that day, a day rarely passed without her drawing the hammer on her slate, and without Orlick's slouching in and standing doggedly before her, as if he knew no more than I did what to make of it.

Chapter 17

I now fell into a regular routine of apprenticeship-life, which was varied, beyond the limits of the village and the marshes, by no more remarkable circumstance than the arrival of my birthday and my paying another visit to Miss Havisham. I found Miss Sarah Pocket still on duty at the gate, I found Miss Havisham just as I had left her, and she spoke of Estella in the very same way, if not in the very same words. The interview lasted but a few minutes, and she gave me a guinea when I was going, and told me to come again on my next birthday. I may mention at once that this became an annual custom. I tried to decline taking the guinea on the first occasion, but with no better effect than causing her to ask me very angrily, if I expected more? Then, and after that, I took it.

So unchanging was the dull old house, the yellow light in the darkened room, the faded spectre in the chair by the dressing-table glass, that I felt as if the stopping of the clocks had stopped Time in that mysterious place, and, while I and everything else outside it grew older, it stood still. Daylight never entered the house as to my thoughts and remembrances of it, any more than as to the actual fact.

It bewildered me, and under its influence I continued at heart to hate my trade and to be ashamed of home.

Imperceptibly I became conscious of a change in Biddy, however. Her shoes came up at the heel, her hair grew bright and neat, her hands were always clean. She was not beautiful—she was common, and could not be like Estella—but she was pleasant and wholesome and sweet-tempered. She had not been with us more than a year (I remember her being newly out of mourning at the time it struck me), when I observed to myself one evening that she had curiously thoughtful and attentive eyes; eyes that were very pretty and very good.

It came of my lifting up my own eyes from a task I was poring at—writing some passages from a book, to improve myself in two ways at once by a sort of stratagem—and seeing Biddy observant of what I was about. I laid down my pen, and Biddy stopped in her needlework without laying it down.

"Biddy," said I, "how do you manage it? Either I am very stupid, or you are very clever."

"What is it that I manage? I don't know," returned Biddy, smiling.

She managed our whole domestic life, and wonderfully too; but I did not mean that, though that made what I did mean, more surprising.

"How do you manage, Biddy," said I, "to learn everything that I learn, and always to keep up with me?" I was beginning to be rather vain of my knowledge, for I spent my birthday guineas on it, and set aside the greater part of my pocket-money for similar investment; though I have no doubt, now, that the little I knew was extremely dear at the price.

"I might as well ask you," said Biddy, "how *you* manage?"

"No; because when I come in from the forge of a night, any one can see me turning to at it. But you never turn to at it, Biddy."

"I suppose I must catch it—like a cough," said Biddy, quietly; and went on with her sewing.

Pursuing my idea as I leaned back in my wooden chair and looked at Biddy sewing away with her head on one side, I began to think her rather an extraordinary girl. For, I called to mind now, that she was equally accomplished in terms of our trade, and the names of our different sorts of work, and our various tools. In short, whatever I knew, Biddy knew. Theoretically, she was already as good a blacksmith as I, or better.

"You are one of those, Biddy," said I, "who make the most of every chance. You never had a chance before you came here, and see how improved you are!"

Biddy looked at me for an instant, and went on with her sewing. "I was your first teacher though; wasn't I?" said she, as she sewed.

"Biddy!" I exclaimed, in amazement. "Why, you are crying!"

"No I am not," said Biddy, looking up and laughing. "What put that in your head?"

What could have put it in my head, but the glistening of a tear as it dropped on her work? I sat silent, recalling what a drudge she had been until Mr. Wopsle's great-aunt successfully overcame that bad habit of living, so highly desirable to be got rid of by some people. I recalled the hopeless circumstances by which she had been surrounded in the miserable little shop and the miserable little noisy evening school, with that miserable old bundle of incompetence always to be dragged and shouldered. I reflected that even in those untoward times there must have been latent in Biddy what was now developing, for, in my first uneasiness and discontent I had turned to her for help, as a matter of course. Biddy sat quietly sewing, shedding no more tears, and while I looked at her and thought about it all, it occurred to me that perhaps I had not been sufficiently grateful to Biddy. I might have been too reserved, and should have patronised her more (though I did not use that precise word in my meditations), with my confidence.

"Yes, Biddy," I observed, when I had done turning it over, "you were my first teacher, and that at a time when we little thought of ever being together like this, in this kitchen."

"Ah, poor thing!" replied Biddy. It was like her self-forgetfulness, to transfer the remark to my sister, and to get up and be busy about her, making her more comfortable; "that's sadly true!"

"Well!" said I, "we must talk together a little more, as we used to do. And I must consult you a little more, as I used to do. Let us have a quiet walk on the marshes next Sunday, Biddy, and a long chat."

My sister was never left alone now; but Joe more than readily undertook the care of her on that Sunday afternoon, and Biddy and I went out together. It was summer-time, and lovely weather. When we had passed the village and the church and the churchyard, and were out on the marshes and began to see the sails of the ships as they sailed on, I began to combine Miss Havisham and Estella with the prospect, in my usual way. When we came to the river-side and sat down on the bank, with the water rippling at our feet, making it all more quiet than it would have been without that sound, I resolved that it was a good time and place for the admission of Biddy into my inner confidence.

"Biddy," said I, after binding her to secrecy, "I want to be a gentleman."

"Oh, I wouldn't, if I was you!" she returned. "I don't think it would answer."

"Biddy," said I, with some severity, "I have particular reasons for wanting to be a gentleman."

"You know best, Pip; but don't you think you are happier as you are?"

"Biddy," I exclaimed, impatiently, "I am not at all happy as I am. I am disgusted with my calling and with my life. I have never taken to either, since I was bound. Don't be absurd."

"Was I absurd?" said Biddy, quietly raising her eyebrows; "I am sorry for that; I didn't mean to be. I only want you to do well, and to be comfortable."

"Well then, understand once for all that I never shall or can be comfortable—or anything but miserable—there, Biddy!—unless I can lead a very different sort of life from the life I lead now."

"That's a pity!" said Biddy, shaking her head with a sorrowful air.

Now, I too had so often thought it a pity, that, in the singular kind of quarrel with myself which I was always carrying on, I was half inclined to shed tears of vexation and distress when Biddy gave utterance to her sentiment and my own. I told her she was right, and I knew it was much to be regretted, but still it was not to be helped.

"If I could have settled down," I said to Biddy, plucking up the short grass within reach, much as I had once upon a time pulled my feelings out of my hair and kicked them into the brewery wall: "if I could have settled down and been but half as fond of the forge as I was when I was little, I know it would have been much better for me. You and I and Joe would have wanted nothing then, and Joe and I would perhaps have gone partners when I was out of my time, and I might even have grown up to keep company with you, and we might have sat on this very bank on a fine Sunday, quite different people. I should have been good enough for *you;* shouldn't I, Biddy?"

Biddy sighed as she looked at the ships sailing on, and returned for answer, "Yes; I am not over-particular." It scarcely sounded flattering, but I knew she meant well.

"Instead of that," said I, plucking up more grass and chewing a blade or two, "see how I am going on. Dissatisfied, and uncomfortable, and—what would it signify to me, being coarse and common, if nobody had told me so!"

Biddy turned her face suddenly towards mine, and looked far more attentively at me than she had looked at the sailing ships.

"It was neither a very true nor a very polite thing to say," she remarked, directing her eyes to the ships again. "Who said it?"

I was disconcerted, for I had broken away without quite seeing where I was going. It was not to be shuffled off now, however, and I answered, "The beautiful young lady at Miss Havisham's, and she's more beautiful than anybody ever was, and I admire her dreadfully, and I want to be a gentleman on her account." Having made this lunatic confession, I began to throw my torn-up grass into the river, as if I had some thoughts of following it.

"Do you want to be a gentleman, to spite her or to gain her over?" Biddy quietly asked me, after a pause.

"I don't know," I moodily answered.

"Because, if it is to spite her," Biddy pursued, "I should think—but you know best—that might be better and more independently done by caring nothing for her words. And if it is to gain her over, I should think—but you know best—she was not worth gaining over."

Exactly what I myself had thought, many times. Exactly what was perfectly manifest to me at the moment. But how could I, a poor dazed village lad, avoid that wonderful inconsistency into which the best and wisest of men fall every day?

"It may be all quite true," said I to Biddy, "but I admire her dreadfully."

In short, I turned over on my face when I came to that, and got a good grasp on the hair on each side of my head, and wrenched it well. All the while knowing the madness of my heart to be so very mad and misplaced, that I was quite conscious it would have served my face right, if I had lifted it up by my hair, and knocked it against the pebbles as a punishment for belonging to such an idiot.

Biddy was the wisest of girls, and she tried to reason no more with me. She put her hand, which was a comfortable hand though roughened by work, upon my hands, one after another, and gently took them out of my hair. Then she softly patted my shoulder in a soothing way, while with my face upon my sleeve I cried a little—exactly as I had done in the brewery yard—and felt vaguely convinced that I was very much ill used by somebody, or by everybody; I can't say which.

"I am glad of one thing," said Biddy, "and that is, that you have felt you could give me your confidence, Pip. And I am glad of another thing, and that is, that of course you know you may depend upon my keeping it and always so far deserving it. If your first teacher (dear! such a poor one, and so much in need of being taught herself!) had been your teacher at the present time, she thinks she knows what lesson she would set. But it would be a hard one to learn, and you have got beyond her, and it's of no use now." So, with a quiet sigh for me, Biddy rose from the bank, and said, with a fresh and pleasant change of voice, "Shall we walk a little further, or go home?"

"Biddy," I cried, getting up, putting my arm round her neck, and giving her a kiss, "I shall always tell you everything."

"Till you're a gentleman," said Biddy.

"You know I never shall be, so that's always. Not that I have any occasion to tell you anything, for you know everything I know—as I told you at home the other night."

"Ah!" said Biddy, quite in a whisper, as she looked away at the ships. And then repeated, with her former pleasant change; "shall we walk a little further, or go home?"

I said to Biddy we would walk a little further, and we did so, and the summer afternoon toned down into the summer evening, and it was very beautiful. I began to consider whether I was not more naturally and wholesomely situated, after all, in these circumstances, than playing beggar my neighbour by candlelight in the room with the stopped clocks, and being despised by Estella. I thought it would be very good for me if I could get her out of my head, with all the rest of those remembrances and fancies, and could go to work determined to relish what I had to do, and stick to it, and make the best of it. I asked myself the question whether I did not surely know that if Estella were beside me at that moment instead of Biddy, she would make me miserable? I was obliged to admit that I did know it for a certainty, and I said to myself, "Pip, what a fool you are!"

We talked a good deal as we walked, and all that Biddy said seemed right. Biddy was never insulting, or capricious, or Biddy to-day and somebody else to-morrow; she would have derived only pain, and no pleasure, from giving me pain; she would far rather have wounded her own breast than mine. How could it be, then, that I did not like her much the better of the two?

"Biddy," said I, when we were walking homeward, "I wish you could put me right."

"I wish I could!" said Biddy.

"If I could only get myself to fall in love with you—you don't mind my speaking so openly to such an old acquaintance?"

"Oh dear, not at all!" said Biddy. "Don't mind me."

"If I could only get myself to do it, *that* would be the thing for me."

"But you never will, you see," said Biddy.

It did not appear quite so unlikely to me that evening, as it would have done if we had discussed it a few hours before. I therefore observed I was not quite sure of that. But Biddy said she *was,* and she said it decisively. In my heart I believed her to be right; and yet I took it rather ill, too, that she should be so positive on the point.

When we came near the churchyard, we had to cross an embankment, and get over a stile near a sluice-gate. There started up, from the gate, or from the rushes, or from the ooze (which was quite in his stagnant way), old Orlick.

"Halloa!" he growled, "where are you two going?"

Where should we be going, but home? "Well then," said he, "I'm jiggered if I don't see you home!"

This penalty of being jiggered was a favourite supposititious case of his. He attached no definite meaning to the word that I am aware of, but used it, like his own pretended christian name, to affront mankind, and convey an idea of something savagely damaging. When I was younger, I had had a general belief that if he had jiggered me personally, he would have done it with a sharp and twisted hook.

Biddy was much against his going with us, and said to me in a whisper, "Don't let him come; I don't like him." As I did not like him either, I took the liberty of saying that we thanked him, but we didn't want seeing home. He received that piece of information with a yell of laughter, and dropped back, but came slouching after us at a little distance.

Curious to know whether Biddy suspected him of having had a hand in that murderous attack of which my sister had never been able to give any account, I asked her why she did not like him?

"Oh!" she replied, glancing over her shoulder as he slouched after us, "because I—I am afraid he likes me."

"Did he ever tell you he liked you?" I asked, indignantly.

"No," said Biddy, glancing over her shoulder again, "he never told me so; but he dances at me, whenever he can catch my eye."

However novel and peculiar this testimony of attachment, I did not doubt the accuracy of the interpretation. I was very hot indeed upon old Orlick's daring to admire her; as hot as if it were an outrage on myself.

"But it makes no difference to you, you know," said Biddy, calmly.

"No, Biddy, it makes no difference to me; only I don't like it; I don't approve of it."

"Nor I neither," said Biddy. "Though *that* makes no difference to you."

"Exactly," said I; "but I must tell you I should have no opinion of you, Biddy, if he danced at you with your own consent."

I kept an eye on Orlick after that night, and, whenever circumstances were favourable to his dancing at Biddy, got before him, to obscure that demonstration. He had struck root in Joe's establishment, by reason of my sister's sudden fancy for him, or I should have tried to get him dismissed. He quite understood and reciprocated my good intentions, as I had reason to know thereafter.

And now, because my mind was not confused enough before, I complicated its confusion fifty thousand-fold, by having states and seasons when I was clear that Biddy was immeasurably better than Estella, and that the plain honest working life to which I was born, had nothing in it to be ashamed of, but offered me sufficient means of self-respect and happiness. At those times, I would decide conclusively that my disaffection to dear old Joe and the forge, was gone, and that I was growing up in a fair way to be partners with Joe and to keep company with Biddy—when all in a moment some confounding remembrance of the Havisham days would fall upon me, like a destructive missile, and scatter my wits again. Scattered wits take a long time picking up; and often, before I had got them well together, they would be dispersed in all directions by one stray thought, that perhaps after all Miss Havisham was going to make my fortune when my time was out.

If my time had run out, it would have left me still at the height of my perplexities, I dare say. It never did run out, however, but was brought to a premature end, as I proceed to relate.

[PART 11]

Chapter 18

It was in the fourth year of my apprenticeship to Joe, and it was a Saturday night. There was a group assembled round the fire at the Three Jolly Bargemen, attentive to Mr. Wopsle as he read the newspaper aloud. Of that group I was one.

A highly popular murder had been committed, and Mr. Wopsle was imbrued in blood to the eyebrows. He gloated over every abhorrent adjective in the description, and identified himself with every witness at the Inquest. He faintly moaned, "I am done for," as the victim, and he barbarously bellowed, "I'll serve you out," as the murderer. He gave the medical testimony, in pointed imitation of our local practitioner; and he piped and shook, as the aged turnpike-keeper who had heard blows, to an extent so very paralytic as to suggest a doubt regarding the mental competency of that witness. The coroner, in Mr. Wopsle's hands, became Timon of Athens; the beadle, Coriolanus.° He enjoyed himself thoroughly, and we all enjoyed ourselves, and were delightfully comfortable. In this cozy state of mind we came to the verdict Wilful Murder.

Then, and not sooner, I became aware of a strange gentleman leaning over the back of the settle opposite me, looking on. There was an expression of contempt on his face, and he bit the side of a great forefinger as he watched the group of faces. "Well!" said the stranger to Mr. Wopsle, when the reading was done, "you have settled it all to your own satisfaction, I have no doubt?"

Everybody started and looked up, as if it were the murderer. He looked at everybody coldly and sarcastically.

"Guilty, of course?" said he. "Out with it. Come!"

"Sir," returned Mr. Wopsle, "without having the honour of your acquaintance, I do say Guilty." Upon this, we all took courage to unite in a confirmatory murmur.

"I know you do," said the stranger; "I knew you would. I told you so. But now I'll ask you a question. Do you know, or do you not know, that the law of England supposes every man to be innocent, until he is proved—proved—to be guilty?"

"Sir," Mr. Wopsle began to reply, "as an Englishman myself, I——"

"Come!" said the stranger, biting his forefinger at him. "Don't evade the question. Either you know it, or you don't know it. Which is it to be?"

He stood with his head on one side and himself on one side, in a bullying interrogative manner, and he threw his forefinger at Mr. Wopsle—as it were to mark him out—before biting it again.

"Now!" said he. "Do you know it, or don't you know it?"

"Certainly I know it," replied Mr. Wopsle.

"Certainly you know it. Then why didn't you say so at first? Now, I'll ask you another question;" taking possession of Mr. Wopsle, as if he had a right to him. "*Do* you know that none of these witnesses have yet been cross-examined?"

Mr. Wopsle was beginning, "I can only say——" when the stranger stopped him.

Timon . . . Coriolanus: Heroic roles from Shakespeare's tragedies.

"What? You won't answer the question, yes or no? Now, I'll try you again." Throwing his finger at him again. "Attend to me. Are you aware, or are you not aware, that none of these witnesses have yet been cross-examined? Come, I only want one word from you. Yes, or no?"

Mr. Wopsle hesitated, and we all began to conceive rather a poor opinion of him.

"Come!" said the stranger, "I'll help you. You don't deserve help, but I'll help you. Look at that paper you hold in your hand. What is it?"

"What is it?" repeated Mr. Wopsle, eyeing it, much at a loss.

"Is it," pursued the stranger in his most sarcastic and suspicious manner, "the printed paper you have just been reading from?"

"Undoubtedly."

"Undoubtedly. Now, turn to that paper, and tell me whether it distinctly states that the prisoner expressly said that his legal advisers instructed him altogether to reserve his defence?"

"I read that just now," Mr. Wopsle pleaded.

"Never mind what you read just now, sir; I don't ask you what you read just now. You may read the Lord's Prayer backwards, if you like—and, perhaps, have done it before to-day. Turn to the paper. No, no, no, my friend; not to the top of the column; you know better than that; to the bottom, to the bottom." (We all began to think Mr. Wopsle full of subterfuge.) "Well? Have you found it?"

"Here it is," said Mr. Wopsle.

"Now, follow that passage with your eye, and tell me whether it distinctly states that the prisoner expressly said that he was instructed by his legal advisers wholly to reserve his defence? Come! Do you make that of it?"

Mr. Wopsle answered, "Those are not the exact words."

"Not the exact words!" repeated the gentleman, bitterly. "Is that the exact substance?"

"Yes," said Mr. Wopsle.

"Yes," repeated the stranger, looking round at the rest of the company with his right hand extended towards the witness, Wopsle. "And now I ask you what you say to the conscience of that man who, with that passage before his eyes, can lay his head upon his pillow after having pronounced a fellow-creature guilty, unheard?"

We all began to suspect that Mr. Wopsle was not the man we had thought him, and that he was beginning to be found out.

"And that same man, remember," pursued the gentleman, throwing his finger at Mr. Wopsle heavily; "that same man might be summoned as a juryman upon this very trial, and, having thus deeply committed himself, might return to the bosom of his family and lay his head upon his pillow, after deliberately swearing that he would well and truly try the issue joined between Our Sovereign Lord the King and the prisoner at the bar, and would a true verdict give according to the evidence, so help him God!"

We were all deeply persuaded that the unfortunate Wopsle had gone too far, and had better stop in his reckless career while there was yet time.

The strange gentleman, with an air of authority not to be disputed, and with a manner expressive of knowing something secret about every one of us that would effectually do for each individual if he chose to disclose it, left the back of the settle, and came into the space between the two settles, in front of the fire, where he remained standing: his left hand in his pocket, and he biting the forefinger of his right.

"From information I have received," said he, looking round at us as we all quailed before him, " I have reason to believe there is a blacksmith among you, by name Joseph—or Joe—Gargery. Which is the man?"

"Here is the man," said Joe.

The strange gentleman beckoned him out of his place, and Joe went.

"You have an apprentice," pursued the stranger, "commonly known as Pip? Is he here?"

"I am here!" I cried.

The stranger did not recognise me, but I recognised him as the gentleman I had met on the stairs, on the occasion of my second visit to Miss Havisham. I had known him the moment I saw him looking over the settle, and now that I stood confronting him with his hand upon my shoulder, I checked off again in detail, his large head, his dark complexion, his deep-set eyes, his bushy black eyebrows, his large watch-chain, his strong black dots of beard and whisker, and even the smell of scented soap on his great hand.

"I wish to have a private conference with you two," said he, when he had surveyed me at his leisure. "It will take a little time. Perhaps we had better go to your place of residence. I prefer not to anticipate my communication here; you will impart as much or as little of it as you please to your friends afterwards; I have nothing to do with that."

Amidst a wondering silence, we three walked out of the Jolly Bargemen, and in a wondering silence walked home. While going along, the strange gentleman occasionally looked at me, and occasionally bit the side of his finger. As we neared home, Joe vaguely acknowledging the occasion as an impressive and ceremonious one, went on ahead to open the front door. Our conference was held in the state parlour, which was feebly lighted by one candle.

It began with the strange gentleman's sitting down at the table, drawing the candle to him, and looking over some entries in his pocket-book. He then put up the pocket-book and set the candle a little aside: after peering round it into the darkness at Joe and me, to ascertain which was which.

"My name," he said, "is Jaggers, and I am a lawyer in London. I am pretty well known. I have unusual business to transact with you, and I commence by explaining that it is not of my originating. If my advice had been asked, I should not have been here. It was not asked, and you see me here. What I have to do as the confidential agent of another, I do. No less, no more."

Finding that he could not see us very well from where he sat, he got up, and threw one leg over the back of a chair and leaned upon it; thus having one foot on the seat of the chair, and one foot on the ground.

"Now, Joseph Gargery, I am the bearer of an offer to relieve you of this young fellow your apprentice. You would not object to cancel his indentures, at his request and for his good? You would not want anything for so doing?"

"Lord forbid that I should want anything for not standing in Pip's way," said Joe, staring.

"Lord forbidding is pious, but not to the purpose," returned Mr. Jaggers. "The question is, Would you want anything? Do you want anything?"

"The answer is," returned Joe, sternly, "No."

I thought Mr. Jaggers glanced at Joe, as if he considered him a fool for his disinterestedness. But I was too much bewildered between breathless curiosity and surprise, to be sure of it.

"Very well," said Mr. Jaggers. "Recollect the admission you have made, and don't try to go from it presently."

"Who's a going to try?" retorted Joe.

"I don't say anybody is. Do you keep a dog?"

"Yes, I do keep a dog."

"Bear in mind then, that Brag is a good dog, but Holdfast is a better.° Bear that in mind, will you?" repeated Mr. Jaggers, shutting his eyes and nodding his head at Joe, as if he were forgiving him something. "Now, I return to this young fellow. And the communication I have got to make is, that he has great expectations."

Joe and I gasped, and looked at one another.

"I am instructed to communicate to him," said Mr. Jaggers, throwing his finger at me, sideways, "that he will come into a handsome property. Further, that it is the desire of the present possessor of that property, that he be immediately removed from his present sphere of life and from this place, and be brought up as a gentleman—in a word, as a young fellow of great expectations."

My dream was out; my wild fancy was surpassed by sober reality; Miss Havisham was going to make my fortune on a grand scale.

"Now, Mr. Pip," pursued the lawyer, "I address the rest of what I have to say, to you. You are to understand, first, that it is the request of the person from whom I take my instructions, that you always bear the name of Pip. You will have no objection, I dare say, to your great expectations being encumbered with that easy condition. But if you have any objection, this is the time to mention it."

My heart was beating so fast, and there was such a singing in my ears, that I could scarcely stammer I had no objection.

"I should think not! Now you are to understand, secondly, Mr. Pip, that the name of the person who is your liberal benefactor remains a profound secret, until the person chooses to reveal it. I am empowered to mention that it is the intention of the person to reveal it at first hand by word of mouth to yourself. When or where that intention may be carried out, I cannot say; no one can say. It may be years hence. Now, you are distinctly to understand that you are most positively prohibited from making any inquiry on this head, or any allusion or reference, however distant, to any individual whomsoever as *the* individual, in all the communications you may have with me. If you have a suspicion in your own breast, keep that suspicion in your own breast. It is not the least to the purpose what the reasons of this prohibition are; they may be the strongest and gravest reasons, or they may be mere whim. That is not for you to inquire into. The condition is laid down. Your acceptance of it, and your observance of it as binding, is the only remaining condition that I am charged with, by the person from whom I take my instructions, and for whom I am not otherwise responsible. That person is the person from whom you derive your

Brag . . . better: A proverb cautioning one to keep one's mouth shut ("held fast").

expectations, and the secret is solely held by that person and by me. Again, not a very difficult condition with which to encumber such a rise in fortune; but if you have any objection to it, this is the time to mention it. Speak out."

Once more, I stammered with difficulty that I had no objection.

"I should think not! Now, Mr. Pip, I have done with stipulations." Though he called me Mr. Pip, and began rather to make up to me, he still could not get rid of a certain air of bullying suspicion; and even now he occasionally shut his eyes and threw his finger at me while he spoke, as much as to express that he knew all kinds of things to my disparagement, if he only chose to mention them. "We come next, to mere details of arrangement. You must know that, although I have used the term 'expectations' more than once, you are not endowed with expectations only. There is already lodged in my hands, a sum of money amply sufficient for your suitable education and maintenance. You will please consider me your guardian. Oh!" for I was going to thank him, "I tell you at once, I am paid for my services, or I shouldn't render them. It is considered that you must be better educated, in accordance with your altered position, and that you will be alive to the importance and necessity of at once entering on that advantage."

I said I had always longed for it.

"Never mind what you have always longed for, Mr. Pip," he retorted; "keep to the record. If you long for it now, that's enough. Am I answered that you are ready to be placed at once, under some proper tutor? Is that it?"

I stammered yes, that was it.

"Good. Now, your inclinations are to be consulted. I don't think that wise, mind, but it's my trust. Have you ever heard of any tutor whom you would prefer to another?"

I had never heard of any tutor but Biddy and Mr. Wopsle's great-aunt; so, I replied in the negative.

"There is a certain tutor, of whom I have some knowledge, who I think might suit the purpose," said Mr. Jaggers. "I don't recommend him, observe; because I never recommend anybody. The gentleman I speak of, is one Mr. Matthew Pocket."

Ah! I caught at the name directly. Miss Havisham's relation. The Matthew whom Mr. and Mrs. Camilla had spoken of. The Matthew whose place was to be at Miss Havisham's head, when she lay dead, in her bride's dress on the bride's table.

"You know the name?" said Mr. Jaggers, looking shrewdly at me, and then shutting up his eyes while he waited for my answer.

My answer was, that I had heard of the name.

"Oh!" said he. "You have heard of the name. But the question is, what do you say of it?"

I said, or tried to say, that I was much obliged to him for his recommendation——

"No, my young friend!" he interrupted, shaking his great head very slowly. "Recollect yourself!"

Not recollecting myself, I began again that I was much obliged to him for his recommendation——

"No, my young friend," he interrupted, shaking his head and frowning and smiling both at once; "no, no, no; it's very well done, but it won't do; you are too young to fix me with it. Recommendation is not the word, Mr. Pip. Try another."

Correcting myself, I said that I was much obliged to him for his mention of Mr. Matthew Pocket——

"*That's* more like it!" cried Mr. Jaggers.

—And (I added), I would gladly try that gentleman.

"Good. You had better try him in his own house. The way shall be prepared for you, and you can see his son first, who is in London. When will you come to London?"

I said (glancing at Joe, who stood looking on, motionless), that I supposed I could come directly.

"First," said Mr. Jaggers, "you should have some new clothes to come in, and they should not be working clothes. Say this day week. You'll want some money. Shall I leave you twenty guineas?"

He produced a long purse, with the greatest coolness, and counted them out on the table and pushed them over to me. This was the first time he had taken his leg from the chair. He sat astride of the chair when he had pushed the money over, and sat swinging his purse and eyeing Joe.

"Well, Joseph Gargery? You look dumb-foundered?"

"I *am!*" said Joe, in a very decided manner.

"It was understood that you wanted nothing for yourself, remember?"

"It were understood," said Joe. "And it are understood. And it ever will be similar according."

"But what," said Mr. Jaggers, swinging his purse, "what if it was in my instructions to make you a present, as compensation?"

"As compensation what for?" Joe demanded.

"For the loss of his services."

Joe laid his hand upon my shoulder with the touch of a woman. I have often thought him since, like the steam-hammer, that can crush a man or pat an eggshell, in his combination of strength with gentleness. "Pip is that hearty welcome," said Joe, "to go free with his services, to honour and fortun', as no words can tell him. But if you think as Money can make compensation to me for the loss of the little child—what come to the forge—and ever the best of friends!——"

O dear good Joe, whom I was so ready to leave and so unthankful to, I see you again, with your muscular blacksmith's arm before your eyes, and your broad chest heaving, and your voice dying away. O dear good faithful tender Joe, I feel the loving tremble of your hand upon my arm, as solemnly this day as if it had been the rustle of an angel's wing!

But I encouraged Joe at the time. I was lost in the mazes of my future fortunes, and could not retrace the by-paths we had trodden together. I begged Joe to be comforted, for (as he said) we had ever been the best of friends, and (as I said) we ever would be so. Joe scooped his eyes with his disengaged wrist, as if he were bent on gouging himself, but said not another word.

Mr. Jaggers had looked on at this, as one who recognised in Joe the village idiot, and in me his keeper. When it was over, he said, weighing in his hand the purse he had ceased to swing:

"Now, Joseph Gargery, I warn you this is your last chance. No half measures with me. If you mean to take a present that I have it in charge to make you, speak out, and you shall have it. If on the contrary you mean to say——" Here, to his great amazement, he was stopped by Joe's suddenly working round him with every demonstration of a fell pugilistic purpose.

"Which I meantersay," cried Joe, "that if you come into my place bull-baiting and badgering me, come out! Which I meantersay as sech if you're a man, come on! Which I meantersay that what I say, I meantersay and stand or fall by!"

I drew Joe away, and he immediately became placable; merely stating to me, in an obliging manner and as a polite expostulatory notice to any one whom it might happen to concern, that he were not a going to be bull-baited and badgered in his own place. Mr. Jaggers had risen when Joe demonstrated, and had backed near the door. Without evincing any inclination to come in again, he there delivered his valedictory remarks. They were these.

"Well, Mr. Pip, I think the sooner you leave here—as you are to be a gentleman—the better. Let it stand for this day week, and you shall receive my printed address in the mean time. You can take a hackney-coach at the stage coach-office in London, and come straight to me. Understand, that I express no opinion, one way or other, on the trust I undertake. I am paid for undertaking it, and I do so. Now, understand that, finally. Understand that!"

He was throwing his finger at both of us, and I think would have gone on, but for his seeming to think Joe dangerous, and going off.

Something came into my head which induced me to run after him, as he was going down to the Jolly Bargemen where he had left a hired carriage.

"I beg your pardon, Mr. Jaggers."

"Halloa!" said he, facing round, "what's the matter?"

"I wish to be quite right, Mr. Jaggers, and to keep to your directions; so I thought I had better ask. Would there be any objection to my taking leave of any one I know, about here, before I go away?"

"No," said he, looking as if he hardly understood me.

"I don't mean in the village only, but up town?"

"No," said he. "No objection."

I thanked him and ran home again, and there I found that Joe had already locked the front door and vacated the state parlour, and was seated by the kitchen fire with a hand on each knee, gazing intently at the burning coals. I too sat down before the fire and gazed at the coals, and nothing was said for a long time.

My sister was in her cushioned chair in her corner, and Biddy sat at her needlework before the fire, and Joe sat next Biddy, and I sat next Joe in the corner opposite my sister. The more I looked into the glowing coals, the more incapable I became of looking at Joe; the longer the silence lasted, the more unable I felt to speak.

At length I got out, "Joe, have you told Biddy?"

"No, Pip," returned Joe, still looking at the fire, and holding his knees tight, as if he had private information that they intended to make off somewhere, "which I left it to yourself, Pip."

"I would rather you told, Joe."

"Pip's a gentleman of fortun' then," said Joe, "and God bless him in it!"

Biddy dropped her work, and looked at me. Joe held his knees and looked at me. I looked at both of them. After a pause, they both heartily congratulated me; but there was a certain touch of sadness in their congratulations, that I rather resented.

I took it upon myself to impress Biddy (and through Biddy, Joe) with the grave obligation I considered my friends under, to know nothing and say nothing about the maker of my fortune. It would all come out in good time, I observed, and in the mean while nothing was to be said, save that I had come into great expectations from a mysterious patron. Biddy nodded her head thoughtfully at the fire as she took up her work again, and said she would be very particular; and Joe, still detaining his knees, said, "Ay, ay, I'll be ekervally partickler, Pip;" and then they congratulated me again, and went on to express so much wonder at the notion of my being a gentleman, that I didn't half like it.

Infinite pains were then taken by Biddy to convey to my sister some idea of what had happened. To the best of my belief, those efforts entirely failed. She laughed and nodded her head a great many times, and even repeated after Biddy, the words "Pip" and "Property." But I doubt if they had more meaning in them than an election cry,° and I cannot suggest a darker picture of her state of mind.

I never could have believed it without experience, but as Joe and Biddy became more at their cheerful ease again, I became quite gloomy. Dissatisfied with my fortune, of course I could not be; but it is possible that I may have been, without quite knowing it, dissatisfied with myself.

Anyhow, I sat with my elbow on my knee and my face upon my hand, looking into the fire, as those two talked about my going away, and about what they should do without me, and all that. And whenever I caught one of them looking at me, though never so pleasantly (and they often looked at me—particularly Biddy), I felt offended: as if they were expressing some mistrust of me. Though Heaven knows they never did by word or sign.

At those times I would get up and look out at the door; for, our kitchen door opened at once upon the night, and stood open on summer evenings to air the room. The very stars to which I then raised my eyes, I am afraid I took to be but poor and humble stars for glittering on the rustic objects among which I had passed my life.

"Saturday night," said I, when we sat at our supper of bread-and-cheese and beer. "Five more days, and then the day before *the* day! They'll soon go."

"Yes, Pip," observed Joe, whose voice sounded hollow in his beer mug. "They'll soon go."

"Soon, soon go," said Biddy.

"I have been thinking, Joe, that when I go down town on Monday, and order my new clothes, I shall tell the tailor that I'll come and

---

election cry: A slogan shouted during a political campaign.

put them on there, or that I'll have them sent to Mr. Pumblechook's. It would be very disagreeable to be stared at by all the people here."

"Mr. and Mrs. Hubble might like to see you in your new gen-teel figure too, Pip," said Joe, industriously cutting his bread, with his cheese on it, in the palm of his left hand, and glancing at my untasted supper as if he thought of the time when we used to compare slices. "So might Wopsle. And the Jolly Bargemen might take it as a compliment."

"That's just what I don't want, Joe. They would make such a business of it—such a coarse and common business—that I couldn't bear myself."

"Ah, that indeed, Pip!" said Joe. "If you couldn't abear yourself——"

Biddy asked me here, as she sat holding my sister's plate, "Have you thought about when you'll show yourself to Mr. Gargery, and your sister, and me? You will show yourself to us; won't you?"

"Biddy," I returned with some resentment, "you are so exceedingly quick that it's difficult to keep up with you."

("She always were quick," observed Joe.)

"If you had waited another moment, Biddy, you would have heard me say that I shall bring my clothes here in a bundle one evening— most likely on the evening before I go away."

Biddy said no more. Handsomely forgiving her, I soon exchanged an affectionate good night with her and Joe, and went up to bed. When I got into my little room, I sat down and took a long look at it, as a mean little room that I should soon be parted from and raised above, for ever. It was furnished with fresh young remembrances too, and even at the same moment I fell into much the same confused division of mind between it and the better rooms to which I was going, as I had been in so often between the forge and Miss Havisham's, and Biddy and Estella.

The sun had been shining brightly all day on the roof of my attic, and the room was warm. As I put the window open and stood looking out, I saw Joe come slowly forth at the dark door below, and take a turn or two in the air; and then I saw Biddy come, and bring him a pipe and light it for him. He never smoked so late, and it seemed to hint to me that he wanted comforting, for some reason or other.

He presently stood at the door immediately beneath me, smoking his pipe, and Biddy stood there too, quietly talking to him, and I knew that they talked of me, for I heard my name mentioned in an endearing tone by both of them more than once. I would not have listened for more, if I could have heard more: so, I drew away from the window, and sat down in my one chair by the bedside, feeling it very sorrowful and strange that this first night of my bright fortunes should be the loneliest I had ever known.

Looking towards the open window, I saw light wreaths from Joe's pipe floating there, and I fancied it was like a blessing from Joe—not obtruded on me or paraded before me, but pervading the air we shared together. I put my light out, and crept into bed; and it was an uneasy bed now, and I never slept the old sound sleep in it any more.

[PART 12]

Chapter 19

Morning made a considerable difference in my general prospect of Life, and brightened it so much that it scarcely seemed the same. What lay heaviest on my mind, was, the consideration that six days intervened between me and the day of departure; for, I could not divest myself of a misgiving that something might happen to London in the mean while, and that, when I got there, it would be either greatly deteriorated or clean gone.

Joe and Biddy were very sympathetic and pleasant when I spoke of our approaching separation; but they only referred to it when I did. After breakfast, Joe brought out my indentures from the press in the best parlour, and we put them in the fire, and I felt that I was free. With all the novelty of my emancipation on me, I went to church with Joe, and thought, perhaps the clergyman wouldn't have read that about the rich man and the kingdom of Heaven, if he had known all.

After our early dinner I strolled out alone, purposing to finish off the marshes at once, and get them done with. As I passed the church, I felt (as I had felt during service in the morning) a sublime compassion for the poor creatures who were destined to go there, Sunday after Sunday, all their lives through, and to lie obscurely at last among the low green mounds. I promised myself that I would do something for them one of these days, and formed a plan in outline for bestowing a dinner of roast beef and plum-pudding, a pint of ale, and a gallon of condescension, upon everybody in the village.

If I had often thought before, with something allied to shame, of my companionship with the fugitive whom I had once seen limping among those graves, what were my thoughts on this Sunday, when the place recalled the wretch, ragged and shivering, with his felon iron and badge! My comfort was, that it happened a long time ago, and that he had doubtless been transported a long way off, and that he was dead to me, and might be veritably dead into the bargain.

No more low wet grounds, no more dykes and sluices, no more of these grazing cattle—though they seemed, in their dull manner, to wear a more respectful air now, and to face round, in order that they might stare as long as possible at the possessor of such great expectations—farewell, monotonous acquaintances of my childhood, henceforth I was for London and greatness: not for smith's work in general and for you! I made my exultant way to the old Battery, and, lying down there to consider the question whether Miss Havisham intended me for Estella, fell asleep.

When I awoke, I was much surprised to find Joe sitting beside me, smoking his pipe. He greeted me with a cheerful smile on my opening my eyes, and said:

"As being the last time, Pip, I thought I'd foller."

"And Joe, I am very glad you did so."

"Thankee, Pip."

"You may be sure, dear Joe," I went on, after we had shaken hands, "that I shall never forget you."

"No, no, Pip!" said Joe, in a comfortable tone, "*I*'m sure of that. Ay, ay, old chap! Bless you, it were only necessary to get it well round in a man's mind, to be certain on it. But it took a bit of time to get it well round, the change come so oncommon plump; didn't it?"

Somehow, I was not best pleased with Joe's being so mightily secure of me. I should have liked him to have betrayed emotion, or to have said, "It does you credit, Pip," or something of that sort. Therefore, I made no remark on Joe's first head: merely saying as to his second, that the tidings had indeed come suddenly, but that I had always wanted to be a gentleman, and had often and often speculated on what I would do, if I were one.

"Have you though?" said Joe. "Astonishing!"

"It's a pity now, Joe," said I, "that you did not get on a little more, when we had our lessons here; isn't it?"

"Well, I don't know," returned Joe. "I'm so awful dull. I'm only master of my own trade. It were always a pity as I was so awful dull; but it's no more of a pity now, than it was—this day twelvemonth—don't you see?"

What I had meant was, that when I came into my property and was able to do something for Joe, it would have been much more agreeable if he had been better qualified for a rise in station. He was so perfectly innocent of my meaning, however, that I thought I would mention it to Biddy in preference.

So, when we had walked home and had had tea, I took Biddy into our little garden by the side of the lane, and, after throwing out in a general way for the elevation of her spirits, that I should never forget her, said I had a favour to ask of her.

"And it is, Biddy," said I, "that you will not omit any opportunity of helping Joe on, a little."

"How helping him on?" asked Biddy, with a steady sort of glance.

"Well! Joe is a dear good fellow—in fact, I think he is the dearest fellow that ever lived—but he is rather backward in some things. For instance, Biddy, in his learning and his manners."

Although I was looking at Biddy as I spoke, and although she opened her eyes very wide when I had spoken, she did not look at me.

"Oh, his manners! Won't his manners do then?" asked Biddy, plucking a black currant leaf.

"My dear Biddy, they do very well here——"

"Oh! they *do* very well here?" interposed Biddy, looking closely at the leaf in her hand.

"Hear me out—but if I were to remove Joe into a higher sphere, as I shall hope to remove him when I fully come into my property, they would hardly do him justice."

"And don't you think he knows that?" asked Biddy.

It was such a very provoking question (for it had never in the most distant manner occurred to me), that I said, snappishly, "Biddy, what do you mean?"

Biddy having rubbed the leaf to pieces between her hands—and the smell of a black currant bush has ever since recalled to me that evening in the little garden by the side of the lane—said, "Have you never considered that he may be proud?"

"Proud?" I repeated, with disdainful emphasis.

"Oh! there are many kinds of pride," said Biddy, looking full at me and shaking her head; "pride is not all of one kind——"

"Well? What are you stopping for?" said I.

"Not all of one kind," resumed Biddy. "He may be too proud to let any one take him out of a place that he is competent to fill, and fills well and with respect. To tell you the truth, I think he is: though it sounds bold in me to say so, for you must know him far better than I do."

"Now, Biddy," said I, "I am very sorry to see this in you. I did not expect to see this in you. You are envious, Biddy, and grudging. You are dissatisfied on account of my rise in fortune, and you can't help showing it."

"If you have the heart to think so," returned Biddy, "say so. Say so over and over again, if you have the heart to think so."

"If you have the heart to be so, you mean, Biddy," said I, in a virtuous and superior tone; "don't put it off upon me. I am very sorry to see it, and it's a—it's a bad side of human nature. I did intend to ask you to use any little opportunities you might have after I was gone, of improving dear Joe. But after this, I ask you nothing. I am extremely sorry to see this in you, Biddy," I repeated. "It's a—it's a bad side of human nature."

"Whether you scold me or approve of me," returned poor Biddy, "you may equally depend upon my trying to do all that lies in my power, here, at all times. And whatever opinion you take away of me, shall make no difference in my remembrance of you. Yet a gentleman should not be unjust neither," said Biddy, turning away her head.

I again warmly repeated that it was a bad side of human nature (in which sentiment, waiving its application, I have since seen reason to think I was right), and I walked down the little path away from Biddy, and Biddy went into the house, and I went out at the garden gate and took a dejected stroll until supper-time; again feeling it very sorrowful and strange that this, the second night of my bright fortunes, should be as lonely and unsatisfactory as the first.

But, morning once more brightened my view, and I extended my clemency to Biddy, and we dropped the subject. Putting on the best clothes I had, I went into town as early as I could hope to find the shops open, and presented myself before Mr. Trabb, the tailor: who was having his breakfast in the parlour behind his shop, and who did not think it worth his while to come out to me, but called me in to him.

"Well!" said Mr. Trabb, in a hail-fellow-well-met kind of way. "How are you, and what can I do for you?"

Mr. Trabb had sliced his hot roll into three feather beds, and was slipping butter in between the blankets, and covering it up. He was a prosperous old bachelor, and his open window looked into a prosperous little garden and orchard, and there was a prosperous iron safe let into the wall at the side of his fireplace, and I did not doubt that heaps of his prosperity were put away in it in bags.

"Mr. Trabb," said I, "it's an unpleasant thing to have to mention, because it looks like boasting; but I have come into a handsome property."

A change passed over Mr. Trabb. He forgot the butter in bed, got up from the bedside, and wiped his fingers on the tablecloth, exclaiming, "Lord bless my soul!"

"I am going up to my guardian in London," said I, casually drawing some guineas out of my pocket and looking at them; "and I want a fashionable suit of clothes to go in. I wish to pay for them," I added—otherwise I thought he might only pretend to make them, "with ready money."

"My dear sir," said Mr. Trabb, as he respectfully bent his body, opened his arms, and took the liberty of touching me on the outside of each elbow, "don't hurt me by mentioning that. May I venture to congratulate you? Would you do me the favour of stepping into the shop?"

Mr. Trabb's boy was the most audacious boy in all that countryside. When I had entered he was sweeping the shop, and he had sweetened his labours by sweeping over me. He was still sweeping when I came out into the shop with Mr. Trabb, and he knocked the broom against all possible corners and obstacles, to express (as I understood it) equality with any blacksmith, alive or dead.

"Hold that noise," said Mr. Trabb, with the greatest sternness, "or I'll knock your head off! Do me the favour to be seated, sir. Now, this," said Mr. Trabb, taking down a roll of cloth, and tiding it out in a flowing manner over the counter, preparatory to getting his hand under it to show the gloss, "is a very sweet article. I can recommend it for your purpose, sir, because it really is extra super. But you shall see some others. Give me Number Four, you!" (To the boy, and with a dreadfully severe stare: foreseeing the danger of that miscreant's brushing me with it, or making some other sign of familiarity.)

Mr. Trabb never removed his stern eye from the boy until he had deposited number four on the counter and was at a safe distance again. Then, he commanded him to bring number five, and number eight. "And let me have none of your tricks here," said Mr. Trabb, "or you shall repent it, you young scoundrel, the longest day you have to live."

Mr. Trabb then bent over number four, and in a sort of deferential confidence recommended it to me as a light article for summer wear, an article much in vogue among the nobility and gentry, an article that it would ever be an honour to him to reflect upon a distinguished fellow-townsman's (if he might claim me for a fellow-townsman) having worn. "Are you bringing numbers five and eight, you vagabond," said Mr. Trabb to the boy after that, "or shall I kick you out of the shop and bring them myself?"

I selected the materials for a suit, with the assistance of Mr. Trabb's judgment, and re-entered the parlour to be measured. For, although Mr. Trabb had my measure already, and had previously been quite contented with it, he said apologetically that it "wouldn't do under existing circumstances, sir—wouldn't do at all." So, Mr. Trabb measured and calculated me, in the parlour, as if I were an estate and he the finest species of surveyor, and gave himself such a world of trouble that I felt that no suit of clothes could possibly remunerate him for his pains. When he had at last done and had appointed to send the articles to Mr. Pumblechook's on the Thursday evening, he said, with his hand upon the parlour lock, "I know, sir, that London gentlemen cannot be expected to patronise local work, as a rule; but if you would give me a turn now and then in the quality of a townsman, I should greatly esteem it. Good morning, sir, much obliged.—Door!"

The last word was flung at the boy, who had not the least notion what it meant. But I saw him collapse as his master rubbed me out with his hands, and my first decided experience of the stupendous power of money, was, that it had morally laid upon his back, Trabb's boy.

After this memorable event, I went to the hatter's, and the boot-maker's, and the hosier's, and felt rather like Mother Hubbard's dog whose outfit required the services of so many trades. I also went to the coach-office and took my place for seven o'clock on Saturday morning. It was not necessary to explain everywhere that I had come into a handsome property; but whenever I said anything to that effect, it followed that the officiating tradesman ceased to have his attention diverted through the window by the High-street, and concentrated his mind upon me. When I had ordered everything I wanted, I directed my steps towards Pumblechook's, and, as I approached that gentleman's place of business, I saw him standing at his door.

He was waiting for me with great impatience. He had been out early with the chaise-cart, and had called at the forge and heard the news. He had prepared a collation for me in the Barnwell parlour, and he too ordered his shopman to "come out of the gangway" as my sacred person passed.

"My dear friend," said Mr. Pumblechook, taking me by both hands, when he and I and the collation were alone, "I give you joy of your good fortune. Well deserved, well deserved!"

This was coming to the point, and I thought it a sensible way of expressing himself.

"To think," said Mr. Pumblechook, after snorting admiration at me for some moments, "that I should have been the humble instrument of leading up to this, is a proud reward."

I begged Mr. Pumblechook to remember that nothing was to be ever said or hinted, on that point.

"My dear young friend," said Mr. Pumblechook, "if you will allow me to call you so——"

I murmured "Certainly," and Mr. Pumblechook took me by both hands again, and communicated a movement to his waistcoat, which had an emotional appearance, though it was rather low down, "My dear young friend, rely upon my doing my little all in your absence, by keeping the fact before the mind of Joseph.—Joseph!" said Mr. Pumblechook, in the way of a compassionate adjuration. "Joseph!! Joseph!!!" Thereupon he shook his head and tapped it, expressing his sense of deficiency in Joseph.

"But my dear young friend," said Mr. Pumblechook, "you must be hungry, you must be exhausted. Be seated. Here is a chicken had round from the Boar, here is a tongue had round from the Boar, here's one or two little things had round from the Boar, that I hope you may not despise. But do I," said Mr. Pumblechook, getting up again the moment after he had sat down, "see afore me, him as I ever sported with in his times of happy infancy? And may I—*may* I——?"

This May I, meant might he shake hands? I consented, and he was fervent, and then sat down again.

"Here is wine," said Mr. Pumblechook. "Let us drink, Thanks to Fortune, and may she ever pick out her favourites with equal judgment! And yet I cannot," said Mr. Pumblechook, getting up again, "see afore me One—and likewise drink to One—without again expressing—May I—*may* I——?"

I said he might, and he shook hands with me again, and emptied his glass and turned it upside down. I did the same; and if I had turned myself upside down before drinking, the wine could not have gone more direct to my head.

Mr. Pumblechook helped me to the liver wing, and to the best slice of tongue (none of those out-of-the-way No Thoroughfares of Pork now), and took, comparatively speaking, no care of himself at all. "Ah! poultry, poultry! You little thought," said Mr. Pumblechook, apostrophising the fowl in the dish, "when you was a young fledgling, what was in store for you. You little thought you was to be refreshment beneath this humble roof for one as—Call it a weakness, if you will," said Mr. Pumblechook, getting up again, "but may I? *may* I——?"

It began to be unnecessary to repeat the form of saying he might, so he did it at once. How he ever did it so often without wounding himself with my knife, I don't know.

"And your sister," he resumed, after a little steady eating, "which had the honour of bringing you up by hand! It's a sad picter, to reflect that she's no longer equal to fully understanding the honour. May——"

I saw he was about to come at me again, and I stopped him.

"We'll drink her health," said I.

"Ah!" cried Mr. Pumblechook, leaning back in his chair, quite flaccid with admiration, "that's the way you know 'em, sir!" (I don't know who Sir was, but he certainly was not I, and there was no third person present); "that's the way you know the noble minded, sir! Ever forgiving and ever affable. It might," said the servile Pumblechook, putting down his untasted glass in a hurry and getting up again, "to a common person, have the appearance of repeating—but *may* I——?"

When he had done it, he resumed his seat and drank to my sister. "Let us never be blind," said Mr. Pumblechook, "to her faults of temper, but it is to be hoped she meant well."

At about this time, I began to observe that he was getting flushed in the face; as to myself, I felt all face, steeped in wine and smarting.

I mentioned to Mr. Pumblechook that I wished to have my new clothes sent to his house, and he was ecstatic on my so distinguishing him. I mentioned my reason for desiring to avoid observation in the village, and he lauded it to the skies. There was nobody but himself, he intimated, worthy of my confidence, and—in short, might he? Then he asked me tenderly if I remembered our boyish games at sums, and how we had gone together to have me bound apprentice, and, in effect, how he had ever been my favourite fancy and my chosen friend? If I had taken ten times as many glasses of wine as I had, I should have known that he never had stood in that relation towards me, and should in my heart of hearts have repudiated the idea. Yet for all that, I remember feeling convinced that I had been much mistaken in him, and that he was a sensible practical good-hearted prime fellow.

By degrees he fell to reposing such great confidence in me, as to ask my advice in reference to his own affairs. He mentioned that there was an opportunity for a great amalgamation and monopoly of the corn and seed trade on those premises, if enlarged, such as had never occurred before in that, or any other neighbourhood. What alone was wanting to the realisation of a vast fortune, he considered to be More Capital. Those were the two little words, more capital. Now it appeared to him (Pumblechook) that if that capital were got into the business, through a sleeping partner, sir—which sleeping partner would have nothing to do but walk in, by self or deputy, whenever he pleased, and examine the books—and walk in twice a year and take his profits away in his pocket, to the tune of fifty per cent—it appeared to him that that might be an opening for a young gentleman of spirit combined with property, which would be worthy of his attention. But what did I think? He had great confidence in my opinion, and what did I think? I gave it as my opinion. "Wait a bit!" The united vastness and distinctness of this view so struck him, that he no longer asked if he might shake hands with me, but said he really must—and did.

We drank all the wine, and Mr. Pumblechook pledged himself over and over again to keep Joseph up to the mark (I don't know what mark), and to render me efficient and constant service (I don't know what service). He also made known to me for the first time in my life, and certainly after having kept his secret wonderfully well, that he had always said of me, "That boy is no common boy, and mark me, his fortun' will be no common fortun'." He said with a tearful smile that it was a singular thing to think of now, and I said so too. Finally, I went out into the air, with a dim perception that there was something unwonted in the conduct of the sunshine, and found that I had slumberously got to the turnpike without having taken any account of the road.

There, I was roused by Mr. Pumblechook's hailing me. He was a long way down the sunny street, and was making expressive gestures for me to stop. I stopped, and he came up breathless.

"No, my dear friend," said he, when he had recovered wind for speech. "Not if I can help it. This occasion shall not entirely pass without that affability on your part.—May I, as an old friend and well-wisher? *May* I?"

We shook hands for the hundredth time at least, and he ordered a young carter out of my way with the greatest indignation. Then, he blessed me and stood waving his hand to me until I had passed the crook in the road; and then I turned into a field and had a long nap under a hedge before I pursued my way home.

I had scant luggage to take with me to London, for little of the little I possessed was adapted to my new station. But, I began packing that same afternoon, and wildly packed up things that I knew I should want next morning, in a fiction that there was not a moment to be lost.

So, Tuesday, Wednesday, and Thursday, passed; and on Friday morning I went to Mr. Pumblechook's, to put on my new clothes and pay my visit to Miss Havisham. Mr. Pumblechook's own room was given up to me to dress in, and was decorated with clean towels expressly for the event. My clothes were rather a disappointment, of course. Probably every new and eagerly expected garment ever put on since clothes came in, fell a trifle short of the wearer's expectation. But after I had had my new suit on, some half an hour, and had gone through an immensity of posturing with Mr. Pumblechook's very limited dressing-glass, in the futile endeavour to see my legs, it seemed to fit me better. It being market morning at a neighbouring town some ten miles off, Mr. Pumblechook was not at home. I had not told him exactly when I meant to leave, and was not likely to shake hands with him again before departing. This was all as it should be, and I went out in my new array: fearfully ashamed of having to pass the shopman, and suspicious after all that I was at a personal disadvantage, something like Joe's in his Sunday suit.

I went circuitously to Miss Havisham's by all the back ways, and rang at the bell constrainedly, on account of the stiff long fingers of my gloves. Sarah Pocket came to the gate, and positively reeled back when she saw me so changed; her walnut-shell countenance likewise, turned from brown to green and yellow.

"You?" said she. "You, good gracious! What do you want?"

"I am going to London, Miss Pocket," said I, "and want to say good-by to Miss Havisham."

I was not expected, for she left me locked in the yard, while she went to ask if I were to be admitted. After a very short delay, she returned and took me up, staring at me all the way.

Miss Havisham was taking exercise in the room with the long spread table, leaning on her crutch stick. The room was lighted as of yore, and at the sound of our entrance, she stopped and turned. She was then just abreast of the rotted bride-cake.

"Don't go, Sarah," she said. "Well, Pip?"

"I start for London, Miss Havisham, to-morrow," I was exceedingly careful what I said, "and I thought you would kindly not mind my taking leave of you."

"This is a gay figure, Pip," said she, making her crutch stick play round me, as if she, the fairy godmother who had changed me, were bestowing the finishing gift.

"I have come into such good fortune since I saw you last, Miss Havisham," I murmured. "And I am so grateful for it, Miss Havisham!"

"Ay, ay!" said she, looking at the discomfited and envious Sarah, with delight. "I have seen Mr. Jaggers. *I* have heard about it, Pip. So you go to-morrow?"

"Yes, Miss Havisham."

"And you are adopted by a rich person?"

"Yes, Miss Havisham."

"Not named?"

"No, Miss Havisham."

"And Mr. Jaggers is made your guardian?"

"Yes, Miss Havisham."

She quite gloated on these questions and answers, so keen was her enjoyment of Sarah Pocket's jealous dismay. "Well!" she went on; "you have a promising career before you. Be good—deserve it—and abide by Mr. Jaggers's instructions." She looked at me, and looked at Sarah, and Sarah's countenance wrung out of her watchful face a cruel smile. "Good-by, Pip!—you will always keep the name of Pip, you know."

"Yes, Miss Havisham."

"Good-by, Pip!"

She stretched out her hand, and I went down on my knee and put it to my lips. I had not considered how I should take leave of her; it came naturally to me at the moment, to do this. She looked at Sarah Pocket with triumph in her weird eyes, and so I left my fairy godmother, with both her hands on her crutch stick, standing in the midst of the dimly lighted room beside the rotten bride-cake that was hidden in cobwebs.

Sarah Pocket conducted me down, as if I were a ghost who must be seen out. She could not get over my appearance, and was in the last degree confounded. I said "Good-by, Miss Pocket;" but she merely stared, and did not seem collected enough to know that I had spoken. Clear of the house, I made the best of my way back to Pumblechook's, took off my new clothes, made them into a bundle, and went back home in my older dress, carrying it—to speak the truth, much more at my ease too, though I had the bundle to carry.

And now, those six days which were to have run out so slowly, had run out fast and were gone, and to-morrow looked me in the face more steadily than I could look at it. As the six evenings had dwindled away, to five, to four, to three, to two, I had become more and more appreciative of the society of Joe and Biddy. On this last evening, I dressed myself out in my new clothes, for their delight, and sat in my splendour until bedtime. We had a hot supper on the occasion, graced by the inevitable roast fowl, and we had some flip to finish with. We were all very low, and none the higher for pretending to be in spirits.

I was to leave our village at five in the morning, carrying my little hand-portmanteau, and I had told Joe that I wished to walk away all alone. I am afraid—sore afraid—that this purpose originated in my sense of the contrast there would be between me and Joe, if we went to the coach together. I had pretended with myself that there was nothing of this taint in the arrangement; but when I went up to my little room on this last night, I felt compelled to admit that it might be so, and had an impulse upon me to go down again and entreat Joe to walk with me in the morning. I did not.

All night there were coaches in my broken sleep, going to wrong places instead of to London, and having in the traces, now dogs, now cats, now pigs, now men—never horses. Fantastic failures of journeys occupied me until the day dawned and the birds were singing. Then, I got up and partly dressed, and sat at the window to take a last look out, and in taking it fell asleep.

Biddy was astir so early to get my breakfast, that, although I did not sleep at the window an hour, I smelt the smoke of the kitchen fire when I started up with a terrible idea that it must be late in the afternoon. But long after that, and long after I had heard the clinking of the teacups and was quite ready, I wanted the resolution to go down stairs. After all, I remained up there, repeatedly unlocking and unstrapping my small portmanteau and locking and strapping it up again, until Biddy called to me that I was late.

It was a hurried breakfast with no taste in it. I got up from the meal, saying with a sort of briskness, as if it had only just occurred to me, "Well! I suppose I must be off!" and then I kissed my sister who was laughing and nodding and shaking in her usual chair, and kissed Biddy, and threw my arms around Joe's neck. Then I took up my little portmanteau and walked out. The last I saw of them, was, when I presently heard a scuffle behind me, and looking back, saw Joe throwing an old shoe after me and Biddy throwing another old shoe. I stopped then, to wave my hat, and dear old Joe waved his strong right arm above his head, crying huskily "Hooroar!" and Biddy put her apron to her face.

I walked away at a good pace, thinking it was easier to go than I had supposed it would be, and reflecting that it would never have done to have had an old shoe thrown after the coach, in sight of all the High-street. I whistled and made nothing of going. But the village was very peaceful and quiet, and the light mists were solemnly rising, as if to show me the world, and I had been so innocent and little there, and all beyond was so unknown and great, that in a moment with a strong heave and sob I broke into tears. It was by the finger-post at the end of the village, and I laid my hand upon it, and said, "Good-by O my dear, dear friend!"

Heaven knows we need never be ashamed of our tears, for they are rain upon the blinding dust of earth, overlaying our hard hearts. I was better after I had cried, than before—more sorry, more aware of my own ingratitude, more gentle. If I had cried before, I should have had Joe with me then.

So subdued I was by those tears, and by their breaking out again in the course of the quiet walk, that when I was on the coach, and it was clear of the town, I deliberated with an aching heart whether I would not get down when we changed horses, and walk back, and have another evening at home, and a better parting. We changed, and I had not made up my mind, and still reflected for my comfort that it would be quite practicable to get down and walk back, when we changed again. And while I was occupied with these deliberations, I would fancy an exact re-semblance to Joe in some man coming along the road towards us, and my heart would beat high.—As if he could possibly be there!

We changed again, and yet again, and it was now too late and too far to go back, and I went on. And the mists had all solemnly risen now, and the world lay spread before me.

THIS IS THE END OF THE FIRST STAGE OF
PIP'S EXPECTATIONS.

[PART 13]

Chapter 20

The journey from our town to the metropolis, was a journey of about five hours. It was a little past mid-day when the four-horse stage-coach by which I was a passenger, got into the ravel of traffic frayed out about the Cross-Keys,° Wood-street, Cheapside, London.

Cross-Keys: An inn located in the center of London, approximately twenty-five miles from Pip's town.

We Britons had at that time particularly settled that it was treasonable to doubt our having and our being the best of everything: otherwise, while I was scared by the immensity of London, I think I might have had some faint doubts whether it was not rather ugly, crooked, narrow, and dirty.

Mr. Jaggers had duly sent me his address; it was, Little Britain,° and he had written after it on his card, "just out of Smithfield, and close by the coach-office." Nevertheless, a hackney-coachman, who seemed to have as many capes to his greasy great-coat as he was years old, packed me up in his coach and hemmed me in with a folding and jingling barrier of steps, as if he were going to take me fifty miles. His getting on his box, which I remember to have been decorated with an old weather-stained pea-green hammercloth motheaten into rags, was quite a work of time. It was a wonderful equipage, with six great coronets outside, and ragged things behind for I don't know how many footmen to hold on by, and a harrow below them, to prevent amateur footmen from yielding to the temptation.

I had scarcely had time to enjoy the coach and to think how like a straw-yard it was, and yet how like a rag-shop, and to wonder why the horses' nose-bags were kept inside, when I observed the coachman beginning to get down, as if we were going to stop presently. And stop we presently did, in a gloomy street, at certain offices with an open door, whereon was painted MR. JAGGERS.

"How much?" I asked the coachman.

The coachman answered, "A shilling—unless you wish to make it more."

I naturally said I had no wish to make it more.

"Then it must be a shilling," observed the coachman. "I don't want to get into trouble. *I* know *him!*" He darkly closed an eye at Mr. Jaggers's name, and shook his head.

When he had got his shilling, and had in course of time completed the ascent to his box, and had got away (which appeared to relieve his mind), I went into the front office with my little portmanteau in my hand and asked, Was Mr. Jaggers at home?

"He is not," returned the clerk. "He is in Court at present. Am I addressing Mr. Pip?"

I signified that he was addressing Mr. Pip.

Little Britain: A street near the Old Bailey, the criminal court, and Smithfield Market, which was both slaughterhouse and cattle-market.

"Mr. Jaggers left word would you wait in his room. He couldn't say how long he might be, having a case on. But it stands to reason, his time being valuable, that he won't be longer than he can help."

With those words, the clerk opened a door, and ushered me into an inner chamber at the back. Here, we found a gentleman with one eye, in a velveteen suit and knee-breeches, who wiped his nose with his sleeve on being interrupted in the perusal of the newspaper.

"Go and wait outside, Mike," said the clerk.

I began to say that I hoped I was not interrupting——when the clerk shoved this gentleman out with as little ceremony as I ever saw used, and tossing his fur cap out after him, left me alone.

Mr. Jaggers's room was lighted by a skylight only, and was a most dismal place; the skylight, eccentrically patched like a broken head, and the distorted adjoining houses looking as if they had twisted themselves to peep down at me through it. There were not so many papers about, as I should have expected to see; and there were some odd objects about, that I should not have expected to see—such as an old rusty pistol, a sword in a scabbard, several strange-looking boxes and packages, and two dreadful casts on a shelf, of faces peculiarly swollen, and twitchy about the nose. Mr. Jaggers's own high-backed chair was of deadly black horsehair, with rows of brass nails round it, like a coffin; and I fancied I could see how he leaned back in it, and bit his forefinger at the clients. The room was but small, and the clients seemed to have had a habit of backing up against the wall: the wall, especially opposite to Mr. Jaggers's chair, being greasy with shoulders. I recalled, too, that the one-eyed gentleman had shuffled forth against the wall when I was the innocent cause of his being turned out.

I sat down in the cliental chair placed over against Mr. Jaggers's chair, and became fascinated by the dismal atmosphere of the place. I called to mind that the clerk had the same air of knowing something to everybody else's disadvantage, as his master had. I wondered how many other clerks there were up-stairs, and whether they all claimed to have the same detrimental mastery of their fellow-creatures. I wondered what was the history of all the odd litter about the room, and how it came there. I wondered whether the two swollen faces were of Mr. Jaggers's family, and, if he were so unfortunate as to have had a pair of such ill-looking relations, why he stuck them on that dusty perch for the blacks° and flies to settle on, instead of giving them a place at home. Of course I had no experience of a London summer

blacks: Soot.

day, and my spirits may have been oppressed by the hot exhausted air, and by the dust and grit that lay thick on everything. But I sat wondering and waiting in Mr. Jaggers's close room, until I really could not bear the two casts on the shelf above Mr. Jaggers's chair, and got up and went out.

When I told the clerk that I would take a turn in the air while I waited, he advised me to go round the corner and I should come into Smithfield. So, I came into Smithfield; and the shameful place, being all asmear with filth and fat and blood and foam, seemed to stick to me. So, I rubbed it off with all possible speed by turning into a street where I saw the great black dome of Saint Paul's bulging at me from behind a grim stone building which a bystander said was Newgate Prison. Following the wall of the jail, I found the roadway covered with straw to deaden the noise of passing vehicles; and from this, and from the quantity of people standing about, smelling strongly of spirits and beer, I inferred that the trials were on.

While I looked about me here, an exceedingly dirty and partially drunk minister of justice° asked me if I would like to step in and hear a trial or so: informing me that he could give me a front place for half-a-crown, whence I should command a full view of the Lord Chief Justice in his wig and robes—mentioning that awful personage like waxwork, and presently offering him at the reduced price of eighteenpence. As I declined the proposal on the plea of an appointment, he was so good as to take me into a yard and show me where the gallows was kept, and also where people were publicly whipped, and then he showed me the Debtors' Door, out of which culprits came to be hanged: heightening the interest of that dreadful portal by giving me to understand that "four on 'em" would come out at that door the day after to-morrow at eight in the morning, to be killed in a row. This was horrible, and gave me a sickening idea of London: the more so as the Lord Chief Justice's proprietor wore (from his hat down to his boots and up again to his pocket-handkerchief inclusive) mildewed clothes, which had evidently not belonged to him originally, and which, I took it into my head, he had bought cheap of the executioner. Under these circumstances I thought myself well rid of him for a shilling.

I dropped into the office to ask if Mr. Jaggers had come in yet, and I found he had not, and I strolled out again. This time, I made the tour of Little Britain, and turned into Bartholomew Close; and now I

minister of justice: Sarcastic title for the gatekeeper.

became aware that other people were waiting about for Mr. Jaggers, as well as I. There were two men of secret appearance lounging in Bartholomew Close, and thoughtfully fitting their feet into the cracks of the pavement as they talked together, one of whom said to the other when they first passed me, that "Jaggers would do it if it was to be done." There was a knot of three men and two women standing at a corner, and one of the women was crying on her dirty shawl, and the other comforted her by saying, as she pulled her own shawl over her shoulders, "Jaggers is for him, 'Melia, and what more *could* you have?" There was a red-eyed little Jew who came into the Close while I was loitering there, in company with a second little Jew whom he sent upon an errand; and while the messenger was gone, I remarked this Jew, who was of a highly excitable temperament, performing a jig of anxiety under a lamp-post, and accompanying himself, in a kind of frenzy, with the words, "Oh Jaggerth, Jaggerth, Jaggerth! all otherth ith Cag-Maggerth,° give me Jaggerth!" These testimonies to the popularity of my guardian made a deep impression on me, and I admired and wondered more than ever.

At length, as I was looking out at the iron gate of Bartholomew Close into Little Britain, I saw Mr. Jaggers coming across the road towards me. All the others who were waiting, saw him at the same time, and there was quite a rush at him. Mr. Jaggers, putting a hand on my shoulder and walking me on at his side without saying anything to me, addressed himself to his followers.

First, he took the two secret men.

"Now, I have nothing to say to *you*," said Mr. Jaggers, throwing his finger at them. "I want to know no more than I know. As to the result, it's a toss-up. I told you from the first it was a toss-up. Have you paid Wemmick?"

"We made the money up this morning, sir," said one of the men, submissively, while the other perused Mr. Jaggers's face.

"I don't ask you when you made it up, or where, or whether you made it up at all. Has Wemmick got it?"

"Yes, sir," said both the men together.

"Very well; then you may go. Now, I won't have it!" said Mr. Jaggers, waving his hand at them to put them behind him. "If you say a word to me, I'll throw up the case."

"We thought, Mr. Jaggers——" one of the men began, pulling off his hat.

Cag-Maggerth: Lisped version of the term *cag-maggers,* sellers of bad meat and refuse.

"That's what I told you not to do," said Mr. Jaggers. "*You* thought! I think for you; that's enough for you. If I want you, I know where to find you; I don't want you to find me. Now I won't have it. I won't hear a word."

The two men looked at one another as Mr. Jaggers waved them behind again, and humbly fell back and were heard no more.

"And now *you!*" said Mr. Jaggers, suddenly stopping, and turning on the two women with the shawls, from whom the three men had meekly separated. — "Oh! Amelia, is it?"

"Yes, Mr. Jaggers."

"And do you remember," retorted Mr. Jaggers, "that but for me you wouldn't be here and couldn't be here?"

"Oh yes, sir!" exclaimed both women together. "Lord bless you, sir, well we knows that!"

"Then why," said Mr. Jaggers, "do you come here?"

"My Bill, sir!" the crying woman pleaded.

"Now, I tell you what!" said Mr. Jaggers. "Once for all. If you don't know that your Bill's in good hands, I know it. And if you come here, bothering about your Bill, I'll make an example of both your Bill and you, and let him slip through my fingers. Have you paid Wemmick?"

"Oh yes, sir! Every farden."

"Very well. Then you have done all you have got to do. Say another word — one single word — and Wemmick shall give you your money back."

This terrible threat caused the two women to fall off immediately. No one remained now but the excitable Jew, who had already raised the skirts of Mr. Jaggers's coat to his lips several times.

"I don't know this man!" said Mr. Jaggers, in the same devastating strain. "What does this fellow want?"

"Ma thear Mithter Jaggerth. Hown brother to Habraham Latharuth!"

"Who's he?" said Mr. Jaggers. "Let go of my coat."

The suitor, kissing the hem of the garment again before relinquishing it, replied, "Habraham Latharuth, on thuthpithion of plate."

"You're too late," said Mr. Jaggers. "I am over the way."

"Holy father, Mithter Jaggerth!" cried my excitable acquaintance, turning white, "don't thay you're again Habraham Latharuth!"

"I am," said Mr. Jaggers, "and there's an end of it. Get out of the way."

"Mithter Jaggerth! Half a moment! My hown cuthen'th gone to Mithter Wemmick at thith prethent minute, to hoffer him hany termth. Mithter Jaggerth! Half a quarter of a moment! If you'd have the condethenthun to be bought off from the t'other thide—at hany thuperior prithe!—money no object!—Mithter Jaggerth— Mithter——!"

My guardian threw his supplicant off with supreme indifference, and left him dancing on the pavement as if it were red-hot. Without further interruption, we reached the front office, where we found the clerk and the man in velveteen with the fur cap.

"Here's Mike," said the clerk, getting down from his stool, and approaching Mr. Jaggers confidentially.

"Oh!" said Mr. Jaggers, turning to the man, who was pulling a lock of hair in the middle of his forehead, like the Bull in Cock Robin° pulling at the bell-rope; "your man comes on this afternoon. Well?"

"Well, Mas'r Jaggers," returned Mike, in the voice of a sufferer from a constitutional cold; "arter a deal o' trouble, I've found one, sir, as might do."

"What is he prepared to swear?"

"Well, Mas'r Jaggers," said Mike, wiping his nose on his fur cap this time; "in a general way, anythink."

Mr. Jaggers suddenly became most irate. "Now, I warned you before," said he, throwing his forefinger at the terrified client, "that if you ever presumed to talk in that way here, I'd make an example of you. You infernal scoundrel, how dare you tell ME that?"

The client looked scared, but bewildered too, as if he were unconscious what he had done.

"Spooney!" said the clerk, in a low voice, giving him a stir with his elbow. "Soft Head! Need you say it face to face?"

"Now, I ask you, you blundering booby," said my guardian, very sternly, "once more and for the last time, what the man you have brought here is prepared to swear?"

Mike looked hard at my guardian, as if he were trying to learn a lesson from his face, and slowly replied, "Ayther to character, or to having been in his company and never left him all the night in question."

"Now, be careful. In what station of life is this man?"

Mike looked at his cap, and looked at the floor, and looked at the ceiling, and looked at the clerk, and even looked at me, before begin-

pulling . . . Cock Robin: A traditional gesture of deference to one's superiors, here compared to the action of the bull who tolls the bell in the nursery rhyme "Who Killed Cock-Robin?"

ning to reply in a nervous manner, "We've dressed him up like——"
when my guardian blustered out:

"What? You WILL, will you?"

("Spooney!" added the clerk again, with another stir.)

After some helpless casting about, Mike brightened and began again:

"He is dressed like a 'spectable pieman. A sort of a pastrycook."

"Is he here?" asked my guardian.

"I left him," said Mike, "a setting on some door-steps round the corner."

"Take him past that window, and let me see him."

The window indicated, was the office window. We all three went to it, behind the wire blind, and presently saw the client go by in an accidental manner, with a murderous-looking tall individual, in a short suit of white linen and a paper cap. This guileless confectioner was not by any means sober, and had a black eye in the green stage of recovery, which was painted over.

"Tell him to take his witness away directly," said my guardian to the clerk, in extreme disgust, "and ask him what he means by bringing such a fellow as that."

My guardian then took me into his own room, and while he lunched, standing, from a sandwich-box and a pocket-flask of sherry (he seemed to bully his very sandwich as he ate it), informed me what arrangements he had made for me. I was to go to "Barnard's Inn,"° to young Mr. Pocket's rooms, where a bed had been sent in for my accommodation; I was to remain with young Mr. Pocket until Monday; on Monday I was to go with him to his father's house on a visit, that I might try how I liked it. Also, I was told what my allowance was to be —it was a very liberal one—and had handed to me from one of my guardian's drawers, the cards of certain tradesmen with whom I was to deal for all kinds of clothes, and such other things as I could in reason want. "You will find your credit good, Mr. Pip," said my guardian, whose flask of sherry smelt like a whole cask-full, as he hastily refreshed himself, "but I shall by this means be able to check your bills, and to pull you up if I find you outrunning the constable.° Of course you'll go wrong somehow, but that's no fault of mine."

After I had pondered a little over this encouraging sentiment, I asked Mr. Jaggers if I could send for a coach? He said it was not worth while, I was so near my destination; Wemmick should walk round with me, if I pleased.

Barnard's Inn: Formerly one of the inns of Chancery, a residence for law students. **outrunning the constable:** Spending beyond one's means and, therefore, running from the law.

I then found that Wemmick was the clerk in the next room. Another clerk was rung down from up-stairs to take his place while he was out, and I accompanied him into the street, after shaking hands with my guardian. We found a new set of people lingering outside, but Wemmick made a way among them by saying coolly yet decisively, "I tell you it's no use; he won't have a word to say to one of you;" and we soon got clear of them, and went on side by side.

Chapter 21

Casting my eyes on Mr. Wemmick as we went along, to see what he was like in the light of day, I found him to be a dry man, rather short in stature, with a square wooden face, whose expression seemed to have been imperfectly chipped out with a dull-edged chisel. There were some marks in it that might have been dimples, if the material had been softer and the instrument finer, but which, as it was, were only dints. The chisel had made three or four of these attempts at embellishment over his nose, but had given them up without an effort to smooth them off. I judged him to be a bachelor from the frayed condition of his linen, and he appeared to have sustained a good many bereavements; for, he wore at least four mourning rings, besides a brooch representing a lady and a weeping willow at a tomb with an urn on it. I noticed, too, that several rings and seals hung at his watch-chain, as if he were quite laden with remembrances of departed friends. He had glittering eyes—small, keen, and black—and thin wide mottled lips. He had had them, to the best of my belief, from forty to fifty years.

"So you were never in London before?" said Mr. Wemmick to me.

"No," said I.

"*I* was new here once," said Mr. Wemmick. "Rum to think of now!"

"You are well acquainted with it now?"

"Why, yes," said Mr. Wemmick. "I know the moves of it."

"Is it a very wicked place?" I asked, more for the sake of saying something than for information.

"You may get cheated, robbed, and murdered, in London. But there are plenty of people anywhere, who'll do that for you."

"If there is bad blood between you and them," said I, to soften it off a little.

"Oh! I don't know about bad blood," returned Mr. Wemmick; "there's not much bad blood about. They'll do it, if there's anything to be got by it."

"That makes it worse."

"You think so?" returned Mr. Wemmick. "Much about the same, I should say."

He wore his hat on the back of his head, and looked straight before him: walking in a self-contained way as if there were nothing in the streets to claim his attention. His mouth was such a post-office of a mouth that he had a mechanical appearance of smiling. We had got to the top of Holborn Hill before I knew that it was merely a mechanical appearance, and that he was not smiling at all.

"Do you know where Mr. Matthew Pocket lives?" I asked Mr. Wemmick.

"Yes," said he, nodding in the direction. "At Hammersmith, west of London."

"Is that far?"

"Well! Say five miles."

"Do you know him?"

"Why, you're a regular cross-examiner!" said Mr. Wemmick, looking at me with an approving air. "Yes, I know him. *I* know him!"

There was an air of toleration or depreciation about his utterance of these words, that rather depressed me; and I was still looking sideways at his block of a face in search of any encouraging note to the text, when he said here we were at Barnard's Inn. My depression was not alleviated by the announcement, for, I had supposed that establishment to be an hotel kept by Mr. Barnard, to which the Blue Boar in our town was mere public-house. Whereas I now found Barnard to be a disembodied spirit, or a fiction, and his inn the dingiest collection of shabby buildings ever squeezed together in a rank corner as a club for Tom-cats.

We entered this haven through a wicket-gate, and were disgorged by an introductory passage into a melancholy little square that looked to me like a flat burying-ground. I thought it had the most dismal trees in it, and the most dismal sparrows, and the most dismal cats, and the most dismal houses (in number half a dozen or so), that I had ever seen. I thought the windows of the sets of chambers into which these houses were divided, were in every stage of dilapidated blind and curtain, crippled flower-pot, cracked glass, dusty decay, and miserable makeshift; while To Let To Let To Let, glared at me from empty rooms, as if no new wretches ever came there, and the vengeance of the soul of Barnard were being slowly appeased by the gradual suicide of the present occupants and their unholy interment under the gravel. A frouzy mourning of soot and smoke attired this forlorn creation of

Barnard, and it had strewn ashes on its head, and was undergoing penance and humiliation as a mere dust-hole. Thus far my sense of sight; while dry rot and wet rot and all the silent rots that rot in neglected roof and cellar—rot of rat and mouse and bug and coaching-stables near at hand besides—addressed themselves faintly to my sense of smell, and moaned, "Try Barnard's Mixture."°

So imperfect was this realisation of the first of my great expectations, that I looked in dismay at Mr. Wemmick. "Ah!" said he, mistaking me; "the retirement reminds you of the country. So it does me."

He led me into a corner and conducted me up a flight of stairs—which appeared to me to be slowly collapsing into sawdust, so that one of those days the upper lodgers would look out at their doors and find themselves without the means of coming down—to a set of chambers on the top floor. Mr. Pocket, Jun., was painted on the door, and there was a label on the letter-box, "Return shortly."

"He hardly thought you'd come so soon," Mr. Wemmick explained. "You don't want me any more?"

"No, thank you," said I.

"As I keep the cash," Mr. Wemmick observed, "we shall most likely meet pretty often. Good day."

"Good day."

I put out my hand, and Mr. Wemmick at first looked at it as if he thought I wanted something. Then he looked at me, and said, correcting himself,

"To be sure! Yes. You're in the habit of shaking hands?"

I was rather confused, thinking it must be out of the London fashion, but said yes.

"I have got so out of it!" said Mr. Wemmick—"except at last. Very glad, I'm sure, to make your acquaintance. Good day!"

When we had shaken hands and he was gone, I opened the staircase window and had nearly beheaded myself, for, the lines had rotted away, and it came down like the guillotine. Happily it was so quick that I had not put my head out. After this escape, I was content to take a foggy view of the Inn through the window's encrusting dirt, and to stand dolefully looking out, saying to myself that London was decidedly over-rated.

Mr. Pocket, Junior's, idea of Shortly was not mine, for I had nearly maddened myself with looking out for half an hour, and had written

***

"**Try Barnard's Mixture**": Probably a reference to an advertisement for a patent medicine.

my name with my finger several times in the dirt of every pane in the window, before I heard footsteps on the stairs. Gradually there arose before me the hat, head, neckcloth, waistcoat, trousers, boots, of a member of society of about my own standing. He had a paper-bag under each arm and a pottle° of strawberries in one hand, and was out of breath.

"Mr. Pip?" said he.

"Mr. Pocket?" said I.

"Dear me!" he exclaimed. "I am extremely sorry; but I knew there was a coach from your part of the country at mid-day, and I thought you would come by that one. The fact is, I have been out on your ac-count—not that that is any excuse—for I thought, coming from the country, you might like a little fruit after dinner, and I went to Covent Garden Market to get it good."

For a reason that I had, I felt as if my eyes would start out of my head. I acknowledged his attention incoherently, and began to think this was a dream.

"Dear me!" said Mr. Pocket, Junior. "This door sticks so!"

As he was fast making jam of his fruit by wrestling with the door while the paper-bags were under his arms, I begged him to allow me to hold them. He relinquished them with an agreeable smile, and combated with the door as if it were a wild beast. It yielded so sud-denly at last, that he staggered back upon me, and I staggered back upon the opposite door, and we both laughed. But still I felt as if my eyes must start out of my head, and as if this must be a dream.

"Pray come in," said Mr. Pocket, Junior. "Allow me to lead the way. I am rather bare here, but I hope you'll be able to make out tolerably well till Monday. My father thought you would get on more agreeably through to-morrow with me than with him, and might like to take a walk about London. I am sure I shall be very happy to show London to you. As to our table, you won't find that bad, I hope, for it will be supplied from our coffee-house here, and (it is only right I should add) at your ex-pense, such being Mr. Jaggers's directions. As to our lodging, it's not by any means splendid, because I have my own bread to earn, and my father hasn't anything to give me, and I shouldn't be willing to take it, if he had. This is our sitting-room—just such chairs and tables and carpet and so forth, you see, as they could spare from home. You mustn't give me credit for the tablecloth and spoons and castors, because they come for you from the coffee-house. This is my little bedroom; rather musty, but

pottle: A small basket.

Barnard's *is* musty. This is your bedroom; the furniture's hired for the occasion, but I trust it will answer the purpose; if you should want anything, I'll go and fetch it. The chambers are retired, and we shall be alone together, but we shan't fight, I dare say. But, dear me, I beg your pardon, you're holding the fruit all this time. Pray let me take these bags from you. I am quite ashamed."

As I stood opposite to Mr. Pocket, Junior, delivering him the bags, One, Two, I saw the starting appearance come into his own eyes that I knew to be in mine, and he said, falling back:

"Lord bless me, you're the prowling boy!"

"And you," said I, "are the pale young gentleman!"

[PART 14]

Chapter 22

The pale young gentleman and I stood contemplating one another in Barnard's Inn, until we both burst out laughing. "The idea of its being you!" said he. "The idea of its being *you!*" said I. And then we contemplated one another afresh, and laughed again. "Well!" said the pale young gentleman, reaching out his hand good humouredly, "it's all over now, I hope, and it will be magnanimous in you if you'll forgive me for having knocked you about so."

I derived from this speech that Mr. Herbert Pocket (for Herbert was the pale young gentleman's name) still rather confounded his intention with his execution. But I made a modest reply, and we shook hands warmly.

"You hadn't come into your good fortune at that time?" said Herbert Pocket.

"No," said I.

"No," he acquiesced: "I heard it had happened very lately. *I* was rather on the look-out for good fortune then."

"Indeed?"

"Yes. Miss Havisham had sent for me, to see if she could take a fancy to me. But she couldn't—at all events, she didn't."

I thought it polite to remark that I was surprised to hear that.

"Bad taste," said Herbert, laughing, "but a fact. Yes, she had sent for me on a trial visit, and if I had come out of it successfully, I suppose I should have been provided for; perhaps I should have been what-you-may-called it to Estella."

"What's that?" I asked, with sudden gravity.

He was arranging his fruit in plates while we talked, which divided his attention, and was the cause of his having made this lapse of a word. "Affianced," he explained, still busy with the fruit. "Betrothed. Engaged. What's-his-named. Any word of that sort."

"How did you bear your disappointment?" I asked.

"Pooh!" said he, "I didn't care much for it. *She's* a Tartar."

"Miss Havisham?" I suggested.

"I don't say no to that, but I meant Estella. That girl's hard and haughty and capricious to the last degree, and has been brought up by Miss Havisham to wreak revenge on all the male sex."

"What relation is she to Miss Havisham?"

"None," said he. "Only adopted."

"Why should she wreak revenge on all the male sex? What revenge?"

"Lord, Mr. Pip!" said he. "Don't you know?"

"No," said I.

"Dear me! It's quite a story, and shall be saved till dinner-time. And now let me take the liberty of asking you a question. How did you come there, that day?"

I told him, and he was attentive until I had finished, and then burst out laughing again, and asked me if I was sore afterwards? I didn't ask him if *he* was, for my conviction on that point was perfectly established.

"Mr. Jaggers is your guardian, I understand?" he went on.

"Yes."

"You know he is Miss Havisham's man of business and solicitor, and has her confidence when nobody else has?"

This was bringing me (I felt) towards dangerous ground. I answered with a constraint I made no attempt to disguise, that I had seen Mr. Jaggers in Miss Havisham's house on the very day of our combat, but never at any other time, and that I believed he had no recollection of having ever seen me there.

"He was so obliging as to suggest my father for your tutor, and he called on my father to propose it. Of course he knew about my father from his connexion with Miss Havisham. My father is Miss Havisham's cousin; not that that implies familiar intercourse between them, for he is a bad courtier and will not propitiate her."

Herbert Pocket had a frank and easy way with him that was very taking. I had never seen any one then, and I have never seen any one since, who more strongly expressed to me, in every look and tone, a natural incapacity to do anything secret and mean. There was something wonderfully hopeful about his general air, and something that at the same time whispered to me he would never be very successful or rich. I don't know how this was. I became imbued with the notion on that first occasion before we sat down to dinner, but I cannot define by what means.

He was still a pale young gentleman, and had a certain conquered languor about him in the midst of his spirits and briskness, that did not seem indicative of natural strength. He had not a handsome face, but it was better than handsome: being extremely amiable and cheerful. His figure was a little ungainly, as in the days when my knuckles had taken such liberties with it, but it looked as if it would always be light and young. Whether Mr. Trabb's local work would have sat more gracefully on him than on me, may be a question; but I am conscious that he carried off his rather old clothes, much better than I carried off my new suit.

As he was so communicative, I felt that reserve on my part would be a bad return unsuited to our years. I therefore told him my small story, and laid stress on my being forbidden to inquire who my benefactor was. I further mentioned that as I had been brought up a blacksmith in a country place, and knew very little of the ways of politeness, I would take it as a great kindness in him if he would give me a hint whenever he saw me at a loss or going wrong.

"With pleasure," said he, "though I venture to prophesy that you'll want very few hints. I dare say we shall be often together, and I should like to banish any needless restraint between us. Will you do me the favour to begin at once to call me by my christian name, Herbert?"

I thanked him, and said I would. I informed him in exchange that my christian name was Philip.

"I don't take to Philip," said he, smiling, "for it sounds like a moral boy out of the spelling-book, who was so lazy that he fell into a pond, or so fat that he couldn't see out of his eyes, or so avaricious that he locked up his cake till the mice ate it, or so determined to go a birds'-nesting that he got himself eaten by bears who lived handy in the neighbourhood. I tell you what I should like. We are so harmonious, and you have been a blacksmith—would you mind it?"

"I shouldn't mind anything that you propose," I answered, "but I don't understand you."

"Would you mind Handel for a familiar name? There's a charming piece of music by Handel, called the Harmonious Blacksmith."

"I should like it very much."

"Then, my dear Handel," said he, turning round as the door opened, "here is the dinner, and I must beg of you to take the top of the table, because the dinner is of your providing."

This I would not hear of, so he took the top, and I faced him. It was a nice little dinner—seemed to me then, a very Lord Mayor's Feast—and it acquired additional relish from being eaten under those independent circumstances, with no old people by, and with London all around us. This again was heightened by a certain gipsy character that set the banquet off: for, while the table was, as Mr. Pumblechook might have said, the lap of luxury—being entirely furnished forth from the coffee-house—the circumjacent region of sitting-room was of a comparatively pastureless and shifty character: imposing on the waiter the wandering habits of putting the covers on the floor (where he fell over them), the melted butter in the arm-chair, the bread on the book-shelves, the cheese in the coal-scuttle, and the boiled fowl into my bed in the next room—where I found much of its parsley and butter in a state of congelation when I retired for the night. All this made the feast delightful, and when the waiter was not there to watch me, my pleasure was without alloy.

We had made some progress in the dinner, when I reminded Herbert of his promise to tell me about Miss Havisham.

"True," he replied. "I'll redeem it at once. Let me introduce the topic, Handel, by mentioning that in London it is not the custom to put the knife in the mouth—for fear of accidents—and that while the fork is reserved for that use, it is not put further in than is necessary. It is scarcely worth mentioning, only it's as well to do as other people do. Also, the spoon is not generally used over-hand, but under. This has two advantages. You get at your mouth better (which after all is the object), and you save a good deal of the attitude of opening oysters, on the part of the right elbow."

He offered these friendly suggestions in such a lively way, that we both laughed and I scarcely blushed.

"Now," he pursued, "concerning Miss Havisham. Miss Havisham, you must know, was a spoilt child. Her mother died when she was a baby, and her father denied her nothing. Her father was a country gentleman down in your part of the world, and was a brewer. I don't know why it should be a crack thing to be a brewer; but it is indisputable that while you cannot possibly be genteel and bake, you may be as genteel as never was and brew. You see it every day."

"Yet a gentleman may not keep a public-house; may he?" said I.

"Not on any account," returned Herbert; "but a public-house may keep a gentleman. Well! Mr. Havisham was very rich and very proud. So was his daughter."

"Miss Havisham was an only child?" I hazarded.

"Stop a moment, I am coming to that. No, she was not an only child; she had a half-brother. Her father privately married again—his cook, I rather think."

"I thought he was proud," said I.

"My good Handel, so he was. He married his second wife privately, because he was proud, and in course of time *she* died. When she was dead, I apprehend he first told his daughter what he had done, and then the son became a part of the family, residing in the house you are acquainted with. As the son grew a young man, he turned out riotous, extravagant, undutiful—altogether bad. At last his father disinherited him; but he softened when he was dying, and left him well off, though not nearly so well off as Miss Havisham. Take another glass of wine, and excuse my mentioning that society as a body does not expect one to be so strictly conscientious in emptying one's glass, as to turn it bottom upwards with the rim on one's nose."

I had been doing this, in an excess of attention to his recital. I thanked him, and apologised. He said, "Not at all," and resumed.

"Miss Havisham was now an heiress, and you may suppose was looked after as a great match. Her half-brother had now ample means again, but what with debts and what with new madness wasted them most fearfully again. There were stronger differences between him and her, than there had been between him and his father, and it is suspected that he cherished a deep and mortal grudge against her, as having influenced the father's anger. Now, I come to the cruel part of the story—merely breaking off, my dear Handel, to remark that a dinner-napkin will not go into a tumbler."

Why I was trying to pack mine into my tumbler, I am wholly unable to say. I only know that I found myself, with a perseverance worthy of a much better cause, making the most strenuous exertions to compress it within those limits. Again I thanked him and apologised, and again he said in the cheerfullest manner, "Not at all, I am sure!" and resumed.

"There appeared upon the scene—say at the races, or the public balls, or anywhere else you like—a certain man, who made love to Miss Havisham. I never saw him, for this happened five-and-twenty years ago (before you and I were, Handel), but I have heard my father

mention that he was a showy-man, and the kind of man for the purpose. But that he was not to be, without ignorance or prejudice, mistaken for a gentleman, my father most strongly asseverates; because it
is a principle of his that no man who was not a true gentleman at
heart, ever was, since the world began, a true gentleman in manner.
He says, no varnish can hide the grain of the wood; and that the more
varnish you put on, the more the grain will express itself. Well! This
man pursued Miss Havisham closely, and professed to be devoted to
her. I believe she had not shown much susceptibility up to that time;
but all she possessed, certainly came out then, and she passionately
loved him. There is no doubt that she perfectly idolised him. He practised on her affection in that systematic way, that he got great sums of
money from her, and he induced her to buy her brother out of a share
in the brewery (which had been weakly left him by his father) at an immense price, on the plea that when he was her husband he must hold
and manage it all. Your guardian was not at that time in Miss Havisham's councils, and she was too haughty and too much in love, to be
advised by any one. Her relations were poor and scheming, with the
exception of my father; he was poor enough, but not time-serving or
jealous. The only independent one among them, he warned her that
she was doing too much for this man, and was placing herself too un-
reservedly in his power. She took the first opportunity of angrily ordering my father out of the house, in his presence, and my father has
never seen her since."

I thought of her having said, "Matthew will come and see me at
last when I am laid dead upon that table;" and I asked Herbert
whether his father was so inveterate against her?

"It's not that," said he, "but she charged him, in the presence of
her intended husband, with being disappointed in the hope of fawning
upon her for his own advancement, and, if he were to go to her now,
it would look true—even to him—and even to her. To return to the
man and make an end of him. The marriage day was fixed, the wedding dresses were bought, the wedding tour was planned out, the
wedding guests were invited. The day came, but not the bridegroom.
He wrote her a letter——"

"Which she received," I struck in, "when she was dressing for her
marriage? At twenty minutes to nine?"

"At the hour and minute," said Herbert, nodding, "at which she
afterwards stopped all the clocks. What was in it, further than that it
most heartlessly broke the marriage off, I can't tell you, because I

don't know. When she recovered from a bad illness that she had, she laid the whole place waste, as you have seen it, and she has never since looked upon the light of day."

"Is that all the story?" I asked, after considering it.

"All I know of it; and indeed I only know so much, through piecing it out for myself; for my father always avoids it, and, even when Miss Havisham invited me to go there, told me no more of it than it was absolutely requisite I should understand. But I have forgotten one thing. It has been supposed that the man to whom she gave her misplaced confidence, acted throughout in concert with her half-brother; that it was a conspiracy between them; and that they shared the profits."

"I wonder he didn't marry her and get all the property," said I.

"He may have been married already, and her cruel mortification may have been a part of her half-brother's scheme," said Herbert. "Mind! I don't know that."

"What became of the two men?" I asked, after again considering the subject.

"They fell into deeper shame and degradation—if there can be deeper—and ruin."

"Are they alive now?"

"I don't know."

"You said just now, that Estella was not related to Miss Havisham, but adopted. When adopted?"

Herbert shrugged his shoulders. "There has always been an Estella, since I have heard of a Miss Havisham. I know no more. And now Handel," said he, finally throwing off the story as it were, "there is a perfectly open understanding between us. All that I know about Miss Havisham, you know."

"And all that I know," I retorted, "you know."

"I fully believe it. So there can be no competition or perplexity between you and me. And as to the condition on which you hold your advancement in life—namely, that you are not to inquire or discuss to whom you owe it—you may be very sure that it will never be encroached upon, or even approached, by me, or by any one belonging to me."

In truth, he said this with so much delicacy, that I felt the subject done with, even though I should be under his father's roof for years and years to come. Yet he said it with so much meaning, too, that I felt he as perfectly understood Miss Havisham to be my benefactress, as I understood the fact myself.

It had not occurred to me before, that he had led up to the theme for the purpose of clearing it out of our way; but we were so much the lighter and easier for having broached it, that I now perceived this to be the case. We were very gay and sociable, and I asked him, in the course of conversation, what he was? He replied, "A capitalist—an Insurer of Ships." I suppose he saw me glancing about the room in search of some tokens of Shipping, or capital, for he added, "In the City."°

I had grand ideas of the wealth and importance of Insurers of Ships in the City, and I began to think with awe, of having laid a young Insurer on his back, blackened his enterprising eye, and cut his responsible head open. But, again, there came upon me, for my relief, that odd impression that Herbert Pocket would never be very successful or rich.

"I shall not rest satisfied with merely employing my capital in insuring ships. I shall buy up some good Life Assurance shares, and cut into the Direction.° I shall also do a little in the mining way. None of these things will interfere with my chartering a few thousand tons on my own account. I think I shall trade," said he, leaning back in his chair, "to the East Indies, for silks, shawls, spices, dyes, drugs, and precious woods. It's an interesting trade."

"And the profits are large?" said I.

"Tremendous!" said he.

I wavered again, and began to think here were greater expectations than my own.

"I think I shall trade, also," said he, putting his thumbs in his waistcoat pockets, "to the West Indies, for sugar, tobacco, and rum. Also to Ceylon, specially for elephants' tusks."

"You will want a good many ships," said I.

"A perfect fleet," said he.

Quite overpowered by the magnificence of these transactions, I asked him where the ships he insured mostly traded to at present?

"I haven't begun insuring yet," he replied. "I am looking about me."

Somehow, that pursuit seemed more in keeping with Barnard's Inn. I said (in a tone of conviction), "Ah-h!"

"Yes. I am in a counting-house, and looking about me."

"Is a counting-house profitable?" I asked.

In the City: The central business section of London.   **cut into the Direction:** Make a place for oneself as a director of a company—in this case, a life-insurance company.

"To——do you mean to the young fellow who's in it?" he asked, in reply.

"Yes; to you."

"Why, n-no: not to me." He said this with the air of one carefully reckoning up and striking a balance. "Not directly profitable. That is, it doesn't pay me anything, and I have to—— keep myself."

This certainly had not a profitable appearance, and I shook my head as if I would imply that it would be difficult to lay by much accumulative capital from such a source of income.

"But the thing is," said Herbert Pocket, "that you look about you. *That's* the grand thing. You are in a counting-house, you know, and you look about you."

It struck me as a singular implication that you couldn't be out of a counting-house, you know, and look about you; but I silently deferred to his experience.

"Then the time comes," said Herbert, "when you see your opening. And you go in, and you swoop upon it and you make your capital, and then there you are! When you have once made your capital, you have nothing to do but employ it."

This was very like his way of conducting that encounter in the garden; very like. His manner of bearing his poverty, too, exactly corresponded to his manner of bearing that defeat. It seemed to me that he took all blows and buffets now, with just the same air as he had taken mine then. It was evident that he had nothing around him but the simplest necessaries, for everything that I remarked upon turned out to have been sent in on my account from the coffee-house or somewhere else.

Yet, having already made his fortune in his own mind, he was so unassuming with it that I felt quite grateful to him for not being puffed up. It was a pleasant addition to his naturally pleasant ways, and we got on famously. In the evening we went out for a walk in the streets, and went half-price to the Theatre;° and next day we went to church at Westminster Abbey, and in the afternoon we walked in the Parks; and I wondered who shod all the horses there, and wished Joe did.

On a moderate computation, it was many months, that Sunday, since I had left Joe and Biddy. The space interposed between myself and them, partook of that expansion, and our marshes were any dis-

---

half-price to the Theatre: The cost of admission was so reduced after a portion of the program had been presented.

tance off. That I could have been at our old church in my old church-going clothes, on the very last Sunday that ever was, seemed a combination of impossibilities, geographical and social, solar and lunar. Yet in the London streets, so crowded with people and so brilliantly lighted in the dusk of evening, there were depressing hints of reproaches for that I had put the poor old kitchen at home so far away; and in the dead of night, the footsteps of some incapable impostor of a porter mooning about Barnard's Inn, under pretence of watching it, fell hollow on my heart.

On the Monday morning at a quarter before nine, Herbert went to the counting-house to report himself—to look about him, too, I suppose—and I bore him company. He was to come away in an hour or two to attend me to Hammersmith, and I was to wait about for him. It appeared to me that the eggs from which young Insurers were hatched, were incubated in dust and heat, like the eggs of ostriches, judging from the places to which those incipient giants repaired on a Monday morning. Nor did the counting-house where Herbert assisted, show in my eyes as at all a good Observatory; being a back second floor up a yard, of a grimy presence in all particulars, and with a look into another back second floor, rather than a look out.

I waited about until it was noon, and I went upon 'Change,° and I saw fluey° men sitting there under the bills about shipping, whom I took to be great merchants, though I couldn't understand why they should all be out of spirits. When Herbert came, we went and had lunch at a celebrated house which I then quite venerated, but now believe to have been the most abject superstition in Europe, and where I could not help noticing, even then, that there was much more gravy on the tablecloths and knives and waiters' clothes, than in the steaks. This collation disposed of at a moderate price (considering the grease: which was not charged for), we went back to Barnard's Inn and got my little portmanteau, and then took coach for Hammersmith. We arrived there at two or three o'clock in the afternoon, and had very little way to walk to Mr. Pocket's house. Lifting the latch of a gate, we passed direct into a little garden overlooking the river, where Mr. Pocket's children were playing about. And unless I deceive myself on a point where my interests or prepossessions are certainly not concerned, I saw that Mr. and Mrs. Pocket's children were not growing up or being brought up, but were tumbling up.

'Change: The Royal Exchange, a stock exchange.   **fluey:** Dusty.

Mrs. Pocket was sitting on a garden chair under a tree, reading, with her legs upon another garden chair; and Mrs. Pocket's two nurse-maids, were looking about them while the children played. "Mamma," said Herbert, "this is young Mr. Pip." Upon which Mrs. Pocket received me with an appearance of amiable dignity.

"Master Alick and Miss Jane," cried one of the nurses to two of the children, "if you go a bouncing up against them bushes you'll fall over into the river and be drownded, and what'll your pa say then!"

At the same time this nurse picked up Mrs. Pocket's handkerchief, and said, "If that don't make six times you've dropped it, Mum!" Upon which Mrs. Pocket laughed and said, "Thank you, Flopson," and settling herself in one chair only, resumed her book. Her countenance immediately assumed a knitted and intent expression as if she had been reading for a week, but before she could have read half a dozen lines, she fixed her eyes upon me, and said, "I hope your mamma is quite well?" This unexpected inquiry put me into such a difficulty that I began saying in the absurdest way that if there had been any such person I had no doubt she would have been quite well and would have been very much obliged and would have sent her compliments, when the nurse came to my rescue.

"Well!" she cried, picking up the pocket-handkerchief, "if that don't make seven times! What ARE you a doing of this afternoon, Mum!" Mrs. Pocket received her property, at first with a look of unut-terable surprise as if she had never seen it before, and then with a laugh of recognition, and said, "Thank you, Flopson," and forgot me, and went on reading.

I found, now I had leisure to count them, that there were no fewer than six little Pockets present, in various stages of tumbling up. I had scarcely arrived at the total when a seventh was heard, as in the region of air, wailing dolefully.

"If there ain't Baby!" said Flopson, appearing to think it most sur-prising. "Make haste up, Millers."

Millers, who was the other nurse, retired into the house, and by degrees the child's wailing was hushed and stopped, as if it were a young ventriloquist with something in its mouth. Mrs. Pocket read all the time, and I was curious to know what the book could be.

We were waiting, I supposed, for Mr. Pocket to come out to us; at any rate we waited there, and so I had an opportunity of observing the remarkable family phenomenon that whenever any of the children strayed near Mrs. Pocket in their play, they always tripped themselves up and tumbled over her—always very much to her momentary astonishment, and their own more enduring lamentation. I was at a loss to account for this surprising circumstance, and could not help giving my mind to speculations about it, until by-and-by Millers came down with the baby, which baby was handed to Flopson, which Flopson was handing it to Mrs. Pocket, when she too went fairly head-foremost over Mrs. Pocket, baby and all, and was caught by Herbert and myself.

"Gracious me, Flopson!" said Mrs. Pocket, looking off her book for a moment, "everybody's tumbling!"

"Gracious you, indeed, Mum!" returned Flopson, very red in the face; "what have you got there?"

"*I* got here, Flopson?" asked Mrs. Pocket.

"Why, if it ain't your footstool!" cried Flopson. "And if you keep it under your skirts like that, who's to help tumbling! Here! Take the baby, Mum, and give me your book."

Mrs. Pocket acted on the advice, and inexpertly danced the infant a little in her lap, while the other children played about it. This had lasted but a very short time, when Mrs. Pocket issued summary orders that they were all to be taken into the house for a nap. Thus I made the second discovery on that first occasion, that the nurture of the little Pockets consisted of alternately tumbling up and lying down.

Under these circumstances, when Flopson and Millers had got the children into the house, like a little flock of sheep, and Mr. Pocket came out of it to make my acquaintance, I was not much surprised to find that Mr. Pocket was a gentleman with a rather perplexed expression of face, and with his very grey hair disordered on his head, as if he didn't quite see his way to putting anything straight.

[PART 15]

Chapter 23

Mr. Pocket said he was glad to see me, and he hoped I was not sorry to see him. "For, I really am not," he added, with his son's smile, "an alarming personage." He was a young-looking-man, in spite of his perplexities and his very grey hair, and his manner seemed quite natural. I use the word natural, in the sense of its being unaffected; there was something comic in his distraught way, as though it would have been downright ludicrous but for his own perception that it was very near being so. When he had talked with me a little, he said to Mrs. Pocket, with a rather anxious contraction of his eyebrows, which were black and handsome, "Belinda, I hope you have welcomed Mr. Pip?" And she looked up from her book, and said, "Yes." She then smiled upon me in an absent state of mind, and asked me if I liked the taste of orange-flower water? As the question had no bearing, near or remote, or any foregone or subsequent transaction, I consider it to have been thrown out, like her previous approaches, in general conversational condescension.

I found out within a few hours, and may mention at once, that Mrs. Pocket was the only daughter of a certain quite accidental deceased Knight,° who had invented for himself a conviction that his deceased father would have been made a Baronet but for somebody's determined opposition arising out of entirely personal motives—I forget whose, if I ever knew—the Sovereign's, the Prime Minister's, the Lord Chancellor's, the Archbishop of Canterbury's, anybody's—and had tacked himself on to the nobles of the earth in right of this quite supposititious fact. I believe he had been knighted himself for storming the English grammar at the point of the pen, in a desperate address engrossed on vellum, on the occasion of the laying of the first stone of some building or other, and for handing some Royal Personage either the trowel or the mortar. Be that as it may, he had directed Mrs. Pocket to be brought up from her cradle as one who in the nature of things must marry a title, and who was to be guarded from the acquisition of plebeian domestic knowledge. So successful a watch and ward had been established over the young lady by this judicious parent, that she had grown up highly ornamental, but perfectly helpless and useless. With her character thus happily formed, in the first bloom of her youth she had encountered Mr. Pocket: who was also in the first bloom of youth, and not quite decided whether to mount to the Woolsack, or to roof himself in with a mitre.° As his doing the one or the other was a mere question of time, he and Mrs. Pocket had taken Time by the forelock (when, to judge from its length, it would seem to have wanted cutting), and had married without the knowledge of the judicious parent. The judicious parent, having nothing to bestow or withhold but his blessing, had handsomely settled that dower upon them after a short struggle, and had informed Mr. Pocket that his wife was "a treasure for a Prince." Mr. Pocket had invested the Prince's treasure in the ways of the world ever since, and it was supposed to

---

accidental . . . Knight: Made a knight by accident. A knighthood is not hereditary; a baronetcy is.   **mount . . . mitre:** To become Lord Chancellor, the highest judicial officer in Great Britain, or to become a bishop.

have brought him in but indifferent interest. Still, Mrs. Pocket was in general the object of a queer sort of respectful pity, because she had not married a title; while Mr. Pocket was the object of a queer sort of forgiving reproach, because he had never got one.

Mr. Pocket took me into the house and showed me my room: which was a pleasant one, and so furnished as that I could use it with comfort for my own private sitting-room. He then knocked at the doors of two other similar rooms, and introduced me to their occupants, by name Drummle and Startop. Drummle, an old-looking young man of a heavy order of architecture, was whistling. Startop, younger in years and appearance, was reading and holding his head, as if he thought himself in danger of exploding it with too strong a charge of knowledge.

Both Mr. and Mrs. Pocket had such a noticeable air of being in somebody else's hands, that I wondered who really was in possession of the house and let them live there, until I found this unknown power to be the servants. It was a smooth way of going on, perhaps, in respect of saving trouble; but it had the appearance of being expensive, for the servants felt it a duty they owed to themselves to be nice in their eating and drinking, and to keep a deal of company down stairs. They allowed a very liberal table to Mr. and Mrs. Pocket, yet it always appeared to me that by far the best part of the house to have boarded in, would have been the kitchen—always supposing the boarder capable of self-defence, for, before I had been there a week, a neighbouring lady with whom the family were personally unacquainted, wrote in to say that she had seen Millers slapping the baby. This greatly distressed Mrs. Pocket, who burst into tears on receiving the note, and said it was an extraordinary thing that the neighbours couldn't mind their own business.

By degrees I learnt, and chiefly from Herbert, that Mr. Pocket had been educated at Harrow and at Cambridge, where he had distinguished himself; but that when he had had the happiness of marrying Mrs. Pocket very early in life, he had impaired his prospects and taken up the calling of a Grinder.° After grinding a number of dull blades—of whom it was remarkable that their fathers, when influential, were always going to help him to preferment, but always forgot to do it when the blades had left the Grindstone—he had wearied of that poor work and had come to London. Here, after gradually failing in loftier hopes, he had "read" with° divers who had lacked opportunities or neglected

---

Grinder: A crammer or coach for students taking examinations.   **"read" with:** Tutored.

them, and had refurbished divers others for special occasions, and had turned his acquirements to the account of literary compilation and correction, and on such means, added to some very moderate private resources, still maintained the house I saw.

Mr. and Mrs. Pocket had a toady neighbour; a widow lady of that highly sympathethic nature that she agreed with everybody, blessed everybody, and shed smiles and tears on everybody, according to circumstances. This lady's name was Mrs. Coiler, and I had the honour of taking her down to dinner on the day of my installation. She gave me to understand on the stairs, that it was a blow to dear Mrs. Pocket that dear Mr. Pocket should be under the necessity of receiving gentlemen to read with him. That did not extend to me, she told me in a gush of love and confidence (at that time, I had known her something less than five minutes); if they were all like Me, it would be quite another thing.

"But dear Mrs. Pocket," said Mrs. Coiler, "after her early disappointment (not that dear Mr. Pocket was to blame in that), requires so much luxury and elegance——"

"Yes, ma'am," I said, to stop her, for I was afraid she was going to cry.

"And she is of so aristocratic a disposition——"

"Yes, ma'am," I said again, with the same object as before.

"——that it *is* hard," said Mrs. Coiler, "to have dear Mr. Pocket's time and attention diverted from dear Mrs. Pocket."

I could not help thinking that it might be harder if the butcher's time and attention were diverted from dear Mrs. Pocket; but I said nothing, and indeed had enough to do in keeping a bashful watch upon my company-manners.

It came to my knowledge, through what passed between Mrs. Pocket and Drummle while I was attentive to my knife and fork, spoon, glasses, and other instruments of self-destruction, that Drummle, whose christian name was Bentley, was actually the next heir but one to a baronetcy. It further appeared that the book I had seen Mrs. Pocket reading in the garden, was all about titles, and that she knew the exact date at which her grandpapa would have come into the book, if he ever had come at all. Drummle didn't say much, but in his limited way (he struck me as a sulky kind of fellow) he spoke as one of the elect, and recognised Mrs. Pocket as a woman and a sister. No one but themselves and Mrs. Coiler the toady neighbour showed any interest in this part of the conversation, and it appeared to me that it was painful to Herbert; but it promised to last a long time, when the page came in with the announcement of a domestic affliction. It was, in effect, that the cook had mislaid the beef. To my unutterable amazement, I now, for the first time, saw Mr. Pocket relieve his mind by going through a performance that struck me as very extraordinary, but which made no impression on anybody else, and with which I soon became as familiar as the rest. He laid down the carving-knife and fork—being engaged in carving, at the moment—put his two hands into his disturbed hair, and appeared to make an extraordinary effort to lift himself up by it. When he had done this, and had not lifted himself up at all, he quietly went on with what he was about.

Mrs. Coiler then changed the subject, and began to flatter me. I liked it for a few moments, but she flattered me so very grossly that the pleasure was soon over. She had a serpentine way of coming close at me when she pretended to be vitally interested in the friends and localities I had left, which was altogether snaky and fork-tongued; and when she made an occasional bounce upon Startop (who said very little to her), or upon Drummle (who said less), I rather envied them for being on the opposite side of the table.

After dinner the children were introduced, and Mrs. Coiler made admiring comments on their eyes, noses, and legs—a sagacious way of improving their minds. There were four little girls, and two little boys, besides the baby who might have been either, and the baby's next successor who was as yet neither. They were brought in by Flopson and Millers, much as though those two non-commissioned officers had been recruiting somewhere for children and had enlisted these: while Mrs. Pocket looked at the young Nobles that ought to have been, as if she rather thought she had had the pleasure of inspecting them before, but didn't quite know what to make of them.

"Here! Give me your fork, Mum, and take the baby," said Flopson. "Don't take it that way, or you'll get its head under the table."

Thus advised, Mrs. Pocket took it the other way, and got its head upon the table; which was announced to all present by a prodigious concussion.

"Dear, dear! Give it me back, Mum," said Flopson; "and Miss Jane, come and dance to baby, do!"

One of the little girls, a mere mite who seemed to have prematurely taken upon herself some charge of the others, stepped out of her place by me, and danced to and from the baby until it left off crying, and laughed. Then, all the children laughed, and Mr. Pocket (who in the mean time had twice endeavoured to lift himself up by the hair) laughed, and we all laughed and were glad.

Flopson, by dint of doubling the baby at the joints like a Dutch doll, then got it safely into Mrs. Pocket's lap, and gave it the nutcrackers to play with: at the same time recommending Mrs. Pocket to take notice that the handles of that instrument were not likely to agree with its eyes, and sharply charging Miss Jane to look after the same. Then, the two nurses left the room, and had a lively scuffle on the staircase with a dissipated page who had waited at dinner, and who had clearly lost half his buttons at the gaming-table.

I was made very uneasy in my mind by Mrs. Pocket's falling into a discussion with Drummle respecting two baronetcies, while she ate a sliced orange steeped in sugar and wine, and forgetting all about the baby on her lap: who did most appalling things with the nutcrackers. At length, little Jane perceiving its young brains to be imperiled, softly left her place, and with many small artifices coaxed the dangerous weapon away. Mrs. Pocket finishing her orange at about the same time, and not approving of this, said to Jane:

"You naughty child, how dare you? Go and sit down this instant!"

"Mamma dear," lisped the little girl, "baby ood have put hith eyeth out."

"How dare you tell me so?" retorted Mrs. Pocket. "Go and sit down in your chair this moment!"

Mrs. Pocket's dignity was so crushing, that I felt quite abashed: as if I myself had done something to rouse it.

"Belinda," remonstrated Mr. Pocket, from the other end of the table, "how can you be so unreasonable? Jane only interfered for the protection of baby."

"I will not allow anybody to interfere," said Mrs. Pocket. "I am surprised, Matthew, that you should expose me to the affront of interference."

"Good God!" cried Mr. Pocket, in an outbreak of desolate desperation. "Are infants to be nutcrackered into their tombs, and is nobody to save them?"

"I will not be interfered with by Jane," said Mrs. Pocket, with a majestic glance at that innocent little offender. "I hope I know my poor grandpapa's position. Jane, indeed!"

Mr. Pocket got his hands in his hair again, and this time really did lift himself some inches out of his chair. "Hear this!" he helplessly exclaimed to the elements. "Babies are to be nutcrackered dead, for people's poor grandpapa's positions!" Then he let himself down again, and became silent.

We all looked awkwardly at the tablecloth while this was going on.

A pause succeeded, during which the honest and irrepressible baby made a series of leaps and crows at little Jane, who appeared to me to be the only member of the family (irrespective of servants) with whom it had any decided acquaintance.

"Mr. Drummle," said Mrs. Pocket, "will you ring for Flopson? Jane, you undutiful little thing, go and lie down. Now, baby darling, come with ma!"

The baby was the soul of honour, and protested with all its might. It doubled itself up the wrong way over Mrs. Pocket's arm, exhibited a pair of knitted shoes and dimpled ankles to the company in lieu of its soft face, and was carried out in the highest state of mutiny. And it gained its point after all, for I saw it through the window within a few minutes, being nursed by little Jane.

It happened that the other five children were left behind at the dinner-table, through Flopson's having some private engagement, and their not being anybody else's business. I thus became aware of the mutual relations between them and Mr. Pocket, which were exemplified in the following manner. Mr. Pocket, with the normal perplexity of his face heightened and his hair rumpled, looked at them for some minutes, as if he couldn't make out how they came to be boarding and lodging in that establishment, and why they hadn't been billeted by Nature on somebody else. Then, in a distant, Missionary way he asked them certain questions—as why little Joe had that hole in his frill: who said, Pa, Flopson was going to mend it when she had time—and how little Fanny came by that whitlow: who said, Pa, Millers was going to poultice it when she didn't forget. Then, he melted into parental tenderness, and gave them a shilling apiece and told them to go and play; and then as they went out, with one very strong effort to lift himself up by the hair he dismissed the hopeless subject.

In the evening there was rowing on the river. As Drummle and Startop had each a boat, I resolved to set up mine, and to cut them both out. I was pretty good at most exercises in which country-boys are adepts, but, as I was conscious of wanting elegance of style for the Thames—not to say for other waters—I at once engaged to place myself under the tuition of the winner of a prize-wherry who plied at our stairs, and to whom I was introduced by my new allies. This practical authority confused me very much, by saying I had the arm of a blacksmith. If he could have known how nearly the compliment lost him his pupil, I doubt if he would have paid it.

There was a supper-tray after we got home at night, and I think we should all have enjoyed ourselves, but for a rather disagreeable domestic occurrence. Mr. Pocket was in good spirits, when a housemaid came in, and said, "If you please, sir, I should wish to speak to you."

"Speak to your master?" said Mrs. Pocket, whose dignity was roused again. "How can you think of such a thing? Go and speak to Flopson. Or speak to me—at some other time."

"Begging your pardon, ma'am?" returned the housemaid, "I should wish to speak at once, and to speak to master."

Hereupon, Mr. Pocket went out of the room, and we made the best of ourselves until he came back.

"This is a pretty thing, Belinda!" said Mr. Pocket, returning with a countenance expressive of grief and despair. "Here's the cook lying insensibly drunk on the kitchen floor, with a large bundle of fresh butter made up in the cupboard ready to sell for grease!"

Mrs. Pocket instantly showed much amiable emotion, and said, "This is that odious Sophia's doing!"

"What do you mean, Belinda?" demanded Mr. Pocket.

"Sophia has told you," said Mrs. Pocket. "Did I not see her with my own eyes and hear her with my own ears, come into the room just now and ask to speak to you?"

"But has she not taken me down stairs, Belinda," returned Mr. Pocket, "and shown me the woman, and the bundle too?"

"And do you defend her, Matthew," said Mrs. Pocket, "for making mischief?"

Mr. Pocket uttered a dismal groan.

"Am I, grandpapa's granddaughter, to be nothing in the house?" said Mrs. Pocket. "Besides, the cook has always been a very nice respectful woman, and said in the most natural manner when she came to look after the situation, that she felt I was born to be a Duchess."

There was a sofa where Mr. Pocket stood, and he dropped upon it in the attitude of the Dying Gladiator.° Still, in that attitude he said, with a hollow voice, "Good night, Mr. Pip," when I deemed it advisable to go to bed and leave him.

Chapter 24

After two or three days, when I had established myself in my room and had gone backwards and forwards to London several times, and had ordered all I wanted of my tradesmen, Mr. Pocket and I had a

---

Dying Gladiator: A well-known Roman sculpture of a reclining warrior raised on one arm.

long talk together. He knew more of my intended career than I knew myself, for he referred to his having been told by Mr. Jaggers that I was not designed for any profession, and that I should be well enough educated for my destiny if I could "hold my own" with the average of young men in prosperous circumstances. I acquiesced, of course, knowing nothing to the contrary.

He advised my attending certain places in London, for the acquisition of such mere rudiments as I wanted, and my investing him with the functions of explainer and director of all my studies. He hoped that with intelligent assistance I should meet with little to discourage me, and should soon be able to dispense with any aid but his. Through his way of saying this, and much more to similar purpose, he placed himself on confidential terms with me in an admirable manner; and I may state at once that he was always so zealous and honourable in fulfilling his compact with me, that he made me zealous and honourable in fulfilling mine with him. If he had shown indifference as a master, I have no doubt I should have returned the compliment as a pupil; he gave me no such excuse, and each of us did the other justice. Nor, did I ever regard him as having anything ludicrous about him — or anything but what was serious, honest, and good—in his tutor communication with me.

When these points were settled, and so far carried out as that I had begun to work in earnest, it occurred to me that if I could retain my bedroom in Barnard's Inn, my life would be agreeably varied, while my manners would be none the worse for Herbert's society. Mr. Pocket did not object to this arrangement, but urged that before any step could possibly be taken in it, it must be submitted to my guardian. I felt that his delicacy arose out of the consideration that the plan would save Herbert some expense, so I went off to Little Britain and imparted my wish to Mr. Jaggers.

"If I could buy the furniture now hired for me," said I, "and one or two other little things, I should be quite at home there."

"Go it!" said Mr. Jaggers, with a short laugh. "I told you you'd get on. Well! How much do you want?"

I said I didn't know how much.

"Come!" retorted Mr. Jaggers. "How much? Fifty pounds?"

"Oh, not nearly so much."

"Five pounds?" said Mr. Jaggers.

This was such a great fall, that I said in discomfiture, "Oh! more than that."

"More than that, eh?" retorted Mr. Jaggers, lying in wait for me, with his hands in his pockets, his head on one side, and his eyes on the wall behind me; "how much more?"

"It is so difficult to fix a sum," said I, hesitating.

"Come!" said Mr. Jaggers. "Let's get at it. Twice five; will that do? Three times five; will that do? Four times five; will that do?"

I said I thought that would do handsomely.

"Four times five will do handsomely, will it?" said Mr. Jaggers, knitting his brows. "Now, what do you make of four times five?"

"What do I make of it?"

"Ah!" said Mr. Jaggers; "how much?"

"I suppose you make it twenty pounds," said I, smiling.

"Never mind what *I* make it, my friend," observed Mr. Jaggers, with a knowing and contradictory toss of his head. "I want to know what *you* make it."

"Twenty pounds, of course."

"Wemmick!" said Mr. Jaggers, opening his office door. "Take Mr. Pip's written order, and pay him twenty pounds."

This strongly marked way of doing business made a strongly marked impression on me, and that not of an agreeable kind. Mr. Jaggers never laughed; but he wore great bright creaking boots, and, in poising himself on these boots, with his large head bent down and his eyebrows joined together, awaiting an answer, he sometimes caused the boots to creak, as if *they* laughed in a dry and suspicious way. As he happened to go out now, and as Wemmick was brisk and talkative, I said to Wemmick that I hardly knew what to make of Mr. Jaggers's manner.

"Tell him that, and he'll take it as a compliment," answered Wemmick; "he don't mean that you *should* know what to make of it.— Oh!" for I looked surprised, "it's not personal; it's professional: only professional."

Wemmick was at his desk, lunching—and crunching—on a dry hard biscuit; pieces of which he threw from time to time into his slit of a mouth, as if he were posting them.

"Always seems to me," said Wemmick, "as if he had set a man-trap and was watching it. Suddenly—click—you're caught!"

Without remarking that man-traps were not among the amenities of life, I said I supposed he was very skilful?

"Deep," said Wemmick, "as Australia." Pointing with his pen at the office floor, to express that Australia was understood, for the purposes of the figure, to be symmetrically on the opposite spot of the globe. "If there was anything deeper," added Wemmick, bringing his pen to paper, "he'd be it."

Then, I said I supposed he had a fine business, and Wemmick said, "Ca-pi-tal!" Then I asked if there were many clerks? to which he replied:

"We don't run much into clerks, because there's only one Jaggers, and people won't have him at second hand. There are only four of us. Would you like to see 'em? You are one of us, as I may say."

I accepted the offer. When Mr. Wemmick had put all the biscuit into the post, and had paid me my money from a cash-box in a safe, the key of which safe he kept somewhere down his back and produced from his coat-collar like an iron pigtail, we went up-stairs. The house was dark and shabby, and the greasy shoulders that had left their mark in Mr. Jaggers's room, seemed to have been shuffling up and down the staircase for years. In the front first floor, a clerk who looked something between a publican and a rat-catcher—a large pale puffed swollen man—was attentively engaged with three or four people of shabby appearance, whom he treated as unceremoniously as everybody seemed to be treated who contributed to Mr. Jaggers's coffers. "Getting evidence together," said Mr. Wemmick, as we came out, "for the Bailey." In the room over that, a little flabby terrier of a clerk with dangling hair (his cropping seemed to have been forgotten when he was a puppy) was similarly engaged with a man with weak eyes, whom Mr. Wemmick presented to me as a smelter who kept his pot always boiling, and who would melt me anything I pleased—and who was in an excessive white-perspiration, as if he had been trying his art on himself. In a back room, a high-shouldered man with a face-ache tied up in dirty flannel, who was dressed in old black clothes that bore the appearance of having been waxed, was stooping over his work of making fair copies of the notes of the other two gentlemen, for Mr. Jaggers's own use.

This was all the establishment. When we went down stairs again, Wemmick led me into my guardian's room, and said, "This you've seen already."

"Pray," said I, as the two odious casts with the twitchy leer upon them caught my sight again, "whose likenesses are those?"

"These?" said Wemmick, getting upon a chair, and blowing the dust off the horrible heads before bringing them down. "These are two celebrated ones. Famous clients of ours that got us a world of credit. This chap (why you must have come down in the night and been peeping into the inkstand, to get this blot upon your eyebrow, you old rascal!) murdered his master, and, considering that he wasn't brought up to evidence, didn't plan it badly."

"Is it like him?" I asked, recoiling from the brute, as Wemmick spat upon his eyebrow and gave it a rub with his sleeve.

"Like him? It's himself, you know. The cast was made in Newgate, directly after he was taken down. You had a particular fancy for me, hadn't you, Old Artful?" said Wemmick. He then explained this affectionate apostrophe, by touching his brooch representing the lady and the weeping willow at the tomb with the urn upon it, and saying, "Had it made for me, express!"

"Is the lady anybody?" said I.

"No," returned Wemmick. "Only his game. (You liked your bit of game, didn't you?) No; deuce a bit of a lady in the case, Mr. Pip, except one—and she wasn't of this slender ladylike sort, and you wouldn't have caught *her* looking after this urn—unless there was something to drink in it." Wemmick's attention being thus directed to his brooch, he put down the cast, and polished the brooch with his pocket-handkerchief.

"Did that other creature come to the same end?" I asked. "He has the same look."

"You're right," said Wemmick; "it's the genuine look. Much as if one nostril was caught up with a horsehair and a little fishhook. Yes, he came to the same end; quite the natural end here, I assure you. He forged wills, this blade did, if he didn't also put the supposed testators to sleep° too. You were a gentlemanly Cove,° though" (Mr. Wemmick was again apostrophising), "and you said you could write Greek. Yah, Bounceable!° What a liar you were. I never met such a liar as you!" Before putting his late friend on his shelf again, Wemmick touched the largest of his mourning rings, and said, "Sent out to buy it for me, only the day before."

While he was putting up the other cast and coming down from the chair, the thought crossed my mind that all his personal jewellery was derived from like sources. As he had shown no diffidence on the subject, I ventured on the liberty of asking him the question, when he stood before me, dusting his hands.

"Oh yes," he returned, "these are all gifts of that kind. One brings another, you see; that's the way of it. I always take 'em. They're cu-

---

put . . . sleep: Kill the people whose wills he forged.   **Cove:** Chap (slang).
Bounceable: Inclined to swagger or boast.

riosities. And they're property. They may not be worth much, but, after all, they're property and portable. It don't signify to you with your brilliant lookout, but as to myself, my guiding-star always is, Get hold of portable property."

When I had rendered homage to this light, he went on to say, in a friendly manner:

"If at any odd time when you have nothing better to do, you wouldn't mind coming over to see me at Walworth,° I could offer you a bed, and I should consider it an honour. I have not much to show you; but such two or three curiosities as I have got, you might like to look over; and I am fond of a bit of garden and a summer-house."

I said I should be delighted to accept his hospitality.

"Thankee," said he; "then we'll consider that it's to come off, when convenient to you. Have you dined with Mr. Jaggers yet?"

"Not yet."

"Well," said Wemmick, "he'll give you wine, and good wine. I'll give you punch, and not bad punch. And now I'll tell you something. When you go to dine with Mr. Jaggers, look at his housekeeper."

"Shall I see something very uncommon?"

"Well," said Wemmick, "you'll see a wild beast tamed. Not so very uncommon, you'll tell me. I reply, that depends on the original wildness of the beast, and the amount of taming. It won't lower your opinion of Mr. Jaggers's powers. Keep your eye on it."

I told him I would do so, with all the interest and curiosity that his preparation awakened. As I was taking my departure, he asked me if I would like to devote five minutes to seeing Mr. Jaggers "at it?"

For several reasons, and not least because I didn't clearly know what Mr. Jaggers would be found to be "at," I replied in the affirmative. We dived into the City, and came up in a crowded police-court, where a blood-relation (in the murderous sense) of the deceased with the fanciful taste in brooches, was standing at the bar, uncomfortably chewing something; while my guardian had a woman under examination or cross-examination—I don't know which—and was striking her, and the bench, and everybody present, with awe. If anybody, of whatsoever degree, said a word that he didn't approve of, he instantly required to have it "taken down." If anybody wouldn't make an admission, he said, "I'll have it out of you!" and if anybody made an admission, he said, "Now I have got you!" The magistrates shivered under a single bite of his finger. Thieves and thief-takers hung in dread

Walworth: A suburb south of London.

rapture on his words, and shrank when a hair of his eyebrows turned in their direction. Which side he was on, I couldn't make out, for he seemed to me to be grinding the whole place in a mill; I only know that when I stole out on tiptoe, he was not on the side of the bench; for, he was making the legs of the old gentleman who presided, quite convulsive under the table, by his denunciations of his conduct as the representative of British law and justice in that chair that day.

[PART 16]

Chapter 25

Bentley Drummle, who was so sulky a fellow that he even took up a book as if its writer had done him an injury, did not take up an acquaintance in a more agreeable spirit. Heavy in figure, movement, and comprehension—in the sluggish complexion of his face, and in the large awkward tongue that seemed to loll about in his mouth as he himself lolled about in a room—he was idle, proud, niggardly, reserved, and suspicious. He came of rich people down in Somersetshire, who had nursed this combination of qualities until they made the discovery that it was just of age and a blockhead. Thus, Bentley Drummle had come to Mr. Pocket when he was a head taller than that gentleman, and half a dozen heads thicker than most gentlemen.

Startop had been spoilt by a weak mother and kept at home when he ought to have been at school, but he was devotedly attached to her, and admired her beyond measure. He had a woman's delicacy of feature, and was—"as you may see, though you never saw her," said Herbert to me—exactly like his mother. It was but natural that I should take to him much more kindly than to Drummle, and that, even in the earliest evenings of our boating, he and I should pull homeward abreast of one another, conversing from boat to boat, while Bentley Drummle came up in our wake alone, under the overhanging banks and among the rushes. He would always creep in-shore like some uncomfortable amphibious creature, even when the tide would have sent him fast upon his way; and I always think of him as coming after us in the dark or by the back-water, when our own two boats were breaking the sunset or the moonlight in mid-stream.

Herbert was my intimate companion and friend. I presented him with a half-share in my boat, which was the occasion of his often coming down to Hammersmith; and my possession of a half-share in his chambers often took me up to London. We used to walk between the two places at all hours. I have an affection for the road yet (though it is not so pleasant a road as it was then), formed in the impressibility of untried youth and hope.

When I had been in Mr. Pocket's family a month or two, Mr. and Mrs. Camilla turned up. Camilla was Mr. Pocket's sister. Georgiana, whom I had seen at Miss Havisham's on the same occasion, also turned up. She was a cousin—an indigestive single woman, who called her rigidity religion, and her liver love. These people hated me with the hatred of cupidity and disappointment. As a matter of course, they fawned upon me in my prosperity with the basest meanness. Towards Mr. Pocket, as a grown-up infant with no notion of his own interests, they showed the complacent forbearance I had heard them express. Mrs. Pocket they held in contempt; but they allowed the poor soul to have been heavily disappointed in life, because that shed a feeble re-flected light upon themselves.

These were the surroundings among which I settled down, and ap-plied myself to my education. I soon contracted expensive habits, and began to spend an amount of money that within a few short months I should have thought almost fabulous; but through good and evil I stuck to my books. There was no other merit in this, than my having sense enough to feel my deficiencies. Between Mr. Pocket and Her-bert I got on fast; and, with one or the other always at my elbow to give me the start I wanted, and clear obstructions out of my road, I must have been as great a dolt as Drummle if I had done less.

I had not seen Mr. Wemmick for some weeks, when I thought I would write him a note and propose to go home with him on a certain evening. He replied that it would give him much pleasure, and that he would expect me at the office at six o'clock. Thither I went, and there I found him, putting the key of his safe down his back as the clock struck.

"Did you think of walking down to Walworth?" said he.

"Certainly," said I, "if you approve."

"Very much," was Wemmick's reply, "for I have had my legs under the desk all day, and shall be glad to stretch them. Now, I'll tell you what I have got for supper, Mr. Pip. I have got a stewed steak—which is of home preparation—and a cold roast fowl—which is from the cook's-shop. I think it's tender, because the master of the shop was a Juryman in some cases of ours the other day, and we let him down easy. I reminded him of it when I bought the fowl, and I said, 'Pick us out a good one, old Briton, because if we had chosen to keep you in the box another day or two, we could easily have done it.' He said to that, 'Let me make you a present of the best fowl in the shop.' I let him, of course. As far as it goes, it's property and portable. You don't object to an aged parent, I hope?"

I really thought he was still speaking of the fowl, until he added, "Because I have got an aged parent at my place." I then said what politeness required.

"So, you haven't dined with Mr. Jaggers yet?" he pursued, as we walked along.

"Not yet."

"He told me so this afternoon when he heard you were coming. I expect you'll have an invitation to-morrow. He's going to ask your pals, too. Three of 'em; ain't there?"

Although I was not in the habit of counting Drummle as one of my intimate associates, I answered, "Yes."

"Well, he's going to ask the whole gang;" I hardly felt complimented by the word; "and whatever he gives you, he'll give you good. Don't look forward to variety, but you'll have excellence. And there's another rum thing in his house," proceeded Wemmick, after a moment's pause, as if the remark followed on the housekeeper understood; "he never lets a door or window be fastened at night."

"Is he never robbed?"

"That's it!" returned Wemmick. "He says, and gives it out publicly, 'I want to see the man who'll rob *me*.' Lord bless you, I have heard him, a hundred times if I have heard him once, say to regular cracksmen in our front office, 'You know where I live; now, no bolt is ever drawn there; why don't you do a stroke of business with me? Come; can't I tempt you?' Not a man of them, sir, would be bold enough to try it on, for love or money."

"They dread him so much?" said I.

"Dread him," said Wemmick. "I believe you they dread him. Not but what he's artful, even in his defiance of them. No silver, sir. Britannia metal,° every spoon."

"So they wouldn't have much," I observed, "even if they——"

"Ah! But *he* would have much," said Wemmick, cutting me short, "and they know it. He'd have their lives,° and the lives of scores of

---

Britannia metal: An inexpensive alloy that can be brightly shined to resemble silver. **He'd . . . lives:** Until 1861, theft of property worth forty shillings was punishable by death.

'em. He'd have all he could get. And it's impossible to say what he couldn't get, if he gave his mind to it."

I was falling into meditation on my guardian's greatness, when Wemmick remarked:

"As to the absence of plate, that's only his natural depth, you know. A river's its natural depth, and he's his natural depth. Look at his watch-chain. That's real enough."

"It's very massive," said I.

"Massive?" repeated Wemmick. "I think so. And his watch is a gold repeater,° and worth a hundred pound if it's worth a penny. Mr. Pip, there are about seven hundred thieves in this town who know all about that watch; there's not a man, a woman, or a child, among them, who wouldn't identify the smallest link in that chain, and drop it as if it was red-hot, if inveigled into touching it."

At first with such discourse, and afterwards with conversation of a more general nature, did Mr. Wemmick and I beguile the time and the road, until he gave me to understand that we had arrived in the district of Walworth.

It appeared to be a collection of back lanes, ditches, and little gardens, and to present the aspect of a rather dull retirement. Wemmick's house was a little wooden cottage in the midst of plots of garden, and the top of it was cut out and painted like a battery mounted with guns.

"My own doing," said Wemmick. "Looks pretty; don't it?"

I highly commended it. I think it was the smallest house I ever saw; with the queerest gothic windows (by far the greater part of them sham), and a gothic door, almost too small to get in at.

"That's a real flagstaff, you see," said Wemmick, "and on Sundays I run up a real flag. Then look here. After I have crossed this bridge, I hoist it up—so—and cut off the communication."

The bridge was a plank, and it crossed a chasm about four feet wide and two deep. But it was very pleasant to see the pride with which he hoisted it up and made it fast; smiling as he did so, with a relish and not merely mechanically.

"At nine o'clock every night, Greenwich time," said Wemmick, "the gun fires. There he is, you see! And when you hear him go, I think you'll say he's a Stinger."

The piece of ordnance referred to, was mounted in a separate fortress, constructed of lattice-work. It was protected from the weather by an ingenious little tarpaulin contrivance in the nature of an umbrella.

repeater: A watch that "repeats" or strikes the hour when a lever is pressed.

"Then, at the back," said Wemmick, "out of sight, so as not to impede the idea of fortifications—for it's a principle with me, if you have an idea, carry it out and keep it up—I don't know whether that's your opinion——"

I said, decidedly.

"At the back, there's a pig, and there are fowls and rabbits; then, I knock together my own little frame, you see, and grow cucumbers; and you'll judge at supper what sort of a salad I can raise. So, sir," said Wemmick, smiling again, but seriously too, as he shook his head, "if you can suppose the little place besieged, it would hold out a devil of a time in point of provisions."

Then, he conducted me to a bower about a dozen yards off, but which was approached by such ingenious twists of path that it took quite a long time to get at; and in this retreat our glasses were already set forth. Our punch was cooling in an ornamental lake, on whose margin the bower was raised. This piece of water (with an island in the middle which might have been the salad for supper) was of a circular form, and he had constructed a fountain in it, which, when you set a little mill going and took a cork out of a pipe, played to that powerful extent that it made the back of your hand quite wet.

"I am my own engineer, and my own carpenter, and my own plumber, and my own gardener, and my own Jack of all Trades," said Wemmick, in acknowledging my compliments. "Well; it's a good thing, you know. It brushes the Newgate cobwebs away, and pleases the Aged. You wouldn't mind being at once introduced to the Aged, would you? It wouldn't put you out?"

I expressed the readiness I felt, and we went into the Castle. There, we found, sitting by a fire, a very old man in a flannel coat: clean, cheerful, comfortable, and well cared for, but intensely deaf.

"Well aged parent," said Wemmick, shaking hands with him in a cordial and jocose way, "how am you?"

"All right, John; all right!" replied the old man.

"Here's Mr. Pip, aged parent," said Wemmick, "and I wish you could hear his name. Nod away at him, Mr. Pip; that's what he likes. Nod away at him, if you please, like winking!"

"This is a fine place of my son's, sir," cried the old man, while I nodded as hard as I possibly could. "This is a pretty pleasure-ground, sir. This spot and these beautiful works upon it ought to be kept together by the Nation, after my son's time, for the people's enjoyment."

"You're as proud of it as Punch; ain't you, Aged?" said Wemmick, contemplating the old man, with his hard face really softened; "*there's* a nod for you;" giving him a tremendous one; "*there's* another for you;" giving him a still more tremendous one; "you like that, don't you? If you're not tired, Mr. Pip—though I know it's tiring to strangers—will you tip him one more? You can't think how it pleases him."

I tipped him several more, and he was in great spirits. We left him bestirring himself to feed the fowls, and we sat down to our punch in the arbour; where Wemmick told me as he smoked a pipe that it had taken him a good many years to bring the property up to its present pitch of perfection.

"Is it your own, Mr. Wemmick?"

"Oh yes," said Wemmick, "I have got hold of it, a bit at a time. It's a freehold, by George!"

"Is it, indeed? I hope Mr. Jaggers admires it?"

"Never seen it," said Wemmick. "Never heard of it. Never seen the Aged. Never heard of him. No; the office is one thing, and private life is another. When I go into the office, I leave the Castle behind me, and when I come into the Castle, I leave the office behind me. If it's not in any way disagreeable to you, you'll oblige me by doing the same. I don't wish it professionally spoken about."

Of course I felt my good faith involved in the observance of his request. The punch being very nice, we sat there drinking it and talking, until it was almost nine o'clock. "Getting near gun-fire," said Wemmick then, as he laid down his pipe; "it's the Aged's treat."

Proceeding into the Castle again, we found the Aged heating the poker, with expectant eyes, as a preliminary to the performance of this great nightly ceremony. Wemmick stood with his watch in his hand, until the moment was come for him to take the red-hot poker from the Aged, and repair to the battery. He took it, and went out, and presently the Stinger went off with a Bang that shook the crazy little box of a cottage as if it must fall to pieces, and made every glass and teacup in it ring. Upon this, the Aged—who I believe would have been blown out of his arm-chair but for holding on by the elbows—cried out exultingly, "He's fired! I heerd him!" and I nodded at the old gentleman until it is no figure of speech to declare that I absolutely could not see him.

The interval between that time and supper, Wemmick devoted to showing me his collection of curiosities. They were mostly of a felonious character; comprising the pen with which a celebrated forgery had been committed, a distinguished razor or two, some locks of hair,

and several manuscript confessions written under condemnation—
upon which Mr. Wemmick set particular value as being, to use his own
words, "every one of 'em Lies, sir." These were agreeably dispersed
among small specimens of china and glass, various neat trifles made by
the proprietor of the museum, and some tobacco-stoppers carved by
the Aged. They were all displayed in that chamber of the Castle into
which I had been first inducted, and which served, not only as the
general sitting-room but as the kitchen too, if I might judge from a
saucepan on the hob, and a brazen bijou over the fireplace designed
for the suspension of a roasting-jack.

There was a neat little girl in attendance, who looked after the
Aged in the day. When she had laid the supper-cloth, the bridge was
lowered to give her means of egress, and she withdrew for the night.
The supper was excellent; and though the Castle was rather subject to
dry-rot insomuch that it tasted like a bad nut, and though the pig
might have been farther off, I was heartily pleased with my whole entertainment. Nor was there any drawback on my little turret bedroom,
beyond there being such a very thin ceiling between me and the
flagstaff, that when I lay down on my back in bed, it seemed as if I had
to balance that pole on my forehead all night.

Wemmick was up early in the morning, and I am afraid I heard
him cleaning my boots. After that, he fell to gardening, and I saw him
from my gothic window pretending to employ the Aged, and nodding
at him in a most devoted manner. Our breakfast was as good as the
supper, and at half-past eight precisely we started for Little Britain. By
degrees, Wemmick got dryer and harder as we went along, and his
mouth tightened into a post-office again. At last, when we got to his
place of business and he pulled out his key from his coat-collar, he
looked as unconscious of his Walworth property as if the Castle and
the drawbridge and the arbour and the lake and the fountain and the
Aged, had all been blown into space together by the last discharge of
the Stinger.

Chapter 26

It fell out as Wemmick had told me it would, that I had an early
opportunity of comparing my guardian's establishment with that of his
cashier and clerk. My guardian was in his room, washing his hands
with his scented soap, when I went into the office from Walworth; and
he called me to him, and gave me the invitation for myself and friends
which Wemmick had prepared me to receive. "No ceremony" he stip-

ulated, "and no dinner dress, and say to-morrow." I asked him where
we should come to (for I had no idea where he lived), and I believe it
was in his general objection to make anything like an admission, that
he replied, "Come here, and I'll take you home with me." I embrace
this opportunity of remarking that he washed his clients off, as if he
were a surgeon or a dentist. He had a closet in his room, fitted up for
the purpose, which smelt of the scented soap like a perfumer's shop. It
had an unusually large jack-towel on a roller inside the door, and he
would wash his hands, and wipe them and dry them all over this towel,
whenever he came in from a police-court or dismissed a client from his
room. When I and my friends repaired to him at six o'clock next day,
he seemed to have been engaged on a case of a darker complexion
than usual, for, we found him with his head butted into this closet, not
only washing his hands, but laving his face and gargling his throat.
And even when he had done all that, and had gone all round the jack-
towel, he took out his penknife and scraped the case out of his nails
before he put his coat on.

There were some people slinking about as usual when we passed
out into the street, who were evidently anxious to speak with him; but
there was something so conclusive in the halo of scented soap which
encircled his presence, that they gave it up for that day. As we walked
along westward, he was recognised ever and again by some face in the
crowd of the streets, and whenever that happened he talked louder to
me; but he never otherwise recognised anybody, or took notice that
anybody recognised him.

He conducted us to Gerrard-street, Soho, to a house on the south
side of that street. Rather a stately house of its kind, but dolefully in
want of painting, and with dirty windows. He took out his key and
opened the door, and we all went into a stone hall, bare, gloomy, and
little used. So, up a dark brown staircase into a series of three dark
brown rooms on the first floor. There were carved garlands on the
panelled walls, and as he stood among them giving us welcome, I
know what kind of loops I thought they looked like.

Dinner was laid in the best of these rooms; the second was his
dressing-room; the third, his bedroom. He told us that he held the
whole house, but rarely used more of it than we saw. The table was
comfortably laid—no silver in the service, of course—and at the side
of his chair was a capacious dumb-waiter, with a variety of bottles and
decanters on it, and four dishes of fruit for dessert. I noticed throughout, that he kept everything under his own hand, and distributed
everything himself.

There was a bookcase in the room; I saw, from the backs of the books, that they were about evidence, criminal law, criminal biography, trials, acts of parliament, and such things. The furniture was all very solid and good, like his watch-chain. It had an official look, however, and there was nothing merely ornamental to be seen. In a corner, was a little table of papers with a shaded lamp: so that he seemed to bring the office home with him in that respect too, and to wheel it out of an evening and fall to work.

As he had scarcely seen my three companions until now—for, he and I had walked together—he stood on the hearth-rug, after ringing the bell, and took a searching look at them. To my surprise, he seemed at once to be principally if not solely interested in Drummle.

"Pip," said he, putting his large hand on my shoulder and moving me to the window, "I don't know one from the other. Who's the Spider!"

"The spider?" said I.

"The blotchy, sprawly, sulky fellow."

"That's Bentley Drummle," I replied; "the one with the delicate face is Startop."

Not making the least account of "the one with the delicate face," he returned. "Bentley Drummle is his name, is it? I like the look of that fellow."

He immediately began to talk to Drummle: not at all deterred by his replying in his heavy reticent way, but apparently led on by it to screw discourse out of him. I was looking at the two, when there came between me and them, the housekeeper, with the first dish for the table.

She was a woman of about forty, I supposed—but I may have thought her younger than she was. Rather tall, of a lithe nimble figure, extremely pale, with large faded eyes, and a quantity of streaming hair. I cannot say whether any diseased affection of the heart caused her lips to be parted as if she were panting, and her face to bear a curious expression of suddenness and flutter; but I know that I had been to see Macbeth at the theatre, a night or two before, and that her face looked to me as if it were all disturbed by fiery air, like the faces I had seen rise out of the Witches' caldron.

She set the dish on, touched my guardian quietly on the arm with a finger to notify that dinner was ready, and vanished. We took our seats at the round table, and my guardian kept Drummle on one side of him, while Startop sat on the other. It was a noble dish of fish that the housekeeper had put on table, and we had a joint of equally choice mutton afterwards, and then an equally choice bird. Sauces, wines, all the accessories we wanted, and all of the best, were given out by our host from his dumb-waiter; and when they had made the circuit of the table, he always put them back again. Similarly, he dealt us clean plates and knives and forks, for each course, and dropped those just disused into two baskets on the ground by his chair. No other attendant than the housekeeper appeared. She set on every dish; and I always saw in her face, a face rising out of the caldron. Years afterwards, I made a dreadful likeness of that woman, by causing a face that had no other natural resemblance to it than it derived from flowing hair, to pass behind a bowl of flaming spirits in a dark room.

Induced to take particular notice of the housekeeper, both by her own striking appearance and by Wemmick's preparation, I observed that whenever she was in the room, she kept her eyes attentively on my guardian, and that she would remove her hands from any dish she put before him, hesitatingly, as if she dreaded his calling her back, and wanted him to speak when she was nigh, if he had anything to say. I fancied that I could detect in his manner a consciousness of this, and a purpose of always holding her in suspense.

Dinner went off gaily, and, although my guardian seemed to follow rather than originate subjects, I knew that he wrenched the weakest part of our dispositions out of us. For myself, I found that I was expressing my tendency to lavish expenditure, and to patronise Herbert, and to boast of my great prospects, before I quite knew that I had opened my lips. It was so with all of us, but with no one more than Drummle: the development of whose inclination to gird in a grudging and suspicious way at the rest, was screwed out of him before the fish was taken off.

It was not then, but when we had got to the cheese, that our conversation turned upon our rowing feats, and that Drummle was rallied for coming up behind of a night in that slow amphibious way of his. Drummle upon this, informed our host that he much preferred our room to our company, and that as to skill he was more than our master, and that as to strength he could scatter us like chaff. By some invisible agency, my guardian wound him up to a pitch little short of ferocity about this trifle; and he fell to baring and spanning his arm to show how muscular it was, and we all fell to baring and spanning our arms in a ridiculous manner.

Now, the housekeeper was at that time clearing the table; my guardian, taking no heed of her, but with the side of his face turned from her, was leaning back in his chair biting the side of his forefinger and showing an interest in Drummle, that, to me, was quite inexplicable. Suddenly, he clapped his large hand on the housekeeper's, like a trap, as she stretched it across the table. So suddenly and smartly did he do this, that we all stopped in our foolish contention.

"If you talk of strength," said Mr. Jaggers, "*I*'ll show you a wrist. Molly, let them see your wrist."

Her entrapped hand was on the table, but she had already put her other hand behind her waist. "Master," she said, in a low voice, with her eyes attentively and entreatingly fixed upon him. "Don't!"

"*I*'ll show you a wrist," repeated Mr. Jaggers, with an immovable determination to show it. "Molly, let them see your wrist."

"Master," she again murmured. "Please!"

"Molly," said Mr. Jaggers, not looking at her, but obstinately looking at the opposite side of the room, "let them see *both* your wrists. Show them. Come!"

He took his hand from hers, and turned that wrist up on the table. She brought her other hand from behind her, and held the two out side by side. The last wrist was much disfigured—deeply scarred and scarred across and across. When she held her hands out, she took her eyes from Mr. Jaggers, and turned them watchfully on every one of the rest of us in succession.

"There's power here," said Mr. Jaggers, coolly tracing out the sinews with his forefinger. "Very few men have the power of wrist that this woman has. It's remarkable what mere force of grip there is in these hands. I have had occasion to notice many hands; but I never saw stronger in that respect, man's or woman's, than these."

While he said these words in a leisurely critical style, she continued to look at every one of us in regular succession as we sat. The moment he ceased, she looked at him again. "That'll do, Molly," said Mr. Jaggers, giving her a slight nod; "you have been admired, and can go." She withdrew her hands and went out of the room, and Mr. Jaggers, putting the decanters on from his dumb-waiter, filled his glass and passed round the wine.

"At half-past nine, gentlemen," said he, "we must break up. Pray make the best use of your time. I am glad to see you all. Mr. Drummle, I drink to you."

If his object in singling out Drummle were to bring him out still more, it perfectly succeeded. In a sulky triumph, Drummle showed his morose depreciation of the rest of us, in a more and more offensive degree until he became downright intolerable. Through all his stages, Mr. Jaggers followed him with the same strange interest. He actually seemed to serve as a zest to Mr. Jaggers's wine.

In our boyish want of discretion I dare say we took too much to drink, and I know we talked too much. We became particularly hot upon some boorish sneer of Drummle's, to the effect that we were too free with our money. It led to my remarking, with more zeal than discretion, that it came with a bad grace from him, to whom Startop had lent money in my presence but a week or so before.

"Well," retorted Drummle; "he'll be paid."

"I don't mean to imply that he won't," said I, "but it might make you hold your tongue about us and our money, I should think."

"*You* should think!" retorted Drummle. "Oh Lord!"

"I dare say," I went on, meaning to be very severe, "that you wouldn't lend money to any of us, if we wanted it."

"You are right," said Drummle. "I wouldn't lend one of you a sixpence. I wouldn't lend anybody a sixpence."

"Rather mean to borrow under those circumstances, I should say."

"*You* should say," repeated Drummle. "Oh Lord!"

This was so very aggravating—the more especially as I found myself making no way against his surly obtuseness—that I said, disregarding Herbert's efforts to check me:

"Come, Mr. Drummle, since we are on the subject, I'll tell you what passed between Herbert here and me, when you borrowed that money."

"*I* don't want to know what passed between Herbert there and you," growled Drummle. And I think he added in a lower growl, that we might both go to the devil and shake ourselves.

"I'll tell you, however," said I, "whether you want to know or not. We said that as you put it in your pocket very glad to get it, you seemed to be immensely amused at his being so weak as to lend it."

Drummle laughed outright, and sat laughing in our faces, with his hands in his pockets and his round shoulders raised: plainly signifying that it was quite true, and that he despised us, as asses all.

Hereupon Startop took him in hand, though with a much better grace than I had shown, and exhorted him to be a little more agreeable. Startop, being a lively bright young fellow, and Drummle being the exact opposite, the latter was always disposed to resent him as a direct personal affront. He now retorted in a coarse lumpish way, and Startop tried to turn the discussion aside with some small pleasantry that made us all laugh. Resenting this little success more than anything, Drummle, without any threat or warning, pulled his hands out of his pockets, dropped his round shoulders, swore, took up a large glass, and would have flung it at his adversary's head, but for our entertainer's dexterously seizing it at the instant when it was raised for that purpose.

"Gentlemen," said Mr. Jaggers, deliberately putting down the glass, and hauling out his gold repeater by its massive chain, "I am exceedingly sorry to announce that it's half-past nine."

On this hint we all rose to depart. Before we got to the street door, Startop was cheerily calling Drummle "old boy," as if nothing had happened. But the old boy was so far from responding, that he would not even walk to Hammersmith on the same side of the way; so, Herbert and I, who remained in town, saw them going down the street on opposite sides; Startop leading, and Drummle lagging behind in the shadow of the houses, much as he was wont to follow in his boat.

As the door was not yet shut, I thought I would leave Herbert there for a moment, and run up-stairs again to say a word to my guardian. I found him in his dressing-room surrounded by his stock of boots, already hard at it, washing his hands of us.

I told him I had come up again, to say how sorry I was that anything disagreeable should have occurred, and that I hoped he would not blame me much.

"Pooh!" said he, sluicing his face, and speaking through the water-drops; "it's nothing, Pip. I like that Spider though."

He had turned towards me now, and was shaking his head, and blowing, and towelling himself.

"I am glad you like him, sir," said I—"but I don't."

"No, no," my guardian assented; "don't have too much to do with him. Keep as clear of him as you can. But I like the fellow, Pip; he is one of the true sort. Why, if I was a fortune-teller——"

Looking out of the towel, he caught my eye.

"But I am not a fortune-teller," he said, letting his head drop into a festoon of towel, and towelling away at his two ears. "You know what I am, don't you? Good night, Pip."

"Good night, sir."

In about a month after that, the Spider's time with Mr. Pocket was up for good, and, to the great relief of all the house but Mrs. Pocket, he went home to the family hole.

[PART 17]

Chapter 27

My Dear Mr. Pip,

I write this by request of Mr. Gargery, for to let you know that he is going to London in company of Mr. Wopsle and would be glad if agreeable to be allowed to see you. He would call at Barnard's Hotel Tuesday morning 9 o'clock, when if not agreeable please leave word. Your poor sister is much the same as when you left. We talk of you in the kitchen every night, and wonder what you are saying and doing. If now considered in the light of a liberty, excuse it for the love of poor old days. No more, dear Mr. Pip, from

Your ever obliged, and affectionate

Servant,

BIDDY.

P.S. He wishes me most particular to write *what larks*. He says you will understand. I hope and do not doubt it will be agreeable to see him even though a gentleman, for you had ever a good heart and he is a worthy worthy man. I have read him all, excepting only the last little sentence, and he wishes me most particular to write again *what larks*.

I received this letter by the post on Monday morning, and therefore its appointment was for next day. Let me confess exactly, with what feelings I looked forward to Joe's coming.

Not with pleasure, though I was bound to him by so many ties; no; with considerable disturbance, some mortification, and a keen sense of incongruity. If I could have kept him away by paying money, I certainly would have paid money. My greatest reassurance was, that he was coming to Barnard's Inn, not to Hammersmith, and consequently would not fall in Bentley Drummle's way. I had little objection to his being seen by Herbert or his father, for both of whom I had a respect; but I had the sharpest sensitiveness as to his being seen by Drummle, whom I held in contempt. So, throughout life, our worst weaknesses and meannesses are usually committed for the sake of the people whom we most despise.

I had begun to be always decorating the chambers in some quite unnecessary and inappropriate way or other, and very expensive those wrestles with Barnard proved to be. By this time, the rooms were vastly different from what I had found them, and I enjoyed the

honour of occupying a few prominent pages in the books of a neighbouring upholsterer. I had got on so fast of late, that I had even
started a boy in boots°—top boots—in bondage and slavery to whom
I might have been said to pass my days. For, after I had made the
monster (out of the refuse of my washerwoman's family) and had
clothed him with a blue coat, canary waistcoat, white cravat, creamy
breeches, and the boots already mentioned, I had to find him a little
to do and a great deal to eat; and with both of those horrible require-
ments he haunted my existence.

This avenging phantom was ordered to be on duty at eight on
Tuesday morning in the hall (it was two feet square, as charged for
floorcloth), and Herbert suggested certain things for breakfast that he
thought Joe would like. While I felt sincerely obliged to him for being
so interested and considerate, I had an odd half-provoked sense of suspicion upon me, that if Joe had been coming to see *him*, he wouldn't
have been quite so brisk about it.

However, I came into town on the Monday night to be ready for
Joe, and I got up early in the morning, and caused the sitting-room
and breakfast-table to assume their most splendid appearance. Unfortunately the morning was drizzly, and an angel could not have concealed the fact that Barnard was shedding sooty tears outside the window, like some weak giant of a Sweep.

As the time approached I should have liked to run away, but the
Avenger pursuant to orders was in the hall, and presently I heard Joe
on the staircase. I knew it was Joe, by his clumsy manner of coming
up-stairs—his state boots being always too big for him—and by the
time it took him to read the names on the other floors in the course of
his ascent. When at last he stopped outside our door, I could hear his
finger tracing over the painted letters of my name, and I afterwards
distinctly heard him breathing in at the keyhole. Finally he gave a faint
single rap, and Pepper—such was the compromising name of the
avenging boy—announced "Mr. Gargery!" I thought he never would
have done wiping his feet, and that I must have gone out to lift him
off the mat, but at last he came in.

"Joe, how are you, Joe?"

"Pip, how AIR you, Pip?"

With his good honest face all glowing and shining, and his hat put
down on the floor between us, he caught both my hands and worked
them straight up and down, as if I had been the last-patented Pump.

started . . . boots: Hired a young servant.

"I am glad to see you, Joe. Give me your hat."

But Joe, taking it up carefully with both hands, like a bird's-nest with eggs in it, wouldn't hear of parting with that piece of property, and persisted in standing talking over it in a most uncomfortable way.

"Which you have that growed," said Joe, "and that swelled, and that gentlefolked;" Joe considered a little before he discovered this word; "as to be sure you are a honour to your king and country."

"And you, Joe, look wonderfully well."

"Thank God," said Joe, "I'm ekerval to most. And your sister, she's no worse than she were. And Biddy, she's ever right and ready. And all friends is no backerder, if not no forarder. 'Ceptin' Wopsle; he's had a drop."

All this time (still with both hands taking great care of the bird's-nest), Joe was rolling his eyes round and round the room, and round and round the flowered pattern of my dressing-gown.

"Had a drop, Joe?"

"Why yes," said Joe, lowering his voice, "he's left the Church, and went into the playacting. Which the playacting have likeways brought him to London along with me. And his wish were," said Joe, getting the bird's-nest under his left arm for the moment and groping in it for an egg with his right; "if no offence, as I would 'and you that."

I took what Joe gave me, and found it to be the crumpled playbill of a small metropolitan theatre, announcing the first appearance, in that very week, of "the celebrated Provincial Amateur of Roscian renown,° whose unique performance in the highest tragic walk of our National Bard has lately occasioned so great a sensation in local dramatic circles."

"Were you at his performance, Joe?" I inquired.

"I *were*," said Joe, with emphasis and solemnity.

"Was there a great sensation?"

"Why," said Joe, "yes, there certainly were a peck of orange-peel.° Partickler, when he see the ghost. Though I put it to yourself, sir, whether it were calc'lated to keep a man up to his work with a good hart, to be continiwally cutting in betwixt him and the Ghost with 'Amen!' A man may have had a misfortun' and been in the Church," said Joe, lowering his voice to an argumentative and feeling tone, "but that is no reason why you should put him out at such a time. Which I

---

of Roscian renown: As famous as the Roman actor Roscius.   peck of orange-peel: In the rowdier theatres, audience members threw refuse from the food they were eating onto the stage or at the actors to show their displeasure with a performance.

meantersay, if the ghost of a man's own father cannot be allowed to claim his attention, what can, Sir? Still more, when his mourning 'at is unfortunately made so small as that the weight of the black feathers brings it off, try to keep it on how you may."

A ghost-seeing effect in Joe's own countenance informed me that Herbert had entered the room. So, I presented Joe to Herbert, who held out his hand; but Joe backed from it, and held on by the bird's-nest.

"Your servant, Sir," said Joe, "which I hope as you and Pip"— here his eye fell on the Avenger, who was putting some toast on table, and so plainly denoted an intention to make that young gentleman one of the family, that I frowned it down and confused him more—"I meantersay, you two gentlemen—which I hope as you get your elths in this close spot? For the present may be a werry good inn, according to London opinions," said Joe, confidentially, "and I believe its character do stand i;° but I wouldn't keep a pig in it myself—not in the case that I wished him to fatten wholesome and to eat with a meller flavour on him."

Having borne this flattering testimony to the merits of our dwelling-place, and having incidentally shown this tendency to call me "sir," Joe, being invited to sit down to table, looked all round the room for a suitable spot on which to deposit his hat—as if it were only on some very few rare substances in nature that it could find a resting-place—and ultimately stood it on an extreme corner of the chimney-piece, from which it ever afterwards fell off at intervals.

"Do you take tea, or coffee, Mr. Gargery?" asked Herbert, who always presided of a morning.

"Thankee, Sir," said Joe, stiff from head to foot, "I'll take whichever is most agreeable to yourself."

"What do you say to coffee?"

"Thankee, Sir," returned Joe, evidently dispirited by the proposal, "since you *are* so kind as make chice of coffee, I will not run contrairy to your own opinions. But don't you never find it a little 'eating?"

"Say tea then," said Herbert, pouring it out.

Here Joe's hat tumbled off the mantel-piece, and he started out of his chair and picked it up, and fitted it to the same exact spot. As if it were an absolute point of good breeding that it should tumble off again soon.

---

its character . . . i: It has a good ("i" for "high") reputation.

"When did you come to town, Mr. Gargery?"

"Were it yesterday afternoon?" said Joe, after coughing behind his hand, as if he had had time to catch the whooping-cough since he came. "No it were not. Yes it were. Yes. It were yesterday afternoon" (with an appearance of mingled wisdom, relief, and strict impartiality).

"Have you seen anything of London, yet?"

"Why, yes, Sir," said Joe, "me and Wopsle went off straight to look at the Blacking Ware'us. But we didn't find that it come up to its likeness in the red bills at the shop doors; which I meantersay," added Joe, in an explanatory manner, "as it is there drawd too architectooralooral."

I really believe Joe would have prolonged this word (mightily expressive to my mind of some architecture that I know) into a perfect Chorus, but for his attention being providentially attracted by his hat, which was toppling. Indeed, it demanded from him a constant attention, and a quickness of eye and hand, very like that exacted by wicket-keeping.° He made extraordinary play with it, and showed the greatest skill; now, rushing at it and catching it neatly as it dropped; now, merely stopping it mid-way, beating it up, and humouring it in various parts of the room and against a good deal of the pattern of the paper on the wall, before he felt it safe to close with it; finally, splashing it into the slop-basin, where I took the liberty of laying hands upon it.

As to his shirt-collar, and his coat-collar, they were perplexing to reflect upon—insoluble mysteries both. Why should a man scrape himself to that extent, before he could consider himself full dressed? Why should he suppose it necessary to be purified by suffering for his holiday clothes? Then he fell into such unaccountable fits of meditation, with his fork mid-way between his plate and his mouth; had his eyes attracted in such strange directions; was afflicted with such remarkable coughs; sat so far from the table, and dropped so much more than he ate, and pretended that he hadn't dropped it; that I was heartily glad when Herbert left us for the City.

I had neither the good sense nor the good feeling to know that this was all my fault, and that if I had been easier with Joe, Joe would have been easier with me. I felt impatient of him and out of temper with him; in which condition he heaped coals of fire on my head.

"Us two being now alone, Sir,——" began Joe.

"Joe," I interrupted, pettishly, "how can you call me, Sir?"

Joe looked at me for a single instant with something faintly like

wicket-keeping: Catching the ball in cricket.

reproach. Utterly preposterous as his cravat was, and as his collars were, I was conscious of a sort of dignity in the look.

"Us two being now alone," resumed Joe, "and me having the intentions and abilities to stay not many minutes more, I will now conclude—leastways begin—to mention what have led to my having had the present honour. For was it not," said Joe, with his old air of lucid exposition, "that my only wish were to be useful to you, I should not have had the honour of breaking wittles in the company and abode of gentlemen."

I was so unwilling to see the look again, that I made no remonstrance against this tone.

"Well, Sir," pursued Joe, "this is how it were. I were at the Bargemen t'other night, Pip;" whenever he subsided into affection, he called me Pip, and whenever he relapsed into politeness he called me Sir; "when there come up in his shay-cart, Pumblechook. Which that same identical," said Joe, going down a new track, "do comb my 'air the wrong way sometimes, awful, by giving out up and down town as it were him which ever had your infant companionation and were looked upon as a playfellow by yourself."

"Nonsense. It was you, Joe."

"Which I fully believed it were, Pip," said Joe, slightly tossing his head, "though it signify little now, Sir. Well, Pip; this same identical, which his manners is given to blusterous, come to me at the Bargemen (wot a pipe and a pint of beer do give refreshment to the working-man, Sir, and do not over stimilate), and his word were, 'Joseph, Miss Havisham she wish to speak to you.'"

"Miss Havisham, Joe?"

"'She wish,' were Pumblechook's word, 'to speak to you.'" Joe sat and rolled his eyes at the ceiling.

"Yes, Joe? Go on, please."

"Next day, Sir," said Joe, looking at me as if I were a long way off, "having cleaned myself, I go and I see Miss A."

"Miss A., Joe? Miss Havisham?"

"Which I say, Sir," replied Joe, with an air of legal formality, as if he were making his will, "Miss A., or otherways Havisham. Her expression air then as follering: 'Mr. Gargery. You air in correspondence with Mr. Pip?' Having had a letter from you, I were able to say 'I am.' (When I married your sister, Sir, I said 'I will;' and when I answered your friend, Pip, I said 'I am.') 'Would you tell him, then,' said she, 'that which Estella has come home and would be glad to see him.'"

I felt my face fire up as I looked at Joe. I hope one remote cause of its firing, may have been my consciousness that if I had known his errand, I should have given him more encouragement.

"Biddy," pursued Joe, "when I got home and asked her fur to write the message to you, a little hung back. Biddy says, 'I know he will be very glad to have it by word of mouth, it is holiday-time, you want to see him, go!' I have now concluded, Sir," said Joe, rising from his chair, "and, Pip, I wish you ever well and ever prospering to a greater and a greater heighth."

"But you are not going now, Joe?"

"Yes I am," said Joe.

"But you are coming back to dinner, Joe?"

"No I am not," said Joe.

Our eyes met, and all the "Sir" melted out of that manly heart as he gave me his hand.

"Pip, dear old chap, life is made of ever so many partings welded together, as I may say, and one man's a blacksmith, and one's a whitesmith,° and one's a goldsmith, and one's a coppersmith. Diwisions among such must come, and must be met as they come. If there's been any fault at all to-day, it's mine. You and me is not two figures to be together in London; nor yet anywheres else but what is private, and beknown, and understood among friends. It ain't that I am proud, but that I want to be right, as you shall never see me no more in these clothes. I'm wrong in these clothes. I'm wrong out of the forge, the kitchen, or off th' meshes. You won't find half so much fault in me if you think of me in my forge dress, with my hammer in my hand, or even my pipe. You won't find half so much fault in me if, supposing as you should ever wish to see me, you come and put your head in at the forge window and see Joe the blacksmith, there, at the old anvil, in the old burnt apron, sticking to the old work. I'm awful dull, but I hope I've beat out something nigh the rights of this at last. And so GOD bless you, dear old Pip, old chap, GOD bless you!"

I had not been mistaken in my fancy that there was a simple dignity in him. The fashion of his dress could no more come in its way when he spoke these words, than it could come in its way in Heaven. He touched me gently on the forehead, and went out. As soon as I could recover myself sufficiently, I hurried out after him and looked for him in the neighbouring streets; but he was gone.

whitesmith: Tinsmith.

Chapter 28

It was clear that I must repair to our town next day, and in the first flow of my repentance it was equally clear that I must stay at Joe's. But, when I had secured my box-place by to-morrow's coach and had been down to Mr. Pocket's and back, I was not by any means convinced on the last point, and began to invent reasons and make excuses for putting up at the Blue Boar. I should be an inconvenience at Joe's; I was not expected, and my bed would not be ready; I should be too far from Miss Havisham's, and she was exacting and mightn't like it. All other swindlers upon earth are nothing to the self-swindlers, and with such pretences did I cheat myself. Surely a curious thing. That I should innocently take a bad half-crown of somebody else's manufacture, is reasonable enough; but that I should knowingly reckon the spurious coin of my own make, as good money! An obliging stranger, under pretence of compactly folding up my bank-notes for security's sake, abstracts the notes and gives me nutshells; but what is his sleight of hand to mine, when I fold up my own nutshells and pass them on myself as notes!

Having settled that I must go the Blue Boar, my mind was much disturbed by indecision whether or no to take the Avenger. It was tempting to think of that expensive Mercenary publicly airing his boots in the archway of the Blue Boar's posting-yard; it was almost solemn to imagine him casually produced in the tailor's shop and confounding the disrespectful senses of Trabb's boy. On the other hand, Trabb's boy might worm himself into his intimacy and tell him things; or, reckless and desperate wretch as I knew he could be, might hoot him in the High-street. My patroness, too, might hear of him, and not approve. On the whole, I resolved to leave the Avenger behind.

It was the afternoon coach by which I had taken my place, and, as winter had now come round, I should not arrive at my destination until two or three hours after dark. Our time of starting from the Cross Keys was two o'clock. I arrived on the ground with a quarter of an hour to spare, attended by the Avenger—if I may connect that expression with one who never attended on me if he could possibly help it.

At that time it was customary to carry Convicts down to the dockyards by stagecoach. As I had often heard of them in the capacity of outside passengers, and had more than once seen them on the high road dangling their ironed legs over the coach roof, I had no cause to be surprised when Herbert, meeting me in the yard, came up and told me there were two convicts going down with me. But I had a reason that was an old reason now, for constitutionally faltering whenever I heard the word convict.

"You don't mind them, Handel?" said Herbert.

"Oh no!"

"I thought you seemed as if you didn't like them?"

"I can't pretend that I do like them, and I suppose you don't particularly. But I don't mind them."

"See! There they are," said Herbert, "coming out of the Tap. What a degraded and vile sight it is!"

They had been treating their guard, I suppose, for they had a gaoler with them, and all three came out wiping their mouths on their hands. The two convicts were handcuffed together, and had irons on their legs—irons of a pattern that I knew well. They wore the dress that I likewise knew well. Their keeper had a brace of pistols, and carried a thick-knobbed bludgeon under his arm; but he was on terms of good understanding with them, and stood, with them beside him, looking on at the putting-to of the horses, rather with an air as if the convicts were an interesting Exhibition not formally open at the moment, and he the Curator. One was a taller and stouter man than the other, and appeared as a matter of course, according to the mysterious ways of the world both convict and free, to have had allotted to him the smaller suit of clothes. His arms and legs were like great pincushions of those shapes, and his attire disguised him absurdly; but I knew his half-closed eye at one glance. There stood the man whom I had seen on the settle at the Three Jolly Bargemen on a Saturday night, and who had brought me down with his invisible gun!

It was easy to make sure that as yet he knew me no more than if he had never seen me in his life. He looked across at me, and his eye appraised my watch-chain, and then he incidentally spat and said something to the other convict, and they laughed and slued themselves round with a clink of their coupling manacle, and looked at something else. The great numbers on their backs, as if they were street doors; their coarse mangy ungainly outer surface, as if they were lower animals; their ironed legs, apologetically garlanded with pocket-handkerchiefs; and the way in which all present looked at them and kept from them; made them (as Herbert had said) a most disagreeable and degraded spectacle.

But this was not the worst of it. It came out that the whole of the back of the coach had been taken by a family removing from London, and that there were no places for the two prisoners but on the seat in front, behind the coachman. Hereupon, a choleric gentleman, who had taken the fourth place on that seat, flew into a most violent passion, and said that it was a breach of contract to mix him up with such villanous company, and that it was poisonous and pernicious and infamous and shameful, and I don't know what else. At this time the coach was ready and the coachman impatient, and we were all preparing to get up, and the prisoners had come over with their keeper— bringing with them that curious flavour of bread-poultice, baize, rope-yarn, and hearth-stone, which attends the convict presence.

"Don't take it so much amiss, sir," pleaded the keeper to the angry passenger; "I'll sit next you myself. I'll put 'em on the outside of the row. They won't interfere with you, sir. You needn't know they're there."

"And don't blame *me*," growled the convict I had recognised. "*I* don't want to go. *I* am quite ready to stay behind. As fur as I am concerned any one's welcome to *my* place."

"Or, mine," said the other, gruffly. "*I* wouldn't have incommoded none of you, if I'd a had *my* way." Then, they both laughed, and began cracking nuts, and spitting the shells about.—As I really think I should have liked to do myself, if I had been in their place and so despised.

At length, it was voted that there was no help for the angry gentleman, and that he must either go in his chance company or remain behind. So, he got into his place, still making complaints, and the keeper got into the place next him, and the convicts hauled themselves up as well as they could, and the convict I had recognised sat behind me with his breath on the hair of my head.

"Good-by, Handel!" Herbert called out as we started. I thought what a blessed fortune it was, that he had found another name for me than Pip.

It is impossible to express with what acuteness I felt the convict's breathing, not only on the back of my head, but all along my spine. The sensation was like being touched in the marrow with some pungent and searching acid, and it set my very teeth on edge. He seemed to have more breathing business to do than another man, and to make more noise in doing it; and I was conscious of growing high-shouldered on one side, in my shrinking endeavours to fend him off.

The weather was miserably raw, and the two cursed the cold. It made us all lethargic before we had gone far, and when we had left the Half-way House behind, we habitually dozed and shivered and were silent. I dozed off, myself, in considering the question whether I ought to restore a couple of pounds sterling to this creature before losing sight of him, and how it could best be done. In the act of dipping forward as if I were going to bathe among the horses, I woke in a fright and took the question up again.

But I must have lost it longer than I had thought, since, although I could recognise nothing in the darkness and the fitful lights and shadows of our lamps, I traced marsh country in the cold damp wind that blew at us. Cowering forward for warmth and to make me a screen against the wind, the convicts were closer to me than before. The very first words I heard them interchange as I became conscious were the words of my own thought, "Two One Pound notes."

"How did he get 'em?" said the convict I had never seen.

"How should I know?" returned the other. "He had 'em stowed away somehows. Giv him by friends, I expect."

"I wish," said the other, with a bitter curse upon the cold, "that I had 'em here."

"Two one pound notes, or friends?"

"Two one pound notes. I'd sell all the friends I ever had, for one, and think it a blessed good bargain. Well? So he says——?"

"So he says," resumed the convict I had recognised—"it was all said and done in half a minute, behind a pile of timber in the Dock-yard—'You're a going to be discharged?' Yes, I was. Would I find out that boy that had fed him and kep his secret, and give him them two one pound notes? Yes, I would. And I did."

"More fool you," growled the other. "I'd have spent 'em on a Man, in wittles and drink. He must have been a green one. Mean to say he knowed nothing of you?"

"Not a ha'porth. Different gangs and different ships. He was tried again for prison breaking, and got made a Lifer."°

"And was that—Honour!—the only time you worked out, in this part of the country?"

"The only time."

"What might have been your opinion of the place?"

"A most beastly place. Mudbank, mist, swamp, and work; work, swamp, mist, and mudbank."

They both execrated the place in very strong language, and gradually growled themselves out, and had nothing left to say.

After overhearing this dialogue, I should assuredly have got down and been left in the solitude and darkness of the highway, but for

Lifer: Transported to Australia for life.

feeling certain that the man had no suspicion of my identity. Indeed, I was not only so changed in the course of nature, but so differently dressed and so differently circumstanced, that it was not at all likely he could have known me without accidental help. Still, the coincidence of our being together on the coach, was sufficiently strange to fill me with a dread that some other coincidence might at any moment connect me, in his hearing, with my name. For this reason, I resolved to alight as soon as we touched the town, and put myself out of his hearing. This device I executed successfully. My little portmanteau was in the boot under my feet; I had but to turn a hinge to get it out; I threw it down before me, got down after it, and was left at the first lamp on the first stones of the town pavement. As to the convicts, they went their way with the coach, and I knew at what point they would be spirited off to the river. In my fancy, I saw the boat with its convict crew waiting for them at the slime-washed stairs,—again heard the gruff "Give way, you!" like an order to dogs—again saw the wicked Noah's Ark lying out on the black water.

I could not have said what I was afraid of, for my fear was altogether undefined and vague, but there was great fear upon me. As I walked on to the hotel, I felt that a dread, much exceeding the mere apprehension of a painful or disagreeable recognition, made me tremble. I am confident that it took no distinctness of shape, and that it was the revival for a few minutes of the terror of childhood.

The coffee-room at the Blue Boar was empty, and I had not only ordered my dinner there, but had sat down to it, before the waiter knew me. As soon as he had apologised for the remissness of his memory, he asked me if he should send Boots for Mr. Pumblechook?

"No," said I, "certainly not."

The waiter (it was he who had brought up the Great Remonstrance from the Commercials, on the day when I was bound) appeared surprised, and took the earliest opportunity of putting a dirty old copy of a local newspaper so directly in my way, that I took it up and read this paragraph:

Our readers will learn, not altogether without interest, in reference to the recent romantic rise in fortune of a young artificer in iron of this neighbourhood (what a theme, by the way, for the magic pen of our as yet not universally acknowledged townsman TOOBY, the poet of our columns!) that the youth's earliest patron, companion, and friend, was a highly-respected individual not entirely unconnected with the corn and seed trade, and whose eminently convenient and commodious business premises are situate within a hundred miles of the High-street. It is not wholly irrespective of our personal feelings that we record HIM as the Mentor of our young Telemachus,° for it is good to know that our town produced the founder of the latter's fortunes. Does the thought-contracted brow of the local Sage or the lustrous eye of local Beauty inquire whose fortunes? We believe that Quintin Matsys was the BLACKSMITH of Antwerp.°   VERB. SAP.°

I entertain a conviction, based upon large experience, that if in the days of my prosperity I had gone to the North Pole, I should have met somebody there, wandering Esquimaux or civilised man, who would have told me that Pumblechook was my earliest patron and the founder of my fortunes.

[PART 18]

Chapter 29

Betimes in the morning I was up and out. It was too early yet to go to Miss Havisham's, so I loitered into the country on Miss Havisham's side of town—which was not Joe's side; I could go there tomorrow—thinking about my patroness, and painting brilliant pictures of her plans for me.

She had adopted Estella, she had as good as adopted me, and it could not fail to be her intention to bring us together. She reserved it for me to restore the desolate house, admit the sunshine into the dark rooms, set the clocks a going and the cold hearths a blazing, tear down the cobwebs, destroy the vermin—in short, do all the shining deeds of the young Knight of romance, and marry the Princess. I had stopped to look at the house as I passed; and its seared red brick walls, blocked windows, and strong green ivy clasping even the stacks of chimneys with its twigs and tendons, as if with sinewy old arms, had made up a rich attractive mystery, of which I was the hero. Estella was the inspiration of it, and the heart of it, of course. But, though she had taken such strong possession of me, though my fancy and my hope were so set upon her, though her influence on my boyish life and character had been all-powerful, I did not, even that romantic

---

Telemachus: While Odysseus is absent from Ithaca, his son Telemachus is guided by Odysseus's friend Mentor.   **Quintin . . . Antwerp:** Matsys became a famous painter after reportedly having been a blacksmith.   **VERB. SAP:** Latin abbreviation for "a word to the wise."

morning, invest her with any attributes save those she possessed. I
mention this in this place, of a fixed purpose, because it is the clue by
which I am to be followed into my poor labyrinth. According to my
experience, the conventional notion of a lover cannot be always true.
The unqualified truth is, that when I loved Estella with the love of a
man, I loved her simply because I found her irresistible. Once for all;
I knew to my sorrow, often and often, if not always, that I loved her
against reason, against promise, against peace, against hope, against
happiness, against all discouragement that could be. Once for all; I
loved her none the less because I knew it, and it had no more influence in restraining me, than if I had devoutly believed her to be
human perfection.

I so shaped out my walk as to arrive at the gate at my old time.
When I had rung at the bell with an unsteady hand, I turned my back
upon the gate, while I tried to get my breath and keep the beating of
my heart moderately quiet. I heard the side door open, and steps come
across the court-yard; but I pretended not to hear, even when the gate
swung on its rusty hinges.

Being at last touched on the shoulder, I started and turned. I
started much more naturally then, to find myself confronted by a man
in a sober grey dress. The last man I should have expected to see in
that place of porter at Miss Havisham's door.

"Orlick!"

"Ah, young master, there's more changes than yours. But come in,
come in. It's opposed to my orders to hold the gate open."

I entered and he swung it, and locked it, and took the key out.
"Yes!" said he, facing round, after doggedly preceding me a few steps
towards the house. "Here I am!"

"How did you come here?"

"I come here," he retorted, "on my legs. I had my box brought
alongside me in a barrow."

"Are you here for good?"

"I ain't here for harm, young master, I suppose?"

I was not so sure of that. I had leisure to entertain the retort in my
mind, while he slowly lifted his heavy glance from the pavement, up
my legs and arms, to my face.

"Then you have left the forge?" I said.

"Do this look like a forge?" replied Orlick, sending his glance all
round him with an air of injury. "Now, do it look like it?"

I asked him how long he had left Gargery's forge?

"One day is so like another here," he replied, "that I don't know without casting it up. However, I come here some time since you left."

"I could have told you that, Orlick."

"Ah!" said he, dryly. "But then you've got to be a scholar."

By this time we had come to the house, where I found his room to be one just within the side door, with a little window in it looking on the court-yard. In its small proportions, it was not unlike the kind of place usually assigned to a gate-porter in Paris. Certain keys were hanging on the wall, to which he now added the gate key; and his patchwork-covered bed was in a little inner division or recess. The whole had a slovenly confined and sleepy look, like a cage for a human dormouse: while he, looming dark and heavy in the shadow of a corner by the window, looked like the human dormouse for whom it was fitted up—as indeed he was.

"I never saw this room before," I remarked; "but there used to be no Porter here."

"No," said he; "not till it got about that there was no protection on the premises, and it come to be considered dangerous, with convicts and Tag and Rag and Bobtail going up and down. And then I was recommended to the place as a man who could give another man as good as he brought, and I took it. It's easier than bellowsing and hammering.—That's loaded, that is."

My eye had been caught by a gun with a brass-bound stock over the chimney-piece, and his eye had followed mine.

"Well," said I, not desirous of more conversation, "shall I go up to Miss Havisham?"

"Burn me, if I know!" he retorted, first stretching himself and then shaking himself; "my orders ends here, young master. I give this here bell a rap with this here hammer, and you go on along the passage till you meet somebody."

"I am expected, I believe?"

"Burn me twice over, if I can say!" said he.

Upon that, I turned down the long passage which I had first trodden in my thick boots, and he made his bell sound. At the end of the passage, while the bell was still reverberating, I found Sarah Pocket: who appeared to have now become constitutionally green and yellow by reason of me.

"Oh!" said she. "You, is it, Mr. Pip?"

"It is, Miss Pocket. I am glad to tell you that Mr. Pocket and family are all well."

"Are they any wiser?" said Sarah, with a dismal shake of her head;

"they had better be wiser, than well. Ah, Matthew, Matthew! You know your way, sir?"

Tolerably, for I had gone up the staircase in the dark, many a time. I ascended it now, in lighter boots than of yore, and tapped in my old way at the door of Miss Havisham's room. "Pip's rap," I heard her say, immediately; "come in, Pip."

She was in her chair near the old table, in the old dress, with her two hands crossed on her stick, her chin resting on them, and her eyes on the fire. Sitting near her, with the white shoe that had never been worn, in her hand, and her head bent as she looked at it, was an elegant lady whom I had never seen.

"Come in, Pip," Miss Havisham continued to mutter, without looking round or up; "come in, Pip, how do you do, Pip? so you kiss my hand as if I were a queen, eh?——Well?"

She looked up at me suddenly, only moving her eyes, and repeated in a grimly playful manner,

"Well?"

"I heard, Miss Havisham," said I, rather at a loss, "that you were so kind as to wish me to come and see you, and I came directly."

"Well?"

The lady whom I had never seen before, lifted up her eyes and looked archly at me, and then I saw that the eyes were Estella's eyes. But she was so much changed, was so much more beautiful, so much more womanly, in all things winning admiration had made such wonderful advance, that I seemed to have made none. I fancied, as I looked at her, that I slipped hopelessly back into the coarse and common boy again. O the sense of distance and disparity that came upon me, and the inaccessibility that came about her!

She gave me her hand. I stammered something about the pleasure I felt in seeing her again, and about my having looked forward to it for a long, long time.

"Do you find her much changed, Pip?" asked Miss Havisham, with her greedy look, and striking her stick upon a chair that stood between them, as a sign to me to sit down there.

"When I came in, Miss Havisham, I thought there was nothing of Estella in the face or figure; but now it all settles down so curiously into the old——"

"What? You are not going to say into the old Estella?" Miss Havisham interrupted. "She was proud and insulting, and you wanted to go away from her. Don't you remember?"

I said confusedly that that was long ago, and that I knew no better then, and the like. Estella smiled with perfect composure, and said she had no doubt of my having been quite right, and of her having been very disagreeable.

"Is *he* changed?" Miss Havisham asked her.

"Very much," said Estella, looking at me.

"Less coarse and common?" said Miss Havisham, playing with Estella's hair.

Estella laughed, and looked at the shoe in her hand, and laughed again, and looked at me, and put the shoe down. She treated me as a boy still, but she lured me on.

We sat in the dreamy room among the old strange influences which had so wrought upon me, and I learnt that she had but just come home from France, and that she was going to London. Proud and wilful as of old, she had brought those qualities into such subjection to her beauty that it was impossible and out of nature—or I thought so—to separate them from her beauty. Truly it was impossible to dissociate her presence from all those wretched hankerings after money and gentility that had disturbed my boyhood—from all those ill-regulated aspirations that had first made me ashamed of home and Joe—from all those visions that had raised her face in the glowing fire, struck it out of the iron on the anvil, extracted it from the darkness of night to look in at the wooden window of the forge and flit away. In a word, it was impossible for me to separate her, in the past or in the present, from the innermost life of my life.

It was settled that I should stay there all the rest of the day, and return to the hotel at night, and to London to-morrow. When we had conversed for a while, Miss Havisham sent us two out to walk in the neglected garden: on our coming in by-and-by, she said, I should wheel her about a little as in times of yore.

So, Estella and I went out into the garden by the gate through which I had strayed to my encounter with the pale young gentleman, now Herbert; I, trembling in spirit and worshipping the very hem of her dress; she, quite composed and most decidedly not worshipping the hem of mine. As we drew near to the place of encounter, she stopped and said:

"I must have been a singular little creature to hide and see that fight that day: but I did, and I enjoyed it very much."

"You rewarded me very much."

"Did I?" she replied, in an incidental and forgetful way. "I remember I entertained a great objection to your adversary, because I took it ill that he should be brought here to pester me with his company."

"He and I are great friends now," said I.

"Are you? I think I recollect though, that you read with his father?"

"Yes."

I made the admission with reluctance, for it seemed to have a boyish look, and she already treated me more than enough like a boy.

"Since your change of fortune and prospects, you have changed your companions," said Estella.

"Naturally," said I.

"And necessarily," she added, in a haughty tone; "what was fit company for you once, would be quite unfit company for you now."

In my conscience, I doubt very much whether I had any lingering intention left, of going to see Joe; but if I had, this observation put it to flight.

"You had no idea of your impending good fortune, in those times?" said Estella, with a slight wave of her hand, signifying in the fighting times.

"Not the least."

The air of completeness and superiority with which she walked at my side, and the air of youthfulness and submission with which I walked at hers, made a contrast that I strongly felt. It would have rankled in me more than it did, if I had not regarded myself as eliciting it by being so set apart for her and assigned to her.

The garden was too overgrown and rank for walking in with ease, and after we had made the round of it twice or thrice, we came out again into the brewery yard. I showed her to a nicety where I had seen her walking on the casks, that first old day, and she said, with a cold and careless look in that direction, "Did I?" I reminded her where she had come out of the house and given me my meat and drink, and she said, "I don't remember." "Not remember that you made me cry?" said I. "No," said she, and shook her head and looked about her. I verily believe that her not remembering and not minding in the least, made me cry again, inwardly—and that is the sharpest crying of all.

"You must know," said Estella, condescending to me as a brilliant and beautiful woman might, "that I have no heart—if that has anything to do with my memory."

I got through some jargon to the effect that I took the liberty of doubting that. That I knew better. That there could be no such beauty without it.

"Oh! I have a heart to be stabbed in or shot in, I have no doubt," said Estella, "and, of course, if it ceased to beat I should cease to be.

But you know what I mean. I have no softness there, no—sympathy—sentiment—nonsense."

What *was* it that was borne in upon my mind when she stood still and looked attentively at me? Anything that I had seen in Miss Havisham? No. In some of her looks and gestures there was that tinge of resemblance to Miss Havisham which may often be noticed to have been acquired by children, from grown persons with whom they have been much associated and secluded, and which, when childhood is past, will produce a remarkable occasional likeness of expression between faces that are otherwise quite different. And yet I could not trace this to Miss Havisham. I looked again, and though she was still looking at me, the suggestion was gone.

What *was* it?

"I am serious," said Estella, not so much with a frown (for her brow was smooth) as with a darkening of her face; "if we are to be thrown much together, you had better believe it at once. No!" imperiously stopping me as I opened my lips. "I have not bestowed my tenderness anywhere. I have never had any such thing."

In another moment we were in the brewery so long disused, and she pointed to the high gallery where I had seen her going out on that same first day, and told me she remembered to have been up there, and to have seen me standing scared below. As my eyes followed her white hand, again the same dim suggestion that I could not possibly grasp, crossed me. My involuntary start occasioned her to lay her hand upon my arm. Instantly the ghost passed once more, and was gone.

What *was* it?

"What is the matter?" asked Estella. "Are you scared again?"

"I should be, if I believed what you said just now," I replied, to turn it off.

"Then you don't? Very well. It is said, at any rate. Miss Havisham will soon be expecting you at your old post, though I think that might be laid aside now, with other old belongings. Let us make one more round of the garden, and then go in. Come! You shall not shed tears for my cruelty to-day; you shall be my Page, and give me your shoulder."

Her handsome dress had trailed upon the ground. She held it in one hand now, and with the other lightly touched my shoulder as we walked. We walked round the ruined garden twice or thrice more, and it was all in bloom for me. If the green and yellow growth of weed in the chinks of the old wall had been the most precious flowers that ever blew, it could not have been more cherished in my remembrance.

There was no discrepancy of years between us, to remove her far from me; we were of nearly the same age, though of course the age told for more in her case than in mine; but the air of inaccessibility which her beauty and her manner gave her, tormented me in the midst of my delight, and at the height of the assurance I felt that our patroness had chosen us for one another. Wretched boy!

At last we went back into the house, and there I heard, with surprise, that my guardian had come down to see Miss Havisham on business, and would come back to dinner. The old wintry branches of chandeliers in the room where the mouldering table was spread, had been lighted while we were out, and Miss Havisham was in her chair and waiting for me.

It was like pushing the chair itself back into the past, when we began the old slow circuit round about the ashes of the bridal feast. But, in the funereal room, with that figure of the grave fallen back in the chair fixing its eyes upon her, Estella looked more bright and beautiful than before, and I was under stronger enchantment.

The time so melted away, that our early dinner-hour drew close at hand, and Estella left us to prepare herself. We had stopped near the centre of the long table, and Miss Havisham, with one of her withered arms stretched out of the chair, rested that clenched hand upon the yellow cloth. As Estella looked back over her shoulder before going out at the door, Miss Havisham kissed that hand to her, with a ravenous intensity that was of its kind quite dreadful.

Then, Estella being gone and we two left alone, she turned to me, and said in a whisper:

"Is she beautiful, graceful, well-grown? Do you admire her?"

"Everybody must who sees her, Miss Havisham."

She drew an arm round my neck, and drew my head close down to hers as she sat in the chair. "Love her, love her, love her! How does she use you?"

Before I could answer (if I could have answered so difficult a question at all), she repeated, "Love her, love her, love her! If she favours you, love her. If she wounds you, love her. If she tears your heart to pieces—and as it gets older and stronger, it will tear deeper—love her, love her, love her!"

Never had I seen such passionate eagerness as was joined to her utterance of these words. I could feel the muscles of the thin arm round my neck, swell with the vehemence that possessed her.

"Hear me, Pip! I adopted her to be loved. I bred her and educated her, to be loved. I developed her into what she is, that she might be loved. Love her!"

She said the word often enough, and there could be no doubt that she meant to say it; but if the often repeated word had been hate instead of love—despair—revenge—dire death—it could not have sounded from her lips more like a curse.

"I'll tell you," said she, in the same hurried passionate whisper, "what real love is. It is blind devotion, unquestioning self-humiliation, utter submission, trust and belief against yourself and against the whole world, giving up your whole heart and soul to the smiter—as I did!"

When she came to that, and to a wild cry that followed that, I caught her round the waist. For she rose up in the chair, in her shroud of a dress, and struck at the air as if she would as soon have struck herself against the wall and fallen dead.

All this passed in a few seconds. As I drew her down into her chair, I was conscious of a scent that I knew, and turning, saw my guardian in the room.

He always carried (I have not yet mentioned it, I think) a pocket-handkerchief of rich silk and of imposing proportions, which was of great value to him in his profession. I have seen him so terrify a client or a witness by ceremoniously unfolding this pocket-handkerchief as if he were immediately going to blow his nose, and then pausing, as if he knew he should not have time to do it before such client or witness committed himself, that the self-committal has followed directly, quite as a matter of course. When I saw him in the room, he had this expressive pocket-handkerchief in both hands, and was looking at us. On meeting my eye, he said plainly, by a momentary and silent pause in that attitude, "Indeed? Singular!" and then put the handkerchief to its right use with wonderful effect.

Miss Havisham had seen him as soon as I, and was (like everybody else) afraid of him. She made a strong attempt to compose herself, and stammered that he was as punctual as ever.

"As punctual as ever," he repeated, coming up to us. "(How do you do, Pip. Shall I give you a ride, Miss Havisham? Once round?) And so you are here, Pip?"

I told him when I had arrived, and how Miss Havisham had wished me to come and see Estella. To which he replied, "Ah! Very fine young lady!" Then he pushed Miss Havisham in her chair before him, with one of his large hands, and put the other in his trousers-pocket as if the pocket were full of secrets.

"Well, Pip! How often have you seen Miss Estella before?" said he, when he came to a stop.

"How often?"

"Ah! How many times. Ten thousand times?"

"Oh! Certainly not so many."

"Twice?"

"Jaggers," interposed Miss Havisham, much to my relief; "leave my Pip alone, and go with him to your dinner."

He complied, and we groped our way down the dark stairs together. While we were still on our way to those detached apartments across the paved yard at the back, he asked me how often I had seen Miss Havisham eat and drink; offering me a breadth of choice, as usual, between a hundred times and once.

I considered, and said, "Never."

"And never will, Pip," he retorted, with a frowning smile. "She has never allowed herself to be seen doing either, since she lived this present life of hers. She wanders about in the night, and then lays hands on such food as she takes."

"Pray, sir," said I, "may I ask you a question?"

"You may," said he, "and I may decline to answer it. Put your question."

"Estella's name. Is it Havisham, or——?" I had nothing to add.

"Or what?" said he.

"Is it Havisham?"

"It is Havisham."

This brought us to the dinner-table, where she and Sarah Pocket awaited us. Mr. Jaggers presided, Estella sat opposite to him, I faced my green and yellow friend. We dined very well, and were waited on by a maid servant whom I had never seen in all my comings and goings, but who, for anything I know, had been in that mysterious house the whole time. After dinner, a bottle of choice old port was placed before my guardian (he was evidently well acquainted with the vintage), and the two ladies left us.

Anything to equal the determined reticence of Mr. Jaggers under that roof, I never saw elsewhere, even in him. He kept his very looks to himself, and scarcely directed his eyes to Estella's face once during dinner. When she spoke to him, he listened, and in due course answered, but never looked at her, that I could see. On the other hand, she often looked at him, with interest and curiosity, if not distrust, but his face never showed the least consciousness. Throughout dinner he took a dry delight in making Sarah Pocket greener and yellower, by often referring in conversation with me to my expectations; but here, again, he showed no consciousness, and even made it appear that he extorted—and even did extort, though I don't know how—those references out of my innocent self.

And when he and I were left alone together, he sat with an air upon him of general lying by in consequence of information he possessed, that really was too much for me. He cross-examined his very wine when he had nothing else in hand. He held it between himself and the candle, tasted the port, rolled it in his mouth, swallowed it, looked at his glass again, smelt the port, tried it, drank it, filled again, and cross-examined the glass again, until I was as nervous as if I had known the wine to be telling him something to my disadvantage. Three or four times I feebly thought I would start conversation; but whenever he saw me going to ask him anything, he looked at me with his glass in his hand, and rolling his wine about in his mouth, as if requesting me to take notice that it was of no use, for he couldn't answer.

I think Miss Pocket was conscious that the sight of me involved her in the danger of being goaded to madness, and perhaps tearing off her cap—which was a very hideous one, in the nature of a muslin mop—and strewing the ground with her hair—which assuredly had never grown on *her* head. She did not appear when we afterwards went up to Miss Havisham's room, and we four played at whist. In the interval, Miss Havisham, in a fantastic way, had put some of the most beautiful jewels from her dressing-table into Estella's hair, and about her bosom and arms; and I saw even my guardian look at her from under his thick eyebrows, and raise them a little, when her loveliness was before him, with those rich flushes of glitter and colour in it.

Of the manner and extent to which he took our trumps into custody, and came out with mean little cards at the ends of hands, before which the glory of our Kings and Queens was utterly abased, I say nothing; nor, of the feeling that I had, respecting his looking upon us personally in the light of three very obvious and poor riddles that he had found out long ago. What I suffered from, was the incompatibility between his cold presence and my feelings towards Estella. It was not that I knew I could never bear to speak to him about her, that I knew I could never bear to hear him creak his boots at her, that I knew I could never bear to see him wash his hands of her; it was, that my admiration should be within a foot or two of him—it was, that my feelings should be in the same place with him—*that,* was the agonising circumstance.

We played until nine o'clock, and then it was arranged that when Estella came to London I should be forewarned of her coming and should meet her at the coach; and then I took leave of her, and touched her and left her.

My guardian lay at the Boar in the next room to mine. Far into the night, Miss Havisham's words, "Love her, love her, love her!" sounded in my ears. I adapted them for my own repetition, and said to my pillow, "I love her, I love her, I love her!" hundreds of times. Then, a burst of gratitude came upon me, that she should be destined for me, once the blacksmith's boy. Then, I thought if she were, as I feared, by no means rapturously grateful for that destiny yet, when would she begin to be interested in me? When should I awaken the heart within her, that was mute and sleeping now?

Ah me! I thought those were high and great emotions. But I never thought there was anything low and small in my keeping away from Joe, because I knew she would be contemptuous of him. It was but a day gone, and Joe had brought the tears into my eyes; they had soon dried, God forgive me! soon dried.

[PART 19]

Chapter 30

After well considering the matter while I was dressing at the Blue Boar in the morning, I resolved to tell my guardian that I doubted Orlick's being the right sort of man to fill a post of trust at Miss Havisham's. "Why, of course he is not the right sort of man, Pip," said my guardian, comfortably satisfied beforehand on the general head, "because the man who fills the post of trust never is the right sort of man." It seemed quite to put him into spirits, to find that this particular post was not exceptionally held by the right sort of man, and he listened in a satisfied manner while I told him what knowledge I had of Orlick. "Very good, Pip," he observed, when I had concluded, "I'll go round presently, and pay our friend off." Rather alarmed by this summary action, I was for a little delay, and even hinted that our friend himself might be difficult to deal with. "Oh no he won't," said my guardian, making his pocket-handkerchief-point, with perfect confidence; "I should like to see him argue the question with *me*."

As we were going back together to London by the mid-day coach, and as I breakfasted under such terrors of Pumblechook that I could scarcely hold my cup, this gave me an opportunity of saying that I wanted a walk, and that I would go on along the London-road while Mr. Jaggers was occupied, if he would let the coachman know that I would get into my place when overtaken. I was thus enabled to fly from the Blue Boar immediately after breakfast. By then making a loop of about a couple of miles into the open country at the back of Pumblechook's premises, I got round into the High-street again, a little beyond that pitfall, and felt myself in comparative security.

It was interesting to be in the quiet old town once more, and it was not disagreeable to be here and there suddenly recognised and stared after. One or two of the trades-people even darted out of their shops and went a little way down the street before me, that they might turn, as if they had forgotten something, and pass me face to face—on which occasions I don't know whether they or I made the worse pretence; they of not doing it, or I of not seeing it. Still my position was a distinguished one, and I was not at all dissatisfied with it, until Fate threw me in the way of that unlimited miscreant, Trabb's boy.

Casting my eyes along the street at a certain point of my progress, I beheld Trabb's boy approaching, lashing himself with an empty blue bag. Deeming that a serene and unconscious contemplation of him would best beseem me, and would be most likely to quell his evil mind, I advanced with that expression of countenance, and was rather congratulating myself on my success, when suddenly the knees of Trabb's boy smote together, his hair uprose, his cap fell off, he trembled violently in every limb, staggered out into the road, and crying to the populace, "Hold me! I'm so frightened!" feigned to be in a paroxysm of terror and contrition, occasioned by the dignity of my appearance. As I passed him, his teeth loudly chattered in his head, and with every mark of extreme humiliation, he prostrated himself in the dust.

This was a hard thing to bear, but this was nothing. I had not advanced another two hundred yards, when, to my inexpressible terror, amazement, and indignation, I again beheld Trabb's boy approaching. He was coming round a narrow corner. His blue bag was slung over his shoulder, honest industry beamed in his eyes, a determination to proceed to Trabb's with cheerful briskness was indicated in his gait. With a shock he became aware of me, and was severely visited as before; but this time his motion was rotatory, and he staggered round and round me with knees more afflicted, and with uplifted hands as if beseeching for mercy. His sufferings were hailed with the greatest joy by a knot of spectators, and I felt utterly confounded.

I had not got as much further down the street as the post-office, when I again beheld Trabb's boy shooting round by a back way. This time, he was entirely changed. He wore the blue bag in the manner of my great-coat, and was strutting along the pavement towards me on the opposite side of the street, attended by a company of delighted young friends to whom he from time to time exclaimed, with a wave of his hand, "Don't know yah!" Words cannot state the amount of aggravation and injury wreaked upon me by Trabb's boy, when, passing abreast of me, he pulled up his shirt-collar, twined his side-hair, stuck an arm akimbo, and smirked extravagantly by, wriggling his elbows and body, and drawling to his attendants, "Don't know yah, don't know yah, pon my soul don't know yah!" The disgrace attendant on his immediately afterwards taking to crowing and pursuing me across the bridge with crows, as from an exceedingly dejected fowl who had known me when I was a blacksmith, culminated the disgrace with which I left the town, and was, so to speak, ejected by it into the open country.

But unless I had taken the life of Trabb's boy on that occasion, I really do not even now see what I could have done save endure. To have struggled with him in the street, or to have exacted any lower recompense from him than his heart's best blood, would have been futile and degrading. Moreover, he was a boy whom no man could hurt; an invulnerable and dodging serpent who, when chased into a corner, flew out again between his captor's legs, scornfully yelping. I wrote, however, to Mr. Trabb by next day's post, to say that Mr. Pip must decline to deal further with one who could so far forget what he owed to the best interests of society, as to employ a boy who excited Loathing in every respectable mind.

The coach, with Mr. Jaggers inside, came up in due time, and I took my box-seat again, and arrived in London safe—but not sound, for my heart was gone. As soon as I arrived, I sent a penitential codfish and barrel of oysters to Joe (as reparation for not having gone myself), and then went on to Barnard's Inn.

I found Herbert dining on cold meat, and delighted to welcome me back. Having despatched The Avenger to the coffee-house for an addition to the dinner, I felt that I must open my breast that very evening to my friend and chum. As confidence was out of the question with The Avenger in the hall, which could merely be regarded in the light of an ante-chamber to the keyhole, I sent him to the Play. A better proof of the severity of my bondage to that taskmaster could scarcely be afforded, than the degrading shifts to which I was constantly driven to find him employment. So mean is extremity, that I sometimes sent him to Hyde Park-corner to see what o'clock it was.

Dinner done and we sitting with our feet upon the fender, I said to Herbert, "My dear Herbert, I have something very particular to tell you."

"My dear Handel," he returned, "I shall esteem and respect your confidence."

"It concerns myself, Herbert," said I, "and one other person."

Herbert crossed his feet, looked at the fire with his head on one side, and having looked at it in vain for some time, looked at me because I didn't go on.

"Herbert," said I, laying my hand upon his knee. "I love—I adore—Estella."

Instead of being transfixed, Herbert replied in an easy matter-of-course way, "Exactly. Well?"

"Well, Herbert? Is that all you say? Well?"

"What next, I mean?" said Herbert. "Of course I know *that*."

"How do you know it?" said I.

"How do I know it, Handel? Why, from you."

"I never told you."

"Told me! You have never told me when you have got your hair cut, but I have had senses to perceive it. You have always adored her, ever since I have known you. You brought your adoration and your portmanteau here, together. Told me! Why, you have always told me all day long. When you told me your own story, you told me plainly that you began adoring her the first time you saw her, when you were very young indeed."

"Very well, then," said I, to whom this was a new and not unwelcome light, "I have never left off adoring her. And she has come back, a most beautiful and most elegant creature. And I saw her yesterday. And if I adored her before, I now doubly adore her."

"Lucky for you then, Handel," said Herbert, "that you are picked out for her and allotted to her. Without encroaching on forbidden ground, we may venture to say that there can be no doubt between ourselves of that fact. Have you any idea yet, of Estella's views on the adoration question?"

I shook my head gloomily. "Oh! She is thousands of miles away, from me," said I.

"Patience, my dear Handel: time enough, time enough. But you have something more to say?"

"I am ashamed to say it," I returned, "and yet it's no worse to say it than to think it. You call me a lucky fellow. Of course, I am. I was a blacksmith's boy but yesterday; I am—what shall I say I am—to-day?"

"Say, a good fellow, if you want a phrase," returned Herbert, smiling, and clapping his hand on the back of mine, "a good fellow, with impetuosity and hesitation, boldness and diffidence, action and dreaming, curiously mixed in him."

I stopped for a moment to consider whether there really was this mixture in my character. On the whole, I by no means recognised the analysis, but thought it not worth disputing.

"When I ask what I am to call myself to-day, Herbert," I went on, "I suggest what I have in my thoughts. You say I am lucky. I know I have done nothing to raise myself in life, and that Fortune alone has raised me; that is being very lucky. And yet, when I think of Estella——"

("And when you don't, you know?" Herbert threw in, with his eyes on fire; which I thought kind and sympathetic of him.)

"—Then, my dear Herbert, I cannot tell you how dependent and uncertain I feel, and how exposed to hundreds of chances. Avoiding forbidden ground, as you did just now, I may still say that on the constancy of one person (naming no person) all my expectations depend. And at the best, how indefinite and unsatisfactory, only to know so vaguely what they are!" In saying this, I relieved my mind of what had always been there, more or less, though no doubt most since yester-day.

"Now, Handel," Herbert replied, in his gay hopeful way, "it seems to me that in the despondency of the tender passion, we are looking into our gift-horse's mouth with a magnifying glass. Likewise, it seems to me that, concentrating our attention on the examination, we altogether overlook one of the best points of the animal. Didn't you tell me that your guardian, Mr. Jaggers, told you in the beginning, that you were not endowed with expectations only? And even if he had not told you so—though that is a very large If, I grant—could you believe that of all men in London, Mr. Jaggers is the man to hold his present relations towards you unless he were sure of his ground?"

I said I could not deny that this was a strong point. I said it (people often do so, in such cases) like a rather reluctant concession to truth and justice;—as if I wanted to deny it!

"I should think it *was* a strong point," said Herbert, "and I should think you would be puzzled to imagine a stronger; as to the rest, you must bide your guardian's time, and he must bide his client's time.

You'll be one-and-twenty before you know where you are, and then perhaps you'll get some further enlightenment. At all events, you'll be nearer getting it, for it must come at last."

"What a hopeful disposition you have!" said I, gratefully admiring his cheery ways.

"I ought to have," said Herbert, "for I have not much else. I must acknowledge, by-the-by, that the good sense of what I have just said is not my own, but my father's. The only remark I ever heard him make on your story, was the final one: 'The thing is settled and done, or Mr. Jaggers would not be in it.' And now before I say anything more about my father, or my father's son, and repay confidence with confidence, I want to make myself seriously disagreeable to you for a moment—positively repulsive."

"You won't succeed," said I.

"Oh yes I shall!" said he. "One, two, three, and now I am in for it. Handel, my good fellow;" though he spoke in this light tone, he was very much in earnest: "I have been thinking since we have been talking with our feet on this fender, that Estella surely cannot be a condition of your inheritance, if she was never referred to by your guardian. Am I right in so understanding what you have told me, as that he never referred to her, directly or indirectly, in any way? Never even hinted, for instance, that your patron might have views as to your marriage ultimately?"

"Never."

"Now, Handel, I am quite free from the flavour of sour grapes, upon my soul and honour! Not being bound to her, can you not detach yourself from her?—I told you I should be disagreeable."

I turned my head aside, for, with a rush and a sweep, like the old marsh winds coming up from the sea, a feeling like that which had subdued me on the morning when I left the forge, when the mists were solemnly rising, and when I laid my hand upon the village finger-post, smote upon my heart again. There was silence between us for a little while.

"Yes; but my dear Handel," Herbert went on, as if we had been talking instead of silent, "its having been so strongly rooted in the breast of a boy whom nature and circumstances made so romantic, renders it very serious. Think of her bringing-up, and think of Miss Havisham. Think of what she is herself (now I am repulsive and you abominate me). This may lead to miserable things."

"I know it, Herbert," said I, with my head still turned away, "but I can't help it."

"You can't detach yourself?"

"No. Impossible!"

"You can't try, Handel?"

"No. Impossible!"

"Well!" said Herbert, getting up with a lively shake as if he had been asleep, and stirring the fire; "now I'll endeavour to make myself agreeable again!"

So he went round the room and shook the curtains out, put the chairs in their places, tidied the books and so forth that were lying about, looked into the hall, peeped into the letter-box, shut the door, and came back to his chair by the fire: where he sat down, nursing his left leg in both arms.

"I was going to say a word or two, Handel, concerning my father and my father's son. I am afraid it is scarcely necessary for my father's son to remark that my father's establishment is not particularly brilliant in its housekeeping."

"There is always plenty, Herbert," said I: to say something encouraging.

"Oh yes! and so the dustman says, I believe, with the strongest approval, and so does the marine store-shop in the back street. Gravely, Handel, for the subject is grave enough, you know how it is, as well as I do. I suppose there was a time once when my father had not given matters up; but if ever there was, the time is gone. May I ask you if you have ever had an opportunity of remarking, down in your part of the country, that the children of not exactly suitable marriages, are always most particularly anxious to be married?"

This was such a singular question, that I asked him in return, "Is it so?"

"I don't know," said Herbert, "that's what I want to know. Because it is decidedly the case with us. My poor sister Charlotte who was next me and died before she was fourteen, was a striking example. Little Jane is the same. In her desire to be matrimonially established, you might suppose her to have passed her short existence in the perpetual contemplation of domestic bliss. Little Alick in a frock has already made arrangements for his union with a suitable young person at Kew. And indeed, I think we are all engaged, except the baby."

"Then you are?" said I.

"I am," said Herbert; "but it's a secret."

I assured him of my keeping the secret, and begged to be favoured with further particulars. He had spoken so sensibly and feelingly of my weakness that I wanted to know something about his strength.

"May I ask the name?" I said.

"Name of Clara," said Herbert.

"Live in London?"

"Yes. Perhaps I ought to mention," said Herbert, who had become curiously crestfallen and meek, since we entered on the interesting theme, "that she is rather below my mother's nonsensical family notions. Her father had to do with the victualling of passenger-ships. I think he was a species of purser."

"What is he now?" said I.

"He's an invalid now," replied Herbert.

"Living on——?"

"On the first floor," said Herbert. Which was not at all what I meant, for I had intended my question to apply to his means. "I have never seen him, for he has always kept his room overhead, since I have known Clara. But I have heard him constantly. He makes tremendous rows—roars, and pegs at the floor with some frightful instrument." In looking at me and then laughing heartily, Herbert for the time recovered his usual lively manner.

"Don't you expect to see him?" said I.

"Oh yes, I constantly expect to see him," returned Herbert, "because I never hear him, without expecting him to come tumbling through the ceiling. But I don't know how long the rafters may hold."

When he had once more laughed heartily, he became meek again, and told me that the moment he began to realise Capital, it was his intention to marry this young lady. He added as a self-evident proposition, engendering low spirits, "But you *can't* marry, you know, while you're looking about you."

As we contemplated the fire, and as I thought what a difficult vision to realise this same Capital sometimes was, I put my hands in my pockets. A folded piece of paper in one of them attracting my attention, I opened it and found it to be the playbill I had received from Joe, relative to the celebrated provincial amateur of Roscian renown. "And bless my heart," I involuntarily added aloud, "it's to-night!"

This changed the subject in an instant, and made us hurriedly resolve to go to the play. So, when I had pledged myself to comfort and abet Herbert in the affair of his heart by all practicable and impracticable means, and when Herbert had told me that his affianced already knew me by reputation and that I should be presented to her, and when we had warmly shaken hands upon our mutual confidence, we blew out our candles, made up our fire, locked our door, and issued forth in quest of Mr. Wopsle and Denmark.

Chapter 31

On our arrival in Denmark, we found the king and queen of that country elevated in two arm-chairs on a kitchen-table, holding a Court. The whole of the Danish nobility were in attendance; consisting of a noble boy in the wash-leather boots of a gigantic ancestor, a venerable Peer with a dirty face who seemed to have risen from the people late in life, and the Danish chivalry with a comb in its hair and a pair of white silk legs, and presenting on the whole a feminine appearance. My gifted townsman stood gloomily apart, with folded arms, and I could have wished that his curls and forehead had been more probable.

Several curious little circumstances transpired as the action proceeded. The late king of the country not only appeared to have been troubled with a cough at the time of his decease, but to have taken it with him to the tomb, and to have brought it back. The royal phantom also carried a ghostly manuscript round its truncheon, to which it had the appearance of occasionally referring, and that, too, with an air of anxiety and a tendency to lose the place of reference which were suggestive of a state of mortality. It was this, I conceive, which led to the Shade's being advised by the gallery to "turn over!"—a recommendation which it took extremely ill. It was likewise to be noted of this majestic spirit that whereas it always appeared with an air of having been out a long time and walked an immense distance, it perceptibly came from a closely contiguous wall. This occasioned its terrors to be received derisively. The Queen of Denmark, a very buxom lady, though no doubt historically brazen, was considered by the public to have too much brass about her; her chin being attached to her diadem by a broad band of that metal (as if she had a gorgeous toothache), her waist being encircled by another, and each of her arms by another, so that she was openly mentioned as "the kettle-drum." The noble boy in the ancestral boots, was inconsistent; representing himself, as it were in one breath, as an able seaman, a strolling actor, a gravedigger, a clergyman, and a person of the utmost importance at a Court fencing-match, on the authority of whose practised eye and nice discrimination the finest strokes were judged. This gradually led to a want of toleration for him, and even—on his being detected in holy orders, and declining to perform the funeral service—to the general indignation taking the form of nuts. Lastly, Ophelia was a prey to such slow musical madness, that when, in course of time, she had taken off her white muslin scarf, folded it up, and buried it, a sulky man who had been long cooling his impatient nose against an iron bar in the front row of the gallery, growled, "Now the baby's put to bed let's have supper!" Which, to say the least of it, was out of keeping.

Upon my unfortunate townsman all these incidents accumulated with playful effect. Whenever that undecided Prince had to ask a question or state a doubt, the public helped him out with it. As for example; on the question whether 'twas nobler in the mind to suffer, some roared yes, and some no, and some inclining to both opinions said "toss up for it;" and quite a Debating Society arose. When he asked what should such fellows as he do crawling between earth and heaven, he was encouraged with loud cries of "Hear, hear!" When he appeared with his stocking disordered (its disorder expressed, according to usage, by one very neat fold in the top, which I suppose to be always got up with a flat iron), a conversation took place in the gallery respecting the paleness of his leg, and whether it was occasioned by the turn the ghost had given him. On his taking the recorders—very like a little black flute that had just been played in the orchestra and handed out at the door—he was called upon unanimously for Rule Britannia. When he recommended the player not to saw the air thus, the sulky man said, "And don't *you* do it, neither; you're a deal worse than *him!*" And I grieve to add that peals of laughter greeted Mr. Wopsle on every one of these occasions.

But his greatest trials were in the churchyard: which had the appearance of a primeval forest, with a kind of small ecclesiastical washhouse on one side, and a turnpike-gate on the other. Mr. Wopsle in a comprehensive black cloak, being descried entering at the turnpike, the gravedigger was admonished in a friendly way, "Look out! Here's the undertaker a coming, to see how you're a getting on with your work!" I believe it is well known in a constitutional country that Mr. Wopsle could not possibly have returned the skull, after moralising over it, without dusting his fingers on a white napkin taken from his breast; but even that innocent and indispensable action did not pass without the comment "Wai-ter!" The arrival of the body for interment (in an empty black box with the lid tumbling open), was the signal for a general joy which was much enhanced by the discovery, among the bearers, of an individual obnoxious to identification. The joy attended Mr. Wopsle through his struggle with Laertes on the brink of the orchestra and the grave, and slackened no more until he had tumbled the king off the kitchen-table, and had died by inches from the ankles upward.

We had made some pale efforts in the beginning to applaud Mr. Wopsle; but they were too hopeless to be persisted in. Therefore we had sat, feeling keenly for him, but laughing, nevertheless, from ear to ear. I laughed in spite of myself all the time, the whole thing was so droll; and yet I had a latent impression that there was something decidedly fine in Mr. Wopsle's elocution—not for old associations' sake, I am afraid, but because it was very slow, very dreary, very up-hill and down-hill, and very unlike any way in which any man in any natural circumstances of life or death ever expressed himself about anything. When the tragedy was over, and he had been called for and hooted, I said to Herbert, "Let us go at once, or perhaps we shall meet him."

We made all the haste we could down stairs, but we were not quick enough either. Standing at the door was a Jewish man with an unnaturally heavy smear of eyebrow, who caught my eye as we advanced, and said, when we came up with him:

"Mr. Pip and friend?"

Identity of Mr. Pip and friend confessed.

"Mr. Waldengarver," said the man, "would be glad to have the honour."

"Waldengarver?" I repeated—when Herbert murmured in my ear, "Probably Wopsle."

"Oh!" said I. "Yes. Shall we follow you?"

"A few steps, please." When we were in a side alley, he turned and asked, "How did you think he looked?—I dressed him."

I don't know what he had looked like, except a funeral; with the addition of a large Danish sun or star hanging round his neck by a blue ribbon, that had given him the appearance of being insured in some extraordinary Fire Office.° But I said he had looked very nice.

"When he come to the grave," said our conductor, "he showed his cloak beautiful. But, judging from the wing, it looked to me that when he see the ghost in the queen's apartment, he might have made more of his stockings."

I modestly assented, and we all fell through a little dirty swing door, into a sort of hot packing-case immediately behind it. Here Mr. Wopsle was divesting himself of his Danish garments, and here there was just room for us to look at him over one another's shoulders, by keeping the packing-case door, or lid, wide open.

"Gentlemen," said Mr. Wopsle, "I am proud to see you. I hope, Mr. Pip, you will excuse my sending round. I had the happiness to

---

large Danish sun. . . Office: Fire insurance companies identified the buildings that they insured with large metal disks or "fire-marks."

know you in former times, and the Drama has ever had a claim which has ever been acknowledged, on the noble and the affluent."

Meanwhile, Mr. Waldengarver, in a frightful perspiration, was trying to get himself out of his princely sables.

"Skin the stockings off, Mr. Waldengarver," said the owner of that property, "or you'll bust 'em. Bust 'em, and you'll bust five-and-thirty shillings. Shakspeare never was complimented with a finer pair. Keep quiet in your chair now, and leave 'em to me."

With that, he went upon his knees, and began to flay his victim; who, on the first stocking coming off, would certainly have fallen over backward with his chair, but for there being no room to fall anyhow.

I had been afraid until then to say a word about the play. But then, Mr. Waldengarver looked up at us complacently, and said:

"Gentlemen, how did it seem to you, to go, in front?"

Herbert said from behind (at the same time poking me), "capitally." So I said "capitally."

"How did you like my reading of the character, gentlemen?" said Mr. Waldengarver, almost, if not quite, with patronage.

Herbert said from behind (again poking me), "massive and concrete." So I said boldly, as if I had originated it, and must beg to insist upon it, "massive and concrete."

"I am glad to have your approbation, gentlemen," said Mr. Waldengarver, with an air of dignity, in spite of his being ground against the wall at the time, and holding on by the seat of the chair.

"But I'll tell you one thing, Mr. Waldengarver," said the man who was on his knees, "in which you're out in your reading. Now mind! I don't care who says contrairy; I tell you so. You're out in your reading of Hamlet when you get your legs in profile. The last Hamlet as I dressed, made the same mistakes in his reading at rehearsal, till I got him to put a large red wafer on each of his shins, and then at that rehearsal (which was the last) I went in front, sir, to the back of the pit, and whenever his reading brought him into profile, I called out 'I don't see no wafers!' And at night his reading was lovely."

Mr. Waldengarver smiled at me, as much as to say "a faithful dependent—I overlook his folly;" and then said aloud, "My view is a little classic and thoughtful for them here; but they will improve, they will improve."

Herbert and I said together, Oh, no doubt they would improve.

"Did you observe, gentlemen," said Mr. Waldengarver, "that there was a man in the gallery who endeavoured to cast derision on the ser-vice—I mean, the representation?"

We basely replied that we rather thought we had noticed such a man. I added, "He was drunk, no doubt."

"Oh dear no, sir," said Mr. Wopsle, "not drunk. His employer would see to that, sir. His employer would not allow him to be drunk."

"You know his employer?" said I.

Mr. Wopsle shut his eyes, and opened them again; performing both ceremonies very slowly. "You must have observed, gentlemen," said he, "an ignorant and a blatant ass, with a rasping throat and a countenance expressive of low malignity, who went through—I will not say sustained—the rôle (if I may use a French expression) of Claudius King of Denmark. That is his employer, gentlemen. Such is the profession!"

Without distinctly knowing whether I should have been more sorry for Mr. Wopsle if he had been in despair, I was so sorry for him as it was, that I took the opportunity of his turning round to have his braces put on—which jostled us out at the doorway—to ask Herbert what he thought of having him home to supper? Herbert said he thought it would be kind to do so; therefore I invited him, and he went to Barnard's with us, wrapped up to the eyes, and we did our best for him, and he sat until two o'clock in the morning, reviewing his success and developing his plans. I forget in detail what they were, but I have a general recollection that he was to begin with reviving the Drama, and to end with crushing it; inasmuch as his decease would leave it utterly bereft and without a chance or hope.

Miserably I went to bed after all, and miserably thought of Estella, and miserably dreamed that my expectations were all cancelled, and that I had to give my hand in marriage to Herbert's Clara, or play Hamlet to Miss Havisham's Ghost, before twenty thousand people, without knowing twenty words of it.

[PART 20]

Chapter 32

One day when I was busy with my books and Mr. Pocket, I re-ceived a note by the post, the mere outside of which threw me into a great flutter; for, though I had never seen the handwriting in which it was addressed, I divined whose hand it was. It had no set beginning, as Dear Mr. Pip, or Dear Pip, or Dear Sir, or Dear Anything, but ran thus:

> I am to come to London the day after to-morrow by the mid-day coach. I believe it was settled you should meet me? At all events Miss Havisham has that impression, and I write in obedience to it. She sends you her regard.
>
> Yours, Estella.

If there had been time, I should probably have ordered several suits of clothes for this occasion; but as there was not, I was fain to be content with those I had. My appetite vanished instantly, and I knew no peace or rest until the day arrived. Not that its arrival brought me either; for, then I was worse than ever, and began haunting the coach-office in Wood-street, Cheapside, before the coach had left the Blue Boar in our town. For all that I knew this perfectly well, I still felt as if it were not safe to let the coach-office be out of my sight longer than five minutes at a time; and in this condition of unreason I had performed the first half-hour of a watch of four or five hours, when Wemmick ran against me.

"Halloa, Mr. Pip," said he; "how do you do? I should hardly have thought this was *your* beat."

I explained that I was waiting to meet somebody who was coming up by coach, and I inquired after the Castle and the Aged.

"Both flourishing, thankye," said Wemmick, "and particularly the Aged. He's in wonderful feather. He'll be eighty-two next birthday. I have a notion of firing eighty-two times, if the neighbourhood shouldn't complain, and that cannon of mine should prove equal to the pressure. However, this is not London talk. Where do you think I am going to?"

"To the office?" said I, for he was tending in that direction.

"Next thing to it," returned Wemmick, "I am going to Newgate. We are in a banker's-parcel case° just at present, and I have been down the road taking a squint at the scene of action, and thereupon must have a word or two with our client."

"Did your client commit the robbery?" I asked.

"Bless your soul and body, no," answered Wemmick, very dryly.

---

banker's-parcel case: A case involving a bank messenger or parcel-carrier.

"But he is accused of it. So might you or I be. Either of us might be accused of it, you know."

"Only neither of us is," I remarked.

"Yah!" said Wemmick, touching me on the breast with his forefinger; "you're a deep one, Mr. Pip! Would you like to have a look at Newgate? Have you time to spare?"

I had so much time to spare, that the proposal came as a relief, notwithstanding its irreconcilability with my latent desire to keep my eye on the coach-office. Muttering that I would make the inquiry whether I had time to walk with him, I went into the office, and ascertained from the clerk with the nicest precision and much to the trying of his temper, the earliest moment at which the coach could be expected—which I knew beforehand, quite as well as he. I then rejoined Mr. Wemmick, and affecting to consult my watch and to be surprised by the information I had received, accepted his offer.

We were at Newgate in a few minutes, and we passed through the lodge where some fetters were hanging up on the bare walls among the prison rules, into the interior of the jail. At that time, jails were much neglected, and the period of exaggerated reaction consequent on all public wrong-doing—and which is always its heaviest and longest punishment—was still far off. So, felons were not lodged and fed better than soldiers (to say nothing of paupers), and seldom set fire to their prisons with the excusable object of improving the flavour of their soup.° It was visiting time when Wemmick took me in; and a potman was going his rounds with beer; and the prisoners, behind bars in yards, were buying beer, and talking to friends; and a frouzy, ugly, disorderly, depressing scene it was.

It struck me that Wemmick walked among the prisoners, much as a gardener might walk among his plants. This was first put into my head by his seeing a shoot that had come up in the night, and saying, "What, Captain Tom? Are *you* there? Ah, indeed!" and also, "Is that Black Bill behind the cistern? Why I didn't look for you these two months; how do you find yourself?" Equally in his stopping at the bars and attending to anxious whisperers—always singly—Wemmick with his post-office in an immovable state, looked at them while in conference, as if he were taking particular notice of the advance they had made, since last observed, towards coming out in full blow at their trial.

He was highly popular, and I found that he took the familiar de-

set fire . . . soup: Probably a reference to the riots at Chatham Convict Prison in February 1861.

partment of Mr. Jaggers's business: though something of the state of Mr. Jaggers hung about him too, forbidding approach beyond certain limits. His personal recognition of each successive client was comprised in a nod, and in his settling his hat a little easier on his head with both hands, and then tightening the post-office, and putting his hands in his pockets. In one or two instances, there was a difficulty respecting the raising of fees, and then Mr. Wemmick, backing as far as possible from the insufficient money produced, said, "It's no use, my boy. I'm only a subordinate. I can't take it. Don't go on in that way with a subordinate. If you are unable to make up your quantum, my boy, you had better address yourself to a principal; there are plenty of principals in the profession, you know, and what is not worth the while of one, may be worth the while of another; that's my recommendation to you, speaking as a subordinate. Don't try on useless measures. Why should you? Now, who's next?"

Thus, we walked through Wemmick's greenhouse, until he turned to me and said, "Notice the man I shall shake hands with." I should have done so, without the preparation, as he had shaken hands with no one yet.

Almost as soon as he had spoken, a portly upright man (whom I can see now, as I write) in a well-worn olive-coloured frock-coat, with a peculiar pallor overspreading the red in his complexion, and eyes that went wandering about when he tried to fix them, came up to a corner of the bars, and put his hand to his hat—which had a greasy and fatty surface like cold broth—with a half-serious and half-jocose military salute.

"Colonel, to you!" said Wemmick; "how are you, Colonel?"

"All right, Mr. Wemmick."

"Everything was done that could be done, but the evidence was too strong for us, Colonel."

"Yes, it was too strong, sir—but *I* don't care."

"No, no," said Wemmick, coolly, "*you* don't care." Then, turning to me, "Served His Majesty this man. Was a soldier in the line and bought his discharge."

I said, "Indeed?" and the man's eyes looked at me, and then looked over my head, and then looked all round me, and then he drew his hand across his lips and laughed.

"I think I shall be out of this on Monday, sir," he said to Wemmick.

"Perhaps," returned my friend, "but there's no knowing."

"I am glad to have the chance of bidding you good-by, Mr. Wemmick," said the man, stretching out his hand between two bars.

"Thankye," said Wemmick, shaking hands with him. "Same to you, Colonel."

"If what I had upon me when taken, had been real, Mr. Wemmick," said the man unwilling to let his hand go, "I should have asked the favour of your wearing another ring—in acknowledgment of your attentions."

"I'll accept the will for the deed," said Wemmick. "By-the-by; you were quite a pigeon-fancier." The man looked up at the sky. "I am told you had a remarkable breed of tumblers. *Could* you commission any friend of yours to bring me a pair, if you've no further use for 'em?"

"It shall be done, sir."

"All right," said Wemmick, "they shall be taken care of. Good afternoon, Colonel. Good-by!" They shook hands again, and as we walked away Wemmick said to me, "A Coiner,° a very good workman. The Recorder's report is made to-day, and he is sure to be executed on Monday. Still you see, as far as it goes, a pair of pigeons are portable property, all the same." With that, he looked back, and nodded at this dead plant, and then cast his eyes about him in walking out of the yard, as if he were considering what other pot would go best in its place.

As we came out of the prison through the lodge, I found that the great importance of my guardian was appreciated by the turnkeys, no less than by those whom they held in charge. "Well, Mr. Wemmick," said the turnkey who kept us between the two studded and spiked lodge gates, and who carefully locked one before he unlocked the other, "what's Mr. Jaggers going to do with that waterside murder? Is he going to make it manslaughter, or what's he going to make of it?"

"Why don't you ask him?" returned Wemmick.

"Oh yes, I dare say!" said the turnkey.

"Now, that's the way with them here, Mr. Pip," remarked Wemmick, turning to me with his post-office elongated. "They don't mind what they ask of me, the subordinate; but you'll never catch 'em asking any questions of my principal."

"Is this young gentleman one of the 'prentices or articled ones of your office?" asked the turnkey, with a grin at Mr. Wemmick's humour.

"There he goes again, you see!" cried Wemmick, "I told you so! Asks another question of the subordinate before his first is dry! Well, supposing Mr. Pip is one of them?"

Coiner: Here, a counterfeiter.

"Why then," said the turnkey, grinning again, "he knows what Mr. Jaggers is."

"Yah!" cried Wemmick, suddenly hitting out at the turnkey in a facetious way, "you're as dumb as one of your own keys when you have to do with my principal, you know you are. Let us out, you old fox, or I'll get him to bring an action against you for false imprisonment."

The turnkey laughed, and gave us good day, and stood laughing at us over the spikes of the wicket when we descended the steps into the street.

"Mind you, Mr. Pip," said Wemmick, gravely in my ear, as he took my arm to be more confidential; "I don't know that Mr. Jaggers does a better thing than the way in which he keeps himself so high. He's always so high. His constant height is of a piece with his immense abilities. That Colonel durst no more take leave of *him*, than that turnkey durst ask him his intentions respecting a case. Then, between his height and them, he slips in his subordinate—don't you see?—and so he has 'em, soul and body."

I was very much impressed, and not for the first time, by my guardian's subtlety. To confess the truth, I very heartily wished, and not for the first time, that I had had some other guardian of minor abilities.

Mr. Wemmick and I parted at the office in Little Britain, where suppliants for Mr. Jaggers's notice were lingering about as usual, and I returned to my watch in the street of the coach-office, with some three hours on hand. I consumed the whole time in thinking how strange it was that I should be encompassed by all this taint of prison and crime; that, in my childhood out on our lonely marshes on a winter evening I should have first encountered it; that, it should have reappeared on two occasions, starting out like a stain that was faded but not gone; that, it should in this new way pervade my fortune and advancement. While my mind was thus engaged, I thought of the beautiful young Estella, proud and refined, coming towards me, and I thought with absolute abhorrence of the contrast between the jail and her. I wished that Wemmick had not met me, or that I had not yielded to him and gone with him, so that, of all days in the year on this day, I might not have had Newgate in my breath and on my clothes. I beat the prison dust off my feet as I sauntered to and fro, and I shook it out of my dress, and I exhaled its air from my lungs. So contaminated did I feel, remembering who was coming, that the coach came quickly after all, and I was not yet free from the soiling consciousness of Mr.

Wemmick's conservatory, when I saw her face at the coach window and her hand waving to me.

What *was* the nameless shadow which again in that one instant had passed?

Chapter 33

In her furred travelling-dress, Estella seemed more delicately beautiful than she had ever seemed yet, even in my eyes. Her manner was more winning that she had cared to let it be to me before, and I thought I saw Miss Havisham's influence in the change.

We stood in the Inn Yard while she pointed out her luggage to me, and when it was all collected I remembered—having forgotten everything but herself in the mean while—that I knew nothing of her destination.

"I am going to Richmond," she told me. "Our lesson is, that there are two Richmonds, one in Surrey and one in Yorkshire, and that mine is the Surrey Richmond. The distance is ten miles. I am to have a carriage, and you are to take me. This is my purse, and you are to pay my charges out of it. Oh, you must take the purse! We have no choice, you and I, but to obey our instructions. We are not free to follow our own devices, you and I."

As she looked at me in giving me the purse, I hoped there was an inner meaning in her words. She said them slightingly, but not with displeasure.

"A carriage will have to be sent for, Estella. Will you rest here a little?"

"Yes, I am to rest here a little, and I am to drink some tea, and you are to take care of me the while."

She drew her arm through mine, as if it must be done, and I requested a waiter who had been staring at the coach like a man who had never seen such a thing in his life, to show us a private sitting-room. Upon that, he pulled out a napkin, as if it were a magic clue without which he couldn't find the way up-stairs, and led us to the black hole of the establishment: fitted up with a diminishing mirror (quite a superfluous article considering the hole's proportions), an anchovy sauce-cruet, and somebody's pattens. On my objecting to this retreat, he took us into another room with a dinner-table for thirty, and in the grate a scorched leaf of a copy-book under a bushel of coal-dust. Having looked at this extinct conflagration and shaken his head, he took my order: which, proving to be merely "Some tea for the lady," sent him out of the room in a very low state of mind.

I was, and I am, sensible that the air of this chamber, in its strong combination of stable with soup-stock, might have led one to infer that the coaching department was not doing well, and that the enterprising proprietor was boiling down the horses for the refreshment department. Yet the room was all in all to me, Estella being in it. I thought that with her I could have been happy there for life. (I was not at all happy there at the time, observe, and I knew it well.)

"Where are you going to, at Richmond?" I asked Estella.

"I am going to live," said she, "at a great expense, with a lady there, who has the power—or says she has—of taking me about, and introducing me, and showing people to me and showing me to people."

"I suppose you will be glad of variety and admiration?"

"Yes, I suppose so."

She answered so carelessly, that I said, "You speak of yourself as if you were some one else."

"Where did you learn how I speak of others? Come, come," said Estella, smiling delightfully, "you must not expect me to go to school to *you;* I must talk in my own way. How do you thrive with Mr. Pocket?"

"I live quite pleasantly there; at least——" It appeared to me that I was losing a chance.

"At least?" repeated Estella.

"As pleasantly as I could anywhere, away from you."

"You silly boy," said Estella, quite composedly, "how can you talk such nonsense? Your friend Mr. Matthew, I believe, is superior to the rest of his family?"

"Very superior indeed. He is nobody's enemy——"

"Don't add but his own," interposed Estella, "for I hate that class of man. But he really is disinterested, and above small jealousy and spite, I have heard?"

"I am sure I have every reason to say so."

"You have not every reason to say so of the rest of his people," said Estella, nodding at me with an expression of face that was at once grave and rallying, "for they beset Miss Havisham with reports and insinuations to your disadvantage. They watch you, misrepresent you, write letters about you (anonymous sometimes), and you are the torment and the occupation of their lives. You can scarcely realise to yourself the hatred those people feel for you."

"They do me no harm, I hope?" said I.

Instead of answering, Estella burst out laughing. This was very singular to me, and I looked at her in considerable perplexity. When she left off—and she had not laughed languidly, but with real enjoyment—I said, in my diffident way with her:

"I hope I may suppose that you would not be amused if they did me any harm."

"No, no, you may be sure of that," said Estella. "You may be certain that I laugh because they fail. Oh, those people with Miss Havisham, and the tortures they undergo!" She laughed again, and even now when she had told me why, her laughter was very singular to me, for I could not doubt its being genuine, and yet it seemed too much for the occasion. I thought there must really be something more here than I knew; she saw the thought in my mind, and answered it.

"It is not easy for even you," said Estella, "to know what satisfaction it gives me to see those people thwarted, or what an enjoyable sense of the ridiculous I have when they are made ridiculous. For you were not brought up in that strange house from a mere baby.—I was. You had not your little wits sharpened by their intriguing against you, suppressed and defenceless, under the mask of sympathy and pity and what not that is soft and soothing.—I had. You did not gradually open your round childish eyes wider and wider to the discovery of that impostor of a woman who calculates her stores of peace of mind for when she wakes up in the night.—I did."

It was no laughing matter with Estella now, nor was she summoning these remembrances from any shallow place. I would not have been the cause of that look of hers, for all my expectations in a heap.

"Two things I can tell you," said Estella. "First, notwithstanding the proverb that constant dropping will wear away a stone, you may set your mind at rest that these people never will—never would, in a hundred years—impair your ground with Miss Havisham, in any particular, great or small. Second, I am beholden to you as the cause of their being so busy and so mean in vain, and there is my hand upon it."

As she gave it me playfully—for her darker mood had been but momentary—I held it and put it to my lips. "You ridiculous boy," said Estella, "will you never take warning? Or do you kiss my hand in the spirit in which I once let you kiss my cheek?"

"What is it?" said I.

"I must think a moment. A spirit of contempt for the fawners and plotters."

"If I say yes, may I kiss the cheek again?"

"You should have asked before you touched the hand. But, yes, if you like."

I leaned down, and her calm face was like a statue's. "Now," said Estella, gliding away the instant I touched her cheek, "you are to take care that I have some tea, and you are to take me to Richmond."

Her reverting to this tone as if our association were forced upon us and we were mere puppets, gave me pain; but everything in our intercourse did give me pain. Whatever her tone with me happened to be, I could put no trust in it, and build no hope on it; and yet I went on against trust and against hope. Why repeat it a thousand times? So it always was.

I rang for the tea, and the waiter, reappearing with his magic clue, brought in by degrees some fifty adjuncts to that refreshment, but of tea not a glimpse. A teaboard, cups and saucers, plates, knives and forks (including carvers), spoons (various), salt-cellars, a meek little muffin confined with the utmost precaution under a strong iron cover, Moses in the bullrushes typified by a soft bit of butter in a quantity of parsley, a pale loaf with a powdered head, two proof impressions of the bars of the kitchen fireplace on triangular bits of bread, and ultimately a fat family urn: which the waiter staggered in with, expressing in his countenance burden and suffering. After a prolonged absence at this stage of the entertainment, he at length came back with a casket of precious appearance containing twigs. These I steeped in hot water, and so from the whole of these appliances extracted one cup of I don't know what, for Estella.

The bill paid, and the waiter remembered, and the ostler not forgotten, and the chambermaid taken into consideration—in a word, the whole house bribed into a state of contempt and animosity, and Estella's purse much lightened—we got into our post-coach and drove away. Turning into Cheapside and rattling up Newgate-street, we were soon under the walls of which I was so ashamed.

"What place is that?" Estella asked me.

I made a foolish pretence of not at first recognising it, and then told her. As she looked at it, and drew in her head again, murmuring "Wretches!" I would not have confessed to my visit for any consideration.

"Mr. Jaggers," said I, by way of putting it neatly on somebody else, "has the reputation of being more in the secrets of that dismal place than any man in London."

"He is more in the secrets of every place, I think," said Estella, in a low voice.

"You have been accustomed to see him often, I suppose?"

"I have been accustomed to see him at uncertain intervals, ever since I can remember. But I know him no better now, than I did before I could speak plainly. What is your own experience of him? Do you advance with him?"

"Once habituated to his distrustful manner," said I, "I have done very well."

"Are you intimate?"

"I have dined with him at his private house."

"I fancy," said Estella, shrinking, "that must be a curious place."

"It is a curious place."

I should have been chary of discussing my guardian too freely even with her; but I should have gone on with the subject so far as to describe the dinner in Gerrard-street, if we had not then come into a sudden glare of gas.° It seemed, while it lasted, to be all alight and alive with that inexplicable feeling I had had before; and when we were out of it, I was as much dazed for a few moments as if I had been in Lightning.

So, we fell into other talk, and it was principally about the way by which we were travelling, and about what parts of London lay on this side of it, and what on that. The great city was almost new to her, she told me, for she had never left Miss Havisham's neighbourhood until she had gone to France, and she had merely passed through London then in going and returning. I asked her if my guardian had any charge of her while she remained here? To that she emphatically said "God forbid!" and no more.

It was impossible for me to avoid seeing that she cared to attract me; that she made herself winning; and would have won me even if the task had needed pains. Yet this made me none the happier, for, even if she had not taken that tone of our being disposed of by others, I should have felt that she held my heart in her hand because she wilfully chose to do it, and not because it would have wrung any tenderness in her, to crush it and throw it away.

When we passed through Hammersmith, I showed her where Mr. Matthew Pocket lived, and said it was no great way from Richmond, and that I hoped I should see her sometimes.

"Oh yes, you are to see me; you are to come when you think

---

sudden glare of gas: Gas light flickering up momentarily.

proper; you are to be mentioned to the family; indeed you are already mentioned."

I inquired was it a large household she was going to be a member of?

"No; there are only two; mother and daughter. The mother is a lady of some station, I believe, though not averse to increasing her income."

"I wonder Miss Havisham could part with you again so soon."

"It is a part of Miss Havisham's plans for me, Pip," said Estella, with a sigh, as if she were tired; "I am to write to her constantly and see her regularly, and report how I go on—I and the jewels—for they are nearly all mine now."

It was the first time she had ever called me by my name. Of course she did so, purposely, and knew that I should treasure it up.

We came to Richmond all too soon, and our destination there, was a house by the Green; a staid old house, where hoops and powder and patches, embroidered coats rolled stockings ruffles and swords, had had their court days many a time. Some ancient trees before the house were still cut into fashions as formal and unnatural as the hoops and wigs and stiff skirts; but their own allotted places in the great procession of the dead were not far off, and they would soon drop into them and go the silent way of the rest.

A bell with an old voice—which I dare say in its time had often said to the house, Here is the green farthingale, Here is the diamond-hilted sword, Here are the shoes with red heels and the blue solitaire,°—sounded gravely in the moonlight, and two cherry-coloured maids came fluttering out to receive Estella. The doorway soon absorbed her boxes, and she gave me her hand and a smile, and said good night, and was absorbed likewise. And still I stood looking at the house, thinking how happy I should be if I lived there with her, and knowing that I never was happy with her, but always miserable.

I got into the carriage to be taken back to Hammersmith, and I got in with a bad heart-ache, and I got out with a worse heart-ache. At our own door, I found little Jane Pocket coming home from a little party escorted by her little lover; and I envied her little lover, in spite of his being subject to Flopson.

Mr. Pocket was out lecturing; for, he was a most delightful lecturer on domestic economy, and his treatises on the management of

---

farthingale . . . solitaire: Items of eighteenth-century dress: a farthingale is a hooped petticoat; a solitaire, a loose necktie.

children and servants were considered the very best text-books on those themes. But, Mrs. Pocket was at home, and was in a little difficulty, on account of the baby's having been accommodated with a needle-case to keep him quiet during the unaccountable absence (with a relative in the Foot Guards) of Millers. And more needles were missing, than it could be regarded as quite wholesome for a patient of such tender years either to apply externally or to take as a tonic.

Mr. Pocket being justly celebrated for giving most excellent practical advice, and for having a clear and sound perception of things and a highly judicious mind, I had some notion in my heart-ache of begging him to accept my confidence. But, happening to look up at Mrs. Pocket as she sat reading her book of dignities after prescribing Bed as a sovereign remedy for baby, I thought—Well—No, I wouldn't.

[PART 21]

Chapter 34

As I had grown accustomed to my expectations, I had insensibly begun to notice their effect upon myself and those around me. Their influence on my own character, I disguised from my recognition as much as possible, but I knew very well that it was not all good. I lived in a state of chronic uneasiness respecting my behaviour to Joe. My conscience was not by any means comfortable about Biddy. When I woke up in the night—like Camilla—I used to think, with a weariness on my spirits, that I should have been happier and better if I had never seen Miss Havisham's face, and had risen to manhood content to be partners with Joe in the honest old forge. Many a time of an evening, when I sat alone looking at the fire, I thought, after all there was no fire like the forge fire and the kitchen fire at home.

Yet Estella was so inseparable from all my restlessness and disquiet of mind, that I really fell into confusion as to the limits of my own part in its production. That is to say, supposing I had had no expectations, and yet had had Estella to think of, I could not make out to my satisfaction that I should have done much better. Now, concerning the influence of my position on others, I was in no such difficulty, and so I perceived—though dimly enough perhaps—that it was not beneficial to anybody, and, above all, that it was not beneficial to Herbert. My lavish habits led his easy nature into expenses that he could not afford, corrupted the simplicity of his life, and disturbed his peace with anxieties and regrets. I was not at all remorseful for having unwittingly set those other branches of the Pocket family to the poor arts they practised: because such littlenesses were their natural bent, and would have been evoked by anybody else, if I had left them slumbering. But Herbert's was a very different case, and it often caused me a twinge to think that I had done him evil service in crowding his sparsely-furnished chambers with incongruous upholstery work, and placing the canary-breasted Avenger at his disposal.

So now, as an infallible way of making little ease great ease, I began to contract a quantity of debt. I could hardly begin but Herbert must begin too, so he soon followed. At Startop's suggestion, we put ourselves down for election into a club called The Finches of the Grove: the object of which institution I have never divined, if it were not that the members should dine expensively once a fortnight, to quarrel among themselves as much as possible after dinner, and to cause six waiters to get drunk on the stairs. I know that these gratifying social ends were so invariably accomplished, that Herbert and I understood nothing else to be referred to in the first standing toast of the society: which ran "Gentlemen, may the present promotion of good feeling ever reign predominant among the Finches of the Grove."

The Finches spent their money foolishly (the Hotel we dined at was in Covent-garden), and the first Finch I saw, when I had the honour of joining the Grove, was Bentley Drummle: at that time floundering about town in a cab of his own, and doing a great deal of damage to the posts at the street corners. Occasionally, he shot himself out of his equipage head-foremost over the apron; and I saw him on one occasion deliver himself at the door of the Grove in this unintentional way—like coals. But here I anticipate a little, for I was not a Finch, and could not be, according to the sacred laws of the society, until I came of age.

In my confidence in my own resources, I would willingly have taken Herbert's expenses on myself; but Herbert was proud, and I could make no such proposal to him. So, he got into difficulties in every direction, and continued to look about him. When we gradually fell into keeping late hours and late company, I noticed that he looked about him with a desponding eye at breakfast-time; that he began to look about him more hopefully about mid-day; that he drooped when he came in to dinner; that he seemed to descry Capital in the distance rather clearly, after dinner; that he all but realised Capital towards midnight; and that at about two o'clock in the morning, he became so deeply despondent again as to talk of buying a rifle and going to America, with a general purpose of compelling buffaloes to make his fortune.

I was usually at Hammersmith about half the week, and when I was at Hammersmith I haunted Richmond: whereof separately by-and-by. Herbert would often come to Hammersmith when I was there, and I think at those seasons his father would occasionally have some passing perception that the opening he was looking for, had not appeared yet. But in the general tumbling up of the family, his tumbling out in life somewhere, was a thing to transact itself some-how. In the mean time Mr. Pocket grew greyer, and tried oftener to lift himself out of his perplexities by the hair. While Mrs. Pocket tripped up the family with her footstool, read her book of dignities, lost her pocket-handkerchief, told us about her grandpapa, and taught the young idea how to shoot,° by shooting it into bed whenever it at-tracted her notice.

As I am now generalising a period of my life with the object of clearing my way before me, I can scarcely do so better than by at once completing the description of our usual manners and customs at Barnard's Inn.

We spent as much money as we could, and got as little for it as people could make up their minds to give us. We were always more or less miserable, and most of our acquaintance were in the same condi-tion. There was a gay fiction among us that we were constantly enjoy-ing ourselves, and a skeleton truth that we never did. To the best of my belief, our case was in the last aspect a rather common one.

Every morning, with an air ever new, Herbert went into the City to look about him. I often paid him a visit in the dark back-room in which he consorted with an ink-jar, a hat-peg, a coal-box, a string-box, an almanack, a desk and stool, and a ruler; and I do not remem-ber that I ever saw him do anything else but look about him. If we all did what we undertake to do, as faithfully as Herbert did, we might live in a Republic of the Virtues. He had nothing else to do, poor fel-low, except at a certain hour of every afternoon to "go to Lloyd's"—in observance of a ceremony of seeing his principal, I think. He never did anything else in connexion with Lloyd's that I could find out, ex-cept come back again. When he felt his case unusually serious, and that he positively must find an opening, he would go on 'Change at a busy

___

taught . . . shoot: An adaptation of a line from *The Seasons* by James Thomson (1700–1748); *to shoot* means to sprout or develop.

time, and walk in and out, in a kind of gloomy country dance figure, among the assembled magnates. "For," says Herbert to me, coming home to dinner on one of those special occasions, "I find the truth to be, Handel, that an opening won't come to one, but one must go to it——so I have been."

If we had been less attached to one another, I think we must have hated one another regularly every morning. I detested the chambers beyond expression at that period of repentance, and could not endure the sight of the Avenger's livery: which had a more expensive and a less remunerative appearance then, than at any other time in the four-and-twenty hours. As we got more and more into debt, breakfast became a hollower and hollower form, and, being on one occasion at breakfast-time threatened (by letter) with legal proceedings, "not unwholly unconnected," as my local paper might put it, "with jewellery," I went to far as to seize the Avenger by his blue collar and shake him off his feet—so that he was actually in the air, like a booted Cupid—for presuming to suppose that we wanted a roll.

At certain times—meaning at uncertain times, for they depended on our humour—I would say to Herbert, as if it were a remarkable discovery:

"My dear Herbert, we are getting on badly."

"My dear Handel," Herbert would say to me, in all sincerity, "if you will believe me, those very words were on my lips, by a strange coincidence."

"Then, Herbert," I would respond, "let us look into our affairs."

We always derived profound satisfaction from making an appointment for this purpose. I always thought this was business, this was the way to confront the thing, this was the way to take the foe by the throat. And I know Herbert thought so too.

We ordered something rather special for dinner, with a bottle of something similarly out of the common way, in order that our minds might be fortified for the occasion, and we might come well up to the mark. Dinner over, we produced a bundle of pens, a copious supply of ink, and a goodly show of writing and blotting paper. For, there was something very comfortable in having plenty of stationery.

I would then take a sheet of paper, and write across the top of it, in a neat hand, the heading, "Memorandum of Pip's debts;" with Barnard's Inn and the date very carefully added. Herbert would also take a sheet of paper, and write across it with similar formalities, "Memorandum of Herbert's debts."

Each of us would then refer to a confused heap of papers at his side, which had been thrown into drawers, worn into holes in pockets, half-burnt in lighting candles, stuck for weeks into the looking-glass, and otherwise damaged. The sound of our pens going, refreshed us exceedingly, insomuch that I sometimes found it difficult to distinguish between this edifying business proceeding and actually paying the money. In point of meritorious character, the two things seemed about equal.

When we had written a little while, I would ask Herbert how he got on? Herbert probably would have been scratching his head in a most rueful manner at the sight of his accumulating figures.

"They are mounting up, Handel," Herbert would say; "upon my life, they are mounting up."

"Be firm, Herbert," I would retort, plying my own pen with great assiduity. "Look the thing in the face. Look into your affairs. Stare them out of countenance."

"So I would, Handel, only they are staring *me* out of countenance."

However, my determined manner would have its effect, and Herbert would fall to work again. After a time he would give up once more, on the plea that he had not got Cobbs's bill, or Lobbs's, or Nobbs's, as the case might be.

"Then, Herbert, estimate; estimate it in round numbers, and put it down."

"What a fellow of resource you are!" my friend would reply, with admiration. "Really your business powers are very remarkable."

I thought so too. I established with myself on these occasions, the reputation of a first-rate man of business—prompt, decisive, energetic, clear, cool-headed. When I had got all my responsibilities down upon my list, I compared each with the bill, and ticked it off. My self-approval when I ticked an entry was quite a luxurious sensation. When I had no more ticks to make, I folded all my bills up uniformly, docketed each on the back, and tied the whole into a symmetrical bundle. Then I did the same for Herbert (who modestly said he had not my administrative genius), and felt that I had brought his affairs into a focus for him.

My business habits had one other bright feature, which I called "leaving a Margin." For example; supposing Herbert's debts to be one hundred and sixty-four pounds four-and-twopence, I would say, "Leave a margin, and put them down at two hundred." Or, supposing my own to be four times as much, I would leave a margin, and put them down at seven hundred. I had the highest opinion of the wisdom of this same Margin, but I am bound to acknowledge that on looking back, I deem it to have been an expensive device. For, we always ran into new debt immediately, to the full extent of the margin, and sometimes in the sense of freedom and solvency it imparted, got pretty far on into another margin.

But there was a calm, a rest, a virtuous hush, consequent on these examinations of our affairs that gave me, for the time, an admirable opinion of myself. Soothed by my exertions, my method, and Herbert's compliments, I would sit with his symmetrical bundle and my own on the table before me among the stationery, and feel like a bank of some sort, rather than a private individual.

We shut our outer door on these solemn occasions, in order that we might not be interrupted. I had fallen into my serene state one evening, when we heard a letter dropped through the slit in the said door, and fall on the ground. "It's for you, Handel," said Herbert, going out and coming back with it, "and I hope there is nothing the matter." This was in allusion to its heavy black seal and border.

The letter was signed TRABB & CO., and its contents were simply, that I was an honoured sir, and that they begged to inform me that Mrs. J. Gargery had departed this life on Monday last, at twenty minutes past six in the evening, and that my attendance was requested at the interment on Monday next at three o'clock in the afternoon.

Chapter 35

It was the first time that a grave had opened in my road of life, and the gap it made in the smooth ground was wonderful. The figure of my sister in her chair by the kitchen fire, haunted me night and day. That the place could possibly be, without her, was something my mind seemed unable to compass; and whereas she had seldom or never been in my thoughts of late, I had now the strangest ideas that she was coming towards me in the street, or that she would presently knock at the door. In my rooms too, with which she had never been at all associated, there was at once the blankness of death and a perpetual suggestion of the sound of her voice or the turn of her face or figure, as if she were still alive and had been often there.

Whatever my fortunes might have been, I could scarcely have recalled my sister with much tenderness. But I suppose there is a shock of regret which may exist without much tenderness. Under its influence (and perhaps to make up for the want of the softer feeling) I was seized with a violent indignation against the assailant from whom she had suffered so much; and I felt that on sufficient proof I could have revengefully pursued Orlick, or any one else, to the last extremity.

Having written to Joe, to offer consolation, and to assure him that I should come to the funeral, I passed the intermediate days in the curious state of mind I have glanced at. I went down early in the morning, and alighted at the Blue Boar in good time to walk over to the forge.

It was fine summer weather again, and, as I walked along, the times when I was a little helpless creature, and my sister did not spare me, vividly returned. But they returned with a gentle tone upon them that softened even the edge of Tickler. For now, the very breath of the beans and clover whispered to my heart that the day must come when it would be well for my memory that others walking in the sunshine should be softened as they thought of me.

At last I came within sight of the house, and saw that Trabb and Co. had put in a funereal execution and taken possession.° Two dismally absurd persons, each ostentatiously exhibiting a crutch done up in black bandage—as if that instrument could possibly communicate any comfort to anybody—were posted at the front door; and in one of them I recognised a postboy discharged from the Boar for turning a young couple into a sawpit on their bridal morning, in consequence of intoxication rendering it necessary for him to ride his horse clasped around the neck with both arms. All the children of the village, and most of the women, were admiring these sable warders and the closed windows of the house and forge; and as I came up, one of the two warders (the postboy) knocked at the door—implying that I was far too much exhausted by grief, to have strength remaining to knock for myself.

Another sable warder (a carpenter, who had once eaten two geese for a wager) opened the door, and showed me into the best parlour. Here, Mr. Trabb had taken unto himself the best table, and had got all the leaves up, and was holding a kind of black Bazaar, with the aid of a quantity of black pins. At the moment of my arrival, he had just finished putting somebody's hat into black long-clothes, like an African baby; so he held out his hand for mine. But I, misled by the action, and confused by the occasion, shook hands with him with every testimony of warm affection.

Poor dear Joe, entangled in a little black cloak tied in a large bow

---

execution . . . possession: By execution of a court order, sheriffs seized the property of a debtor.

under his chin, was seated apart at the upper end of the room; where, as chief mourner, he had evidently been stationed by Trabb. When I bent down and said to him, "Dear Joe, how are you?" he said, "Pip, old chap, you knowed her when she were a fine figure and a——" and clasped my hand and said no more.

Biddy, looking very neat and modest in her black dress, went quietly here and there, and was very helpful. When I had spoken to Biddy, as I thought it not a time for talking I went and sat down near Joe, and there began to wonder in what part of the house it—she—my sister—was. The air of the parlour being faint with the smell of sweet cake, I looked about for the table of refreshments; it was scarcely visible until one had got accustomed to the gloom, but there was a cut-up plum-cake upon it, and there were cut-up oranges, and sandwiches, and biscuits, and two decanters that I knew very well as ornaments, but had never seen used in all my life; one full of port, and one of sherry. Standing at this table, I became conscious of the servile Pumblechook in a black cloak and several yards of hatband, who was alternately stuffing himself, and making obsequious movements to catch my attention. The moment he succeeded, he came over to me (breathing sherry and crumbs), and said in a subdued voice, "May I, dear sir?" and did. I then descried Mr. and Mrs. Hubble; the last-named in a decent speechless paroxysm in a corner. We were all going to "follow," and were all in course of being tied up separately (by Trabb) into ridiculous bundles.

"Which, I meantersay, Pip," Joe whispered me, as we were being what Mr. Trabb called "formed" in the parlour, two and two—and it was dreadfully like a preparation for some grim kind of dance; "which I meantersay, sir, as I would in preference have carried her to the church myself, along with three or four friendly ones wot come to it with willing harts and arms, but it were considered wot the neighbours would look down on such and would be of opinions as it were wanting in respect."

"Pocket-handkerchiefs out, all!" cried Mr. Trabb at this point, in a depressed business-like voice. "Pocket-handkerchiefs out! We are ready!"

So, we all put our pocket-handkerchiefs to our faces, as if our noses were bleeding; and filed out two and two; Joe and I; Biddy and Pumblechook; Mr. and Mrs. Hubble. The remains of my poor sister had been brought round by the kitchen door, and, it being a point of Undertaking ceremony that the six bearers must be stifled and blinded under a horrible black velvet housing with a white border, the whole looked like a blind monster with twelve human legs, shuffling and blundering along, under the guidance of two keepers—the postboy and his comrade.

The neighbourhood, however, highly approved of these arrangements, and we were much admired as we went through the village; the more youthful and vigorous part of the community making dashes now and then to cut us off, and lying in wait to intercept us at points of vantage. At such times the more exuberant among them called out in an excited manner on our emergence round some corner of expectancy, "*Here* they come!" "*Here* they are!" and we were all but cheered. In this progress I was much annoyed by the abject Pumblechook, who, being behind me, persisted all the way as a delicate attention in arranging my streaming hatband, and smoothing my cloak. My thoughts were further distracted by the excessive pride of Mr. and Mrs. Hubble, who were surpassingly conceited and vainglorious in being members of so distinguished a procession.

And now, the range of marshes lay clear before us, with the sails of the ships on the river growing out of it; and we went into the churchyard, close to the graves of my unknown parents, Philip Pirrip, late of this parish, and Also Georgiana, Wife of the Above. And there, my sister was laid quietly in the earth while the larks sang high above it, and the light wind strewed it with beautiful shadows of clouds and trees.

Of the conduct of the worldly-minded Pumblechook while this was doing, I desire to say no more than that it was all addressed to me; and that even when those noble passages were read which remind humanity how it brought nothing into the world and can take nothing out, and how it fleeth like a shadow and never continueth long in one stay, I heard him cough a reservation of the case of a young gentleman who came unexpectedly into large property. When we got back, he had the hardihood to tell me that he wished my sister could have known I had done her so much honour, and to hint that she would have considered it reasonably purchased at the price of her death. After that, he drank all the rest of the sherry, and Mr. Hubble drank the port, and the two talked (which I have since observed to be customary in such cases) as if they were of quite another race from the deceased, and were notoriously immortal. Finally, he went away with Mr. and Mr. Hubble—to make an evening of it, I felt sure, and to tell the Jolly Bargemen that he was the founder of my fortunes and my earliest benefactor.

When they were all gone, and when Trabb and his men—but not his boy: I looked for him—had crammed their mummery into bags, and were gone too, the house felt wholesomer. Soon afterwards, Biddy, Joe, and I, had a cold dinner together; but we dined in the best parlour, not in the old kitchen, and Joe was so exceedingly particular what he did with his knife and fork and the salt-cellar and what not, that there was great restraint upon us. But after dinner, when I made him take his pipe, and when I had loitered with him about the forge, and when we sat down together on the great block of stone outside it, we got on better. I noticed that after the funeral Joe changed his clothes so far, as to make a compromise between his Sunday dress and working dress: in which the dear fellow looked natural, and like the Man he was.

He was very much pleased by my asking if I might sleep in my own little room, and I was pleased too; for, I felt that I had done rather a great thing in making the request. When the shadows of evening were closing in, I took an opportunity of getting into the garden with Biddy for a little talk.

"Biddy," said I, "I think you might have written to me about these sad matters."

"Do you, Mr. Pip?" said Biddy. "I should have written if I had thought that."

"Don't suppose that I mean to be unkind, Biddy, when I say I consider that you ought to have thought that."

"Do you, Mr. Pip?"

She was so quiet and had such an orderly, good, and pretty way with her, that I did not like the thought of making her cry again. After looking a little at her downcast eyes as she walked beside me, I gave up that point.

"I suppose it will be difficult for you to remain here now, Biddy dear?"

"Oh! I can't do so, Mr. Pip," said Biddy, in a tone of regret, but still of quiet conviction. "I have been speaking to Mrs. Hubble, and I am going to her to-morrow. I hope we shall be able to take some care of Mr. Gargery, together, until he settles down."

"How are you going to live, Biddy? If you want any mo——"

"How am I going to live?" repeated Biddy, striking in, with a momentary flush upon her face. "I'll tell you, Mr. Pip. I am going to try to get the place of mistress in the new school nearly finished here. I can be well recommended by all the neighbours, and I hope I can be industrious and patient, and teach myself while I teach others. You know, Mr. Pip," pursued Biddy, with a smile, as she raised her eyes to my face, "the new schools are not like the old, but I learnt a good deal from you after that time, and have had time since then to improve."

"I think you would always improve, Biddy, under any circumstances."

"Ah! Except in my bad side of human nature," murmured Biddy.

It was not so much a reproach, as an irresistible thinking aloud. Well! I thought I would give up that point too. So, I walked a little further with Biddy, looking silently at her downcast eyes.

"I have not heard the particulars of my sister's death, Biddy."

"They are very slight, poor thing. She had been in one of her bad states—though they had got better of late, rather than worse—for four days, when she came out of it in the evening, just at tea-time, and said quite plainly, 'Joe.' As she had never said any word for a long while, I ran and fetched in Mr. Gargery from the forge. She made signs to me that she wanted him to sit down close to her, and wanted me to put her arms around his neck. So I put them round his neck, and she laid her head down on his shoulder quite content and satisfied. And so she presently said 'Joe' again, and once 'Pardon,' and once 'Pip.' And so she never lifted her head up any more, and it was just an hour later when we laid it down on her own bed, because we found she was gone."

Biddy cried; the darkening garden, and the lane, and the stars that were coming out, were blurred in my own sight.

"Nothing was ever discovered, Biddy?"

"Nothing."

"Do you know what is become of Orlick?"

"I should think from the colour of his clothes that he is working in the quarries."

"Of course you have seen him then?—Why are you looking at that dark tree in the lane?"

"I saw him there, on the night she died."

"That was not the last time either, Biddy?"

"No; I have seen him there, since we have been walking here.—It is of no use," said Biddy, laying her hand upon my arm, as I was for running out, "you know I would not deceive you; he was not there a minute, and he is gone."

It revived my utmost indignation to find that she was still pursued by this fellow, and I felt inveterate against him. I told her so, and told her that I would spend any money or take any pains to drive him out of that country. By degrees she led me into more temperate talk, and she told me how Joe loved me, and how Joe never complained of anything—she didn't say, of me; she had no need; I knew what she meant—but ever did his duty in his way of life, with a strong hand, a quiet tongue, and a gentle heart.

"Indeed, it would be hard to say too much for him," said I; "and Biddy, we must often speak of these things, for of course I shall be often down here now. I am not going to leave poor Joe alone."

Biddy said never a single word.

"Biddy, don't you hear me?"

"Yes, Mr. Pip."

"Not to mention your calling me Mr. Pip—which appears to me to be in bad taste, Biddy—what do you mean?"

"What do I mean?" asked Biddy, timidly.

"Biddy," said I, in a virtuously self-asserting manner, "I must request to know what you mean by this?"

"By this?" said Biddy.

"Now, don't echo," I retorted. "You used not to echo, Biddy."

"Used not!" said Biddy. "O Mr. Pip! Used!"

Well! I rather thought I would give up that point too. After another silent turn in the garden, I fell back on the main position.

"Biddy," said I, "I made a remark respecting my coming down here often, to see Joe, which you received with a marked silence. Have the goodness, Biddy, to tell me why."

"Are you quite sure, then, that you WILL come to see him often?" asked Biddy, stopping in the narrow garden walk, and looking at me under the stars with a clear and honest eye.

"Oh dear me!" said I, as if I found myself compelled to give up Biddy in despair. "This really is a very bad side of human nature! Don't say any more, if you please, Biddy. This shocks me very much."

For which cogent reason I kept Biddy at a distance during supper, and, when I went up to my own old little room, took as stately a leave of her as I could, in my murmuring soul, deem reconcilable with the churchyard and the event of the day. As often as I was restless in the night, and that was every quarter of an hour, I reflected what an unkindness, what an injury, what an injustice, Biddy had done me.

Early in the morning, I was to go. Early in the morning, I was out, and, looking in, unseen, at one of the wooden windows of the forge. There I stood, for minutes, looking at Joe, already at work with a glow of health and strength upon his face that made it show as if the bright sun of the life in store for him were shining on it.

"Good-by, dear Joe!—No, don't wipe it off—for God's sake, give me your blackened hand!—I shall be down soon, and often."

"Never too soon, sir," said Joe, "and never too often, Pip!"

Biddy was waiting for me at the kitchen door, with a mug of new milk and a crust of bread. "Biddy," said I, when I gave her my hand at parting, "I am not angry, but I am hurt."

"No, don't be hurt," she pleaded quite pathetically; "let only me be hurt, if I have been ungenerous."

Once more, the mists were rising as I walked away. If they disclosed to me, as I suspect they did, that I should not come back, and that Biddy was quite right, all I can say is—they were quite right too.

[PART 22]

Chapter 36

Herbert and I went on from bad to worse, in the way of increasing our debts, looking into our affairs, leaving Margins, and the like exemplary transactions; and Time went on, whether or no, as he has a way of doing; and I came of age—in fulfilment of Herbert's prediction, that I should do so before I knew where I was.

Herbert himself had come of age, eight months before me. As he had nothing else than his majority to come into, the event did not make a profound sensation in Barnard's Inn. But we had looked forward to my one-and-twentieth birthday, with a crowd of speculations and anticipations, for we had both considered that my guardian could hardly help saying something definite on that occasion.

I had taken care to have it well understood in Little Britain, when my birthday was. On the day before it, I received an official note from Wemmick, informing me that Mr. Jaggers would be glad if I would call upon him at five in the afternoon of the auspicious day. This convinced us that something great was to happen, and threw me into an unusual flutter when I repaired to my guardian's office, a model of punctuality.

In the outer office Wemmick offered me his congratulations, and incidentally rubbed the side of his nose with a folded piece of tissue-paper that I liked the look of. But he said nothing respecting it, and motioned me with a nod into my guardian's room. It was November, and my guardian was standing before his fire leaning his back against the chimney-piece, with his hands under his coat-tails.

"Well, Pip," said he, "I must call you Mr. Pip to-day. Congratulations, Mr. Pip."

We shook hands—he was always a remarkably short shaker—and I thanked him.

"Take a chair, Mr. Pip," said my guardian.

As I sat down, and he preserved his attitude and bent his brows at his boots, I felt at a disadvantage, which reminded me of that old time when I had been put upon a tombstone. The two ghastly casts on the shelf were not far from him, and their expression was as if they were making a stupid apoplectic attempt to attend to the conversation.

"Now my young friend," my guardian began, as if I were a witness in the box, "I am going to have a word or two with you."

"If you please, sir."

"What do you suppose," said Mr. Jaggers, bending forward to look at the ground, and then throwing his head back to look at the ceiling, "what do you suppose you are living at the rate of?"

"At the rate of, sir?"

"At," repeated Mr. Jaggers, still looking at the ceiling, "the—rate—of?" And then looked all round the room, and paused with his pocket-handkerchief in his hand, half way to his nose.

I had looked into my affairs so often, that I had thoroughly destroyed any slight notion I might ever have had of their bearings. Reluctantly, I confessed myself quite unable to answer the question. This reply seemed agreeable to Mr. Jaggers, who said, "I thought so!" and blew his nose with an air of satisfaction.

"Now, I have asked *you* a question, my friend," said Mr. Jaggers. "Have you anything to ask *me?*"

"Of course it would be a great relief to me to ask you several questions, sir; but I remember your prohibition."

"Ask one," said Mr. Jaggers.

"Is my benefactor to be made known to me to-day?"

"No. Ask another."

"Is that confidence to be imparted to me soon?"

"Waive that, a moment," said Mr. Jaggers, "and ask another."

I looked about me, but there appeared to be now no possible escape from the inquiry, "Have—I—anything to receive, sir?" On that, Mr. Jaggers said, triumphantly, "I thought we should come to it!" and called to Wemmick to give him that piece of paper. Wemmick appeared, handed it in, and disappeared.

"Now, Mr. Pip," said Mr. Jaggers, "attend, if you please. You have been drawing pretty freely here; your name occurs pretty often in Wemmick's cash-book; but you are in debt, of course?"

"I am afraid I must say yes, sir."

"You know you must say yes; don't you?" said Mr. Jaggers.

"Yes, sir."

"I don't ask you what you owe, because you don't know; and if you did know, you wouldn't tell me; you would say less. Yes, yes, my friend," cried Mr. Jaggers, waving his forefinger to stop me, as I made a show of protesting: "it's likely enough that you think you wouldn't, but you would. You'll excuse me, but I know better than you. Now, take this piece of paper in your hand. You have got it? Very good. Now, unfold it and tell me what it is."

"This is a bank-note," said I, "for five hundred pounds."

"That is a bank-note," repeated Mr. Jaggers, "for five hundred pounds. And a very handsome sum of money too, I think. You consider it so?"

"How could I do otherwise!"

"Ah! But answer the question," said Mr. Jaggers.

"Undoubtedly."

"You consider it, undoubtedly, a handsome sum of money. Now, that handsome sum of money, Pip, is your own. It is a present to you on this day, in earnest of your expectations. And at the rate of that handsome sum of money per annum, and at no higher rate, you are to live until the donor of the whole appears. That is to say, you will now take your money affairs entirely into your own hands, and you will draw from Wemmick one hundred and twenty-five pounds per quarter, until you are in communication with the fountainhead, and no longer with the mere agent. As I have told you before, I am the mere agent. I execute my instructions, and I am paid for doing so. I think them injudicious, but I am not paid for giving any opinion on their merits."

I was beginning to express my gratitude to my benefactor for the great liberality with which I was treated, when Mr. Jaggers stopped me. "I am not paid, Pip," said he, coolly, "to carry your words to any one;" and then gathered up his coat-tails, as he had gathered up the subject, and stood frowning at his boots as if he suspected them of designs against him.

After a pause, I hinted:

"There was a question just now, Mr. Jaggers, which you desired me to waive for a moment. I hope I am doing nothing wrong in asking it again?"

"What is it?" said he.

I might have known that he would never help me out; but it took me aback to have to shape the question afresh, as if it were quite new. "Is it likely," I said, after hesitating, "that my patron, the fountainhead you have spoken of, Mr. Jaggers, will soon—" there I delicately stopped.

"Will soon what?" asked Mr. Jaggers. "That's no question as it stands, you know."

"Will soon come to London," said I, after casting about for a precise form of words, "or summon me anywhere else?"

"Now here," replied Mr. Jaggers, fixing me for the first time with his dark deep-set eyes, "we must revert to the evening when we first encountered one another in your village. What did I tell you then, Pip?"

"You told me, Mr. Jaggers, that it might be years hence when that person appeared."

"Just so," said Mr. Jaggers; "that's my answer."

As we looked full at one another, I felt my breath come quicker in my strong desire to get something out of him. And as I felt that it came quicker, and as I felt that he saw that it came quicker, I felt that I had less chance than ever of getting anything out of him.

"Do you suppose it will still be years hence, Mr. Jaggers?"

Mr. Jaggers shook his head—not in negativing the question, but in altogether negativing the notion that he could anyhow be got to answer it—and the two horrible casts of the twitched faces looked, when my eyes strayed up to them, as if they had come to a crisis in their suspended attention, and were going to sneeze.

"Come!" said Mr. Jaggers, warming the backs of his legs with the backs of his warmed hands, "I'll be plain with you, my friend Pip. That's a question I must not be asked. You'll understand that, better, when I tell you it's a question that might compromise *me*. Come! I'll go a little further with you; I'll say something more."

He bent down so low to frown at his boots, that he was able to rub the calves of his legs in the pause he made.

"When that person discloses," said Mr. Jaggers, straightening himself, "you and that person will settle your own affairs. When that person discloses, my part in this business will cease and determine. When that person discloses, it will not be necessary for me to know anything about it. And that's all I have got to say."

We looked at one another until I withdrew my eyes, and looked thoughtfully at the floor. From this last speech I derived the notion that Miss Havisham, for some reason or no reason, had not taken him into her confidence as to her designing me for Estella; that he resented this, and felt a jealousy about it; or that he really did object to that scheme, and would have nothing to do with it. When I raised my eyes again, I found that he had been shrewdly looking at me all the time, and was doing so still.

"If that is all you have to say, sir," I remarked, "there can be nothing left for me to say."

He nodded assent, and pulled out his thief-dreaded watch, and asked me where I was going to dine? I replied at my own chambers, with Herbert. As a necessary sequence, I asked him if he would favour us with his company, and he promptly accepted the invitation. But he insisted on walking home with me, in order that I might make no extra preparation for him, and first he had a letter or two to write, and (of course) had his hands to wash. So, I said I would go into the outer office and talk to Wemmick.

The fact was, that when the five hundred pounds had come into my pocket, a thought had come into my head which had been often there before; and it appeared to me that Wemmick was a good person to advise with, concerning such thought.

He had already locked up his safe, and made preparations for going home. He had left his desk, brought out his two greasy office candlesticks and stood them in line with the snuffers on a slab near the door, ready to be extinguished; he had raked his fire low, put his hat and great-coat ready, and was beating himself all over the chest with his safe-key, as an athletic exercise after business.

"Mr. Wemmick," said I, "I want to ask your opinion. I am very desirous to serve a friend."

Wemmick tightened his post-office and shook his head, as if his opinion were dead against any fatal weakness of that sort.

"This friend," I pursued, "is trying to get on in commercial life, but has no money, and finds it difficult and disheartening to make a beginning. Now, I want somehow to help him to a beginning."

"With money down?" said Wemmick, in a tone drier than any saw-dust.

"With *some* money down," I replied, for an uneasy remembrance shot across me of that symmetrical bundle of papers at home; "with *some* money down, and perhaps some anticipation of my expectations."

"Mr. Pip," said Wemmick, "I should like just to run over with you on my fingers, if you please, the names of the various bridges up as high as Chelsea Reach. Let's see; there's London, one; Southwark, two; Blackfriars, three; Waterloo, four; Westminster, five; Vauxhall, six." He had checked off each bridge in its turn, with the handle of his safe-key on the palm of his hand. "There's as many as six, you see, to choose from."

"I don't understand you," said I.

"Choose your bridge, Mr. Pip," returned Wemmick, "and take a walk upon your bridge, and pitch your money into the Thames over the centre arch of your bridge, and you know the end of it. Serve a friend with it, and you may know the end of it too—but it's a less pleasant and profitable end."

I could have posted a newspaper in his mouth, he made it so wide after saying this.

"This is very discouraging," said I.

"Meant to be so," said Wemmick.

"Then is it your opinion," I inquired, with some little indignation, "that a man should never——"

"——Invest portable property in a friend?" said Wemmick. "Certainly he should not. Unless he wants to get rid of the friend—and then it becomes a question how much portable property it may be worth to get rid of him."

"And that," said I, "is your deliberate opinion, Mr. Wemmick?"

"That," he returned, "is my deliberate opinion in this office."

"Ah!" said I, pressing him, for I thought I saw him near a loophole here; "but would that be your opinion at Walworth?"

"Mr. Pip," he replied, with gravity, "Walworth is one place, and this office is another. Much as the Aged is one person, and Mr. Jaggers is another. They must not be confounded together. My Walworth sentiments must be taken at Walworth; none but my official sentiments can be taken in this office."

"Very well," said I, much relieved, "then I shall look you up at Walworth, you may depend upon it."

"Mr. Pip," he returned, "you will be welcome there, in a private and personal capacity."

We had held this conversation in a low voice, well knowing my guardian's ears to be the sharpest of the sharp. As he now appeared in his doorway, towelling his hands, Wemmick got on his great-coat and stood by to snuff out the candles. We all three went into the street together, and from the door-step Wemmick turned his way, and Mr. Jaggers and I turned ours.

I could not help wishing more than once that evening, that Mr. Jaggers had had an Aged in Gerrard-street, or a Stinger, or a Something, or a Somebody, to unbend his brows a little. It was an uncomfortable consideration on a twenty-first birthday, that coming of age at all seemed hardly worth while in such a guarded and suspicious world as he made of it. He was a thousand times better informed and cleverer than Wemmick, and yet I would a thousand times rather have had Wemmick to dinner. And Mr. Jaggers made not me alone intensely melancholy, because, after he was gone, Herbert said of himself, with his eyes fixed on the fire, that he thought he must have committed a felony and forgotten the details of it, he felt so dejected and guilty.

Chapter 37

Deeming Sunday the best day for taking Mr. Wemmick's Walworth sentiments, I devoted the next ensuing Sunday afternoon to a pilgrimage to the Castle. On arriving before the battlements, I found the Union Jack flying and the drawbridge up; but undeterred by this show of defiance and resistance, I rang at the gate, and was admitted in a most pacific manner by the Aged.

"My son, sir," said the old man, after securing the drawbridge, "rather had it in his mind that you might happen to drop in, and he left word that he would soon be home from his afternoon's walk. He is very regular in his walks, is my son. Very regular in everything, is my son."

I nodded at the old gentleman as Wemmick himself might have nodded, and we went in and sat down by the fireside.

"You made acquaintance with my son, sir," said the old man, in his chirping way, while he warmed his hands at the blaze, "at his office, I expect?" I nodded. "Hah! I have heerd that my son is a wonderful hand at his business, sir?" I nodded hard. "Yes; so they tell me. His business is the Law?" I nodded harder. "Which makes it more surprising in my son," said the old man, "for he was not brought up to the Law, but to the Wine-Coopering."°

Curious to know how the old gentleman stood informed concerning the reputation of Mr. Jaggers, I roared that name at him. He threw me into the greatest confusion by laughing heartily and replying in a very sprightly manner, "No, to be sure; you're right." And to this hour I have not the faintest notion what he meant, or what joke he thought I had made.

As I could not sit there nodding at him perpetually, without making some other attempt to interest him, I shouted an inquiry whether his own calling in life had been "the Wine-Coopering." By dint of straining that term out of myself several times and tapping the old

Wine-Coopering: Maker of wine barrels.

gentleman on the chest to associate it with him, I at last succeeded in making my meaning understood.

"No," said the old gentleman; "the warehousing, the warehousing. First, over yonder;" he appeared to mean up the chimney, but I believe he intended to refer me to Liverpool; "and then in the City of London here. However, having an infirmity—for I am hard of hearing, sir——"

I expressed in pantomime the greatest astonishment.

"—Yes, hard of hearing; having the infirmity coming upon me, my son he went into the Law, and he took charge of me, and he by little and little made out this elegant and beautiful property. But returning to what you said, you know," pursued the old man, again laughing heartily, "what I say is, No to be sure; you're right."

I was modestly wondering whether my utmost ingenuity would have enabled me to say anything that would have amused him half as much as this imaginary pleasantry, when I was startled by a sudden click in the wall on one side of the chimney, and the ghostly tumbling open of a little wooden flap with "JOHN" upon it. The old man, following my eyes, cried with great triumph, "My son's come home!" and we both went out to the drawbridge.

It was worth any money to see Wemmick waving a salute to me from the other side of the moat, when we might have shaken hands across it with the greatest ease. The Aged was so delighted to work the drawbridge, that I made no offer to assist him, but stood quiet until Wemmick had come across, and had presented me to Miss Skiffins: a lady by whom he was accompanied.

Miss Skiffins was of a wooden appearance, and was, like her escort, in the post-office branch of the service. She might have been some two or three years younger than Wemmick, and I judged her to stand possessed of portable property. The cut of her dress from the waist upward, both before and behind, made her figure very like a boy's kite; and I might have pronounced her gown a little too decidedly orange, and her gloves a little too intensely green. But she seemed to be a good sort of fellow, and showed a high regard for the Aged. I was not long in discovering that she was a frequent visitor at the Castle; for, on our going in, and my complimenting Wemmick on his ingenious contrivance for announcing himself to the Aged, he begged me to give my attention for a moment to the other side of the chimney, and disappeared. Presently another click came, and another little door tumbled open with "Miss Skiffins" on it; then Miss Skiffins shut up and John tumbled open; then Miss Skiffins and John both tumbled open together, and finally shut up together. On

Wemmick's return from working these mechanical appliances, I expressed the great admiration with which I regarded them, and he said, "Well, you know, they're both pleasant and useful to the Aged. And by George, sir, it's a thing worth mentioning, that of all the people who come to this gate, the secret of those pulls is only known to the Aged, Miss Skiffins, and me!"

"And Mr. Wemmick made them," added Miss Skiffins, "with his own hands out of his own head."

While Miss Skiffins was taking off her bonnet (she retained her green gloves during the evening as an outward and visible sign that there was company), Wemmick invited me to take a walk with him round the property, and see how the island looked in winter-time. Thinking that he did this to give me an opportunity of taking his Walworth sentiments, I seized the opportunity as soon as we were out of the Castle.

Having thought of the matter with care, I approached my subject as if I had never hinted at it before. I informed Wemmick that I was anxious in behalf of Herbert Pocket, and I told him how we had first met, and how we had fought. I glanced at Herbert's home, and at his character, and at his having no means but such as he was dependent on his father for: those, uncertain and unpunctual. I alluded to the advantages I had derived in my first rawness and ignorance from his society, and I confessed that I feared I had but ill repaid them, and that he might have done better without me and my expectations. Keeping Miss Havisham in the background at a great distance, I still hinted at the possibility of my having competed with him in his prospects, and at the certainty of his possessing a generous soul, and being far above any mean distrusts, retaliations, or designs. For all these reasons (I told Wemmick), and because he was my young companion and friend, and I had a great affection for him, I wished my own good fortune to reflect some rays upon him, and therefore I sought advice from Wemmick's experience and knowledge of men and affairs, how I could best try with my resources to help Herbert to some present income—say of a hundred a year, to keep him in good hope and heart—and gradually to buy him on to some small partnership. I begged Wemmick, in conclusion, to understand that my help must always be rendered without Herbert's knowledge or suspicion, and that there was no one else in the world with whom I could advise. I wound up by laying my hand upon his shoulder, and saying, "I can't help confiding in you, though I know it must be troublesome to you; but that is your fault, in having ever brought me here."

Wemmick was silent for a little while, and then said with a kind of start, "Well you know, Mr. Pip, I must tell you one thing. This is devilish good of you."

"Say you'll help me to be good then," said I.

"Ecod,"° replied Wemmick, shaking his head, "that's not my trade."

"Nor is this your trading-place," said I.

"You are right," he returned. "You hit the nail on the head. Mr. Pip, I'll put on my considering-cap, and I think all you want to do, may be done by degrees. Skiffins (that's her brother) is an accountant and agent. I'll look him up and go to work for you."

"I thank you ten thousand times."

"On the contrary," said he, "I thank you, for though we are strictly in our private and personal capacity, still it may be mentioned that there *are* Newgate cobwebs about, and it brushes them away."

After a little further conversation to the same effect, we returned into the Castle where we found Miss Skiffins preparing tea. The responsible duty of making the toast was delegated to the Aged, and that excellent old gentleman was so intent upon it that he seemed to me in some danger of melting his eyes. It was no nominal meal that we were going to make, but a vigorous reality. The Aged prepared such a haystack of buttered toast, that I could scarcely see him over it as it simmered on an iron stand hooked on to the top-bar; while Miss Skiffins brewed such a jorum of tea, that the pig in the back premises became strongly excited, and repeatedly expressed his desire to participate in the entertainment.

The flag had been struck, and the gun had been fired, at the right moment of time, and I felt as snugly cut off from the rest of Walworth as if the moat were thirty feet wide by as many deep. Nothing disturbed the tranquillity of the Castle, but the occasional tumbling open of John and Miss Skiffins: which little doors were a prey to some spasmodic infirmity that made me sympathetically uncomfortable until I got used to it. I inferred from the methodical nature of Miss Skiffins's arrangements that she made tea there every Sunday night; and I rather suspected that a classic brooch she wore, representing the profile of an undesirable female with a very straight nose and a very new moon, was a piece of portable property that had been given her by Wemmick.

We ate the whole of the toast, and drank tea in proportion, and it was delightful to see how warm and greasy we all got after it. The

---

Ecod: A mild oath ("egad" or "by god").

Aged especially, might have passed for some clean old chief of a savage tribe, just oiled. After a short pause of repose, Miss Skiffins—in the absence of the little servant who, it seemed, retired to the bosom of her family on Sunday afternoons—washed up the tea-things, in a trifling lady-like amateur manner that compromised none of us. Then, she put on her gloves again, and we drew round the fire, and Wemmick said, "Now Aged Parent, tip us the paper."

Wemmick explained to me while the Aged got his spectacles out, that this was according to custom, and that it gave the old gentleman infinite satisfaction to read the news aloud. "I won't offer an apology," said Wemmick, "for he isn't capable of many pleasures—are you, Aged P.?"

"All right, John, all right," returned the old man, seeing himself spoken to.

"Only tip him a nod every now and then when he looks off his paper," said Wemmick, "and he'll be as happy as a king. We are all attention, Aged One."

"All right, John, all right!" returned the cheerful old man: so busy and so pleased, that it really was quite charming.

The Aged's reading reminded me of the classes at Mr. Wopsle's great-aunt's, with the pleasanter peculiarity that it seemed to come through a keyhole. As he wanted the candles close to him, and as he was always on the verge of putting either his head or the newspaper into them, he required as much watching as a powder-mill. But Wemmick was equally untiring and gentle in his vigilance, and the Aged read on, quite unconscious of his many rescues. Whenever he looked at us, we all expressed the greatest interest and amazement, and nodded until he resumed again.

As Wemmick and Miss Skiffins sat side by side, and as I sat in a shadowy corner, I observed a slow and gradual elongation of Mr. Wemmick's mouth, powerfully suggestive of his slowly and gradually stealing his arm round Miss Skiffins's waist. In course of time I saw his hand appear on the other side of Miss Skiffins; but at that moment Miss Skiffins neatly stopped him with the green glove, unwound his arm again as if it were an article of dress, and with the greatest deliberation laid it on the table before her. Miss Skiffins's composure while she did this was one of the most remarkable sights I have ever seen, and if I could have thought the act consistent with abstraction of mind, I should have deemed that Miss Skiffins performed it mechanically.

By-and-by, I noticed Wemmick's arm beginning to disappear

again, and gradually fading out of view. Shortly afterwards, his mouth began to widen again. After an interval of suspense on my part that was quite enthralling and almost painful, I saw his hand appear on the other side of Miss Skiffins. Instantly, Miss Skiffins stopped it with the neatness of a placid boxer, took off that girdle or cestus° as before, and laid it on the table. Taking the table to represent the path of virtue, I am justified in stating that during the whole time of the Aged's reading, Wemmick's arm was straying from the path of virtue and being re-called to it by Miss Skiffins.

At last, the Aged read himself into a light slumber. This was the time for Wemmick to produce a little kettle, a tray of glasses, and a black bottle with a porcelain-topped cork, representing some clerical dignitary of a rubicund and social aspect. With the aid of these appliances we all had something warm to drink: including the Aged, who was soon awake again. Miss Skiffins mixed, and I observed that she and Wemmick drank out of one glass. Of course I knew better than to offer to see Miss Skiffins home, and under the circumstances I thought I had best go first: which I did, taking a cordial leave of the Aged, and having passed a pleasant evening.

Before a week was out, I received a note from Wemmick, dated Walworth, stating that he hoped he had made some advance in that matter appertaining to our private and personal capacities, and that he would be glad if I could come and see him again upon it. So, I went out to Walworth again, and yet again, and yet again, and I saw him by appointment in the City several times, but never held any communication with him on the subject in or near Little Britain. The upshot was, that we found a worthy young merchant or shipping-broker, not long established in business, who wanted intelligent help, and who wanted capital, and who in due course of time and receipt would want a part-ner. Between him and me, secret articles were signed of which Herbert was the subject, and I paid him half of my five hundred pounds down, and engaged for sundry other payments: some, to fall due at certain dates out of my income: some, contingent on my coming into my property. Miss Skiffins's brother conducted the negotiation. Wemmick pervaded it throughout, but never appeared in it.

The whole business was so cleverly managed, that Herbert had not the least suspicion of my hand being in it. I never shall forget the radi-ant face with which he came home one afternoon, and told me, as a

cestus: A belt or girdle, often specifically that worn by a bride or by Venus; alternatively, the heavy leather hand-covering or glove worn by boxers.

mighty piece of news, of his having fallen in with one Clarriker (the young merchant's name), and of Clarriker's having shown an extraordinary inclination towards him, and of his belief that the opening had come at last. Day by day as his hopes grew stronger and his face brighter, he must have thought me a more and more affectionate friend, for I had the greatest difficulty in restraining my tears of triumph when I saw him so happy. At length, the thing being done, and he having that day entered Clarriker's House, and he having talked to me for a whole evening in a flush of pleasure and success, I did really cry in good earnest when I went to bed, to think that my expectations had done some good to somebody.

A great event in my life, the turning point of my life, now opens on my view. But, before I proceed to narrate it, and before I pass on to all the changes it involved, I must give one chapter to Estella. It is not much to give to the theme that so long filled my heart.

[PART 23]

Chapter 38

If that staid old house near the Green at Richmond should ever come to be haunted when I am dead, it will be haunted, surely, by my ghost. O the many, many nights and days through which the unquiet spirit within me haunted that house when Estella lived there! Let my body be where it would, my spirit was always wandering, wandering, wandering, about that house.

The lady with whom Estella was placed, Mrs. Brandley by name, was a widow, with one daughter several years older than Estella. The mother looked young, and the daughter looked old; the mother's complexion was pink, and the daughter's was yellow; the mother set up for frivolity, and the daughter for theology. They were in what is called a good position, and visited, and were visited by, numbers of people. Little, if any, community of feeling subsisted between them and Estella, but the understanding was established that they were necessary to her, and that she was necessary to them. Mrs. Brandley had been a friend of Miss Havisham's before the time of her seclusion.

In Mrs. Brandley's house and out of Mrs. Brandley's house, I suffered every kind and degree of torture that Estella could cause me. The nature of my relations with her, which placed me on terms of familiarity without placing me on terms of favour, conduced to my distraction. She made use of me to tease other admirers, and she turned the very familiarity between herself and me, to the account of putting a constant slight on my devotion to her. If I had been her secretary, steward, half-brother, poor relation—if I had been a younger brother of her appointed husband—I could not have seemed to myself, further from my hopes when I was nearest to her. The privilege of calling her by her name and hearing her call me by mine, became under the circumstances an aggravation of my trials; and while I think it likely that it almost maddened her other lovers, I know too certainly that it almost maddened me.

She had admirers without end. No doubt my jealousy made an admirer of every one who went near her; but there were more than enough of them without that.

I saw her often at Richmond, I heard of her often in town, and I used often to take her and the Brandleys on the water; there were picnics, fête days, plays, operas, concerts, parties, all sorts of pleasures, through which I pursued her—and they were all miseries to me. I never had one hour's happiness in her society, and yet my mind all round the four-and-twenty hours was harping on the happiness of having her with me unto death.

Throughout this part of our intercourse—and it lasted, as will presently be seen, for what I then thought a long time—she habitually reverted to that tone which expressed that our association was forced upon us. There were other times when she would come to a sudden check in this tone and in all her many tones, and would seem to pity me.

"Pip, Pip," she said one evening, coming to such a check, when we sat apart at a darkening window of the house in Richmond; "will you never take warning?"

"Of what?"

"Of me."

"Warning not to be attracted by you, do you mean, Estella?"

"Do I mean! If you don't know what I mean, you are blind."

I should have replied that Love was commonly reputed blind, but for the reason that I always was restrained—and this was not the least of my miseries—by a feeling that it was ungenerous to press myself upon her, when she knew that she could not choose but obey Miss Havisham. My dread always was, that this knowledge on her part laid me under a heavy disadvantage with her pride, and made me the subject of a rebellious struggle in her bosom.

"At any rate," said I, "I have no warning given me just now, for you wrote to me to come to you, this time."

"That's true," said Estella, with a cold careless smile that always chilled me.

After looking at the twilight without, for a little while, she went on to say:

"The time has come round when Miss Havisham wishes to have me for a day at Satis. You are to take me there, and bring me back, if you will. She would rather I did not travel alone, and objects to receiving my maid, for she has a sensitive horror of being talked of by such people. Can you take me?"

"Can I take you, Estella!"

"You can then? The day after to-morrow, if you please. You are to pay all charges out of my purse. You hear the condition of your going?"

"And must obey," said I.

This was all the preparation I received for that visit, or for others like it: Miss Havisham never wrote to me, nor had I ever so much as seen her handwriting. We went down on the next day but one, and we found her in the room where I had first beheld her, and it is needless to add that there was no change in Satis House.

She was even more dreadfully fond of Estella than she had been when I last saw them together; I repeat the word advisedly, for there was something positively dreadful in the energy of her looks and embraces. She hung upon Estella's beauty, hung upon her words, hung upon her gestures, and sat mumbling her own trembling fingers while she looked at her, as though she were devouring the beautiful creature she had reared.

From Estella she looked at me, with a searching glance that seemed to pry into my heart and probe its wounds. "How does she use you, Pip; how does she use you?" she asked me again, with her witch-like eagerness, even in Estella's hearing. But, when we sat by her flickering fire at night, she was most weird; for then, keeping Estella's hand drawn through her arm and clutched in her own hand, she extorted from her, by dint of referring back to what Estella had told her in her regular letters, the names and conditions of the men whom she had fascinated; and as Miss Havisham dwelt upon this roll, with the intensity of a mind mortally hurt and diseased, she sat with her other hand on her crutch stick, and her chin on that, and her wan bright eyes glaring at me, a very spectre.

I saw in this, wretched though it made me, and bitter the sense of dependence and even of degradation that it awakened—I saw in this, that Estella was set to wreak Miss Havisham's revenge on men, and that she was not to be given to me until she had gratified it for a term. I saw in this, a reason for her being beforehand assigned to me. Sending her out to attract and torment and do mischief, Miss Havisham sent her with the malicious assurance that she was beyond the reach of all admirers, and that all who staked upon that cast were secured to lose. I saw in this, that I, too, was tormented by a perversion of ingenuity, even while the prize was reserved for me. I saw in this, the reason for my being staved off so long, and the reason for my late guardian's declining to commit himself to the formal knowledge of such a scheme. In a word, I saw in this, Miss Havisham as I had her then and there before my eyes, and always had had her before my eyes; and I saw in this, the distinct shadow of the darkened and unhealthy house in which her life was hidden from the sun.

The candles that lighted that room of hers were placed in sconces on the wall. They were high from the ground, and they burnt with the steady dulness of artificial light in air that is seldom renewed. As I looked round at them, and at the pale gloom they made, and at the stopped clock, and at the withered articles of bridal dress upon the table and the ground, and at her own awful figure with its ghostly reflection thrown large by the fire upon the ceiling and the wall, I saw in everything the construction that my mind had come to, repeated and thrown back to me. My thoughts passed into the great room across the landing where the table was spread, and I saw it written, as it were, in the falls of the cobwebs from the centre-piece, in the crawlings of the spiders on the cloth, in the tracks of the mice as they betook their little quickened hearts behind the panels, and in the gropings and pausings of the beetles on the floor.

It happened on the occasion of this visit that some sharp words arose between Estella and Miss Havisham. It was the first time I had ever seen them opposed.

We were seated by the fire, as just now described, and Miss Havisham still had Estella's arm drawn through her own, and still clutched Estella's hand in hers, when Estella gradually began to detach herself. She had shown a proud impatience more than once before, and had rather endured that fierce affection than accepted or returned it.

"What!" said Miss Havisham, flashing her eyes upon her, "are you tired of me?"

"Only a little tired of myself," replied Estella, disengaging her arm, and moving to the great chimney-piece, where she stood looking down at the fire.

"Speak the truth, you ingrate!" cried Miss Havisham, passionately striking her stick upon the floor; "you are tired of me."

Estella looked at her with perfect composure, and again looked down at the fire. Her graceful figure and her beautiful face expressed a self-possessed indifference to the wild heat of the other, that was almost cruel.

"You stock and stone!" exclaimed Miss Havisham. "You cold, cold heart!"

"What?" said Estella, preserving her attitude of indifference as she leaned against the great chimney-piece and only moving her eyes; "do you reproach me for being cold? You?"

"Are you not?" was the fierce retort.

"You should know," said Estella. "I am what you have made me. Take all the praise, take all the blame; take all the success, take all the failure; in short, take me."

"O, look at her, look at her!" cried Miss Havisham, bitterly. "Look at her, so hard and thankless, on the hearth where she was reared! Where I took her into this wretched breast when it was first bleeding from its stabs, and where I have lavished years of tenderness upon her!"

"At least I was no party to the compact," said Estella, "for if I could walk and speak, when it was made, it was as much as I could do. But what would you have? You have been very good to me, and I owe everything to you. What would you have?"

"Love," replied the other.

"You have it."

"I have not," said Miss Havisham.

"Mother by adoption," retorted Estella, never departing from the easy grace of her attitude, never raising her voice as the other did, never yielding either to anger or tenderness, "Mother by adoption, I have said I owe everything to you. All I possess is freely yours. All that you have given me, is at your command to have again. Beyond that, I have nothing. And if you ask me to give you what you never gave me, my gratitude and duty cannot do impossibilities."

"Did I never give her, love!" cried Miss Havisham, turning wildly to me. "Did I never give her a burning love, inseparable from jealousy at all times, and from sharp pain, while she speaks thus to me! Let her call me mad, let her call me mad!"

"Why should I call you mad," returned Estella, "I, of all people? Does any one live, who knows what set purposes you have, half as well as I do? Does any one live, who knows what a steady memory you have, half as well as I do? I who have sat on this same hearth on the little stool that is even now beside you there, learning your lessons and looking up into your face, when your face was strange and frightened me!"

"Soon forgotten!" moaned Miss Havisham. "Times soon forgotten!"

"No, not forgotten," retorted Estella. "Not forgotten, but treasured up in my memory. When have you found me false to your teaching? When have you found me unmindful of your lessons? When have you found me giving admission here," she touched her bosom with her hand, "to anything that you excluded? Be just to me."

"So proud, so proud!" moaned Miss Havisham, pushing away her grey hair with both her hands.

"Who taught me to be proud?" returned Estella. "Who praised me when I learnt my lesson?"

"So hard, so hard!" moaned Miss Havisham, with her former action.

"Who taught me to be hard?" returned Estella. "Who praised me when I learnt my lesson?"

"But to be proud and hard to *me!*" Miss Havisham quite shrieked, as she stretched out her arms. "Estella, Estella, Estella, to be proud and hard to *me!*"

Estella looked at her for a moment with a kind of calm wonder, but was not otherwise disturbed; when the moment was past, she looked down at the fire again.

"I cannot think," said Estella, raising her eyes after a silence, "why you should be so unreasonable when I come to see you after a separation. I have never forgotten your wrongs and their causes. I have never been unfaithful to you or your schooling. I have never shown any weakness that I can charge myself with."

"Would it be weakness to return my love?" exclaimed Miss Havisham. "But yes, yes, she would call it so!"

"I begin to think," said Estella, in a musing way, after another moment of calm wonder, "that I almost understand how this comes about. If you had brought up your adopted daughter wholly in the dark confinement of these rooms, and had never let her know that there was such a thing as the daylight by which she has never once seen your face—if you had done that, and then, for a purpose had wanted her to understand the daylight and know all about it, you would have been disappointed and angry?"

Miss Havisham, with her head in her hands, sat making a low moaning, and swaying herself on her chair, but gave no answer.

"Or," said Estella, "—which is a nearer case—if you had taught her, from the dawn of her intelligence, with your utmost energy and might, that there was such a thing as daylight, but that it was made to be her enemy and destroyer, and she must always turn against it, for it had blighted you and would else blight her;—if you had done this, and then, for a purpose, had wanted her to take naturally to the daylight and she could not do it, you would have been disappointed and angry?"

Miss Havisham sat listening (or it seemed so, for I could not see her face), but still made no answer.

"So," said Estella, "I must be taken as I have been made. The success is not mine, the failure is not mine, but the two together make me."

Miss Havisham had settled down, I hardly knew how, upon the floor, among the faded bridal relics with which it was strewn. I took advantage of the moment—I had sought one from the first—to leave the room, after beseeching Estella's attention to her, with a movement of my hand. When I left, Estella was yet standing by the great chimney-piece, just as she had stood throughout. Miss Havisham's grey hair was all adrift upon the ground, among the other bridal wrecks, and was a miserable sight to see.

It was with a depressed heart that I walked in the starlight for an hour and more, about the court-yard, and about the brewery, and about the ruined garden. When I at last took courage to return to the room, I found Estella sitting at Miss Havisham's knee, taking up some stitches in one of those old articles of dress that were dropping to pieces, and of which I have often been reminded since by the faded tatters of old banners that I have seen hanging up in cathedrals. Afterwards, Estella and I played cards, as of yore—only we were skilful now, and played French games—and so the evening wore away, and I went to bed.

I lay in that separate building across the court-yard. It was the first time I had ever lain down to rest in Satis House, and sleep refused to come near me. A thousand Miss Havishams haunted me. She was on this side of my pillow, on that, at the head of the bed, at the foot, behind the half-opened door of the dressing-room, in the dressing-room, in the room overhead, in the room beneath—everywhere. At last, when the night was slow to creep on towards two o'clock, I felt that I absolutely could no longer bear the place as a place to lie down in, and that I must get up. I therefore got up and put on my clothes, and went out across the yard into the long stone passage, designing to gain the outer court-yard and walk there for the relief of my mind. But, I was no sooner in the passage than I extinguished my candle; for, I saw Miss Havisham going along it in a ghostly manner, making a low cry. I followed her at a distance, and saw her go up the staircase. She carried a bare candle in her hand, which she had probably taken from one of the sconces in her own room, and was a most unearthly object by its light. Standing at the bottom of the staircase, I felt the mildewed air of the feast-chamber, without seeing her open the door, and I heard her walking there, and so across into her own room, and so across again into that, never ceasing the low cry. After a time, I tried in the dark both to get out, and to go back, but I could do neither until some streaks of day strayed in and showed me where to lay my hands. During the whole interval, whenever I went to the bottom of the staircase, I heard her footstep, saw her light pass above, and heard her ceaseless low cry.

Before we left next day, there was no revival of the difference between her and Estella, nor was it ever revived on any similar occasion; and there were four similar occasions, to the best of my remembrance. Nor, did Miss Havisham's manner towards Estella in anywise change, except that I believed it to have something like fear infused among its former characteristics.

It is impossible to turn this leaf of my life, without putting Bentley Drummle's name upon it; or I would, very gladly.

On a certain occasion when the Finches were assembled in force, and when good feeling was being promoted in the usual manner by nobody's agreeing with anybody else, the presiding Finch called the Grove to order, forasmuch as Mr. Drummle had not yet toasted a lady; which, according to the solemn constitution of the society, it was the brute's turn to do that day. I thought I saw him leer in an ugly way at me while the decanters were going round, but as there was no love lost between us, that might easily be. What was my indignant surprise when he called upon the company to pledge him to "Estella"!

"Estella who?" said I.

"Never you mind," retorted Drummle.

"Estella of where?" said I. "You are bound to say of where." Which he was, as a Finch.

"Of Richmond, gentlemen," said Drummle, putting me out of the question, "and a peerless beauty."

Much he knew about peerless beauties, a mean miserable idiot! I whispered Herbert.

"I know that lady," said Herbert, across the table, when the toast had been honoured.

"*Do* you?" said Drummle.

"And so do I," I added, with a scarlet face.

"*Do* you?" said Drummle. "*Oh*, Lord!"

This was the only retort—except glass or crockery—that the heavy creature was capable of making; but, I became as highly incensed by it as if it had been barbed with wit, and I immediately rose in my place and said that I could not but regard it as being like the honourable Finch's impudence to come down to that Grove—we always talked about coming down to that Grove, as a neat Parliamentary turn of expression—down to that Grove, proposing a lady of whom he knew nothing. Mr. Drummle upon this, starting up, demanded what I meant by that? Whereupon, I made him the extreme reply that I believed he knew where I was to be found.

Whether it was possible in a Christian country to get on without blood, after this, was a question on which the Finches were divided. The debate upon it grew so lively, indeed, that at least six more honourable members told six more, during the discussion, that they believed *they* knew where *they* were to be found. However, it was decided at last (the Grove being a Court of Honour) that if Mr. Drummle would bring never so slight a certificate from the lady, importing that he had the honour of her acquaintance, Mr. Pip must express his regret, as a gentleman and a Finch, for "having been betrayed into a warmth which." Next day was appointed for the production (lest our honour should take cold from delay), and next day Drummle appeared with a polite little avowal in Estella's hand, that she had had the honour of dancing with him several times. This left me no course but to regret that I had been "betrayed into a warmth which," and on the whole to repudiate, as untenable, the idea that I was to be found anywhere. Drummle and I then sat snorting at one another for an hour, while the Grove engaged in indiscriminate contradiction, and finally the promotion of good feeling was declared to have gone ahead at an amazing rate.

I tell it lightly, but it was no light thing to me. For, I cannot adequately express what pain it gave me to think that Estella should show any favour to a contemptible, clumsy, sulky booby, so very far below the average. To the present moment, I believe it to have been referable to some pure fire of generosity and disinterestedness in my love for her, that I could not endure the thought of her stooping to that hound. No doubt I should have been miserable whomsoever she had favoured; but a worthier object would have caused me a different kind and degree of distress.

It was easy for me to find out, and I did soon find out, that Drummle had begun to follow her closely, and that she allowed him to do it. A little while, and he was always in pursuit of her, and he and I crossed one another every day. He held on, in a dull persistent way, and Estella held him on; now with encouragement, now with discouragement, now almost flattering him, now openly despising him, now knowing him very well, now scarcely remembering who he was.

The Spider, as Mr. Jaggers had called him, was used to lying in wait, however, and had the patience of his tribe. Added to that, he had a blockhead confidence in his money and in his family greatness, which sometimes did him good service—almost taking the place of concentration and determined purpose. So, the Spider, doggedly watching Estella, outwatched many brighter insects, and would often uncoil himself and drop at the right nick of time.

At a certain Assembly Ball° at Richmond (there used to be Assembly Balls at most places then), where Estella had outshone all other beauties, this blundering Drummle so hung about her, and with so much toleration on her part, that I resolved to speak to her concerning him. I took the next opportunity: which was when she was waiting for Mrs. Brandley to take her home, and was sitting apart among some flowers, ready to go. I was with her, for I almost always accompanied them to and from such places.

"Are you tired, Estella?"

"Rather, Pip."

"You should be."

"Say rather, I should not be; for I have my letter to Satis House to write, before I go to sleep."

"Recounting to-night's triumph?" said I. "Surely a very poor one, Estella."

"What do you mean? I didn't know there had been any."

"Estella," said I, "do look at that fellow in the corner yonder, who is looking over here at us."

"Why should I look at him?" returned Estella, with her eyes on me instead. "What is there in that fellow in the corner yonder—to use your words—that I need look at?"

Assembly Ball: Fashionable ball held in a public room of, for example, an inn.

"Indeed, that is the very question I want to ask you," said I. "For he has been hovering about you all night."

"Moths, and all sorts of ugly creatures," replied Estella, with a glance towards him, "hover about a lighted candle. Can the candle help it?"

"No," I returned; "but cannot the Estella help it?"

"Well!" said she, laughing, after a moment, "perhaps. Yes. Anything you like."

"But, Estella, do hear me speak. It makes me wretched that you should encourage a man so generally despised as Drummle. You know he is despised."

"Well?" said she.

"You know he is as ungainly within, as without. A deficient, ill-tempered, lowering, stupid fellow."

"Well?" said she.

"You know he has nothing to recommend him but money, and a ridiculous roll of addle-headed predecessors; now, don't you?"

"Well?" said she again; and each time she said it, she opened her lovely eyes the wider.

To overcome the difficulty of getting past that monosyllable, I took it from her, and said, repeating it with emphasis, "Well! Then, that is why it makes me wretched."

Now, if I could have believed that she favoured Drummle with any idea of making me—me—wretched, I should have been in better heart about it; but in that habitual way of hers, she put me so entirely out of the question, that I could believe nothing of the kind.

"Pip," said Estella, casting her glance over the room, "don't be foolish about its effect on you. It may have its effect on others, and may be meant to have. It's not worth discussing."

"Yes it is," said I, "because I cannot bear that people should say, 'she throws away her graces and attractions on a mere boor, the lowest in the crowd.'"

"I can bear it," said Estella.

"Oh! don't be so proud, Estella, and so inflexible."

"Calls me proud and inflexible in this breath!" said Estella, opening her hands. "And in his last breath reproached me for stooping to a boor!"

"There is no doubt you do," said I, something hurriedly, "for I have seen you give him looks and smiles this very night, such as you never give to—me."

"Do you want me then," said Estella, turning suddenly with a fixed and serious, if not angry, look, "to deceive and entrap you?"

"Do you deceive and entrap him, Estella?"

"Yes, and many others—all of them but you. Here is Mrs. Brandley. I'll say no more."

And now that I have given the one chapter to the theme that so filled my heart, and so often made it ache and ache again, I pass on, unhindered, to the event that had impended over me longer yet; the event that had begun to be prepared for, before I knew that the world held Estella, and in the days when her baby intelligence was receiving its first distortions from Miss Havisham's wasting hands.

In the Eastern story,° the heavy slab that was to fall on the bed of state in the flush of conquest was slowly wrought out of the quarry, the tunnel for the rope to hold it in its place was slowly carried through the leagues of rock, the slab was slowly raised and fitted in the roof, the rope was rove to it and slowly taken through the miles of hollow to the great iron ring. All being made ready with much labour, and the hour come, the sultan was aroused in the dead of the night, and the sharpened axe that was to sever the rope from the great iron ring was put into his hand, and he struck with it, and the rope parted and rushed away, and the ceiling fell. So, in my case; all the work, near and afar, that tended to the end, had been accomplished; and in an instant the blow was struck, and the roof of my stronghold dropped upon me.

[PART 24]

Chapter 39

I was three-and-twenty years of age. Not another word had I heard to enlighten me on the subject of my expectations, and my twenty-third birthday was a week gone. We had left Barnard's Inn more than a year, and lived in the Temple.° Our chambers were in Garden-court, down by the river.

Mr. Pocket and I had for some time parted company as to our

Eastern story: From "The Enchanter, or the Sultan of Misnar," *Tales of the Genii* (1764), by James Ridley.   **the Temple:** A group of buildings, housing residences and legal chambers, between the Thames and Fleet Street.

original relations, though we continued on the best terms. Notwithstanding my inability to settle to anything—which I hope arose out of the restless and incomplete tenure on which I held my means—I had a taste for reading, and read regularly so many hours a day. That matter of Herbert's was still progressing, and everything with me was as I have brought it down to the close of the last chapter.

Business had taken Herbert on a journey to Marseilles. I was alone, and had a dull sense of being alone. Dispirited and anxious, long hoping that to-morrow or next week would clear my way, and long disappointed, I sadly missed the cheerful face and ready response of my friend.

It was wretched weather; stormy and wet, stormy and wet; and mud, mud, mud, deep in all the streets. Day after day, a vast heavy veil had been driving over London from the East, and it drove still, as if in the East there were an Eternity of cloud and wind. So furious had been the gusts, that high buildings in town had had the lead stripped off their roofs; and in the country, trees had been torn up, and sails of windmills carried away; and gloomy accounts had come in from the coast, of shipwreck and death. Violent blasts of rain had accompanied these rages of wind, and the day just closed as I sat down to read had been the worst of all.

Alterations have been made in that part of the Temple since that time, and it has not now so lonely a character as it had then, nor is it so exposed to the river. We lived at the top of the last house, and the wind rushing up the river shook the house that night, like discharges of cannon, or breakings of a sea. When the rain came with it and dashed against the windows, I thought, raising my eyes to them as they rocked, that I might have fancied myself in a storm-beaten lighthouse. Occasionally, the smoke came rolling down the chimney as though it could not bear to go out into such a night; and when I set the doors open and looked down the staircase, the staircase lamps were blown out; and when I shaded my face with my hands and looked through the black windows (opening them ever so little, was out of the question in the teeth of such wind and rain) I saw that the lamps in the court were blown out, and that the lamps on the bridges and the shore were shuddering, and that the coal fires in barges on the river were being carried away before the wind like red-hot splashes in the rain.

I read with my watch upon the table, purposing to close my book at eleven o'clock. As I shut it, Saint Paul's, and all the many church-clocks in the City—some leading, some accompanying, some following—struck that hour. The sound was curiously flawed by the wind; and I was listening, and thinking how the wind assailed and tore it, when I heard a footstep on the stair.

What nervous folly made me start, and awfully connect it with the footstep of my dead sister, matters not. It was past in a moment, and I listened again, and heard the footstep stumble in coming on. Remembering then, that the staircase-lights were blown out, I took up my reading-lamp and went out to the stair-head. Whoever was below had stopped on seeing my lamp, for all was quiet.

"There is some one down there, is there not?" I called out, looking down.

"Yes," said a voice from the darkness beneath.

"What floor do you want?"

"The top. Mr. Pip."

"That is my name.—There is nothing the matter?"

"Nothing the matter," returned the voice. And the man came on.

I stood with my lamp held out over the stair-rail, and he came slowly within its light. It was a shaded lamp, to shine upon a book, and its circle of light was very contracted; so that he was in it for a mere instant, and then out of it. In the instant, I had seen a face that was strange to me, looking up with an incomprehensible air of being touched and pleased by the sight of me.

Moving the lamp as the man moved, I made out that he was substantially dressed, but roughly; like a voyager by sea. That he had long iron grey hair. That his age was about sixty. That he was a muscular man, strong on his legs, and that he was browned and hardened by exposure to weather. As he ascended the last stair or two, and the light of my lamp included us both, I saw, with a stupid kind of amazement, that he was holding out both his hands to me.

"Pray what is your business?" I asked him.

"My business?" he repeated, pausing. "Ah! Yes. I will explain my business, by your leave."

"Do you wish to come in?"

"Yes," he replied; "I wish to come in, Master."

I had asked him the question inhospitably enough, for I resented the sort of bright and gratified recognition that still shone in his face. I resented it, because it seemed to imply that he expected me to respond to it. But, I took him into the room I had just left, and, having set the lamp on the table, asked him as civilly as I could, to explain himself.

He looked about him with the strangest air—an air of wondering pleasure, as if he had some part in the things he admired—and he pulled off a rough outer coat, and his hat. Then, I saw that his head was furrowed and bald, and that the long iron grey hair grew only on its sides. But, I saw nothing that in the least explained him. On the contrary, I saw him next moment, once more holding out both his hands to me.

"What do you mean?" said I, half suspecting him to be mad.

He stopped in his looking at me, and slowly rubbed his right hand over his head. "It's disapinting to a man," he said, in a coarse broken voice, "arter having looked for'ard so distant, and come so fur; but you're not to blame for that—neither on us is to blame for that. I'll speak in half a minute. Give me half a minute, please."

He sat down on a chair that stood before the fire, and covered his forehead with his large brown veinous hands. I looked at him attentively then, and recoiled a little from him; but I did not know him.

"There's no one nigh," said he, looking over his shoulder; "is there?"

"Why do you, a stranger coming into my rooms at this time of the night, ask that question?" said I.

"You're a game one," he returned, shaking his head at me with a deliberate affection, at once most unintelligible and most exasperating; "I'm glad you've grow'd up, a game one! But don't catch hold of me. You'd be sorry arterwards to have done it."

I relinquished the intention he had detected, for I knew him! Even yet, I could not recal a single feature, but I knew him! If the wind and the rain had driven away the intervening years, had scattered all the intervening objects, had swept us to the churchyard where we first stood face to face on such different levels, I could not have known my convict more distinctly than I knew him now, as he sat in the chair before the fire. No need to take a file from his pocket and show it to me; no need to take the handkerchief from his neck and twist it round his head; no need to hug himself with both his arms, and take a shivering turn across the room, looking back at me for recognition. I knew him before he gave me one of those aids, though, a moment before, I had not been conscious of remotely suspecting his identity.

He came back to where I stood, and again held out both his hands. Not knowing what to do—for, in my astonishment I had lost my self-possession—I reluctantly gave him my hands. He grasped them heartily, raised them to his lips, kissed them, and still held them.

"You acted noble, my boy," said he. "Noble, Pip! And I have never forgot it!"

At a change in his manner as if he were even going to embrace me, I laid a hand upon his breast and put him away.

"Stay!" said I. "Keep off! If you are grateful to me for what I did when I was a little child, I hope you have shown your gratitude by mending your way of life. If you have come here to thank me, it was not necessary. Still, however, you have found me out, there must be something good in the feeling that has brought you here, and I will not repulse you; but surely you must understand that—I——"

My attention was so attracted by the singularity of his fixed look at me, that the words died away on my tongue.

"You was a saying," he observed, when we had confronted one another in silence, "that surely I must understand. What, surely must I understand?"

"That I cannot wish to renew that chance intercourse with you of long ago, under these different circumstances. I am glad to believe you have repented and recovered yourself. I am glad to tell you so. I am glad that, thinking I deserve to be thanked, you have come to thank me. But our ways are different ways, none the less. You are wet, and you look weary. Will you drink something before you go?"

He had replaced his neckerchief loosely, and had stood, keenly observant of me, biting a long end of it. "I think," he answered, still with the end at his mouth and still observant of me, "that I *will* drink (I thank you) afore I go."

There was a tray ready on a side-table. I brought it to the table near the fire, and asked him what he would have? He touched one of the bottles without looking at it or speaking, and I made him some hot rum-and-water. I tried to keep my hand steady while I did so, but his look at me as he leaned back in his chair with the long draggled end of his neckerchief between his teeth—evidently forgotten—made my hand very difficult to master. When at last I put the glass to him, I saw with amazement that his eyes were full of tears.

Up to this time I had remained standing, not to disguise that I wished him gone. But I was softened by the softened aspect of the man, and felt a touch of reproach. "I hope," said I, hurriedly putting something into a glass for myself, and drawing a chair to the table, "that you will not think I spoke harshly to you just now. I had no intention of doing it, and I am sorry for it if I did. I wish you well, and happy!"

As I put my glass to my lips, he glanced with surprise at the end of his neckerchief, dropping from his mouth when he opened it, and stretched out his hand. I gave him mine, and then he drank, and drew his sleeve across his eyes and forehead.

"How are you living?" I asked him.

"I've been a sheep-farmer, stock-breeder, other trades besides, away in the new world,"° said he: "many a thousand mile of stormy water off from this."

"I hope you have done well?"

"I've done wonderful well. There's others went out alonger me as has done well too, but no man has done nigh as well as me. I'm famous for it."

"I am glad to hear it."

"I hope to hear you say so, my dear boy."

Without stopping to try to understand those words or the tone in which they were spoken, I turned off to a point that had just come into my mind.

"Have you ever seen a messenger you once sent to me," I inquired, "since he undertook that trust?"

"Never set eyes upon him. I warn't likely to it."

"He came faithfully, and he brought me the two one-pound notes. I was a poor boy then, as you know, and to a poor boy they were a little fortune. But, like you, I have done well since, and you must let me pay them back. You can put them to some other poor boy's use." I took out my purse.

He watched me as I laid my purse upon the table and opened it, and he watched me as I separated two one-pound notes from its contents. They were clean and new, and I spread them out and handed them over to him. Still watching me, he laid them one upon the other, folded them long-wise, gave them a twist, set fire to them at the lamp, and dropped the ashes into the tray.

"May I make so bold," he said then, with a smile that was like a frown, and with a frown that was like a smile, "as ask you *how* you have done well, since you and me was out on them lone shivering marshes?"

"How?"

"Ah!"

He emptied his glass, got up, and stood at the side of the fire, with his heavy brown hand on the mantelshelf. He put a foot up to the bars, to dry and warm it, and the wet boot began to steam; but, he

new world: Australia.

neither looked at it, nor at the fire, but steadily looked at me. It was only now that I began to tremble.

When my lips had parted, and had shaped some words that were without sound, I forced myself to tell him (though I could not do it distinctly), that I had been chosen to succeed to some property.

"Might a mere warmint ask what property?" said he.

I faltered, "I don't know."

"Might a mere warmint ask whose property?" said he.

I faltered again, "I don't know."

"Could I make a guess, I wonder," said the Convict, "at your income since you come of age! As to the first figure now. Five?"

With my heart beating like a heavy hammer of disordered action, I rose out of my chair, and stood with my hand upon the back of it, looking wildly at him.

"Concerning a guardian," he went on. "There ought to have been some guardian, or such-like, whiles you was a minor. Some lawyer, maybe. As to the first letter of that lawyer's name now. Would it be J?"

All the truth of my position came flashing on me; and its disappointments, dangers, disgraces, consequences of all kinds, rushed in in such a multitude that I was borne down by them and had to struggle for every breath I drew.

"Put it," he resumed, "as the employer of that lawyer whose name begun with a J, and might be Jaggers—put it as he had come over sea to Portsmouth, and had landed there, and had wanted to come on to you. 'However, you have found me out,' you says just now. Well! However did I find you out? Why, I wrote from Portsmouth to a person in London, for particulars of your address. That person's name? Why, Wemmick."

I could not have spoken one word, though it had been to save my life. I stood, with a hand on the chair-back and a hand on my breast, where I seemed to be suffocating—I stood so, looking wildly at him, until I grasped at the chair, when the room began to surge and turn. He caught me, drew me to the sofa, put me up against the cushions, and bent on one knee before me: bringing the face that I now well remembered, and that I shuddered at, very near to mine.

"Yes, Pip, dear boy, I've made a gentleman on you! It's me wot has done it! I swore that time, sure as ever I earned a guinea, that guinea should go to you. I swore arterwards, sure as ever I spec'lated and got rich, you should get rich. I lived rough, that you should live smooth; I worked hard, that you should be above work. What odds, dear boy? Do

I tell it, fur you to feel a obligation? Not a bit. I tell it, fur you to know as that there hunted dunghill dog wot you kep life in, got his head so high that he could make a gentleman—and, Pip, you're him!"

The abhorrence in which I held the man, the dread I had of him, the repugnance with which I shrank from him, could not have been exceeded if he had been some terrible beast.

"Look'ee here, Pip. I'm your second father. You're my son— more to me nor any son. I've put away money, only for you to spend. When I was a hired-out shepherd in a solitary hut, not seeing no faces but faces of sheep till I half forgot wot men's and women's faces wos like, I see yourn. I drops my knife many a time in that hut when I was a eating my dinner or my supper, and I says, 'Here's the boy again, a looking at me whiles I eats and drinks!' I see you there a many times, as plain as ever I see you on them misty marshes. 'Lord strike me dead!' I says each time—and I goes out in the air to say it under the open heavens—'but wot, if I gets liberty and money, I'll make that boy a gentleman!' And I done it. Why, look at you, dear boy! Look at these here lodgings o' yourn, fit for a lord! A lord? Ah! You shall show money with lords for wagers, and beat 'em!"

In his heat and triumph, and in his knowledge that I had been nearly fainting, he did not remark on my reception of all this. It was the one grain of relief I had.

"Look'ee here!" he went on, taking my watch out of my pocket, and turning towards him a ring on my finger, while I recoiled from his touch as if he had been a snake, "a gold 'un and a beauty: *that's* a gentleman's, I hope! A diamond all set round with rubies; *that's* a gentleman's, I hope! Look at your linen; fine and beautiful! Look at your clothes; better ain't to be got! And your books too," turning his eyes round the room, "mounting up, on their shelves, by hundreds! And you read 'em; don't you? I see you'd been a reading of 'em when I come in. Ha, ha, ha! You shall read 'em to me, dear boy! And if they're in foreign languages wot I don't understand, I shall be just as proud as if I did."

Again he took both my hands and put them to his lips, while my blood ran cold within me.

"Don't you mind talking, Pip," said he, after again drawing his sleeve over his eyes and forehead, as the click came in his throat which I well remembered—and he was all the more horrible to me that he was so much in earnest; "you can't do better nor keep quiet, dear boy. You ain't looked slowly forward to this as I have; you wosn't prepared for this, as I wos. But didn't you never think it might be me?"

"O no, no, no," I returned. "Never, never!"

"Well, you see it *wos* me, and single-handed. Never a soul in it but my own self and Mr. Jaggers."

"Was there no one else?" I asked.

"No," said he, with a glance of surprise: "who else should there be? And, dear boy, how good-looking you have growed! There's bright eyes somewheres—eh? Isn't there bright eyes somewheres, wot you love the thoughts on?"

O Estella, Estella!

"They shall be yourn, dear boy, if money can buy 'em. Not that a gentleman like you, so well set up as you, can't win 'em off of his own game; but money shall back you! Let me finish wot I was a telling you, dear boy. From that there hut and that there hiring-out, I got money left me by my master (which died, and had been the same as me), and got my liberty and went for myself. In every single thing I went for, I went for you. 'Lord strike a blight upon it,' I says, wotever it was I went for, 'if it ain't for him!' It all prospered wonderful. As I giv' you to understand just now, I'm famous for it. It was the money left me, and the gains of the first few year wot I sent home to Mr. Jaggers—all for you—when he first come arter you, agreeable to my letter."

O, that he had never come! That he had left me at the forge—far from contented, yet, by comparison, happy!

"And then, dear boy, it was a recompense to me, look'ee here, to know in secret that I was making a gentleman. The blood horses of them colonists might fling up the dust over me as I was walking; what do I say? I says to myself, 'I'm making a better gentleman nor ever *you*'ll be!' When one of 'em says to another, 'He was a convict, a few year ago, and is a ignorant common fellow now, for all he's lucky,' what do I say? I says to myself, 'If I ain't a gentleman, nor yet ain't got no learning, I'm the owner of such. All on you owns stock and land; which on you owns a brought-up London gentleman?' This way I kep myself a going. And this way I held steady afore my mind that I would for certain come one day and see my boy, and make myself known to him, on his own ground."

He laid his hand on my shoulder. I shuddered at the thought that for anything I knew, his hand might be stained with blood.

"It warn't easy, Pip, for me to leave them parts, nor yet it warn't safe. But I held to it, and the harder it was, the stronger I held, for I was determined, and my mind firm made up. At last I done it. Dear boy, I done it!"

I tried to collect my thoughts, but I was stunned. Throughout, I had seemed to myself to attend more to the wind and the rain than to him; even now, I could not separate his voice from those voices, though those were loud and his was silent.

"Where will you put me?" he asked, presently. "I must be put somewheres, dear boy."

"To sleep?" said I.

"Yes. And to sleep long and sound," he answered; "for I've been sea-tossed and sea-washed, months and months."

"My friend and companion," said I, rising from the sofa, "is absent; you must have his room."

"He won't come back to-morrow; will he?"

"No," said I, answering almost mechanically, in spite of my utmost efforts; "not to-morrow."

"Because, look'ee here, dear boy," he said, dropping his voice, and laying a long finger on my breast in an impressive manner, "caution is necessary."

"How do you mean? Caution?"

"By G—, it's Death!"

"What's death?"

"I was sent for life. It's death to come back. There's been over-much coming back of late years, and I should of a certainty be hanged if took."°

Nothing was needed but this; the wretched man, after loading wretched me with his gold and silver chains for years, had risked his life to come to me, and I held it there in my keeping! If I had loved him instead of abhorring him; if I had been attracted to him by the strongest admiration and affection, instead of shrinking from him with the strongest repugnance; it could have been no worse. On the contrary, it would have been better, for his preservation would then have naturally and tenderly addressed my heart.

My first care was to close the shutters, so that no light might be seen from without, and then to close and make fast the doors. While I did so, he stood at the table drinking rum and eating biscuit; and when I saw him thus engaged, I saw my convict on the marshes at his meal again. It almost seemed to me as if he must stoop down presently, to file at his leg.

When I had gone into Herbert's room, and had shut off any other communication between it and the staircase than through the room in

---

I . . . took: Returning to Britain was, until 1835, a capital offense for convicts who had been transported for life, although no such executions were carried out after 1810.

which our conversation had been held, I asked him if he would go to bed? He said yes, but asked me for some of my "gentleman's linen" to put on in the morning. I brought it out, and laid it ready for him, and my blood again ran cold when he again took me by both hands to give me good night.

I got away from him, without knowing how I did it, and mended the fire in the room where we had been together, and sat down by it, afraid to go to bed. For an hour or more, I remained too stunned to think; and it was not until I began to think, that I began fully to know how wrecked I was, and how the ship in which I had sailed was gone to pieces.

Miss Havisham's intentions towards me, all a mere dream; Estella not designed for me; I only suffered in Satis House as a convenience, a sting for the greedy relations, a model with a mechanical heart to practise on when no other practice was at hand; those were the first smarts I had. But, sharpest and deepest pain of all—it was for the convict, guilty of I knew not what crimes, and liable to be taken out of those rooms where I sat thinking, and hanged at the Old Bailey door, that I had deserted Joe.

I would not have gone back to Joe now, I would not have gone back to Biddy now, for any consideration: simply, I suppose, because my sense of my own worthless conduct to them was greater than every consideration. No wisdom on earth could have given me the comfort that I should have derived from their simplicity and fidelity; but I could never, never, never, undo what I had done.

In every rage of wind and rush of rain, I heard pursuers. Twice, I could have sworn there was a knocking and whispering at the outer door. With these fears upon me, I began either to imagine or recal that I had had mysterious warnings of this man's approach. That, for weeks gone by, I had passed faces in the streets which I had thought like his. That, these likenesses had grown more numerous, as he, coming over the sea, had drawn nearer. That, his wicked spirit had somehow sent these messengers to mine, and that now on this stormy night he was as good as his word, and with me.

Crowding up with these reflections came the reflection that I had seen him with my childish eyes to be a desperately violent man; that I had heard that other convict reiterate that he had tried to murder him; that I had seen him down in the ditch tearing and fighting like a wild beast. Out of such remembrances I brought into the light of the fire, a half-formed terror that it might not be safe to be shut up there with him in the dead of the wild solitary night. This dilated until it filled the

room, and impelled me to take a candle and go in and look at my
dreadful burden.

He had rolled a handkerchief round his head, and his face was set
and lowering in his sleep. But he was asleep, and quietly too, though
he had a pistol lying on the pillow. Assured of this, I softly removed
the key to the outside of his door, and turned it on him before I again
sat down by the fire. Gradually I slipped from the chair and lay on the
floor. When I awoke, without having parted in my sleep with the perception of my wretchedness, the clocks of the Eastward churches were
striking five, the candles were wasted out, the fire was dead, and the
wind and rain intensified the thick black darkness.

THIS IS THE END OF THE SECOND STAGE
OF PIP'S EXPECTATIONS.

[PART 25]

Chapter 40

It was fortunate for me that I had to take precautions to ensure (so
far as I could) the safety of my dreaded visitor; for, this thought pressing on me when I awoke, held other thoughts in a confused concourse
at a distance.

The impossibility of keeping him concealed in the chambers was
self-evident. It could not be done, and the attempt to do it would inevitably engender suspicion. True, I had no Avenger in my service
now, but I was looked after by an inflammatory old female, assisted by
an animated rag-bag whom she called her niece, and to keep a room
secret from them would be to invite curiosity and exaggeration. They
both had weak eyes, which I had long attributed to their chronically
looking in at keyholes, and they were always at hand when not
wanted; indeed that was their only reliable quality besides larceny. Not
to get up a mystery with these people, I resolved to announce in the
morning that my uncle had unexpectedly come from the country.

This course I decided on while I was yet groping about in the
darkness for the means of getting a light. Not stumbling on the means
after all, I was fain to go out to the adjacent Lodge and get the watch-

man there to come with his lantern. Now, in groping my way down the black staircase I fell over something, and that something was a man crouching in a corner.

As the man made no answer when I asked him what he did there, but eluded my touch in silence, I ran to the Lodge and urged the watchman to come quickly: telling him of the incident on the way back. The wind being as fierce as ever, we did not care to endanger the light in the lantern by rekindling the extinguished lamps on the staircase, but we examined the staircase from the bottom to the top and found no one there. It then occurred to me as possible that the man might have slipped into my rooms; so, lighting my candle at the watchman's, and leaving him standing at the door, I examined them carefully, including the room in which my dreaded guest lay asleep. All was quiet, and assuredly no other man was in those chambers.

It troubled me that there should have been a lurker on the stairs, on that night of all nights in the year, and I asked the watchman, on the chance of eliciting some hopeful explanation as I handed him a dram at the door, whether he had admitted at his gate any gentleman who had perceptibly been dining out? Yes, he said; at different times of the night, three. One lived in Fountain Court, and the other two lived in the Lane, and he had seen them all go home. Again, the only other man who dwelt in the house of which my chambers formed a part, had been in the country for some weeks; and he certainly had not returned in the night, because we had seen his door with his seal on it as we came upstairs.

"The night being so bad, sir," said the watchman, as he gave me back my glass, "uncommon few have come in at my gate. Besides them three gentlemen that I have named, I don't call to mind another since about eleven o'clock, when a stranger asked for you."

"My uncle," I muttered. "Yes."

"You saw him, sir?'

"Yes. Oh yes."

"Likewise the person with him?"

"Person with him!" I repeated.

"I judged the person to be with him," returned the watchman. "The person stopped, when he stopped to make inquiry of me, and the person took this way when he took this way."

"What sort of person?"

The watchman had not particularly noticed; he should say a working person; to the best of his belief, he had a dust-coloured kind of clothes on, under a dark coat. The watchman made more light of the matter than I did, and naturally; not having my reason for attaching weight to it.

When I had got rid of him, which I thought it well to do without prolonging explanations, my mind was much troubled by these two circumstances taken together. Whereas they were easy of innocent so-lution apart—as, for instance, some diner-out or diner-at-home, who had not gone near this watchman's gate, might have strayed to my staircase and dropped asleep there—and my nameless visitor might have brought some one with him to show him the way—still, joined, they had an ugly look to one as prone to distrust and fear as the changes of a few hours had made me.

I lighted my fire, which burnt with a raw pale flare at that time of the morning, and fell into a doze before it. I seemed to have been dozing a whole night when the clocks struck six. As there was full an hour and a half between me and daylight, I dozed again; now, waking up uneasily, with prolix conversations about nothing, in my ears; now, making thunder of the wind in the chimney; at length, falling off into a profound sleep from which the daylight woke me with a start.

All this time I had never been able to consider my own situation, nor could I do so yet. I had not the power to attend to it. I was greatly dejected and distressed, but in an incoherent wholesale sort of way. As to forming any plan for the future, I could as soon have formed an ele-phant. When I opened the shutters and looked out at the wet wild morning, all of a leaden hue; when I walked from room to room; when I sat down again shivering, before the fire, waiting for my laun-dress to appear; I thought how miserable I was, but hardly knew why, or how long I had been so, or on what day of the week I made the re-flection, or even who I was that made it.

At last, the old woman and the niece came in—the latter with a head not easily distinguishable from her dusty broom—and testified surprise at sight of me and the fire. To whom I imparted how my uncle had come in the night and was then asleep, and how the break-fast preparations were to be modified accordingly. Then, I washed and dressed while they knocked the furniture about and made a dust; and so, in a sort of dream or sleep-waking, I found myself sitting by the fire again, waiting for—Him—to come to breakfast.

By-and-by, his door opened and he came out. I could not bring myself to bear the sight of him, and I thought he had a worse look by daylight.

"I do not even know," said I, speaking low as he took his seat at the table, "by what name to call you. I have given out that you are my uncle."

"That's it, dear boy! Call me uncle."

"You assumed some name, I suppose, on board ship?"

"Yes, dear boy. I took the name of Provis."

"Do you mean to keep that name?"

"Why, yes, dear boy, it's as good as another—unless you'd like another."

"What is your real name?" I asked him in a whisper.

"Magwitch," he answered, in the same tone; "chrisen'd Abel."

"What were you brought up to be?"

"A warmint, dear boy."

He answered quite seriously, and used the word as if it denoted some profession.

"When you came into the Temple last night——" said I, pausing to wonder whether that could really have been last night, which seemed so long ago.

"Yes, dear boy?"

"When you came in at the gate and asked the watchman that way here, had you any one with you?"

"With me? No, dear boy."

"But there was some one there?"

"I didn't take particular notice," he said, dubiously, "not knowing the ways of the place. But I think there *was* a person, too, come in alonger me."

"Are you known in London?"

"I hope not!" said he, giving his neck a jerk with his forefinger that made me turn hot and sick.

"Were you known in London, once?"

"Not over and above, dear boy. I was in the provinces mostly."

"Were you—tried—in London?"

"Which time?" said he, with a sharp look.

"The last time."

He nodded. "First knowed Mr. Jaggers that way. Jaggers was for me."

It was on my lips to ask him what he was tried for, but he took up a knife, gave it a flourish, and with the words, "And what I done is worked out and paid for!" fell to at his breakfast.

He ate in a ravenous way that was very disagreeable, and all his actions were uncouth, noisy, and greedy. Some of his teeth had failed him since I saw him eat on the marshes, and as he turned his food in his mouth, and turned his head sideways to bring his strongest fangs to bear upon it, he looked terribly like a hungry old dog. If I had begun with any appetite, he would have taken it away, and I should have sat much as I did—repelled from him by an insurmountable aversion, and gloomily looking at the cloth.

"I'm a heavy grubber, dear boy," he said, as a polite kind of apology when he had made an end of his meal, "but I always was. If it had been in my constitution to be a lighter grubber, I might ha' got into lighter trouble. Similarly, I must have my smoke. When I was first hired out as shepherd t'other side the world, it's my belief I should ha' turned into a molloncolly-mad sheep myself, if I hadn't a had my smoke."

As he said so, he got up from table, and putting his hand into the breast of the peacoat he wore, brought out a short black pipe, and a handful of loose tobacco of the kind that is called Negro-head. Having filled his pipe, he put the surplus tobacco back again, as if his pocket were a drawer. Then, he took a live coal from the fire with the tongs, and lighted his pipe at it, and then turned round on the hearth-rug with his back to the fire, and went through his favourite action of holding out both his hands for mine.

"And this," said he, dandling my hands up and down in his, as he puffed at his pipe; "and this is the gentleman what I made! The real genuine One! It does me good fur to look at you, Pip. All I stip'late, is, to stand by and look at you, dear boy!"

I released my hands as soon as I could, and found that I was beginning slowly to settle down to the contemplation of my condition. What I was chained to, and how heavily, became intelligible to me, as I heard his hoarse voice, and sat looking up at his furrowed bald head with its iron grey hair at the sides.

"I mustn't see my gentleman a footing it in the mire of the streets; there mustn't be no mud on *his* boots. My gentleman must have horses, Pip! Horses to ride, and horses to drive, and horses for his servant to ride and drive as well. Shall colonists have their horses (and blood 'uns, if you please, good Lord!) and not my London gentleman? No, no. We'll show 'em another pair of shoes than that, Pip; won't us?"

He took out of his pocket a great thick pocket-book, bursting with papers, and tossed it on the table.

"There's something worth spending in that there book, dear boy. It's yourn. All I've got ain't mine; it's yourn. Don't you be afeerd on it. There's more where that come from. I've come to the old country fur to see my gentleman spend his money *like* a gentleman. That'll be *my* pleasure. *My* pleasure 'ull be fur to see him do it. And blast you all!" he wound up, looking round the room and snapping his fingers once with a loud snap, "blast you every one, from the judge in his wig, to the colonist a stirring up the dust, I'll show a better gentleman than the whole kit on you put together!"

"Stop!" said I, almost in a frenzy of fear and dislike, "I want to speak to you. I want to know what is to be done. I want to know how you are to be kept out of danger, how long you are going to stay, what projects you have."

"Look'ee here, Pip," said he, laying his hand on my arm in a suddenly altered and subdued manner; "first of all, look'ee here. I forgot myself half a minute ago. What I said was low; that's what it was; low. Look'ee here, Pip. Look over it. I ain't a going to be low."

"First," I resumed, half groaning, "what precautions can be taken against your being recognised and seized?"

"No, dear boy," he said, in the same tone as before, "that don't go first. Lowness goes first. I ain't took so many year to make a gentleman, not without knowing what's due to him. Look'ee here, Pip. I was low; that's what I was; low. Look over it, dear boy."

Some sense of the grimly-ludicrous moved me to a fretful laugh, as I replied, "I *have* looked over it. In Heaven's name, don't harp upon it!"

"Yes, but look'ee here," he persisted. "Dear boy, I ain't come so fur to be low. Now, go on, dear boy. You was a saying——"

"How are you to be guarded from the danger you have incurred?"

"Well, dear boy, the danger ain't so great. Without I was informed agen, the danger ain't so much to signify. There's Jaggers, and there's Wemmick, and there's you. Who else is there to inform?"

"Is there no chance person who might identify you in the street?" said I.

"Well," he returned, "there ain't many. Nor yet I don't intend to advertise myself in the newspapers by the name of A. M. come back from Botany Bay;° and years have rolled away, and who's to gain by it? Still, look'ee here, Pip. If the danger had been fifty times as great, I should ha' come to see you, mind you, just the same."

"And how long do you remain?"

"How long?" said he, taking his black pipe from his mouth, and dropping his jaw as he stared at me. "I'm not a going back. I've come for good."

Botany Bay: The penal colony near Sydney in New South Wales, Australia.

"Where are you to live?" said I. "What is to be done with you? Where will you be safe?"

"Dear boy," he returned, "there's disguising wigs can be bought for money, and there's hair powder, and spectacles, and black clothes—shorts° and what not. Others has done it safe afore; and what others has done afore, others can do agen. As to the where and how of living, dear boy, give me your own opinions on it."

"You take it smoothly now," said I, "but you were very serious last night, when you swore it was Death."

"And so I swear it is Death," said he, putting his pipe back in his mouth, "and Death by the rope, in the open street not fur from this, and it's serious that you should fully understand it to be so. What then, when that's once done? Here I am. To go back now, 'ud be as bad as to stand ground—worse. Besides, Pip, I'm here, because I've meant it by you, years and years. As to what I dare, I'm a old bird now, as has dared all manner of traps since first he was fledged, and I'm not afeerd to perch upon a scarecrow. If there's Death hid inside of it, there is, and let him come out, and I'll face him, and then I'll believe in him and not afore. And now let me have a look at my gentleman agen."

Once more, he took me by both hands and surveyed me with an air of admiring proprietorship: smoking with great complacency all the while.

It appeared to me that I could do no better than secure him some quiet lodging hard by, of which he might take possession when Herbert returned: whom I expected in two or three days. That the secret must be confided to Herbert as a matter of unavoidable necessity, even if I could have put the immense relief I should derive from sharing it with him out of the question, was plain to me. But it was by no means so plain to Mr. Provis (I resolved to call him by that name), who reserved his consent to Herbert's participation until he should have seen him and formed a favourable judgment of his physiognomy. "And even then, dear boy," said he, pulling a greasy little clasped black Testament out of his pocket, "we'll have him on his oath."

To state that my terrible patron carried this little black book about the world solely to swear people on in cases of emergency, would be to state what I never quite established—but this I can say, that I never knew him put it to any other use. The book itself had the appearance of having been stolen from some court of justice, and perhaps his knowl-

---

shorts: Knee breeches, which had been worn earlier by professional men.

edge of its antecedents, combined with his own experience in that wise, gave him a reliance on its powers as a sort of legal spell or charm. On this first occasion of his producing it, I recalled how he had made me swear fidelity in the churchyard long ago, and how he had described himself last night as always swearing to his resolutions in his solitude.

As he was at present dressed in a seafaring slop suit, in which he looked as if he had some parrots and cigars to dispose of, I next discussed with him what dress he should wear. He cherished an extraordinary belief in the virtues of "shorts" as a disguise, and had in his own mind sketched a dress for himself that would have made him something between a dean and a dentist. It was with considerable difficulty that I won him over to the assumption of a dress more like a prosperous farmer's; and we arranged that he should cut his hair close, and wear a little powder. Lastly, as he had not yet been seen by the laundress or her niece, he was to keep himself out of their view until his change of dress was made.

It would seem a simple matter to decide on these precautions; but in my dazed, not to say distracted, state, it took so long, that I did not get out to further them, until two or three in the afternoon. He was to remain shut up in the chambers while I was gone, and was on no account to open the door.

There being to my knowledge a respectable lodging-house in Essex-street, the back of which looked into the Temple, and was almost within hail of my windows, I first of all repaired to that house, and was so fortunate as to secure the second floor for my uncle, Mr. Provis. I then went from shop to shop, making such purchases as were necessary to the change in his appearance. This business transacted, I turned my face, on my own account, to Little Britain. Mr. Jaggers was at his desk, but, seeing me enter, got up immediately and stood before his fire.

"Now, Pip," said he, "be careful."

"I will, sir," I returned. For, I had thought well of what I was going to say coming along.

"Don't commit yourself," said Mr. Jaggers, "and don't commit any one. You understand—any one. Don't tell me anything: I don't want to know anything; I am not curious."

Of course I saw that he knew the man was come.

"I merely want, Mr. Jaggers," said I, "to assure myself that what I have been told, is true. I have no hope of its being untrue, but at least I may verify it."

Mr. Jaggers nodded. "But did you say 'told' or 'informed'?" he asked me, with his head on one side, and not looking at me, but looking in a listening way at the floor. "Told would seem to imply verbal communication. You can't have verbal communication with a man in New South Wales, you know."

"I will say, informed, Mr. Jaggers."

"Good."

"I have been informed by a person named Abel Magwitch, that he is the benefactor so long unknown to me."

"That is the man," said Mr. Jaggers, "—in New South Wales."

"And only he?" said I.

"And only he," said Mr. Jaggers.

"I am not so unreasonable, sir, as to think you at all responsible for my mistakes and wrong conclusions; but I always supposed it was Miss Havisham."

"As you say, Pip," returned Mr. Jaggers, turning his eyes upon me coolly, and taking a bite at his forefinger, "I am not at all responsible for that."

"And yet it looked so like it, sir," I pleaded with a downcast heart.

"Not a particle of evidence, Pip," said Mr. Jaggers, shaking his head and gathering up his skirts. "Take nothing on its looks; take everything on evidence. There's no better rule."

"I have no more to say," said I, with a sigh, after standing silent for a little while. "I have verified my information, and there an end."

"And Magwitch—in New South Wales—having at last disclosed himself," said Mr. Jaggers, "you will comprehend, Pip, how rigidly throughout my communication with you, I have always adhered to the strict line of fact. There has never been the least departure from the strict line of fact. You are quite aware of that?"

"Quite, sir."

"I communicated to Magwitch—in New South Wales—when he first wrote to me—from New South Wales—the caution that he must not expect me ever to deviate from the strict line of fact. I also communicated to him another caution. He appeared to me to have obscurely hinted in his letter at some distant idea he had of seeing you in England here. I cautioned him that I must hear no more of that; that he was not at all likely to obtain a pardon; that he was expatriated for the term of his natural life; and that his presenting himself in this country would be an act of felony, rendering him liable to the extreme penalty of the law. I gave Magwitch that caution," said Mr. Jaggers, looking hard at me; "I wrote it to New South Wales. He guided himself by it, no doubt."

"No doubt," said I.

"I have been informed by Wemmick," pursued Mr. Jaggers, still looking hard at me, "that he has received a letter, under date Portsmouth, from a colonist of the name of Purvis, or ——"

"Or Provis," I suggested.

"Or Provis—thank you, Pip. Perhaps it *is* Provis? Perhaps you know it's Provis?"

"Yes," said I.

"You know it's Provis. A letter, under date Portsmouth, from a colonist of the name of Provis, asking for the particulars of your address, on behalf of Magwitch. Wemmick sent him the particulars, I understand, by return of post. Probably it is through Provis that you have received the explanation of Magwitch—in New South Wales?"

"It came through Provis," I replied.

"Good day, Pip," said Mr. Jaggers, offering his hand; "glad to have seen you. In writing by post to Magwitch—in New South Wales—or in communicating with him through Provis, have the goodness to mention that the particulars and vouchers of our long account shall be sent to you, together with the balance; for there is still a balance remaining. Good day, Pip!"

We shook hands, and he looked hard at me as long as he could see me. I turned at the door, and he was still looking hard at me, while the two vile casts on the shelf seemed to be trying to get their eyelids open, and to force out of their swollen throats, "O, what a man he is!"

Wemmick was out, and though he had been at his desk he could have done nothing for me. I went straight back to the Temple, where I found the terrible Provis drinking rum-and-water and smoking negro-head, in safety.

Next day the clothes I had ordered, all came home, and he put them on. Whatever he put on, became him less (it dismally seemed to me) than what he had worn before. To my thinking, there was something in him that made it hopeless to attempt to disguise him. The more I dressed him and the better I dressed him, the more he looked like the slouching fugitive on the marshes. This effect on my anxious fancy was partly referable, no doubt, to his old face and manner growing more familiar to me; but I believe too that he dragged one of his legs as if there were still a weight of iron on it, and that from head to foot there was Convict in the very grain of the man.

The influences of his solitary hut-life were upon him besides, and gave him a savage air that no dress could tame; added to these, were the influences of his subsequent branded life among men, and, crowning all, his consciousness that he was dodging and hiding now. In all his ways of sitting and standing, and eating and drinking—of brooding about, in a high-shouldered reluctant style—of taking out his great horn-handled jack-knife and wiping it on his legs and cutting his food—of lifting light glasses and cups to his lips, as if they were clumsy pannikins—of chopping a wedge off his bread, and soaking up with it the last fragments of gravy round and round his plate, as if to make the most of an allowance, and then drying his finger-ends on it, and then swallowing it—in these ways and a thousand other small nameless instances arising every minute in the day, there was Prisoner, Felon, Bondsman, plain as plain could be.

It had been his own idea to wear that touch of powder, and I had conceded the powder after overcoming the shorts. But I can compare the effect of it, when on, to nothing but the probable effect of rouge upon the dead; so awful was the manner in which everything in him that it was most desirable to repress, started through that thin layer of pretence, and seemed to come blazing out at the crown of his head. It was abandoned as soon as tried, and he wore his grizzled hair cut short.

Words cannot tell what a sense I had, at the same time, of the dreadful mystery that he was to me. When he fell asleep of an evening, with his knotted hands clenching the sides of the easy-chair, and his bald head tattooed with deep wrinkles falling forward on his breast, I would sit and look at him, wondering what he had done, and loading him with all the crimes in the Calendar,° until the impulse was powerful on me to start up and fly from him. Every hour so increased my abhorrence of him, that I even think I might have yielded to this impulse in the first agonies of being so haunted, notwithstanding all he had done for me, and the risk he ran, but for the knowledge that Herbert must soon come back. Once, I actually did start out of bed in the night, and begin to dress myself in my worst clothes, hurriedly intending to leave him there with everything else I possessed, and enlist for India as a private soldier.

I doubt if a ghost could have been more terrible to me, up in those lonely rooms in the long evenings and long nights, with the wind and the rain always rushing by. A ghost could not have been taken and

Calendar: *The Newgate Calendar,* a collection of biographies of criminals.

hanged on my account, and the consideration that he could be, and the dread that he would be, were no small addition to my horrors. When he was not asleep, or playing a complicated kind of Patience with a ragged pack of cards of his own—a game that I never saw before or since, and in which he recorded his winnings by sticking his jack-knife into the table—when he was not engaged in either of these pursuits, he would ask me to read to him—"Foreign language, dear boy!" While I complied, he, not comprehending a single word, would stand before the fire surveying me with the air of an Exhibitor,° and I would see him, between the fingers of the hand with which I shaded my face, appealing in dumb show to the furniture to take notice of my proficiency. The imaginary student pursued by the misshapen creature he had impiously made,° was not more wretched than I, pursued by the creature who had made me, and recoiling from him with a stronger repulsion, the more he admired me and the fonder he was of me.

This is written of, I am sensible, as if it had lasted a year. It lasted about five days. Expecting Herbert all the time, I dared not go out, except when I took Provis for an airing after dark. At length, one evening when dinner was over and I had dropped into a slumber quite worn out—for my nights had been agitated and my rest broken by fearful dreams—I was roused by the welcome footstep on the staircase. Provis, who had been asleep too, staggered up at the noise I made, and in an instant I saw his jack-knife shining in his hand.

"Quiet! It's Herbert!" I said; and Herbert came bursting in, with the airy freshness of six hundred miles of France upon him.

"Handel, my dear fellow, how are you, and again how are you, and again how are you? I seem to have been gone a twelve-month! Why, so I must have been, for you have grown quite thin and pale! Handel, my——Halloa! I beg your pardon."

He was stopped in his running on and in his shaking hands with me, by seeing Provis. Provis, regarding him with a fixed attention, was slowly putting up his jack-knife, and groping in another pocket for something else.

"Herbert, my dear friend," said I, shutting the double doors, while Herbert stood staring and wondering, "something very strange has happened. This is—a visitor of mine."

Exhibitor: Manager of an exhibition or sideshow.   **imaginary . . . made:** Frankenstein is pursued and finally destroyed by the "misshapen creature" he has made in Mary Shelley's *Frankenstein* (1818).

"It's all right, dear boy!" said Provis coming forward, with his little clasped black book, and then addressing himself to Herbert. "Take it in your right hand. Lord strike you dead on the spot, if ever you split in any way sumever! Kiss it!"

"Do so, as he wishes it," I said to Herbert. So, Herbert, looking at me with a friendly uneasiness and amazement, complied, and Provis immediately shaking hands with him, said, "Now you're on your oath, you know. And never believe me on mine, if Pip shan't make a gentleman on you!"

[PART 26]

Chapter 41

In vain should I attempt to describe the astonishment and disquiet of Herbert, when he and I and Provis sat down before the fire, and I recounted the whole of the secret. Enough, that I saw my own feelings reflected in Herbert's face, and, not least among them, my repugnance towards the man who had done so much for me.

What would alone have set a division between that man and us, if there had been no other dividing circumstance, was his triumph in my story. Saving his troublesome sense of having been "low" on one occasion since his return—on which point he began to hold forth to Herbert, the moment my revelation was finished—he had no perception of the possibility of my finding any fault with my good fortune. His boast that he had made me a gentleman, and that he had come to see me support the character on his ample resources, was made for me quite as much as for himself; and that it was a highly agreeable boast to both of us, and that we must both be very proud of it, was a conclusion quite established in his own mind.

"Though, look'ee here, Pip's comrade," he said to Herbert, after having discoursed for some time, "I know very well that once since I come back—for half a minute—I've been low. I said to Pip, I knowed as I had been low. But don't you fret yourself on that score. I ain't made Pip a gentleman, and Pip ain't agoing to make you a gentleman, not fur me not to know what's due to ye both. Dear boy, and Pip's comrade, you two may count upon me always having a gen-teel muzzle on. Muzzled I have been since that half a minute when I was betrayed into lowness, muzzled I am at the present time, muzzled I ever will be."

Herbert said, "Certainly," but looked as if there were no specific consolation in this, and remained perplexed and dismayed. We were anxious for the time when he would go to his lodging, and leave us together, but he was evidently jealous of leaving us together, and sat late. It was midnight before I took him round to Essex-street, and saw him safely in at his own dark door. When it closed upon him, I experienced the first moment of relief I had known since the night of his arrival.

Never quite free from an uneasy remembrance of the man on the stairs, I had always looked about me in taking my guest out after dark, and in bringing him back; and I looked about me now. Difficult as it is in a large city to avoid the suspicion of being watched, when the mind is conscious of danger in that regard, I could not persuade myself that any of the people within sight cared about my movements. The few who were passing, passed on their several ways, and the street was empty when I turned back into the Temple. Nobody had come out at the gate with us, nobody went in at the gate with me. As I crossed by the fountain, I saw his lighted back windows looking bright and quiet, and, when I stood for a few moments in the doorway of the building where I lived, before going up the stairs, Garden-court was as still and lifeless as the staircase was when I ascended it.

Herbert received me with open arms, and I had never felt before, so blessedly, what it is to have a friend. When he had spoken some sound words of sympathy and encouragement, we sat down to consider the question, What was to be done?

The chair that Provis had occupied still remaining where it had stood—for he had a barrack way with him of hanging about one spot, in one unsettled manner, and going through one round of observances with his pipe and his negro-head and his jack-knife and his pack of cards, and what not, as if it were all put down for him on a slate—I say, his chair remaining where it had stood, Herbert unconsciously took it, but next moment started out of it, pushed it away, and took another. He had no occasion to say, after that, that he had conceived an aversion for my patron, neither had I occasion to confess my own. We interchanged that confidence without shaping a syllable.

"What," said I to Herbert, when he was safe in another chair, "what is to be done?"

"My poor dear Handel," he replied, holding his head, "I am too stunned to think."

"So was I, Herbert, when the blow first fell. Still, something must be done. He is intent upon various new expenses—horses, and carriages, and lavish appearances of all kinds. He must be stopped somehow."

"You mean that you can't accept——?"

"How can I?" I interposed, as Herbert paused. "Think of him! Look at him!"

An involuntary shudder passed over both of us.

"Yet I am afraid the dreadful truth is, Herbert, that he is attached to me, strongly attached to me. Was there ever such a fate!"

"My poor dear Handel," Herbert repeated.

"Then," said I, "after all, stopping short here, never taking another penny from him, think what I owe him already! Then again: I am heavily in debt—very heavily for me, who have now no expectations—and I have been bred to no calling, and I am fit for nothing."

"Well, well, well!" Herbert remonstrated. "Don't say fit for nothing."

"What am I fit for? I know only one thing that I am fit for, and that is, to go for a soldier. And I might have gone, my dear Herbert, but for the prospect of taking counsel with your friendship and affection."

Of course I broke down there; and of course Herbert, beyond seizing a warm grip of my hand, pretended not to know it.

"Anyhow, my dear Handel," said he presently, "soldiering won't do. If you were to renounce this patronage and these favours, I suppose you would do so with some faint hope of one day repaying what you have already had. Not very strong, that hope, if you went soldiering! Besides, it's absurd. You would be infinitely better in Clarriker's house, small as it is. I am working up towards a partnership, you know."

Poor fellow! He little suspected with whose money.

"But there is another question," said Herbert. "This is an ignorant determined man, who has long had one fixed idea. More than that, he seems to me (I may misjudge him) to be a man of a desperate and fierce character."

"I know he is," I returned. "Let me tell you what evidence I have seen of it." And I told him what I had not mentioned in my narrative; of that encounter with the other convict.

"See, then," said Herbert; "think of this! He comes here at the peril of his life, for the realisation of his fixed idea. In the moment of realisation, after all his toil and waiting, you cut the ground from under his feet, destroy his idea, and make his gains worthless to him. Do you see nothing that he might do, under the disappointment?"

"I have seen it, Herbert, and dreamed of it, ever since the fatal night of his arrival. Nothing has been in my thoughts so distinctly, as his putting himself in the way of being taken."

"Then you may rely upon it," said Herbert, "that there would be great danger of his doing it. That is his power over you as long as he remains in England, and that would be his reckless course if you forsook him."

I was so struck by the horror of this idea, which had weighed upon me from the first, and the working out of which would make me regard myself, in some sort, as his murderer, that I could not rest in my chair but began pacing to and fro. I said to Herbert, meanwhile, that even if Provis were recognised and taken, in spite of himself, I should be wretched as the cause, however innocently. Yes; even though I was so wretched in having him at large and near me, and even though I would far far rather have worked at the forge all the days of my life than I would ever have come to this!

But there was no raving off the question, What was to be done?

"The first and the main thing to be done," said Herbert, "is to get him out of England. You will have to go with him, and then he may be induced to go."

"But get him where I will, could I prevent his coming back?"

"My good Handel, is it not obvious that with Newgate in the next street, there must be far greater hazard in your breaking your mind to him and making him reckless, here, than elsewhere. If a pretext to get him away could be made out of that other convict, or out of anything else in his life, now."

"There, again!" said I, stopping before Herbert, with my open hands held out, as if they contained the desperation of the case. "I know nothing of his life. It has almost made me mad to sit here of a night and see him before me, so bound up with my fortunes and misfortunes, and yet so unknown to me, except as the miserable wretch who terrified me two days in my childhood!"

Herbert got up, and linked his arm in mine, and we slowly walked to and fro together, studying the carpet.

"Handel," said Herbert, stopping, "you feel convinced that you can take no further benefits from him; do you?"

"Fully. Surely you would, too, if you were in my place?"

"And you feel convinced that you must break with him?"

"Herbert, can you ask me?"

"And you have, and are bound to have, that tenderness for the life he has risked on your account, that you must save him, if possible, from throwing it away. Then you must get him out of England before you stir a finger to extricate yourself. That done, extricate yourself, in Heaven's name, and we'll see it out together, dear old boy."

It was a comfort to shake hands upon it, and walk up and down again, with only that done.

"Now, Herbert," said I, "with reference to gaining some knowledge of his history. There is but one way that I know of. I must ask him point-blank."

"Yes. Ask him," said Herbert, "when we sit at breakfast in the morning." For, he had said, on taking leave of Herbert, that he would come to breakfast with us.

With this project formed, we went to bed. I had the wildest dreams concerning him, and woke unrefreshed; I woke, too, to recover the fear which I had lost in the night, of his being found out as a returned transport. Waking, I never lost that fear.

He came round at the appointed time, took out his jack-knife, and sat down to his meal. He was full of plans "for his gentleman's coming out strong, and like a gentleman," and urged me to begin speedily upon the pocket-book, which he had left in my possession. He considered the chambers and his own lodging as temporary residences, and advised me to look out at once for a "fashionable crib" near Hyde Park, in which he could have "a shake-down."° When he had made an end of his breakfast, and was wiping his knife on his leg, I said to him, without a word of preface:

"After you were gone last night, I told my friend of the struggle that the soldiers found you engaged in on the marshes, when we came up. You remember?"

"Remember!" said he. "I think so!"

"We want to know something about that man—and about you. It is strange to know no more about either, and particularly you, than I was able to tell last night. Is not this as good a time as another for our knowing more?"

"Well!" he said, after consideration. "You're on your oath, you know, Pip's comrade?"

"Assuredly," replied Herbert.

"As to anything I say, you know," he insisted. "The oath applies to all."

"I understand it to do so."

"And look'ee here! Wotever I done, is worked out and paid for," he insisted again.

---

crib . . . shake-down: A residence ("crib") and a bed ("shake-down").

"So be it."

He took out his black pipe and was going to fill it with negro-head, when, looking at the tangle of tobacco in his hand, he seemed to think it might perplex the thread of his narrative. He put it back again, stuck his pipe in a button-hole of his coat, spread a hand on each knee, and, after turning an angry eye on the fire for a few silent moments, looked round at us and said what follows.

Chapter 42

"Dear boy and Pip's comrade. I am not a going fur to tell you my life, like a song or a story-book. But to give it you short and handy, I'll put it at once into a mouthful of English. In jail and out of jail, in jail and out of jail, in jail and out of jail. There, you've got it. That's *my* life pretty much, down to such times as I got shipped off, arter Pip stood my friend.

"I've been done everything to, pretty well—except hanged. I've been locked up, as much as a silver tea-kettle. I've been carted here and carted there, and put out of this town and put out of that town, and stuck in the stocks, and whipped and worried and drove. I've no more notion where I was born, than you have—if so much. I first become aware of myself, down in Essex, a thieving turnips for my living. Summun had run away from me—a man—a tinker—and he'd took the fire with him, and left me wery cold.

"I know'd my name to be Magwitch, chrisen'd Abel. How did I know it? Much as I know'd the birds' names in the hedges to be chaffinch, sparrer, thrush. I might have thought it was all lies together, only as the birds' names come out true, I supposed mine did.

"So fur as I could find, there warn't a soul that see young Abel Magwitch, with as little on him as in him, but wot caught fright at him, and either drove him off, or took him up. I was took up,° took up, took up, to that extent that I reg'larly grow'd up took up.

"This is the way it was, that when I was a ragged little creetur as much to be pitied as ever I see (not that I looked in the glass, for there warn't many insides of furnished houses known to me), I got the name of being hardened. 'This is a terrible hardened one,' they says to prison wisitors, picking out me. 'May be said to live in jails, this boy.' Then they looked at me, and I looked at them, and they measured my head,° some on 'em—they had better a measured my stomach—and

---

took up: Arrested.   **measured my head:** Phrenologists measured skulls to judge mental and moral capacities.

others on 'em giv me tracts what I couldn't read, and made me speeches what I couldn't unnerstand. They always went on agen me about the Devil. But what the Devil was I to do? I must put something into my stomach, mustn't I?—Howsomever, I'm a getting low, and I know what's due. Dear boy and Pip's comrade, don't you be afeerd of me being low.

"Tramping, begging, thieving, working sometimes when I could—though that warn't as often as you may think, till you put the question whether you would ha' been over ready to give me work yourselves—a bit of a poacher, a bit of a labourer, a bit of a waggoner, a bit of a haymaker, a bit of a hawker, a bit of most things that don't pay and lead to trouble, I got to be a man. A deserting soldier in a Travellers' Rest, what lay hid up to the chin under a lot of taturs, learnt me to read; and a travelling Giant what signed his name at a penny a time learnt me to write. I warn't locked up as often now as formerly, but I wore out my good share of key-metal still.

"At Epsom races, a matter of over twenty year ago, I got acquainted wi' a man whose skull I'd crack wi' this poker, like the claw of a lobster, if I'd got it on this hob. His right name was Compeyson; and that's the man, dear boy, what you see me a pounding in the ditch, according to what you truly told your comrade arter I was gone last night.

"He set up fur a gentleman, this Compeyson, and he'd been to a public boarding-school and had learning. He was a smooth one to talk, and was a dab at the ways of gentlefolks. He was good-looking too. It was the night afore the great race, when I found him on the heath, in a booth that I know'd on. Him and some more was a sitting among the tables when I went in, and the landlord (which had a knowledge of me, and was a sporting one) called him out, and said, 'I think this is a man that might suit you'—meaning I was.

"Compeyson, he looks at me very noticing, and I look at him. He has a watch and a chain and a ring and a breast-pin and a handsome suit of clothes.

"'To judge from appearances, you're out of luck,' says Compeyson to me.

"'Yes, master, and I've never been in it much.' (I had come out of Kingston Jail last on a vagrancy committal. Not but what it might have been for something else; but it warn't.)

"'Luck changes,' says Compeyson; 'perhaps yours is going to change.'

"I says, 'I hope it may be so. There's room.'

"'What can you do?' says Compeyson.

"'Eat and drink,' I says; 'if you'll find the materials.'

"Compeyson laughed, looked at me again very noticing, giv me five shillings, and appointed me for next night. Same place.

"I went to Compeyson next night, same place, and Compeyson took me on to be his man and pardner. And what was Compeyson's business in which we was to go pardners? Compeyson's business was the swindling, handwriting forging, stolen bank-note passing, and such-like. All sorts of traps as Compeyson could set with his head, and keep his own legs out of and get the profits from and let another man in for, was Compeyson's business. He'd no more heart than a iron file, he was as cold as death, and he had the head of the Devil afore mentioned.

"There was another in with Compeyson, as was called Arthur— not as being so chrisen'd, but as a surname. He was in a Decline, and was a shadow to look at. Him and Compeyson had been in a bad thing with a rich lady some years afore, and they'd made a pot of money by it; but Compeyson betted and gamed, and he'd have run through the king's taxes. So, Arthur was a dying, and a dying poor and with the horrors° on him, and Compeyson's wife (which Compeyson kicked mostly) was a having pity on him when she could, and Compeyson was a having pity on nothing and nobody.

"I might a took warning by Arthur, but I didn't; and I won't pretend I was partick'ler—for where 'ud be the good on it, dear boy and comrade? So I begun wi' Compeyson, and a poor tool I was in his hands. Arthur lived at the top of Compeyson's house (over nigh Brentford° it was), and Compeyson kept a careful account agen him for board and lodging, in case he should ever get better to work it out. But Arthur soon settled the account. The second or third time as ever I see him, he come a tearing down into Compeyson's parlour late at night, in only a flannel gown, with his hair all in a sweat, and he says to Compeyson's wife, 'Sally, she really is up-stairs alonger me, now, and I can't get rid of her. She's all in white,' he says, 'wi' white flowers in her hair, and she's awful mad, and she's got a shroud hanging over her arm, and she says she'll put it on me at five in the morning.'

"Says Compeyson: 'Why, you fool, don't you know she's got a living body? And how should she be up there, without coming through the door, or in at the window, and up the stairs?'

horrors: Delirium tremens.   **Brentford:** A town eight miles from London.

"'I don't know how she's there,' says Arthur, shivering dreadful with the horrors, 'but she's standing in the corner at the foot of the bed, awful mad. And over where her heart's broke—*you* broke it!—there's drops of blood.'

"Compeyson spoke hardy, but he was always a coward. 'Go up alonger this drivelling sick man,' he says to his wife, 'and Magwitch, lend her a hand, will you?' But he never come nigh himself.

"Compeyson's wife and me took him up to bed agen, and he raved most dreadful. 'Why look at her!' he cries out. 'She's a shaking the shroud at me! Don't you see her? Look at her eyes! Ain't it awful to see her so mad?' Next, he cries, 'She'll put it on me, and then I'm done for! Take it away from her, take it away!' And then he catched hold of us, and kep on a talking to her, and answering of her, till I half believed I see her myself.

"Compeyson's wife, being used to him, giv him some liquor to get the horrors off, and by-and-by he quieted. 'Oh, she's gone! Has her keeper been for her?' he says. 'Yes,' says Compeyson's wife. 'Did you tell him to lock her and bar her in?' 'Yes.' 'And to take that ugly thing away from her?' 'Yes, yes, all right.' 'You're a good creetur,' he says, 'don't leave me, whatever you do, and thank you!'

"He rested pretty quiet till it might want a few minutes of five, and then he starts up with a scream, and screams out, 'Here she is! She's got the shroud again. She's unfolding it. She's coming out of the corner. She's coming to the bed. Hold me, both on you—one of each side—don't let her touch me with it. Hah! she missed me that time. Don't let her throw it over my shoulders. Don't let her lift me up to get it round me. She's lifting me up. Keep me down!' Then he lifted himself up hard, and was dead.

"Compeyson took it easy as a good riddance for both sides. Him and me was soon busy, and first he swore me (being ever artful) on my own book—this here little black book, dear boy, what I swore your comrade on.

"Not to go into the things that Compeyson planned, and I done—which 'ud take a week—I'll simply say to you, dear boy, and Pip's comrade, that that man got me into such nets as made me his black slave. I was always in debt to him, always under his thumb, always a working, always a getting into danger. He was younger than me, but he'd got craft, and he'd got learning, and he overmatched me five hundred times told and no mercy. My Missis as I had the hard time wi'——Stop though! I ain't brought *her* in——"

He looked about him in a confused way, as if he had lost his place in the book of his remembrance; and he turned his face to the fire, and spread his hands broader on his knees, and lifted them off and put them on again.

"There ain't no need to go into it," he said, looking round once more. "The time wi' Compeyson was a'most as hard a time as ever I had; that said, all's said. Did I tell you as I was tried, alone, for misdemeanour, while with Compeyson?"

I answered, No.

"Well!" he said, "I *was,* and got convicted. As to took up on suspicion, that was twice or three times in the four or five year that it lasted; but evidence was wanting. At last, me and Compeyson was both committed for felony—on a charge of putting stolen notes in circulation—and there was other charges behind. Compeyson says to me, 'Separate defences, no communication,' and that was all. And I was so miserable poor, that I sold all the clothes I had, except what hung on my back, afore I could get Jaggers.

"When we was put in the dock, I noticed first of all what a gentleman Compeyson looked, wi' his curly hair and his black clothes and his white pocket-handkercher, and what a common sort of wretch I looked. When the prosecution opened and the evidence was put short, aforehand, I noticed how heavy it all bore on me, and how light on him. When the evidence was giv in the box, I noticed how it was always me that had come for'ard, and could be swore to, how it was always me that the money had been paid to, how it was always me that had seemed to work the thing and get the profit. But, when the defence come on, then I see the plan plainer; for, says the counsellor for Compeyson, 'My lord and gentlemen, here you has afore you, side by side, two persons as your eyes can separate wide; one, the younger, well brought up, who will be spoke to as such; one, the elder, ill brought up, who will be spoke to as such; one, the younger, seldom if ever seen in these here transactions, and only suspected; t'other, the elder, always seen in 'em and always wi' his guilt brought home. Can you doubt, if there is but one in it, which is the one, and, if there is two in it, which is much the worst one?' And such-like. And when it come to character, warn't it Compeyson as had been to the school, and warn't it his schoolfellows as was in this position and in that, and warn't it him as had been know'd by witnesses in such clubs and societies, and nowt to his disadvantage? And warn't it me as had been tried afore, and as had been know'd up hill and down dale in

Bridewells and Lock-Ups?° And when it come to speech-making, warn't it Compeyson as could speak to 'em wi' his face dropping every now and then into his white pocket-handkercher—ah! and wi' verses in his speech, too—and warn't it me as could only say, 'Gentlemen, this man at my side is a most precious rascal'? And when the verdict come, warn't it Compeyson as was recommended to mercy on account of good character and bad company, and giving up all the information he could agen me, and warn't it me as got never a word but Guilty? And when I says to Compeyson, 'Once out of this court, I'll smash that face o' yourn?' ain't it Compeyson as prays the Judge to be protected, and gets two turnkeys stood betwixt us? And when we're sentenced, ain't it him as gets seven year, and me fourteen, and ain't it him as the Judge is sorry for, because he might a done so well, and ain't it me as the Judge perceives to be a old offender of wiolent passion, likely to come to worse?"

He had worked himself into a state of great excitement, but he checked it, took two or three short breaths, swallowed as often, and stretching out his hand towards me said, in a reassuring manner, "I ain't a going to be low, dear boy!"

He had so heated himself that he took out his handkerchief and wiped his face and head and neck and hands, before he could go on.

"I had said to Compeyson that I'd smash that face of his, and I swore Lord smash mine! to do it. We was in the same prison-ship, but I couldn't get at him for long, though I tried. At last I come behind him and hit him on the cheek to turn him round and get a smashing one at him, when I was seen and seized. The black-hole of that ship warn't a strong one, to a judge of black-holes that could swim and dive. I escaped to the shore, and I was a hiding among the graves there, envying them as was in 'em and all over, when I first see my boy!"

He regarded me with a look of affection that made him almost abhorrent to me again, though I had felt great pity for him.

"By my boy, I was giv to understand as Compeyson was out on them marshes too. Upon my soul, I half believe he escaped in his terror, to get quit of me, not knowing it was me as had got ashore. I hunted him down. I smashed his face. 'And now,' says I, 'as the worst thing I can do, caring nothing for myself, I'll drag you back.' And I'd have swum off, towing him by the hair, if it had come to that, and I'd a got him aboard without the soldiers.

Bridewells and Lock-Ups: Prisons (generalized from the London prison called Bridewell) and local jails.

"Of course he'd much the best of it to the last—his character was so good. He had escaped when he was made half wild by me and my murderous intentions; and his punishment was light. I was put in irons, brought to trial again, and sent for life. I didn't stop for life, dear boy and Pip's comrade, being here."

He wiped himself again, as he had done before, and then slowly took his tangle of tobacco from his pocket, and plucked his pipe from his button-hole, and slowly filled it, and began to smoke.

"Is he dead?" I asked, after a silence.

"Is who dead, dear boy?"

"Compeyson."

"He hopes *I* am, if he's alive, you may be sure," with a fierce look. "I never heerd no more of him."

Herbert had been writing with his pencil in the cover of a book. He softly pushed the book over to me, as Provis stood smoking with his eyes on the fire, and I read in it:

> Young Havisham's name was Arthur. Compeyson is the man who professed to be Miss Havisham's lover.

I shut the book and nodded slightly to Herbert, and put the book by; but we neither of us said anything, and both looked at Provis as he stood smoking by the fire.

[PART 27]

Chapter 43

Why should I pause to ask how much of my shrinking from Provis might be traced to Estella? Why should I loiter on my road, to compare the state of mind in which I had tried to rid myself of the stain of the prison before meeting her at the coach-office, with the state of mind in which I now reflected on the abyss between Estella in her pride and beauty, and the returned transport whom I harboured? The road would be none the smoother for it, the end would be none the better for it, he would not be helped, nor I extenuated.

A new fear had been engendered in my mind by his narrative; or rather, his narrative had given form and purpose to the fear that was already there. If Compeyson were alive and should discover his return, I could hardly doubt the consequence. That, Compeyson stood in mortal fear of him, neither of the two could know much better than I;

and that, any such man as that man had been described to be, would hesitate to release himself for good from a dreaded enemy by the safe means of becoming an informer, was scarcely to be imagined.

Never had I breathed, and never would I breathe—or so I resolved—a word of Estella to Provis. But, I said to Herbert that before I could go abroad, I must see both Estella and Miss Havisham. This was when we were left alone on the night of the day when Provis told us his story. I resolved to go out to Richmond next day, and I went.

On my presenting myself at Mrs. Brandley's, Estella's maid was called to tell me that Estella had gone into the country. Where? To Satis House, as usual. Not as usual, I said, for she had never yet gone there without me; when was she coming back? There was an air of reservation in the answer which increased my perplexity, and the answer was, that her maid believed she was only coming back at all for a little while. I could make nothing of this, except that it was meant that I should make nothing of it, and I went home again in complete discomfiture.

Another night-consultation with Herbert after Provis was gone home (I always took him home, and always looked well about me), led us to the conclusion that nothing should be said about going abroad until I came back from Miss Havisham's. In the mean time, Herbert and I were to consider separately what it would be best to say; whether we should devise any pretence of being afraid that he was under suspicious observation; or whether I, who had never yet been abroad, should propose an expedition. We both knew that I had but to propose anything, and he would consent. We agreed that his remaining many days in his present hazard was not to be thought of.

Next day, I had the meanness to feign that I was under a binding promise to go down to Joe; but I was capable of almost any meanness towards Joe or his name. Provis was to be strictly careful while I was gone, and Herbert was to take the charge of him that I had taken. I was to be absent only one night, and, on my return, the gratification of his impatience for my starting as a gentleman on a greater scale, was to be begun. It occurred to me then, and as I afterwards found to Herbert also, that he might be best got away across the water, on that pretence—as, to make purchases, or the like.

Having thus cleared the way for my expedition to Miss Havisham's, I set off by the early morning coach before it was yet light, and was out on the open country-road when the day came creeping on, halting and whimpering and shivering, and wrapped in patches of cloud and rags of mist, like a beggar. When we drove up to the Blue

Boar after a drizzly ride, whom should I see come out under the gateway, toothpick in hand, to look at the coach, but Bentley Drummle!

As he pretended not to see me, I pretended not to see him. It was a very lame pretence on both sides; the lamer, because we both went into the coffee-room, where he had just finished his breakfast, and where I ordered mine. It was poisonous to me to see him in the town, for I very well knew why he had come there.

Pretending to read a smeary newspaper long out of date, which had nothing half so legible in its local news, as the foreign matter of coffee, pickles, fish sauces, gravy, melted butter, and wine, with which it was sprinkled all over, as if it had taken the measles in a highly irregular form, I sat at my table while he stood before the fire. By degrees it became an enormous injury to me that he stood before the fire, and I got up, determined to have my share of it. I had to put my hand behind his legs for the poker when I went up to the fireplace to stir the fire, but still pretended not to know him.

"Is this a cut?" said Mr. Drummle.

"Oh!" said I, poker in hand; "it's you, is it? How do you do? I was wondering who it was, who kept the fire off."

With that, I poked tremendously, and having done so, planted myself side by side with Mr. Drummle, my shoulders squared and my back to the fire.

"You have just come down?" said Mr. Drummle, edging me a little away with his shoulder.

"Yes," said I, edging *him* a little away with *my* shoulder.

"Beastly place," said Drummle. — "Your part of the country, I think?"

"Yes," I assented. "I am told it's very like your Shropshire."

"Not in the least like it," said Drummle.

Here Mr. Drummle looked at his boots, and I looked at mine, and then Mr. Drummle looked at my boots, and I looked at his.

"Have you been here long?" I asked, determined not to yield an inch of the fire.

"Long enough to be tired of it," returned Drummle, pretending to yawn, but equally determined.

"Do you stay here long?"

"Can't say," answered Mr. Drummle. "Do you?"

"Can't say," said I.

I felt here, through a tingling in my blood, that if Mr. Drummle's shoulder had claimed another hair's breadth of room, I should have jerked him into the window; equally, that if my own shoulder had urged a similar claim, Mr. Drummle would have jerked me into the nearest box. He whistled a little. So did I.

"Large tract of marshes about here, I believe?" said Drummle.

"Yes. What of that?" said I.

Mr. Drummle looked at me, and then at my boots, and then said, "Oh!" and laughed.

"Are you amused, Mr. Drummle?"

"No," said he, "not particularly. I am going out for a ride in the saddle. I mean to explore those marshes for amusement. Out-of-the-way villages there, they tell me. Curious little public-houses—and smithies—and that. Waiter!"

"Yes, sir."

"Is that horse of mine ready?"

"Brought round to the door, sir."

"I say. Look here, you sir. The lady won't ride to-day; the weather won't do."

"Very good, sir."

"And I don't dine, because I'm going to dine at the lady's."

"Very good, sir."

Then, Drummle glanced at me, with an insolent triumph on his great-jowled face that cut me to the heart, dull as he was, and so exasperated me, that I felt inclined to take him in my arms (as the robber in the story-book is said to have taken the old lady), and seat him on the fire.

One thing was manifest to both of us, and that was, that until relief came, neither of us could relinquish the fire. There we stood, well squared up before it, shoulder to shoulder and foot to foot, with our hands behind us, not budging an inch. The horse was visible outside in the drizzle at the door, my breakfast was put on table, Drummle's was cleared away, the waiter invited me to begin, I nodded, we both stood our ground.

"Have you been to the Grove since?" said Drummle.

"No," said I, "I had quite enough of the Finches the last time I was there."

"Was that when we had a difference of opinion?"

"Yes," I replied, very shortly.

"Come, come! They let you off easily enough," sneered Drummle. "You shouldn't have lost your temper."

"Mr. Drummle," said I, "you are not competent to give advice on that subject. When I lose my temper (not that I admit having done so on that occasion), I don't throw glasses."

"I do," said Drummle.

After glancing at him once or twice, in an increased state of smouldering ferocity, I said:

"Mr. Drummle, I did not seek this conversation, and I don't think it an agreeable one."

"I am sure it's not," said he, superciliously over his shoulder; "I don't think anything about it."

"And therefore," I went on, "with your leave, I will suggest that we hold no kind of communication in future."

"Quite my opinion," said Drummle, "and what I should have suggested myself, or done—more likely—without suggesting. But don't lose your temper. Haven't you lost enough without that?"

"What do you mean, sir?"

"Wai-ter!" said Drummle, by way of answering me.

The waiter reappeared.

"Look here, you sir. You quite understand that the young lady don't ride to-day, and that I dine at the young lady's?"

"Quite so, sir."

When the waiter had felt my fast-cooling tea-pot with the palm of his hand, and had looked imploringly at me, and had gone out, Drummle, careful not to move the shoulder next me, took a cigar from his pocket and bit the end off, but showed no sign of stirring. Choking and boiling as I was, I felt that we could not go a word further, without introducing Estella's name, which I could not endure to hear him utter; and therefore I looked stonily at the opposite wall, as if there were no one present, and forced myself to silence. How long we might have remained in this ridiculous position it is impossible to say, but for the incursion of three thriving farmers—laid on by the waiter, I think—who came into the coffee-room unbuttoning their great-coats and rubbing their hands, and before whom, as they charged at the fire, we were obliged to give way.

I saw him through the window, seizing his horse's mane, and mounting in his blundering brutal manner, and sidling and backing away. I thought he was gone, when he came back, calling for a light for the cigar in his mouth, which he had forgotten. A man in a dust-coloured dress appeared with what was wanted—I could not have said from where: whether from the inn yard, or the street, or where not—and as Drummle leaned down from the saddle and lighted his cigar and laughed, with a jerk of his head towards the coffee-room windows, the slouching shoulders and ragged hair of this man, whose back was towards me, reminded me of Orlick.

Too heavily out of sorts to care much at the time whether it were he or no, or after all to touch the breakfast, I washed the weather and the journey from my face and hands, and went out to the memorable old house that it would have been so much the better for me never to have entered, never to have seen.

Chapter 44

In the room where the dressing-table stood, and where the wax candles burnt on the wall, I found Miss Havisham and Estella; Miss Havisham seated on a settee near the fire, and Estella on a cushion at her feet. Estella was knitting, and Miss Havisham was looking on. They both raised their eyes as I went in, and both saw an alteration in me. I derived that, from the look they interchanged.

"And what wind," said Miss Havisham, "blows you here, Pip?"

Though she looked steadily at me, I saw that she was rather confused. Estella, pausing for a moment in her knitting with her eyes upon me, and then going on, I fancied that I read in the action of her fingers, as plainly as if she had told me in the dumb alphabet, that she perceived I had discovered my real benefactor.

"Miss Havisham," said I, "I went to Richmond yesterday, to speak to Estella; and finding that some wind had blown *her* here, I followed."

Miss Havisham motioning to me for the third or fourth time to sit down, I took the chair by the dressing-table, which I had often seen her occupy. With all that ruin at my feet and about me, it seemed a natural place for me, that day.

"What I had to say to Estella, Miss Havisham, I will say before you, presently—in a few moments. It will not surprise you, it will not displease you. I am as unhappy as you can ever have meant me to be."

Miss Havisham continued to look steadily at me. I could see in the action of Estella's fingers as they worked, that she attended to what I said: but she did not look up.

"I have found out who my patron is. It is not a fortunate discovery, and is not likely ever to enrich me in reputation, station, fortune, anything. There are reasons why I must say no more of that. It is not my secret, but another's."

As I was silent for a while, looking at Estella and considering how to go on, Miss Havisham repeated, "It is not your secret, but another's. Well?"

"When you first caused me to be brought here, Miss Havisham;

when I belonged to the village over yonder, that I wish I had never left; I suppose I did really come here, as any other chance boy might have come—as a kind of servant, to gratify a want or a whim, and to be paid for it?"

"Ay, Pip," replied Miss Havisham, steadily nodding her head; "you did."

"And that Mr. Jaggers——"

"Mr. Jaggers," said Miss Havisham, taking me up in a firm tone, "had nothing to do with it, and knew nothing of it. His being my lawyer, and his being the lawyer of your patron, is a coincidence. He holds the same relation towards numbers of people, and it might easily arise. Be that as it may, it did arise, and was not brought about by any one."

Any one might have seen in her haggard face that there was no suppression or evasion so far.

"But when I fell into the mistake I have so long remained in, at least you led me on?" said I.

"Yes," she returned, again nodding steadily, "I let you go on."

"Was that kind?"

"Who am I," cried Miss Havisham, striking her stick upon the floor and flashing into wrath so suddenly that Estella glanced up at her in surprise, "who am I, for God's sake, that I should be kind!"

It was a weak complaint to have made, and I had not meant to make it. I told her so, as she sat brooding after this outburst.

"Well, well, well!" she said. "What else?"

"I was liberally paid for my old attendance here," I said, to soothe her, "in being apprenticed, and I have asked these questions only for my own information. What follows has another (and I hope more disinterested) purpose. In humouring my mistake, Miss Havisham, you punished—practised on—perhaps you will supply whatever term expresses your intention, without offence—your self-seeking relations?"

"I did. Why, they would have it so! So would you. What has been my history, that I should be at the pains of entreating either them, or you, not to have it so! You made your own snares. *I* never made them."

Waiting until she was quiet again—for this, too, flashed out of her in a wild and sudden way—I went on.

"I have been thrown among one family of your relations, Miss Havisham, and have been constantly among them since I went to London. I know them to have been as honestly under my delusion as I myself. And I should be false and base if I did not tell you, whether it

is acceptable to you or no, and whether you are inclined to give cre-
dence to it or no, that you deeply wrong both Mr. Matthew Pocket
and his son Herbert, if you suppose them to be otherwise than generous, upright, open, and incapable of anything designing or mean."

"They are your friends," said Miss Havisham.

"They made themselves my friends," said I, "when they supposed
me to have superseded them; and when Sarah Pocket, Miss Georgiana,
and Mistress Camilla, were not my friends, I think."

This contrasting of them with the rest seemed, I was glad to see, to
do them good with her. She looked at me keenly for a little while, and
then said quietly:

"What do you want for them?"

"Only," said I, "that you would not confound them with the others. They may be of the same blood, but, believe me, they are not of
the same nature."

Still looking at me keenly, Miss Havisham repeated:

"What do you want for them?"

"I am not so cunning, you see," I said, in answer, conscious that I
reddened a little, "as that I could hide from you, even if I desired, that
I do want something. Miss Havisham, if you would spare the money
to do my friend Herbert a lasting service in life, but which from the
nature of the case must be done without his knowledge, I could show
you how."

"Why must it be done without his knowledge?" she asked, settling
her hands upon her stick, that she might regard me the more attentively.

"Because," said I, "I began the service myself, more than two years
ago, without his knowledge, and I don't want to be betrayed. Why I
fail in my ability to finish it, I cannot explain. It is a part of the secret
which is another person's and not mine."

She gradually withdrew her eyes from me, and turned them on the
fire. After watching it for what appeared in the silence and by the light
of the slowly wasting candles to be a long time, she was roused by the
collapse of some of the red coals, and looked towards me again—at
first, vacantly—then, with a gradually concentrating attention. All this
time, Estella knitted on. When Miss Havisham had fixed her attention
on me, she said, speaking as if there had been no lapse in our
dialogue:

"What else?"

"Estella," said I, turning to her now, and trying to command my trembling voice, "you know I love you. You know that I have loved you long and dearly."

She raised her eyes to my face, on being thus addressed, and her fingers plied their work, and she looked at me with an unmoved countenance. I saw that Miss Havisham glanced from me to her, and from her to me.

"I should have said this sooner, but for my long mistake. It induced me to hope that Miss Havisham meant us for one another. While I thought you could not help yourself, as it were, I refrained from saying it. But I must say it now."

Preserving her unmoved countenance, and with her fingers still going, Estella shook her head.

"I know," said I, in answer to that action; "I know. I have no hope that I shall ever call you mine, Estella. I am ignorant what may become of me very soon, how poor I may be, or where I may go. Still, I love you. I have loved you ever since I first saw you in this house."

Looking at me perfectly unmoved and with her fingers busy, she shook her head again.

"It would have been cruel in Miss Havisham, horribly cruel, to practise on the susceptibility of a poor boy, and to torture me through all these years with a vain hope and an idle pursuit, if she had reflected on the gravity of what she did. But I think she did not. I think that in the endurance of her own trial, she forgot mine, Estella."

I saw Miss Havisham put her hand to her heart and hold it there, as she sat looking by turns at Estella and at me.

"It seems," said Estella, very calmly, "that there are sentiments, fancies—I don't know how to call them—which I am not able to comprehend. When you say you love me, I know what you mean, as a form of words; but nothing more. You address nothing in my breast, you touch nothing there. I don't care for what you say at all. I have tried to warn you of this; now, have I not?"

I said in a miserable manner, "Yes."

"Yes. But you would not be warned, for you thought I did not mean it. Now, did you not think so?"

"I thought and hoped you could not mean it. You, so young, untried, and beautiful, Estella! Surely it is not in Nature."

"It is in *my* nature," she returned. And then she added, with a stress upon the words, "It is in the nature formed within me. I make a great difference between you and all other people when I say so much. I can do no more."

"Is it not true," said I, "that Bentley Drummle is in town here, and pursuing you?"

"It is quite true," she replied, referring to him with the indifference of utter contempt.

"That you encourage him, and ride out with him, and that he dines with you this very day?"

She seemed a little surprised that I should know it, but again replied, "Quite true."

"You cannot love him, Estella!"

Her fingers stopped for the first time, as she retorted rather angrily, "What have I told you? Do you still think, in spite of it, that I do not mean what I say?"

"You would never marry him, Estella?"

She looked towards Miss Havisham, and considered for a moment with her work in her hands. Then she said, "Why not tell you the truth? I am going to be married to him."

I dropped my face into my hands, but was able to control myself better than I could have expected, considering what agony it gave me to hear her say those words. When I raised my face again, there was such a ghastly look upon Miss Havisham's, that it impressed me, even in my passionate hurry and grief.

"Estella, dearest dearest Estella, do not let Miss Havisham lead you into this fatal step. Put me aside for ever—you have done so, I well know—but bestow yourself on some worthier person than Drummle. Miss Havisham gives you to him, as the greatest slight and injury that could be done to the many far better men who admire you, and to the few who truly love you. Among those few, there may be one who loves you even as dearly, though he has not loved you as long, as I. Take him, and I can bear it better, for your sake!"

My earnestness awoke a wonder in her that seemed as if it would have been touched with compassion, if she could have rendered me at all intelligible to her own mind.

"I am going," she said again, in a gentler voice, "to be married to him. The preparations for my marriage are making, and I shall be married soon. Why do you injuriously introduce the name of my mother by adoption? It is my own act."

"Your own act, Estella, to fling yourself away upon a brute?"

"On whom should I fling myself away?" she retorted, with a smile. "Should I fling myself away upon the man who would the soonest feel (if people do feel such things) that I took nothing to him? There! It is done. I shall do well enough, and so will my husband. As to leading me into what you call this fatal step, Miss Havisham would have had me wait, and not marry yet; but I am tired of the life I have led, which has very few charms for me, and I am willing enough to change it. Say no more. We shall never understand each other."

"Such a mean brute, such a stupid brute!" I urged in despair.

"Don't be afraid of my being a blessing to him," said Estella; "I shall not be that. Come! Here is my hand. Do we part on this, you visionary boy——or man?"

"O Estella!" I answered, as my bitter tears fell fast on her hand, do what I would to restrain them; "even if I remained in England and could hold my head up with the rest, how could I see you Drummle's wife!"

"Nonsense," she returned, "nonsense. This will pass in no time."

"Never, Estella!"

"You will get me out of your thoughts in a week."

"Out of my thoughts! You are part of my existence, part of myself. You have been in every line I have ever read, since I first came here, the rough common boy whose poor heart you wounded even then. You have been in every prospect I have ever seen since—on the river, on the sails of the ships, on the marshes, in the clouds, in the light, in the darkness, in the wind, in the woods, in the sea, in the streets. You have been the embodiment of every graceful fancy that my mind has ever become acquainted with. The stones of which the strongest London buildings are made, are not more real, or more impossible to be displaced by your hands, than your presence and influence have been to me, there and everywhere, and will be. Estella, to the last hour of my life, you cannot choose but remain part of my character, part of the little good in me, part of the evil. But, in this separation I associate you only with the good, and I will faithfully hold you to that always, for you must have done me far more good than harm, let me feel now what sharp distress I may. O God bless you, God forgive you!"

In what ecstasy of unhappiness I got these broken words out of myself, I don't know. The rhapsody welled up within me, like blood from an inward wound, and gushed out. I held her hand to my lips some lingering moments, and so I left her. But ever afterwards, I remembered—and soon afterwards with stronger reason—that while Estella looked at me merely with incredulous wonder, the spectral figure of Miss Havisham, her hand still covering her heart, seemed all resolved into a ghastly stare of pity and remorse.

All done, all gone! So much was done and gone, that when I went out at the gate, the light of the day seemed of a darker colour than when I went in. For a while, I hid myself among some lanes and by-paths, and then struck off to walk all the way to London. For, I had by that time come to myself so far, as to consider that I could not go back to the inn and see Drummle there; that I could not bear to sit upon the coach and be spoken to; that I could do nothing half so good for myself as tire myself out.

It was past midnight when I crossed London Bridge. Pursuing the narrow intricacies of the streets which at that time tended westward near the Middlesex shore of the river, my readiest access to the Temple was close by the river-side, through Whitefriars. I was not expected till to-morrow, but I had my keys, and, if Herbert were gone to bed, could get to bed myself without disturbing him.

As it seldom happened that I came in at that Whitefriars gate after the Temple was closed, and as I was very muddy and weary, I did not take it ill that the night-porter examined me with much attention as he held the gate a little way open for me to pass in. To help his memory I mentioned my name.

"I was not quite sure, sir, but I thought so. Here's a note, sir. The messenger that brought it, said would you be so good as read it by my lantern."

Much surprised by the request, I took the note. It was directed to Philip Pip, Esquire, and on the top of the superscription were the words, "PLEASE READ THIS, HERE." I opened it, the watchman holding up his light, and read inside, in Wemmick's writing:

"DON'T GO HOME."

[PART 28]

Chapter 45

Turning from the Temple gate as soon as I had read the warning, I made the best of my way to Fleet-street, and there got a late hackney chariot and drove to the Hummums° in Covent Garden. In those times a bed was always to be got there at any hour of the night, and the chamberlain, letting me in at his ready wicket, lighted the candle next in order on his shelf, and showed me straight into the bedroom next in order on his list. It was a sort of vault on the ground floor at the back, with a despotic monster of a four-post bedstead in it,

Hummums: A hotel named for its location on the former site of a Turkish bath ("hammam").

straddling over the whole place, putting one of his arbitrary legs into the fireplace and another into the doorway, and squeezing the wretched little washing-stand in quite a Divinely Righteous manner.

As I had asked for a night-light, the chamberlain had brought me in, before he left me, the good old constitutional rush-light of those virtuous days—an object like the ghost of a walking-cane, which instantly broke its back if it were touched, which nothing could ever be lighted at, and which was placed in solitary confinement at the bottom of a high tin tower, perforated with round holes that made a staringly wide-awake pattern on the walls. When I had got into bed, and lay there footsore, weary, and wretched, I found that I could no more close my own eyes than I could close the eyes of this foolish Argus. And thus, in the gloom and death of the night, we stared at one another.

What a doleful night! How anxious, how dismal, how long! There was an inhospitable smell in the room, of cold soot and hot dust; and, as I looked up into the corners of the tester over my head, I thought what a number of bluebottle flies from the butchers', and earwigs from the market, and grubs from the country, must be holding on up there, lying by for next summer. This led me to speculate whether any of them ever tumbled down, and then I fancied that I felt light falls on my face—a disagreeable turn of thought, suggesting other and more objectionable approaches up my back. When I had lain awake a little while, those extraordinary voices with which silence teems, began to make themselves audible. The closet whispered, the fireplace sighed, the little washing-stand ticked, and one guitar-string played occasionally in the chest of drawers. At about the same time, the eyes on the wall acquired a new expression, and in every one of those staring rounds I saw written, DON'T GO HOME.

Whatever night-fancies and night-noises crowded on me, they never warded off this DON'T GO HOME. It plaited itself into whatever I thought of, as a bodily pain would have done. Not long before, I had read in the newspapers, how a gentleman unknown had come to the Hummums in the night, and had gone to bed, and had destroyed himself, and had been found in the morning weltering in blood. It came into my head that he must have occupied this very vault of mine, and I got out of bed to assure myself that there were no red marks about; then opened the door to look out into the passages, and cheer myself with the companionship of a distant light, near which I knew the chamberlain to be dozing. But all this time, why I was not to go home, and what had happened at home, and when I should go home, and whether Provis was safe at home, were questions occupying my mind so busily, that one might have supposed there could be no more room in it for any other theme. Even when I thought of Estella, and how we had parted that day for ever, and when I recalled all the circumstances of our parting, and all her looks and tones, and the action of her fingers while she knitted—even then I was pursuing, here and there and everywhere, the caution Don't go home. When at last I dozed, in sheer exhaustion of mind and body, it became a vast shadowy verb which I had to conjugate. Imperative mood, present tense: Do not thou go home, let him not go home, let us not go home, do not ye or you go home, let not them go home. Then, potentially: I may not and I cannot go home; and I might not, could not, would not, and should not go home; until I felt that I was going distracted, and rolled over on the pillow, and looked at the staring rounds upon the wall again.

I had left directions that I was to be called at seven; for it was plain that I must see Wemmick before seeing any one else, and equally plain that this was a case in which his Walworth sentiments, only, could be taken. It was a relief to get out of the room where the night had been so miserable, and I needed no second knocking at the door to startle me from my uneasy bed.

The Castle battlements arose upon my view at eight o'clock. The little servant happening to be entering the fortress with two hot rolls, I passed through the postern and crossed the drawbridge, in her company, and so came without announcement into the presence of Wemmick as he was making tea for himself and the Aged. An open door afforded a perspective view of the Aged in bed.

"Halloa, Mr. Pip!" said Wemmick. "You did come home, then?"

"Yes," I returned; "but I didn't go home."

"That's all right," said he, rubbing his hands. "I left a note for you at each of the Temple gates, on the chance. Which gate did you come to?"

I told him.

"I'll go round to the others in the course of the day and destroy the notes," said Wemmick; "it's a good rule never to leave documentary evidence if you can help it, because you don't know when it may be put in. I'm going to take a liberty with you.— *Would* you mind toasting this sausage for the Aged P.?"

I said I should be delighted to do it.

"Then you can go about your work, Mary Anne," said Wemmick

to the little servant; "which leaves us to ourselves, don't you see, Mr. Pip?" he added, winking, as she disappeared.

I thanked him for his friendship and caution, and our discourse proceeded in a low tone, while I toasted the Aged's sausage and he buttered the crumb of the Aged's roll.

"Now, Mr. Pip, you know," said Wemmick, "you and I understand one another. We are in our private and personal capacities, and we have been engaged in a confidential transaction before to-day. Official sentiments are one thing. We are extra official."

I cordially assented. I was so very nervous, that I had already lighted the Aged's sausage like a torch, and been obliged to blow it out.

"I accidentally heard, yesterday morning," said Wemmick, "being in a certain place where I once took you—even between you and me, it's as well not to mention names when avoidable——"

"Much better not," said I. "I understand you."

"I heard there by chance, yesterday morning," said Wemmick, "that a certain person not altogether of uncolonial pursuits, and not unpossessed of portable property—I don't know who it may really be—we won't name this person——"

"Not necessary," said I.

"—had made some little stir in a certain part of the world where a good many people go, not always in gratification of their own inclinations, and not quite irrespective of the government expense——"

In watching his face, I made quite a fire-work of the Aged's sausage, and greatly discomposed both my own attention and Wemmick's; for which I apologised.

"—by disappearing from such place, and being no more heard of thereabouts. From which," said Wemmick, "conjectures had been raised and theories formed. I also heard that you at your chambers in Garden-court, Temple, had been watched, and might be watched again."

"By whom?" said I.

"I wouldn't go into that," said Wemmick, evasively, "it might clash with official responsibilities. I heard it, as I have in my time heard other curious things in the same place. I don't tell it you on information received. I heard it."

He took the toasting-fork and sausage from me as he spoke, and set forth the Aged's breakfast neatly on a little tray. Previous to placing it before him, he went into the Aged's room with a clean white cloth, and tied the same under the old gentleman's chin, and propped him up, and put his nightcap on one side, and gave him quite a rakish air. Then, he placed his breakfast before him with great care, and said, "All right, ain't you, Aged P.?" To which the cheerful Aged replied, "All right, John, my boy, all right!" As there seemed to be a tacit understanding that the Aged was not in a presentable state, and was therefore to be considered invisible, I made a pretence of being in complete ignorance of these proceedings.

"This watching of me at my chambers (which I have once had reason to suspect)," I said to Wemmick when he came back, "is inseparable from the person to whom you have adverted; is it?"

Wemmick looked very serious. "I couldn't undertake to say that, of my own knowledge. I mean, I couldn't undertake to say it was at first. But it either is, or it will be, or it's in great danger of being."

As I saw that he was restrained by fealty to Little Britain from saying as much as he could, and as I knew with thankfulness to him how far out of his way he went to say what he did, I could not press him. But I told him, after a little meditation over the fire, that I would like to ask him a question, subject to his answering or not answering, as he deemed right, and sure that his course would be right. He paused in his breakfast, and crossing his arms, and pinching his shirt-sleeves (his notion of in-door comfort was to sit without any coat), he nodded to me once, to put my question.

"You have heard of a man of bad character, whose true name is Compeyson?"

He answered with one other nod.

"Is he living?"

One other nod.

"Is he in London?"

He gave me one other nod, compressed the post-office exceedingly, gave me one last nod, and went on with his breakfast.

"Now," said Wemmick, "questioning being over;" which he emphasised and repeated for my guidance; "I come to what I did, after hearing what I heard. I went to Garden-court to find you; not finding you, I went to Clarriker's to find Mr. Herbert."

"And him you found?" said I, with great anxiety.

"And him I found. Without mentioning any names or going into any details, I gave him to understand that if he was aware of anybody—Tom, Jack, or Richard—being about the chambers, or about the immediate neighbourhood, he had better get Tom, Jack, or Richard, out of the way while you were out of the way."

"He would be greatly puzzled what to do?"

"He *was* puzzled what to do; not the less, because I gave him my opinion that it was not safe to try to get Tom, Jack, or Richard, too far out of the way at present. Mr. Pip, I'll tell you something. Under existing circumstances there is no place like a great city when you are once in it. Don't break cover too soon. Lie close. Wait till things slacken, before you try the open, even for foreign air."

I thanked him for his valuable advice, and asked him what Herbert had done?

"Mr. Herbert," said Wemmick, "after being all of a heap for half an hour, struck out a plan. He mentioned to me as a secret, that he is courting a young lady who has, as no doubt you are aware, a bedridden Pa. Which Pa, having been in the Purser line of life, lies a-bed in a bow-window where he can see the ships sail up and down the river. You are acquainted with the young lady, most probably?"

"Not personally," said I.

The truth was, that she had objected to me as an expensive companion who did Herbert no good, and that, when Herbert had first proposed to present me to her, she had received the proposal with such very moderate warmth, that Herbert had felt himself obliged to confide the state of the case to me, with a view to the lapse of a little time before I made her acquaintance. When I had begun to advance Herbert's prospects by stealth, I had been able to bear this with cheerful philosophy; he and his affianced, for their part, had naturally not been very anxious to introduce a third person into their interviews; and thus, although I was assured that I had risen in Clara's esteem, and although the young lady and I had long regularly interchanged messages and remembrances by Herbert, I had never seen her. However, I did not trouble Wemmick with these particulars.

"The house with the bow-window," said Wemmick, "being by the river-side, down the Pool° there between Limehouse and Greenwich, and being kept, it seems, by a very respectable widow who has a furnished upper floor to let, Mr. Herbert put it to me, what did I think of that as a temporary tenement for Tom, Jack, or Richard? Now, I thought very well of it, for three reasons I'll give you. That is to say. Firstly. It's altogether out of all your beats, and is well away from the usual heap of streets great and small. Secondly. Without going near it yourself, you could always hear of the safety of Tom, Jack, or Richard,

Pool: Section of the Thames, filled with docks and shipping, between Greenwich and London Bridge.

through Mr. Herbert. Thirdly. After a while and when it might be prudent, if you should want to slip Tom, Jack, or Richard, on board a foreign packet-boat, there he is—ready."

Much comforted by these considerations, I thanked Wemmick again and again, and begged him to proceed.

"Well, sir! Mr. Herbert threw himself into the business with a will, and by nine o'clock last night he housed Tom, Jack, or Richard—whichever it may be—you and I don't want to know—quite success-fully. At the old lodgings it was understood that he was summoned to Dover, and in fact he was taken down the Dover road and cornered out of it. Now, another great advantage of all this, is, that it was done without you, and when, if any one was concerning himself about your movements, you must be known to be ever so many miles off and quite otherwise engaged. This diverts suspicion and confuses it; and for the same reason I recommended that even if you came back last night, you should not go home. It brings in more confusion, and you want confusion."

Wemmick, having finished his breakfast, here looked at his watch, and began to get his coat on.

"And now, Mr. Pip," said he, with his hands still in the sleeves, "I have probably done the most I can do; but if I can ever do more—from a Walworth point of view, and in a strictly private and personal capacity—I shall be glad to do it. Here's the address. There can be no harm in your going here to-night and seeing for yourself that all is well with Tom, Jack, or Richard, before you go home—which is another reason for your not going home last night. But after you have gone home, don't go back here. You are very welcome, I am sure, Mr. Pip;" his hands were now out of his sleeves, and I was shaking them; "and let me finally impress one important point upon you." He laid his hands upon my shoulders, and added in a solemn whisper: "Avail yourself of this evening to lay hold of his portable property. You don't know what may happen to him. Don't let anything happen to the portable property."

Quite despairing of making my mind clear to Wemmick on this point, I forbore to try.

"Time's up," said Wemmick, "and I must be off. If you had nothing more pressing to do than to keep here till dark, that's what I should advise. You look very much worried, and it would do you good to have a perfectly quiet day with the Aged—he'll be up presently—and a little bit of——you remember the pig?"

"Of course," said I.

"Well; and a little bit of *him*. That sausage you toasted was his, and he was in all respects a first-rater. Do try him, if it is only for old acquaintance sake. Good-by, Aged Parent!" in a cheery shout.

"All right, John; all right, my boy!" piped the old man from within.

I soon fell asleep before Wemmick's fire, and the Aged and I enjoyed one another's society by falling asleep before it more or less all day. We had loin of pork for dinner, and greens grown on the estate, and I nodded at the Aged with a good intention whenever I failed to do it drowsily. When it was quite dark, I left the Aged preparing the fire for toast; and I inferred from the number of teacups, as well as from his glances at the two little doors in the wall, that Miss Skiffins was expected.

Chapter 46

Eight o'clock had struck before I got into the air that was scented, not disagreeably, by the chips and shavings of the long-shore boat-builders, and mast oar and block makers. All that water-side region of the upper and lower Pool below Bridge, was unknown ground to me, and when I struck down by the river, I found that the spot I wanted was not where I had supposed it to be, and was anything but easy to find. It was called Mill Pond Bank, Chinks's Basin; and I had no other guide to Chinks's Basin than the Old Green Copper Rope-Walk.°

It matters not what stranded ships repairing in dry docks I lost myself among, what old hulls of ships in course of being knocked to pieces, what ooze and slime and other dregs of tide, what yards of ship-builders and ship-breakers, what rusty anchors blindly biting into the ground though for years off duty, what mountainous country of accumulated casks and timber, how many rope-walks that were not the Old Green Copper. After several times falling short of my destination and as often overshooting it, I came unexpectedly round a corner, upon Mill Pond Bank. It was a fresh kind of place, all circumstances considered, where the wind from the river had room to turn itself round; and there were two or three trees in it, and there was the stump of a ruined windmill, and there was the Old Green Copper Rope-Walk—whose long and narrow vista I could trace in the moonlight,

---

Rope-Walk: A long, roofed alley where rope was made.

along a series of wooden frames set in the ground, that looked like su-
perannuated haymaking-rakes which had grown old and lost most of
their teeth.

Selecting from the few queer houses upon Mill Pond Bank, a
house with a wooden front and three stories of bow-window (not bay-
window, which is another thing), I looked at the plate upon the door,
and read there, Mrs. Whimple. That being the name I wanted, I
knocked, and an elderly woman of a pleasant and thriving appearance
responded. She was immediately deposed, however, by Herbert, who
silently led me into the parlour and shut the door. It was an odd sensation to see his very familiar face established quite at home in that very
unfamiliar room and region; and I found myself looking at him, much
as I looked at the corner-cupboard with the glass and china, the shells
upon the chimney-piece, and the coloured engravings on the wall, representing the death of Captain Cook, a ship-launch, and his Majesty
King George the Third in a state-coachman's wig, leather-breeches,
and top-boots, on the terrace at Windsor.

"All is well, Handel," said Herbert, "and he is quite satisfied,
though eager to see you. My dear girl is with her father; and if you'll
wait till she comes down, I'll make you known to her, and then we'll
go up-stairs.——*That's* her father."

I had become aware of an alarming growling overhead, and had
probably expressed the fact in my countenance.

"I am afraid he is a sad old rascal," said Herbert, smiling, "but I
have never seen him. Don't you smell rum? He is always at it."

"At rum?" said I.

"Yes," returned Herbert, "and you may suppose how mild it
makes his gout. He persists, too, in keeping all the provisions up-stairs
in his room, and serving them out. He keeps them on shelves over his
head, and *will* weigh them all. His room must be like a chandler's
shop."

While he thus spoke, the growling noise became a prolonged roar,
and then died away.

"What else can be the consequence," said Herbert, in explanation,
"if he *will* cut the cheese? A man with the gout in his right hand—and
everywhere else—can't expect to get through a Double Gloucester°
without hurting himself."

He seemed to have hurt himself very much, for he gave another
furious roar.

Double Gloucester: A cheese weighing up to thirty pounds.

"To have Provis for an upper lodger is quite a godsend to Mrs. Whimple," said Herbert, "for of course people in general won't stand that noise. A curious place, Handel; isn't it?"

It was a curious place, indeed; but remarkably well kept and clean.

"Mrs. Whimple," said Herbert, when I told him so, "is the best of housewives, and I really do not know what my Clara would do without her motherly help. For, Clara has no mother of her own, Handel, and no relation in the world but old Gruffandgrim."

"Surely that's not his name, Herbert?"

"No, no," said Herbert, "that's my name for him. His name is Mr. Barley. But what a blessing it is for the son of my father and mother, to love a girl who has no relations, and who can never bother herself, or anybody else, about her family!"

Herbert had told me on former occasions, and now reminded me, that he first knew Miss Clara Barley when she was completing her education at an establishment at Hammersmith, and that on her being recalled home to nurse her father, he and she had confided their affection to the motherly Mrs. Whimple, by whom it had been fostered and regulated with equal kindness and discretion, ever since. It was understood that nothing of a tender nature could possibly be confided to old Barley, by reason of his being totally unequal to the consideration of any subject more psychological than Gout, Rum, and Purser's stores.

As we were thus conversing in a low tone while Old Barley's sustained growl vibrated in the beam that crossed the ceiling, the room door opened, and a very pretty slight dark-eyed girl of twenty or so, came in with a basket in her hand: whom Herbert tenderly relieved of the basket, and presented blushing, as "Clara." She really was a most charming girl, and might have passed for a captive fairy, whom that truculent Ogre, Old Barley, had pressed into his service.

"Look here," said Herbert, showing me the basket, with a compassionate and tender smile after we had talked a little; "here's poor Clara's supper, served out every night. Here's her allowance of bread, and here's her slice of cheese, and here's her rum—which I drink. This is Mr. Barley's breakfast for to-morrow, served out to be cooked. Two mutton chops, three potatoes, some split peas, a little flour, two ounces of butter, a pinch of salt, and all this black pepper. It's stewed up together, and taken hot, and it's a nice thing for the gout, I should think!"

There was something so natural and winning in Clara's resigned way of looking at these stores in detail, as Herbert pointed them out,—and something so confiding, loving, and innocent, in her modest manner of yielding herself to Herbert's embracing arm—and something so gentle in her, so much needing protection on Mill Pond Bank, by Chinks's Basin, and the Old Green Copper Rope-Walk, with Old Barley growling in the beam—that I would not have undone the engagement between her and Herbert, for all the money in the pocket-book I had never opened.

I was looking at her with pleasure and admiration, when suddenly the growl swelled into a roar again, and a frightful bumping noise was heard above, as if a giant with a wooden leg were trying to bore it through the ceiling to come at us. Upon this Clara said to Herbert, "Papa wants me, darling!" and ran away.

"There is an unconscionable old shark for you!" said Herbert. "What do you suppose he wants now, Handel?"

"I don't know," said I. "Something to drink?"

"That's it!" cried Herbert, as if I had made a guess of extraordinary merit. "He keeps his grog ready-mixed in a little tub on the table. Wait a moment, and you'll hear Clara lift him up to take some.— There he goes!" Another roar, with a prolonged shake at the end. "Now," said Herbert, as it was succeeded by silence, "he's drinking. Now," said Herbert, as the growl resounded in the beam once more, "he's down again on his back!"

Clara returned soon afterwards, and Herbert accompanied me upstairs to see our charge. As we passed Mr. Barley's door, he was heard hoarsely muttering within, in a strain that rose and fell like wind, the following Refrain; in which I substitute good wishes for something quite the reverse.

"Ahoy! Bless your eyes, here's old Bill Barley. Here's old Bill Barley, bless your eyes. Here's old Bill Barley on the flat of his back, by the Lord. Lying on the flat of his back, like a drifting old dead flounder, here's your old Bill Barley, bless your eyes. Ahoy! Bless you."

In this strain of consolation, Herbert informed me the invisible Barley would commune with himself by the day and night together; often while it was light, having, at the same time, one eye at a telescope which was fitted on his bed for the convenience of sweeping the river.

In his two cabin rooms at the top of the house, which were fresh and airy, and in which Mr. Barley was less audible than below, I found Provis comfortably settled. He expressed no alarm, and seemed to feel none that was worth mentioning; but it struck me that he was soft-

ened—indefinably, for I could not have said how, and could never afterwards recal how when I tried; but certainly.

The opportunity that the day's rest had given me for reflection,
had resulted in my fully determining to say nothing to him respecting
Compeyson. For anything I knew, his animosity towards the man
might otherwise lead to his seeking him out and rushing on his own
destruction. Therefore, when Herbert and I sat down with him by his
fire, I asked him first of all whether he relied on Wemmick's judgment
and sources of information?

"Ay, ay, dear boy!" he answered, with a grave nod, "Jaggers's
knows."

"Then, I have talked with Wemmick," said I, "and have come to
tell you what caution he gave me and what advice."

This I did accurately, with the reservation just mentioned; and I
told him how Wemmick had heard, in Newgate prison (whether from
officers or prisoners I could not say), that he was under some suspicion, and that my chambers had been watched; how Wemmick had
recommended his keeping close for a time, and my keeping away from
him; and what Wemmick had said about getting him abroad. I added,
that of course, when the time came, I should go with him, or should
follow close upon him, as might be safest in Wemmick's judgment.
What was to follow that, I did not touch upon; neither indeed was I at
all clear or comfortable about it in my own mind, now that I saw him
in that softer condition, and in declared peril for my sake. As to alter-
ing my way of living, by enlarging my expenses, I put it to him
whether in our present unsettled and difficult circumstances, it would
not be simply ridiculous, if it were no worse?

He could not deny this, and indeed was very reasonable throughout. His coming back was a venture, he said, and he had always known
it to be a venture. He would do nothing to make it a desperate venture, and he had very little fear of his safety with such good help.

Herbert, who had been looking at the fire and pondering, here
said that something had come into his thoughts arising out of Wemmick's suggestion, which it might be worth while to pursue. "We are
both good watermen, Handel, and could take him down the river ourselves when the right time comes. No boat would then be hired for
the purpose, and no boatmen; that would save at least a chance of suspicion, and any chance is worth saving. Never mind the season; don't
you think it might be a good thing if you began at once to keep a boat
at the Temple stairs, and were in the habit of rowing up and down the

river? You fall into that habit, and then who notices or minds? Do it twenty or fifty times, and there is nothing special in your doing it the twenty-first or fifty-first."

I liked this scheme, and Provis was quite elated by it. We agreed that it should be carried into execution, and that Provis should never recognise us if we came below Bridge and rowed past Mill Pond Bank. But, we further agreed that he should pull down the blind in that part of his window which gave upon the east, whenever he saw us and all was right.

Our conference being now ended, and everything arranged, I rose to go; remarking to Herbert that he and I had better not go home together, and that I would take half an hour's start of him. "I don't like to leave you here," I said to Provis, "though I cannot doubt your being safer here than near me. Good-by!"

"Dear boy," he answered, clasping my hands, "I don't know when we may meet again, and I don't like Good-by. Say Good Night!"

"Good night! Herbert will go regularly between us, and when the time comes you may be certain I shall be ready. Good night, Good night!"

We thought it best that he should stay in his own rooms, and we left him on the landing outside his door, holding a light over the stair-rail to light us down stairs. Looking back at him, I thought of the first night of his return when our positions were reversed, and when I little supposed my heart could ever be as heavy and anxious at parting from him as it was now.

Old Barley was growling and swearing when we repassed his door, with no appearance of having ceased or of meaning to cease. When we got to the foot of the stairs, I asked Herbert whether he had preserved the name of Provis? He replied, certainly not, and that the lodger was Mr. Campbell. He also explained that the utmost known of Mr. Campbell there, was, that he (Herbert) had Mr. Campbell consigned to him, and felt a strong personal interest in his being well cared for, and living a secluded life. So, when we went into the parlour where Mrs. Whimple and Clara were seated at work, I said nothing of my own interest in Mr. Campbell, but kept it to myself.

When I had taken leave of the pretty gentle dark-eyed girl, and of the motherly woman who had not outlived her honest sympathy with a little affair of true love, I felt as if the Old Green Copper Rope-Walk had grown quite a different place. Old Barley might be as old as the hills, and might swear like a whole field of troopers, but there were re-deeming youth and trust and hope enough in Chinks's Basin to fill it to overflowing. And then I thought of Estella, and of our parting, and went home very sadly.

All things were as quiet in the Temple as ever I had seen them. The windows of the rooms on that side, lately occupied by Provis, were dark and still, and there was no lounger in Garden-court. I walked past the fountain twice or thrice before I descended the steps that were between me and my rooms, but I was quite alone. Herbert coming to my bedside when he came in—for I went straight to bed, dispirited and fatigued—made the same report. Opening one of the windows after that, he looked out into the moonlight, and told me that the pavement was as solemnly empty as the pavement of any Cathedral at that same hour.

Next day, I set myself to get the boat. It was soon done, and the boat was brought round to the Temple-stairs, and lay where I could reach her within a minute or two. Then, I began to go out as for train- ing and practice: sometimes alone, sometimes with Herbert. I was often out in cold, rain, and sleet, but nobody took much note of me after I had been out a few times. At first, I kept above Blackfriars Bridge; but as the hours of the tide changed, I took towards London Bridge. It was Old London Bridge in those days,° and at certain states of the tide there was a race and a fall of water there which gave it a bad reputation. But I knew well enough how to "shoot" the bridge° after seeing it done, and so began to row about among the shipping in the Pool, and down to Erith.° The first time I passed Mill Pond Bank, Herbert and I were pulling a pair of oars; and, both in going and re- turning, we saw the blind towards the east come down. Herbert was rarely there less frequently than three times in a week, and he never brought me a single word of intelligence that was at all alarming. Still, I knew that there was cause for alarm, and I could not get rid of the notion of being watched. Once received, it is a haunting idea; how many undesigning persons I suspected of watching me, it would be hard to calculate.

In short, I was always full of fears for the rash man who was in hid- ing. Herbert had sometimes said to me that he found it pleasant to stand at one of our windows after dark, when the tide was running down, and to think that it was flowing, with everything it bore, to- wards Clara. But I thought with dread that it was flowing towards

---

Old . . . days: That is, before 1831, when the "old" London Bridge was demolished. **"shoot" the bridge:** Judge the current so as to pass safely through the arches of the bridge.   **Erith:** A port in Kent twelve miles east of London.

Magwitch, and that any black mark on its surface might be his pursuers, going swiftly, silently, and surely, to take him.

[PART 29]

Chapter 47

Some weeks passed without bringing any change. We waited for Wemmick, and he made no sign. If I had never known him out of Little Britain, and had never enjoyed the privilege of being on a familiar footing at the Castle, I might have doubted him; not so for a moment, knowing him as I did.

My worldly affairs began to wear a gloomy appearance, and I was pressed for money by more than one creditor. Even I myself began to know the want of money (I mean of ready money in my own pocket), and to relieve it by converting some easily spared articles of jewellery into cash. But I had quite determined that it would be a heartless fraud to take more money from my patron in the existing state of my uncertain thoughts and plans. Therefore, I had sent him the unopened pocket-book by Herbert, to hold in his own keeping, and I felt a kind of satisfaction—whether it was a false kind or a true, I hardly know— in not having profited by his generosity since his revelation of himself.

As the time wore on, an impression settled heavily upon me that Estella was married. Fearful of having it confirmed, though it was all but a conviction, I avoided the newspapers, and begged Herbert (to whom I had confided the circumstances of our last interview) never to speak of her to me. Why I hoarded up this last wretched little rag of the robe of hope that was rent and given to the winds, how do I know! Why did you who read this, commit that not dissimilar inconsistency of your own, last year, last month, last week?

It was an unhappy life that I lived, and its one dominant anxiety, towering over all its other anxieties like a high mountain above a range of mountains, never disappeared from my view. Still, no new cause for fear arose. Let me start from my bed as I would, with the terror fresh upon me that he was discovered; let me sit listening as I would, with dread, for Herbert's returning step at night, lest it should be fleeter than ordinary, and winged with evil news; for all that, and much more to like purpose, the round of things went on. Condemned to inaction and a state of constant restlessness and suspense, I rowed about in my boat, and waited, waited, waited, as I best could.

There were states of the tide when, having been down the river, I could not get back through the eddy-chafed arches and starlings of old London Bridge; then, I left my boat at a wharf near the Custom House, to be brought up afterwards to the Temple stairs. I was not averse to doing this, as it served to make me and my boat a commoner incident among the water-side people there. From this slight occasion, sprang two meetings that I have now to tell of.

One afternoon, late in the month of February, I came ashore at the wharf at dusk. I had pulled down as far as Greenwich with the ebb tide, and had turned with the tide. It had been a fine bright day, but had become foggy as the sun dropped, and I had had to feel my way back among the shipping, pretty carefully. Both in going and returning, I had seen the signal in his window, All well.

As it was a raw evening and I was cold, I thought I would comfort myself with dinner at once; and as I had hours of dejection and solitude before me if I went home to the Temple, I thought I would afterwards go to the play. The theatre where Mr. Wopsle had achieved his questionable triumph, was in that waterside neighbourhood (it is nowhere now), and to that theatre I resolved to go. I was aware that Mr. Wopsle had not succeeded in reviving the Drama, but, on the contrary, had rather partaken of its decline. He had been ominously heard of, through the playbills, as a faithful Black,° in connexion with a little girl of noble birth, and a monkey. And Herbert had seen him as a predatory Tartar° of comic propensities, with a face like a red brick, and an outrageous hat all over bells.

I dined at what Herbert and I used to call a Geographical chop-house—where there were maps of the world in porter-pot rims on every half-yard of the tablecloths, and charts of gravy on every one of the knives—to this day there is scarcely a single chop-house within the Lord Mayor's dominions which is not Geographical—and wore out the time in dozing over crumbs, staring at gas, and baking in a hot blast of dinners. By-and-by, I roused myself and went to the play.

There, I found a virtuous boatswain in his Majesty's service—a most excellent man, though I could have wished his trousers not so tight in some places and not quite so loose in others—who knocked all the little men's hats over their eyes, though he was very generous and brave, and who wouldn't hear of anybody's paying taxes, though he was very patriotic. He had a bag of money in his pocket, like a

Black: A black man, presumably here a servant or slave.   **Tartar:** A native of Central Asia, stereotypically a savage or violent person.

pudding in the cloth, and on that property married a young person in bed-furniture,° with great rejoicings; the whole population of Portsmouth (nine in number at the last Census) turning out on the beach, to rub their own hands and shake everybody else's, and sing "Fill, fill!" A certain dark-complexioned Swab,° however, who would-n't fill, or do anything else that was proposed to him, and whose heart was openly stated (by the boatswain) to be as black as his figure-head, proposed to two other Swabs to get all mankind into difficulties; which was so effectually done (the Swab family having considerable political influence) that it took half the evening to set things right, and then it was only brought about through an honest little grocer with a white hat, black gaiters, and red nose, getting into a clock, with a grid-iron, and listening, and coming out, and knocking everybody down from behind with the gridiron whom he couldn't confute with what he had overheard. This led to Mr. Wopsle's (who had never been heard of before) coming in with a star and garter° on, as a plenipoten-tiary of great power direct from the Admiralty, to say that the Swabs were all to go to prison on the spot, and that he had brought the boatswain down the Union Jack, as a slight acknowledgment of his public services. The boatswain, unmanned for the first time, respect-fully dried his eyes on the Jack, and then cheering up and addressing Mr. Wopsle as Your Honour, solicited permission to take him by the fin. Mr. Wopsle conceding his fin with a gracious dignity, was immedi-ately shoved into a dusty corner while everybody danced a hornpipe; and from that corner, surveying the public with a discontented eye, became aware of me.

The second piece was the last new grand comic Christmas pan-tomime, in the first scene of which, it pained me to suspect that I de-tected Mr. Wopsle with red worsted legs under a highly magnified phosphoric countenance and a shock of red curtain-fringe for his hair, engaged in the manufacture of thunderbolts in a mine, and displaying great cowardice when his gigantic master came home (very hoarse) to dinner. But he presently presented himself under worthier circum-stances; for, the Genius of Youthful Love being in want of assistance—on account of the parental brutality of an ignorant farmer who op-posed the choice of his daughter's heart, by purposely falling upon the object, in a flour sack, out of the first-floor window—summoned a sententious Enchanter; and he, coming up from the antipodes rather

---

in bed-furniture: In a costume made from bed-curtains.   **Swab:** Derogatory term for sailor.   **star and garter:** Emblems of noble rank.

unsteadily, after an apparently violent journey, proved to be Mr. Wopsle in a high-crowned hat, with a necromantic work in one volume under his arm. The business of this enchanter on earth, being principally to be talked at, sung at, butted at, danced at, and flashed at with fires of various colours, he had a good deal of time on his hands. And I observed with great surprise, that he devoted it to staring in my direction as if he were lost in amazement.

There was something so remarkable in the increasing glare of Mr. Wopsle's eye, and he seemed to be turning so many things over in his mind and to grow so confused, that I could not make it out. I sat thinking of it, long after he had ascended to the clouds in a large watch-case, and still I could not make it out. I was still thinking of it when I came out of the theatre an hour afterwards, and found him waiting for me near the door.

"How do you do?" said I, shaking hands with him as we turned down the street together. "I saw that you saw me."

"Saw you, Mr. Pip!" he returned. "Yes, of course I saw you. But who else was there?"

"Who else?"

"It is the strangest thing," said Mr. Wopsle, drifting into his lost look again; "and yet I could swear to him."

Becoming alarmed, I entreated Mr. Wopsle to explain his meaning.

"Whether I should have noticed him at first but for your being there," said Mr. Wopsle, going on in the same lost way, "I can't be positive; yet I think I should."

Involuntarily I looked round me, as I was accustomed to look round me when I went home; for, these mysterious words gave me a chill.

"Oh! He can't be in sight," said Mr. Wopsle. "He went out, before I went off, I saw him go."

Having the reason that I had, for being suspicious, I even suspected this poor actor. I mistrusted a design to entrap me into some admission. Therefore, I glanced at him as we walked on together, but said nothing.

"I had a ridiculous fancy that he must be with you, Mr. Pip, till I saw that you were quite unconscious of him, sitting behind you there, like a ghost."

My former chill crept over me again, but I was resolved not to speak yet, for it was quite consistent with his words that he might be set on to induce me to connect these references with Provis. Of course, I was perfectly sure and safe that Provis had not been there.

"I dare say you wonder at me, Mr. Pip; indeed I see you do. But it is so very strange! You'll hardly believe what I am going to tell you. I could hardly believe it myself, if you told me."

"Indeed?" said I.

"No, indeed. Mr. Pip, you remember in old times a certain Christmas Day, when you were quite a child, and I dined at Gargery's, and some soldiers came to the door to get a pair of handcuffs mended?"

"I remember it very well."

"And you remember that there was a chase after two convicts, and that we joined in it, and that Gargery took you on his back, and that I took the lead and you kept up with me as well as you could?"

"I remember it all very well." Better than he thought—except the last clause.

"And you remember that we came up with the two in a ditch, and that there was a scuffle between them, and that one of them had been severely handled and much mauled about the face, by the other?"

"I see it all before me."

"And that the soldiers lighted torches, and put the two in the centre, and that we went on to see the last of them, over the black marshes, with the torchlight shining on their faces—I am particular about that; with the torchlight shining on their faces, when there was an outer ring of dark night all about us?"

"Yes," said I. "I remember all that."

"Then, Mr. Pip, one of those two prisoners sat behind you to-night. I saw him over your shoulder."

"Steady!" I thought. I asked him then, "Which of the two do you suppose you saw?"

"The one who had been mauled," he answered readily, "and I'll swear I saw him! The more I think of him, the more certain I am of him."

"This is very curious!" said I, with the best assumption I could put on, of its being nothing more to me. "Very curious indeed!"

I cannot exaggerate the enhanced disquiet into which this conversation threw me, or the special and peculiar terror I felt at Compeyson's having been behind me "like a ghost." For, if he had ever been out of my thoughts for a few moments together since the hiding had begun, it was in those very moments when he was closest to me; and to think that I should be so unconscious and off my guard after all my care, was as if I had shut an avenue of a hundred doors to keep him out, and then had found him at my elbow. I could not doubt either that he was there, because I was there, and that however slight an appearance of danger there might be about us, danger was always near and active.

I put such questions to Mr. Wopsle as, When did the man come in? He could not tell me that; he saw me, and over my shoulder he saw the man. It was not until he had seen him for some time that he began to identify him; but he had from the first vaguely associated him with me, and known him as somehow belonging to me in the old village time. How was he dressed? Prosperously, but not noticeably otherwise; he thought, in black. Was his face at all disfigured? No, he believed not. I believed not, too, for, although in my brooding state I had taken no especial notice of the people behind me, I thought it likely that a face at all disfigured would have attracted my attention.

When Mr. Wopsle had imparted to me all that he could recal or I extract, and when I had treated him to a little appropriate refreshment after the fatigues of the evening, we parted. It was between twelve and one o'clock when I reached the Temple, and the gates were shut. No one was near me when I went in and went home.

Herbert had come in, and we held a very serious council by the fire. But there was nothing to be done, saving to communicate to Wemmick what I had that night found out, and to remind him that we waited for his hint. As I thought that I might compromise him if I went too often to the Castle, I made this communication by letter. I wrote it before I went to bed, and went out and posted it; and again no one was near me. Herbert and I agreed that we could do nothing else but be very cautious. And we were very cautious indeed—more cautious than before, if that were possible—and I for my part never went near Chinks's Basin, except when I rowed by, and then I only looked at Mill Pond Bank as I looked at anything else.

Chapter 48

The second of the two meetings referred to in the last chapter, occurred about a week after the first. I had again left my boat at the wharf below Bridge; the time was an hour earlier in the afternoon; and, undecided where to dine, I had strolled up into Cheapside, and was strolling along it, surely the most unsettled person in all the busy concourse, when a large hand was laid upon my shoulder, by some one overtaking me. It was Mr. Jaggers's hand, and he passed it through my arm.

"As we are going in the same direction, Pip, we may walk together. Where are you bound for?"

"For the Temple, I think," said I.

"Don't you know?" said Mr. Jaggers.

"Well," I returned, glad for once to get the better of him in cross-examination, "I do *not* know, for I have not made up my mind."

"You are going to dine?" said Mr. Jaggers. "You don't mind admitting that, I suppose?"

"No," I returned, "I don't mind admitting that."

"And are not engaged?"

"I don't mind admitting also, that I am not engaged."

"Then," said Mr. Jaggers, "come and dine with me."

I was going to excuse myself, when he added, "Wemmick's coming." So, I changed my excuse into an acceptance—the few words I had uttered, serving for the beginning of either—and we went along Cheapside and slanted off to Little Britain, while the lights were springing up brilliantly in the shop windows, and the street lamplighters, scarcely finding ground enough to plant their ladders on in the midst of the afternoon's bustle, were skipping up and down and running in and out, opening more red eyes in the gathering fog than my rush-light tower at the Hummums had opened white eyes in the ghostly wall.

At the office in Little Britain there was the usual letter-writing, hand-washing, candle-snuffing, and safe-locking, that closed the business of the day. As I stood idle by Mr. Jaggers's fire, its rising and falling flame made the two casts on the shelf look as if they were playing a diabolical game at bo-peep with me; while the pair of coarse fat office candles that dimly lighted Mr. Jaggers as he wrote in a corner, were decorated with dirty winding-sheets,° as if in remembrance of a host of hanged clients.

We went to Gerrard-street, all three together, in a hackney-coach: and as soon as we got there, dinner was served. Although I should not have thought of making, in that place, the most distant reference by so much as a look to Wemmick's Walworth sentiments, yet I should have had no objection to catching his eye now and then in a friendly way. But it was not to be done. He turned his eyes on Mr. Jaggers whenever he raised them from the table, and was as dry and distant to me as if there were twin Wemmicks and this was the wrong one.

"Did you send that note of Miss Havisham's to Mr. Pip, Wemmick?" Mr. Jaggers asked, soon after we began dinner.

winding-sheets: Shrouds.

"No, sir," returned Wemmick; "it was going by post, when you brought Mr. Pip into the office. Here it is." He handed it to his principal, instead of to me.

"It's a note of two lines, Pip," said Mr. Jaggers, handing it on, "sent up to me by Miss Havisham, on account of her not being sure of your address. She tells me that she wants to see you on a little matter of business you mentioned to her. You'll go down?"

"Yes," said I, casting my eyes over the note, which was exactly in those terms.

"When do you think of going down?"

"I have an impending engagement," said I, glancing at Wemmick, who was putting fish into the post-office, "that renders me rather uncertain of my time. At once, I think."

"If Mr. Pip has the intention of going at once," said Wemmick to Mr. Jaggers, "he needn't write an answer, you know."

Receiving this as an intimation that it was best not to delay, I settled that I would go to-morrow, and said so. Wemmick drank a glass of wine and looked with a grimly satisfied air at Mr. Jaggers, but not at me.

"So, Pip! Our friend the Spider," said Mr. Jaggers, "has played his cards. He has won the pool."

It was as much as I could do to assent.

"Hah! He is a promising fellow—in his way—but he may not have it all his own way. The stronger will win in the end, but the stronger has to be found out first. If he should turn to, and beat her——"

"Surely," I interrupted, with a burning face and heart, "you do not seriously think that he is scoundrel enough for that, Mr. Jaggers?"

"I didn't say so, Pip. I am putting a case. If he should turn to and beat her, he may possibly get the strength on his side; if it should be a question of intellect, he certainly will not. It would be chance work to give an opinion how a fellow of that sort will turn out in such circumstances, because it's a toss-up between two results."

"May I ask what they are?"

"A fellow like our friend the Spider," answered Mr. Jaggers, "either beats, or cringes. He may cringe and growl, or cringe and not growl; but he either beats or cringes. Ask Wemmick *his* opinion."

"Either beats or cringes," said Wemmick, not at all addressing himself to me.

"So, here's to Mrs. Bentley Drummle," said Mr. Jaggers, taking a decanter of choicer wine from his dumb-waiter, and filling for each of us and for himself, "and may the question of supremacy be settled to the lady's satisfaction! To the satisfaction of the lady *and* the gentleman, it never will be. Now, Molly, Molly, Molly, Molly, how slow you are to-day!"

She was at his elbow when he addressed her, putting a dish upon the table. As she withdrew her hands from it, she fell back a step or two, nervously muttering some excuse. And a certain action of her fingers as she spoke arrested my attention.

"What's the matter?" said Mr. Jaggers.

"Nothing. Only the subject we were speaking of," said I, "was rather painful to me."

The action of her fingers was like the action of knitting. She stood looking at her master, not understanding whether she was free to go, or whether he had more to say to her and would call her back if she did go. Her look was very intent. Surely, I had seen exactly such eyes and such hands, on a memorable occasion very lately!

He dismissed her, and she glided out of the room. But she remained before me, as plainly as if she were still there. I looked at those hands, I looked at those eyes, I looked at that flowing hair; and I compared them with other hands, other eyes, other hair, that I knew of, and with what those might be after twenty years of a brutal husband and a stormy life. I looked again at those hands and eyes of the housekeeper, and thought of the inexplicable feeling that had come over me when I last walked—not alone—in the ruined garden, and through the deserted brewery. I thought how the same feeling had come back when I saw a face looking at me, and a hand waving to me, from a stage-coach window; and how it had come back again and had flashed about me like Lightning, when I had passed in a carriage— not alone—through a sudden glare of light in a dark street. I thought how one link of association had helped that identification in the theatre, and how such a link, wanting before, had been riveted for me now, when I had passed by a chance swift from Estella's name to the fingers with their knitting action, and the attentive eyes. And I felt absolutely certain that this woman was Estella's mother.

Mr. Jaggers had seen me with Estella, and was not likely to have missed the sentiments I had been at no pains to conceal. He nodded when I said the subject was painful to me, clapped me on the back, put round the wine again, and went on with his dinner.

Only twice more, did the housekeeper reappear, and then her stay in the room was very short, and Mr. Jaggers was sharp with her. But her hands were Estella's hands, and her eyes were Estella's eyes, and if she had reappeared a hundred times I could have been neither more sure nor less sure that my conviction was the truth.

It was a dull evening, for Wemmick drew his wine when it came round, quite as a matter of business—just as he might have drawn his salary when that came round—and with his eyes on his chief, sat in a state of perpetual readiness for cross-examination. As to the quantity of wine, his post-office was as indifferent and ready as any other post-office for its quantity of letters. From my point of view, he was the wrong twin all the time, and only externally like the Wemmick of Walworth.

We took our leave early, and left together. Even when we were groping among Mr. Jaggers's stock of boots for our hats, I felt that the right twin was on his way back; and we had not gone half a dozen yards down Gerrard-street in the Walworth direction before I found that I was walking arm-in-arm with the right twin, and that the wrong twin had evaporated into the evening air.

"Well!" said Wemmick, "that's over! He's a wonderful man, without his living likeness; but I feel that I have to screw myself up when I dine with him—and I dine more comfortably unscrewed."

I felt that this was a good statement of the case, and told him so.

"Wouldn't say it to anybody but yourself," he answered. "I know that what is said between you and me, goes no further."

I asked him if he had ever seen Miss Havisham's adopted daughter, Mrs. Bentley Drummle? He said no. To avoid being too abrupt, I then spoke of the Aged, and of Miss Skiffins. He looked rather sly when I mentioned Miss Skiffins, and stopped in the street to blow his nose, with a roll of the head and a flourish not quite free from latent boastfulness.

"Wemmick," said I, "do you remember telling me before I first went to Mr. Jaggers's private house, to notice that housekeeper?"

"Did I?" he replied. "Ah, I dare say I did. Deuce take me," he added, suddenly, "I know I did. I find I am not quite unscrewed yet."

"A wild beast tamed, you called her."

"And what do *you* call her?"

"The same. How did Mr. Jaggers tame her, Wemmick?"

"That's his secret. She has been with him many a long year."

"I wish you would tell me her story. I feel a particular interest in being acquainted with it. You know that what is said between you and me goes no further."

"Well!" Wemmick replied, "I don't know her story—that is, I don't know all of it. But what I do know, I'll tell you. We are in our private and personal capacities, of course."

"Of course."

"A score or so of years ago, that woman was tried at the Old Bailey for murder, and was acquitted. She was a very handsome young woman, and I believe had some gipsy blood in her. Anyhow, it was hot enough when it was up, as you may suppose."

"But she was acquitted."

"Mr. Jaggers was for her," pursued Wemmick, with a look full of meaning, "and worked the case in a way quite astonishing. It was a desperate case, and it was comparatively early days with him then, and he worked it to general admiration; in fact, it may almost be said to have made him. He worked it himself at the police-office, day after day for many days, contending against even a committal; and at the trial where he couldn't work it himself, sat under Counsel, and—every one knew—put in all the salt and pepper.° The murdered person was a woman; a woman, a good ten years older, very much larger, and very much stronger. It was a case of jealousy. They both led tramping lives, and this woman in Gerrard-street here had been married very young, over the broomstick° (as we say), to a tramping man, and was a perfect fury in point of jealousy. The murdered woman—more a match for the man, certainly, in point of years—was found dead in a barn near Hounslow Heath.° There had been a violent struggle, perhaps a fight. She was bruised and scratched and torn, and had been held by the throat at last and choked. Now, there was no reasonable evidence to implicate any person but this woman, and, on the improbabilities of her having been able to do it, Mr. Jaggers principally rested his case. You may be sure," said Wemmick, touching me on the sleeve, "that he never dwelt upon the strength of her hands then, though he sometimes does now."

I had told Wemmick of his showing us her wrists, that day of the dinner party.

"Well, sir!" Wemmick went on; "it happened—happened, don't

---

put . . . pepper: Provided all the strategy and information ("salt and pepper" or "spice"). As an attorney, Jaggers can represent his clients directly only in the lower courts; here, his client is represented by a barrister ("Counsel"), "under" whom Jaggers serves. **over the broomstick:** Not legally married. **Hounslow Heath:** Twelve miles west of London.

you see?—that this woman was so very artfully dressed from the time of her apprehension, that she looked much slighter than she really was; in particular, her sleeves are always remembered to have been so skilfully contrived that her arms had quite a delicate look. She had only a bruise or two about her—nothing for a tramp—but the backs of her hands were lacerated, and the question was, was it with finger-nails? Now, Mr. Jaggers showed that she had struggled through a great lot of brambles which were not as high as her face; but which she could not have got through and kept her hands out of; and bits of those brambles were actually found in her skin and put in evidence, as well as the fact that the brambles in question were found on exam-ination to have been broken through, and to have little shreds of her dress and little spots of blood upon them here and there. But the boldest point he made, was this. It was attempted to be set up in proof of her jealousy, that she was under strong suspicion of having, at about the time of the murder, frantically destroyed her child by this man—some three years old—to revenge herself upon him. Mr. Jag-gers worked that, in this way. 'We say these are not marks of finger-nails, but marks of brambles, and we show you the brambles. You say they are marks of finger-nails, and you set up the hypothesis that she destroyed her child. You must accept all consequences of that hy-pothesis. For anything we know, she may have destroyed her child, and the child in clinging to her may have scratched her hands. What then? You are not trying her for the murder of her child; why don't you? As to this case, if you *will* have scratches, we say that, for any-thing we know, you may have accounted for them, assuming for the sake of argument that you have not invented them?' To sum up, sir," said Wemmick, "Mr. Jaggers was altogether too many for the Jury, and they gave in."

"Has she been in his service ever since?"

"Yes; but not only that," said Wemmick. "She went into his service immediately after her acquittal, tamed as she is now. She has since been taught one thing and another in the way of her duties, but she was tamed from the beginning."

"Do you remember the sex of the child?"

"Said to have been a girl."

"You have nothing more to say to me to-night?"

"Nothing. I got your letter and destroyed it. Nothing."

We exchanged a cordial Good Night, and I went home, with new matter for my thoughts, though with no relief from the old.

[PART 30]

Chapter 49

Putting Miss Havisham's note in my pocket, that it might serve as my credentials for so soon reappearing at Satis House, in case her waywardness should lead her to express any surprise at seeing me, I went down again by the coach next day. But, I alighted at the Halfway House, and breakfasted there, and walked the rest of the distance; for, I sought to get into the town quietly by the unfrequented ways, and to leave it in the same manner.

The best light of the day was gone when I passed along the quiet echoing courts behind the High-street. The nooks of ruin where the old monks had once had their refectories and gardens, and where the strong walls were now pressed into the service of humble sheds and stables, were almost as silent as the old monks in their graves. The cathedral chimes had at once a sadder and a more remote sound to me, as I hurried on avoiding observation, than they had ever had before; so, the swell of the old organ was borne to my ears like funeral music; and the rooks, as they hovered about the grey tower and swung in the bare high trees of the priory-garden, seemed to call to me that the place was changed, and that Estella was gone out of it for ever.

An elderly woman whom I had seen before as one of the servants who lived in the supplementary house across the back court-yard, opened the gate. The lighted candle stood in the dark passage within, as of old, and I took it up and ascended the staircase alone. Miss Havisham was not in her own room, but was in the larger room across the landing. Looking in at the door, after knocking in vain, I saw her sitting on the hearth in a ragged chair, close before, and lost in the contemplation of, the ashy fire.

Doing as I had often done, I went in, and stood, touching the old chimney-piece, where she could see me when she raised her eyes. There was an air of utter loneliness upon her, that would have moved me to pity though she had wilfully done me a deeper injury than I could charge her with. As I stood compassionating her, and thinking how in the progress of time I too had come to be a part of the wrecked fortunes of that house, her eyes rested on me. She stared, and said in a low voice, "Is it real!"

"It is I, Pip. Mr. Jaggers gave me your note yesterday, and I have lost no time."

"Thank you. Thank you."

As I brought another of the ragged chairs to the hearth and sat down, I remarked a new expression on her face, as if she were afraid of me.

"I want," she said, "to pursue that subject you mentioned to me when you were last here, and to show you that I am not all stone. But perhaps you can never believe, now, that there is anything human in my heart?"

When I said some reassuring words, she stretched out her tremulous right hand, as though she was going to touch me; but she recalled it again before I understood the action, or knew how to receive it.

"You said, speaking for your friend, that you could tell me how to do something useful and good. Something that you would like done, is it not?"

"Something that I would like done very very much."

"What is it?"

I began explaining to her that secret history of the partnership. I had not got far into it, when I judged from her looks that she was thinking in a discursive way of me, rather than of what I said. It seemed to be so, for, when I stopped speaking, many moments passed before she showed that she was conscious of the fact.

"Do you break off," she asked then, with her former air of being afraid of me, "because you hate me too much to bear to speak to me?"

"No, no," I answered, "how can you think so, Miss Havisham! I stopped because I thought you were not following what I said."

"Perhaps I was not," she answered, putting a hand to her head. "Begin again, and let me look at something else. Stay! Now tell me."

She set her hand upon her stick, in the resolute way that sometimes was habitual to her, and looked at the fire with a strong expression of forcing herself to attend. I went on with my explanation, and told her how I had hoped to complete the transaction out of my means, but how in this I was disappointed. That part of the subject (I reminded her) involved matters which could form no part of my explanation, for they were the weighty secrets of another.

"So!" said she, assenting with her head, but not looking at me. "And how much money is wanting to complete the purchase?"

I was rather afraid of stating it, for it sounded a large sum. "Nine hundred pounds."

"If I give you the money for this purpose, will you keep my secret as you have kept your own?"

"Quite as faithfully."

"And your mind will be more at rest?"

"Much more at rest."

"Are you very unhappy now?"

She asked this question, still without looking at me, but in an unwonted tone of sympathy. I could not reply at the moment, for my voice failed me. She put her left arm across the head of her stick, and softly laid her forehead on it.

"I am far from happy, Miss Havisham; but I have other causes of disquiet than any you know of. They are the secrets I have mentioned."

After a little while, she raised her head and looked at the fire again.

"It is noble in you to tell me that you have other causes of unhappiness. Is it true?"

"Too true."

"Can I only serve you, Pip, by serving your friend? Regarding that as done, is there nothing I can do for you yourself?"

"Nothing. I thank you for the question. I thank you even more for the tone of the question. But, there is nothing."

She presently rose from her seat, and looked about the blighted room for the means of writing. There were none there, and she took from her pocket a yellow set of ivory tablets, mounted in tarnished gold, and wrote upon them with a pencil in a case of tarnished gold that hung from her neck.

"You are still on friendly terms with Mr. Jaggers?"

"Quite. I dined with him yesterday."

"This is an authority to him to pay you that money, to lay out at your irresponsible discretion for your friend. I keep no money here; but if you would rather Mr. Jaggers knew nothing of the matter, I will send it to you."

"Thank you, Miss Havisham; I have not the least objection to receiving it from him."

She read me what she had written, and it was direct and clear, and evidently intended to absolve me from any suspicion of profiting by the receipt of the money. I took the tablets from her hand, and it trembled again, and it trembled more as she took off the chain to which the pencil was attached, and put it in mine. All this she did, without looking at me.

"My name is on the first leaf. If you can ever write under my name, 'I forgive her,' though ever so long after my broken heart is dust—pray do it!"

"O Miss Havisham," said I, "I can do it now. There have been sore mistakes; and my life has been a blind and thankless one; and I want forgiveness and direction far too much, to be bitter with you."

She turned her face to me for the first time since she had averted it, and, to my amazement, I may even add to my terror, dropped on her knees at my feet; with her folded hands raised to me in the manner in which, when her poor heart was young and fresh and whole, they must often have been raised to heaven from her mother's side.

To see her with her white hair and her worn face kneeling at my feet, gave me a shock through all my frame. I entreated her to rise, and got my arms about her to help her up; but she only pressed that hand of mine which was nearest to her grasp, and hung her head over it and wept. I had never seen her shed a tear before, and, in the hope that the relief might do her good, I bent over her without speaking. She was not kneeling now, but was down upon the ground.

"O!" she cried, despairingly. "What have I done! What have I done!"

"If you mean, Miss Havisham, what have you done to injure me, let me answer. Very little. I should have loved her under any circumstances. — Is she married?"

"Yes."

It was a needless question, for a new desolation in the desolate house had told me so.

"What have I done! What have I done!" She wrung her hands, and crushed her white hair, and returned to this cry over and over again. "What have I done!"

I knew not how to answer, or how to comfort her. That she had done a grievous thing in taking an impressionable child to mould into the form that her wild resentment, spurned affection, and wounded pride, found vengeance in, I knew full well. But that, in shutting out the light of day, she had shut out infinitely more; that, in seclusion, she had secluded herself from a thousand natural and healing influences; that, her mind, brooding solitary, had grown diseased, as all minds do and must and will that reverse the appointed order of their Maker; I knew equally well. And could I look upon her without compassion, seeing her punishment in the ruin she was, in her profound unfitness for this earth on which she was placed, in the vanity of sorrow which had become a master mania, like the vanity of penitence, the vanity of remorse, the vanity of unworthiness, and other monstrous vanities that have been curses in this world?

"Until you spoke to her the other day, and until I saw in you a looking-glass that showed me what I once felt myself, I did not know what I had done. What have I done! What have I done!" And so again, twenty, fifty times over, What had she done!

"Miss Havisham," I said, when her cry had died away, "you may dismiss me from your mind and conscience. But Estella is a different case, and if you can ever undo any scrap of what you have done amiss in keeping a part of her right nature away from her, it will be better to do that, than to bemoan the past through a hundred years."

"Yes, yes, I know it. But, Pip—my Dear!" There was an earnest womanly compassion for me in her new affection. "My Dear! Believe this: when she first came to me, I meant to save her from misery like my own. At first I meant no more."

"Well, well!" said I. "I hope so."

"But as she grew, and promised to be very beautiful, I gradually did worse, and with my praises, and with my jewels, and with my teachings, and with this figure of myself always before her a warning to back and point my lessons, I stole her heart away and put ice in its place."

"Better," I could not help saying, "to have left her a natural heart, even to be bruised or broken."

With that, Miss Havisham looked distractedly at me for a while, and then burst out again, What had she done!

"If you knew all my story," she pleaded, "you would have some compassion for me and a better understanding of me."

"Miss Havisham," I answered, as delicately as I could, "I believe I may say that I do know your story, and have known it ever since I first left this neighbourhood. It has inspired me with great commiseration, and I hope I understand it and its influences. Does what has passed between us give me any excuse for asking you a question relative to Estella? Not as she is, but as she was when she first came here?"

She was seated on the ground, with her arms on the ragged chair, and her head leaning on them. She looked full at me when I said this, and replied, "Go on."

"Whose child was Estella?"

She shook her head.

"You don't know?"

She shook her head again.

"But Mr. Jaggers brought her here, or sent her here?"

"Brought her here."

"Will you tell me how that came about?"

She answered in a low whisper and with caution: "I had been shut up in these rooms a long time (I don't know how long; you know what time the clocks keep here), when I told him that I wanted a little girl to rear and love, and save from my fate. I had first seen him when

I sent for him to lay this place waste for me; having read of him in the newspapers, before I and the world parted. He told me that he would look about him for such an orphan child. One night he brought her here asleep, and I called her Estella."

"Might I ask her age then?"

"Two or three. She herself knows nothing, but that she was left an orphan and I adopted her."

So convinced I was of that woman's being her mother, that I wanted no evidence to establish the fact in my own mind. But, to any mind, I thought, the connexion here was clear and straight.

What more could I hope to do by prolonging the interview? I had succeeded on behalf of Herbert, Miss Havisham had told me all she knew of Estella, I had said and done what I could to ease her mind. No matter with what other words we parted; we parted.

Twilight was closing in when I went down stairs into the natural air. I called to the woman who had opened the gate when I entered, that I would not trouble her just yet, but would walk round the place before leaving. For, I had a presentiment that I should never be there again, and I felt that the dying light was suited to my last view of it.

By the wilderness of casks that I had walked on long ago, and on which the rain of years had fallen since, rotting them in many places, and leaving miniature swamps and pools of water upon those that stood on end, I made my way to the ruined garden. I went all round it; round by the corner where Herbert and I had fought our battle; round by the paths where Estella and I had walked. So cold, so lonely, so dreary all!

Taking the brewery on my way back, I raised the rusty latch of a little door at the garden end of it, and walked through. I was going out at the opposite door—not easy to open now, for the damp wood had started and swelled, and the hinges were yielding, and the threshold was encumbered with a growth of fungus—when I turned my head to look back. A childish association revived with wonderful force in the moment of the slight action, and I fancied that I saw Miss Havisham hanging to the beam. So strong was the impression, that I stood under the beam shuddering from head to foot before I knew it was a fancy—though to be sure I was there in an instant.

The mournfulness of the place and time, and the great terror of this illusion, though it was but momentary, caused me to feel an indescribable awe as I came out between the open wooden gates where I had once wrung my hair after Estella had wrung my heart. Passing on into the front court-yard, I hesitated whether to call the woman to let me out at the locked gate of which she had the key, or first to go up-stairs and assure myself that Miss Havisham was as safe and well as I had left her. I took the latter course and went up.

I looked into the room where I had left her, and I saw her seated in the ragged chair upon the hearth close to the fire, with her back to-wards me. In the moment when I was withdrawing my head to go qui-etly away, I saw a great flaming light spring up. In the same moment, I saw her running at me, shrieking, with a whirl of fire blazing all about her, and soaring at least as many feet above her head as she was high.

I had a double-caped great-coat on, and over my arm another thick coat. That I got them off, closed with her, threw her down, and got them over her; that I dragged the great cloth from the table for the same purpose, and with it dragged down the heap of rottenness in the midst, and all the ugly things that sheltered there; that we were on the ground struggling like desperate enemies, and that the closer I covered her, the more wildly she shrieked and tried to free herself; that this occurred I knew through the result, but not through anything I felt, or thought, or knew I did. I knew nothing until I knew that we were on the floor by the great table, and that patches of tinder yet alight were floating in the smoky air, which, a moment ago, had been her faded bridal dress.

Then, I looked round and saw the disturbed beetles and spiders running away over the floor, and the servants coming in with breath-less cries at the door. I still held her forcibly down with all my strength, like a prisoner who might escape; and I doubt if I even knew who she was, or why we had struggled, or that she had been in flames, or that the flames were out, until I saw the patches of tinder that had been her garments, no longer alight but falling in a black shower around us.

She was insensible, and I was afraid to have her moved, or even touched. Assistance was sent for and I held her until it came, as if I un-reasonably fancied (I think I did) that if I let her go, the fire would break out again and consume her. When I got up, on the surgeon's coming to her with other aid, I was astonished to see that both my hands were burnt; for, I had no knowledge of it through the sense of feeling.

On examination it was pronounced that she had received serious hurts, but that they of themselves were far from hopeless; the danger lay mainly in the nervous shock. By the surgeon's directions, her bed was carried into that room and laid upon the great table: which hap-pened to be well suited to the dressing of her injuries. When I saw her again, an hour afterwards, she lay indeed where I had seen her strike her stick, and had heard her say that she would lie one day.

Though every vestige of her dress was burnt, as they told me, she still had something of her old ghastly bridal appearance; for, they had covered her to the throat with white cotton-wool, and as she lay with a white sheet loosely overlying that, the phantom air of something that had been and was changed, was still upon her.

I found, on questioning the servants, that Estella was in Paris, and I got a promise from the surgeon that he would write to her by the next post. Miss Havisham's family I took upon myself; intending to communicate with Mr. Matthew Pocket only, and leave him to do as he liked about informing the rest. This I did next day, through Herbert, as soon as I returned to town.

There was a stage, that evening, when she spoke collectedly of what had happened, though with a certain terrible vivacity. Towards midnight she began to wander in her speech, and after that it gradually set in that she said innumerable times in a low solemn voice, "What have I done!" And then, "When she first came, I meant to save her from misery like mine." And then, "Take the pencil and write under my name, 'I forgive her!'" She never changed the order of these three sentences, but she sometimes left out a word in one or other of them; never putting in another word, but always leaving a blank and going on to the next word.

As I could do no service there, and as I had, nearer home, that pressing reason for anxiety and fear which even her wanderings could not drive out of my mind, I decided in the course of the night that I would return by the early morning coach: walking on a mile or so, and being taken up clear of the town. At about six o'clock of the morning, therefore, I leaned over her and touched her lips with mine, just as they said, not stopping for being touched, "Take the pencil and write under my name, 'I forgive her.'"

Chapter 50

My hands had been dressed twice or thrice in the night, and again in the morning. My left arm was a good deal burned to the elbow, and, less severely, as high as the shoulder; it was very painful, but the flames had set in that direction, and I felt thankful it was no worse. My right hand was not so badly burnt but that I could move the fingers. It was bandaged, of course, but much less inconveniently than my left hand and arm; those I carried in a sling; and I could only wear my coat like a cloak, loose over my shoulders and fastened at the neck. My hair had been caught by the fire, but not my head or face.

When Herbert had been down to Hammersmith and seen his father, he came back to me at our chambers, and devoted the day to attending on me. He was the kindest of nurses, and at stated times took off the bandages, and steeped them in the cooling liquid that was kept ready, and put them on again, with a patient tenderness that I was deeply grateful for.

At first, as I lay quiet on the sofa, I found it painfully difficult, I might say impossible, to get rid of the impression of the glare of the flames, their hurry and noise, and the fierce burning smell. If I dozed for a minute, I was awakened by Miss Havisham's cries, and by her running at me with all that height of fire above her head. This pain of the mind was much harder to strive against than any bodily pain I suffered; and Herbert, seeing that, did his utmost to hold my attention engaged.

Neither of us spoke of the boat, but we both thought of it. That was made apparent by our avoidance of the subject, and by our agreeing—without agreement—to make my recovery of the use of my hands, a question of so many hours, not of so many weeks.

My first question when I saw Herbert had been of course, whether all was well down the river? As he replied in the affirmative, with perfect confidence and cheerfulness, we did not resume the subject until the day was wearing away. But then, as Herbert changed the bandages, more by the light of the fire than by the outer light, he went back to it spontaneously.

"I sat with Provis last night, Handel, two good hours."

"Where was Clara?"

"Dear little thing!" said Herbert. "She was up and down with Gruffandgrim all the evening. He was perpetually pegging at the floor, the moment she left his sight. I doubt if he can hold out long though. What with rum and pepper—and pepper and rum—I should think his pegging must be nearly over."

"And then you will be married, Herbert?"

"How can I take care of the dear child otherwise?—Lay your arm out upon the back of the sofa, my dear boy, and I'll sit down here, and get the bandage off so gradually that you shall not know when it comes. I was speaking of Provis. Do you know, Handel, he improves?"

"I said to you I thought he was softened when I last saw him."

"So you did. And so he is. He was very communicative last night, and told me more of his life. You remember his breaking off here about some woman that he had had great trouble with. — Did I hurt you?"

I had started, but not under his touch. His words had given me a start.

"I had forgotten that, Herbert, but I remember it now you speak of it."

"Well! He went into that part of his life, and a dark wild part it is. Shall I tell you? Or would it worry you just now?"

"Tell me by all means. Every word."

Herbert bent forward to look at me more nearly, as if my reply had been rather more hurried or more eager than he could quite account for. "Your head is cool?" he said, touching it.

"Quite," said I. "Tell me what Provis said, my dear Herbert."

"It seems," said Herbert, "—there's a bandage off most charmingly, and now comes the cool one—makes you shrink at first, my poor dear fellow, don't it? but it will be comfortable presently—it seems that the woman was a young woman, and a jealous woman, and a revengeful woman; revengeful, Handel, to the last degree."

"To what last degree?"

"Murder.—Does it strike too cold on that sensitive place?"

"I don't feel it. How did she murder? Whom did she murder?"

"Why, the deed may not have merited quite so terrible a name," said Herbert, "but, she was tried for it, and Mr. Jaggers defended her, and the reputation of that defence first made his name known to Provis. It was another and a stronger woman who was the victim, and there had been a struggle—in a barn. Who began it, or how fair it was, or how unfair, may be doubtful; but how it ended, is certainly not doubtful, for the victim was found throttled."

"Was the woman brought in guilty?"

"No; she was acquitted. — My poor Handel, I hurt you!"

"It is impossible to be gentler, Herbert. Yes? What else?"

"This acquitted young woman and Provis," said Herbert, "had a little child: a little child of whom Provis was exceedingly fond. On the evening of the very night when the object of her jealousy was strangled as I tell you, the young woman presented herself before Provis for one moment, and swore that she would destroy the child (which was in her possession), and he should never see it again; then, she vanished. — There's the worst arm comfortably in the sling once more, and now there remains but the right hand, which is a far easier job. I can do it better by this light than by a stronger, for my hand is steadiest when I don't see the poor blistered patches too distinctly.—You don't think your breathing is affected, my dear boy? You seem to breathe quickly."

"Perhaps I do, Herbert. Did the woman keep her oath?"

"There comes the darkest part of Provis's life. She did."

"That is, he says she did."

"Why, of course, my dear boy," returned Herbert, in a tone of surprise, and again bending forward to get a nearer look at me. "He says it all. I have no other information."

"No, to be sure."

"Now, whether," pursued Herbert, "he had used the child's mother ill, or whether he had used the child's mother well, Provis doesn't say; but, she had shared some four or five years of the wretched life he described to us at this fireside, and he seems to have felt pity for her, and forbearance towards her. Therefore, fearing he should be called upon to depose about this destroyed child, and so be the cause of her death, he hid himself (much as he grieved for the child), kept himself dark, as he says, out of the way and out of the trial, and was only vaguely talked of as a certain man called Abel, out of whom the jealousy arose. After the acquittal she disappeared, and thus he lost the child and the child's mother."

"I want to ask——"

"A moment, my dear boy," said Herbert, "and I have done. That evil genius, Compeyson, the worst of scoundrels among many scoundrels, knowing of his keeping out of the way at that time, and of his reasons for doing so, of course afterwards held the knowledge over his head as a means of keeping him poorer, and working him harder. It was clear last night that this barbed the point of Provis's animosity."

"I want to know," said I, "and particularly, Herbert, whether he told you when this happened?"

"Particularly? Let me remember, then, what he said as to that. His expression was, 'a round score o' year ago, and a'most directly after I took up wi' Compeyson.' How old were you when you came upon him in the little churchyard?"

"I think in my seventh year."

"Ay. It had happened some three or four years then, he said, and you brought into his mind the little girl so tragically lost, who would have been about your age."

"Herbert," said I, after a short silence, in a hurried way, "can you see me best by the light of the window, or the light of the fire?"

"By the firelight," answered Herbert, coming close again.

"Look at me."

"I do look at you, my dear boy."

"Touch me."

"I do touch you, my dear boy."

"You are not afraid that I am in any fever, or that my head is much disordered by the accident of last night?"

"N-no, my dear boy," said Herbert, after taking time to examine me. "You are rather excited, but you are quite yourself."

"I know I am quite myself. And the man we have in hiding down the river, is Estella's Father."

[PART 31]

Chapter 51

What purpose I had in view when I was hot on tracing out and proving Estella's parentage, I cannot say. It will presently be seen that the question was not before me in a distinct shape, until it was put before me by a wiser head than my own.

But, when Herbert and I had held our momentous conversation, I was seized with a feverish conviction that I ought to hunt the matter down—that I ought not to let it rest, but that I ought to see Mr. Jaggers, and come at the bare truth. I really do not know whether I felt that I did this for Estella's sake, or whether I was glad to transfer to the man in whose preservation I was so much concerned, some rays of the romantic interest that had so long surrounded her. Perhaps the latter possibility may be the nearer to the truth.

Any way, I could scarcely be withheld from going out to Gerrard-street that night. Herbert's representations that if I did, I should probably be laid up and stricken useless, when our fugitive's safety would depend upon me, alone restrained my impatience. On the understanding, again and again reiterated, that come what would, I was to go to Mr. Jaggers to-morrow, I at length submitted to keep quiet, and to have my hurts looked after, and to stay at home. Early next morning we went out together, and at the corner of Giltspur-street by Smithfield, I left Herbert to go his way into the City, and took my way to Little Britain.

There were periodical occasions when Mr. Jaggers and Wemmick went over the office accounts, and checked off the vouchers, and put all things straight. On those occasions Wemmick took his books and papers into Mr. Jaggers's room, and one of the up-stairs clerks came down into the outer office. Finding such clerk on Wemmick's post that morning, I knew what was going on; but, I was not sorry to have Mr. Jaggers and Wemmick together, as Wemmick would then hear for himself that I said nothing to compromise him.

My appearance with my arm bandaged and my coat loose over my shoulders, favoured my object. Although I had sent Mr. Jaggers a brief account of the accident as soon as I had arrived in town, yet I had to give him all the details now; and the speciality of the occasion caused our talk to be less dry and hard, and less strictly regulated by the rules of evidence, than it had been before. While I described the disaster, Mr. Jaggers stood, according to his wont, before the fire. Wemmick leaned back in his chair, staring at me, with his hands in the pockets of his trousers, and his pen put horizontally into the post. The two brutal casts, always inseparable in my mind from the official proceedings, seemed to be congestively considering whether they didn't smell fire at the present moment.

My narrative finished, and their questions exhausted, I then produced Miss Havisham's authority to receive the nine hundred pounds for Herbert. Mr. Jaggers's eyes retired a little deeper into his head when I handed him the tablets, but he presently handed them over to Wemmick, with instructions to draw the cheque for his signature. While that was in course of being done, I looked on at Wemmick as he wrote, and Mr. Jaggers, poising and swaying himself on his well-polished boots, looked on at me. "I am sorry, Pip," said he, as I put the cheque in my pocket, when he had signed it, "that we do nothing for *you*."

"Miss Havisham was good enough to ask me," I returned, "whether she could do nothing for me, and I told her No."

"Everybody should know his own business," said Mr. Jaggers. And I saw Wemmick's lips form the words "portable property."

"I should *not* have told her No, if I had been you," said Mr. Jaggers; "but every man ought to know his own business best."

"Every man's business," said Wemmick, rather reproachfully towards me, "is portable property."

As I thought the time was now come for pursuing the theme I had at heart, I said, turning on Mr. Jaggers:

"I did ask something of Miss Havisham, however, sir. I asked her to give me some information relative to her adopted daughter, and she gave me all she possessed."

"Did she?" said Mr. Jaggers, bending forward to look at his boots and then straightening himself. "Hah! I don't think I should have done so, if I had been Miss Havisham. But *she* ought to know her own business best."

"I know more of the history of Miss Havisham's adopted child, than Miss Havisham herself does, sir. I know her mother."

Mr. Jaggers looked at me inquiringly, and repeated "Mother?"

"I have seen her mother within these three days."

"Yes?" said Mr. Jaggers.

"And so have you, sir. And you have seen her still more recently."

"Yes?" said Mr. Jaggers.

"Perhaps I know more of Estella's history than even you do," said I. "I know her father too."

A certain stop that Mr. Jaggers came to in his manner—he was too self-possessed to change his manner, but he could not help its being brought to an indefinably attentive stop—assured me that he did not know who her father was. This I had strongly suspected from Provis's account (as Herbert had repeated it) of his having kept himself dark; which I pieced on to the fact that he himself was not Mr. Jaggers's client until some four years later, and when he could have no reason for claiming his identity. But, I could not be sure of this unconsciousness on Mr. Jaggers's part before, though I was quite sure of it now.

"So! You know the young lady's father, Pip?" said Mr. Jaggers.

"Yes," I replied, "And his name is Provis—from New South Wales."

Even Mr. Jaggers started when I said those words. It was the slightest start that could escape a man, the most carefully repressed and the soonest checked, but he did start, though he made it a part of the action of taking out his pocket-handkerchief. How Wemmick received the announcement I am unable to say, for I was afraid to look at him just then, lest Mr. Jaggers's sharpness should detect that there had been some communication unknown to him between us.

"And on what evidence, Pip?" asked Mr. Jaggers, very coolly, as he paused with his handkerchief half way to his nose, "does Provis make this claim?"

"He does not make it," said I, "and has never made it, and has no knowledge or belief that his daughter is in existence."

For once, the powerful pocket-handkerchief failed. My reply was so unexpected that Mr. Jaggers put the handkerchief back into his pocket without completing the usual performance, folded his arms, and looked with stern attention at me, though with an immovable face.

Then I told him all I knew, and how I knew it; with the one reservation that I left him to infer that I knew from Miss Havisham what I in fact knew from Wemmick. I was very careful indeed as to that. Nor, did I look towards Wemmick until I had finished all I had to tell, and had been for some time silently meeting Mr. Jaggers's look. When I did at last turn my eyes in Wemmick's direction, I found that he had unposted his pen, and was intent upon the table before him.

"Hah!" said Mr. Jaggers at last, as he moved towards the papers on the table. "—What item was it you were at, Wemmick, when Mr. Pip came in?"

But I could not submit to be thrown off in that way, and I made a passionate, almost an indignant, appeal to him to be more frank and manly with me. I reminded him of the false hopes into which I had lapsed, the length of time they had lasted, and the discovery I had made: and I hinted at the danger that weighed upon my spirits. I represented myself as being surely worthy of some little confidence from him, in return for the confidence I had just now imparted. I said that I did not blame him, or suspect him, or mistrust him, but I wanted assurance of the truth from him. And if he asked me why I wanted it and why I thought I had any right to it, I would tell him, little as he cared for such poor dreams, that I had loved Estella dearly and long, and that, although I had lost her and must live a bereaved life, whatever concerned her was still nearer and dearer to me than anything else in the world. And seeing that Mr. Jaggers stood quite still and silent, and apparently quite obdurate, under this appeal, I turned to Wemmick, and said, "Wemmick, I know you to be a man with a gentle heart. I have seen your pleasant home, and your old father, and all the innocent cheerful playful ways with which you refresh your business life. And I entreat you to say a word for me to Mr. Jaggers, and to represent to him that, all circumstances considered, he ought to be more open with me!"

I have never seen two men look more oddly at one another than Mr. Jaggers and Wemmick did after this apostrophe. At first, a misgiving crossed me that Wemmick would be instantly dismissed from his employment; but, it melted as I saw Mr. Jaggers relax into something like a smile, and Wemmick become bolder.

"What's all this?" said Mr. Jaggers. "You with an old father, and you with pleasant and playful ways?"

"Well!" returned Wemmick. "If I don't bring 'em here, what does it matter?"

"Pip," said Mr. Jaggers, laying his hand upon my arm, and smiling openly, "this man must be the most cunning impostor in all London."

"Not a bit of it," returned Wemmick, growing bolder and bolder. "I think you're another."

Again they exchanged their former odd looks, each apparently still distrustful that the other was taking him in.

"*You* with a pleasant home?" said Mr. Jaggers.

"Since it don't interfere with business," returned Wemmick, "let it be so. Now, I look at you, sir, I shouldn't wonder if *you* might be planning and contriving to have a pleasant home of your own, one of these days, when you're tired of all this work."

Mr. Jaggers nodded his head retrospectively two or three times, and actually drew a sigh. "Pip," said he, "we won't talk about 'poor dreams;' you know more about such things than I, having much fresher experience of that kind. But now, about this other matter. I'll put a case to you. Mind! I admit nothing."

He waited for me to declare that I quite understood that he expressly said that he admitted nothing.

"Now, Pip," said Mr. Jaggers, "put this case. Put the case that a woman, under such circumstances as you have mentioned, held her child concealed, and was obliged to communicate the fact to her legal adviser, on his representing to her that he must know, with an eye to the latitude of his defence, how the fact stood about that child. Put the case that at the same time he held a trust to find a child for an eccentric rich lady to adopt and bring up."

"I follow you, sir."

"Put the case that he lived in an atmosphere of evil, and that all he saw of children, was, their being generated in great numbers for certain destruction. Put the case that he often saw children solemnly tried at a criminal bar, where they were held up to be seen; put the case that he habitually knew of their being imprisoned, whipped, transported, neglected, cast out, qualified in all ways for the hangman, and growing up to be hanged. Put the case that pretty nigh all the children he saw in his daily business life, he had reason to look upon as so much spawn, to develop into the fish that were to come to his net—to be prosecuted, defended, forsworn, made orphans, be-devilled somehow."

"I follow you, sir."

"Put the case, Pip, that here was one pretty little child out of the heap, who could be saved; whom the father believed dead, and dared make no stir about; as to whom, over the mother, the legal adviser had this power: 'I know what you did, and how you did it. You came so and so, this was your manner of attack and this the manner of resistance, you went so and so, you did such and such things to divert suspicion. I have tracked you through it all, and I tell it you all. Part with the child, unless it should be necessary to produce it to clear you, and then it shall be produced. Give the child into my hands, and I will do my best to bring you off. If you are saved, your child is saved too; if you are lost, your child is still saved.' Put the case that this was done, and that the woman was cleared."

"I understand you perfectly."

"But that I make no admissions?"

"That you make no admissions." And Wemmick repeated, "No admissions."

"Put the case, Pip, that passion and the terror of death had a little shaken the woman's intellects, and that when she was set at liberty, she was scared out of the ways of the world and went to him to be sheltered. Put the case that he took her in, and that he kept down the old wild violent nature whenever he saw an inkling of its breaking out, by asserting his power over her in the old way. Do you comprehend the imaginary case?"

"Quite."

"Put the case that the child grew up, and was married for money. That the mother was still living. That the father was still living. That the mother and father unknown to one another, were dwelling within so many miles, furlongs, yards if you like, of one another. That the secret was still a secret, except that you had got wind of it. Put that last case to yourself very carefully."

"I do."

"I ask Wemmick to put it to *him*self very carefully."

And Wemmick said, "I do."

"For whose sake would you reveal the secret? For the father's? I think he would not be much the better for the mother. For the mother's? I think if she had done such a deed she would be safer where she was. For the daughter's? I think it would hardly serve her, to establish her parentage for the information of her husband, and to drag her back to disgrace, after an escape of twenty years, pretty secure to last for life. But, add the case that you had loved her, Pip, and had made her the subject of those 'poor dreams' which have, at one time or another, been in the heads of more men than you think likely, then

I tell you that you had better—and would much sooner when you had thought well of it—chop off that bandaged left hand of yours with your bandaged right hand, and then pass the chopper on to Wemmick there, to cut *that* off, too."

I looked at Wemmick, whose face was very grave. He gravely touched his lips with his forefinger. I did the same. Mr. Jaggers did the same. "Now, Wemmick," said the latter then, resuming his usual manner, "what item was it you were at, when Mr. Pip came in?"

Standing by for a little, while they were at work, I observed that the odd looks they had cast at one another were repeated several times: with this difference now, that each of them seemed suspicious, not to say conscious, of having shown himself in a weak and unprofessional light to the other. For this reason, I suppose, they were now inflexible with one another; Mr. Jaggers being highly dictatorial, and Wemmick obstinately justifying himself whenever there was the smallest point in abeyance for a moment. I had never seen them on such ill terms; for generally they got on very well indeed together.

But, they were both happily relieved by the opportune appearance of Mike, the client with the fur cap and the habit of wiping his nose on his sleeve, whom I had seen on the very first day of my appearance within those walls. This individual, who, either in his own person or in that of some member of his family, seemed to be always in trouble (which in that place meant Newgate), called to announce that his eldest daughter was taken up on suspicion of shoplifting. As he imparted this melancholy circumstance to Wemmick, Mr. Jaggers standing magisterially before the fire and taking no share in the proceedings, Mike's eye happened to twinkle with a tear.

"What are you about?" demanded Wemmick, with the utmost indignation. "What do you come snivelling here for?"

"I did't go to do it, Mr. Wemmick."

"You did," said Wemmick. "How dare you? You're not in a fit state to come here, if you can't come here without spluttering like a bad pen. What do you mean by it?"

"A man can't help his feelings, Mr. Wemmick," pleaded Mike.

"His what?" demanded Wemmick, quite savagely. "Say that again!"

"Now, look here my man," said Mr. Jaggers, advancing a step, and pointing to the door. "Get out of this office. I'll have no feelings here. Get out."

"It serves you right," said Wemmick. "Get out."

So the unfortunate Mike very humbly withdrew, and Mr. Jaggers and Wemmick appeared to have re-established their good understanding, and went to work again with an air of refreshment upon them as if they had just had lunch.

Chapter 52

From Little Britain, I went, with my cheque in my pocket, to Miss Skiffins's brother, the accountant; and Miss Skiffins's brother, the accountant, going straight to Clarriker's and bringing Clarriker to me, I had the great satisfaction of concluding that arrangement. It was the only good thing I had done, and the only completed thing I had done, since I was first apprised of my great expectations.

Clarriker informing me on that occasion that the affairs of the House were steadily progressing, that he would now be able to establish a small branch-house in the East which was much wanted for the extension of the business, and that Herbert in his new partnership capacity would go out and take charge of it, I found that I must have prepared for a separation from my friend, even though my own affairs had been more settled. And now indeed I felt as if my last anchor were loosening its hold, and I should soon be driving with the winds and waves.

But, there was recompense in the joy with which Herbert would come home of a night and tell me of these changes, little imagining that he told me no news, and would sketch airy pictures of himself conducting Clara Barley to the land of the Arabian Nights, and of me going out to join them (with a caravan of camels, I believe), and of our all going up the Nile and seeing wonders. Without being sanguine as to my own part in these bright plans, I felt that Herbert's way was clearing fast, and that old Bill Barley had but to stick to his pepper and rum, and his daughter would soon be happily provided for.

We had now got into the month of March. My left arm, though it presented no bad symptoms, took in the natural course so long to heal that I was still unable to get a coat on. My right arm was tolerably restored;—disfigured, but fairly serviceable.

On a Monday morning, when Herbert and I were at breakfast, I received the following letter from Wemmick by the post.

> Walworth. Burn this as soon as read. Early in the week, or say Wednesday, you might do what you know of, if you felt disposed to try it. Now burn.

When I had shown this to Herbert and had put it in the fire—but not before we had both got it by heart—we considered what to do. For, of course my being disabled could now be no longer kept out of view.

"I have thought it over, again and again," said Herbert, "and I think I know a better course than taking a Thames waterman. Take Startop. A good fellow, a skilled hand, fond of us, and enthusiastic and honourable."

I had thought of him, more than once.

"But how much would you tell him, Herbert?"

"It is necessary to tell him very little. Let him suppose it a mere freak, but a secret one, until the morning comes: then let him know that there is urgent reason for your getting Provis aboard and away. You go with him?"

"No doubt."

"Where?"

It had seemed to me, in the many anxious considerations I had given the point, almost indifferent what port we made for—Hamburg, Rotterdam, Antwerp—the place signified little, so that he was got out of England. Any foreign steamer that fell in our way and would take us up, would do. I had always proposed to myself to get him well down the river in the boat: certainly well beyond Gravesend,° which was a critical place for search or inquiry if suspicion were afoot. As foreign steamers would leave London at about the time of high-water, our plan would be to get down the river by a previous ebb-tide, and lie by in some quiet spot until we could pull off to one. The time when one would be due where we lay, wherever that might be, could be calculated pretty nearly, if we made inquiries beforehand.

Herbert assented to all this, and we went out immediately after breakfast to pursue our investigations. We found that a steamer for Hamburg was likely to suit our purpose best, and we directed our thoughts chiefly to that vessel. But we noted down what other foreign steamers would leave London with the same tide, and we satisfied ourselves that we knew the build and colour of each. We then separated for a few hours; I, to get at once such passports as were necessary; Herbert, to see Startop at his lodgings. We both did what we had to do without any hindrance, and when we met again at one o'clock reported it done. I, for my part, was prepared with passports; Herbert had seen Startop, and he was more than ready to join.

Those two should pull a pair of oars, we settled, and I would steer;

Gravesend: A port in Kent twenty-five miles from London.

our charge would be sitter, and keep quiet; as speed was not our ob-ject, we should make way enough. We arranged that Herbert should not come home to dinner before going to Mill Pond Bank that evening; that he should not go there at all, to-morrow evening, Tues-day; that he should prepare Provis to come down to some Stairs hard by the house, on Wednesday, when he saw us approach, and not sooner; that all the arrangements with him should be concluded that Monday night; and that he should be communicated with no more in any way, until we took him on board.

These precautions well understood by both of us, I went home.

On opening the outer door of our chambers with my key, I found a letter in the box, directed to me; a very dirty letter, though not ill-written. It had been delivered by hand (of course since I left home), and its contents were these:

> If you are not afraid to come to the old marshes to-night or to-morrow night at Nine, and to come to the little sluice-house by the limekiln, you had better come. If you want information re-garding *your uncle Provis,* you had much better come and tell no one and lose no time. *You must come alone.* Bring this with you.

I had had load enough upon my mind before the receipt of this strange letter. What to do now, I could not tell. And the worst was, that I must decide quickly, or I should miss the afternoon coach, which would take me down in time for to-night. To-morrow night I could not think of going, for it would be too close upon the time of the flight. And again, for anything I knew, the proffered information might have some important bearing on the flight itself.

If I had had ample time for consideration, I believe I should still have gone. Having hardly any time for consideration—my watch showing me that the coach started within half an hour—I resolved to go. I should certainly not have gone, but for the reference to my Uncle Provis; that, coming on Wemmick's letter and the morning's busy preparation, turned the scale.

It is so difficult to become clearly possessed of the contents of al-most any letter, in a violent hurry, that I had to read this mysterious epistle again, twice, before its injunction to me to be secret got me-chanically into my mind. Yielding to it in the same mechanical kind of way, I left a note in pencil for Herbert, telling him that as I should be so soon going away, I knew not for how long, I had decided to hurry down and back, to ascertain for myself how Miss Havisham was faring. I had then barely time to get my great-coat, lock up the chambers, and make for the coach-office by the short by-ways. If I had taken a hackney-chariot and gone by the streets, I should have missed my aim; going as I did, I caught the coach just as it came out of the yard. I was the only inside passenger, jolting away knee-deep in straw, when I came to myself.

For, I really had not been myself since the receipt of the letter; it had so bewildered me ensuing on the hurry of the morning. The morning hurry and flutter had been great, for, long and anxiously as I had waited for Wemmick, his hint had come like a surprise at last. And now, I began to wonder at myself for being in the coach, and to doubt whether I had sufficient reason for being there, and to consider whether I should get out presently and go back, and to argue against ever heeding an anonymous communication, and, in short, to pass through all those phases of contradiction and indecision to which I suppose very few hurried people are strangers. Still, the reference to Provis by name, mastered everything. I reasoned as I had reasoned already without knowing it—if that be reasoning—in case any harm should befal him through my not going, how could I ever forgive myself!

It was dark before we got down, and the journey seemed long and dreary to me who could see little of it inside, and who could not go outside in my disabled state. Avoiding the Blue Boar, I put up at an inn of minor reputation down the town, and ordered some dinner. While it was preparing, I went to Satis House and inquired for Miss Havisham; she was still very ill, though considered something better.

My inn had once been a part of an ancient ecclesiastical house, and I dined in a little octagonal common-room, like a font. As I was not able to cut my dinner, the old landlord with a shining bald head did it for me. This bringing us into conversation, he was so good as to entertain me with my own story—of course with the popular feature that Pumblechook was my earliest benefactor and the founder of my fortunes.

"Do you know the young man?" said I.

"Know him!" repeated the landlord. "Ever since he was—no height at all."

"Does he ever come back to this neighbourhood?"

"Ay, he comes back," said the landlord, "to his great friends, now and again, and gives the cold shoulder to the man that made him."

"What man is that?"

"Him that I speak of," said the landlord. "Mr. Pumblechook."

"Is he ungrateful to no one else?"

"No doubt he would be, if he could," returned the landlord, "but he can't. And why? Because Pumblechook done everything for him."

"Does Pumblechook say so?"

"Say so!" replied the landlord. "He han't no call to say so."

"But does he say so?"

"It would turn a man's blood to white wine winegar to hear him tell of it, sir," said the landlord.

I thought, "Yet Joe, dear Joe, *you* never tell of it. Long-suffering and loving Joe, *you* never complain. Nor you, sweet-tempered Biddy!"

"Your appetite's been touched like, by your accident," said the landlord, glancing at the bandaged arm under my coat. "Try a tenderer bit."

"No thank you," I replied, turning from the table to brood over the fire. "I can eat no more. Please take it away."

I had never been struck at so keenly, for my thanklessness to Joe, as through the brazen impostor Pumblechook. The falser he, the truer Joe; the meaner he, the nobler Joe.

My heart was deeply and most deservedly humbled as I mused over the fire for an hour or more. The striking of the clock aroused me, but not from my dejection or remorse, and I got up and had my coat fastened round my neck, and went out. I had previously sought in my pockets for the letter, that I might refer to it again, but I could not find it, and was uneasy to think that it must have been dropped in the straw of the coach. I knew very well, however, that the appointed place was the little sluice-house by the limekiln on the marshes, and the hour nine. Towards the marshes I now went straight, having no time to spare.

[PART 32]

Chapter 53

It was a dark night, though the full moon rose as I left the enclosed lands, and passed out upon the marshes. Beyond their dark line there was a ribbon of clear sky, hardly broad enough to hold the red large moon. In a few minutes she had ascended out of that clear field, in among the piled mountains of cloud.

There was a melancholy wind, and the marshes were very dismal. A stranger would have found them insupportable, and even to me they were so oppressive that I hesitated, half inclined to go back. But, I knew them well, and could have found my way on a far darker night, and had no excuse for returning, being there. So, having come there against my inclination, I went on against it.

The direction that I took, was not that in which my old home lay, nor that in which we had pursued the convicts. My back was turned towards the distant Hulks as I walked on, and, though I could see the old lights away on the spits of sand, I saw them over my shoulder. I knew the limekiln as well as I knew the old Battery, but they were miles apart; so that if a light had been burning at each point that night, there would have been a long strip of the blank horizon between the two bright specks.

At first, I had to shut some gates after me, and now and then to stand still while the cattle that were lying in the banked-up pathway, arose and blundered down among the grass and reeds. But after a little while, I seemed to have the whole flats to myself.

It was another half-hour before I drew near to the kiln. The lime was burning with a sluggish stifling smell, but the fires were made up and left, and no workmen were visible. Hard by, was a small stone-quarry. It lay directly in my way, and had been worked that day, as I saw by the tools and barrows that were lying about.

Coming up again to the marsh level out of this excavation—for the rude path lay through it—I saw a light in the old sluice-house. I quickened my pace, and knocked at the door with my hand. Waiting for some reply, I looked about me, noticing how the sluice was abandoned and broken, and how the house—of wood with a tiled roof—would not be proof against the weather much longer, if it were so even now, and how the mud and ooze were coated with lime, and how the choking vapour of the kiln crept in a ghostly way towards me. Still there was no answer, and I knocked again. No answer still, and I tried the latch.

It rose under my hand, and the door yielded. Looking in, I saw a lighted candle on a table, a bench, and a mattress on a truckle bedstead. As there was a loft above, I called, "Is there any one here?" but no voice answered. Then, I looked at my watch, and, finding that it was past nine, called again, "Is there any one here?" There being still no answer, I went out at the door, irresolute what to do.

It was beginning to rain fast. Seeing nothing save what I had seen already, I turned back into the house, and stood just within the shelter of the doorway, looking out into the night. While I was considering that some one must have been there lately and must soon be coming back, or the candle would not be burning, it came into my head to look if the wick were long. I turned round to do so, and had taken up the candle in my hand, when it was extinguished by some violent shock, and the next thing I comprehended, was, that I had been caught in a strong running noose, thrown over my head from behind.

"Now," said a suppressed voice with an oath, "I've got you!"

"What is this?" I cried, struggling. "Who is it? Help, help, help!"

Not only were my arms pulled close to my sides, but the pressure on my bad arm caused me exquisite pain. Sometimes, a strong man's hand, sometimes a strong man's breast, was set against my mouth to deaden my cries, and with a hot breath always close to me, I struggled ineffectually in the dark, while I was fastened tight to the wall. "And now," said the suppressed voice with another oath, "call out again, and I'll make short work of you!"

Faint and sick with the pain of my injured arm, bewildered by the surprise, and yet conscious how easily this threat could be put in execution, I desisted, and tried to ease my arm were it ever so little. But, it was bound too tight for that. I felt as if, having been burnt before, it were now being boiled.

The sudden exclusion of the night and the substitution of black darkness in its place, warned me that the man had closed a shutter. After groping about for a little, he found the flint and steel he wanted, and began to strike a light. I strained my sight upon the sparks that fell among the tinder, and upon which he breathed and breathed, match in hand, but I could only see his lips, and the blue point of the match; even those, but fitfully. The tinder was damp—no wonder there—and one after another the sparks died out.

The man was in no hurry, and struck again with the flint and steel. As the sparks fell thick and bright around him, I could see his hands, and touches of his face, and could make out that he was seated and bending over the table; but nothing more. Presently I saw his blue lips again, breathing on the tinder, and then a flare of light flashed up, and showed me Orlick.

Whom I had looked for, I don't know. I had not looked for him. Seeing him, I felt that I was in a dangerous strait indeed, and I kept my eyes upon him.

He lighted the candle from the flaring match with great deliberation, and dropped the match, and trod it out. Then, he put the candle away from him on the table, so that he could see me, and sat with his arms folded on the table and looked at me. I made out that I was fastened to a stout perpendicular ladder a few inches from the wall—a fixture there—the means of ascent to the loft above.

"Now," said he, when we had surveyed one another for some time, "I've got you."

"Unbind me. Let me go!"

"Ah!" he returned, "*I*'ll let you go. I'll let you go to the moon, I'll let you go to the stars. All in good time."

"Why have you lured me here?"

"Don't you know?" said he, with a deadly look.

"Why have you set upon me in the dark?"

"Because I mean to do it all myself. One keeps a secret better than two. Oh you enemy, you enemy!"

His enjoyment of the spectacle I furnished, as he sat with his arms folded on the table, shaking his head at me and hugging himself, had a malignity in it that made me tremble. As I watched him in silence, he put his hand into the corner at his side, and took up a gun with a brass-bound stock.

"Do you know this?" said he, making as if he would take aim at me. "Do you know where you saw it afore? Speak, wolf!"

"Yes," I answered.

"You cost me that place. You did. Speak!"

"What else could I do?"

"You did that, and that would be enough, without more. How dared you to come betwixt me and a young woman I liked?"

"When did I?"

"When didn't you? It was you as always give Old Orlick a bad name to her."

"You gave it to yourself; you gained it for yourself. I could have done you no harm, if you had done yourself none."

"You're a liar. And you'll take any pains, and spend any money, to drive me out of this country, will you?" said he, repeating my words to Biddy in the last interview I had with her. "Now, I'll tell you a piece of information. It was never so well worth your while to get me out of this country as it is to-night. Ah! If it was all your money twenty times told, to the last brass farden!" As he shook his heavy hand at me, with his mouth snarling like a tiger's, I felt that it was true.

"What are you going to do to me?"

"I'm a going," said he, bringing his fist down upon the table with a heavy blow, and rising as the blow fell, to give it greater force, "I'm a going to have your life!"

He leaned forward staring at me, slowly unclenched his hand and drew it across his mouth as if his mouth watered for me, and sat down again.

"You was always in Old Orlick's way since ever you was a child. You goes out of his way, this present night. He'll have no more on you. You're dead."

I felt that I had come to the brink of my grave. For a moment I looked wildly round my trap for any chance of escape; but there was none.

"More than that," said he, folding his arms on the table again, "I won't have a rag of you, I won't have a bone of you, left on earth. I'll put your body in the kiln—I'd carry two such to it, on my shoulders—and, let people suppose what they may of you, they shall never know nothing."

My mind, with inconceivable rapidity, followed out all the consequences of such a death. Estella's father would believe I had deserted him, would be taken, would die accusing me; even Herbert would doubt me, when he compared the letter I had left for him, with the fact that I had called at Miss Havisham's gate for only a moment; Joe and Biddy would never know how sorry I had been that night; none would ever know what I had suffered, how true I had meant to be, what an agony I had passed through. The death close before me was terrible, but far more terrible than death was the dread of being misremembered after death. And so quick were my thoughts, that I saw myself despised by unborn generations—Estella's children, and their children—while the wretch's words were yet on his lips.

"Now, wolf," said he, "afore I kill you like any other beast—which is wot I mean to do and wot I have tied you up for—I'll have a good look at you and a good goad at you. Oh, you enemy!"

It had passed through my thoughts to cry out for help again; though few could know better than I, the solitary nature of the spot, and the hopelessness of aid. But as he sat gloating over me, I was supported by a scornful detestation of him that sealed my lips. Above all things, I resolved that I would not entreat him, and that I would die making some last poor resistance to him. Softened as my thoughts of all the rest of men were in that dire extremity; humbly beseeching pardon, as I did, of Heaven; melted at heart, as I was, by the thought that I had taken no farewell, and never never now could take farewell, of those who were dear to me, or could explain myself to them, or ask for their compassion on my miserable errors; still, if I could have killed him, even in dying, I would have done it.

He had been drinking, and his eyes were red and bloodshot. Around his neck was slung a tin bottle, as I had often seen his meat and drink slung about him in other days. He brought the bottle to his lips, and took a fiery drink from it; and I smelt the strong spirits that I saw flash into his face.

"Wolf!" said he, folding his arms again, "Old Orlick's a going to tell you somethink. It was you as did for your shrew sister."

Again my mind, with its former inconceivable rapidity, had exhausted the whole subject of the attack upon my sister, her illness, and her death, before his slow and hesitating speech had formed those words.

"It was you, villain," said I.

"I tell you it was your doing—I tell you it was done through you," he retorted, catching up the gun, and making a blow with the stock at the vacant air between us. "I come upon her from behind, as I come upon you to-night. *I* giv' it her! I left her for dead, and if there had been a limekiln as nigh her as there is now nigh you, she shouldn't have come to life again. But it warn't Old Orlick as did it; it was you. You was favoured, and he was bullied and beat. Old Orlick bullied and beat, eh? Now you pays for it. You done it; now you pays for it."

He drank again, and became more ferocious. I saw by his tilting of the bottle that there was no great quantity left in it. I distinctly understood that he was working himself up with its contents, to make an end of me. I knew that every drop it held, was a drop of my life. I knew that when I was changed into a part of the vapour that had crept towards me but a little while before, like my own warning ghost, he would do as he had done in my sister's case—make all haste to the town, and be seen slouching about there, drinking at the ale-houses. My rapid mind pursued him to the town, made a picture of the street with him in it, and contrasted its lights and life with the lonely marsh and the white vapour creeping over it, into which I should have dissolved.

It was not only that I could have summed up years and years and years while he said a dozen words, but that what he did say presented pictures to me, and not mere words. In the excited and exalted state of my brain, I could not think of a place without seeing it, or of persons without seeing them. It is impossible to over-state the vividness of these images, and yet I was so intent, all the time, upon him himself—who would not be intent on the tiger crouching to spring!—that I knew of the slightest action of his fingers.

When he had drunk this second time, he rose from the bench on which he sat, and pushed the table aside. Then, he took up the candle, and shading it with his murderous hand so as to throw its light on me, stood before me, looking at me and enjoying the sight.

"Wolf, I'll tell you something more. It was Old Orlick as you tumbled over on your stairs that night."

I saw the staircase with its extinguished lamps. I saw the shadows of the heavy stair-rails, thrown by the watchman's lantern on the wall. I saw the rooms that I was never to see again; here, a door half open; there, a door closed; all the articles of furniture around.

"And why was Old Orlick there? I'll tell you something more, wolf. You and her *have* pretty well hunted me out of this country, so far as getting a easy living in it goes, and I've took up with new companions, and new masters. Some of 'em writes my letters when I wants 'em wrote—do you mind?—writes my letters, wolf! They writes fifty hands; they're not like sneaking you, as writes but one. I've had a firm mind and a firm will to have your life, since you was down here at your sister's burying. I han't seen a way to get you safe, and I've looked arter you to know your ins and outs. For, says Old Orlick to himself, 'Somehow or another I'll have him!' What! When I looks for you, I finds your uncle Provis, eh?"

Mill Pond Bank, and Chinks's Basin, and the Old Green Copper Rope-Walk, all so clear and plain! Provis in his rooms, the signal whose use was over, pretty Clara, the good motherly woman, old Bill Barley on his back, all drifting by, as on the swift stream of my life fast running out to sea!

"*You* with a uncle too! Why, I know'd you at Gargery's when you was so small a wolf that I could have took your weazen° betwixt this finger and thumb and chucked you away dead (as I'd thoughts o' doing, odd times, when I see you loitering amongst the pollards on a Sunday), and you hadn't found no uncles then. No, not you! But when Old Orlick come for to hear that your uncle Provis had mostlike wore the leg-iron wot Old Orlick had picked up, filed asunder, on these meshes ever so many year ago, and wot he kep by him till he dropped your sister with it, like a bullock, as he means to drop you— hey?—when he come for to hear that—hey?——"

In his savage taunting, he flared the candle so close at me, that I turned my face aside, to save it from the flame.

"Ah!" he cried, laughing, after doing it again, "the burnt child dread the fire! Old Orlick knowed you was burnt, Old Orlick knowed

---

weazen: Throat (slang).

you was a smuggling your uncle Provis away, Old Orlick's a match for you and knowed you'd come to-night! Now I'll tell you something more, wolf, and this ends it. There's them that's as good a match for your uncle Provis as Old Orlick has been for you. Let him 'ware them, when he's lost his nevvy! Let him 'ware them, when no man can't find a rag of his dear relation's clothes, nor yet a bone of his body? There's them that can't and that won't have Magwitch—yes, *I* know the name!—alive in the same land with them, and that's had such sure information of him when he was alive in another land, as that he couldn't and shouldn't leave it unbeknown and put them in danger. P'raps it's them that writes fifty hands, and that's not like sneaking you as writes but one. 'Ware Compeyson, Magwitch, and the gallows!"

He flared the candle at me again, smoking my face and hair, and for an instant blinding me, and turned his powerful back as he replaced the light on the table. I had thought a prayer, and had been with Joe and Biddy and Herbert, before he turned towards me again.

There was a clear space of a few feet between the table and the opposite wall. Within this space, he now slouched backwards and forwards. His great strength seemed to sit stronger upon him than ever before, as he did this with his hands hanging loose and heavy at his sides, and with his eyes scowling at me. I had no grain of hope left. Wild as my inward hurry was, and wonderful the force of the pictures that rushed by me instead of thoughts, I could yet clearly understand that unless he had resolved that I was within a few moments of surely perishing out of all human knowledge, he would never have told me what he had told.

Of a sudden, he stopped, took the cork out of his bottle, and tossed it away. Light as it was, I heard it fall like a plummet. He swallowed slowly, tilting up the bottle by little and little, and now he looked at me no more. The last few drops of liquor he poured into the palm of his hand, and licked up. Then, with a sudden hurry of violence and swearing horribly, he threw the bottle from him, and stooped; and I saw in his hand a stone-hammer with a long heavy handle.

The resolution I had made did not desert me, for, without uttering one vain word of appeal to him, I shouted out with all my might, and struggled with all my might. It was only my head and my legs that I could move, but to that extent I struggled with all the force, until then unknown, that was within me. In the same instant I heard responsive shouts, saw figures and a gleam of light dash in at the door, heard voices and tumult, and saw Orlick emerge from a struggle of men, as if it were tumbling water, clear the table at a leap, and fly out into the night.

After a blank, I found that I was lying unbound, on the floor, in the same place, with my head on some one's knee. My eyes were fixed on the ladder against the wall, when I came to myself—had opened on it before my mind saw it—and thus as I recovered consciousness, I knew that I was in the place where I had lost it.

Too indifferent at first, even to look round and ascertain who supported me, I was lying looking at the ladder, when there came between me and it, a face. The face of Trabb's boy!

"I think he's all right!" said Trabb's boy, in a sober voice; "but ain't he just pale though!"

At these words, the face of him who supported me looked over into mine, and I saw my supporter to be——

"Herbert! Great Heaven!"

"Softly," said Herbert. "Gently, Handel. Don't be too eager."

"And our old comrade, Startop!" I cried, as he too bent over me.

"Remember what he is going to assist us in," said Herbert, "and be calm."

The allusion made me spring up; though I dropped again from the pain in my arm. "The time has not gone by, Herbert, has it? What night is to-night? How long have I been here?" For, I had a strange and strong misgiving that I had been lying there a long time—a day and a night—two days and nights—more.

"The time has not gone by. It is still Monday night."

"Thank God!"

"And you have all to-morrow, Tuesday, to rest in," said Herbert. "But you can't help groaning, my dear Handel. What hurt have you got? Can you stand?"

"Yes, yes," said I, "I can walk. I have no hurt but in this throbbing arm."

They laid it bare, and did what they could. It was violently swollen and inflamed, and I could scarcely endure to have it touched. But, they tore up their handkerchiefs to make fresh bandages, and carefully replaced it in the sling, until we could get to the town and obtain some cooling lotion to put upon it. In a little while we had shut the door of the dark and empty sluice-house, and were passing through the quarry on our way back. Trabb's boy—Trabb's overgrown young man now—went before us with a lantern, which was the light I had seen come in at the door. But, the moon was a good two hours higher than when I had last seen the sky, and the night though rainy was much lighter. The white vapour of the kiln was passing from us as we went by, and, as I had thought a prayer before, I thought a thanksgiving now.

Entreating Herbert to tell me how he had come to my rescue—which at first he had flatly refused to do, but had insisted on my remaining quiet—I learnt that I had in my hurry dropped the letter, open, in our chambers, where he, coming home to bring with him Startop whom he had met in the street on his way to me, found it, very soon after I was gone. Its tone made him uneasy, and the more so because of the inconsistency between it and the hasty letter I had left for him. His uneasiness increasing instead of subsiding after a quarter of an hour's consideration, he set off for the coach-office, with Startop, who volunteered his company, to make inquiry when the next coach went down. Finding that the afternoon coach was gone, and finding that his uneasiness grew into positive alarm, as obstacles came in his way, he resolved to follow in a post-chaise. So, he and Startop arrived at the Blue Boar, fully expecting there to find me, or tidings of me; but, finding neither, went on to Miss Havisham's, where they lost me. Hereupon they went back to the hotel (doubtless at about the time when I was hearing the popular local version of my own story), to refresh themselves and to get some one to guide them out upon the marshes. Among the loungers under the Boar's archway, happened to be Trabb's boy—true to his ancient habit of happening to be everywhere where he had no business—and Trabb's boy had seen me passing from Miss Havisham's in the direction of my dining-place. Thus, Trabb's boy became their guide, and with him they went out to the sluice-house: though by the town way to the marshes, which I had avoided. Now, as they went along, Herbert reflected, that I might, after all, have been brought there on some genuine and serviceable errand tending to Provis's safety, and, bethinking himself that in that case interruption must be mischievous, left his guide and Startop on the edge of the quarry, and went on by himself, and stole round the house two or three times, endeavouring to ascertain whether all was right within. As he could hear nothing but indistinct sounds of one deep rough voice (this was while my mind was so busy), he even at last began to doubt whether I was there, when suddenly I cried out loudly, and he answered the cries, and rushed in, closely followed by the other two.

When I told Herbert what had passed within the house, he was for our immediately going before a magistrate in the town, late at night as it was, and getting out a warrant. But, I had already considered that such a course, by detaining us there, or binding us to come back, might be fatal to Provis. There was no gainsaying this difficulty, and we relinquished all thoughts of pursuing Orlick at that time. For the present, under the circumstances, we deemed it prudent to make rather light of the matter to Trabb's boy; who I am convinced would have been much affected by disappointment, if he had known that his intervention saved me from the limekiln. Not that Trabb's boy was of a malignant nature, but that he had too much spare vivacity, and that it was in his constitution to want variety and excitement at anybody's expense. When we parted, I presented him with two guineas (which seemed to meet his views), and told him that I was sorry ever to have had an ill opinion of him (which made no impression on him at all).

Wednesday being so close upon us, we determined to go back to London that night, three in the post-chaise; the rather, as we should then be clear away, before the night's adventure began to be talked of. Herbert got a large bottle of stuff for my arm, and by dint of having this stuff dropped over it all the night through, I was just able to bear its pain on the journey. It was daylight when we reached the Temple, and I went at once to bed, and lay in bed all day.

My terror, as I lay there, of falling ill and being unfitted for to-morrow, was so besetting, that I wonder it did not disable me of itself. It would have done so, pretty surely, in conjunction with the mental wear and tear I had suffered, but for the unnatural strain upon me that to-morrow was. So anxiously looked forward to, charged with such consequences, its results so impenetrably hidden though so near.

No precaution could have been more obvious than our refraining from communication with him that day; yet this again increased my restlessness. I started at every footstep and every sound, believing that he was discovered and taken, and this was the messenger to tell me so. I persuaded myself that I knew he was taken; that there was something more upon my mind than a fear or a presentiment; that the fact had occurred, and I had a mysterious knowledge of it. As the day wore on and no ill news came, as the day closed in and darkness fell, my over-shadowing dread of being disabled by illness before to-morrow morning, altogether mastered me. My burning arm throbbed, and my burning head throbbed, and I fancied I was beginning to wander. I counted up to high numbers, to make sure of myself, and repeated passages that I knew in prose and verse. It happened sometimes that in the mere escape of a fatigued mind, I dozed for some moments or forgot; then I would say to myself with a start, "Now it has come, and I am turning delirious!"

They kept me very quiet all day, and kept my arm constantly dressed, and gave me cooling drinks. Whenever I fell asleep, I awoke with the notion I had had in the sluice-house, that a long time had elapsed and the opportunity to save him was gone. About midnight I got out of bed and went to Herbert, with the conviction that I had been asleep for four-and-twenty hours, and that Wednesday was past. It was the last self-exhausting effort of my fretfulness, for, after that, I slept soundly.

Wednesday morning was dawning when I looked out of window. The winking lights upon the bridges were already pale, the coming sun was like a marsh of fire on the horizon. The river, still dark and mysterious, was spanned by bridges that were turning coldly grey, with here and there at top a warm touch from the burning in the sky. As I looked along the clustered roofs, with Church towers and spires shooting into the unusually clear air, the sun rose up, and a veil seemed to be drawn from the river, and millions of sparkles burst out upon its waters. From me too, a veil seemed to be drawn, and I felt strong and well.

Herbert lay asleep in his bed, and our old fellow-student lay asleep on the sofa. I could not dress myself without help, but I made up the fire, which was still burning, and got some coffee ready for them. In good time they too started up strong and well, and we admitted the sharp morning air at the windows, and looked at the tide that was still flowing towards us.

"When it turns at nine o'clock," said Herbert, cheerfully, "look out for us, and stand ready, you over there at Mill Pond Bank!"

[PART 33]

Chapter 54

It was one of those March days when the sun shines hot and the wind blows cold: when it is summer in the light, and winter in the shade. We had our pea-coats with us, and I took a bag. Of all my worldly possessions I took no more than the few necessaries that filled the bag. Where I might go, what I might do, or when I might return, were questions utterly unknown to me; nor did I vex my mind with them, for it was wholly set on Provis's safety. I only wondered for the passing moment, as I stopped at the door and looked back, under what altered circumstances I should next see those rooms, if ever.

We loitered down to the Temple stairs, and stood loitering there, as if we were not quite decided to go upon the water at all. Of course I had taken care that the boat should be ready and everything in order. After a little show of indecision, which there were none to see but the two or three amphibious creatures belonging to our Temple stairs, we went on board and cast off; Herbert in the bow, I steering. It was then about high-water—half-past eight.

Our plan was this. The tide, beginning to run down at nine, and being with us until three, we intended still to creep on after it had turned, and row against it until dark. We should then be well in those long reaches below Gravesend, between Kent and Essex, where the river is broad and solitary, where the water-side inhabitants are very few, and where lone public-houses are scattered here and there, of which we could choose one for a resting-place. There, we meant to lie by, all night. The steamer for Hamburg, and the steamer for Rotterdam, would start from London at about nine on Thursday morning. We should know at what time to expect them, according to where we were, and would hail the first; so that if by any accident we were not taken aboard, we should have another chance. We knew the distinguishing marks of each vessel.

The relief of being at last engaged in the execution of the purpose, was so great to me that I felt it difficult to realise the condition in which I had been a few hours before. The crisp air, the sunlight, the movement on the river, and the moving river itself—the road that ran with us, seeming to sympathise with us, animate us, and encourage us on—freshened me with new hope. I felt mortified to be of so little use in the boat; but, there were few better oarsmen than my two friends, and they rowed with a steady stroke that was to last all day.

At that time, the steam-traffic on the Thames was far below its present extent, and watermen's boats were far more numerous. Of barges, sailing colliers, and coasting-traders, there were perhaps as many as now; but, of steam-ships, great and small, not a tithe or a twentieth part so many. Early as it was, there were plenty of scullers going here and there that morning, and plenty of barges dropping down with the tide; the navigation of the river between bridges, in an open boat, was a much easier and commoner matter in those days than it is in these; and we went ahead among many skiffs and wherries, briskly.

Old London Bridge was soon passed, and old Billingsgate market with its oyster-boats and Dutchmen, and the White Tower and Traitors' Gate, and we were in among the tiers of shipping. Here, were the Leith, Aberdeen, and Glasgow steamers, loading and unloading goods, and looking immensely high out of the water as we passed alongside; here, were colliers by the score and score, with the coal-whippers plunging off stages on deck, as counterweights to measures of coal swinging up, which were then rattled over the side into barges; here, at her moorings was to-morrow's steamer for Rotterdam, of which we took good notice; and here to-morrow's for Hamburg, under whose bowsprit we crossed. And now I, sitting in the stern, could see with a faster beating heart, Mill Pond Bank and Mill Pond stairs.

"Is he there?" said Herbert.

"Not yet."

"Right! He was not to come down till he saw us. Can you see his signal?"

"Not well from here; but I think I see it.—Now, I see him! Pull both. Easy, Herbert. Oars!"

We touched the stairs lightly for a single moment, and he was on board and we were off again. He had a boat-cloak with him, and a black canvas bag, and he looked as like a river-pilot as my heart could have wished.

"Dear boy!" he said, putting his arm on my shoulder as he took his seat. "Faithful dear boy, well done. Thankye, thankye!"

Again among the tiers of shipping, in and out, avoiding rusty chain-cables, frayed hempen hawsers and bobbing buoys, sinking for the moment floating broken baskets, scattering floating chips of wood and shaving, cleaving floating scum of coal, in and out, under the figure-head of the John of Sunderland making a speech to the winds (as is done by many Johns), and the Betsy of Yarmouth with a firm formality of bosom and her knobby eyes starting two inches out of her head, in and out, hammers going in ship-builders' yards, saws going at timber, clashing engines going at things unknown, pumps going in leaky ships, capstans going, ships going out to sea, and unintelligible sea-creatures roaring curses over the bulwarks at respondent lighter-men, in and out—out at last upon the clearer river, where the ships' boys might take their fenders in, no longer fishing in troubled waters with them over the side, and where the festooned sails might fly out to the wind.

At the Stairs where we had taken him aboard, and ever since, I had looked warily for any token of our being suspected. I had seen none. We certainly had not been, and at that time as certainly we were not, either attended or followed by any boat. If we had been waited on by any boat, I should have run in to shore, and have obliged her to go on, or to make her purpose evident. But, we held our own, without any appearance of molestation.

He had his boat-cloak on him, and looked, as I have said, a natural part of the scene. It was remarkable (but perhaps the wretched life he had led, accounted for it), that he was the least anxious of any of us. He was not indifferent, for he told me that he hoped to live to see his gentleman one of the best of gentlemen in a foreign country; he was not disposed to be passive or resigned, as I understood it; but he had no notion of meeting danger half way. When it came upon him, he confronted it, but it must come before he troubled himself.

"If you knowed, dear boy," he said to me, "what it is to sit here alonger my dear boy and have my smoke, arter having been day by day betwixt four walls, you'd envy me. But you don't know what it is."

"I think I know the delights of freedom," I answered.

"Ah," said he, shaking his head gravely. "But you don't know it equal to me. You must have been under lock and key, dear boy, to know it equal to me—but I ain't a going to be low."

It occurred to me as inconsistent, that for any mastering idea, he should have endangered his freedom and even his life. But I reflected that perhaps freedom without danger was too much apart from all the habit of his existence to be to him what it would be to another man. I was not far out, since he said, after smoking a little:

"You see, dear boy, when I was over yonder, t'other side the world, I was always a looking to this side; and it come flat to be there, for all I was a growing rich. Everybody knowed Magwitch, and Magwitch could come, and Magwitch could go, and nobody's head would be troubled about him. They ain't so easy concerning me here, dear boy—wouldn't be, leastwise, if they knowed where I was."

"If all goes well," said I, "you will be perfectly free and safe again, within a few hours."

"Well," he returned, drawing a long breath, "I hope so."

"And think so?"

He dipped his hand in the water over the boat's gunwale, and said, smiling with that softened air upon him which was not new to me:

"Ay, I s'pose I think so, dear boy. We'd be puzzled to be more quiet and easy-going than we are at present. But—it's a flowing so soft and pleasant through the water, p'raps, as makes me think it—I was a thinking through my smoke just then, that we can no more see to the bottom of the next few hours, than we can see to the bottom of this river what I catches hold of. Nor yet we can't no more hold their tide than I can hold this. And it's run through my fingers and gone, you see!" holding up his dripping hand.

"But for your face, I should think you were a little despondent," said I.

"Not a bit on it, dear boy! It comes of flowing on so quiet, and of that there rippling at the boat's head making a sort of a Sunday tune. Maybe I'm a growing a trifle old besides."

He put his pipe back in his mouth with an undisturbed expression of face, and sat as composed and contented as if we were already out of England. Yet he was as submissive to a word of advice as if he had been in constant terror, for, when we ran ashore to get some bottles of beer into the boat, and he was stepping out, I hinted that I thought he would be safest where he was, and he said, "Do you, dear boy?" and quietly sat down again.

The air felt cold upon the river, but it was a bright day, and the sunshine was very cheering. The tide ran strong, I took care to lose none of it, and our steady stroke carried us on thoroughly well. By imperceptible degrees, as the tide ran out, we lost more and more of the nearer woods and hills, and dropped lower and lower between the muddy banks, but the tide was yet with us when we were off Gravesend. As our charge was wrapped in his cloak, I purposely passed within a boat or two's length of the floating Custom House,° and so out to catch the stream, alongside of two emigrant ships, and under the bows of a large transport with troops on the forecastle looking down at us. And soon the tide began to slacken, and the craft lying at anchor to swing, and presently they had all swung round, and the ships that were taking advantage of the new tide to get up to the Pool, began to crowd upon us in a fleet, and we kept under the shore, as much out of the strength of the tide now as we could, standing carefully off from low shallows and mud-banks.

Our oarsmen were so fresh, by dint of having occasionally let her drive with the tide for a minute or two, that a quarter of an hour's rest proved full as much as they wanted. We got ashore among some slippery stones while we ate and drank what we had with us, and looked about. It was like my own marsh country, flat and monotonous, and with a dim horizon; while the winding river turned and turned, and the great floating buoys upon it turned and turned, and everything

---

floating Custom House: Officials of the Custom House used boats to board ships coming up the Thames.

else seemed stranded and still. For, now, the last of the fleet of ships was round the last low point we had headed; and the last green barge, straw-laden, with a brown sail, had followed; and some ballast-lighters, shaped like a child's first rude imitation of a boat, lay low in the mud; and a little squat shoal-lighthouse on open piles, stood crippled in the mud on stilts and crutches; and slimy stakes stuck out of the mud, and slimy stones stuck out of the mud, and red landmarks and tidemarks stuck out of the mud, and an old landing-stage and an old roofless building slipped into the mud, and all about us was stagnation and mud.

We pushed off again, and made what way we could. It was much harder work now, but Herbert and Startop persevered, and rowed, and rowed, and rowed, until the sun went down. By that time the river had lifted us a little, so that we could see above the bank. There was the red sun, on the low level of the shore, in a purple haze, fast deepening into black; and there was the solitary flat marsh; and far away there were the rising grounds, between which and us there seemed to be no life, save here and there in the foreground a melancholy gull.

As the night was fast falling, and as the moon, being past the full, would not rise early, we held a little council: a short one, for clearly our course was to lie by at the first lonely tavern we could find. So, they plied their oars once more, and I looked out for anything like a house. Thus we held on, speaking little, for four or five dull miles. It was very cold, and, a collier coming by us, with her galley-fire smoking and flaring, looked like a comfortable home. The night was as dark by this time as it would be until morning; and what light we had, seemed to come more from the river than the sky, as the oars in their dipping struck at a few reflected stars.

At this dismal time we were evidently all possessed by the idea that we were followed. As the tide made, it flapped heavily at irregular intervals against the shore; and whenever such a sound came, one or other of us was sure to start and look in that direction. Here and there, the set of the current had worn down the bank into a little creek, and we were all suspicious of such places, and eyed them nervously. Sometimes, "What was that ripple!" one of us would say in a low voice. Or another, "Is that a boat yonder?" And afterwards, we would fall into a dead silence, and I would sit impatiently thinking with what an unusual amount of noise the oars worked in the thowels.

At length we descried a light and a roof, and presently afterwards ran alongside a little causeway made of stones that had been picked up hard-by. Leaving the rest in the boat, I stepped ashore, and found the light to be in a window of a public-house. It was a dirty place enough, and I dare say not unknown to smuggling adventurers; but there was a good fire in the kitchen, and there were eggs and bacon to eat, and various liquors to drink. Also, there were two double-bedded rooms— "such as they were," the landlord said. No other company was in the house than the landlord, his wife, and a grizzled male creature, the "Jack"° of the little causeway, who was as slimy and smeary as if he had been low-water mark too.

With this assistant, I went down to the boat again, and we all came ashore, and brought out the oars, and rudder, and boat-hook, and all else, and hauled her up for the night. We made a very good meal by the kitchen fire, and then apportioned the bedrooms: Herbert and Startop were to occupy one; I and our charge the other. We found the air as carefully excluded from both, as if air were fatal to life; and there were more dirty clothes and bandboxes under the beds than I should have thought the family possessed. But, we considered ourselves well off, notwithstanding, for a more solitary place we could not have found.

While we were comforting ourselves by the fire after our meal, the Jack—who was sitting in a corner, and who had a bloated pair of shoes on, which he had exhibited while we were eating our eggs and bacon, as interesting relics that he had taken a few days ago from the feet of a drowned seaman washed ashore—asked me if we had seen a four-oared galley going up with the tide? When I told him No, he said she must have gone down then, and yet she "took up too," when she left there.

"They must ha' thought better on't for some reason or another," said the Jack, "and gone down."

"A four-oared galley, did you say?" said I.

"A four," said the Jack, "and two sitters."

"Did they come ashore here?"

"They put in with a stone two-gallon jar, for some beer. I'd ha' been glad to pison the beer myself," said the Jack, "or put some rattling physic° in it."

"Why?"

"*I* know why," said the Jack. He spoke in a slushy voice, as if much mud had washed into his throat.

"He thinks," said the landlord: a weakly meditative man with a

"Jack": Here, a man who does odd jobs.   **rattling physic:** Fast-acting purgative medicine; laxative.

pale eye, who seemed to rely greatly on his Jack: "he thinks they was, what they wasn't."

"*I* knows what I thinks," observed the Jack.

"*You* thinks Custum 'Us, Jack?" said the landlord.

"I do," said the Jack.

"Then you're wrong, Jack."

"Am I!"

In the infinite meaning of his reply and his boundless confidence in his views, the Jack took one of his bloated shoes off, looked into it, knocked a few stones out of it on the kitchen floor, and put it on again. He did this with the air of a Jack who was so right that he could afford to do anything.

"Why, what do you make out that they done with their buttons then, Jack?" asked the landlord, vacillating weakly.

"Done with their buttons?" returned the Jack. "Chucked 'em overboard. Swallered 'em. Sowed 'em, to come up small salad. Done with their buttons!"

"Don't be cheeky, Jack," remonstrated the landlord, in a melancholy and pathetic way.

"A Custum 'Us officer knows what to do with his Buttons," said the Jack, repeating the obnoxious word with the greatest contempt, "when they comes betwixt him and his own light. A Four and two sitters don't go hanging and hovering, up with one tide and down with another, and both with and against another, without there being Custum 'Us at the bottom of it." Saying which he went out in disdain; and the landlord, having no one to rely upon, found it impracticable to pursue the subject.

This dialogue made us all uneasy, and me very uneasy. The dismal wind was muttering round the house, the tide was flapping at the shore, and I had a feeling that we were caged and threatened. A four-oared galley hovering about in so unusual a way as to attract this notice, was an ugly circumstance that I could not get rid of. When I had induced Provis to go up to bed, I went outside with my two companions (Startop by this time knew the state of the case), and held another council. Whether we should remain at the house until near the steamer's time, which would be about one in the afternoon; or whether we should put off early in the morning; was the question we discussed. On the whole we deemed it the better course to lie where we were, until within an hour or so of the steamer's time, and then to get out in her track, and drift easily with the tide. Having settled to do this, we returned into the house and went to bed.

I lay down with the greater part of my clothes on, and slept well for a few hours. When I awoke, the wind had risen, and the sign of the house (the Ship) was creaking and banging about, with noises that startled me. Rising softly, for my charge lay fast asleep, I looked out of the window. It commanded the causeway where we had hauled up our boat, and, as my eyes adapted themselves to the light of the clouded moon, I saw two men looking into her. They passed by under the window, looking at nothing else, and they did not go down to the landing-place which I could discern to be empty, but struck across the marsh in the direction of the Nore.°

My first impulse was to call up Herbert, and show him the two men going away. But, reflecting before I got into his room, which was at the back of the house and adjoined mine, that he and Startop had had a harder day than I, and were fatigued, I forbore. Going back to my window, I could see the two men moving over the marsh. In that light, however, I soon lost them, and feeling very cold, lay down to think of the matter, and fell asleep again.

We were up early. As we walked to and fro, all four together, before breakfast, I deemed it right to recount what I had seen. Again our charge was the least anxious of the party. It was very likely that the men belonged to the Custom House, he said quietly, and that they had no thought of us. I tried to persuade myself that it was so — as, indeed, it might easily be. However, I proposed that he and I should walk away together to a distant point we could see, and that the boat should take us aboard there, or as near there as might prove feasible, at about noon. This being considered a good precaution, soon after breakfast he and I set forth, without saying anything at the tavern.

He smoked his pipe as we went along, and sometimes stopped to clap me on the shoulder. One would have supposed that it was I who was in danger, not he, and that he was reassuring me. We spoke very little. As we approached the point, I begged him to remain in a sheltered place, while I went on to reconnoitre; for, it was towards it that the men had passed in the night. He complied, and I went on alone. There was no boat off the point, nor any boat drawn up anywhere near it, nor were there any signs of the men having embarked there. But, to be sure the tide was high, and there might have been some footprints under water.

When he looked out from his shelter in the distance, and saw that I waved my hat to him to come up, he rejoined me, and there we

Nore: A sandbar at the mouth of the Thames.

waited: sometimes lying on the bank wrapped in our coats, and sometimes moving about to warm ourselves: until we saw our boat coming round. We got aboard easily, and rowed out into the track of the steamer. By that time it wanted but ten minutes of one o'clock, and we began to look out for her smoke.

But, it was half-past one before we saw her smoke, and soon afterwards we saw behind it the smoke of another steamer. As they were coming on at full speed, we got the two bags ready, and took that opportunity of saying good-by to Herbert and Startop. We had all shaken hands cordially, and neither Herbert's eyes nor mine were quite dry, when I saw a four-oared galley shoot out from under the bank but a little way ahead of us, and row out into the same track.

A stretch of shore had been as yet between us and the steamer's smoke, by reason of the bend and wind of the river; but now she was visible, coming head on. I called to Herbert and Startop to keep before the tide, that she might see us lying by for her, and I adjured Provis to sit quite still, wrapped in his cloak. He answered cheerily, "Trust to me, dear boy," and sat like a statue. Meantime the galley, which was very skilfully handled, had crossed us, let us come up with her, and fallen alongside. Leaving just room enough for the play of the oars, she kept alongside, drifting when we drifted, and pulling a stroke or two when we pulled. Of the two sitters, one held the rudder lines, and looked at us attentively—as did all the rowers; the other sitter was wrapped up, much as Provis was, and seemed to shrink, and whisper some instruction to the steerer as he looked at us. Not a word was spoken in either boat.

Startop could make out, after a few minutes, which steamer was first, and gave me the word "Hamburg," in a low voice as we sat face to face. She was nearing us very fast, and the beating of her paddles grew louder and louder. I felt as if her shadow were absolutely upon us, when the galley hailed us. I answered.

"You have a returned Transport there," said the man who held the lines. "That's the man, wrapped in the cloak. His name is Abel Magwitch, otherwise Provis. I apprehend that man, and call upon him to surrender, and you to assist."

At the same moment, without giving any audible direction to his crew, he ran the galley aboard of us. They had pulled one sudden stroke ahead, had got their oars in, had run athwart us, and were holding on to our gunwale, before we knew what they were doing. This caused great confusion on board the steamer, and I heard them calling to us, and heard the order given to stop the paddles, and heard them stop, but felt her driving down upon us irresistibly. In the same moment, I saw the steersman of the galley lay his hand on his prisoner's shoulder, and saw that both boats were swinging round with the force of the tide, and saw that all hands on board the steamer were running forward quite frantically. Still in the same moment, I saw the prisoner start up, lean across his captor, and pull the cloak from the neck of the shrinking sitter in the galley. Still in the same moment, I saw that the face disclosed, was the face of the other convict of long ago. Still in the same moment, I saw the face tilt backward with a white terror on it that I shall never forget, and heard a great cry on board the steamer and a loud splash in the water, and felt the boat sink from under me.

It was but for an instant that I seemed to struggle with a thousand mill-weirs° and a thousand flashes of light; that instant past, I was taken on board the galley. Herbert was there, and Startop was there; but our boat was gone, and the two convicts were gone.

What with the cries aboard the steamer, and the furious blowing-off of her steam, and her driving on, and our driving on, I could not at first distinguish sky from water or shore from shore; but, the crew of the galley righted her with great speed, and, pulling certain swift strong strokes ahead, lay upon their oars, every man looking silently and eagerly at the water astern. Presently a dark object was seen in it, bearing towards us on the tide. No man spoke, but the steersman held up his hand, and all softly backed water, and kept the boat straight and true before it. As it came nearer, I saw it to be Magwitch, swimming, but not swimming freely. He was taken on board, and instantly manacled at the wrists and ankles.

The galley was kept steady, and the silent eager look-out at the water was resumed. But, the Rotterdam steamer now came up, and apparently not understanding what had happened, came on at speed. By the time she had been hailed and stopped, both steamers were drifting away from us, and we were rising and falling in a troubled wake of water. The look-out was kept, long after all was still again and the two steamers were gone; but, everybody knew that it was hopeless now.

At length we gave it up, and pulled under the shore towards the tavern we had lately left, where we were received with no little surprise. Here, I was able to get some comforts for Magwitch—Provis no longer—who had received some very severe injury in the chest and a deep cut in the head.

He told me that he believed himself to have gone under the keel of

---

mill-weirs: Mill-dams and perhaps the mill-wheels associated with them.

the steamer, and to have been struck on the head in rising. The injury to his chest (which rendered his breathing extremely painful) he thought he had received against the side of the galley. He added that he did not pretend to say what he might or might not have done to Compeyson, but, that in the moment of his laying his hand on his cloak to identify him, that villain had staggered up and staggered back, and they had both gone overboard together; when the sudden wrenching of him (Magwitch) out of our boat, and the endeavour of his captor to keep him in it, had capsized us. He told me in a whisper that they had gone down, fiercely locked in each other's arms, and that there had been a struggle under water, and that he had disengaged himself, struck out, and swum away.

I never had any reason to doubt the exact truth of what he thus told me. The officer who steered the galley gave the same account of their going overboard.

When I asked this officer's permission to change the prisoner's wet clothes by purchasing any spare garments I could get at the public-house, he gave it readily: merely observing that he must take charge of everything his prisoner had about him. So the pocket-book which had once been in my hands, passed into the officer's. He further gave me leave to accompany the prisoner to London; but, declined to accord that grace to my two friends.

The Jack at the Ship was instructed where the drowned man had gone down, and undertook to search for the body in the places where it was likeliest to come ashore. His interest in its recovery seemed to me to be much heightened when he heard that it had stockings on. Probably, it took about a dozen drowned men to fit him out completely; and that may have been the reason why the different articles of his dress were in various stages of decay.

We remained at the public-house until the tide turned, and then Magwitch was carried down to the galley and put on board. Herbert and Startop were to get to London by land, as soon as they could. We had a doleful parting, and when I took my place by Magwitch's side, I felt that that was my place henceforth while he lived.

For now, my repugnance to him had all melted away, and in the hunted wounded shackled creature who held my hand in his, I only saw a man who had meant to be my benefactor, and who had felt affectionately, gratefully, and generously, towards me with great constancy through a series of years. I only saw in him a much better man than I had been to Joe.

His breathing became more difficult and painful as the night drew on, and often he could not repress a groan. I tried to rest him on the arm I could use, in any easy position; but, it was dreadful to think that I could not be sorry at heart for his being badly hurt, since it was unquestionably best that he should die. That there were, still living, people enough who were able and willing to identify him, I could not doubt. That he would be leniently treated, I could not hope. He who had been presented in the worst light at his trial, who had since broken prison and been tried again, who had returned from transportation under a life sentence, and who had occasioned the death of the man who was the cause of his arrest.

As we returned towards the setting sun we had yesterday left behind us, and as the stream of our hopes seemed all running back, I told him how grieved I was to think that he had come home for my sake.

"Dear boy," he answered, "I'm quite content to take my chance. I've seen my boy, and he can be a gentleman without me."

No. I had thought about that, while we had been there side by side. No. Apart from any inclinations of my own, I understood Wemmick's hint now. I foresaw that, being convicted, his possessions would be forfeited to the Crown.

"Lookee here, dear boy," said he. "It's best as a gentleman should not be knowed to belong to me now. Only come to see me as if you come by chance alonger Wemmick. Sit where I can see you when I am swore to, for the last o' many times, and I don't ask no more."

"I will never stir from your side," said I, "when I am suffered to be near you. Please God, I will be as true to you, as you have been to me!"

I felt his hand tremble as it held mine, and he turned his face away as he lay in the bottom of the boat, and I heard that old sound in his throat—softened now, like all the rest of him. It was a good thing that he had touched this point, for it put into my mind what I might not otherwise have thought of until too late: That he need never know how his hopes of enriching me had perished.

[PART 34]

Chapter 55

He was taken to the Police Court next day, and would have been immediately committed for trial, but that it was necessary to send down for an old officer of the prison-ship from which he had once escaped, to speak to his identity. Nobody doubted it; but, Compeyson, who had meant to depose to it, was tumbling on the tides, dead, and it happened that there was not at that time any prison officer in London who could give the required evidence. I had gone direct to Mr. Jaggers at his private house, on my arrival over-night, to retain his assistance, and Mr. Jaggers on the prisoner's behalf would admit nothing. It was the sole resource, for he told me that the case must be over in five minutes when the witness was there, and that no power on earth could prevent its going against us.

I imparted to Mr. Jaggers my design of keeping him in ignorance of the fate of his wealth. Mr. Jaggers was querulous and angry with me for having "let it slip through my fingers," and said we must memorialise° by-and-by, and try at all events for some of it. But, he did not conceal from me that although there might be many cases in which the forfeiture would not be exacted, there were no circumstances in this case to make it one of them. I understood that, very well. I was not related to the outlaw, or connected with him by any recognisable tie; he had put his hand to no writing or settlement in my favour before his apprehension, and to do so now would be idle. I had no claim, and I finally resolved, and ever afterwards abided by the resolution, that my heart should never be sickened with the hopeless task of attempting to establish one.

There appeared to be reason for supposing that the drowned informer had hoped for a reward out of this forfeiture, and had obtained some accurate knowledge of Magwitch's affairs. When his body was found, many miles from the scene of his death, and so horribly disfigured that he was only recognisable by the contents of his pockets, notes were still legible, folded in a case he carried. Among these, were the name of a banking-house in New South Wales where a sum of money was, and the designation of certain lands of considerable value. Both these heads of information were in a list that Magwitch, while in prison, gave to Mr. Jaggers, of the possessions he supposed I should inherit. His ignorance, poor fellow, at last served him; he never mistrusted but that my inheritance was quite safe, with Mr. Jaggers's aid.

After three days' delay, during which the crown prosecution stood over for the production of the witness from the prison-ship, the witness came, and completed the easy case. He was committed to take his trial at the next Sessions, which would come on in a month.

memorialise: Petition in writing.

It was at this dark time of my life that Herbert returned home one evening, a good deal cast down, and said:

"My dear Handel, I fear I shall soon have to leave you."

His partner having prepared me for that, I was less surprised than he thought.

"We shall lose a fine opportunity if I put off going to Cairo, and I am very much afraid I must go, Handel, when you most need me."

"Herbert, I shall always need you, because I shall always love you; but my need is no greater now, than at another time."

"You will be so lonely."

"I have not leisure to think of that," said I. "You know that I am always with him to the full extent of the time allowed, and that I should be with him all day long, if I could. And when I come away from him, you know that my thoughts are with him."

The dreadful condition to which he was brought, was so appalling to both of us, that we could not refer to it in plainer words.

"My dear fellow," said Herbert, "let the near prospect of our separation—for, it is very near—be my justification for troubling you about yourself. Have you thought of your future?"

"No, for I have been afraid to think of any future."

"But yours cannot be dismissed; indeed, my dear dear Handel, it must not be dismissed. I wish you would enter on it now, as far as a few friendly words go, with me."

"I will," said I.

"In this branch house of ours, Handel, we must have a——"

I saw that his delicacy was avoiding the right word, so I said, "A clerk."

"A clerk. And I hope it is not at all unlikely that he may expand (as a clerk of your acquaintance has expanded) into a partner. Now, Handel——in short, my dear boy, will you come to me?"

There was something charmingly cordial and engaging in the manner in which after saying "Now, Handel," as if it were the grave beginning of a portentous business exordium, he had suddenly given up that tone, stretched out his honest hand, and spoken like a schoolboy.

"Clara and I have talked about it again and again," Herbert pursued, "and the dear little thing begged me only this evening, with tears in her eyes, to say to you that if you will live with us when we come together, she will do her best to make you happy, and to convince her husband's friend that he is her friend too. We should get on so well, Handel!"

I thanked her heartily, and I thanked him heartily, but said I could not yet make sure of joining him as he so kindly offered. Firstly, my mind was too preoccupied to be able to take in the subject clearly. Secondly——Yes! Secondly, there was a vague something lingering in my thoughts that will come out very near the end of this slight narrative.

"But if you thought, Herbert, that you could, without doing any injury to your business, leave the question open for a little while——"

"For any while," cried Herbert. "Six months, a year!"

"Not so long as that," said I. "Two or three months at most."

Herbert was highly delighted when we shook hands on this arrangement, and said he could now take courage to tell me that he believed he must go away at the end of the week.

"And Clara?" said I.

"The dear little thing," returned Herbert, "holds dutifully to her father as long as he lasts; but he won't last long. Mrs. Whimple confides to me that he is certainly going."

"Not to say an unfeeling thing," said I, "he cannot do better than go."

"I am afraid that must be admitted," said Herbert: "and then I shall come back for the dear little thing, and the dear little thing and I will walk quietly into the nearest church. Remember! The blessed darling comes of no family, my dear Handel, and never looked into the red book,° and hasn't a notion about her grandpapa. What a fortune for the son of my mother!"

On the Saturday in that same week, I took my leave of Herbert— full of bright hope, but sad and sorry to leave me—as he sat on one of the seaport mail coaches. I went into a coffee-house to write a little note to Clara, telling her he had gone off, sending his love to her over and over again, and then went to my lonely home—if it deserved the name, for it was now no home to me, and I had no home anywhere.

On the stairs I encountered Wemmick, who was coming down, after an unsuccessful application of his knuckles to my door. I had not seen him alone, since the disastrous issue of the attempted flight; and he had come, in his private and personal capacity, to say a few words of explanation in reference to that failure.

"The late Compeyson," said Wemmick, "had by little and little got at the bottom of half of the regular business now transacted, and it was from the talk of some of his people in trouble (some of his people being always in trouble) that I heard what I did. I kept my ears open,

---

red book: Guide to the aristocracy such as Debrett's *Peerage.*

seeming to have them shut, until I heard that he was absent, and I thought that would be the best time for making the attempt. I can only suppose now, that it was a part of his policy, as a very clever man, habitually to deceive his own instruments. You don't blame me, I hope, Mr. Pip? I am sure I tried to serve you, with all my heart."

"I am as sure of that, Wemmick, as you can be, and I thank you most earnestly for all your interest and friendship."

"Thank you, thank you very much. It's a bad job," said Wemmick, scratching his head, "and I assure you I haven't been so cut up for a long time. What I look at, is the sacrifice of so much portable property. Dear me!"

"What *I* think of, Wemmick, is the poor owner of the property."

"Yes, to be sure," said Wemmick. "Of course there can be no objection to your being sorry for him, and I'd put down a five-pound note myself to get him out of it. But what I look at, is this. The late Compeyson having been beforehand with him in intelligence of his return, and being so determined to bring him to book, I do not think he could have been saved. Whereas, the portable property certainly could have been saved. That's the difference between the property and the owner, don't you see?"

I invited Wemmick to come up-stairs, and refresh himself with a glass of grog before walking to Walworth. He accepted the invitation. While he was drinking his moderate allowance, he said, with nothing to lead up to it, and after having appeared rather fidgety:

"What do you think of my meaning to take a holiday on Monday, Mr. Pip?"

"Why, I suppose you have not done such a thing these twelve months."

"These twelve years, more likely," said Wemmick. "Yes. I'm going to take a holiday. More than that; I'm going to take a walk. More than that; I'm going to ask you to take a walk with me."

I was about to excuse myself, as being but a bad companion just then, when Wemmick anticipated me.

"I know your engagements," said he, "and I know you are out of sorts, Mr. Pip. But if you *could* oblige me, I should take it as a kindness. It ain't a long walk, and it's an early one. Say it might occupy you (including breakfast on the walk) from eight to twelve. Couldn't you stretch a point and manage it?"

He had done so much for me at various times, that this was very little to do for him. I said I could manage it—would manage it—and he was so very much pleased by my acquiescence, that I was pleased too. At his particular request, I appointed to call for him at the Castle at half-past eight on Monday morning, and so we parted for the time.

Punctual to my appointment, I rang at the Castle gate on the Monday morning, and was received by Wemmick himself: who struck me as looking tighter than usual, and having a sleeker hat on. Within, there were two glasses of rum-and-milk prepared, and two biscuits. The Aged must have been stirring with the lark, for, glancing into the perspective of his bedroom, I observed that his bed was empty.

When we had fortified ourselves with the rum-and-milk and biscuits, and were going out for the walk with that training preparation on us, I was considerably surprised to see Wemmick take up a fishing-rod, and put it over his shoulder. "Why, we are not going fishing!" said I. "No," returned Wemmick, "but I like to walk with one."

I thought this odd; however, I said nothing, and we set off. We went towards Camberwell Green, and when we were thereabouts, Wemmick said suddenly:

"Halloa! Here's a church!"

There was nothing very surprising in that; but again, I was rather surprised, when he said, as if he were animated by a brilliant idea:

"Let's go in!"

We went in, Wemmick leaving his fishing-rod in the porch, and looked all round. In the mean time, Wemmick was diving into his coat-pockets, and getting something out of paper there.

"Halloa!" said he. "Here's a couple of pair of gloves! Let's put 'em on!"

As the gloves were white kid gloves, and as the post-office was widened to its utmost extent, I now began to have my strong suspicions. They were strengthened into certainty when I beheld the Aged enter at a side door, escorting a lady.

"Halloa!" said Wemmick. "Here's Miss Skiffins! Let's have a wedding."

That discreet damsel was attired as usual, except that she was now engaged in substituting for her green kid gloves, a pair of white. The Aged was likewise occupied in preparing a similar sacrifice for the altar of Hymen. The old gentleman, however, experienced so much difficulty in getting his gloves on, that Wemmick found it necessary to put him with his back against a pillar, and then to get behind the pillar himself and pull away at them, while I for my part held the old gentleman round the waist, that he might present an equal and safe resistance. By dint of this ingenious scheme, his gloves were got on to perfection.

The clerk and clergyman then appearing, we were ranged in order at those fatal rails. True to his notion of seeming to do it all without preparation, I heard Wemmick say to himself as he took something out of his waistcoat-pocket before the service began, "Halloa! Here's a ring!"

I acted in the capacity of backer, or best-man, to the bridegroom; while a little limp pew opener in a soft bonnet like a baby's, made a feint of being the bosom friend of Miss Skiffins. The responsibility of giving the lady away, devolved upon the Aged, which led to the clergyman's being unintentionally scandalised, and it happened thus. When he said, "Who giveth this woman to be married to this man?" the old gentleman, not in the least knowing what point of the ceremony we had arrived at, stood most amiably beaming at the ten commandments. Upon which, the clergyman said again, "WHO giveth this woman to be married to this man?" The old gentleman being still in a state of most estimable unconsciousness, the bridegroom cried out in his accustomed voice, "Now Aged P. you know; who giveth?" To which the Aged replied with great briskness, before saying that *he* gave, "All right, John, all right, my boy!" And the clergyman came to so gloomy a pause upon it, that I had doubts for the moment whether we should get completely married that day.

It was completely done, however, and when we were going out of church, Wemmick took the cover off the font, and put his white gloves in it, and put the cover on again. Mrs. Wemmick, more heedful of the future, put her white gloves in her pocket and assumed her green. "*Now,* Mr. Pip," said Wemmick, triumphantly shouldering the fishing-rod as we came out, "let me ask you whether anybody would suppose this to be a wedding party!"

Breakfast had been ordered at a pleasant little tavern, a mile or so away upon the rising-ground beyond the Green; and there was a bagatelle board in the room, in case we should desire to unbend our minds after the solemnity. It was pleasant to observe that Mrs. Wemmick no longer unwound Wemmick's arm when it adapted itself to her figure, but sat in a high-backed chair against the wall, like a violoncello in its case, and submitted to be embraced as that melodious instrument might have done.

We had an excellent breakfast, and when any one declined anything on table, Wemmick said, "Provided by contract, you know; don't be afraid of it!" I drank to the new couple, drank to the Aged, drank to the Castle, saluted the bride at parting, and made myself as agreeable as I could.

Wemmick came down to the door with me, and I again shook hands with him, and wished him joy.

"Thankee!" said Wemmick, rubbing his hands. "She's such a manager of fowls you have no idea. You shall have some eggs, and judge for yourself. I say, Mr. Pip!" calling me back, and speaking low. "This is altogether a Walworth sentiment, please."

"I understand. Not to be mentioned in Little Britain," said I.

Wemmick nodded. "After what you let out the other day, Mr. Jaggers may as well not know of it. He might think my brain was softening, or something of the kind."

Chapter 56

He lay in prison very ill, during the whole interval between his committal for trial, and the coming round of the Sessions. He had broken two ribs, they had wounded one of his lungs, and he breathed with great pain and difficulty, which increased daily. It was a consequence of his hurt, that he spoke so low as to be scarcely audible; therefore, he spoke very little. But, he was ever ready to listen to me, and it became the first duty of my life to say to him, and read to him, what I knew he ought to hear.

Being far too ill to remain in the common prison, he was removed, after the first day or so, into the infirmary. This gave me opportunities of being with him that I could not otherwise have had. And but for his illness he would have been put in irons, for he was regarded as a determined prison-breaker, and I know not what else.

Although I saw him every day, it was for only a short time; hence, the regularly recurring spaces of our separation were long enough to record on his face any slight changes that occurred in his physical state. I do not recollect that I once saw any change in it for the better; he wasted, and became slowly weaker and worse, day by day, from the day when the prison door closed upon him.

The kind of submission or resignation that he showed, was that of a man who was tired out. I sometimes derived an impression, from his manner or from a whispered word or two which escaped him, that he pondered over the question whether he might have been a better man under better circumstances. But, he never justified himself by a hint tending that way, or tried to bend the past out of its eternal shape.

It happened on two or three occasions in my presence, that his desperate reputation was alluded to by one or other of the people in attendance on him. A smile crossed his face then, and he turned his eyes on me with a trustful look, as if he were confident that I had seen some small redeeming touch in him, even so long ago as when I was a little child. As to all the rest, he was humble and contrite, and I never knew him complain.

When the Sessions came round, Mr. Jaggers caused an application to be made for the postponement of his trial until the following Sessions. It was obviously made with the assurance that he could not live so long, and was refused. The trial came on at once, and, when he was put to the bar, he was seated in a chair. No objection was made to my getting close to the dock, on the outside of it, and holding the hand that he stretched forth to me.

The trial was very short and very clear. Such things as could be said for him, were said—how he had taken to industrious habits, and had thriven lawfully and reputably. But, nothing could unsay the fact that he had returned, and was there in presence of the Judge and Jury. It was impossible to try him for that, and do otherwise than find him Guilty.

At that time, it was the custom (as I learnt from my terrible experience of that Sessions) to devote a concluding day to the passing of Sentences, and to make a finishing effect with the Sentence of Death. But for the indelible picture that my remembrance now holds before me, I could scarcely believe, even as I write these words, that I saw two-and-thirty men and women put before the Judge to receive that sentence together. Foremost among the two-and-thirty, was he; seated, that he might get breath enough to keep life in him.

The whole scene starts out again in the vivid colours of the moment, down to the drops of April rain on the windows of the court, glittering in the rays of April sun. Penned in the dock, as I again stood outside it at the corner with his hand in mine, were the two-and-thirty men and women; some defiant, some stricken with terror, some sobbing and weeping, some covering their faces, some staring gloomily about. There had been shrieks from among the women convicts, but they had been stilled, and a hush had succeeded. The sheriffs with their great chains and nosegays,° other civic gewgaws and monsters, criers, ushers, a great gallery full of people—a large theatrical audience—looked on, as the two-and-thirty and the Judge were solemnly confronted. Then, the Judge addressed them. Among the wretched

---

nosegays: Flowers to ward off the smell of the prisoners and their diseases.

creatures before him whom he must single out for special address, was one who almost from his infancy had been an offender against the laws; who, after repeated imprisonments and punishments, had been at length sentenced to exile for a term of years; and who, under circumstances of great violence and daring had made his escape and been re-sentenced to exile for life. That miserable man would seem for a time to have become convinced of his errors, when far removed from the scenes of his old offences, and to have lived a peaceable and honest life. But in a fatal moment, yielding to those propensities and passions, the indulgence of which had so long rendered him a scourge to society, he had quitted his haven of rest and repentance, and had come back to the country where he was proscribed. Being here presently denounced, he had for a time succeeded in evading the officers of Justice, but being at length seized while in the act of flight, he had resisted them, and had—he best knew whether by express design, or in the blindness of his hardihood—caused the death of his denouncer, to whom his whole career was known. The appointed punishment for his return to the land that had cast him out, being Death, and his case being this aggravated case, he must prepare himself to Die.

The sun was striking in at the great windows of the court, through the glittering drops of rain upon the glass, and it made a broad shaft of light between the two-and-thirty and the Judge, linking both together, and perhaps reminding some among the audience, how both were passing on, with absolute equality, to the greater Judgment that knoweth all things and cannot err. Rising for a moment, a distinct speck of face in this way of light, the prisoner said, "My Lord, I have received my sentence of Death from the Almighty, but I bow to yours," and sat down again. There was some hushing, and the Judge went on with what he had to say to the rest. Then, they were all formally doomed, and some of them were supported out, and some of them sauntered out with a haggard look of bravery, and a few nodded to the gallery, and two or three shook hands, and others went out chewing the fragments of herb they had taken from the sweet herbs lying about. He went last of all, because of having to be helped from his chair and to go very slowly; and he held my hand while all the others were removed, and while the audience got up (putting their dresses right, as they might at church or elsewhere) and pointed down at this criminal or at that, and most of all at him and me.

I earnestly hoped and prayed that he might die before the Recorder's

Report° was made, but, in the dread of his lingering on, I began that night to write out a petition to the Home Secretary of State, setting forth my knowledge of him, and how it was that he had come back for my sake. I wrote it as fervently and pathetically as I could, and when I had finished it and sent it in, I wrote out other petitions to such men in authority as I hoped were the most merciful, and drew up one to the Crown itself. For several days and nights after he was sentenced I took no rest except when I fell asleep in my chair, but was wholly absorbed in these appeals. And after I had sent them in, I could not keep away from the places where they were, but felt as if they were more hopeful and less desperate when I was near them. In this unreasonable restlessness and pain of mind, I would roam the streets of an evening, wandering by those offices and houses where I had left the petitions. To the present hour, the weary western streets of London on a cold dusty spring night, with their ranges of stern shut-up mansions and their long rows of lamps, are melancholy to me from this association.

The daily visits I could make him were shortened now, and he was more strictly kept. Seeing, or fancying, that I was suspected of an intention of carrying poison to him, I asked to be searched before I sat down at his bedside, and told the officer who was always there, that I was willing to do anything that would assure him of the singleness of my designs. Nobody was hard with him, or with me. There was duty to be done, and it was done, but not harshly. The officer always gave me the assurance that he was worse, and some other sick prisoners in the room, and some other prisoners who attended on them as sick nurses (malefactors, but not incapable of kindness, GOD be thanked!), always joined in the same report.

As the days went on, I noticed more and more that he would lie placidly looking at the white ceiling, with an absence of light in his face, until some word of mine brightened it for an instant, and then it would subside again. Sometimes he was almost, or quite, unable to speak; then, he would answer me with slight pressures on my hand, and I grew to understand his meaning very well.

The number of the days had risen to ten, when I saw a greater change in him than I had seen yet. His eyes were turned towards the door, and lighted up as I entered.

"Dear boy," he said, as I sat down by his bed: "I thought you was late. But I knowed you couldn't be that."

Recorder's Report: The report of the judge in charge of the trial.

"It is just the time," said I. "I waited for it at the gate."

"You always waits at the gate; don't you, dear boy?"

"Yes. Not to lose a moment of the time."

"Thank'ee dear boy, thank'ee. God bless you! You've never deserted me, dear boy."

I pressed his hand in silence, for I could not forget that I had once meant to desert him.

"And what's the best of all," he said, "you've been more comfortable alonger me, since I was under a dark cloud, than when the sun shone. That's best of all."

He lay on his back, breathing with great difficulty. Do what he would, and love me though he did, the light left his face ever and again, and a film came over the placid look at the white ceiling.

"Are you in much pain to-day?"

"I don't complain of none, dear boy."

"You never do complain."

He had spoken his last words. He smiled, and I understood his touch to mean that he wished to lift my hand, and lay it on his breast. I laid it there, and he smiled again, and put both his hands upon it.

The allotted time ran out, while we were thus; but, looking round, I found the governor of the prison standing near me, and he whispered, "You needn't go yet." I thanked him gratefully, and asked, "Might I speak to him, if he can hear me?"

The governor stepped aside, and beckoned the officer away. The change, though it was made without noise, drew back the film from the placid look at the white ceiling, and he looked most affectionately at me.

"Dear Magwitch, I must tell you, now at last. You understand what I say?"

A gentle pressure on my hand.

"You had a child once, whom you loved and lost."

A stronger pressure on my hand.

"She lived and found powerful friends. She is living now. She is a lady and very beautiful. And I love her!"

With a last faint effort, which would have been powerless but for my yielding to it and assisting it, he raised my hand to his lips. Then, he gently let it sink upon his breast again, with his own hands lying on it. The placid look at the white ceiling came back, and passed away, and his head dropped quietly on his breast.

Mindful, then, of what we had read together, I thought of the two men who went up into the Temple to pray,° and I knew there were no better words that I could say beside his bed, than "O Lord, be merciful to him, a sinner!"

[PART 35]

Chapter 57

Now that I was left wholly to myself, I gave notice of my intention to quit the chambers in the Temple as soon as my tenancy could legally determine, and in the mean while to underlet them. At once I put bills up in the windows; for, I was in debt, and had scarcely any money, and began to be seriously alarmed by the state of my affairs. I ought rather to write that I should have been alarmed if I had had energy and concentration enough to help me to the clear perception of any truth beyond the fact that I was falling very ill. The late stress upon me had enabled me to put off illness, but not to put it away; I knew that it was coming on me now, and I knew very little else, and was even careless as to that.

For a day or two, I lay on the sofa, or on the floor—anywhere, according as I happened to sink down—with a heavy head and aching limbs, and no purpose, and no power. Then there came, one night which appeared of great duration, and which teemed with anxiety and horror; and when in the morning I tried to sit up in my bed and think of it, I found I could not do so.

Whether I really had been down in Garden-court in the dead of the night, groping about for the boat that I supposed to be there; whether I had two or three times come to myself on the staircase with great terror, not knowing how I had got out of bed; whether I had found myself lighting the lamp, possessed by the idea that he was coming up the stairs, and that the lights were blown out; whether I had been inexpressibly harassed by the distracted talking, laughing, and groaning, of some one, and had half suspected those sounds to be of my own making; whether there had been a closed iron furnace in a dark corner of the room, and a voice had called out over and over

two . . . pray: Luke 18:10–13. In this parable, a highly religious man prays by congratulating himself on his virtue, and a tax-gatherer abases himself by praying "God be merciful to me a sinner." Jesus praises the latter, "for . . . he that humbleth himself shall be exalted."

again that Miss Havisham was consuming within it; these were things that I tried to settle with myself and get into some order, as I lay that morning on my bed. But, the vapour of a limekiln would come between me and them, disordering them all, and it was through the vapour at last that I saw two men looking at me.

"What do you want?" I asked, starting; "I don't know you."

"Well, sir," returned one of them, bending down and touching me on the shoulder, "this is a matter that you'll soon arrange, I dare say, but you're arrested."

"What is the debt?"

"Hundred and twenty-three pound, fifteen, six. Jeweller's account, I think."

"What is to be done?"

"You had better come to my house,"° said the man. "I keep a very nice house."

I made some attempt to get up and dress myself. When I next attended to them, they were standing a little off from the bed, looking at me. I still lay there.

"You see my state," said I. "I would come with you if I could; but indeed I am quite unable. If you take me from here, I think I shall die by the way."

Perhaps they replied, or argued the point, or tried to encourage me to believe that I was better than I thought. Forasmuch as they hang in my memory by only this one slender thread, I don't know what they did, except that they forbore to remove me.

That I had a fever and was avoided, that I suffered greatly, that I often lost my reason, that the time seemed interminable, that I confounded impossible existences with my own identity; that I was a brick in the house-wall, and yet entreating to be released from the giddy place where the builders had set me; that I was a steel beam of a vast engine, clashing and whirling over a gulf, and yet that I implored in my own person to have the engine stopped, and my part in it hammered off; that I passed through these phases of disease, I know of my own remembrance, and did in some sort know at the time. That I sometimes struggled with real people, in the belief that they were murderers, and that I would all at once comprehend that they meant to do me good, and would then sink exhausted in their arms, and suffer

---

house: A sponging-house, run for profit by a bailiff, where persons arrested for debt were taken so that they would have opportunities to pay their debts or appease their creditors and therefore avoid being sent to prison.

them to lay me down, I also knew at the time. But, above all, I knew that there was a constant tendency in all these people—who, when I was very ill, would present all kinds of extraordinary transformations of the human face, and would be much dilated in size—above all, I say, I knew that there was an extraordinary tendency in all these people, sooner or later to settle down into the likeness of Joe.

After I had turned the worst point of my illness, I began to notice that while all its other features changed, this one consistent feature did not change. Whoever came about me, still settled down into Joe. I opened my eyes in the night, and I saw in the great chair at the bed-side, Joe. I opened my eyes in the day, and, sitting on the window-seat, smoking his pipe in the shaded open window, still I saw Joe. I asked for cooling drink, and the dear hand that gave it me was Joe's. I sank back on my pillow after drinking, and the face that looked so hopefully and tenderly upon me was the face of Joe.

At last, one day, I took courage, and said, "*Is* it Joe?"

And the dear old home-voice answered, "Which it air, old chap."

"O Joe, you break my heart! Look angry at me, Joe. Strike me, Joe. Tell me of my ingratitude. Don't be so good to me!"

For, Joe had actually laid his head down on the pillow at my side and put his arm round my neck, in his joy that I knew him.

"Which dear old Pip, old chap," said Joe, "you and me was ever friends. And when you're well enough to go out for a ride—what larks!"

After which, Joe withdrew to the window, and stood with his back towards me, wiping his eyes. And as my extreme weakness prevented me from getting up and going to him, I lay there, penitently whispering, "O God bless him! O God bless this gentle Christian man!"

Joe's eyes were red when I next found him beside me; but, I was holding his hand, and we both felt happy.

"How long, dear Joe?"

"Which you meantersay, Pip, how long have your illness lasted, dear old chap?"

"Yes, Joe."

"It's the end of May, Pip. To-morrow is the first of June."

"And have you been here all the time, dear Joe?"

"Pretty nigh, old chap. For, as I says to Biddy when the news of your being ill were brought by letter, which it were brought by the post and being formerly single he is now married though underpaid for a deal of walking and shoe-leather, but wealth were not a object on his part, and marriage were the great wish of his hart——"

"It is so delightful to hear you, Joe! But I interrupt you in what you said to Biddy."

"Which it were," said Joe, "that how you might be amongst strangers, and that how you and me having been ever friends, a wisit at such a moment might not prove unacceptabobble. And Biddy, her word were, 'Go to him, without loss of time.' That," said Joe, summing up with his judicial air, "were the word of Biddy. 'Go to him,' Biddy say, 'without loss of time.' In short, I shouldn't greatly deceive you," Joe added, after a little grave reflection, "if I represented to you that the word of that young woman were, 'without a minute's loss of time.'"

There Joe cut himself short, and informed me that I was to be talked to in great moderation, and that I was to take a little nourishment at stated frequent times, whether I felt inclined for it or not, and that I was to submit myself to all his orders. So, I kissed his hand, and lay quiet, while he proceeded to indite a note to Biddy, with my love in it.

Evidently, Biddy had taught Joe to write. As I lay in bed looking at him, it made me, in my weak state, cry again with pleasure to see the pride with which he set about his letter. My bedstead, divested of its curtains, had been removed, with me upon it, into the sitting-room, as the airiest and largest, and the carpet had been taken away, and the room kept always fresh and wholesome night and day. At my own writing-table, pushed into a corner and cumbered with little bottles, Joe now sat down to his great work, first choosing a pen from the pentray as if it were a chest of large tools, and tucking up his sleeves as if he were going to wield a crowbar or sledge-hammer. It was necessary for Joe to hold on heavily to the table with his left elbow, and to get his right leg well out behind him, before he could begin, and when he did begin, he made every down-stroke so slowly that it might have been six feet long, while at every up-stroke I could hear his pen spluttering extensively. He had a curious idea that the inkstand was on the side of him where it was not, and constantly dipped his pen into space, and seemed quite satisfied with the result. Occasionally, he was tripped up by some orthographical stumbling-block, but on the whole he got on very well indeed, and when he had signed his name, and had removed a finishing blot from the paper to the crown of his head with his two forefingers, he got up and hovered about the table, trying the effect of his performance from various points of view as it lay there, with unbounded satisfaction.

Not to make Joe uneasy by talking too much, even if I had been able to talk much, I deferred asking him about Miss Havisham until next day. He shook his head when I then asked him if she had recovered.

"Is she dead, Joe?"

"Why you see, old chap," said Joe, in a tone of remonstrance, and by way of getting at it by degrees, "I wouldn't go so far as to say that, for that's a deal to say; but she ain't——"

"Living, Joe?"

"That's nigher where it is," said Joe; "she ain't living."

"Did she linger long, Joe?"

"Arter you was took ill, pretty much about what you might call (if you was put to it) a week," said Joe; still determined, on my account, to come at everything by degrees.

"Dear Joe, have you heard what becomes of her property?"

"Well, old chap," said Joe, "it do appear that she had settled the most of it, which I meantersay tied it up, on Miss Estella. But she had wrote out a little coddleshell in her own hand a day or two afore the accident, leaving a cool four thousand to Mr. Matthew Pocket. And why, do you suppose, above all things, Pip, she left that cool four thousand unto him? 'Because of Pip's account of him the said Matthew.' I am told by Biddy, that air the writing," said Joe, repeating the legal turn as if it did him infinite good, "'account of him the said Matthew.' And a cool four thousand, Pip!"

I never discovered from whom Joe derived the conventional temperature of the four thousand pounds, but it appeared to make the sum of money more to him, and he had a manifest relish in insisting on its being cool.

This account gave me great joy, as it perfected the only good thing I had done. I asked Joe whether he had heard if any of the other relations had any legacies?

"Miss Sarah," said Joe, "she have twenty-five pound perannium fur to buy pills, on account of being bilious. Miss Georgiana, she have twenty pound down. Mrs.——what's the name of them wild beasts with humps, old chap?"

"Camels?" said I, wondering why he could possibly want to know.

Joe nodded. "Mrs. Camels," by which I presently understood he meant Camilla, "she have five pound fur to buy rushlights to put her in spirits when she wake up in the night."

The accuracy of these recitals was sufficiently obvious to me, to give me great confidence in Joe's information. "And now," said Joe, "you ain't that strong yet, old chap, that you can take in more nor one additional shovel-full to-day. Old Orlick he's been a bustin' open a dwelling-ouse."

"Whose?" said I.

"Not, I grant you, but what his manners is given to blusterous," said Joe, apologetically; "still, a Englishman's ouse is his Castle, and castles must not be busted 'cept when done in war time. And wot-sume'er the failings on his part, he were a corn and seedsman in his hart."

"Is it Pumblechook's house that has been broken into, then?"

"That's it, Pip," said Joe; "and they took his till, and they took his cash-box, and they drinked his wine, and they partook of his wittles, and they slapped his face, and they pulled his nose, and they tied him up to his bedpust, and they giv' him a dozen, and they stuffed his mouth full of flowering annuals to prewent his crying out. But he knowed Orlick, and Orlick's in the county jail."

By these approaches we arrived at unrestricted conversation. I was slow to gain strength, but I did slowly and surely become less weak, and Joe stayed with me, and I fancied I was little Pip again.

For, the tenderness of Joe was so beautifully proportioned to my need, that I was like a child in his hands. He would sit and talk to me in the old confidence, and with the old simplicity, and in the old unassertive protecting way, so that I would half believe that all my life since the days of the old kitchen was one of the mental troubles of the fever that was gone. He did everything for me except the household work, for which he had engaged a very decent woman, after paying off the laundress on his first arrival. "Which I do assure you, Pip," he would often say, in explanation of that liberty; "I found her a tapping the spare bed, like a cask of beer, and drawing off the feathers in a bucket, for sale. Which she would have tapped yourn next, and draw'd it off with you a laying on it, and was then a carrying away the coals gradiwally in the soup-tureen and wegetable-dishes, and the wine and spirits in your Wellington boots."

We looked forward to the day when I should go out for a ride, as we had once looked forward to the day of my apprenticeship. And when the day came, and an open carriage was got into the Lane, Joe wrapped me up, took me in his arms, carried me down to it, and put me in, as if I were still the small helpless creature to whom he had so abundantly given of the wealth of his great nature.

And Joe got in beside me, and we drove away together into the country, where the rich summer growth was already on the trees and

on the grass, and sweet summer scents filled all the air. The day happened to be Sunday, and when I looked on the loveliness around me,
and thought how it had grown and changed, and how the little wild
flowers had been forming, and the voices of the birds had been
strengthening, by day and by night, under the sun and under the stars,
while poor I lay burning and tossing on my bed, the mere remembrance of having burned and tossed there, came like a check upon my
peace. But, when I heard the Sunday bells, and looked around a little
more upon the outspread beauty, I felt that I was not nearly thankful
enough—that I was too weak yet, to be even that—and I laid my
head on Joe's shoulder, as I had laid it long ago when he had taken me
to the Fair or where not, and it was too much for my young senses.

More composure came to me after a while, and we talked as we
used to talk, lying on the grass at the Old Battery. There was no
change whatever in Joe. Exactly what he had been in my eyes then, he
was in my eyes still; just as simply faithful, and as simply right.

When we got back again and he lifted me out, and carried me—so
easily—across the court and up the stairs, I thought of that eventful
Christmas Day when he had carried me over the marshes. We had not
yet made any allusion to my change of fortune, nor did I know how
much of my late history he was acquainted with. I was so doubtful of
myself now, and put so much trust in him, that I could not satisfy myself whether I ought to refer to it when he did not.

"Have you heard, Joe," I asked him that evening, upon further
consideration, as he smoked his pipe at the window, "who my patron
was?"

"I heerd," returned Joe, "as it were not Miss Havisham, old chap."

"Did you hear who it was, Joe?"

"Well! I heerd as it were a person what sent the person what giv'
you the bank-notes at the Jolly Bargemen, Pip."

"So it was."

"Astonishing!" said Joe, in the placidest way.

"Did you hear that he was dead, Joe?" I presently asked, with increasing diffidence.

"Which? Him as sent the bank-notes, Pip?"

"Yes."

"I think," said Joe, after meditating a long time, and looking
rather evasively at the window-seat, "as I *did* hear tell that how he
were something or another in a general way in that direction."

"Did you hear anything of his circumstances, Joe?"

"Not partickler, Pip."

"If you would like to hear, Joe——" I was beginning, when Joe got up and came to my sofa.

"Lookee here, old chap," said Joe, bending over me. "Ever the best of friends; ain't us, Pip?"

I was ashamed to answer him.

"Wery good, then," said Joe, as if I *had* answered; "that's all right; that's agreed upon. Then why go into subjects, old chap, which as betwixt two sech must be for ever onnecessary? There's subjects enough as betwixt two sech, without onnecessary ones. Lord! To think of your poor sister and her Rampages! And don't you remember Tickler?"

"I do indeed, Joe."

"Lookee here, old chap," said Joe. "I done what I could to keep you and Tickler in sunders, but my power were not always fully equal to my inclinations. For when your poor sister had a mind to drop into you, it were not so much," said Joe, in his favourite argumentative way, "that she dropped into me too, if I put myself in opposition to her but that she dropped into you always heavier for it. I noticed that. It ain't a grab at a man's whisker, nor yet a shake or two of a man (to which your sister was quite welcome), that 'ud put a man off from getting a little child out of punishment. But when that little child is dropped into, heavier, for that grab of whisker or shaking, then that man naterally up and says to himself, 'Where is the good as you are a doing? I grant you I see the 'arm,' says the man, 'but I don't see the good. I call upon you, sir, theerfore, to pint out the good.'"

"The man says?" I observed, as Joe waited for me to speak.

"The man says," Joe assented. "Is he right, that man?"

"Dear Joe, he is always right."

"Well, old chap," said Joe, "then abide by your words. If he's always right (which in general he's more likely wrong), he's right when he says this:—Supposing ever you kep any little matter to yourself, when you was a little child, you kep it mostly because you know'd as J. Gargery's power to part you and Tickler in sunders, were not fully equal to his inclinations. Theerfore, think no more of it as betwixt two sech, and do not let us pass remarks upon onnecessary subjects. Biddy giv' herself a deal o' trouble with me afore I left (for I am most awful dull), as I should view it in this light, and, viewing it in this light, as I should so put it. Both of which," said Joe, quite charmed with his logical arrangement, "being done, now this to you a true friend, say. Namely. You mustn't go a over-doing on it, but you must have your supper and your wine-and-water, and you must be put betwixt the sheets."

The delicacy with which Joe dismissed this theme, and the sweet tact and kindness with which Biddy—who with her woman's wit had found me out so soon—had prepared him for it, made a deep impression on my mind. But whether Joe knew how poor I was, and how my great expectations had all dissolved, like our own marsh mists before the sun, I could not understand.

Another thing in Joe that I could not understand when it first began to develop itself, but which I soon arrived at a sorrowful comprehension of, was this: As I became stronger and better, Joe became a little less easy with me. In my weakness and entire dependence on him, the dear fellow had fallen into the old tone, and called me by the old names, the dear "old Pip, old chap," that now were music in my ears. I too had fallen into the old ways, only happy and thankful that he let me. But, imperceptibly, though I held by them fast, Joe's hold upon them began to slacken; and whereas I wondered at this, at first, I soon began to understand that the cause of it was in me, and that the fault of it was all mine.

Ah! Had I given Joe no reason to doubt my constancy, and to think that in prosperity I should grow cold to him and cast him off? Had I given Joe's innocent heart no cause to feel instinctively that as I got stronger, his hold upon me would be weaker, and that he had better loosen it in time and let me go, before I plucked myself away?

It was on the third or fourth occasion of my going out walking in the Temple Gardens leaning on Joe's arm, that I saw this change in him very plainly. We had been sitting in the bright warm sunlight, looking at the river, and I chanced to say as we got up:

"See, Joe! I can walk quite strongly. Now, you shall see me walk back by myself."

"Which do not over-do it, Pip," said Joe; "but I shall be happy fur to see you able, sir."

The last word grated on me; but how could I remonstrate! I walked no further than the gate of the gardens, and then pretended to be weaker than I was, and asked Joe for his arm. Joe gave it me, but was thoughtful.

I, for my part, was thoughtful too; for, how best to check this growing change in Joe, was a great perplexity to my remorseful thoughts. That I was ashamed to tell him exactly how I was placed, and what I had come down to, I do not seek to conceal; but, I hope my reluctance was not quite an unworthy one. He would want to help me out of his little savings, I knew, and I knew that he ought not to help me, and that I must not suffer him to do it.

It was a thoughtful evening with both of us. But, before we went to bed, I had resolved that I would wait over to-morrow, to-morrow being Sunday, and would begin my new course with the new week. On Monday morning I would speak to Joe about this change, I would lay aside this last vestige of reserve, I would tell him what I had in my thoughts (that Secondly, not yet arrived at), and why I had not decided to go out to Herbert, and then the change would be conquered for ever. As I cleared, Joe cleared, and it seemed as though he had sympathetically arrived at a resolution too.

We had a quiet day on the Sunday, and we rode out into the country, and then walked in the fields.

"I feel thankful that I have been ill, Joe," I said.

"Dear old Pip, old chap, you're a'most come round, sir."

"It has been a memorable time for me, Joe."

"Likeways for myself, sir," Joe returned.

"We have had a time together, Joe, that I can never forget. There were days once, I know, that I did for a while forget; but I never shall forget these."

"Pip," said Joe, appearing a little hurried and troubled, "there has been larks. And, dear sir, what have been betwixt us—have been."

At night, when I had gone to bed, Joe came into my room, as he had done all through my recovery. He asked me if I felt sure that I was as well as in the morning?

"Yes, dear Joe, quite."

"And are always a getting stronger, old chap?"

"Yes, dear Joe, steadily."

Joe patted the coverlet on my shoulder with his great good hand, and said, in what I thought a husky voice, "Good night!"

When I got up in the morning, refreshed and stronger yet, I was full of my resolution to tell Joe all, without delay. I would tell him before breakfast. I would dress at once and go to his room and surprise him; for, it was the first day I had been up early. I went to his room, and he was not there. Not only was he not there, but his box was gone.

I hurried then to the breakfast-table, and on it found a letter. These were its brief contents.

> Not wishful to intrude I have departured fur you are well again dear Pip and will do better without
>
> Jo.
>
> P.S. Ever the best of friends.

Enclosed in the letter, was a receipt for the debt and costs on which I had been arrested. Down to that moment I had vainly supposed that my creditor had withdrawn or suspended proceedings until I should be quite recovered. I had never dreamed of Joe's having paid the money; but, Joe had paid it, and the receipt was in his name.

What remained for me now, but to follow him to the dear old forge, and there to have out my disclosure to him, and my penitent remonstrance with him, and there to relieve my mind and heart of that reserved Secondly, which had begun as a vague something lingering in my thoughts, and had formed into a settled purpose?

The purpose was, that I would go to Biddy, that I would show her how humbled and repentant I came back, that I would tell her how I had lost all I once hoped for, that I would remind her of our old confidences in my first unhappy time. Then, I would say to her, "Biddy, I think you once liked me very well, when my errant heart, even while it strayed away from you, was quieter and better with you than it ever has been since. If you can like me only half as well once more, if you can take me with all my faults and disappointments on my head, if you can receive me like a forgiven child (and indeed I am as sorry, Biddy, and have as much need of a hushing voice and a soothing hand), I hope I am a little worthier of you than I was—not much, but a little. And, Biddy, it shall rest with you to say whether I shall work at the forge with Joe, or whether I shall try for any different occupation down in this country, or whether we shall go away to a distant place where an opportunity awaits me, which I set aside when it was offered, until I knew your answer. And now, dear Biddy, if you can tell me that you will go through the world with me, you will surely make it a better world for me, and me a better man for it, and I will try hard to make it a better world for you."

Such was my purpose. After three days more of recovery, I went down to the old place, to put it in execution; and how I sped in it, is all I have left to tell.

[PART 36]

Chapter 58

The tidings of my high fortunes having had a heavy fall, had got down to my native place and its neighbourhood, before I got there. I found the Blue Boar in possession of the intelligence, and I found that

it made a great change in the Boar's demeanour. Whereas the Boar
had cultivated my good opinion with warm assiduity when I was coming into property, the Boar was exceedingly cool on the subject now
that I was going out of property.

It was evening when I arrived, much fatigued by the journey I had
so often made so easily. The Boar could not put me into my usual
bedroom, which was engaged (probably by some one who had expectations), and could only assign me a very indifferent chamber among
the pigeons and post-chaises up the yard. But, I had as sound a sleep
in that lodging as in the most superior accommodation the Boar could
have given me, and the quality of my dreams was about the same as in
the best bedroom.

Early in the morning while my breakfast was getting ready, I
strolled round by Satis House. There were printed bills on the gate,
and on bits of carpet hanging out of the windows, announcing a sale
by auction of the Household Furniture and Effects, next week. The
House itself was to be sold as old building materials and pulled down.
LOT 1 was marked in whitewashed knock-knee letters on the brew-
house; LOT 2 on that part of the main building which had been so
long shut up. Other lots were marked off on other parts of the structure, and the ivy had been torn down to make room for the inscriptions, and much of it trailed low in the dust and was withered already.
Stepping in for a moment at the open gate and looking around me
with the uncomfortable air of a stranger who had no business there, I
saw the auctioneer's clerk walking on the casks and telling them off for
the information of a catalogue-compiler, pen in hand, who made a
temporary desk of the wheeled chair I had so often pushed along to
the tune of Old Clem.

When I got back to my breakfast in the Boar's coffee-room, I
found Mr. Pumblechook conversing with the landlord. Mr. Pumblechook (not improved in appearance by his late nocturnal adventure)
was waiting for me, and addressed me in the following terms.

"Young man, I am sorry to see you brought low. But what else
could be expected! What else could be expected!"

As he extended his hand with a magnificently forgiving air, and as
I was broken by illness and unfit to quarrel, I took it.

"William," said Mr. Pumblechook to the waiter, "put a muffin on
table. And has it come to this! Has it come to this!"

I frowningly sat down to my breakfast. Mr. Pumblechook stood
over me and poured out my tea—before I could touch the teapot—
with the air of a benefactor who was resolved to be true to the last.

"William," said Mr. Pumblechook, mournfully, "put the salt on. In happier times," addressing me, "I think you took sugar? And did you take milk? You did. Sugar and milk. William, bring a watercress."

"Thank you," said I, shortly, "but I don't eat watercresses."

"You don't eat 'em," returned Mr. Pumblechook, sighing and nodding his head several times, as if he might have expected that, and as if abstinence from watercresses were consistent with my downfal. "True. The simple fruits of the earth. No. You needn't bring any, William."

I went on with my breakfast, and Mr. Pumblechook continued to stand over me, staring fishily and breathing noisily, as he always did.

"Little more than skin and bone!" mused Mr. Pumblechook, aloud. "And yet when he went away from here (I may say with my blessing), and I spread afore him my humble store, like the Bee, he was as plump as a Peach!"

This reminded me of the wonderful difference between the servile manner in which he had offered his hand in my new prosperity, saying, "May I?" and the ostentatious clemency with which he had just now exhibited the same fat five fingers.

"Hah!" he went on, handing me the bread-and-butter. "And air you a going to Joseph?"

"In Heaven's name," said I, firing in spite of myself, "what does it matter to you where I am going? Leave that teapot alone."

It was the worst course I could have taken, because it gave Pumblechook the opportunity he wanted.

"Yes, young man," said he, releasing the handle of the article in question, retiring a step or two from my table, and speaking for the behoof of the landlord and waiter at the door, "I *will* leave that teapot alone. You are right, young man. For once, you are right. I forgit myself when I take such an interest in your breakfast, as to wish your frame, exhausted by the debilitating effects of prodigygality, to be stimilated by the 'olesome nourishment of your forefathers. And yet," said Pumblechook, turning to the landlord and waiter, and pointing me out at arm's length, "this is him as I ever sported with in his days of happy infancy! Tell me not it cannot be; I tell you this is him!"

A low murmur from the two replied. The waiter appeared to be particularly affected.

"This is him," said Pumblechook, "as I have rode in my shay-cart. This is him as I have seen brought up by hand. This is him untoe the sister of which I was uncle by marriage, as her name was Georgiana M'ria from her own mother, let him deny it if he can!"

The waiter seemed convinced that I could not deny it, and that it gave the case a black look.

"Young man," said Pumblechook, screwing his head at me in the old fashion, "you air a going to Joseph. What does it matter to me, you ask me, where you air a going? I say to you, Sir, you air a going to Joseph."

The waiter coughed, as if he modestly invited me to get over that.

"Now," said Pumblechook, and all this with a most exasperating air of saying in the cause of virtue what was perfectly convincing and conclusive, "I will tell you what to say to Joseph. Here is Squires of the Boar present, known and respected in this town, and here is William, which his father's name was Potkins if I do not deceive myself."

"You do not, sir," said William.

"In their presence," pursued Pumblechook, "I will tell you, young man, what to say to Joseph. Says you, 'Joseph, I have this day seen my earliest benefactor and the founder of my fortun's. I will name no names, Joseph, but so they are pleased to call him up-town, and I have seen that man.'"

"I swear I don't see him here," said I.

"Say that likewise," retorted Pumblechook. "Say you said that, and even Joseph will probably betray surprise."

"There you quite mistake him," said I. "I know better."

"Says you," Pumblechook went on, "'Joseph, I have seen that man, and that man bears you no malice and bears me no malice. He knows your character, Joseph, and is well acquainted with your pigheadedness and ignorance; and he knows my character, Joseph, and he knows my want of gratitoode. Yes, Joseph,' says you," here Pumblechook shook his head and hand at me, "'he knows my total deficiency of common human gratitoode. *He* knows it, Joseph, as none can. *You* do not know it, Joseph, having no call to know it, but that man do.'"

Windy donkey as he was, it really amazed me that he could have the face to talk thus to mine.

"Says you, 'Joseph, he gave me a little message, which I will now repeat. It was, that in my being brought low, he saw the finger of Providence. He knowed that finger when he saw it, Joseph, and he saw it plain. It pinted out this writing, Joseph. *Reward of ingratitoode to his earliest benefactor, and founder of fortun's.* But that man said that he did not repent of what he had done, Joseph. Not at all. It was right to do it, it was kind to do it, it was benevolent to do it, and he would do it again.'"

"It's a pity," said I, scornfully, as I finished my interrupted break-fast, "that the man did not say what he had done and would do again."

"Squires of the Boar!" Pumblechook was now addressing the land-lord, "and William! I have no objections to your mentioning, either up-town or down-town, if such should be your wishes, that it was right to do it, kind to do it, benevolent to do it, and that I would do it again."

With those words the Impostor shook them both by hand, with an air, and left the house; leaving me much more astonished than de-lighted by the virtues of that same indefinite "it." I was not long after him in leaving the house too, and when I went down the High-street I saw him holding forth (no doubt to the same effect) at his shop door to a select group, who honoured me with very unfavourable glances as I passed on the opposite side of the way.

But, it was only the pleasanter to turn to Biddy and to Joe, whose great forbearance shone more brightly than before, if that could be, contrasted with this brazen pretender. I went towards them slowly, for my limbs were weak, but with a sense of increasing relief as I drew nearer to them, and a sense of leaving arrogance and untruthfulness further and further behind.

The June weather was delicious. The sky was blue, the larks were soaring high over the green corn, I thought all that countryside more beautiful and peaceful by far than I had ever known it to be yet. Many pleasant pictures of the life that I would lead there, and of the change for the better that would come over my character when I had a guid-ing spirit at my side whose simple faith and clear home-wisdom I had proved, beguiled my way. They awakened a tender emotion in me; for, my heart was softened by my return, and such a change had come to pass, that I felt like one who was toiling home barefoot from distant travel, and whose wanderings had lasted many years.

The schoolhouse where Biddy was mistress, I had never seen; but, the little roundabout lane by which I entered the village for quietness' sake, took me past it. I was disappointed to find that the day was a hol-iday; no children were there, and Biddy's house was closed. Some hopeful notion of seeing her busily engaged in her daily duties, before she saw me, had been in my mind and was defeated.

But, the forge was a very short distance off, and I went towards it under the sweet green limes, listening for the clink of Joe's hammer. Long after I ought to have heard it, and long after I had fancied I heard it and found it but a fancy, all was still. The limes were there, and the white thorns were there, and the chestnut-trees were there, and their leaves rustled harmoniously when I stopped to listen; but, the clink of Joe's hammer was not in the midsummer wind.

Almost fearing, without knowing why, to come in view of the forge, I saw it at last, and saw that it was closed. No gleam of fire, no glittering shower of sparks, no roar of bellows; all shut up, and still.

But, the house was not deserted, and the best parlour seemed to be in use, for there were white curtains fluttering in its window, and the window was open and gay with flowers. I went softly towards it, meaning to peep over the flowers, when Joe and Biddy stood before me, arm in arm.

At first Biddy gave a cry, as if she thought it was my apparition, but in another moment she was in my embrace. I wept to see her, and she wept to see me; I, because she looked so fresh and pleasant; she, because I looked so worn and white.

"But dear Biddy, how smart you are!"

"Yes, dear Pip."

"And Joe, how smart *you* are!"

"Yes, dear old Pip, old chap."

I looked at both of them, from one to the other, and then——

"It's my wedding-day," cried Biddy, in a burst of happiness, "and I am married to Joe!"

They had taken me into the kitchen, and I had laid my head down on the old deal table. Biddy held one of my hands to her lips, and Joe's restoring touch was on my shoulder. "Which he warn't strong enough, my dear, fur to be surprised," said Joe. And Biddy said, "I ought to have thought of it, dear Joe, but I was too happy." They were both so overjoyed to see me, so proud to see me, so touched by my coming to them, so delighted that I should have come by accident to make their day complete!

My first thought was one of great thankfulness that I had never breathed this last baffled hope to Joe. How often, while he was with me in my illness, had it risen to my lips. How irrevocable would have been his knowledge of it, if he had remained with me but another hour!

"Dear Biddy," said I, "you have the best husband in the whole world, and if you could have seen him by my bed you would have—— But no, you couldn't love him better than you do."

"No, I couldn't indeed," said Biddy.

"And, dear Joe, you have the best wife in the whole world, and she will make you as happy as even you deserve to be, you dear, good, noble Joe!"

Joe looked at me with a quivering lip, and fairly put his sleeve before his eyes.

"And Joe and Biddy both, as you have been to church to-day, and are in charity and love with all mankind, receive my humble thanks for all you have done for me, and all I have so ill repaid! And when I say that I am going away within the hour, for I am soon going abroad, and that I shall never rest until I have worked for the money with which you have kept me out of prison, and have sent it to you, don't think, dear Joe and Biddy, that if I could repay it a thousand times over, I suppose I could cancel a farthing of the debt I owe you, or that I would do so if I could!"

They were both melted by these words, and both entreated me to say no more.

"But I must say more. Dear Joe, I hope you will have children to love, and that some little fellow will sit in this chimney corner of a winter night, who may remind you of another little fellow gone out of it for ever. Don't tell him, Joe, that I was thankless; don't tell him, Biddy, that I was ungenerous and unjust; only tell him that I honoured you both, because you were both so good and true, and that, as your child, I said it would be natural to him to grow up a much better man than I did."

"I ain't a going," said Joe, from behind his sleeve, "to tell him no-think o' that natur, Pip. Nor Biddy ain't. Nor yet no one ain't."

"And now, though I know you have already done it in your own kind hearts, pray tell me, both, that you forgive me! Pray let me hear you say the words, that I may carry the sound of them away with me, and then I shall be able to believe that you can trust me, and think better of me, in the time to come!"

"O dear old Pip, old chap," said Joe. "God knows as I forgive you, if I have anythink to forgive!"

"Amen! And God knows I do!" echoed Biddy.

"Now let me go up and look at my old little room, and rest there a few minutes by myself, and then when I have eaten and drunk with you, go with me as far as the finger-post, dear Joe and Biddy, before we say good-by!"

I sold all I had, and put aside as much as I could, for a composition with my creditors—who gave me ample time to pay them in full—and I went out and joined Herbert. Within a month, I had quitted England, and within two months I was clerk to Clarriker and Co., and within four months I assumed my first undivided responsibility. For, the beam across the parlour ceiling at Mill Pond Bank, had then ceased to tremble under old Bill Barley's growls and was at peace, and Herbert had gone away to marry Clara, and I was left in sole charge of the Eastern Branch until he brought her back.

Many a year went round, before I was a partner in the House; but, I lived happily with Herbert and his wife, and lived frugally, and paid my debts, and maintained a constant correspondence with Biddy and Joe. It was not until I became third in the Firm, that Clarriker betrayed me to Herbert; but, he then declared that the secret of Herbert's partnership had been long enough upon his conscience, and he must tell it. So, he told it, and Herbert was as much moved as amazed, and the dear fellow and I were not the worse friends for the long concealment. I must not leave it to be supposed that we were ever a great House, or that we made mints of money. We were not in a grand way of business, but we had a good name, and worked for our profits, and did very well. We owed so much to Herbert's ever cheerful industry and readiness, that I often wondered how I had conceived that old idea of his inaptitude, until I was one day enlightened by the reflection, that perhaps the inaptitude had never been in him at all, but had been in me.

Chapter 59

For eleven years, I had not seen Joe nor Biddy with my bodily eyes—though they had both been often before my fancy in the East—when, upon an evening in December, an hour or two after dark, I laid my hand softly on the latch of the old kitchen door. I touched it so softly that I was not heard, and looked in unseen. There, smoking his pipe in the old place by the kitchen firelight, as hale and as strong as ever though a little grey, sat Joe; and there, fenced into the corner with Joe's leg, and sitting on my own little stool looking at the fire, was——I again!

"We giv' him the name of Pip for your sake, dear old chap," said Joe, delighted when I took another stool by the child's side (but I did *not* rumple his hair), "and we hoped he might grow a little bit like you, and we think he do."

I thought so too, and I took him out for a walk next morning, and we talked immensely, understanding one another to perfection. And I took him down to the churchyard, and set him on a certain tombstone there, and he showed me from that elevation which stone was sacred to the memory of Philip Pirrip, late of this Parish, and Also Georgiana, Wife of the Above.

"Biddy," said I, when I talked with her after dinner, as her little girl lay sleeping in her lap, "you must give Pip to me, one of these days; or lend him, at all events."

"No, no," said Biddy, gently. "You must marry."

"So Herbert and Clara say, but I don't think I shall, Biddy. I have so settled down in their home, that it's not at all likely. I am already quite an old bachelor."

Biddy looked down at her child, and put its little hand to her lips, and then put the good matronly hand with which she had touched it, into mine. There was something in the action and in the light pressure of Biddy's wedding-ring, that had a very pretty eloquence in it.

"Dear Pip," said Biddy, "you are sure you don't fret for her?"

"O no—I think not, Biddy."

"Tell me as an old, old friend. Have you quite forgotten her?"

"My dear Biddy, I have forgotten nothing in my life that ever had a foremost place there, and little that ever had any place there. But that poor dream, as I once used to call it, has all gone by, Biddy, all gone by!"

Nevertheless, I knew while I said those words, that I secretly intended to revisit the site of the old house that evening, alone, for her sake. Yes even so. For Estella's sake.

I had heard of her as leading a most unhappy life, and as being separated from her husband, who had used her with great cruelty, and who had become quite renowned as a compound of pride, avarice, brutality, and meanness. And I had heard of the death of her husband, from an accident consequent on his ill-treatment of a horse. This release had befallen her some two years before; for anything I knew, she was married again.

The early dinner-hour at Joe's, left me abundance of time, without hurrying my talk with Biddy, to walk over to the old spot before dark. But, what with loitering on the way, to look at old objects and to think of old times, the day had quite declined when I came to the place.

There was no house now, no brewery, no building whatever left, but the wall of the old garden. The cleared space had been enclosed with a rough fence, and, looking over it, I saw that some of the old ivy had struck root anew, and was growing green on low quiet mounds of ruin. A gate in the fence standing ajar, I pushed it open, and went in.

A cold silvery mist had veiled the afternoon, and the moon was not yet up to scatter it. But, the stars were shining beyond the mist, and the moon was coming, and the evening was not dark. I could trace out where every part of the old house had been, and where the brewery had been, and where the gates, and where the casks. I had done so, and was looking along the desolate garden-walk, when I beheld a solitary figure in it.

The figure showed itself aware of me, as I advanced. It had been moving towards me, but it stood still. As I drew nearer, I saw it to be the figure of a woman. As I drew nearer yet, it was about to turn away, when it stopped, and let me come up with it. Then, it faltered as if much surprised, and uttered my name, and I cried out:

"Estella!"

"I am greatly changed. I wonder you know me."

The freshness of her beauty was indeed gone, but its indescribable majesty and its indescribable charm remained. Those attractions in it, I had seen before; what I had never seen before, was the saddened softened light of the once proud eyes; what I had never felt before, was the friendly touch of the once insensible hand.

We sat down on a bench that was near, and I said, "After so many years, it is strange that we should thus meet again, Estella, here where our first meeting was! Do you often come back?"

"I have never been here since."

"Nor I."

The moon began to rise, and I thought of the placid look at the white ceiling, which had passed away. The moon began to rise, and I thought of the pressure on my hand when I had spoken the last words he had heard on earth.

Estella was the next to break the silence that ensued between us.

"I have very often hoped and intended to come back, but have been prevented by many circumstances. Poor, poor old place!"

The silvery mist was touched with the first rays of the moonlight, and the same rays touched the tears that dropped from her eyes. Not knowing that I saw them, and setting herself to get the better of them, she said quietly:

"Were you wondering, as you walked along, how it came to be left in this condition?"

"Yes, Estella."

"The ground belongs to me. It is the only possession I have not relinquished. Everything else has gone from me, little by little, but I have kept this. It was the subject of the only determined resistance I made in all the wretched years."

"Is it to be built on?"

"At last it is. I came here to take leave of it before its change. And you," she said, in a voice of touching interest to a wanderer, "you live abroad still?"

"Still."

"And do well, I am sure?"

"I work pretty hard for a sufficient living, and therefore—Yes, I do well."

"I have often thought of you," said Estella.

"Have you?"

"Of late, very often. There was a long hard time when I kept far from me, the remembrance of what I had thrown away when I was quite ignorant of its worth. But, since my duty has not been incompatible with the admission of that remembrance, I have given it a place in my heart."

"You have always held your place in my heart," I answered. And we were silent again, until she spoke.

"I little thought," said Estella, "that I should take leave of you in taking leave of this spot. I am very glad to do so."

"Glad to part again, Estella? To me, parting is a painful thing. To me, the remembrance of our last parting has been ever mournful and painful."

"But you said to me," returned Estella, very earnestly, "'God bless you, God forgive you!' And if you could say that to me then, you will not hesitate to say that to me now—now, when suffering has been stronger than all other teaching, and has taught me to understand what your heart used to be. I have been bent and broken, but—I hope—into a better shape. Be as considerate and good to me as you were, and tell me we are friends."

"We are friends," said I, rising and bending over her, as she rose from the bench.

"And will continue friends apart," said Estella.

I took her hand in mine, and we went out of the ruined place; and, as the morning mists had risen long ago when I first left the forge, so, the evening mists were rising now, and in all the broad expanse of tranquil light they showed to me, I saw the shadow of no parting from her.

THE END.

THE ENDINGS OF *GREAT EXPECTATIONS*

The ending of *Great Expectations* published in 1861 in *All the Year Round* and in the three-volume edition—the one that appears in this text—was not the ending that Dickens originally wrote for the novel. As the biographical introduction explains (see pp. 17–18), he showed the ending that he fully intended to publish to Bulwer-Lytton, who successfully urged Dickens to change it. Critics typically distinguish, therefore, between what they call the "original," unpublished ending and the "revised" version published in 1861.

In the original ending, there is no Chapter 59; immediately after Pip's words to Biddy in the original Chapter 58 ("But that poor dream, as I once used to call it, has all gone by, Biddy, all gone by!" [437]) are the following paragraphs:

> It was four years more, before I saw herself. I had heard of her as leading a most unhappy life, and as being separated from her husband who had used her with great cruelty, and who had become quite renowned as a compound of pride, brutality, and meanness. I had heard of the death of her husband (from an accident consequent on ill-treating a horse), and of her being married again to a Shropshire doctor, who, against his interest, had once very manfully interposed, on an occasion when he was in professional attendance on Mr. Drummle, and had witnessed some outrageous treatment of her. I had heard that the Shropshire doctor was not rich, and that they lived on her own personal fortune.
>
> I was in England again—in London, and walking along Piccadilly with little Pip—when a servant came running after me to ask would I step back to a lady in a carriage who wished to speak to me. It was a little pony carriage, which the lady was driving; and the lady and I looked sadly enough on one another.
>
> "I am greatly changed, I know; but I thought you would like to shake hands with Estella too, Pip. Lift up that pretty child and let me kiss it!" (She supposed the child, I think, to be my child.)
>
> I was very glad afterwards to have had the interview; for, in her face and in her voice, and in her touch, she gave me the assurance, that suffering had been stronger than Miss Havisham's teaching, and had given her a heart to understand what my heart used to be.

When Dickens canceled this ending, he wrote a longer and quite different account of Pip's meeting with Estella. He created a separate chapter for the revised ending, Chapter 59, which begins with the last section of the original Chapter 58, in which Pip recounts his return to the forge, now set at eleven, rather than eight, years since he has last been there. Dickens then described Pip's evening walk to the grounds of Satis House and his conversation with Estella there.

The revised ending had undergone and continued to undergo yet other revisions. In manuscript and in proof, the last part of the last sentence of the novel is

. . . I saw the shadow of no parting from her but one.

Dickens removed the last two words at the proof stage, and the line as it appears in *All the Year Round* and the 1861 three-volume edition (and in this edition) is

. . . I saw the shadow of no parting from her.

In the 1862 one-volume edition, the line was once again revised to read

. . . I saw no shadow of another parting from her.

It appears in that form in all subsequent editions in Dickens's lifetime, including the Charles Dickens Edition of 1868.

The alternate endings of *Great Expectations* have received a great deal of critical commentary. Listed here are particularly useful discussions devoted solely to the questions that they raise:

Eigner, Edwin M. "Bulwer-Lytton and the Changed Endings of *Great Expectations.*" *Nineteenth-Century Fiction* 25 (1970): 107–08.

Meisel, Martin. "The Ending of *Great Expectations.*" *Essays in Criticism* 15 (1965): 326–31.

Millhauser, Milton. *"Great Expectations:* The Three Endings." *Dickens Studies Annual* 2 (1972): 267–77.

Rosenberg, Edgar. "Last Words on *Great Expectations:* A Textual Brief on the Six Endings." *Dickens Studies Annual* 9 (1981): 87–115.

Sadrin, Anny. "The Sense of Two Endings." *Great Expectations.* Unwin Critical Library. London: Unwin Hyman, 1988. 167–80.

PART TWO

Great Expectations:
A Case Study in
Contemporary Criticism

A Critical History of
Great Expectations

Less than one month into the serial publication of *Great Expectations*, Dickens wrote to one of his friends: "Pray read Great Expectations. . . . It is a very great success, and seems universally liked" (*Letters* 3: 196). Even if one discounts some of the characteristic bravado of this claim, Dickens was right. When it was halfway through its run in *All the Year Round*, the novel had accomplished precisely what he had hoped for it: the magazine was selling approximately one hundred thousand copies a week; as he boasted, that figure represented "probably several thousands" more copies than the daily circulation of the London *Times* (*Letters* 3: 218). The value of his "property," as he called the magazine, seemed now secure. Subsequently, *Great Expectations,* unlike any other Dickens novel, was published in three volumes at the relatively high price then standard for sale to lending libraries, where it reached many more readers (Patten 291–92).

The success story of *Great Expectations* has since then had its reverses and revivals. By 1882, when a reviewer estimated that over four million copies of Dickens's novels had been sold since his death in 1870, *Pickwick Papers* and *David Copperfield* were the most popular; *A Tale of Two Cities* and *Great Expectations* the least popular (Collins, *Dickens* 599). By 1968, however, these positions had changed: among American readers, *A Tale of Two Cities* was selling more copies than any other novel, with *Great Expectations* a close second (Patten 332).

Because it is now one of the most widely taught of all the Victorian novels, *Great Expectations* remains clearly one of the most widely purchased and most frequently read.

The fact that the value placed on different Dickens novels has changed so greatly over one hundred years suggests some of the complexities inherent in the history of the responses to *Great Expectations.* Tastes, standards of judgment, even attention spans have, of course, altered greatly over that period of time. Because Victorian readers were always eager for involved plots and engaging characters—the more of both, the merrier—they often favored Dickens's longer, earlier novels over any of the shorter, later ones. Yet one fact has not changed between the Victorian period and our own: a writer's or a work's reputation at any given time reflects specific reading practices that result, in turn, from a complex interplay of institutions and professions—education, publishing, printing, criticism. This interplay creates possibilities for one kind of popularity or another, and the individual writer or individual text is either able or unable to make the most of those possibilities.

The responses of contemporary readers of *Great Expectations* provide a case in point. In conceiving the story of Pip as a serial novel, Dickens was responding, as I have explained in the biographical introduction, to quite specific financial pressures that made him even more than usually aware of the interests and tastes of his readers. The obvious humor of Pip's storytelling, the updating of the Dick Whittington story in the contemporary form of the *Bildungsroman* or novel of growth and development, the construction of the novel in weekly parts that "made Suspense count the days till the next number appeared—again to be baulked, and anew to count" (Chorley 43), were all factors upon which Dickens could depend to appeal to his readers. Despite setting the story earlier in the century, moreover, Dickens engaged a number of questions of topical interest to his readers: What defines a gentleman? Should one's social position be earned or inherited? Addressing such questions allowed Dickens to renew and tighten his hold on his original readers.

Beyond such factors, however, Dickens made one artistic choice that seems to have had the greatest effect on both the contemporary reception of the novel and its critical reputation since then: his choice of Pip as the teller of his own tale. As I have suggested, the decision to write a fictional autobiography may have resulted directly from Dickens's decision not to write a longer, twenty-number monthly serial. The subsequent critical history of the novel reveals that Pip's role as narrator has often coordinated nicely with the varying standards of critics writing at different times. By making the "I" of this novel its most prominent feature, whether that "I" refers to the young boy acting in the story or the older man telling it, Dickens identified the psychology of the main character as his chief subject, just as he relegated to the background the social world in which he placed that subject. Both Victorian and modern critics have largely approved that choice of focus.

In Pip, Dickens succeeded in creating an almost mesmerizing performance of character, and it has been hard for critics to resist the charm of that performance, even when, as was the case with the contemporary reviewers, they were disposed to hold any novel by Dickens to exacting standards. Throughout its long critical history since the 1860s, the novel has almost invariably worked its charm, even when Dickens's fiction fell out of favor at the end of the nineteenth century. In fact, until quite recently, although there have been some exceptions, the form of *Great Expectations* has protected it against the kind of resistant readings that are now so highly prized in academic criticism. If a critical history of *Great Expectations* reveals the continued success of the novel, it demonstrates that such success can be measured not only in terms of sales and sustained popularity, but also in terms of the novel's ability to determine the kind of critical commentary that it has received.

The responses of contemporary reviewers to the publication of *Great Expectations* in 1860 and 1861 might seem, by some standards, less than wildly enthusiastic, but in relation to Dickens's standing among the critics and his popularity as a novelist, they were more than satisfying. Although Dickens, like Thackeray and George Eliot, wrote for a relatively homogeneous audience—and the emphasis here is clearly on the word *relatively*—Dickens's standing in the 1850s was one of the first signs of a development that became more apparent several decades later: the distinction between critical and popular audiences. Although reviewers in the 1850s found more and more fault with Dickens's novels, his readers kept buying them in greater and greater numbers. Largely as a result of the popularity of *David Copperfield* (1849–50), the parts of *Bleak House* (1852–53) sold more copies than its predecessor, approximately thirty-four thousand a month. *Little Dorrit* (1855–57) had even higher sales. *Hard Times* (1854) doubled the circulation of *Household Words*, the magazine in which it appeared, to eighty thousand a week; and *A Tale of Two Cities*

(1859), which was pointedly ignored by the critics, tripled the sales records that had been set by *Household Words* when it appeared in Dickens's new magazine, *All the Year Round*. Although the sales of the novels in monthly numbers in the 1850s were still less than those of a novel like *The Old Curiosity Shop* in the 1840s, which had reached one hundred thousand an issue (Collins, *Dickens* 619–20), Dickens in the 1850s could—and did—feel that he was regaining some of the magic of his early career.

Yet during this time of increasing sales, Dickens's reviewers complained often and vociferously that the novels published after *David Copperfield* were depressing, humorless, and unappealing—too committed to portraying social problems to be entertaining or even, despite their obvious social missions, enlightening. For clearly political reasons, some more conservative reviewers found Dickens wanting: after all, his crusading tones, his chosen role as "champion of the people," had helped make him widely popular. Added to this source of disfavor was Dickens's propensity for sentimentality and for vulgarity, proof to certain reviewers that his background was not of the right kind.

Chief among the faultfinders in the 1850s was James Fitzjames Stephen, who wrote frequently for the newly established *Saturday Review*. Criticism of contemporary literature in the mid-nineteenth century was much more a public matter, less an academic specialty, than it is now. Criticism was largely the province of reviewers who were frequently paid for their often elaborate assessments of new books but who typically made their livelihood through other means. Literature written in English, even the admittedly "classic" work of Shakespeare and Milton, had no place in the curricula at Oxford and Cambridge until much later in the century. Reviews were published anonymously, so their writers often saw themselves as representatives of a particular journal's religious, political, or class affiliations. Stephen, a lawyer with family ties to the civil service, was typical of the kind of writer to whom the job of assessing a new novel might fall. In 1857 he complained that Dickens had "a very wide and a very pernicious political and social influence" because he took on serious political questions without any of the training or experience that would justify such a role: "To [men of sense and cultivation] Mr. Dickens is nothing more than any other public performer—enjoying an extravagantly high reputation, and rewarded for his labours, both in purse and in credit, at an extravagantly high rate" (Collins, *Dickens* 346, 345). The quarrel between Dickens and his reviewers became one of the standard topics of the day, with some reviewers defending the novelist and others defending his critics.

In this context even the sometimes mixed responses of the reviewers to *Great Expectations* were a distinct and early mark of its success. The writer for the *Saturday Review*, the journal most often identified with contempt for Dickens, begins his analysis in a manner still palpably condescending by granting the novelist permission to be pleased with his work: "Mr. Dickens may be reasonably proud of these volumes. After the long series of his varied works—after passing under the cloud of *Little Dorrit* and *Bleak House*—he has written a story that is new, original, powerful, and very entertaining" ("Great Expectations" 69). After the response to *A Tale of Two Cities*, which, according to the *Eclectic Review*, "pleased nobody" (Collins, *Dickens* 421), this was high praise indeed.

The humor of the novel was frequently noted as its chief and most appealing quality. Dickens had promised his friend John Forster, "you will not have to complain of the want of humour [in *Great Expectations*] as in the Tale of Two Cities" (*Letters* 3: 186), and many reviewers responded as if they were so many Forsters proving that Dickens had kept his promise. The writer in the *Times* declared, "Mr. Dickens has good-naturedly granted to his hosts of readers the desire of their hearts [for] the old *Pickwick* style" (Collins, *Dickens* 430). Identifying the distinctive quality of Dickens's fiction as his "perception of the purely farcical, ludicrous, and preposterously funny," the writer in the *Rambler* was pleased to find in *Great Expectations* at least the "partial flickering up of this bright gift" (Collins, *Dickens* 438).

In writing *Great Expectations*, Dickens had been as intent on devising an engaging plot as he had been on making the novel amusing, and he ascribed its success to this dual approach to satisfying his readers' tastes. When he declared the first installments of the novel to be "a very great success," he attributed that result to these two qualities: "I suppose [it is] because it opens funnily, and with an interest too" (*Letters* 3: 196). The reviewers largely agreed with this analysis. The *Atlantic Monthly* found the plot of *Great Expectations* "universally admitted to be the best that Dickens has ever invented" (Collins, *Dickens* 428). A number of writers played on the relation between the noun in the title of the novel, *expectations*, and the high value placed on suspenseful fiction that could raise and then satisfy a reader's expectations. One reviewer, boasting that he had been able to read no more than half of *Little Dorrit*, confessed, "After a careful reading of *Great Expectations*, we must own to having found the book in most ways better than our very small expectations could have foreboded" (Collins, *Dickens* 435). In contrast to the frequent condemnations of Dickens's work in the reviews of the 1850s and in contrast to this particular reviewer's "very small expectations," the novel was clearly a critical success. As one writer announced, *Great Expectations* was "the imaginative book of the year" (Chorley 43).

Contemporary notices of *Great Expectations* focused, as Victorian reviews typically did, on the novelist's treatment of his characters. In this specific regard, the judgments were more mixed. Some reviewers referred to Dickens's characters, and particularly to Miss Havisham and Wemmick, as examples of his "worst mannerisms" or "the poverty of [his] imagination" (Collins, *Dickens* 433, 437). To the *Westminster Review,* Miss Havisham seemed a "galvanized puppet" ("Belles Lettres" 288); to Margaret Oliphant, a fellow novelist writing in *Blackwood's Magazine,* the depiction of Miss Havisham was simply evidence of "fancy run mad" (Collins, *Dickens* 439). Yet other reviewers disagreed. While the *Saturday Review* analyzed precisely the "melodramatic exaggeration" that other reviewers found in Dickens's characters—the propensity to make one trait the basis of an entire characterization—it also deemed Wemmick, roundly condemned by others, as "the great comic creation of the book," and it called Magwitch "a character that attracts us equally by its originality and naturalness." Even so, the reviewer had little patience with the depiction of Miss Havisham, dismissing it as "too exceptional, too nearly bordering on the monstrous and loathsome, to be appropriately introduced in the midst of a story of ordinary English life" ("Great Expectations" 69–70).

That *Great Expectations,* a novel of fantastical coincidences and wildly imaginative characterizations, could be described by the *Saturday Review* as a "story of ordinary English life" can be attributed, I think, to its autobiographical form. Indeed, the *Saturday Review* juxtaposes its commendation of the "more profound study of the general nature of human character than Dickens usually betrays" to an account of its form: "The hero writes an autobiography of his own life, tells the story of his childhood, of his struggles with poverty, and of his gradual rise in the world until he attains what, in Mr. Dickens' novels, is the very vague position of a gentleman" ("Great Expectations" 69). Although one must note the revealing distortions in this account—Pip is never really poor, and his rise is meteoric rather than gradual—it does put the emphasis where Dickens put it, on Pip as character and storyteller. The writer in the *Atlantic Monthly* makes a similar point. After praising the novel as an "artistic creation" producing on the reader "a unity of impression," he explains that Dickens filters the "poetical element of [his] genius . . . through the medium of an imagined mind," Pip's mind (Collins, *Dickens* 429–30). In fact, one might attribute to the creation of Pip as the teller of his own tale almost all that Victorian reviewers found to praise: the humor with which he retells his adventures is made appropriate by his distance in time from them, and the "unity of impression" that they found so refreshing after the sprawling earlier novels results not only from its compressed installments but also from the links between them created by the power of one "imagined mind."

In the decades following Dickens's death, the favor that *Great Expectations* had earlier found with reviewers disappeared as a new generation of critics became more and more intent on deploring the novelist's continuing popularity with the general reader. Instead of providing commentary on a particular novel like *Great Expectations*, they focused on the case to be made against Dickens's fiction as a whole. On the occasion of Dickens's death, his fellow novelist Anthony Trollope offered the kind of evaluation that became typical later on. He noted that Dickens's novels were popular "from the highest to the lowest, among all classes that read." Trollope clearly indicates that such popularity is not universal: "When the masses of English readers, in all English-speaking countries, have agreed to love the writings of any writer, their verdict will be stronger than that of any one judge, let that judge be ever so learned and thoughtful" (Collins, *Dickens* 324). The judge's ruling here is very clear: to "love" Dickens is to identify oneself as neither learned nor thoughtful. Dickens had made it his business—it was literally his business—to engage the interest and loyalty of as many readers as possible. At his death, *All the Year Round* was selling three hundred thousand copies a week and reaching, by one estimate, half the population of London, even though half its copies were sold outside the city (Sutherland 168). During his lifetime, reviewers sometimes complained that Dickens's extraordinary imaginative gifts had been spoiled by his popularity. After his death, such complaints became routine.

In the closing decades of the century, changes in patterns of reading and education as well as developments in the technology and economic conditions of publishing came together to make such widespread popularity less possible and even less desirable from an aesthetic perspective than it had been earlier. The year in which Dickens died was also the year in which the first compulsory education act was passed by the British Parliament; its effect, like that of subsequent education bills, was not only to enlarge the number of readers, but also to emphasize the differences between barely literate readers and more highly educated readers. At the same time new printing technologies made possible the publication of serialized fiction in specialized magazines that catered profitably to smaller and more highly differentiated groups of readers than those for whom mid-Victorian novelists had written. The three-volume novel was superseded by cheaper one-volume novels sold directly to the public, not to lending libraries. Publishers, who by the 1880s and 1890s viewed novelists as their employees and readers as consumers, were more fully in control of the "relations of production" in a "fully capitalist" system of publication (Feltes 78, 89). Novelists who wanted to define their work as serious art sought to appeal to a highly educated, elite audience of critical readers. It was obviously to the advantage of such novelists and readers to confirm their sense of their own status by disdaining as "merely popular" Dickens's earlier success with a larger and relatively more homogeneous audience.

The contrast between this disdain and Dickens's current standing among professional critics—academics now rather than reviewers—could not be greater than it is. Dickens, like Shakespeare, continues to have a popular reputation—both authors are public institutions, common cultural property in the English-speaking world—and academic critics have restored Dickens's reputation so that it is among them as almost universally favorable as his popular reputation was at the beginning of his career. *Great Expectations* has shared in this revival more fully than most of Dickens's novels, and it has once again largely succeeded in determining the kind of commentary that it has received.

The dark night of Dickens's reputation, from the 1880s well into the 1940s, was also the nadir of other Victorian reputations. During that time claims for the value of his work came principally and most prominently from other creative writers, not from reviewers or academics, and a number of them lavished on *Great Expectations* a great deal of generous attention. The poet Algernon Swinburne, essayists and novelists G. K. Chesterton and George Gissing, and the playwright George Bernard Shaw all attempted to prove that Dickens was indeed worth the attention of serious-minded, well-educated, and artistically demanding readers. Calling *Great Expectations* "nearly perfect" in his book-length study of Dickens first published in 1898, George Gissing found the novel full of psychological insight and "harsh truth"—the harshest, perhaps, being that only by half-murdering a shrew like Mrs. Joe can one make her quiet (Cotsell 24, 27). Calling *Great Expectations* a "masterpiece," Swinburne made what was surely in 1902 a previously unheard-of claim: in terms of its story, "there is none superior, if there is anything equal to it, in the whole range of English fiction" (Cotsell 22). G. K. Chesterton applied other superlatives to the novel in the two books he published on Dickens: in 1906 Chesterton called it "a fine story . . . told with a consistency and quietude of individuality which is rare in Dickens"; by 1911 Chesterton was speaking of its "quality of serene irony and even sadness, which puts it quite alone among [Dickens's] other works" (Cotsell 27, 28). The praise continued when George Bernard Shaw, in an introduction to *Great Expectations* (1937), called the novel Dickens's "most compactly perfect book" (Cotsell 34).

Such praise did not become commonplace among academic critics until the 1950s and 1960s. Credit for reviving Dickens's reputation and inaugurating the sustained attention that his works have received since then belongs to two books first published in 1941: *The Wound and the Bow*, by Edmund Wilson, an essayist and journalist, and *The Dickens World*, by Humphry House, an Oxford scholar. Wilson's essay "Dickens: The Two Scrooges" focuses on the novelist's biography; and Dickens emerges as a gloomy, difficult artist whose conflicted nature manifested itself in the ghost stories of his early fiction and the darkness of his later novels. House's book is a work of historical scholarship. It attempts to connect Dickens's novels to the specific historical conditions of the times in which they were written, and its chapters treat such subjects as charity, economics, religion, and politics. These seminal works focus on the two aspects of their subject that would come to distinguish the orientation of later criticism: Dickens the artist and Dickens the social critic. These two books also epitomize past and future forms of the professionalization of critical writing: Wilson's points back to the nineteenth-century mode of more general criticism ("The Two Scrooges" appeared first in the *Atlantic Monthly* and the *New Republic*), and House's points ahead to the rise of specialized academic criticism that occurred once the study of fairly recent literature written in English became part of the curricula of colleges and universities. Yet both works proved that Dickens's fiction repays the kind of critical attention that it had not often received.

Although a few others had made such points about Dickens before (Nisbet 74–83), Wilson and House opened up a field of critical possibilities that were quickly recognized by the growing number of academic writers. The rise in Dickens's stock took place in the context of a number of significant trends inside and outside academia. By 1978 Philip Collins noted that more than one hundred books on Dickens had appeared in print from 1962 to 1974, and he explained that fact by referring to the great explosion in publishing in general: "two-thirds of all the books ever published have appeared since 1952," in less, that is, than a quarter of a century. *Great Expectations* has been the particular beneficiary of the correspondingly increased interest in Dickens. According to Collins, "as a candidate for the most discussed of Dickens' novels, [it] rivals or surpasses *Bleak House*" ("Dickens" 34–35, 104). By the 1980s there was sufficient commentary on *Great Expectations* to justify the publication of an annotated bibliography devoted solely to this one novel. George J. Worth divides the sections on "criticisms and appreciations" in his bibliography into three historical periods—1870–1939, 1940–1969, and 1970–1983—and the last, the shortest period, contains the most entries, a total of 365 entries for only fourteen years.

If Dickens were able to come back to life and flip through the pages of Worth's bibliography, he might be tempted to talk again of the "very great success" of his *Great Expectations*. He might also wonder why this particular novel has received so much attention, and he would need to look at the practices of academic publishing to understand why this is so. Criticism in the nineteenth century was, as I have explained, the professional province of the reviewer. By the second half of the twentieth century, criticism had become the province of the academic, although important reviews of contemporary writing, of course, continued to appear in journals and newspapers. Not only has nineteenth- and twentieth-century literature become a respectable academic subject, but the vastly increased number of students attending college, particularly in the United States, has led to a great increase in the number of academics for whom publication is a professional requirement.

As Gerald Graff has demonstrated, the growing numbers of students in colleges and universities made necessary the development of a way of teaching literature that would be accessible and therefore effective (ch. 10). The New Criticism, which had its greatest influence in the 1950s and 1960s, offered such a method for the classroom, but it also provided academic critics with a methodology that encouraged the writing of what soon became and, to some extent, still is the standard unit of academic criticism: the analysis of one literary work in an article written for publication in an increasing number of academic

journals. New Criticism involves formal analysis of aesthetic structures—for the New Critic, the most sublime literary form is the lyric
poem—and it champions a conception of the organic unity of the autonomous work of art. It is therefore a critical approach that might
not seem appropriate for dealing with Dickens's longer novels. But
Great Expectations, recognized as the most obviously unified of Dickens's novels by even skeptical contemporary reviewers, became the
equally obvious subject of New Critical analysis. In the 1960s and
even into the 1970s, there appeared numerous essays on the unifying
imagery of *Great Expectations.* Images of fire and water, prisons,
marshes, and gardens were analyzed as keys to its artistic success. As
Jerome H. Buckley noted, "the whole [novel] is as much unified by
recurrent symbols and chains of imagery as by solidity of structure"
(47). By 1965, when Robert Garis attempted to develop a new way of
reading Dickens by concentrating on his novels as performances, he
complained that the emphasis on Dickens's work as "seriously symbolic and prophetic" had "hardened into the new orthodoxy" (1).

Throughout the 1950s and 1960s, critical assumptions about the
ideal of the autonomous work of art were frequently accompanied by
the often less openly acknowledged ideal of the unified, autonomous
individual. Because *Great Expectations* purports to portray a
"progress" in three "stages," its action has often been analyzed in
terms of its main character's growth into a self-aware and self-
determined individual. Since even as powerful a reading technique as
New Criticism could never entirely transform a novel like *Great Expectations,* with its obvious references to the facts of Victorian social life,
into a lyric poem, the search for the unity of Pip's character was during
this period even more frequently pursued than the search for the aesthetic unity of the novel. The two endeavors often went hand in hand,
however, one signifying the other.

Throughout the 1960s and 1970s and into the 1980s, therefore,
much of the criticism of the novel has dealt with Pip's character by exploring the relation between public and private, social and personal,
and by emphasizing, as Dickens does, the latter of those pairs of terms.
In short, the autobiographical form of the novel once again determined the nature of the critical perspectives on it. If *Great Expectations* is a *Bildungsroman,* a novel in which the main character comes to
know himself and his place in his world, most twentieth-century critics
have used their energies to retrace that development and to explicate
its significance, often in the service of humanistic ideals of individual-

ity. How encompassing a context in which they set this pattern—how general or how specific its implications—is, I think, the central question to ask about such commentaries.

In one of the earliest and most influential studies of Dickens's fiction from this period, *Charles Dickens: The World of His Novels* (1958), J. Hillis Miller treats Pip as "the universal Dickensian hero" (250) who exists within a specific Victorian "social order" obsessed by class distinctions (262), but Miller posits against this social order a realm of "true selfhood" that is the goal of each individual (271). In the end, according to Miller's reading of Dickens, this selfhood involves the Christian paradox of self-fulfillment through self-denial: Pip discovers that love provides "the only successful escape from . . . the unhappiness of being this unique and isolated individual, Pip," and he proves his capacity for love through his "change in his attitude toward Magwitch" (274). Ultimately, Pip finds "selfhood" in a realm apart from "social eminence" and "social judgments" (277).

Similar conclusions characterize quite dissimilar readings of *Great Expectations* during this period. In *The Dickens World*, Humphry House included a brief analysis of Pip's story as a "snob's progress" (156), a plot specifically characteristic of attitudes current in the late 1850s and early 1860s. When Q. D. Leavis came to write her own account of the novel, "How We Must Read *Great Expectations*" (1970), she rejected the characterization of Pip as a snob and called his story a "successful progress towards spiritual freedom" (287). Although she herself pays attention to historical issues in her furious attacks on previous critics and on American critics in particular for not understanding the niceties of the British class system, Leavis finds in the story a universal message. Pip's ability to acknowledge his debt to Joe and Biddy offers a "convincing proof of a change of heart, and . . . of the understanding of what spiritual health is" (324). According to Leavis, "Dickens shows, in spite of our having to live blindfolded, and in spite of being handicapped by nature and fettered by the social condition, we *can* achieve contentment and self-respect if not happiness" (313).

In an analysis that places *Great Expectations* more specifically in its historical context than Leavis's does, Robin Gilmour examines the novel in relation to *The Idea of the Gentleman in the Victorian Novel* (1981), but his analysis concludes much as hers does. Gilmour is interested in *Great Expectations* as a "fable of cultural emergence" (135), the story of the evolution of the middle class from the violence of Regency England to its position of prominence in the "relatively stable, relatively prosperous" and respectable world of the 1860s (124). Yet, according to Gilmour, what the novel "unequivocally affirms," what Dickens affirms, is the concept of "the gentle man who [lives] by Christian ideals of love and forgiveness" (143).

These three readings—by Miller and Leavis and Gilmour—are typical of most of the readings of *Great Expectations* through the 1980s: the novel, whatever its historical setting is conceived to be, affirms the universal humanistic ideals of love, charity, and fellow-feeling as well as the value of the integrated individual who can learn to put those ideals into practice.

In one sense such readings seem simply to prove that these values were central to Victorian culture and to a writer like Dickens; he is the one, after all, who wrote the line praising Joe as a "gentle Christian man" (421). From another perspective, however, the persistence of such readings, given new currency by Fred Kaplan in his recent biography of Dickens, is all the more remarkable because their prominence coincides with the emergence of critical theory as the dominant trend in literary criticism. The effect of such theory has often been to question the ability of a text, any text, to serve as an unproblematic repository of humanistic values.

Exemplary of the gradual changes in the criticism of *Great Expectations* and of the sustained attention accorded it by academic critics is the eleventh volume of the *Dickens Studies Annual* (*DSA*) (1983). It devotes to the novel five of its twelve regular articles, all essays that had originally been read as papers at the 1981 conference of the newly founded University of California Dickens Institute at Santa Cruz. The institute, now known as the Dickens Project, pays homage to the novelist's continued popularity with the general public by offering a "general education course" devoted to one Dickens novel along with a yearly scholarly conference. (In 1995 the chosen text is *Great Expectations,* as it was for the first meeting, in 1981.) The foundation of the project marks the institutional coming of age of Dickens studies in the United States, and three of the essays in the 1983 *DSA* offer evidence of the critical tendencies that would become more pronounced over the next decade.

These three essays treat *Great Expectations* as a meditation on writing. Robert Tracy examines "Reading Dickens' Writing" to reveal the novelist's anxieties about "the tainted—or at any rate, suspect—art of writing fiction" (56). In "Calligraphy and Code: Writing in *Great Expectations,*" Murray Baumgarten argues that Dickens presents positive and negative accounts of both reading and writing: as calligraphy "whereby the imagination can envision . . . experience in all its fullness" and as code whereby the imagination is imprisoned in rules (62). In the following essay, John O. Jordan explores "The Medium of *Great Expectations*" by picking up on Dickens's mocking reference in the novel to the 1860s craze for spiritualists. Pip is the novel's medium because he is a seer of ghosts and because he tells his own story, but Jordan also identifies the language of the novel as its medium. His conclusion coordinates with those of the two other essays: "We learn . . . that we too, like Pip, are caught in the web of language and writing—that labyrinth into which he invites us but from which there is no exit, no liberation, no redemption" (87). Although none of these essays refers directly to poststructuralist theory, its influence on their conclusions seems obvious. The emphasis on writing as writing, the treatment of *Great Expectations* as a self-referential text that calls into question its own affirmations—these critical moves are characteristic of literary analysis as it has been informed by theory since the 1970s.

Whether one praises or bemoans that influence, its primary effect has been clear: theory renders possible, sometimes even seems to require, readings of literary texts that resist, contradict, or invalidate the terms, assumptions, and implications that the texts themselves seem to authorize. While a poststructuralist theory like deconstruction has put into question New Criticism's ideal of a unified and autonomous work of art, more recent theories of the "subject" have put into question the ideal of the coherent and self-determining individual. Persons do not achieve unity of being or autonomy; rather, they create illusions of such wholeness and freedom so that they can avoid recognizing the extent to which they are self-contradictory productions of cultural and economic forces beyond their control. According to such theories, talk of selfhood or identity—much of the critical talk about Pip, in short—is simply misconceived or delusional. Until quite recently, however, readings of *Great Expectations* have remained relatively innocent of such theoretical concerns.

The difference in this regard between *Great Expectations* and the other "most discussed" of Dickens's novels, *Bleak House*, is revealing. Early on, *Bleak House* attracted to it a number of prominent poststructuralist commentators: J. Hillis Miller inaugurated a series of deconstructive readings with his 1971 introduction to the Penguin edition; in 1983 D. A. Miller offered an influential new historicist reading; and Judith Newton, responding to D. A. Miller's work, chose the novel as the subject of an essay that attempts to place feminist criticism in relation to Marxist and new historical approaches. In short, *Bleak House* is a novel whose richness has been found to be conducive to the most innovative literary theoretical analysis. In a sense this recent history simply repeats trends evident in the previous criticism: in the early 1960s, when Arnold Kettle offered a Marxist reading of Dickens, he chose to discuss *Bleak House* and noted specifically the ways in which then-current readings of *Great Expectations* had obstructed a "just assessment of Dickens's art" (144, 167 n. 1). The difference in the critical histories of the two novels is, I think, another instance of the way in which the form of *Great Expectations* has determined its critical history. The very emphasis on the personal and the private, which the prominence of the autobiographical voice makes almost inescapable, has made it difficult to conceive of the novel in any other terms.

There have been some exceptions to this rule. The first was certainly Julian Moynahan's shrewd psychoanalytic account of Pip's guilt (1960), which challenges the reader of the novel to "work his [or her] way into the narrative from a different angle than the narrator's" (Cotsell 81). More recently, Daniel Cottom has used *Great Expectations* to demonstrate his interest in the "politics of interpretation," and Jeremy Tambling found that the novel illustrates the theories set forth by Michel Foucault in *Discipline and Punish*. These two essays question some of the more cherished traditional conceptions about the affirmations offered by *Great Expectations*. Daniel Cottom proposes "to explore the inescapability of politics in reading: the contest over forms of power that constitutes the reading and understanding of texts in any form" (138). In doing so, he challenges, among other things, any stable or essentialized notion of origins, individuality, and desire. Approaching the novel from a more obviously historical perspective, Jeremy Tambling sees *Great Expectations* as a reflection of the kind of modern social and political power that Foucault found epitomized in Bentham's panopticon, a model for a prison in which isolated inmates are always subjected to the possibility of surveillance and therefore become self-disciplining constructs of disciplinary power. Foucault's conception of the "carceral society," society as prison, has little room for the traditional readings accorded Pip's "progress." According to Tambling, Pip's autobiography is a form of inevitable "self-oppression" (24) rather than liberating self-expression. Moreover, *Great Expectations* is a *Bildungsroman* that presents "a development [of its main character] that can be no development" (29). Both critics directly counter the text's "authority" by offering readings that resist its apparent logic.

The essays reprinted or published for the first time in this edition all propose resistant readings of *Great Expectations*, and they are all informed by poststructuralist theory. Peter Brooks, the effect of whose approach is as much deconstructive as its intent is psychoanalytic, posits a "decentering of [Pip as a] subject in regard to himself" and "an evident subversion and futilization of the very concept of plot." Deconstruction is represented by selections from the work of Edward W. Said; in the first he uses a passage from *Great Expectations* to illustrate the theories of deconstruction; and in the second he employs a deconstructive form of interpretation to provide a postcolonial perspective on *Great Expectations*. For all the differences between their various approaches, the other contributors to this volume—Hilary Schor (feminist criticism), William A. Cohen (gender and sexuality criticism), and Jay Clayton (cultural criticism)—all read the novel "against itself," against the interpretations that the text apparently authorizes. Taken together, these essays demonstrate the richness and vitality of *Great Expectations*, in short, its success, even in the context of the most challenging of contemporary theoretical approaches.

In fact, an account of the recent critical history leads one to something of the same conclusion reached by K. J. Fielding in 1961 when he described the "critical revolution" that had taken place in Dickens studies over the previous twenty years: "One of the merits of the novel is that it allows the reader a teasing variety of interpretations." Despite Q. D. Leavis's pontifications on "How We Must Read *Great Expectations*," there is no one way in which one "must read" the novel. Fielding attributes this effect to the lack of authorial commentary available on *Great Expectations*, in part the result of Dickens's decision to let Pip tell his own tale: "Dickens succeeded in creating a world of his own which he left to express itself. . . . [He] deliberately detached himself from his work, . . . offering the reader what he can make of it for himself" (78). Referring to House's account, Fielding adds, "The whole novel is not merely 'a snob's progress,' but one in which we can never be sure just what progress has been made" (84). As Fielding suggests, *Great Expectations* provides apparently endless opportunities for interpretation, for different formulations of and answers to the question, "Just what progress has been made?" Yet if the novel itself seems to invite a plurality of readings, its critical history suggests that all such acts of interpretation—from those of the reviewers of the

1860s to the readings that critics currently offer—result from a complex interplay among text, readers, and historical circumstances. Ultimately, a text will continue to be the subject of such readings only if it, like Pip's story, continues to satisfy, in one way or another, its audience's expectations.

Janice Carlisle

WORKS CITED

Baumgarten, Murray. "Calligraphy and Code: Writing in *Great Expectations*." *Dickens Studies Annual* 11 (1983): 61–72.

"Belles Lettres." *Westminster Review* ns 21 (Jan. 1862): 288–89.

Buckley, Jerome Hamilton. *Season of Youth: The Bildungsroman from Dickens to Golding*. Cambridge: Harvard UP, 1974.

Chorley, H. F. "*Great Expectations*." *Athenaeum* 13 July 1861: 43–45.

Collins, Philip. "Charles Dickens." *Victorian Fiction: A Second Guide to Research*. Ed. George H. Ford. New York: MLA, 1978. 34–113.

———, ed. *Dickens: The Critical Heritage*. New York: Barnes, 1971.

Cotsell, Michael, ed. *Critical Essays on Charles Dickens's* Great Expectations. Boston: G. K. Hall, 1990.

Cottom, Daniel. *Text and Culture: The Politics of Interpretation*. Theory and History of Literature, vol. 62. Minneapolis: U of Minnesota P, 1989.

Dickens, Charles. *The Letters of Charles Dickens*. Ed. Walter Dexter. Nonesuch Dickens. 3 vols. Bloomsbury: Nonesuch, 1938.

Feltes, N. N. *Modes of Production of Victorian Novels*. Chicago: U of Chicago P, 1986.

Fielding, K. J. "The Critical Autonomy of 'Great Expectations.'" *Review of English Literature* 2 (1961): 75–88.

Garis, Robert. *The Dickens Theatre*. Oxford: Clarendon, 1965.

Gilmour, Robin. *The Idea of the Gentleman in the Victorian Novel*. London: Allen, 1981.

Graff, Gerald. *Professing Literature: An Institutional History*. Chicago: U of Chicago P, 1987.

"Great Expectations." *Saturday Review* 20 July 1861: 69–70.

House, Humphry. *The Dickens World*. London: Oxford UP, 1941.

Jordan, John O. "The Medium of *Great Expectations.*" *Dickens Studies Annual* 11 (1983): 73–88.

Kaplan, Fred. *Dickens: A Biography.* New York: Morrow, 1988.

Kettle, Arnold. "Dickens and the Popular Tradition." 1961. *Literature and Liberation: Selected Essays.* Ed. Graham Martin and W. R. Owens. Manchester: Manchester UP, 1988. 140–67.

Leavis, Q. D. "How We Must Read 'Great Expectations.'" F. R. Leavis and Q. D. Leavis. *Dickens the Novelist.* New York: Pantheon, 1970. 277–331.

Miller, D. A. "Discipline in Different Voices: Bureaucracy, Police, Family, and *Bleak House.*" *The Novel and the Police.* Berkeley: U of California P, 1988. 58–106.

Miller, J. Hillis. *Charles Dickens: The World of His Novels.* 1958. Bloomington: Indiana UP, 1969.

———. "Introduction." *Bleak House.* Ed. Norman Page. Harmondsworth: Penguin, 1971.

Moynahan, Julian. "The Hero's Guilt: The Case of *Great Expectations.*" 1960. Rpt. in Cotsell, ed., 73–87.

Newton, Judith. "Historicism Old and New: 'Charles Dickens' Meets Marxism, Feminism, and West Coast Foucault." *Feminist Studies* 16 (1990): 449–70.

Nisbet, Ada. "Charles Dickens." *Victorian Fiction: A Guide to Research.* Ed. Lionel Stevenson. Cambridge: Harvard UP, 1964. 44–153.

Patten, Robert L. *Charles Dickens and His Publishers.* Oxford: Clarendon, 1978.

Sutherland, J. A. *Victorian Novelists and Publishers.* Chicago: U of Chicago P, 1976.

Tambling, Jeremy. "Prison-Bound: Dickens and Foucault." *Essays in Criticism* 37 (1986): 11–31.

Tracy, Robert. "Reading Dickens' Writing." *Dickens Studies Annual* 11 (1983): 37–59.

Wilson, Edmund. "Dickens: The Two Scrooges." *The Wound and the Bow: Seven Studies in Literature.* New York: Oxford UP, 1947. 1–104.

Worth, George J. *Great Expectations: An Annotated Bibliography.* New York: Garland, 1986.

Psychoanalytic Criticism
and
Great Expectations

WHAT IS PSYCHOANALYTIC CRITICISM?

It seems natural to think about literature in terms of dreams. Like dreams, literary works are fictions, inventions of the mind that, although based on reality, are by definition not literally true. Like a literary work, a dream may have some truth to tell, but, like a literary work, it may need to be interpreted before that truth can be grasped. We can live vicariously through romantic fictions, much as we can through daydreams. Terrifying novels and nightmares affect us in much the same way, plunging us into an atmosphere that continues to cling, even after the last chapter has been read—or the alarm clock has sounded.

The notion that dreams allow such psychic explorations, of course, like the analogy between literary works and dreams, owes a great deal to the thinking of Sigmund Freud, the famous Austrian psychoanalyst who in 1900 published a seminal essay *The Interpretation of Dreams*. But is the reader who feels that Emily Brontë's *Wuthering Heights* is dreamlike—who feels that Mary Shelley's *Frankenstein* is nightmarish—necessarily a Freudian literary critic? To some extent the answer has to be yes. We are all Freudians, really, whether or not we have read a single work by Freud. At one time or another, most of us have referred to ego, libido, complexes, unconscious desires, and sexual repression. The premises of Freud's thought have changed the way the Western world thinks about itself. Psychoanalytic criticism has influenced the teachers our teachers studied with, the works of scholarship and criticism they read, and the critical and creative writers *we* read as well.

What Freud did was develop a language that described, a model that explained, a theory that encompassed human psychology. Many of the elements of psychology he sought to describe and explain are present in the literary works of various ages and cultures, from Sophocles' *Oedipus Rex* to Shakespeare's *Hamlet* to works being written in our own day. When the great novel of the twenty-first century is written, many of these same elements of psychology will probably inform its discourse as well. If, by understanding human psychology according to Freud, we can appreciate literature on a new level, then we should acquaint ourselves with his insights.

Freud's theories are either directly or indirectly concerned with the nature of the unconscious mind. Freud didn't invent the notion of the unconscious; others before him had suggested that even the supposedly "sane" human mind was conscious and rational only at times, and even then at possibly only one level. But Freud went further, suggesting that the powers motivating men and women are *mainly* and *normally* unconscious.

Freud, then, powerfully developed an old idea: that the human mind is essentially dual in nature. He called the predominantly passional, irrational, unknown, and unconscious part of the psyche the *id*, or "it." The *ego*, or "I," was his term for the predominantly rational, logical, orderly, conscious part. Another aspect of the psyche, which he called the *superego*, is really a projection of the ego. The superego almost seems to be outside of the self, making moral judgments, telling us to make sacrifices for good causes even though self-sacrifice may not be quite logical or rational. And, in a sense, the superego *is* "outside," since much of what it tells us to do or think we have learned from our parents, our schools, or our religious institutions.

What the ego and superego tell us *not* to do or think is repressed, forced into the unconscious mind. One of Freud's most important contributions to the study of the psyche, the theory of repression, goes something like this: much of what lies in the unconscious mind has been put there by consciousness, which acts as a censor, driving underground unconscious or conscious thoughts or instincts that it deems unacceptable. Censored materials often involve infantile sexual desires,

Freud postulated. Repressed to an unconscious state, they emerge only in disguised forms: in dreams, in language (so-called Freudian slips), in creative activity that may produce art (including literature), and in neurotic behavior.

According to Freud, all of us have repressed wishes and fears; we all have dreams in which repressed feelings and memories emerge disguised, and thus we are all potential candidates for dream analysis. One of the unconscious desires most commonly repressed is the childhood wish to displace the parent of our own sex and take his or her place in the affections of the parent of the opposite sex. This desire really involves a number of different but related wishes and fears. (A boy—and it should be remarked in passing that Freud here concerns himself mainly with the male—may fear that his father will castrate him, and he may wish that his mother would return to nursing him.) Freud referred to the whole complex of feelings by the word "oedipal," naming the complex after the Greek tragic hero Oedipus, who unwittingly killed his father and married his mother.

Why are oedipal wishes and fears repressed by the conscious side of the mind? And what happens to them after they have been censored? As Roy P. Basler puts it in *Sex, Symbolism, and Psychology in Literature* (1975), "from the beginning of recorded history such wishes have been restrained by the most powerful religious and social taboos, and as a result have come to be regarded as 'unnatural,'" even though "Freud found that such wishes are more or less characteristic of normal human development":

> In dreams, particularly, Freud found ample evidence that such wishes persisted. . . . Hence he conceived that natural urges, when identified as "wrong," may be repressed but not obliterated. . . .
> In the unconscious, these urges take on symbolic garb, regarded as nonsense by the waking mind that does not recognize their significance. (14)

Freud's belief in the significance of dreams, of course, was no more original than his belief that there is an unconscious side to the psyche. Again, it was the extent to which he developed a theory of how dreams work—and the extent to which that theory helped him, by analogy, to understand far more than just dreams—that made him unusual, important, and influential beyond the perimeters of medical schools and psychiatrists' offices.

The psychoanalytic approach to literature not only rests on the theories of Freud; it may even be said to have *begun* with Freud, who was interested in writers, especially those who relied heavily on symbols. Such writers regularly cloak or mystify ideas in figures that make sense only when interpreted, much as the unconscious mind of a neurotic disguises secret thoughts in dream stories or bizarre actions that need to be interpreted by an analyst. Freud's interest in literary artists led him to make some unfortunate generalizations about creativity; for example, in the twenty-third lecture in *Introductory Lectures on Psycho-Analysis* (1922), he defined the artist as "one urged on by instinctive needs that are too clamorous" (314). But it also led him to write creative literary criticism of his own, including an influential essay on "The Relation of a Poet to Daydreaming" (1908) and "The Uncanny" (1919), a provocative psychoanalytic reading of E. T. A. Hoffmann's supernatural tale "The Sandman."

Freud's application of psychoanalytic theory to literature quickly caught on. In 1909, only a year after Freud had published "The Relation of a Poet to Daydreaming," the psychoanalyst Otto Rank published *The Myth of the Birth of the Hero*. In that work, Rank subscribes to the notion that the artist turns a powerful, secret wish into a literary fantasy, and he uses Freud's notion about the oedipal complex to explain why the popular stories of so many heroes in literature are so similar. A year after Rank had published his psychoanalytic account of heroic texts, Ernest Jones, Freud's student and eventual biographer, turned his attention to a tragic text: Shakespeare's *Hamlet*. In an essay first published in the *American Journal of Psychology*, Jones, like Rank, makes use of the oedipal concept: he suggests that Hamlet is a victim of strong feelings toward his mother, the queen.

Between 1909 and 1949 numerous other critics decided that psychological and psychoanalytic theory could assist in the understanding of literature. I. A. Richards, Kenneth Burke, and Edmund Wilson were among the most influential to become interested in the new approach. Not all of the early critics were committed to the approach; neither were all of them Freudians. Some followed Alfred Adler, who believed that writers wrote out of inferiority complexes, and others applied the ideas of Carl Gustav Jung, who had broken with Freud over Freud's emphasis on sex and who had developed a theory of the *collective* unconscious. According to Jungian theory, a great work of literature is not a disguised expression of its author's personal, repressed wishes; rather, it is a manifestation of desires once held by the whole human race but now repressed because of the advent of civilization.

It is important to point out that among those who relied on Freud's models were a number of critics who were poets and novelists as well. Conrad Aiken wrote a Freudian study of American literature, and poets such as Robert Graves and W. H. Auden applied Freudian insights when writing critical prose. William Faulkner, Henry James, James Joyce, D. H. Lawrence, Marcel Proust, and Toni Morrison are only a few of the novelists who have either written criticism influenced by Freud or who have written novels that conceive of character, conflict, and creative writing itself in Freudian terms. The poet H. D. (Hilda Doolittle) was actually a patient of Freud's and provided an account of her analysis in her book *Tribute to Freud*. By giving Freudian theory credibility among students of literature that only they could bestow, such writers helped to endow earlier psychoanalytic criticism with a largely Freudian orientation that has only begun to be challenged in the last two decades.

The willingness, even eagerness, of writers to use Freudian models in producing literature and criticism of their own consummated a relationship that, to Freud and other pioneering psychoanalytic theorists, had seemed fated from the beginning; after all, therapy involves the close analysis of language. René Wellek and Austin Warren included "psychological" criticism as one of the five "extrinsic" approaches to literature described in their influential book, *Theory of Literature* (1942). Psychological criticism, they suggest, typically attempts to do at least one of the following: provide a psychological study of an individual writer; explore the nature of the creative process; generalize about "types and laws present within works of literature"; or theorize about the psychological "effects of literature upon its readers" (81). Entire books on psychoanalytic criticism began to appear, such as Frederick J. Hoffman's *Freudianism and the Literary Mind* (1945).

Probably because of Freud's characterization of the creative mind as "clamorous" if not ill, psychoanalytic criticism written before 1950 tended to psychoanalyze the individual author. Poems were read as fantasies that allowed authors to indulge repressed wishes, to protect themselves from deep-seated anxieties, or both. A perfect example of author analysis would be Marie Bonaparte's 1933 study of Edgar Allan Poe. Bonaparte found Poe to be so fixated on his mother that his repressed longing emerges in his stories in images such as the white spot on a black cat's breast, said to represent mother's milk.

A later generation of psychoanalytic critics often paused to analyze the characters in novels and plays before proceeding to their authors—but not for long, since characters, both evil and good, tended to be seen by these critics as the author's potential selves or projections of various repressed aspects of his or her psyche. For instance, in *A*

Psychoanalytic Study of the Double in Literature (1970), Robert Rogers begins with the view that human beings are double or multiple in nature. Using this assumption, along with the psychoanalytic concept of "dissociation" (best known by its result, the dual or multiple personality), Rogers concludes that writers reveal instinctual or repressed selves in their books, often without realizing that they have done so.

In the view of critics attempting to arrive at more psychological insights into an author than biographical materials can provide, a work of literature is a fantasy or a dream—or at least so analogous to daydream or dream that Freudian analysis can help explain the nature of the mind that produced it. The author's purpose in writing is to gratify secretly some forbidden wish, in particular an infantile wish or desire that has been repressed into the unconscious mind. To discover what the wish is, the psychoanalytic critic employs many of the terms and procedures developed by Freud to analyze dreams.

The literal surface of a work is sometimes spoken of as its "manifest content" and treated as a "manifest dream" or "dream story" would be treated by a Freudian analyst. Just as the analyst tries to figure out the "dream thought" behind the dream story—that is, the latent or hidden content of the manifest dream—so the psychoanalytic literary critic tries to expose the latent, underlying content of a work. Freud used the words *condensation* and *displacement* to explain two of the mental processes whereby the mind disguises its wishes and fears in dream stories. In condensation several thoughts or persons may be condensed into a single manifestation or image in a dream story; in displacement, an anxiety, a wish, or a person may be displaced onto the image of another, with which or whom it is loosely connected through a string of associations that only an analyst can untangle. Psychoanalytic critics treat metaphors as if they were dream condensations; they treat metonyms—figures of speech based on extremely loose, arbitrary associations—as if they were dream displacements. Thus figurative literary language in general is treated as something that evolves as the writer's conscious mind resists what the unconscious tells it to picture or describe. A symbol is, in Daniel Weiss's words, "a meaningful concealment of truth as the truth promises to emerge as some frightening or forbidden idea" (20).

In a 1970 article entitled "The 'Unconscious' of Literature," Norman Holland, a literary critic trained in psychoanalysis, succinctly sums up the attitudes held by critics who would psychoanalyze authors, but without quite saying that it is the *author* that is being analyzed by the psychoanalytic critic. "When one looks at a poem psychoanalytically," he writes, "one considers it as though it were a dream or as though some ideal patient [were speaking] from the couch in iambic pentameter." One "looks for the general level or levels of fantasy associated with the language. By level I mean the familiar stages of childhood development—oral [when desires for nourishment and infantile sexual desires overlap], anal [when infants receive their primary pleasure from defecation], urethral [when urinary functions are the locus of sexual pleasure], phallic [when the penis or, in girls, some penis substitute is of primary interest], oedipal." Holland continues by analyzing not Robert Frost but Frost's poem "Mending Wall" as a specifically oral fantasy that is not unique to its author. "Mending Wall" is "about breaking down the wall which marks the separated or individuated self so as to return to a state of closeness to some Other"—including and perhaps essentially the nursing mother ("Unconscious" 136, 139).

While not denying the idea that the unconscious plays a role in creativity, psychoanalytic critics such as Holland began to focus more on the ways in which authors create works that appeal to *our* repressed wishes and fantasies. Consequently, they shifted their focus away from the psyche of the author and toward the psychology of the reader and the text. Holland's theories, which have concerned themselves more with the reader than with the text, have helped to establish another school of critical theory: reader-response criticism. Elizabeth Wright explains Holland's brand of modern psychoanalytic criticism in this way: "What draws us as readers to a text is the secret expression of what we desire to hear, much as we protest we do not. The disguise must be good enough to fool the censor into thinking that the text is respectable, but bad enough to allow the unconscious to glimpse the unrespectable" (117).

Holland is one of dozens of critics who have revised Freud significantly in the process of revitalizing psychoanalytic criticism. Another such critic is R. D. Laing, whose controversial and often poetical writings about personality, repression, masks, and the double or "schizoid" self have (re)blurred the boundary between creative writing and psychoanalytic discourse. Yet another is D. W. Winnicott, an "object-relations" theorist who has had a significant impact on literary criticism. Critics influenced by Winnicott and his school have questioned the tendency to see reader/text as an either/or construct; instead, they have seen reader and text (or audience and play) in terms of a *relationship* taking place in what Winnicott calls a "transitional" or "potential space"—space in which binary terms like real and illusory, objective and subjective, have little or no meaning.

Psychoanalytic theorists influenced by Winnicott see the transitional or potential reader/text (or audience/play) space as being *like* the space entered into by psychoanalyst and patient. More important, they also see it as being similar to the space between mother and infant: a space characterized by trust in which categorizing terms such as *knowing* and *feeling* mix and merge and have little meaning apart from one another.

Whereas Freud saw the mother-son relationship in terms of the son and his repressed oedipal complex (and saw the analyst-patient relationship in terms of the patient and the repressed "truth" that the analyst could scientifically extract), object-relations analysts see both relationships as *dyadic*—that is, as being dynamic in both directions. Consequently, they don't depersonalize analysis or their analyses. It is hardly surprising, therefore, that contemporary literary critics who apply object-relations theory to the texts they discuss don't depersonalize critics or categorize their interpretations as "truthful," at least, not in any objective or scientific sense. In the view of such critics, interpretations are made of language—itself a transitional object—and are themselves the mediating terms or transitional objects of a relationship.

Like critics of the Winnicottian School, the French structuralist theorist Jacques Lacan focuses on language and language-related issues. He treats the unconscious *as* a language and, consequently, views the dream not as Freud did (that is, as a form and symptom of repression) but rather as a form of discourse. Thus we may study dreams psychoanalytically in order to learn about literature, even as we may study literature in order to learn more about the unconscious. In Lacan's seminar on Poe's "The Purloined Letter," a pattern of repetition like that used by psychoanalysts in their analyses is used to arrive at a reading of the story. According to Wright, "the new psychoanalytic structural approach to literature" employs "analogies from psychoanalysis . . . to explain the workings of the text as distinct from the workings of a particular author's, character's, or even reader's mind" (125).

Lacan, however, did far more than extend Freud's theory of dreams, literature, and the interpretation of both. More significantly, he took Freud's whole theory of psyche and gender and added to it a crucial third term—that of language. In the process, he both used and significantly developed Freud's ideas about the oedipal stage and complex.

Lacan points out that the pre-oedipal stage, in which the child at first does not even recognize its independence from its mother, is also a pre*verbal* stage, one in which the child communicates without the medium of language, or—if we insist on calling the child's communications a language—in a language that can only be called *literal.* ("Coos," certainly, cannot be said to be figurative or symbolic.) Then, while still in the pre-oedipal stage, the child enters the *mirror* stage.

During the mirror period, the child comes to view itself and its mother, later other people as well, *as* independent selves. This is the stage in which the child is first able to fear the aggressions of another, to desire what is recognizably beyond the self (initially the mother), and, finally, to want to compete with another for the same, desired object. This is also the stage at which the child first becomes able to feel sympathy with another being who is being hurt by a third, to cry when another cries. All of these developments, of course, involve projecting beyond the self and, by extension, constructing one's own self (or "ego" or "I") as others view one—that is, as *another.* Such constructions, according to Lacan, are just that: constructs, products, artifacts—fictions of coherence that in fact hide what Lacan calls the "absence" or "lack" of being.

The mirror stage, which Lacan also refers to as the *imaginary* stage, is fairly quickly succeeded by the oedipal stage. As in Freud, this stage begins when the child, having come to view itself as self and the father and mother as separate selves, perceives gender and gender differences between its parents and between itself and one of its parents. For boys, gender awareness involves another, more powerful recognition, for the recognition of the father's phallus as the mark of his difference from the mother involves, at the same time, the recognition that his older and more powerful father is also his rival. That, in turn, leads to the understanding that what once seemed wholly his and even indistinguishable from himself is in fact someone else's: something properly desired only at a distance and in the form of socially acceptable *substitutes.*

The fact that the oedipal stage roughly coincides with the entry of the child into language is extremely important for Lacan. For the linguistic order is essentially a figurative or "Symbolic order"; words are not the things they stand for but are, rather, stand-ins or substitutes for those things. Hence boys, who in the most critical period of their development have had to submit to what Lacan calls the "Law of the Father"—a law that prohibits direct desire for and communicative intimacy with what has been the boy's whole world—enter more easily into the realm of language and the Symbolic order than do girls, who have never really had to renounce that which once seemed continuous with the self: the mother. The gap that has been opened up for boys, which includes the gap between signs and what they substitute—the gap marked by the phallus and encoded with the boy's sense of his maleness—has not opened up for girls, or has not opened up in the same way, to the same degree.

For Lacan, the father need not be present to trigger the oedipal stage; nor does his phallus have to be seen to catalyze the boy's (easier) transition into the Symbolic order. Rather, Lacan argues, a child's recognition of its gender is intricately tied up with a growing recognition of the system of names and naming, part of the larger system of substitutions we call language. A child has little doubt about who its mother is, but who is its father, and how would one know? The father's claim rests on the mother's *word* that he is in fact the father; the father's relationship to the child is thus established through language and a system of marriage and kinship—names—that in turn is basic to rules of everything from property to law. The name of the father (*nom du père,* which in French sounds like *non du père*) involves, in a sense, nothing of the father—nothing, that is, except his word or name.

Lacan's development of Freud has had several important results. First, his sexist-seeming association of maleness with the Symbolic order, together with his claim that women cannot therefore enter easily into the order, has prompted feminists not to reject his theory out of hand but, rather, to look more closely at the relation between language and gender, language and women's inequality. Some feminists have gone so far as to suggest that the social and political relationships between male and female will not be fundamentally altered until language itself has been radically changed. (That change might begin dialectically, with the development of some kind of "feminine language" grounded in the presymbolic, literal-to-imaginary, communication between mother and child.)

Second, Lacan's theory has proved of interest to deconstructors and other poststructuralists, in part because it holds that the ego (which in Freud's view is as necessary as it is natural) is a product or construct. The ego-artifact, produced during the mirror stage, *seems* at once unified, consistent, and organized around a determinate center.

But the unified self, or ego, is a fiction, according to Lacan. The yoking together of fragments and destructively dissimilar elements takes its psychic toll, and it is the job of the Lacanian psychoanalyst to "deconstruct," as it were, the ego, to show its continuities to be contradictions as well.

Ross C Murfin

PSYCHOANALYTIC CRITICISM: A SELECTED BIBLIOGRAPHY

Some Short Introductions to Psychological and Psychoanalytic Criticism

Holland, Norman. "The 'Unconscious' of Literature." *Contemporary Criticism*. Ed. Norman Bradbury and David Palmer. Stratford-upon-Avon Series 12. New York: St. Martin's, 1970. 131–54.

Natoli, Joseph, and Frederik L. Rusch, comps. *Psychocriticism: An Annotated Bibliography*. Westport: Greenwood, 1984.

Scott, Wilbur. *Five Approaches to Literary Criticism*. London: Collier-Macmillan, 1962. See the essays by Burke and Gorer as well as Scott's introduction to the section "The Psychological Approach: Literature in the Light of Psychological Theory."

Wellek, René, and Austin Warren. *Theory of Literature*. New York: Harcourt, 1942. See the chapter "Literature and Psychology" in pt. 3, "The Extrinsic Approach to the Study of Literature."

Wright, Elizabeth. "Modern Psychoanalytic Criticism." *Modern Literary Theory: A Comparative Introduction*. Ed. Ann Jefferson and David Robey. Totowa: Barnes, 1982. 113–33.

Freud, Lacan, and Their Influence

Basler, Roy P. *Sex, Symbolism, and Psychology in Literature*. New York: Octagon, 1975. See especially 13–19.

Clément, Catherine. *The Lives and Legends of Jacques Lacan*. Trans. Arthur Goldhammer. New York: Columbia UP, 1983.

Freud, Sigmund. *Introductory Lectures on Psycho-Analysis*. Trans. Joan Riviere. London: Allen, 1922.

Gallop, Jane. *Reading Lacan*. Ithaca: Cornell UP, 1985.

Hoffman, Frederick J. *Freudianism and the Literary Mind*. Baton Rouge: Louisiana State UP, 1945.

Hogan, Patrick Colm, and Lalita Pandit, eds. *Lacan and Criticism: Essays and Dialogue on Language, Structure, and the Unconscious*. Athens: U of Georgia P, 1990.

Kazin, Alfred. "Freud and His Consequences." *Contemporaries*. Boston: Little, 1962. 351–93.

Lacan, Jacques. *Écrits: A Selection*. Trans. Alan Sheridan. New York: Norton, 1977.

———. *Feminine Sexuality: Lacan and the école freudienne*. Ed. Juliet Mitchell and Jacqueline Rose. Trans. Rose. New York: Norton, 1982.

———. *The Four Fundamental Concepts of Psychoanalysis*. Trans. Alan Sheridan. London: Penguin, 1980.

Macey, David. *Lacan in Contexts*. New York: Verso, 1988.

Meisel, Perry, ed. *Freud: A Collection of Critical Essays*. Englewood Cliffs: Prentice, 1981.

Muller, John P., and William J. Richardson. *Lacan and Language: A Reader's Guide to "Écrits."* New York: International, 1982.

Porter, Laurence M. *"The Interpretation of Dreams": Freud's Theories Revisited*. Twayne's Masterwork Studies Series. Boston: G. K. Hall, 1986.

Reppen, Joseph, and Maurice Charney. *The Psychoanalytic Study of Literature*. Hillsdale: Analytic, 1985.

Schneiderman, Stuart. *Jacques Lacan: The Death of an Intellectual Hero*. Cambridge: Harvard UP, 1983.

———. *Returning to Freud: Clinical Psychoanalysis in the School of Lacan*. New Haven: Yale UP, 1980.

Selden, Raman. *A Reader's Guide to Contemporary Literary Theory*. 2nd ed. Lexington: U of Kentucky P, 1989. See "Jacques Lacan: Language and the Unconscious."

Sullivan, Ellie Ragland. *Jacques Lacan and the Philosophy of Psychoanalysis*. Champaign: U of Illinois P, 1986.

Sullivan, Ellie Ragland, and Mark Bracher, eds. *Lacan and the Subject of Language*. New York: Routledge, 1991.

Trilling, Lionel. "Art and Neurosis." *The Liberal Imagination*. New York: Scribner's, 1950. 160–80.

Wilden, Anthony. "Lacan and the Discourse of the Other." In Lacan, *Speech and Language in Psychoanalysis*. Trans. Wilden. Baltimore: Johns Hopkins UP, 1981. (Published as *The Language of the Self* in 1968.) 159–311.

Psychoanalysis, Feminism, and Literature

Chodorow, Nancy. *The Reproduction of Mothering: Psychoanalysis and the Sociology of Gender.* Berkeley: U of California P, 1978.

Gallop, Jane. *The Daughter's Seduction: Feminism and Psychoanalysis.* Ithaca: Cornell UP, 1982.

Garner, Shirley Nelson, Claire Kahane, and Madelon Sprengnether. *The (M)other Tongue: Essays in Feminist Psychoanalytic Interpretation.* Ithaca: Cornell UP, 1985.

Irigaray, Luce. *This Sex Which Is Not One.* Trans. Catherine Porter. Ithaca: Cornell UP, 1985.

———. *The Speculum of the Other Woman.* Trans. Gillian C. Gill. Ithaca: Cornell UP, 1985.

Jacobus, Mary. "Is There a Woman in This Text?" *New Literary History* 14 (1982): 117–41.

Kristeva, Julia. *The Kristeva Reader.* Ed. Toril Moi. New York: Columbia UP, 1986. See especially the selection from *Revolution in Poetic Language,* 89–136.

Mitchell, Juliet. *Psychoanalysis and Feminism.* New York: Random, 1974.

Mitchell, Juliet, and Jacqueline Rose. "Introduction I" and "Introduction II." Lacan, *Feminine Sexuality: Jacques Lacan and the école freudienne.* New York: Norton, 1985. 1–26, 27–57.

Sprengnether, Madelon. *The Spectral Mother: Freud, Feminism, and Psychoanalysis.* Ithaca: Cornell UP, 1990.

Psychological and Psychoanalytic Studies of Literature

Bettelheim, Bruno. *The Uses of Enchantment: The Meaning and Importance of Fairy Tales.* New York: Knopf, 1976. Although this book is about fairy tales instead of literary works written for publication, it offers model Freudian readings of well-known stories.

Crews, Frederick C. *Out of My System: Psychoanalysis, Ideology, and Critical Method.* New York: Oxford UP, 1975.

———. *Relations of Literary Study.* New York: MLA, 1967. See the chapter "Literature and Psychology."

Diehl, Joanne Feit. "Re-Reading *The Letter:* Hawthorne, the Fetish, and the (Family) Romance." *Nathaniel Hawthorne, "The Scarlet Letter."* Ed. Ross C Murfin. Case Studies in Contemporary Criticism Series. Ed. Ross C Murfin. Boston: Bedford–St. Martin's, 1991. 235–51.

Hallman, Ralph. *Psychology of Literature: A Study of Alienation and Tragedy.* New York: Philosophical Library, 1961.

Hartman, Geoffrey, ed. *Psychoanalysis and the Question of the Text.* Baltimore: Johns Hopkins UP, 1978. See especially the essays by Hartman, Johnson, Nelson, and Schwartz.

Hertz, Neil. *The End of the Line: Essays on Psychoanalysis and the Sublime.* New York: Columbia UP, 1985.

Holland, Norman N. *Dynamics of Literary Response.* New York: Oxford UP, 1968.

———. *Poems in Persons: An Introduction to the Psychoanalysis of Literature.* New York: Norton, 1973.

Kris, Ernest. *Psychoanalytic Explorations in Art.* New York: International, 1952.

Lucas, F. L. *Literature and Psychology.* London: Cassell, 1951.

Natoli, Joseph, ed. *Psychological Perspectives on Literature: Freudian Dissidents and Non-Freudians: A Casebook.* Hamden: Archon Books–Shoe String, 1984.

Phillips, William, ed. *Art and Psychoanalysis.* New York: Columbia UP, 1977.

Rogers, Robert. *A Psychoanalytic Study of the Double in Literature.* Detroit: Wayne State UP, 1970.

Skura, Meredith. *The Literary Use of the Psychoanalytic Process.* New Haven: Yale UP, 1981.

Strelka, Joseph P. *Literary Criticism and Psychology.* University Park: Pennsylvania State UP, 1976. See especially the essays by Lerner and Peckham.

Weiss, Daniel. *The Critic Agonistes: Psychology, Myth, and the Art of Fiction.* Ed. Eric Solomon and Stephen Arkin. Seattle: U of Washington P, 1985.

Lacanian Psychoanalytic Studies of Literature

Collings, David. "The Monster and the Imaginary Mother: A Lacanian Reading of *Frankenstein.*" *Mary Shelley, "Frankenstein."* Ed. Johanna M. Smith. Case Studies in Contemporary Criticism Series. Ed. Ross C Murfin. Boston: Bedford–St. Martin's, 1992. 245–58.

Davis, Robert Con, ed. *The Fictional Father: Lacanian Readings of the Text.* Amherst: U of Massachusetts P, 1981.

———. "Lacan and Narration." *Modern Language Notes* 5 (1983): 843–1063.

Felman, Shoshana, ed. *Literature and Psychoanalysis: The Question of Reading: Otherwise.* Baltimore: Johns Hopkins UP, 1982.

————, ed. *Jacques Lacan and the Adventure of Insight: Psychoanalysis in Contemporary Culture.* Cambridge: Harvard UP, 1987.

Froula, Christine. "When Eve Reads Milton: Undoing the Canonical Economy." *Canons.* Ed. Robert von Hallberg. Chicago: U of Chicago P, 1984. 149–75.

Homans, Margaret. *Bearing the Word: Language and Female Experience in Nineteenth-Century Women's Writing.* Chicago: U of Chicago P, 1986.

Muller, John P., and William J. Richardson, eds. *The Purloined Poe: Lacan, Derrida, and Psychoanalytic Reading.* Baltimore: Johns Hopkins UP, 1988. Includes Lacan's seminar on Poe's "The Purloined Letter."

Psychoanalytic Criticism of *Great Expectations*

Connor, Steven. *"Great Expectations." Charles Dickens.* Rereading Literature. Oxford: Basil Blackwell, 1985. 109–44.

Sadoff, Dianne F. "The Dead Father." *Monsters of Affection: Dickens, Eliot, and Brontë on Fatherhood.* Baltimore: Johns Hopkins UP, 1982. 22–38.

Thomas, Ronald R. "Capitalizing the Unconscious: Nineteenth-Century Fictional Autobiography." *Dreams of Authority: Freud and the Fictions of the Unconscious.* Ithaca: Cornell UP, 1990. 137–91.

A PSYCHOANALYTIC PERSPECTIVE

Introduction

Great Expectations, with its frequently hallucinatory effects and its focus on an individual mind, is a text that invites psychoanalytic readings; and, not surprisingly, the novel has often been the subject of such analysis. Julian Moynahan's classic essay "The Hero's Guilt: The Case of *Great Expectations*" (1960) takes Pip as its "case" to uncover the mechanisms by which he both expresses and represses his desires for social advancement and romantic fulfillment. In a chapter from *Reading for the Plot* (1984), Peter Brooks offers a more contemporary version of literary-critical psychoanalysis by analyzing, not the author or the characters or the readers of *Great Expectations*, but the text itself as a psychic structure. His goal is to reveal "how textual dynamics work" (90), and he does so by positing an analogical equivalence be-tween the "functioning of the psychic apparatus [of an individual] and the functioning of the text." In this relation Brooks finds anew "the possibility of a psychoanalytic criticism" (112).

Central to this investigation is Freud's concept of the relation be-tween the conscious and the unconscious, the ego and the id. If a novel is structured like a psyche, it has conscious or manifest plots and unconscious or repressed plots. But far more important to Brooks than this static, spatial model of psychic life is the dynamic, temporal model that he finds in Freud's *Beyond the Pleasure Principle* (1920). In the chapter that precedes Brooks's analysis of *Great Expectations*, he reads this relatively late and highly speculative work by Freud "as a text con-cerning textuality" (112). Interestingly, Brooks, whose analysis has a decidedly deconstructive turn, casts Freud as a similarly inclined thinker who "feels obliged to deconstruct the illusion of a human drive toward perfection, an impulsion forward and upward" (105).

According to Brooks, Freud substitutes for this illusion a "master-plot" involving the complex and sometimes apparently self-contradic-tory relations between the pleasure principle, the life or sexual instinct, and the death instinct. In Freud's words, the basic human drive is "to return to the quiescence of the inorganic world"— *"the aim of all life is death"* (qtd. at 107, 102). Death, in this scheme, is seen as the same state of inanimate existence as that from which life issues; death is sim-ply the organism's return to its beginnings. What Freud calls the plea-sure principle—the tendency to relieve tension, to reduce pain, to achieve peace—both moves toward and delays the achievement of the goal of the death instinct. This model of psychic life also depends on what Freud labels the "repetition compulsion," the need to return to past traumas and to induce the tensions that the pleasure principle seeks to relieve. Only when there have been sufficient opportunities for the repetition compulsion to be satisfied can the "organism" reach the "right" and "proper" end it has been seeking (107).

In this masterplot Brooks finds a powerful explanatory model for the functioning of plot in narrative. Plots begin and end in the nonnarratable, and they have a kind of death instinct that impels them to seek the end that is at one with their beginning. The "shortest dis-tance" between those two points would be "the straight line . . . the collapse of one into the other, of life into immediate death" (104). Plot, however, "stands as a kind of divergence or deviance, a post-ponement in the discharge which leads back to the inanimate" (103), and the main form of that postponement is repetition, the return of the repressed and the return to the past. As Brooks sums up his approach:

> We emerge from reading *Beyond the Pleasure Principle* with a dynamic model that structures ends (death, quiescence, nonnarratability) against beginnings (Eros, stimulation into tension, the desire of narrative) in a manner that necessitates the middle as detour, as struggle toward the end under the compulsion of imposed delay, as arabesque in the dilatory space of the text. The model proposes that we live in order to die, hence that the intentionality of plot lies in its orientation toward the end even while the end must be achieved only through detour. (107–08)

Just as Brooks credits Freud with deconstructing the "illusion" of the drive toward perfection, Brooks's model allows him to deconstruct the myth of narrative as essentially progressive, a myth in which plot is presumed to reach an end that is better, more stable, more satisfying (even when tragically so) than its beginning. Rather, Brooks's conception of plot is regressive: it continues to return to the past so that it can reach an end that is actually its beginning. For this movement Brooks finds an appropriate emblem in the name of the hero of *Great Expectations:* the name that Pip gives himself, a palindrome, is the same whether read backward or forward. (The same is true, of course, of his family name, Pirrip.)

To demonstrate the pertinence of Freud's dynamic model to *Great Expectations*, Brooks suggests that two "'official' or censoring" plots—the story of education and the fairy tale of Satis House— "stand over" two unconscious or "repressed" plots—the story of criminality and the witch tale of Satis House. Brooks shows how these plots are put into play in *Great Expectations* through the complex mechanism of repetition, which both looks back to the past and moves the plot forward into the future. He sees the novel as "exemplary" of his theory because it is dominated by "repetition and working through, the . . . effort to master painful material from the insistent past." *Great Expectations*, moreover, constantly probes the ways in which the problems of "identity, self-consciousness, naming, and language" participate in the movements of repetition and return.

Like the other readings of *Great Expectations* collected in this edition, Brooks's essay points to negation and frustration as the hallmarks of the novel. Pip, who fails in his attempt to make his past a part of his present, tries to discover for Estella a past that he can reveal to her, but he fails again. Plots and plotting succeed no better than Pip does: "If the chosen plots turn out to be erroneous, unauthorized, self-delusive, the deep plots when brought to light turn out to be criminally tainted, deviant, and thus unusable." Such outcomes, however, prove the necessity of the deviance that constitutes plot: without its delays and diversions, the end and the beginning would already be one. At the denouement of *Great Expectations*, Magwitch, whose relation to Pip provides, according to Brooks, "the central energy of the text," dies; and Pip is "cured" of plot and demonstrates at least his understanding of its limitations through his "acceptance of a continuing existence without plot, as celibate clerk for Clarrikers." For Brooks, such acceptance is perhaps the height of wisdom in a world devoid of "divine masterplots," a world whose life and art are therefore illuminated by Freud's "masterplot."

In his introduction to his discussion of *Great Expectations*, Peter Brooks reiterates the definition of plot that he has offered in his preface to *Reading for the Plot:*

> We have defined plot, for our purposes, as a structuring operation deployed by narratives, or activated in the reading of narratives: as the logic and syntax of those meanings that develop only through sequence and succession. . . . The range of meanings assigned to the word plot in the dictionary includes the sense of the scheme or machination to the accomplishment of some end—the sense apparently derived from the "contamination" of the French *complot.*

He goes on to note that his preceding analysis has "suggested that nineteenth-century novels regularly conceive plot as *complot:* they are structured by a plotting for and toward something, a machination of desire" (113). He then turns to Dickens's novel to demonstrate both the interpretive power of Freud's "masterplot" and the significance of plot as *complot.*

Janice Carlisle

Works Cited

Brooks, Peter. *Reading for the Plot: Design and Intention in Narrative.* New York: Vintage, 1984.

Moynahan, Julian. "The Hero's Guilt: The Case of *Great Expectations.*" *Essays in Criticism* 10 (1960): 60–79. Rpt. in Cotsell, Michael, ed. *Critical Essays on Charles Dickens's* Great Expectations. Boston: G. K. Hall, 1990. 73–87.

PETER BROOKS

Repetition, Repression, and Return: The Plotting of *Great Expectations*

. . . *Great Expectations* is a novel that stands firmly within the golden age of plot, one that is centrally, unashamedly, and—at first glance—unsuspiciously concerned with issues of plot and plotting. It is indeed plotting, as an activity, as a dynamic machination, that may provide our best way into the reading of a fully achieved plot. And this activity of plotting may be most readily discernible in a retrospective first-person narrative. When we ask the questions, How do we find significant plots for our lives? How do we make life narratable? we find that the answers are most clearly dramatized in narratives of an autobiographical cast, since these cannot evade an explicit concern with problems of closure, authority, and narratability. As Sartre argued, autobiographical narration must necessarily be "obituary"—must in any event explicitly show margins outside the narratable, leftover spaces which allow the narrating *I* to objectify and look back at the narrated *I*, and to see the plotted middle as shaped by and as shaping its margins. . . . *Great Expectations* . . . gives in the highest degree the impression that its central meanings depend on the workings-out of its plot. For in this fictional pseudo-autobiography, Dickens adopts the revealing strategy of taking a "life" and creating the demarcations of a "plot" within it. The novel will indeed be concerned with finding a plot and losing it, with the precipitations of the sense of plottedness around its hero, and his eventual "cure" from plot. The novel images in its structure the kind of structuring operation of reading that plot is.

I

Great Expectations is exemplary for a discourse on plot in many respects, not least of all for its beginning. For what the novel chooses to present at its outset is precisely the search for a beginning. As in so many nineteenth-century novels, the hero is an orphan, thus undetermined by any visible inheritance, apparently unauthored. . . . There may be sociological and sentimental reasons to account for the high incidence of orphans in the nineteenth-century novel, but clearly the parentless protagonist frees an author from struggle with preexisting authorities, allowing him to create afresh all the determinants of plot within his text. He thus profits from what Gide called the "lawlessness" of the novel by starting with an undefined, rule-free character and then bringing the law to bear upon him—creating the rules—as the text proceeds. With Pip, Dickens begins as it were with a life that is for the moment precedent to plot, and indeed necessarily in search of plot. Pip when we first see him is himself in search of the "authority"—the word stands in the second paragraph of the novel— that would define and justify—authorize—the plot of his ensuing life.

The "authority" to which Pip refers here is that of the tombstone which bears the names of his dead parents, the names that have already been displaced, condensed, and superseded in the first paragraph, where Pip describes how his "infant tongue" (literally, a speechless tongue: a catachresis that points to a moment of emergence, of entry into language) could only make of the name, Philip Pirrip, left to him by the dead parents, the monosyllabic Pip. "So, I called myself Pip, and came to be called Pip" (23). This originating moment of Pip's narration and his narrative is a self-naming that already subverts whatever authority could be found in the text of the tombstones. The process of reading that text is described by Pip the narrator as "unreasonable," in that it interprets the appearance of the lost father and mother from the shape of the letters of their names. The tracing of the name—which he has already distorted in its application to self—involves a misguided attempt to remotivate the graphic symbol, to make it directly mimetic, mimetic specifically of origin. Loss of origin, misreading, and the problematic of identity are bound up here in ways we will further explore later on. The question of reading and writing—of learning to compose and to decipher texts—is persistently thematized in the novel.[1]

The decipherment of the tombstone text as confirmation of loss of origin—as unauthorization—is here at the start of the novel the prelude to Pip's *cogito*, the moment in which his consciousness seizes his existence as other, alien, forlorn:

> My first most vivid and broad impression of the identity of things, seems to me to have been gained on a memorable raw afternoon towards evening. At such a time I found out for certain, that this bleak place overgrown with nettles was the churchyard; and that Philip Pirrip, late of this parish, and also Georgiana wife of the above, were dead and buried . . . and that the small bundle of shivers growing afraid of it all and beginning to cry, was Pip. (24)

---

[1]On the theme of reading in the novel, see Max Byrd, " 'Reading' in *Great Expectations*."

The repeated verbs of existence—"was" and "were"—perform an elementary phenomenology of Pip's world, locating its irreducible objects and leading finally to the individual subject as other, as aware of his existence through the emotion of fear, fear that then appears as the origin of voice, or articulated sound, as Pip begins to cry: a cry that is immediately censored by the command of the convict Magwitch, the father-to-be, the fearful intrusive figure of future authorship who will demand of Pip: "Give us your name."

The scenario is richly suggestive of the problem of identity, self-consciousness, naming, and language that will accompany Pip throughout the novel, and points to the original decentering of the subject in regard to himself. For purposes of my study of plot, it is important to note how this beginning establishes Pip as an existence without a plot, at the very moment of occurrence of that event which will prove to be decisive for the plotting of his existence, as he will discover only two-thirds of the way through the novel. Alien, unauthorized, self-named, at the point of entry into the language code and the social systems it implies, Pip will in the first part of the novel be in search of a plot, and the novel will recount the gradual precipitation of a sense of plot around him, the creation of portents of direction and intention.

Schematically, we can identify four lines of plot that begin to crystallize around the young Pip, the Pip of Part One, before the arrival of his "Expectations":

1. Communion with the convict/criminal deviance.
2. Naterally wicious/bringing up by hand.
3. The dream of Satis House/the fairy tale.
4. The nightmare of Satis House/the witch tale.

These plots, we will see in a moment, are paired as follows: $2/1 = 3/4$. That is, there is in each case an "official" and censoring plot [2 or 3] standing over a "repressed" plot [1 or 4]. In terms of Pip's own choices, we could rewrite the formula: $3/4/2/1$, to show (in accordance with one of Freud's favorite models) the archaeological layering of strata of repressed material.[2] When the Expectations are announced by Jaggers at the end of part one, they will apparently coincide with Pip's choices

[2]On the archaeological model in Freud, see in particular the use he makes of Pompeii in "Delusions and Dreams in Jensen's *Gradiva*" [*Der Wahn und die Träume in W. Jensens* Gradiva] (1907), in *The Standard Edition of the Complete Psychological Works of Sigmund Freud,* 9: 3–95.

("My dream was out; my wild fancy was surpassed by sober reality" [141]), and will thus appear to take care of the question of plot. But this will be so only on the level of official plots; the Expectations will in fact only mask further the problem of the repressed plots.

I choose the term "communion" for the first plot because its characteristic symbolic gesture is Pip's pity for the convict as he swallows the food Pip has brought him, a moment of sympathetic identification which focuses a series of suggestive sympathies and identifications with the outlaw: the bread and butter that Pip puts down his leg, which makes him walk like the chained convict; Mrs. Joe's belief that he is on his way to the Hulks; Pip's flight from the Christmas dinner table into the arms of a soldier holding out handcuffs, to give a few examples. Pip is concerned to assure "his" convict that he is not responsible for his recapture, a point he conveys in a mute exchange of glances which the convict understands and which leads him to make a public statement in exoneration of Pip, taking responsibility for stealing the food. This in turn provokes an overt statement of community with the outlaw, which comes from Joe: "We don't know what you have done, but we wouldn't have you starved to death for it, poor miserable fellow-creatur.—Would us, Pip?" (56).

The fellowship with the convict here stated by Joe will remain with Pip, but in a state of repression, as what he will later call "that spell of my childhood" (126)—an unavowable memory. It finds its official, adult, repressive version in the conviction—shared by all the adults in Pip's life, with the exception of the childlike Joe—that children are naturally depraved and need to be corrected, kept in line with the Tickler, brought up by hand lest their natural willfulness assert itself in plots that are deviant, transgressive. Pumblechook and the Hubbles, in their Christmas dinner dialogue, give the theme a choric statement (43). The "nateral wiciousness" of children legitimates communion with the outlaw, but legitimates it as that which must be repressed, forced into other plots—including, as we shall see, "binding" Pip as an apprentice.

The dream of Satis House is properly a daydream, in which "His Majesty, the Ego" pleasures himself with the phantasy of social ascension and gentility. Miss Havisham is made to play the role of Fairy Godmother, her crutch become a magic wand, explicitly evoked twice near the close of Part One.[3] This plot has adult sanction; its first ex-

---

[3]See *Great Expectations,* 157–58. Miss Havisham is thus seemingly cast in the role of the "Donor," who provides the hero with a magical agent, one of the seven *dramatis personae* of the fairy tale identified by Vladimir Propp in *The Morphology of the Folktale.*

pression comes from Pumblechook and Mrs. Joe when they surmise
that Miss Havisham intends to "do something" for Pip, and Pip comes
to believe in it, so that when the "Expectations" arrive he accepts
them as the logical fulfillment of the daydream, of his "longings." Yet
to identify Satis House with the daydream is to perform a repression of
all else that Satis House suggests and represents—all that clusters
around the central emblem of the rotting bride cake and its crawling
things. The craziness and morbidity of Satis House repose on desire
fixated, become fetishistic and sadistic, on a deviated eroticism that has
literally shut out the light, stopped the clocks, and made the forward
movement of plot impossible. Satis House, as the circular journeys of
the wheelchair to the rhythm of the blacksmith's song "Old Clem"
may best suggest, constitutes repetition without variation, pure reproduction, a collapsed metonymy where cause and effect have become
identical, the same-as-same. It is significant that when Pip returns from
his first visit to Satis House, he responds to the interrogations of Pumblechook and Mrs. Joe with an elaborate lie—the story of the coach,
the flags, the dogs fighting for "weal cutlets" from a silver basket—a
phantasy that we can read as his response to what he calls a "smart
without a name, that needed counteraction" (75). All the attempts to
read Satis House as a text speaking of gentility and social ascension
may be subverted from the outset, in the passage that describes Pip's
first impression of Miss Havisham: "It was not in the first moments
that I saw all these things. . . . But, I saw that everything within my
view which ought to be white, had been white. . . . Once, I had been
taken to see some ghastly wax-work at the Fair. . . . Now, waxwork
and skeleton seemed to have dark eyes that moved. . . ." (71). The
passage records the formation of a memory trace from a moment of
unmastered horror, itself formed in repetition of moments of past visual impression, a trace that forces its way through the mind without
being grasped by consciousness and is refused outlet in a cry. Much
later in the novel, Pip—and also Miss Havisham herself—will have to
deal with the return of this repressed.

We have, then, a quadripartite scheme of plots, organized into two
pairs, each with an "official" plot, or interpretation of plot, standing
over a repressed plot. The scheme may lead us in the first instance to
reflect on the place of repression as one of the large "orders" of the
novel. Repression plays a dominant role in the theme of education
which is so important to the novel, from Mrs. Joe's bringing up by
hand, through Mr. Wopsle's great-aunt's schoolroom, to Mr. Pocket's
career as a "grinder" of dull blades (while his own children meanwhile

are "tumbling up"). Bringing up by hand in turn suggests Jaggers's hands, representation of accusation and the law, which in turn suggest all the instances of censorship in the name of high authorities evoked from the first scene of the novel onward: censorship is repression in the name of the Law.[4] Jaggers's sinister hand-washings point to the omnipresent taint of Newgate, which echoes the earlier presence of the Hulks, to which Mrs. Joe verbally assigns Pip. Then there is the moment when Pip is "bound" as apprentice blacksmith before the magistrates, in a scene of such repressive appearance that a well-meaning philanthropist is moved to hand Pip a pamphlet entitled *To Be Read in My Cell*. There is a constant association of education, repression, the threat of prison, criminality, the fear of deviance. We might note in passing Dickens's capacity to literalize the metaphors of education—"bringing up by hand," "grinding"—in a manner that subverts the order that ought to assure their figural validity. The particularly sinister version of the *Bildungsroman* presented by *Great Expectations* derives in some measure from the literalization of metaphors pertaining to education and upbringing. Societal repression and censorship are, of course, reinforced by Pip's own, his internalization of the law and the denial of what he calls the "old taint" of his association with the criminal. The whole theme of gentility, as represented by the Finches of the Grove, for instance, or the punishment of Trabb's boy, consistently suggests an aggressivity based on denial. One could reflect here on the splendid name of Pip's superfluous valet: the Avenger.

The way in which the Expectations are instituted, in seeming realization of the Satis House dream, comprehends "bringing up by hand" (the other official plot) in that it includes the disciplines necessary to gentility: grinding with Mr. Pocket, lessons in manners from Herbert, learning to spend one's time and money in appropriate gentlemanly pursuits. There is in this manner a blurring of plot lines, useful to the processes of wish fulfillment in that education and indeed repression itself can be interpreted as agencies necessary to the pursuit of the dream. Realization of the dream permits acceptance of society's interpretations, and in fact requires the abandonment of any effort at personal interpretation: Pip is now enjoined from seeking to know more about the intentions of his donor, disallowed the role of detec-

---

[4]On the role of the law as one of the formal orders of the novel, see Moshe Ron, "Autobiographical Narration and Formal Closure in *Great Expectations*." The importance of criminality in Dickens has, of course, been noted by many critics, including Edmund Wilson in his seminal essay "Dickens: The Two Scrooges" in *The Wound and the Bow*.

tive which so much animates him in Part Three of the novel—when the Expectations have proved false—and is already incipiently present in Part One.

Taking our terminology from the scene where Pip is bound as apprentice, we may consider that education and repression operate in the novel as one form of "binding": official ways of channeling and tying up the mobile energies of life. It is notable that after he has become apprenticed to Joe, Pip goes through a stage of purely iterative existence—presented in Chapter 14—where the direction and movement of plot appear to be finished, where all life's "interest and romance" appear shut out as by a "thick curtain," time reduced to repetitive duration. Conversely, when the Expectations have arrived, Miss Havisham is apparently identified as the fairy-tale donor, and the Satis House plot appears securely bound, Pip need only wait for the next stage of the plot to become manifest. Yet it is clear that for the reader neither binding as an apprentice (the first accomplishment of an upbringing by hand) nor the tying up of Satis House as a fairy-tale plot constitutes valid and adequate means of dealing with and disposing of the communion with the convict and the nightmare of Satis House. The energy released in the text by its liminary "primal scene"—in the graveyard—and by the early visits to Satis House, creating that "smart without a name," simply is not and cannot be bound by the bindings of the official, repressive plots. As readers we know that there has been created in the text an intensive level of energy that cannot be discharged through these official plots.

In fact, the text has been working simultaneously to bind these disavowed energies in other ways, ways over which Pip's ego, and the societal superego, have no control, and of which they have no knowledge, through repetitions that, for the reader, prepare an inevitable return of the repressed. Most striking are the periodic fragmentary returns of the convict-communion material: the leg iron used to bludgeon Mrs. Joe, guns firing from the Hulks to signal further escapes, and especially the reappearance of Joe's file, the dramatic stage property used by Magwitch's emissary in a "proceeding in dumb show . . . pointedly addressed at me." His stirring and tasting his rum and water "pointedly at" Pip suggests the establishment of an aim (Pip calls his proceeding "a shot"), a direction, an intention in Pip's life: the first covert announcement of another plot which will come to govern Pip's life, but of course misinterpreted as to its true aim. With the nightmare energies of Satis House, binding may be at work in those repetitive journeys around the rotting bridal cake, suggestive of the reproduction or working through of the traumatic neurotic whose affects remain fixed on the past, on the traumatic moment that never can be mastered. For Miss Havisham herself, these energies can never be plotted to effective discharge; and we will have occasion to doubt whether they are ever fully bound for Pip as well. The compulsive reproductive repetition that characterizes every detail of Satis House lets us perceive how the returns of the convict-communion suggest a more significant working through of an unmastered past, a repetition that can alter the form of the repeated. In both instances—but ultimately with different results—the progressive, educative plots, the plots of repression and social advancement, are threatened by a repetitive process obscurely going on underneath and beyond them. We sense that forward progress will have to recover markings from the beginning through a dialectic of return.

II

In my references to the work of repetition as the binding of energies, I have been implicitly assuming that one can make a transfer from the model of psychic functioning proposed in *Beyond the Pleasure Principle* to the literary text, an assumption that no doubt can never be "proved" and must essentially find its justification in the illumination it can bring to texts. . . . Texts represent themselves as inhabited by energies, which are ultimately images of desire, and correspond to the arousals, expectations, doubts, suspense, reversals, revaluations, disappointments, embarrassments, fulfillments, and even the incoherences animated by reading. If we can accept the idea of a textual energetics, we can see that in any well-plotted novel the energies released and aroused in the text, especially in its early moments, will not be lost: the text is a kind of thermodynamic plenum, obeying the law of the conservation of energy (as well, no doubt, as the law of entropy). Repetition is clearly a major operative principle of the system, shaping energy, giving it perceptible form, form that the text and the reader can work with in the construction of thematic wholes and narrative orders. Repetition conceived as binding, the creation of cohesion . . . may allow us to see how the text and the reader put energy into forms where it can be mastered, both by the logics set in motion by the plot, and by interpretive effort.

Repetition is, of course, a complex phenomenon, and one that has its history of commentary in philosophical as well as psychoanalytic thought. Is repetition sameness or difference? To repeat evidently implies resemblance, yet can we speak of resemblance unless there is difference? Without difference, repetition would be identity, which would not usually appear to be the case, if only because the chronological context of the repeated occurrence differs from that of the "original" occurrence (the "original" is thus a concept that repetition puts into question). In this sense, repetition always includes the idea of variation in time, and may ever be potentially a progressive act. As Kierkegaard writes near the beginning of *Repetition*, "Repetition and recollection are the same movement, only in opposite directions; for what is recollected has been, is repeated backwards, whereas repetition properly is repeated forwards."[5] Freud . . . considers repetition to be a form of recollection, brought into play when conscious mental rememoration has been blocked by repression. Lacan argues that Freud distinguishes between repeating (*wiederholen*) and reproducing (*reproduzieren*): reproduction would be the full reliving, of the original traumatic scene, for instance, that Freud aimed at early in his career, when he still believed in "catharsis"; whereas repetition always takes place in the realm of the symbolic—in the transference, in language—where the affects and figures of the past are confronted in symbolic form.[6] We can thus perhaps say that for Freud repetition is a symbolic enactment referring back to unconscious determinants, progressive in that it belongs to the forward thrust of desire and is known by way of desire's workings in the signifying chain, but regressive in its points of reference.

We cannot and should not attempt to reduce and resolve the ambiguities of repetition since they are indeed inherent to our experience of repetition, part of what creates its "uncanny" effect and allows us to think about the intractable problem of temporal form, in our lives and in our fictions. In *Great Expectations*, the repetitions associated with Satis House, particularly as played out by Miss Havisham herself, suggest the reproductive in that they aim to restore in all its detail the traumatic moment—recorded by the clocks stopped at twenty minutes to nine—when erotic wishes were abruptly foreclosed by Compeyson's rupture of faith. On the other hand, the repetitions of the convict material experienced by Pip all imply something to

[5]Søren Kierkegaard, *Repetition*, 3–4. For other discussions of repetition in literature, see Gilles Deleuze, *Logique du sens*, and J. Hillis Miller, *Fiction and Repetition*.

[6]See Freud, "The Dynamics of the Transference" and "Remembering, Repeating and Working Through," in *Standard Edition*, 12: 99–108 and 12: 147–56; and Jacques Lacan, *Le Séminaire, Livre XI: Les Quatre Concepts fondamentaux de la psychanalyse*, 49–50.

come—something to come that, as we shall see, will take him back, painfully, to the primal scene, yet take him back in the context of difference. Repetition in the text is a return, a calling back or a turning back. And as I suggested earlier, repetitions are thus both returns to and returns of: for instance, returns to origins and returns of the repressed, moving us forward in Pip's journey toward elucidation, disillusion, and maturity by taking us back, as if in obsessive reminder that we cannot really move ahead until we have understood that still enigmatic past, yet ever pushing us forward, since revelation, tied to the past, belongs to the future.

The novelistic middle, which is perhaps the most difficult of Aristotle's "parts" of a plot to talk about, is in this case notably characterized by the return. Quite literally: it is Pip's repeated returns from London to his home town that constitute the organizing device of the whole of the London period, the time of the Expectations and their aftermath. Pip's returns are always ostensibly undertaken to make reparation to the neglected Joe, an intention never realized; and always implicitly an attempt to discover the intentions of the putative donor in Satis House, to bring her plot to completion. Yet the returns also always bring his regression, in Satis House, to the status of the "coarse and common boy" (224) whose social ascension is hallucinatorily denied, his return to the nightmare of unprogressive repetition; and, too, a revival of the repressed convict association, the return of the childhood spell. Each return suggests that Pip's official plots, which seem to speak of progress, ascent, and the satisfaction of desire, are in fact subject to a process of repetition of the yet unmastered past, the true determinant of his life's direction.

The pattern of the return is established in Pip's first journey back from London, in Chapter 28. His decision to visit Joe is quickly thrown into the shade by the presence on the stagecoach of two convicts, one of whom Pip recognizes as the man of the file and the rum and water, Magwitch's emissary. There is a renewed juxtaposition of official, genteel judgment on the convicts, voiced by Herbert Pocket—"What a vile and degraded spectacle"—and Pip's inward avowal that he feels sympathy for their alienation. On the roof of the coach, seated in front of the convicts, Pip dozes off while pondering whether he ought to restore the two one-pound notes that the convict of the file had passed him so many years before. Upon regaining consciousness, the first two words he hears, continuing his dream thoughts, are: "Two one-pound notes." There follows the convict's account of his embassy from "Pip's convict" to the boy who had saved him. Although Pip is certain that the convict cannot recognize him, so changed in age, circumstance, and even name (since Herbert Pocket calls him "Handel"), the dreamlike experience forces a kind of recognition of a forgotten self, refound in fear and pain: "I could not have said what I was afraid of. . . . I am confident that it took no distinctness of shape, and that it was the revival for a few minutes of the terror of childhood" (220). The return to origins has led to the return of the repressed, and vice versa. Repetition as return becomes a reproduction and reenactment of infantile experience: not simply a recall of the primal moment, but a reliving of its pain and terror, suggesting the impossibility of escape from the originating scenarios of childhood, the condemnation forever to replay them.

This first example may stand for the other returns of the novel's middle, which all follow the same pattern, which all double return to with return of and show Pip's ostensible progress in the world to be subverted by the irradicable presence of the convict-communion and the Satis House nightmare. It is notable that toward the end of the middle—as the novel's denouement approaches—there is an acceleration in the rhythm of these returns, as if to affirm that all the clues to Pip's future, the forward movement of his plot, in fact lie in the past. Repetition as return speaks as a textual version of the death instinct, plotting the text, beyond the seeming dominance of the pleasure principle, toward its proper end, imaging this end as necessarily a time before the beginning. In the moment of crisis before the climax of the novel's action, Pip is summoned back to the marshes associated with his infancy to face extinction at the hands of Orlick—who has throughout the novel acted the role of Pip's "bad double," a hateful and sadistic version of the hero—in a threatened short-circuit of the text, as Pip indicates when he thinks how he will be misunderstood by others if he dies prematurely, without explanation: "Misremembered after death . . . despised by unborn generations" (388). Released from this threat, Pip attempts to escape from England, but even this voyage out to another land and another life leads him back: the climax of Magwitch's discovery and recapture are played out in the Thames estuary, where "it was like my own marsh country, flat and monotonous, and with a dim horizon" (399). We are back in the horizontal perspectives and muddy tidal flats that are so much a part of our perception of the childhood Pip.

But before speaking further of resolutions, I must say a word about the novel's great "recognition scene," the moment at which the latent becomes manifest, the repressed convict plot is forcibly brought to consciousness, a scene that decisively reenacts both a return of the repressed and a return to the primal moment of childhood. The recognition scene comes in Chapter 39, and it is preceded by two curious paragraphs at the end of Chapter 38 in which Pip as narrator suggests that the pages he has just written, concerning his frustrated courtship of Estella, constitute, on the plane of narration itself, a last binding of that plot in its overt version, as a plot of romance, and that now he must move on to a deeper level of plot—reaching further back— which subsumes as it subverts all the other plots of the novel: "All the work, near and afar, that tended to the end had been accomplished." That this long-range plot is presented as analogous to "the Eastern story" in which a heavy slab of stone is carved out and fitted into the roof in order that it may fall on "the bed of state in the flush of conquest" seems in coded fashion to suggest punishment for erotic transgression, which we may want to read as return of the nightmare plot of Satis House, forcing its way through the fairy tale, speaking of the perverse, sadistic eroticism that Pip has covered over with his erotic object choice—Estella, who in fact represents the wrong choice of plot and another danger of short-circuit. To anticipate later revelations, we should note that Estella will turn out to be approximately Pip's sister—natural daughter of Magwitch as he is Magwitch's adoptive son—which lends force to the idea that she, like so many Romantic maidens, is marked by the interdict, as well as the seduction, of incest, which, as the perfect androgynous coupling, is precisely the short-circuit of desire.[7]

The scene of Magwitch's return operates for Pip as a painful forcing through of layers of repression, an analogue of analytic work, compelling Pip to recognize that what he calls "that chance encounter of long ago" is no chance, and cannot be assigned to the buried past but must be repeated, reenacted, worked through in the present. The scene replays numerous details of their earlier encounter, and the central moment of recognition comes as a reenactment and revival of the novel's primal scene, played in dumb show, a mute text which the more effectively stages recognition as a process of return to the in-

---

[7]The pattern of the incestuous couple, where the implication of the brother-sister relation serves as both attraction and prohibition, has been noted by several critics. See especially Harry Stone, "The Love Pattern in Dickens' Novels," and Albert J. Guerard, *The Triumph of the Novel*, 70. *Great Expectations* gives particular weight to the figure of the father as source of the law: Magwitch, assuming in different registers the role of father both to Estella and to Pip, becomes not a figure of authority so much as a principle of interdiction, of prohibition.

escapable past: "Even yet, I could not recal a single feature, but I knew him! . . . No need to take a file from his pocket and show it to me; no need to take the handkerchief from his neck. . . . I knew him before he gave me one of those aids" (294). The preterition on which the passage is constructed—"no need . . . no need"—marks the gradual retrieval of the past as its involuntary repetition within the present. The repetition takes place—as Magwitch's effective use of indicative signs may suggest—in the mode of the symbolic, offering a persuasive instance of Freud's conception of repetition as a form of recollection brought into action by repression and resistance to its removal. It becomes clear that the necessity for Pip to repeat and work through everything associated with his original communion with Magwitch is a factor of his "forgetting" this communion: a forgetting that is merely conscious. The reader has undergone a similar process through textual repetition and return, one that in his case has had the function of not permitting him to forget.

The scene of Magwitch's return is an important one for any study of plot since it demonstrates so well how such a novelist as Dickens can make plotting the central vehicle and armature of meaning in the narrative text. All the issues raised in the novel—social, ethical, interpretive—are here simultaneously brought to climax through the peripety of the plot. Exposure of the "true" plot of Pip's life brings with it instantaneous consequences for all the other "codes" of the novel, as he recognizes with the statement, "All the truth of my position came *flashing* on me; and its disappointments, dangers, disgraces, consequences of all kinds" (297, my italics). The return of the repressed—the repressed as knowledge of the self's other story, the true history of its misapprehended desire—forces a total revision of the subject's relation to the orders within which it constitutes meaning.

Magwitch poses unanswerable questions, about the origins of Pip's property and the means of his social ascent, which force home to Pip that he has covered over a radical lack of original authority. Like Oedipus—who cannot answer Tiresias's final challenge: Who are your parents?—Pip does not know where he stands. The result has been the intrusion of an aberrant, contingent authorship—Magwitch's—in the story of the self. Education and training in gentility turn out to be merely an agency in the repression of the determinative convict plot. Likewise, the daydream/fairy tale of Satis House stands revealed as a repression, or perhaps a "secondary revision," of the nightmare. That it should be the criminally deviant, transgressive plot that is shown to have priority over all the others stands within the logic of the model derived from *Beyond the Pleasure Principle*, since it is precisely this plot that most markedly constitutes the detour from inorganic quiescence: the arabesque of the narratable. One could almost derive a narratological law here: the true plot will be the most deviant. We might be tempted to see this deviant arabesque as gratuitous, the figure of "pure narration." Yet we are obliged to remotivate it, for the return of the repressed shows that the story Pip would tell about himself has all along been undermined and rewritten by the more complex history of unconscious desire, unavailable to the conscious subject but at work in the text. Pip has in fact misread the plot of his life.

III

The misreading of plots and the question of authority bring us back to the question of reading with which the novel began. Pip's initial attempt to decipher his parents' appearance and character from the letters traced on their tombstones has been characterized as "childish" and "unreasonable." Pip's decipherment in fact appears as an attempt to motivate the arbitrary sign, to interpret signs as if they were mimetic and thus naturally tied to the object for which they stand. Deriving from the shape of the letters on the tombstones that his father "was a square, stout, dark man, with curly hair," and that his mother was "freckled and sickly," for all its literal fidelity to the graphic trace, constitutes a dangerously figural reading, a metaphorical process unaware of itself, the making of a fiction unaware of its status as fiction making. Pip is here claiming natural authority for what is in fact conventional, arbitrary, dependent on interpretations.

The question of texts, reading, and interpretation is, as we earlier noted, consistently thematized in the novel: in Pip's learning to read (using that meager text, Mr. Wopsle's great-aunt's catalogue of prices), and his attempts to transmit the art of writing to Joe; the expressive dumb shows between Pip and Joe; messages written on the slate, by Pip to Joe, and then (in minimum symbolic form) by the aphasic Mrs. Joe; the uncanny text of Estella's visage, always reminding Pip of a repetition of something else which he cannot identify; Molly's wrists, cross-hatched with scratches, a text for the judge, and eventually for Pip as detective, to decipher; Mr. Wopsle's declamations of *George Barnwell* and *Richard III*. The characters appear to be ever on the watch for ways in which to textualize the world, so that they can give their readings of it: a situation thematized early in the novel, at the

Christmas dinner table, as Pumblechook and Wopsle criticize the sermon of the day and propose other "subjects":

> Mr. Pumblechook added, after a short interval of reflection, "Look at Pork alone. There's a subject! . . ."
> "True, sir. Many a moral for the young," returned Mr. Wopsle; and I knew he was going to lug me in, before he said it; "might be deduced from that text. . . . Swine," pursued Mr. Wopsle. . . . "Swine were the companions of the prodigal." (44)

The scene suggests a mad proliferation of textuality, where literal and figural switch places, where any referent can serve as an interpretant, become the sign of another message, in a wild process of semiosis which seems to be anchored only insofar as all texts eventually speak of Pip himself as an unjustified presence, a presence demanding interpretation. . . . [Here follows an analysis of the ways in which Wopsle, particularly in his playing of Hamlet, makes clear "the lack of authorship and authority in texts" (*Reading* 132–34).]

Mr. Wopsle's career may stand as a figure for Pip's. Whereas the model of the *Bildungsroman* seems to imply progress, a leading forth, and developmental change, Pip's story—and this may be true of other nineteenth-century educative plots as well—becomes more and more as it nears its end the working through of past history, an attempted return to the origin as the motivation of all the rest, the clue to what must else appear, as Pip puts it to Miss Havisham, a "blind and thankless" life (364). The past needs to be incorporated *as past* within the present, mastered through the play of repetition in order for there to be an escape from repetition: in order for there to be difference, change, progress. In the failure ever to recover his own origin, Pip comes to concern himself with the question of Estella's origin, searching for her patronymics where knowledge of his own is ever foreclosed. Estella's story in fact eventually links all the plots of the novel: Satis House, the aspiration to gentility, the convict identity, "naterally wicious" (the status from which Jaggers rescued her), bringing up by hand, the law. Pip's investigation of her origins as substitute for knowledge of his own has a certain validity in that, we discover, he appeared originally to Magwitch as a substitute for the lost Estella, his great expectations a compensation for the impossibility of hers: a chiasmus of the true situation. Yet when Pip has proved himself to be the successful detective in this quest, when he has uncovered the convergence of lines of plot that previously appeared distinct and indeed proved himself more penetrating even than Jaggers, he discovers the knowledge he has gained to be radically unusable. When he has imparted his knowledge to Jaggers and Wemmick, he reaches a kind of standoff between what he has called his "poor dreams" and the deep plot he has now exposed. As Jaggers puts it to him, there is no gain to be had from knowledge. We are in the heart of darkness, and the articulation of its meaning must simply be repressed. In this novel full of mysteries and hidden connections, detective work turns out to be both necessary and useless. It can offer no comfort and no true illumination to the detective himself. Like deciphering the letters on the tombstone, it produces no authority for the plot of life.

The novel in fact toward its end appears to record a generalized breakdown of plots: none of the schemes machinated by the characters manages to accomplish its aims. The proof *a contrario* may be the "oversuccessful" result of Miss Havisham's plot, which has turned Estella into so heartless a creature that she cannot even experience emotional recognition of her benefactress. Miss Havisham's plotting has been a mechanical success but an intentional failure, as her final words, during her delirium following the fire, may suggest: "'What have I done!' And then, 'When she first came, I meant to save her from misery like mine.' And then, 'Take the pencil and write under my name, "I forgive her!"'" (369). The cycle of three statements suggests a metonymic movement in search of arrest, a plot that can never find satisfactory resolution, that unresolved must play over its insistent repetitions, until silenced by death. Miss Havisham's deathbed scene transmits a "wisdom" that is in the deconstructive mode, a warning against plot.

We confront the paradox that in this most highly plotted of novels, where Dickens performs all his thematic demonstrations through the manipulation of plot, we witness an evident subversion and futilization of the very concept of plot. If the chosen plots turn out to be erroneous, unauthorized, self-delusive, the deep plots when brought to light turn out to be criminally tainted, deviant, and thus unusable. Plot as direction and intention in existence appears ultimately to be as evanescent as Magwitch's money, the product of immense labor, deprivation, and planning, which is in the end forfeit to the Crown. Like money in its role as universal modern (capitalist) signifier as described by Roland Barthes in *S/Z*, tied to no referent (such as land), defined only by its exchange value, capable of unlimited metonymic circulation, the expectations of fortune, as both plot and its aim or intention, as vehicle and object of representation, circulate through inflation to devaluation.

The ultimate situation of plot in the novel may suggest an approach to the vexed question of Dickens's two endings to the novel: the one he originally wrote and the revision (substituted at Bulwer Lytton's suggestion) that was in fact printed. I think it is entirely legitimate to prefer the original ending, with its flat tone and refusal of romantic expectation, and find that the revision, with its tentative promise of reunion between Pip and Estella, "unbinds" energies that we thought had been thoroughly bound and indeed discharged from the text. We may also feel that choice between the two endings is somewhat arbitrary and unimportant in that the decisive moment has already occurred before either of these finales begins. The real ending may take place with Pip's recognition and acceptance of Magwitch after his recapture—this is certainly the ethical denouement—and his acceptance of a continuing existence without plot, as celibate clerk for Clarrikers. The pages that follow may simply be *obiter dicta*.

If we acknowledge Pip's experience of and with Magwitch to be the central energy of the text, it is significant that the climax of this experience, the moment of crisis and reversal in the attempted escape from England, bears traces of a hallucinatory repetition of the childhood spell—indeed, of that first recapture of Magwitch already repeated in Mr. Wopsle's [account of seeing Compeyson in the audience behind Pip as Wopsle plays a role in a Christmas pantomime (353)]: "In the same moment, I saw the steersman of the galley lay his hand on the prisoner's shoulder. . . . Still in the same moment, I saw the prisoner start up. . . ." (354). If this scene marks the beginning of a resolution—which it does in that it brings the death of the arch-villain Compeyson and the death sentence for Magwitch, hence the disappearance from the novel of its most energetic plotters—it is resolution in the register of repetition and working through, the final effort to master painful material from the insistent past. Pip emerges from this scene with an acceptance of the determinative past as both determinative and as *past*, which prepares us for the final escape *from* plot. It is interesting to note that where the "dream" plot of Estella is concerned, Pip's stated resolution has none of the compulsive energetic force of the passage just quoted, but is rather a conventional romantic fairy-tale ending, a conscious fiction designed, of course, to console the dying Magwitch, but possibly also a last effort at self-delusion: "You had a child once, whom you loved and lost. . . . She lived and found powerful friends. She is living now. She is a lady and very beautiful. And I love her!" (418). If taken as anything other than a conscious fiction—if taken as part of the "truth" discovered by Pip's detections—this version of Pip's experience leads straight to what is most troubling in Dickens's revised version of the ending: the suggestion of an unbinding of what has already been bound up and disposed of, an unbinding that is indeed perceptible in the rather embarrassed prose with which the revision begins: "Nevertheless, I knew while I said these words, that I secretly intended to revisit the site of the old house that evening, alone, for her sake. Yes even so. For Estella's sake," (437). Are we to understand that the experience of Satis House has never really been mastered? Is its nightmare energy still present in the text as well? The original end may have an advantage in denying to Pip's text the possibility of any reflux of energy, any new aspirations, the undoing of anything already done, the unbinding of energy that has been bound and led to discharge.

As at the start of the novel we had the impression of a life not yet subject to plot—a life in search of the sense of plot that would only gradually begin to precipitate around it—so at the end we have the impression of a life that has outlived plot, renounced plot, been cured of it: life that is left over. What follows the recognition of Magwitch is left over, and any renewal of expectation and plotting—such as a revived romance with Estella—would have to belong to another story. It is with the image of a life bereft of plot, of movement and desire, that the novel most appropriately leaves us. Indeed, we have at the end what could appropriately be called a "cure" from plot, in Pip's recognition of the general forfeiture of plotting, his renunciation of any attempt to direct his life. Plot comes to resemble a diseased, fevered state of the organism caught in the machinery of a desire which must eventually be renounced. Plot, we come to understand, was a state of abnormality or deviance, suggested thematically by its uneasy position between Newgate and Old Bailey, between criminality and the law. The nineteenth-century novel in general—and especially that highly symptomatic development, the detective story—regularly conceives plot as a condition of deviance and abnormality, the product of cities and social depths, of a world where *récit* is *complot*, where all stories are the result of plotting, and plotting is very much machination. Deviance is the very condition for life to be "narratable": the state of normality is devoid of interest, energy, and the possibility for narration. In between a beginning prior to plot and an end beyond plot, the middle—the plotted text—has been in a state of *error:* wandering and misinterpretation.

IV

That plot should prove to be deviance and error is fully consonant with Freud's model in *Beyond the Pleasure Principle*, where the narratable life of the organism is seen as detour, a deviance from the quiescence of the inorganic which has been maintained through the dynamic interaction of Eros and the death instinct. What Pip at one point has called his "ill-regulated aspirations" (225) is the figure of plot as desire: Eros as the force that binds integers together in ever-larger wholes, totalizing, metaphoric, the desire for possession of the world and for the integration of meaning—whereas, concomitantly, repetition and return have spoken of the death instinct, the drive to return to the quiescence of the inorganic, of the nontextual. Yet the repetitions, which have served to bind the various plots, both prolonging the detour and more effectively preparing the final discharge, have created that delay necessary to incorporate the past within the present and to let us understand end in relation to beginning. Through the erotics of the text, we have inexorably been led to its end, which is precisely quiescence: a time after which is an image of the time before. We have reached the non-narratable. Adducing the argument of "Remembering, Repeating and Working Through" to that of *Beyond the Pleasure Principle*, we perceive that repetition is a kind of remembering, and thus a way of reorganizing a story whose connective links have been obscured and lost. If repetition speaks of the death instinct, the finding of the right end, then what is being played out in repetition is necessarily the proper vector of the drive toward the end. That is, once you have determined the right plot, plot is over. Plot itself is working-through.

Great Expectations is exemplary in demonstrating both the need for plot and its status as deviance, both the need for narration and the necessity to be cured from it. The deviance and error of plot may necessarily result from the interplay of desire in its history with the narrative insistence on explanatory form: the desire to wrest beginnings and ends from the uninterrupted flow of middles, from temporality itself; the search for that significant closure that would illuminate the sense of an existence, the meaning of life. The desire for meaning is ultimately the reader's, who must mime Pip's acts of reading but do them better. Both using and subverting the systems of meaning discovered or postulated by its hero, *Great Expectations* exposes for its reader the very reading process itself: the way the reader goes about finding meaning in the narrative text, and the limits of that meaning as the limits of narrative.

In the terms of the problematic of reading which the novel thematizes from its opening page, we could say that Pip, continuously returning toward origins in order to know the plot whose authority would lead him to the right end but never recovering origins and never finding the authoritative plot, never succeeds in going behind his self-naming to a reading of the missing patronymic. He is ever returned to a rereading of the unauthorized text of his self-given name, Pip. "Pip" sounded like a beginning, a seed. But, of course, when you reach the end of the name "Pip," you can return backward, and it is just the same: a repetitive text without variation or point of fixity, a return that leads to an unarrested shuttling back and forth. The name is in fact a palindrome. In the rereading of the palindrome the novel may offer its final comment on its expectative plot.

What, finally, do we make of the fact that Dickens, masterplotter in the history of the novel, in this most tightly and consistently plotted of his novels seems to expose plot as a kind of necessary error? Dickens's most telling comment on the question may be at the moment of Magwitch's sentencing. The judge gives a legalistic and moralistic version of Magwitch's life story, his violence, his crimes, the passions that made him a "scourge to society" and led him to escape from deportation, thus calling upon his head the death sentence: [with a "broad shaft of light . . . linking" the judge and the prisoners, Magwitch rises to say, "My Lord, I have received my sentence of Death from the Almighty, but I bow to yours" (416).] This passage is sentimental but also, I think, effective. It juxtaposes human plots—including those of the law—to eternal orders that render human attempts to plot, and to interpret plot, not only futile but ethically unacceptable. The greater Judgment makes human plots mere shadows. There is another end that recuperates passing human time, and its petty chronologies, to the timeless. Yet despite the narrator's affirmations, this other end is not visible, the other orders are not available. . . . If there is a divine masterplot for human existence, it is radically unknowable.

In the absence or silence of divine masterplots, the organization and interpretation of human plots remains as necessary as it is problematic. Reading the signs of intention in life's actions is the central act of existence, which in turn legitimizes the enterprise of reading for the reader of *Great Expectations*—or perhaps, vice versa, since the reading of plot within the text and as the text are perfectly analogous, mirrors of one another. If there is by the end of the narrative an abandonment of the attempt to read plot, this simply mirrors the fact that the process of narration has come to a close—or, again, vice versa. But that there should be a cure from the reading of plot within the text—before its very end—and the creation of a leftover, suggests a critique of reading itself, which is possibly like the judge's sentence: human interpretation in ignorance of the true vectors of the true text. . . . But if the mastertext is not available, we are condemned to the reading of erroneous plots, granted insight only insofar as we can gain disillusion from them. We are condemned to repetition, rereading, in the knowledge that what we discover will always be that there was nothing to be discovered. Yet the process remains necessary if we are not to be caught perpetually in the "blind and thankless" existence, in the illusory middle. Like Oedipus, like Pip, we are condemned to reinterpretation of our names. But it is rare that the name coincide so perfectly with a fullness and a negation of identity as in the case of Oedipus. In a post-tragic universe, our situation is more likely to be that of Pip, compelled to reinterpret the meaning of the name he assigned to himself with his infant tongue, the history of an infinitely repeatable palindrome.

WORKS CITED

Byrd, Max. "'Reading' in *Great Expectations.*" *PMLA* 91 (1976): 259–65.

Deleuze, Gilles. *Logique du sens.* Paris: Editions de Minuit, 1969.

Freud, Sigmund. *The Standard Edition of the Complete Psychological Works of Sigmund Freud.* Ed. James Strachey. London: Hogarth, 1953–74.

Guerard, Albert J. *The Triumph of the Novel.* New York: Oxford UP, 1976.

Kierkegaard, Søren. *Repetition.* Trans. Walter Lowrie. Princeton: Princeton UP, 1941.

Lacan, Jacques. *Le Séminaire, Livre XI: Les Quatre Concepts fondamentaux de la psychoanalyse.* Paris: Editions de Seuil, 1973.

Miller, J. Hillis. *Fiction and Repetition.* Cambridge: Harvard UP, 1982.

Ron, Moshe. "Autobiographical Narration and Formal Closure in *Great Expectations.*" *Hebrew University Studies in Literature* 5 (1977): 37–66.

Stone, Harry. "The Love Pattern in Dickens' Novels." *Dickens the Craftsman.* Ed. Robert B. Partlow, Jr. Carbondale: Southern Illinois UP, 1970. 1–20.

Wilson, Edmund. "Dickens: The Two Scrooges." *The Wound and the Bow.* Boston: Houghton, 1941. 1–104.

Deconstruction
and
Great Expectations

WHAT IS DECONSTRUCTION?

Deconstruction has a reputation for being the most complex and forbidding of contemporary critical approaches to literature, but in fact almost all of us have, at one time, either deconstructed a text or badly wanted to deconstruct one. Sometimes when we hear a lecturer effectively marshal evidence to show that a book means primarily one thing, we long to interrupt and ask what he or she would make of other, conveniently overlooked passages, passages that seem to contradict the lecturer's thesis. Sometimes, after reading a provocative critical article that *almost* convinces us that a familiar work means the opposite of what we assumed it meant, we may wish to make an equally convincing case for our former reading of the text. We may not think that the poem or novel in question better supports our interpretation, but we may recognize that the text can be used to support *both* readings. And sometimes we simply want to make that point: texts can be used to support seemingly irreconcilable positions.

To reach this conclusion is to feel the deconstructive itch. J. Hillis Miller, the preeminent American deconstructor, puts it this way: "Deconstruction is not a dismantling of the structure of a text, but a demonstration that it has already dismantled itself. Its apparently solid ground is no rock but thin air" ("Stevens' Rock" 341). To deconstruct a text isn't to show that all the high old themes aren't there to be found in it. Rather, it is to show that a text—not unlike DNA with its double helix—can have intertwined, opposite "discourses"— strands of narrative, threads of meaning.

Ultimately, of course, deconstruction refers to a larger and more complex enterprise than the practice of demonstrating that a text means contradictory things. The term refers to a way of reading texts practiced by critics who have been influenced by the writings of the French philosopher Jacques Derrida. It is important to gain some understanding of Derrida's project and of the historical backgrounds of his work before reading the deconstruction that follows, let alone attempting to deconstruct a text. But it is important, too, to approach deconstruction with anything but a scholar's sober and almost worshipful respect for knowledge and truth. Deconstruction offers a playful alternative to traditional scholarship, a confidently adversarial alternative, and deserves to be approached in the spirit that animates it.

Derrida, a philosopher of language who coined the term "deconstruction," argues that we tend to think and express our thoughts in terms of opposites. Something is black but not white, masculine and therefore not feminine, a cause rather than an effect, and so forth. These mutually exclusive pairs or dichotomies are too numerous to list but would include beginning/end, conscious/unconscious, presence/absence, speech/writing, and construction/destruction (the last being the opposition that Derrida's word *deconstruction* tries to contain and subvert). If we think hard about these dichotomies, Derrida suggests, we will realize that they are not simply oppositions; they are also hierarchies in miniature. In other words, they contain one term that our culture views as being superior and one term viewed as negative or inferior. Sometimes the superior term seems only subtly superior (*speech, masculine, cause*), whereas sometimes we know immediately which term is culturally preferable (*presence* and *beginning* and *consciousness* are easy choices). But the hierarchy always exists.

Of particular interest to Derrida, perhaps because it involves the language in which all the other dichotomies are expressed, is the hierarchical opposition speech/writing. Derrida argues that the "privileging" of speech, that is, the tendency to regard speech in positive terms and writing in negative terms, cannot be disentangled from the privileging of presence. (Postcards are written by absent friends; we read Plato because he cannot speak from beyond the grave.) Furthermore, according to Derrida, the tendency to privilege both speech and presence is part of the Western tradition of *logocentrism*, the belief that in some ideal beginning were creative *spoken* words, words such as "Let there be light," spoken by an ideal, *present* God. According to logocentric tradition, these words can now only be represented in unoriginal speech or writing (such as the written phrase in quotation marks above). Derrida doesn't seek to reverse the hierarchized opposition between speech and writing, or presence and absence, or early and late, for to do so would be to fall into a trap of perpetuating the same forms of thought and expression that he seeks to deconstruct. Rather, his goal is to erase the boundary between oppositions such as speech and writing, and to do so in such a way as to throw the order and values implied by the opposition into question.

Returning to the theories of Ferdinand de Saussure, who invented the modern science of linguistics, Derrida reminds us that the association of speech with present, obvious, and ideal meaning and writing with absent, merely pictured, and therefore less reliable meaning is suspect, to say the least. As Saussure demonstrated, words are *not* the things they name and, indeed, they are only arbitrarily associated with those things. Neither spoken nor written words have present, positive, identifiable attributes themselves; they have meaning only by virtue of their difference from other words *(red, read, reed)*. In a sense, meanings emerge from the gaps or spaces between them. Take *read* as an example. To know whether it is the present or past tense of the verb— whether it rhymes with *red* or *reed*—we need to see it in relation to some other word (for example, *yesterday*).

Because the meanings of words lie in the differences between them and in the differences between them and the things they name, Derrida suggests that all language is constituted by *différance,* a word he has coined that puns on two French words meaning "to differ" and "to defer": words are the deferred presences of the things they "mean," and their meaning is grounded in difference. Derrida, by the way, changes the *e* in the French word *différence* to an *a* in his neologism *différance;* the change, which can be seen in writing but cannot be heard in spoken French, is itself a playful, witty challenge to the notion that writing is inferior or "fallen" speech.

In *De la grammatologie* [*Of Grammatology*] (1967) and *Dissemination* (1972), Derrida begins to redefine writing by deconstructing some old definitions. In *Dissemination,* he traces logocentrism back to Plato, who in the *Phaedrus* has Socrates condemn writing and who, in all the great dialogues, powerfully postulates that metaphysical longing for origins and ideals that permeates Western thought. "What Derrida does in his reading of Plato," Barbara Johnson points out, "is to unfold dimensions of Plato's *text* that work against the grain of (Plato's own) Platonism" (xxiv). Remember: that is what deconstruction does according to Miller; it shows a text dismantling itself.

In *Of Grammatology,* Derrida turns to the *Confessions* of Jean-Jacques Rousseau and exposes a grain running against the grain. Rousseau, another great Western idealist and believer in innocent, noble origins, on one hand condemned writing as mere representation, a corruption of the more natural, childlike, direct, and therefore undevious speech. On the other hand, Rousseau admitted his own tendency to lose self-presence and blurt out exactly the wrong thing in public. He confesses that, by writing at a distance from his audience, he often expressed himself better: "If I were present, one would never know what I was worth," Rousseau admitted (Derrida, *Of Grammatology* 142). Thus, writing is a *supplement* to speech that is at the same time *necessary.* Barbara Johnson, sounding like Derrida, puts it this way: "Recourse to writing . . . is necessary to recapture a presence whose lack has not been preceded by any fullness" (Derrida, *Dissemination* xii). Thus, Derrida shows that one strand of Rousseau's discourse made writing seem a secondary, even treacherous supplement, while another made it seem necessary to communication.

Have Derrida's deconstructions of *Confessions* and the *Phaedrus* explained these texts, interpreted them, opened them up and shown us what they mean? Not in any traditional sense. Derrida would say that anyone attempting to find a single, correct meaning in a text is simply imprisoned by that structure of thought that would oppose two readings and declare one to be right and not wrong, correct rather than incorrect. In fact, any work of literature that we interpret defies the laws of Western logic, the laws of opposition and noncontradiction. In the views of poststructuralist critics, texts don't say "A and not B." They say "A and not-A," as do texts written by literary critics, who are also involved in producing creative writing.

Miller has written that the purpose of deconstruction is to show "the existence in literature of structures of language which contradict the law of non-contradiction." Why find the grain that runs against the grain? To restore what Miller has called "the strangeness of literature," to reveal the "capacity of each work to surprise the reader," to demonstrate that "literature continually exceeds any formula or theory with which the critic is prepared to encompass it" (Miller, *Fiction* 5).

Although its ultimate aim may be to critique Western idealism and logic, deconstruction began as a response to structuralism and to formalism, another structure-oriented theory of reading. (Deconstruction, which is really only one kind of a poststructuralist criticism, is sometimes referred to as poststructuralist criticism, or even as poststructuralism.)

Structuralism, Robert Scholes tells us, may now be seen as a reaction to modernist alienation and despair (3). Using Saussure's theory as Derrida was to do later, European structuralists attempted to create a *semiology,* or science of signs, that would give humankind at once a scientific and a holistic way of studying the world and its human inhabitants. Roland Barthes, a structuralist who later shifted toward poststructuralism, hoped to recover literary language from the isolation in which it had been studied and to show that the laws that govern it govern all signs, from road signs to articles of clothing. Claude Lévi-Strauss, a structural anthropologist who studied everything from village structure to the structure of myths, found in myths what he called *mythemes,* or building blocks, such as basic plot elements. Recognizing that the same mythemes occur in similar myths from different cultures, he suggested that all myths may be elements of one great myth being written by the collective human mind.

Derrida could not accept the notion that structuralist thought might someday explain the laws governing human signification and thus provide the key to understanding the form and meaning of everything from an African village to a Greek myth to Rousseau's *Confessions.* In his view, the scientific search by structural anthropologists for what unifies humankind amounts to a new version of the old search for the lost ideal, whether that ideal be Plato's bright realm of the Idea or the Paradise of Genesis or Rousseau's unspoiled Nature. As for the structuralist belief that texts have "centers" of meaning, in Derrida's view that derives from the logocentric belief that there is a reading of the text that accords with "the book as seen by God." Jonathan Culler, who thus translates a difficult phrase from Derrida's *L'Écriture et la différence* [*Writing and Difference*] (1967) in his book *Structuralist Poetics* (1975), goes on to explain what Derrida objects to in structuralist literary criticism:

> [When] one speaks of the structure of a literary work, one does so from a certain vantage point: one starts with notions of the meaning or effects of a poem and tries to identify the structures responsible for those effects. Possible configurations or patterns that make no contribution are rejected as irrelevant. That is to say, an intuitive understanding of the poem functions as the "centre" . . . : it is both a starting point and a limiting principle. (244)

For these reasons, Derrida and his poststructuralist followers reject the very notion of "linguistic competence" introduced by Noam Chomsky, a structural linguist. The idea that there is a competent reading "gives a privileged status to a particular set of rules of reading, . . . granting preeminence to certain conventions and excluding from the realm of language all the truly creative and productive violations of those rules" (Culler, *Structuralist Poetics* 241).

Poststructuralism calls into question assumptions made about literature by formalist, as well as by structuralist, critics. Formalism, or the New Criticism as it was once commonly called, assumes a work of literature to be a freestanding, self-contained object, its meanings found in the complex network of relations that constitute its parts (images, sounds, rhythms, allusions, and so on). To be sure, deconstruction is somewhat like formalism in several ways. Both the formalist and the deconstructor focus on the literary text; neither is likely to interpret a poem or a novel by relating it to events in the author's life, letters, historical period, or even culture. And formalists, long before deconstructors, discovered counterpatterns of meaning in the same text. Formalists find ambiguity and irony, deconstructors find contradiction and undecidability.

Undecidability, as Paul de Man came to define it, is a complex notion easily misunderstood. There is a tendency to assume it refers to readers who, when forced to decide between two or more equally plausible and conflicting readings motivated by the same text, throw up their hands and decide that the choice can't be made. But undecidability in fact debunks this whole notion of reading as a decision-making process carried out on texts by readers. To say we are forced to choose or decide—or that we are unable to do so—is to locate the problem of undecidability falsely outside ourselves, and to make it reside within a text to which we come as an Other. The poststructuralist concept of undecidability, we might say, deconstructs the either/or type distinction or opposition that structuralists and formalists have made between reader and text. It entails what de Man calls the "mutual obliteration" not only of propositions apparently opposed but also of the subject/object relation.

Undecidability is thus rather different from ambiguity, as understood by formalists. Formalists believe a complete understanding of a literary work is possible, an understanding in which even the ambiguities will fulfill a definite, meaningful function. Deconstructors confront the apparently limitless possibilities for the production of meaning that develop when the language of the critic enters the language of the text. They cannot accept the formalist view that a work of literary art has organic unity (therefore, structuralists would say, a "center"), if only we could find it. The formalist critic ultimately makes sense of ambiguity; undecidability, by contrast, is never reduced, let alone resolved, by deconstructive reading.

Poststructuralists break with formalists, too, over an issue they have debated with structuralists. The issue involves metaphor and metonymy, two terms for different kinds of rhetorical *tropes,* or figures of speech. *Metonymy* refers to a figure that is chosen to stand for something that it is commonly associated with, or with which it happens to be contiguous or juxtaposed. When said to a waitress, "I'll have the cold plate today" is a metonymic figure of speech for "I'll eat the cold food you're serving today." We refer to the food we want as a plate simply because plates are what food happens to be served on and because everyone understands that by *plate* we mean food. A *metaphor,* on the other hand, is a figure of speech that involves a special, intrinsic, nonarbitrary relationship with what it represents. When you say you are blue, if you believe that there is an intrinsic, timeless likeness between that color and melancholy feeling—a likeness that just doesn't exist between sadness and yellow—then you are using the word *blue* metaphorically.

Although both formalists and structuralists make much of the difference between metaphor and metonymy, Derrida, Miller, and de Man have contended with the distinction deconstructively. They have questioned not only the distinction but also, and perhaps especially, the privilege we grant to metaphor, which we tend to view as the positive and superior figure of speech. De Man, in *Allegories of Reading* (1979), analyzes a passage from Proust's *Swann's Way,* arguing that it is about the nondistinction between metaphor and metonymy—and that it makes its claim metonymically. In *Fiction and Repetition: Seven English Novels* (1982), Miller connects the belief in metaphorical correspondences with other metaphysical beliefs, such as those in origins, endings, transcendence, and underlying truths. Isn't it likely, deconstructors keep implicitly asking, that every metaphor was once a metonym, but that we have simply forgotten what arbitrary juxtaposition or contiguity gave rise to the association that now seems mysteriously special?

The hypothesis that what we call metaphors are really old metonyms may perhaps be made clearer by the following example. We used the word *Watergate* as a metonym to refer to a political scandal that began in the Watergate building complex. Recently, we have used part of the building's name *(gate)* to refer to more recent scandals *(Irangate).* However, already there are people who use and "understand" these terms who are unaware that Watergate is the name of a building. In the future, isn't it possible that *gate,* which began as part of a simple metonym, will seem like the perfect metaphor for scandal—a word that suggests corruption and wrongdoing with a strange and inexplicable rightness?

This is how deconstruction works: by showing that what was prior and privileged in the old hierarchy (for instance, metaphor and speech) can just as easily seem secondary, the deconstructor causes the formerly privileged term to exchange properties with the formerly devalued one. Causes become effects and (d)evolutions become origins, but the result is neither the destruction of the old order or hierarchy nor the construction of a new one. It is, rather, *deconstruction.* In Robert Scholes's words, "If either cause or effect can occupy the position of an origin, then origin is no longer originary; it loses its metaphorical privilege" (88).

Once deconstructed, literal and figurative can exchange properties, so that the prioritizing between them is erased: all words, even *dog* and *cat,* are understood to be figures. It's just that we have used some of them so long that we have forgotten how arbitrary and metonymic they are. And, just as literal and figurative can exchange properties, criticism can exchange properties with literature, in the process coming to be seen not merely as a supplement—the second, negative, and inferior term in the binary opposition creative writing/literary criticism—but rather as an equally creative form of work. Would we write if there were not critics—intelligent readers motivated and able to make sense of what is written? Who, then, depends on whom?

"It is not difficult to see the attractions" of deconstructive reading, Jonathan Culler has commented. "Given that there is no ultimate or absolute justification for any system or for the interpretations from it," the critic is free to value "the activity of interpretation itself, . . . rather than any results which might be obtained" (*Structuralist Poetics* 248). Not everyone, however, has so readily seen the attractions of deconstruction. Two eminent critics, M. H. Abrams and Wayne Booth, have observed that a deconstructive reading "is plainly and simply parasitical" on what Abrams calls "the obvious or univocal meaning" (Abrams 457–58). In other words, there would be no deconstructors if critics did not already exist who can see and show central and definite meanings in texts. Miller responded in an essay entitled "The Critic as Host," in which he deconstructed not only the oppositional hierarchy (host/parasite) but also the two terms themselves, showing that each derives from two definitions meaning nearly opposite things. *Host* means "hospitable welcomer" and "military horde." *Parasite* originally had a positive connotation; in Greek, *parasitos* meant "beside the grain" and referred to a friendly guest. Finally, Miller suggests, the words *parasite* and *host* are inseparable, depending on one another for their meaning in a given work, much as do hosts and parasites, authors and critics, structuralists and poststructuralists.

In telling "The Story of Deconstruction" in his book on contemporary American literature and theory, Jay Clayton assesses the current status of this unique approach to texts. Although he notes how frequently deconstructive critics have been cited for their lack of political engagement, he contends that deconstruction, "a movement accused of formalism and arid intellectualism, participates in the political turn of contemporary culture" (34). He proves his point by explaining that what began as theory in the late 1960s and 1970s has developed into a method employed by a variety of different critical approaches: "The practice of deconstruction has come to displace the very theoretical enterprise that gave birth to its procedures" (58–59). Deconstruction is now a tool used by practitioners of a wide range of literary critical approaches—ethnic, feminist, new historicist, Marxist—and by those outside of literary studies who are involved in critical race theory and critical legal studies (34). Clayton cites the work of Edward W. Said as a case in point. As early as the publication of *Beginnings: Intention and Method,* in 1975, Said was employing a form of deconstructive criticism that emphasizes the "power" of texts "to initiate projects in the real world" (45–46), and this emphasis has become even more insistent in his subsequent work. Such criticism attests to the expanding role that deconstruction currently plays in developing contemporary understandings of literature and culture.

Ross C Murfin

DECONSTRUCTION:
A SELECTED BIBLIOGRAPHY

Deconstruction, Poststructuralism, and Structuralism: Introductions, Guides, and Surveys

Arac, Jonathan, Wlad Godzich, and Wallace Martin, eds. *The Yale Critics: Deconstruction in America*. Minneapolis: U of Minnesota P, 1983. See especially the essays by Bové, Godzich, Pease, and Corngold.

Berman, Art. *From the New Criticism to Deconstruction: The Reception of Structuralism and Post-Structuralism.* Urbana: U of Illinois P, 1988.

Butler, Christopher. *Interpretation, Deconstruction, and Ideology: An Introduction to Some Current Issues in Literary Theory.* Oxford: Oxford UP, 1984.

Cain, William E. "Deconstruction in America: The Recent Literary Criticism of J. Hillis Miller." *College English* 41 (1979): 367–82.

Clayton, Jay. *The Pleasures of Babel: Contemporary American Literature and Theory.* New York: Oxford UP, 1993.

Culler, Jonathan. *On Deconstruction: Theory and Criticism After Structuralism.* Ithaca: Cornell UP, 1982.

———. *Structuralist Poetics: Structuralism, Linguistics, and the Study of Literature.* Ithaca: Cornell UP, 1975. See especially ch. 10.

Esch, Deborah. "Deconstruction." *Redrawing the Boundaries: The Transformation of English and American Literary Studies.* Ed. Stephen Greenblatt and Giles Gunn. New York: MLA, 1992. 374–91.

Gasché, Rodolphe. "Deconstruction as Criticism." *Glyph* 6 (1979): 177–215.

Jay, Gregory. *America the Scrivener: Deconstruction and the Subject of Literary History.* Ithaca: Cornell UP, 1990.

Jefferson, Ann. "Structuralism and Post Structuralism." *Modern Literary Theory: A Comparative Introduction.* Totowa, NJ: Barnes, 1982. 84–112.

Leitch, Vincent B. *American Literary Criticism from the Thirties to the Eighties.* New York: Columbia UP, 1988. See especially ch. 10, "Deconstructive Criticism."

———. *Deconstructive Criticism: An Advanced Introduction and Survey.* New York: Columbia UP, 1983.

Lentricchia, Frank. *After the New Criticism.* Chicago: U of Chicago P, 1981.

Melville, Stephen W. *Philosophy Beside Itself: On Deconstruction and Modernism.* Vol. 27 of *Theory and History of Literature.* Minneapolis: U of Minnesota P, 1986.

Norris, Christopher. *Deconstruction and the Interests of Theory.* Vol. 4 of *Oklahoma Project for Discourse and Theory.* Norman: U of Oklahoma P, 1989.

———. *Deconstruction: Theory and Practice.* London: Methuen, 1982. Rev. ed. London: Routledge, 1991.

Raval, Suresh. *Metacriticism*. Athens: U of Georgia P, 1981.

Scholes, Robert. *Structuralism in Literature: An Introduction*. New Haven: Yale UP, 1974.

Sturrock, John. *Structuralism and Since*. New York: Oxford UP, 1975.

Selected Works by Jacques Derrida and Paul de Man

de Man, Paul. *Allegories of Reading*. New Haven: Yale UP, 1979. See especially ch. 1, "Semiology and Rhetoric."

—————. *Blindness and Insight*. New York: Oxford UP, 1971. Minneapolis: U of Minnesota P, 1983. The 1983 edition contains important essays not included in the original edition.

—————. *The Resistance to Theory*. Minneapolis: U of Minnesota P, 1986.

Derrida, Jacques. *Acts of Literature*. Ed. Derek Attridge. New York: Routledge, 1992. Includes a helpful editor's introduction on Derrida and literature.

—————. *Dissemination*. 1972. Trans. Barbara Johnson. Chicago: U of Chicago P, 1981. See especially the concise, incisive "Translator's Introduction," which provides a useful point of entry into this work and others by Derrida.

—————. *Margins of Philosophy*. Trans. Alan Bass. Chicago: U of Chicago P, 1982.

—————. *Of Grammatology*. Trans. Gayatri C. Spivak. Baltimore: Johns Hopkins UP, 1976. Trans. of *De la Grammatologie*. 1967.

—————. *The Postcard: From Socrates to Freud and Beyond*. Trans. with intro. Alan Bass. Chicago: U of Chicago P, 1987.

—————. *Writing and Difference*. 1967. Trans. Alan Bass. Chicago: U of Chicago P, 1978.

Essays in Deconstruction and Poststructuralism

Barthes, Roland. *S/Z*. Trans. Richard Miller. New York: Hill, 1974. In this influential work, Barthes turns from a structuralist to a poststructuralist approach.

Bloom, Harold, et al., eds. *Deconstruction and Criticism*. New York: Seabury, 1979. Includes essays by Bloom, de Man, Derrida, Miller, and Hartman.

Chase, Cynthia. *Decomposing Figures*. Baltimore: Johns Hopkins UP, 1986.

Harari, Josué, ed. *Textual Strategies: Perspectives in Post-Structuralist Criticism*. Ithaca: Cornell UP, 1979.

Johnson, Barbara. *The Critical Difference: Essays in the Contemporary Rhetoric of Reading*. Baltimore: Johns Hopkins UP, 1980.

_____. *A World of Difference*. Baltimore: Johns Hopkins UP, 1987.

Krupnick, Mark, ed. *Displacement: Derrida and After*. Bloomington: Indiana UP, 1987.

Miller, J. Hillis. *Ariadne's Thread: Story Lines*. New Haven: Yale UP, 1992.

_____. *The Ethics of Reading: Kant, de Man, Eliot, Trollope, James, and Benjamin*. New York: Columbia UP, 1987.

_____. *Fiction and Repetition: Seven English Novels*. Cambridge: Harvard UP, 1982.

_____. *Hawthorne and History, Defacing It*. Cambridge: Basil Blackwell, 1991. Contains a bibliography of Miller's work from 1955 to 1990.

_____. "Stevens' Rock and Criticism as Cure." *Georgia Review* 30 (1976): 5–31, 330–48.

Said, Edward W. *Beginnings: Intention and Method*. New York: Columbia UP, 1975.

Ulmer, Gregory L. *Applied Grammatology*. Baltimore: Johns Hopkins UP, 1985.

Other Work Referred to in "What Is Deconstruction?"

Abrams, M. H. "Rationality and the Imagination in Cultural History." *Critical Inquiry* 2 (1976): 447–64.

Deconstructive Criticism of *Great Expectations*

Hara, Eiichi. "Stories Present and Absent in *Great Expectations*." *ELH* (1986): 593–614.

Morris, Christopher. "The Bad Faith of Pip's Bad Faith: Deconstructing *Great Expectations*." *ELH* 54 (1987): 941–55.

Ron, Moshe. "Autobiographical Narration and Formal Closure in *Great Expectations*." *Hebrew University Studies in Literature* 5 (1977): 37–66.

DECONSTRUCTIVE AND POSTCOLONIAL PERSPECTIVES

Introduction

Although the term *deconstruction* does not appear in the index to Edward W. Said's *Culture and Imperialism* (1993), his most recent work suggests that he remains a committed deconstructive critic. Said might not wish to claim such a title, but he continues to demonstrate that the methods of deconstruction can be central to the practice of a politically engaged criticism. In fact, the following excerpts from his work chart the movement of deconstruction from the realm of theory to that of practice (Clayton 34), and they identify their author as one of the critics most responsible for this development. Both of the larger works from which these excerpts are taken explicitly outline the limitations of deconstruction precisely as they put into practice its methodology. In the process they demonstrate how deconstructive readings are now used to encourage readers to confront historical realities such as imperialism, the "actual contests over land and the land's people" that Said finds central to centuries of Western culture (7).

The first excerpt, here entitled "Dickens and Derrida," comes from "Criticism Between Culture and System," an essay in *The World, the Text, and the Critic* (1983). Said uses a passage from *Great Expectations* to illustrate Derrida's theories about representation. Said argues that what Dickens achieves in his description of Wopsle's performance, or representation, of *Hamlet* is analogous to what Derrida does when he writes about a classic text by Plato: both writers "allow . . . the very notion of representation to represent itself." The discrepancy between the reader's idea of what *Hamlet* is ideally and Wopsle's botched enactment of it or between a text by Plato and Derrida's rewriting of it demonstrates a number of theories central to deconstruction: there is no "original" text, but only representations of it; and these representations refer not to "a transcendental signified outside them" but only to themselves.

Dickens, therefore, in "a most unphilosophic way"—and, of course, in a most unconscious way—illustrates in this scene from *Great Expectations* Derrida's ideas about language, presence, and representation. The comic incompetence of Wopsle and his colleagues, therefore, has quite serious and even profound implications: even though we may want to think of Shakespeare's *Hamlet* as a sublime instance of its author's imperishable genius, Wopsle's representation of it, according to Said, exemplifies the play's fragility; and its incompetence to control its own representation breaks down the binary distinction between original and copy, represented and representation. In this sense, then, what Said calls the "double scene" in *Great Expectations* simply reveals what an examination of any text would reveal: Dickens, without knowing it, was practicing deconstruction. What Dickens proves in the case of *Hamlet* is, of course, what recent deconstructionist readers have argued in the case of *Great Expectations.*

Said's analysis, however, has a much larger purpose than reaching such a conclusion. In this essay, he uses *Great Expectations* to present what he calls an "extremely bald summary" of Derrida's theories so that he can critique them along with the very different theories of Michel Foucault (see introduction to Cultural Criticism). These writers exemplify for Said the "central" contemporary intellectual crisis, "the problem of knowledge, of *how* we know what we know" (182). Both thinkers, Said claims, are interested in problems of textuality, and both have profitably and effectively opposed quasi-scientific conceptions of a work's unity and stability. Ultimately, however, Said finds the thought of both Derrida and Foucault lacking, and his critique of their work provides a basis for the application of his own deconstructive practice.

In both cases, Said finds problematic the theorists' recognition or understanding of history. Derrida's interest in the instability, contradictions, and undecidability of every text, according to Said, ignores a text's "historical density, specificity, and weight" (210–11):

> Certainly any reading method like Derrida's, whose main ambition is both to reveal one or another undecidable elements in a text in lieu of some simple reductive message the text is supposed to contain and, on the other hand, to shy away from making each reading of a text part of some cumulatively built explicit thesis about the historical persistence of Western metaphysical thought, certainly any method like that will finally be unable to get hold of the local material density and power of ideas as historical actuality. (212)

The verdict here is clear: although deconstruction provides "a particularly alert and influential reading method," in isolation it exhibits an "inhibiting and crippling" ahistoricity (214). In the case of Foucault, the problem is an insufficient understanding of the significance of historical change, even though, Said concedes, Foucault focused throughout his career on "texts as an integral . . . part . . . of social processes" (215). Particularly troubling in Foucault's thought from this perspective is his tendency to view history as "a homogeneous French-speaking territory," when it is more accurately understood as "a complex interaction between uneven economies, societies, and ideologies" (222).

Said's analysis of both Derrida and Foucault, therefore, leads to one conclusion: critics must move beyond their theories if they are to "account for, and rationally to discover and know, the force of statements in texts"—"statements and texts [that do] something more or less effective, with consequences that criticism should make it its business to reveal. For if texts are a form of impressive human activity, they must be correlated with (not reduced to) other forms of impressive, perhaps even repressive, and displacing forms of human activity" (224–25). In *Culture and Imperialism* (1993)—from which the second excerpt below is taken—Said tries to "account for the force of statements in texts," and he does so by employing a method of reading that is deconstructive in intent and in effect, but he places it within a global perspective that conceives of a text as having "a lasting historical, actual imprint on human life" (*World* 211). What is now called his postcolonial approach to texts, in fact, takes deconstruction as a way of reaching his critical and political goals, not as an end in itself.

Said has had a central role in announcing and defining the emerging field of postcolonial studies. His book *Orientalism* (1978) was a powerful and relatively early challenge to Eurocentric conceptions of the colonial Other, and *Culture and Imperialism* continued that project. As Said explains in the latter work,

> In British culture, for instance, one may discover a consistency of concern in Spenser, Shakespeare, Defoe, and Austen that fixes socially desirable, empowered space in metropolitan England or Europe and connects it by design, motive, and development to distant and peripheral worlds (Ireland, Venice, Africa, Jamaica), conceived of as desirable but subordinate. And with these meticulously maintained references come attitudes — about rule, control, profit and enhancement and suitability — that grow with astonishing power from the seventeenth to the end of the nineteenth century. These structures do not arise from preexisting (semi-conspiratorial) design that the writers then manipulate, but are bound up with the development of Britain's cultural identity, as that identity imagines itself in a geographically conceived world. (52)

Said argues that the novel was the literary form in Great Britain most responsible for articulating and consolidating this imperialistic "structure of attitude and reference" (62). To deconstruct this "structure," Said depends on such binary oppositions as metropolis and colony, Europe and non–Europe, so that he can undermine those oppositions by pointing out their unacknowledged incorporation of "overlapping experience" (Introduction xx). In fact, Said proposes a form of what deconstruction calls "double reading" of classic Western texts—what Ross Murfin calls A and non-A—but Said labels it "contrapuntal" reading (51): Said's counterpoint sees the text in its metropolitan context—the way it is usually read—but also in the context created by its role within the history of empire. In typical deconstructive fashion, neither reading erases the other; both, according to Said, deserve our attention.

In his introduction to *Culture and Imperialism*, Said again turns briefly to *Great Expectations* to use it as an example, this time as an example of "contrapuntal" reading. He first grants that the novel is usually read "squarely within the metropolitan history of British fiction," that it is a novel taken to be about England and English attitudes and concerns. He then contrasts *Great Expectations* to works by twentieth-century historians, Robert Hughes and Paul Carter, so that he can indicate some of the richness of the history of colonial Australia, which Dickens treats merely as a convenience. In this sense, Said sees Dickens's depiction of Australia as typical of mid-nineteenth-century British fiction: the "outlying territories are available for use, at will, at the novelist's discretion, usually for relatively simple purposes such as immigration, fortune, or exile" (74). Said's analysis points to another binary opposition, this one between Australia as a penal colony created to house the socially unacceptable and Egypt as a "normal" colony created to increase trade between the metropolis and the rest of the world. Implicit in his analysis is a further binary, not raised by his references to Carter and Hughes, between the colonizer and the colonized, between the British convicts and the indigenous peoples not so much as even mentioned in *Great Expectations*.

By setting these binary oppositions in play, Said's brief glance at the novel—which is not meant, of course, to provide a full reading of it—raises many questions. Are the oppositions that he outlines undermined in the novel? Do Pip's and Magwitch's very different experiences as colonists "overlap" with other? If so, how? What is the relation in *Great Expectations* between the metropolis, which in this case is literally London, and the colonies? Why was Dickens writing about a convict in Australia even as transportation to its penal colonies was being ended? Does Australia serve merely as a convenience of the plot or does it identify Dickens as a "participant" in the history of colonialism? (Said would answer "yes" to both those questions.) What, finally, was and is the "force" of the "statement" that Dickens made in writing *Great Expectations*? How can one gauge its "lasting historical, actual imprint on human life"? If one is to read the novel "contrapuntally," as Said hopes its readers will do, these are the sorts of questions that deserve consideration.

Janice Carlisle

Works Cited

Clayton, Jay. *The Pleasures of Babel: Contemporary American Literature and Theory.* New York: Oxford UP, 1993.

Said, Edward W. "Criticism Between Culture and System." *The World, the Text, and the Critic.* Cambridge: Harvard UP, 1983. 178–225.

———. *Culture and Imperialism.* New York: Knopf, 1993.

EDWARD W. SAID

Two Commentaries on *Great Expectations*: From Deconstruction to Postcolonialism

I. DICKENS AND DERRIDA [from *The World, the Text, and the Critic* (1983)]

[At the beginning of chapter 31 in *Great Expectations*,] Pip and Herbert go off to watch a performance of *Hamlet* in which Mr. Wopsle, Pip's fellow townsman, has the leading role. The performance comes before Pip finds out who his benefactor is, so the near farce of what he and Herbert see on the stage is meant to be a mocking allusion to Pip's own pretensions to be a gentleman.

> On our arrival in Denmark, we found the king and queen of that country elevated in two arm-chairs on a kitchen-table, holding a Court. The whole of the Danish nobility were in attendance; consisting of a noble boy in the wash-leather boots of a gigantic ancestor, a venerable Peer with a dirty face, who seemed to have risen from the people late in life, and the Danish chivalry with a

comb in its hair and a pair of white silk legs, and presenting on the whole a feminine appearance. My gifted townsman stood gloomily apart, with folded arms, and I could have wished that his curls and forehead had been more probable.

Several curious little circumstances transpired as the action proceeded. The late king of the country not only appeared to have been troubled with a cough at the time of his decease, but to have taken it with him to the tomb, and to have brought it back. The royal phantom also carried a ghostly manuscript round its truncheon, to which it had the appearance of occasionally referring, and that, too, with an air of anxiety and a tendency to lose the place of reference which were suggestive of a state of mortality. It was this, I conceive, which led to the Shade's being advised by the gallery to "turn over!" —a recommendation which it took extremely ill. . . . The Queen of Denmark, a very buxom lady, though no doubt historically brazen, was considered by the public to have too much brass about her; her chin being attached to her diadem by a broad band of that metal (as if she had a gorgeous toothache), her waist being encircled by another, and each of her arms by another, so that she was openly mentioned as the "kettledrum." . . . Lastly, Ophelia was a prey to such slow musical madness, that when, in course of time, she had taken off her white muslin scarf, folded it up, and buried it, a sulky man who had been long cooling his impatient nose against an iron bar in the front row of the gallery, growled, "Now the baby's put to bed, let's have supper!" Which, to say the least of it, was out of keeping.

Upon my unfortunate townsman all these incidents accumulated with playful effect. Whenever that undecided Prince had to ask a question or state a doubt, the public helped him out with it. As for example; on the question whether 'twas nobler in the mind to suffer, some roared yes, and some no, and some inclining to both opinions said "toss up for it;" and quite a Debating Society arose. When he asked what should such fellows as he do crawling between earth and heaven, he was encouraged with loud cries of "Hear, hear!" . . . On his taking the recorders . . . he was called upon unanimously for Rule Britannia. When he recommended the player not to saw the air thus, the sulky man said, "And don't *you* do it, neither; you're a deal worse than *him!*" (240–41)

The comedy of this is immediately obvious: Dickens takes a well-known play, never mentions it by name, and proceeds to describe the somewhat demeaning incongruities that occur when it is being staged by an incompetent and ridiculous company. The technique of Dickens's description, however, bears a little more analysis. In the first place,

several levels of action are formed in a scene that, because Dickens describes a staged performance at a theater, is expected to keep all those
levels distinct from one another. There are Pip and Herbert; there is
an audience; there are several vociferous members of the audience who
stand out; there are bad actors; there is a stage setting that is supposed
to be Denmark; and finally, very far away it seems, there is supposed to
be a play written by Shakespeare, commanding the entire proceedings
(although the actor playing the part of the ghost carries the text with
him).

Now, in the second place, these levels are hardly distinct from one
another during the performance, which is why the whole business is so
funny. Since nothing and no one—actors, spectators, setting, Pip and
Herbert—does what is expected, we come to realize without much
difficulty that no one and nothing fits the part assigned. The fit between actor and role, between audience and performer, between
speaker and words, between supposed setting and actual scene: all
these are out of joint and behave differently than they would if, for example, actor and part were perfectly matched. In short, nothing during this hilariously inept performance perfectly represents what we expect to be represented. In our heads we have a picture telling us that
Hamlet ought to look noble, that the audience ought to be quiet, that
the ghost be ghostlike. The effect of these foiled expectations is a trav-
esty of a great play that, despite its abuses, nevertheless manages to
weave its way more or less into everything Dickens describes, informing the entire proceedings. Indeed it would be quite accurate to say
that Shakespeare's play, its text, is there offstage, and what happens
onstage is a result of the text's imperfect or insufficient power to command this particular performance. For what goes wrong is in some
measure due not only to the company's and the audience's incompetence but also to the text's insufficient authority to make a representation or performance of itself work "properly."

One more thing. Not only are the levels scrambled, not only is
there no correspondence between original text and its realization;
there is also the fact that *Hamlet* the play is everywhere in Dickens' account of this disastrous evening. What Dickens gives us is in fact a
double scene or, to use a musical analogy, a theme and variations in
which one text or theme and a confused, new version of it take place
simultaneously in Dickens' prose. His narrative somehow manages to
portray *Hamlet* and *Hamlet* travestied, together, not so much only as
montage but as criticism, opening the venerated masterpiece to its
own vulnerability, letting a monument of literature accept and actually

accommodate the fact of its written, and hence unprotected, consequence, which is that each time it is performed the performance is a substitute for the original, and so on to infinity, with the original becoming a more and more hypothetical "original." So at one and the same time Dickens narrates a dramatic text in the process of its performance as it was intended to be performed, as well as the same text in a new configuration, as it is being performed and grossly travestied. The old and the new can cohabit this way for us only because Dickens puts the two together and lets them happen together in his text, according to a relatively strict method of comic exfoliation. If we say that *Hamlet* as Shakespeare wrote it is at the center or origin of the whole episode, then what Dickens gives us is a comically literal account of the center not only unable to hold, but *being* unable to hold, producing instead a number of new, devastatingly eccentric multiples of the play. Thus . . . the text commands and indeed permits, invents, all its misinterpretations and misreadings, which are functions of the text.

From the beginning of his career Derrida has been fascinated with the possibilities of this sort of thing. Some of his philosophic ideas about presence, about the privilege given by Western metaphysics to voice over writing, about the disappearance of the idea of center or origin in modern thought, are assumed in a most unphilosophic way by Dickens, for whom the simple incontrovertible fact that Shakespeare may have been the author of a great play called *Hamlet*, but who is not around to prevent *Hamlet* from being taken over and literally redone by anyone who has a mind to do so, is an assumption resembling Derrida's notion that ideas of voice, presence, and metaphysical "origins" are simply inadequate for the performative actualities of language. The other side of this view is the paradoxical one that Shakespeare's *text* is about its travesties of course, but those have to do with the text's powers, which are tied to its written state and the exigencies of performance and not to Shakespeare's presence as a once alive human being.

The technique of showing how these myths about voice and presence persist in our thinking and in much writing (whose whole status is undermined by the idea that writing is simply a reflection for something, like thought or a voice, which it is expected to represent) is Derrida's, as much as it is Dickens' in this scene and—to mention another example—Mark Twain's in *A Connecticut Yankee in King Arthur's Court.* Derrida himself has made the point that such debunkings as his in a sense revalidate the old myths, just as Dickens' parody of *Hamlet* is an act of homage to Shakespeare. . . . For Derrida the reason for this "hold" (the word he uses in *La Voix et le phénomène* is *prise*) on us and him of the old ideas is that they have preempted our thinking almost but not quite completely, they have caused certain notions (*impensés*) to become uncritically accepted, and—this is more important—as a philosopher he has been unable to discover a new way of thinking that totally liberates us from old ideas. Derrida has been extremely scrupulous about saying that he is not attempting to replace the old ideas with new ones, since he apparently does not intend to become the promulgator of a new orthodoxy to replace the old one. Whether this new orthodoxy emerges or not in his work is an important question, I think deliberately ignored by Derrida and his disciples.

But what is Derrida's philosophic strategy of deconstruction, as he calls it, and why are its techniques helpfully illuminated by the scene in *Great Expectations?* Let us start with representation, which is one of the key problems in all criticism and philosophy. Most accounts of representation, including Plato's, involve an original and a copy or representation, the first coming first in time and higher in value, the second later and lower in time and value, the first determining the second. In principle, a representative representation is meant to be a sometimes unavoidable, sometimes merely convenient substitute for the original, which for any number of reasons cannot be present to be itself and act itself. The representative or substitute is thus qualitatively different from the original, in part because an original is itself and is not contaminated by its difference. I simplify greatly of course, but Derrida's philosophic position is that difference—as between original and representative—is not a quality merely added to a representation or secondary object, in the way language is often considered to be a substitute for the real thing (since, for example, it is commonly supposed that language represents an idea or a person not immediately present). Rather, Derrida says that difference on one level is added to objects when they are designated as representative, but on another level, the strictly verbal level of designation itself, difference is already differed and therefore cannot be thought of as a quality or an idea or a concept having originals and copies. Difference is something wholly intrinsic to language, which is diacritical and is the very activity of language itself when it is perceived not phonetically but graphically. For this purely linguistic activity Derrida invents the word *différance*, an unnameable (or unpronounceable) name. "What is unnameable here is not some ineffable being that cannot be approached by a name; like God, for example. What is unnameable is the play that brings about the nominal effects, the relatively unitary or atomic structures we call names, or chains or substitutions for names" (159).

To name something is to specify an idea, object, or concept with some priority to the very activity of naming and to the name. Derrida wants us to see—if not to understand—that so long as we believe that language is mainly a representation of something else, we cannot see what language does; so long as we are expecting to understand language in terms of some primitive essence to which it is a functional addition, then we cannot see that any use of language means not only representation but, paradoxically, the end or permanent deferring of representation and the beginning or something else, which he calls writing. So long as we do not see that writing more accurately and materially than speaking signifies language being used not simply as a substitute for something better than itself but as an activity all its own, we cannot recognize that "something better" is a fundamental illusion (for if it could be there, it would be there). In short, we will remain in the grip of metaphysics.

Written language involves representation, just as the play that Pip sees is a representation; yet to say that language—or rather writing, since that is what Derrida is talking about always—and the performance are representations is not to say that they could be something else. They cannot be because, the play called *Hamlet* by Shakespeare is also an instance of writing, and all writing is not a replacement for anything, but an admission that there is only writing when language is to be used, at least so far as the possibility of sustained, repeatable representation is concerned. All of a sudden we see that the very notion of representation acquires a new uncertainty, just as every performance of *Hamlet*—no matter how zany—confirms the play's own verbal and even thematic instability. What we find Derrida doing is what we saw Dickens doing, allowing the very notion of representation to represent itself, on a stage (which is a profoundly apt locale, obviously) where at least two versions of a familiar text get in each other's way and on top of each other, one reversing the other, the new version supplementing the old, and the whole thing happening within Dickens's own prose, which is where and only where it can happen. Thus Derrida's endless worrying of representation involves him in a kind of permanent but highly economical tautology. He uses his own prose to represent certain ideas of presence, as well as their representations, at work in a whole series of texts from Plato to Heidegger; then in representing these texts he rereads and rewrites them, enabling us to see them not as representations of something, as references to a transcendental signified outside them, but as texts representing only themselves in, for a text, perfectly representative ways.

II. DICKENS AND AUSTRALIA
[from *Culture and Imperialism* (1993)]

Let me say a little here about what I have in mind, using [a] well-known and very great novel. . . . Dickens's *Great Expectations* (1861) is primarily a novel about self-delusion, about Pip's vain attempts to become a gentleman with neither the hard work nor the aristocratic source of income required for such a role. Early in life he helps a condemned convict, Abel Magwitch, who, after being transported to Australia, pays back his young benefactor with large sums of money; because the lawyer involved says nothing as he disburses the money, Pip persuades himself that an elderly gentlewoman, Miss Havisham, has been his patron. Magwitch then reappears illegally in London, unwelcomed by Pip because everything about the man reeks of delinquency and unpleasantness. In the end, though, Pip is reconciled to Magwitch and to his reality: he finally acknowledges Magwitch—hunted, apprehended, and fatally ill—as his surrogate father, not as someone to be denied or rejected, though Magwitch is in fact unacceptable, being from Australia, a penal colony designed for the rehabilitation but not the repatriation of transported English criminals.

Most, if not all, readings of this remarkable work situate it squarely within the metropolitan history of British fiction, whereas I believe that it belongs in a history both more inclusive and more dynamic than such interpretations allow. It has been left to two more recent books than Dickens's—Robert Hughes's magisterial *The Fatal Shore* and Paul Carter's brilliantly speculative *The Road to Botany Bay*—to reveal a vast history of speculation about the experience of Australia, a "white" colony like Ireland, in which we can locate Magwitch and Dickens not as mere coincidental references in that history, but as participants in it, through the novel and through a much older and wider experience between England and its overseas territories.

Australia was established as a penal colony in the late eighteenth century mainly so that England could transport an irredeemable, unwanted excess population of felons to a place, originally charted by Captain Cook, that would also function as a colony replacing those lost in America. The pursuit of profit, the building of empire, and what Hughes calls social *apartheid* together produced modern Australia, which by the time Dickens first took an interest in it during the

1840s (in *David Copperfield* Wilkins Micawber happily immigrates there) had progressed somewhat into profitability and a sort of "free system" where laborers could do well on their own if allowed to do so. Yet in Magwitch "Dickens knotted several strands in the English perception of convicts in Australia at the end of transportation. They could succeed, but they could hardly, in the real sense, return. They could expiate their crimes in a technical, legal sense, but what they suffered there warped them into permanent outsiders. And yet they were capable of redemption—as long as they stayed in Australia" (Hughes 586).

Carter's exploration of what he calls Australia's spatial history offers us another version of that same experience. Here explorers, convicts, ethnographers, profiteers, soldiers chart the vast and relatively empty continent each in a discourse that jostles, displaces, or incorporates the others. Botany Bay is therefore first of all an Enlightenment discourse of travel and discovery, then a set of travelling narrators (including Cook) whose words, charts, and intentions accumulate the strange territories and gradually turn them into "home." The adjacence between the Benthamite organization of space (which produced the city of Melbourne) and the apparent disorder of the Australian bush is shown by Carter to have become an optimistic transformation of social space, which produced an Elysium for gentlemen, an Eden for laborers in the 1840s (Carter 202–60). What Dickens envisions for Pip, being Magwitch's "London gentleman," is roughly equivalent to what was envisioned by English benevolence for Australia, one social space authorizing another.

But *Great Expectations* was not written with anything like the concern for native Australian accounts that Hughes or Carter has, nor did it presume or forecast a tradition of Australian writing, which in fact came later to include the literary works of David Malouf, Peter Carey, and Patrick White. The prohibition placed on Magwitch's return is not only penal but imperial: subjects can be taken to places like Australia, but they cannot be allowed a "return" to metropolitan space, which, as all Dickens's fiction testifies, is meticulously charted, spoken for, inhabited by a hierarchy of metropolitan personages. So on the one hand, interpreters like Hughes and Carter expand on the relatively attenuated presence of Australia in nineteenth-century British writing, expressing the fullness and earned integrity of an Australian history that became independent from Britain's in the twentieth century; yet, on the other, an accurate reading of *Great Expectations* must note that after Magwitch's delinquency is expiated, so to speak, after Pip redemptively acknowledges his debt to the old, bitterly energized, and vengeful convict, Pip himself collapses and is revived in two explicitly positive ways. A new Pip appears, less laden than the old Pip with the chains of the past—he is glimpsed in the form of a child, also called Pip; and the old Pip takes on a new career with his boyhood friend Herbert Pocket, this time not as an idle gentleman but as a hardworking trader in the East, where Britain's other colonies offer a sort of normality that Australia never could.

Thus even as Dickens settles the difficulty with Australia, another structure of attitude and reference emerges to suggest Britain's imperial intercourse through trade and travel with the Orient. In his new career as colonial businessman, Pip is hardly an exceptional figure, since nearly all of Dickens's businessmen, wayward relatives, and frightening outsiders have a fairly normal and secure connection with the empire. But it is only in recent years that these connections have taken on interpretative importance. A new generation of scholars and critics—the children of decolonization in some instances, the beneficiaries (like sexual, religious, and racial minorities) of advances in human freedom at home—have seen in such great texts of Western literature a standing interest in what was considered a lesser world, populated with lesser people of color, portrayed as open to the intervention of so many Robinson Crusoes. . . .

To lose sight of or ignore the national and international context of, say, Dickens's representations of Victorian businessmen, and to focus only on the internal coherence of their roles in his novels is to miss an essential connection between his fiction and its historical world. And understanding that connection does not reduce or diminish the novels' value as works of art: on the contrary, because of their *worldliness*, because of their complex affiliations with their real setting, they are *more* interesting and *more* valuable as works of art.

WORKS CITED

Carter, Paul. *The Road to Botany Bay: An Exploration of Landscape and History.* New York: Knopf, 1988.

Derrida, Jacques. *Speech and Phenomena, and Other Essays on Husserl's Theory of Signs.* Trans. David B. Allison. Evanston: Northwestern UP, 1973.

Hughes, Robert. *The Fatal Shore: The Epic of Australia's Founding.* New York: Knopf, 1987.

Feminist Criticism
and
Great Expectations

WHAT IS FEMINIST CRITICISM?

Feminist criticism comes in many forms, and feminist critics have a variety of goals. Some have been interested in rediscovering the works of women writers overlooked by a masculine-dominated culture. Others have revisited books by male authors and reviewed them from a woman's point of view to understand how they both reflect and shape the attitudes that have held women back. A number of contemporary feminists have turned to topics as various as women in postcolonial societies, women's autobiographical writings, lesbians and literature, womanliness as masquerade, and the role of film and other popular media in the construction of the feminine gender.

Until a few years ago, however, feminist thought tended to be classified not according to topic but, rather, according to country of origin. This practice reflected the fact that, during the 1970s and early 1980s, French, American, and British feminists wrote from somewhat different perspectives.

French feminists tended to focus their attention on language, analyzing the ways in which meaning is produced. They concluded that language as we commonly think of it is a decidedly male realm. Drawing on the ideas of the psychoanalytic philosopher Jacques Lacan, they

reminded us that language is a realm of public discourse. A child enters the linguistic realm just as it comes to grasp its separateness from
its mother, just about the time that boys identify with their father, the
family representative of culture. The language learned reflects a binary
logic that opposes such terms as active/passive, masculine/feminine,
sun/moon, father/mother, head/heart, son/daughter, intelligent/
sensitive, brother/sister, form/matter, phallus/vagina, reason/emo-
tion. Because this logic tends to group with masculinity such qualities
as light, thought, and activity, French feminists said that the structure
of language is phallocentric: it privileges the phallus and, more generally, masculinity by associating them with things and values more appreciated by the (masculine-dominated) culture. Moreover, French
feminists suggested, "masculine desire dominates speech and posits
woman as an idealized fantasy-fulfillment for the incurable emotional
lack caused by separation from the mother" (Jones, "Writing" 83).

French feminists associated language with separation from the
mother. Its distinctions, they argued, represent the world from the
male point of view. Language systematically forces women to choose:
either they can imagine and represent themselves as men imagine and
represent them (in which case they may speak, but will speak as men)
or they can choose "silence," becoming in the process "the invisible
and unheard sex" (Jones, "Writing" 83).

But some influential French feminists maintained that language
only *seems* to give women such a narrow range of choices. There is another possibility, namely that women can develop a *feminine* language.
In various ways, early French feminists such as Annie Leclerc, Xavière
Gauthier, and Marguerite Duras suggested that there is something
that may be called *l'écriture féminine:* women's writing. More recently, Julia Kristeva has said that feminine language is "semiotic," not
"symbolic." Rather than rigidly opposing and ranking elements of reality, rather than symbolizing one thing but not another in terms of a
third, feminine language is rhythmic and unifying. If from the male
perspective it seems fluid to the point of being chaotic, that is a fault of
the male perspective.

According to Kristeva, feminine language is derived from the pre-
oedipal period of fusion between mother and child. Associated with
the maternal, feminine language is not only a threat to culture, which
is patriarchal, but also a medium through which women may be creative in new ways. But Kristeva paired her central, liberating claim—
that truly feminist innovation in all fields requires an understanding of
the relation between maternity and feminine creation—with a warn-

ing. A feminist language that refuses to participate in "masculine" discourse, that places its future entirely in a feminine, semiotic discourse, risks being politically marginalized by men. That is to say, it risks being relegated to the outskirts (pun intended) of what is considered socially and politically significant.

Kristeva, who associated feminine writing with the female body, was joined in her views by other leading French feminists. Hélène Cixous, for instance, also posited an essential connection between the woman's body, whose sexual pleasure has been repressed and denied expression, and women's writing. "Write your self. Your body must be heard," Cixous urged; once they learn to write their bodies, women will not only realize their sexuality but enter history and move toward a future based on a "feminine" economy of giving rather than the "masculine" economy of hoarding (Cixous 880). For Luce Irigaray, women's sexual pleasure (*jouissance*) cannot be expressed by the dominant, ordered, "logical," masculine language. Irigaray explored the connection between women's sexuality and women's language through the following analogy: as women's *jouissance* is more multiple than men's unitary, phallic pleasure ("woman has sex organs just about everywhere"), so "feminine" language is more diffusive than its "masculine" counterpart. ("That is undoubtedly the reason . . . her language . . . goes off in all directions and . . . he is unable to discern the coherence," Irigaray writes [*This Sex* 101–03].)

Cixous's and Irigaray's emphasis on feminine writing as an expression of the female body drew criticism from other French feminists. Many argued that an emphasis on the body either reduces "the feminine" to a biological essence or elevates it in a way that shifts the valuation of masculine and feminine but retains the binary categories. For Christine Fauré, Irigaray's celebration of women's difference failed to address the issue of masculine dominance, and a Marxist-feminist, Catherine Clément, warned that "poetic" descriptions of what constitutes the feminine will not challenge that dominance in the realm of production. The boys will still make the toys, and decide who gets to use them. In her effort to redefine women as political rather than as sexual beings, Monique Wittig called for the abolition of the sexual categories that Cixous and Irigaray retained and revalued as they celebrated women's writing.

American feminist critics of the 1970s and early 1980s shared with French critics both an interest in and a cautious distrust of the concept of feminine writing. Annette Kolodny, for instance, worried that the "richness and variety of women's writing" will be missed if we see in it only its "feminine mode" or "style" ("Some Notes" 78). And yet Kolodny herself proceeded, in the same essay, to point out that women *have* had their own style, which includes reflexive constructions ("she found herself crying") and particular, recurring themes (clothing and self-fashioning are mentioned by Kolodny; other American feminists have focused on madness, disease, and the demonic).

Interested as they became in the "French" subject of feminine style, American feminist critics began by analyzing literary texts rather than philosophizing abstractly about language. Many reviewed the great works by male writers, embarking on a revisionist rereading of literary tradition. These critics examined the portrayals of women characters, exposing the patriarchal ideology implicit in such works and showing how clearly this tradition of systematic masculine dominance is inscribed in our literary tradition. Kate Millett, Carolyn Heilbrun, and Judith Fetterley, among many others, created this model for American feminist criticism, a model that Elaine Showalter came to call "the feminist critique" of "male-constructed literary history" ("Poetics" 128).

Meanwhile another group of critics including Sandra Gilbert, Susan Gubar, Patricia Meyer Spacks, and Showalter herself created a somewhat different model. Whereas feminists writing "feminist critique" analyzed works by men, practitioners of what Showalter used to refer to as "gynocriticism" studied the writings of those women who, against all odds, produced what she calls "a literature of their own." In *The Female Imagination* (1975), Spacks examined the female literary tradition to find out how great women writers across the ages have felt, perceived themselves, and imagined reality. Gilbert and Gubar, in *The Madwoman in the Attic* (1979), concerned themselves with well-known women writers of the nineteenth century, but they too found that general concerns, images, and themes recur, because the authors that they wrote about lived "in a culture whose fundamental definitions of literary authority were both overtly and covertly patriarchal" (45).

If one of the purposes of gynocriticism was to (re)study well-known women authors, another was to rediscover women's history and culture, particularly women's communities that nurtured female creativity. Still another related purpose was to discover neglected or forgotten women writers and thus to forge an alternative literary tradition, a canon that better represents the female perspective by better representing the literary works that have been written by women. Showalter, in *A Literature of Their Own* (1977), admirably began to fulfill this purpose, providing a remarkably comprehensive overview of women's writing through three of its phases. She defined these as the "Feminine, Feminist, and Female" phases, phases during which women first imitated a masculine tradition (1840–80), then protested against its standards and values (1880–1920), and finally advocated their own autonomous, female perspective (1920 to the present).

With the recovery of a body of women's texts, attention returned to a question raised in 1978 by Lillian Robinson: Shouldn't feminist criticism need to formulate a theory of its own practice? Won't reliance on theoretical assumptions, categories, and strategies developed by men and associated with nonfeminist schools of thought prevent feminism from being accepted as equivalent to these other critical discourses? Not all American feminists came to believe that a special or unifying theory of feminist practice was urgently needed; Showalter's historical approach to women's culture allowed a feminist critic to use theories based on nonfeminist disciplines. Kolodny advocated a "playful pluralism" that encompasses a variety of critical schools and methods. But Jane Marcus and others responded that if feminists adopt too wide a range of approaches, they may relax the tensions between feminists and the educational establishment necessary for political activism.

The question of whether feminism weakens or fortifies itself by emphasizing its separateness—and by developing unity through separateness—was one of several areas of debate within American feminism during the 1970s and early 1980s. Another area of disagreement touched on earlier, between feminists who stress universal feminine attributes (the feminine imagination, feminine writing) and those who focus on the political conditions experienced by certain groups of women at certain times in history, paralleled a larger distinction between American feminist critics and their British counterparts.

While it gradually became customary to refer to an Anglo-American tradition of feminist criticism, British feminists tended to distinguish themselves from what they saw as an American overemphasis on texts linking women across boundaries and decades and an underemphasis on popular art and culture. They regarded their own critical practice as more political than that of North American feminists, whom they sometimes faulted for being uninterested in historical detail. They joined such American critics as Myra Jehlen in suggesting that a continuing preoccupation with women writers may bring about the dangerous result of placing women's texts outside the history that conditions them.

British feminists felt that the American opposition to male

stereotypes that denigrate women often leads to counterstereotypes of feminine virtue that ignore real differences of race, class, and culture among women. In addition, they argued that American celebrations of individual heroines falsely suggest that powerful individuals may be immune to repressive conditions and may even imply that *any* individual can go through life unconditioned by the culture and ideology in which she or he lives.

Similarly, the American endeavor to recover women's history—for example, by emphasizing that women developed their own strategies to gain power within their sphere—was seen by British feminists like Judith Newton and Deborah Rosenfelt as an endeavor that "mystifies" male oppression, disguising it as something that has created for women a special world of opportunities. More important from the British standpoint, the universalizing and "essentializing" tendencies in both American practice and French theory disguise women's oppression by highlighting sexual difference, suggesting that a dominant system is impervious to political change. By contrast, British feminist theory emphasized an engagement with historical process in order to promote social change.

By now the French, American, and British approaches have so thoroughly critiqued, influenced, and assimilated one another that the work of most Western practitioners is no longer easily identifiable along national boundary lines. Instead, it tends to be characterized according to whether the category of *woman* is the major focus in the exploration of gender and gender oppression or, alternatively, whether the interest in sexual difference encompasses an interest in other differences that also define identity. The latter paradigm encompasses the work of feminists of color, Third World (preferably called postcolonial) feminists, and lesbian feminists, many of whom have asked whether the universal category of woman constructed by certain French and North American predecessors is appropriate to describe women in minority groups or non-Western cultures.

These feminists stress that, while all women are female, they are something else as well (such as African-American, lesbian, Muslim Pakistani). This "something else" is precisely what makes them, their problems, and their goals different from those of other women. As Armit Wilson has pointed out, Asian women living in Britain are expected by their families and communities to preserve Asian cultural traditions; thus, the expression of personal identity through clothing involves a much more serious infraction of cultural rules than it does for a Western woman. Gloria Anzaldúa has spoken personally and eloquently about the experience of many women on the margins of Eurocentric North American culture. "I am a border woman," she writes in *Borderlands: La Frontera = The New Mestiza* (1987). "I grew up between two cultures, the Mexican (with a heavy Indian influence) and the Anglo. . . . Living on the borders and in margins, keeping intact one's shifting and multiple identity and integrity is like trying to swim in a new element, an 'alien' element" (i).

Instead of being divisive and isolating, this evolution of feminism into femin*isms* has fostered a more inclusive, global perspective. The era of recovering women's texts—especially texts by white Western women—has been succeeded by a new era in which the goal is to recover entire cultures of women. Two important figures of this new era are Trinh T. Minh-ha and Gayatri Spivak. Spivak, in works such as *In Other Worlds: Essays in Cultural Politics* (1987) and *Outside in the Teaching Machine* (1993), has shown how political independence (generally looked upon by metropolitan Westerners as a simple and beneficial historical and political reversal) has complex implications for "subaltern" or subproletarian women.

The understanding of woman not as a single, deterministic category but rather as the nexus of diverse experiences has led some white, Western, "majority" feminists like Jane Tompkins and Nancy K. Miller to advocate and practice "personal" or "autobiographical" criticism. Once reluctant to inject themselves into their analyses for fear of being labeled idiosyncratic, impressionistic, and subjective by men, some feminists are now openly skeptical of the claims to reason, logic, and objectivity that have been made in the past by male critics. With the advent of more personal feminist critical styles has come a powerful new interest in women's autobiographical writings.

Shari Benstock, who has written personal criticism in her book *Textualizing the Feminine* (1991), was one of the first feminists to argue that traditional autobiography is a gendered, "masculinist" genre. Its established conventions, feminists have recently pointed out, call for a life-plot that turns on action, triumph through conflict, intellectual self-discovery, and often public renown. The body, reproduction, children, and intimate interpersonal relationships are generally well in the background and often absent. Arguing that the lived experiences of women and men differ—women's lives, for instance, are often characterized by interruption and deferral—Leigh Gilmore has developed a theory of women's self-representation in her book *Autobiographics: A Feminist Theory of Self-Representation* (1994).

Autobiographics and personal criticism are only two of a number of recent developments in contemporary feminist criticism. Others alluded to in the first paragraph of this introduction—lesbian studies, performance or "masquerade" theory, and studies of the role played by film and various other "technologies" in shaping gender today—are so prominent in contemporary *gender* criticism that they are discussed in a separate introduction (see "What Is Gender Criticism?" pp. 558–66). Although that introduction will outline several of the differences between the feminist and gender approaches, the fact of this overlap should remind us that categories obscure similarities even as they help us make distinctions. Feminist criticism is, after all, a form of gender criticism, and gender criticism as we have come to know it could never have developed without feminist criticism.

Ross C Murfin

FEMINIST CRITICISM: A SELECTED BIBLIOGRAPHY

French Feminist Theory

Cixous, Hélène. "The Laugh of the Medusa." Trans. Keith Cohen and Paula Cohen. *Signs* 1 (1976): 875–93.

Cixous, Hélène, and Catherine Clément. *The Newly Born Woman.* Trans. Betsy Wing. Minneapolis: U of Minnesota P, 1986.

Irigaray, Luce. *An Ethics of Sexual Difference.* Trans. Carolyn Burke and Gillian C. Gill. Ithaca: Cornell UP, 1993.

———. *This Sex Which Is Not One.* Trans. Catherine Porter. Ithaca: Cornell UP, 1985.

Jones, Ann Rosalind. "Inscribing Femininity: French Theories of the Feminine." *Making a Difference: Feminist Literary Criticism.* Ed. Gayle Green and Coppélia Kahn. London: Methuen, 1985. 80–112.

———. "Writing the Body: Toward an Understanding of *L'Écriture féminine.*" Showalter, ed., *The New Feminist Criticism.* New York: Pantheon, 1985. 361–77.

Kristeva, Julia. *Desire in Language: A Semiotic Approach to Literature and Art.* Ed. Leon S. Roudiez. Trans. Thomas Gora, Alice Jardine, and Roudiez. New York: Columbia UP, 1980.

Marks, Elaine, and Isabelle de Courtivron, eds. *New French Feminisms: An Anthology.* Amherst: U of Massachusetts P, 1980.

Moi, Toril, ed. *French Feminist Thought: A Reader*. Oxford: Basil Blackwell, 1987.

Feminist Theory: Classic Texts, General Approaches, Collections

Abel, Elizabeth, and Emily K. Abel, eds. *The "Signs" Reader: Women, Gender, and Scholarship*. Chicago: U of Chicago P, 1983.

Barrett, Michèle, and Anne Phillips. *Destabilizing Theory: Contemporary Feminist Debates*. Stanford: Stanford UP, 1992.

Beauvoir, Simone de. *The Second Sex*. 1953. Trans. and ed. H. M. Parshley. New York: Bantam, 1961.

Benstock, Shari. *Textualizing the Feminine: On the Limits of Genre*. Norman: U of Oklahoma P, 1991.

Butler, Judith. *Gender Trouble: Feminism and the Subversion of Identity*. New York: Routledge, 1990.

de Lauretis, Teresa, ed. *Feminist Studies/Critical Studies*. Bloomington: Indiana UP, 1986.

Felman, Shoshana. "Women and Madness: The Critical Phallacy." *Diacritics* 5 (1975): 2–10.

Fetterley, Judith. *The Resisting Reader: A Feminist Approach to American Fiction*. Bloomington: Indiana UP, 1978.

Fuss, Diana. *Essentially Speaking: Feminism, Nature and Difference*. New York: Routledge, 1989.

Gallop, Jane. *The Daughter's Seduction: Feminism and Psychoanalysis*. Ithaca: Cornell UP, 1982.

hooks, bell. *Feminist Theory: From Margin to Center*. Boston: South End P, 1984.

Kolodny, Annette. "Dancing Through the Minefield: Some Observations on the Theory, Practice, and Politics of a Feminist Literary Criticism." Showalter, ed., *The New Feminist Criticism*. New York: Pantheon, 1985. 144–67.

———. "Some Notes on Defining a 'Feminist Literary Criticism.'" *Critical Inquiry* 2 (1975): 78.

Lovell, Terry, ed. *British Feminist Thought: A Reader*. Oxford: Basil Blackwell, 1990.

Meese, Elizabeth, and Alice Parker, eds. *The Difference Within: Feminism and Critical Theory*. Philadelphia: John Benjamins, 1989.

Miller, Nancy K., ed. *The Poetics of Gender*. New York: Columbia UP, 1986.

Millett, Kate. *Sexual Politics*. Garden City, NJ: Doubleday, 1970.

Rich, Adrienne. *On Lies, Secrets, and Silence: Selected Prose, 1966–1979*. New York: Norton, 1979.

Showalter, Elaine, ed. *The New Feminist Criticism: Essays on Women, Literature, and Theory.* New York: Pantheon, 1985.

———. "Toward a Feminist Poetics." Showalter, ed., *The New Feminist Criticism.* New York: Pantheon, 1985. 125–43.

Stimpson, Catherine R. "Feminist Criticism." *Redrawing the Boundaries: The Transformation of English and American Literary Studies.* Ed. Stephen Greenblatt and Giles Gunn. New York: MLA, 1992. 251–70.

Warhol, Robyn R., and Diane Price Herndl, eds. *Feminisms: An Anthology of Literary Theory and Criticism.* New Brunswick, NJ: Rutgers UP, 1991.

Weed, Elizabeth, ed. *Coming to Terms: Feminism, Theory, Politics.* New York: Routledge, 1989.

Woolf, Virginia. *A Room of One's Own.* New York: Harcourt, 1929.

Women's Writing and Creativity

Abel, Elizabeth, ed. *Writing and Sexual Difference.* Chicago: U of Chicago P, 1982.

DuPlessis, Rachel Blau. *The Pink Guitar: Writing as Feminist Practice.* New York: Routledge, 1990.

Finke, Laurie. *Feminist Theory, Women's Writing.* Ithaca: Cornell UP, 1992.

Gilbert, Sandra M., and Susan Gubar. *The Madwoman in the Attic: The Woman Writer and the Nineteenth-Century Literary Imagination.* New Haven: Yale UP, 1979.

Homans, Margaret. *Bearing the Word: Language and Female Experience in Nineteenth-Century Women's Writing.* Chicago: U of Chicago P, 1986.

Jacobus, Mary, ed. *Women Writing and Writing about Women.* New York: Barnes, 1979.

Miller, Nancy K. *Subject to Change: Reading Feminist Writing.* New York: Columbia UP, 1988.

Newton, Judith Lowder. *Women, Power and Subversion: Social Strategies in British Fiction, 1778–1860.* Athens: U of Georgia P, 1981.

Poovey, Mary. *The Proper Lady and the Woman Writer: Ideology as Style in the Works of Mary Wollstonecraft, Mary Shelley, and Jane Austen.* Chicago: U of Chicago P, 1984.

Showalter, Elaine. *A Literature of Their Own: British Women Novelists from Brontë to Lessing.* Princeton: Princeton UP, 1977.

Spacks, Patricia Meyer. *The Female Imagination.* New York: Knopf, 1975.

Feminism, Race, Class, and Nationality

Anzaldúa, Gloria. *Borderlands: La Frontera = The New Mestiza*. San Francisco: Spinsters/Aunt Lute, 1987.

Christian, Barbara. *Black Feminist Criticism: Perspectives on Black Women Writers*. New York: Pergamon, 1985.

hooks, bell. *Ain't I a Woman?: Black Women and Feminism*. Boston: South End P, 1981.

———. *Black Looks: Race and Representation*. Boston: South End P, 1992.

Kaplan, Cora. *Sea Changes: Essays on Culture and Feminism*. London: Verso, 1986.

Moraga, Cherrie, and Gloria Anzaldúa. *This Bridge Called My Back: Writings by Radical Women of Color*. New York: Kitchen Table, 1981.

Newton, Judith, and Deborah Rosenfelt, eds. *Feminist Criticism and Social Change: Sex, Class, and Race in Literature and Culture*. New York: Methuen, 1985.

Pryse, Marjorie, and Hortense Spillers, eds. *Conjuring: Black Women, Fiction, and Literary Tradition*. Bloomington: Indiana UP, 1985.

Robinson, Lillian S. *Sex, Class, and Culture*. 1978. New York: Methuen, 1986.

Smith, Barbara. "Towards a Black Feminist Criticism." Showalter, ed., *The New Feminist Criticism*. New York: Pantheon, 1985. 168–85.

Feminism and Postcoloniality

Emberley, Julia. *Thresholds of Difference: Feminist Critique, Native Women's Writings, Postcolonial Theory*. Toronto: U of Toronto P, 1993.

Mohanty, Chandra Talpade, Ann Russo, and Lourdes Torres, eds. *Third World Women and the Politics of Feminism*. Bloomington: Indiana UP, 1991.

Schipper, Mineke, ed. *Unheard Words: Women and Literature in Africa, the Arab World, Asia, the Caribbean, and Latin America*. London: Allison, 1985.

Spivak, Gayatri Chakravorty. *In Other Worlds: Essays in Cultural Politics*. New York: Methuen, 1987.

———. *Outside in the Teaching Machine*. New York: Routledge, 1993.

Trinh T. Minh-ha. *Woman, Native, Other: Writing Postcoloniality and Feminism*. Bloomington: Indiana UP, 1989.

Wilson, Armit. *Finding a Voice: Asian Women in Britain*. 1979. London: Virago, 1980.

Women's Self-Representation and Personal Criticism

Benstock, Shari, ed. *The Private Self: Theory and Practice of Women's Autobiographical Writings*. Chapel Hill: U of North Carolina P, 1988.

Gilmore, Leigh. *Autobiographics: A Feminist Theory of Self-Representation*. Ithaca: Cornell UP, 1994.

Martin, Biddy, and Chandra Talpade Mohanty. "Feminist Politics: What's Home Got to Do with It?" *Life/Lines: Theorizing Women's Autobiography*. Ed. Bella Brodski and Celeste Schenck. Ithaca: Cornell UP, 1988.

Miller, Nancy K. *Getting Personal: Feminist Occasions and Other Autobiographical Acts*. New York: Routledge, 1991.

Smith, Sidonie. *A Poetics of Women's Autobiography: Marginality and the Fictions of Self-Representation*. Bloomington: Indiana UP, 1988.

Feminist Film Theory

de Lauretis, Teresa. *Alice Doesn't: Feminism, Semiotics, Cinema*. Bloomington: Indiana UP, 1986.

Doane, Mary Ann. *Re-vision: Essays in Feminist Film Criticism*. Frederick, MD: U Publications of America, 1984.

Modleski, Tania. *Feminism without Women: Culture and Criticism in a "Postfeminist" Age*. New York: Routledge, 1991.

Mulvey, Laura. *Visual and Other Pleasures*. Bloomington: Indiana UP, 1989.

Penley, Constance, ed. *Feminism and Film Theory*. New York: Routledge, 1988.

Feminist Criticism of *Great Expectations*

Langbauer, Laurie. "Streetwalkers and Homebodies: Dickens's Romantic Women." *Women and Romance: The Consolations of Gender in the English Novel*. Ithaca: Cornell UP, 1990. 127–87.

Raphael, Linda. "A Re-Vision of Miss Havisham: Her Expectations and Our Responses." *Studies in the Novel* 21 (1989): 400–12.

Walsh, Susan. "Bodies of Capital: *Great Expectations* and the Climateric Economy." *Victorian Studies* 37 (1993): 73–98.

A FEMINIST PERSPECTIVE

Introduction

Hilary Schor's essay on *Great Expectations* approaches the novel from the perspectives of both the American and the French brands of feminism as Ross Murfin has defined them in his introduction to feminist criticism. On one hand, the essay participates in the classic mode of American feminism by reading "the woman's story" in a man's text, Pip's autobiography and the novel that Dickens has written in the guise of that autobiography. The woman in question is, of course, Estella; and Schor notes quite accurately how often Estella's role in the novel is simply taken for granted, never interrogated or viewed as problematic. Schor points to Estella as the principal and most significant of a series of "shadowy women, half-women, victimized women, women whom Pip cannot see clearly, women who hide from the light." These women "haunt" *Great Expectations*, and Schor's primary goal is to understand their meaning in the novel and, perhaps more important, to themselves. In this way, Schor attempts to reread or "revise" a canonical novel by restoring to our sense of it the importance of its female figures.

On the other hand, Schor's interest in language, in the constitution of subjectivity through language, places her essay clearly in the tradition of French feminists and their American counterparts, feminists whose use of deconstructive techniques and psychoanalytic insights have illuminated female subjectivity. If it is Schor's goal to "read" Estella's story, the methodology at work in that reading is drawn from poststructuralist theories about the nature of language, desire, and the cultural construction of individuality.

In fact, like the selections from Edward Said's work presented in this edition, Hilary Schor's essay also demonstrates Jay Clayton's contention that many different brands of criticism now use deconstructive methods (34). Schor argues that *Great Expectations* is a novel that both obscures and depends upon a woman's story. The "vision" of the novel contains its own "countervision." Her reading of the revised ending of the novel, like Said's reading of Wopsle's *Hamlet*, casts Dickens as a deconstructionist: the revised ending improves on the original one in that it offers two contradictory and mutually exclusive endings, Pip's and Estella's; but it does not choose between them by giving one priority over the other.

Schor takes the title of her essay from Jaggers's speculations about the kind of married life that Estella will have with her intended husband, Drummle. Jaggers assumes that the marriage will be a contest between the two, but he imagines that Drummle may have the upper hand if he literally uses his hands to "turn to and beat" Estella. Schor takes this linking of violence and sexuality as the hallmark of the construction of subjectivity, male and female, in the novel. She demonstrates this point first by analyzing how violence, language, and desire—the last of these often figured in economic terms—come together to constitute Pip's subjectivity. Estella's role, as the object of Pip's desire, is, of course, central to this construction, and Schor explains that Estella's casting as the "smiter" of Pip's heart defines him as female, passive, and dependent. Schor, however, turns this formulation around by turning to the question of Estella's subjectivity. If Pip must use Estella—even abuse her by making her his tormenter—to be who he is, who is Estella?

At this point, Schor rejects the idea that questioning "Estella's value apart from Pip's valuation of her" is "a deliberate perversity," an "anachronistic reading possible only from the perspective of contemporary feminism." Rather, Schor demonstrates that Dickens creates in Estella the novel's most acute critic of Pip and therefore affords her an important place in this man's story. In turning again to questions of language, however, Schor returns to the issue of violence, locating it in both the plots of the novel and in the metaphoric language that Pip uses to "subsume" Estella into his own story. Although Schor posits a similarity between rape and metaphor, although she points to Pip's mistreatment of Estella, both in his life and in his telling of it, Schor suggests that at the end of the novel, *Great Expectations* "separates itself from this pattern of abuse and usurpation." She concludes her essay by asking a version of K. J. Fielding's question about Pip—"Just what progress has been made?"—but she turns away from this traditional interest in the male hero of the novel to assert Estella's primacy in *Great Expectations:* in effect, by giving Estella words to say, Dickens allows her story at least to stand next to, if not in place of, a man's story.

Janice Carlisle

Work Cited

Clayton, Jay. *The Pleasures of Babel: Contemporary American Literature and Theory.* New York: Oxford UP, 1993.

HILARY SCHOR

"If He Should Turn to and Beat Her": Violence, Desire, and the Woman's Story in *Great Expectations*

Of all Dickens's fantastic accounts of boys' lives, each part fairy tale and part horror story, none more insistently plays with the story of the fairy princess, or more insistently rewrites its darker side, than does *Great Expectations*. Pip casts his own story as a romance, with Estella as at once the beautiful, cold, distant "light" of his existence and the reward for his trials; as he carefully positions her (the star by which he can navigate), so she must remain, in order for his story to have coherence. We, too, mark our positions by her distance: to the extent that we are ironic readers of the novel, we will focus on her unsuitability and Pip's obsession; if we choose to value Dickensian sentiment, we will emphasize her changed heart and her altered form, and we will, with Pip, look for no "shadow" of a further parting. The Estella who has been "bent and broken" will in either case monitor *our* progress and wisdom and our assessment of Pip's growth.

But one of the persistent problematics of *Great Expectations*—the real shadow that haunts its ending—is not whether Pip ever marries Estella but whether Pip ever *sees* Estella: Does he ever free her from her fixed place as the guiding light of his existence? This question matters as an emblem not only of Pip's maturity but of Dickens's relation to his hero—his narrator—throughout the novel. Pip, as everyone knows, is an insufferable young man, but fewer readers have commented on the ways in which he remains insufferable to the end of the novel. No character points out his shallowness throughout more effectively than Estella, questioning and teasing him, mocking his efforts to be his own hero. But more to the purpose here, no character so writes her own novel, escaping Pip's monomaniacal obsession, than Estella, who throughout is wiser, sadder, and funnier than Pip—and who is the character most entirely "bent and broken" by the novel into another form.

To try to read Estella's novel—with its bitter realism and its own change of heart—through Pip's narration is not only to illuminate the way Dickens constructs narratives-within-narratives, the way autobiographical narrative is always questioning itself, but to question again the nature of the two endings. Reading for Estella's "end" is to make of the famous "second ending" two quite different endings, suggesting that Dickensian closure—like Dickensian "art"—writes it-self through (the fear of) the woman's story.

I

Although not a novelist, Pip is one of Dickens's greatest fabulists, and his favorite story is that he is designed to marry Estella, and she him. She, however, is his most critical reader: from her initial valuation of him ("what coarse hands") through her most honest moments ("Do you want me, then, to deceive and entrap you?"), she has the ability to put him off balance, to begin his story again. More dis-turbingly, she questions the notion of autonomous heroics his story depends on, reminding him that "We have no choice, you and I, but to obey our instructions. We are not free to follow our own devices, you and I" (250). Her tone, he recounts, was "as if our association were forced upon us and we were mere puppets [and it] gave me pain; but everything in our intercourse did give me pain" (253). In fact, though, Estella is right, and they are both puppets: if Pip's tragedy is his assumption of authority where none exists, Estella's is her knowl-edge that she is powerless and her realization that knowing this will in no way change her story.

Pip's story, like most critical accounts of it, begins with him alone, trying to trace out of linguistic fragments his own history, probing the "authority of tombstones" in order to generate out of them a family, a personality, a past.[1] Facing the emptiness of the marshes and himself, a "small bundle of shivers growing afraid of it all and beginning to cry," he is grabbed, shaken, tumbled upside down, released prematurely from his examination of "the identity of things" and set loose in the world that Dickens describes as that of the "Accoucheur Policeman" ready to abduct people for the effrontery of having been born (23–24, 41). Pip, that foundling, seedling, blossom, who has been "brought up by hand," "ram-paged" upon, "dosed" and "examined," will spend the rest of the book trying to escape the world he has been abandoned into and to fill in the pictures behind those words in the graveyard, for without those words he is empty and might as well, as Mrs. Joe wishes, have been buried in the graveyard. Having "called myself Pip and [having come] to be called Pip," he must write himself a story and find his own way out of the marshes.

[1]The best discussion of this problem in the novel remains Peter Brooks's "Repeti-tion, Repression, and Return" (pp. 481–501).

This version of Pip's story is one often rehearsed by critics, in part because it is a readerly explanation. What Pip sees as the way out is suggested to him in the first chapter: it is primarily linguistic, for he can read the tombstone; he can invent his lost family; he can "give it mouth!" as the convict orders. But that narrative of linguistic self-creation is linked to human re-creation: Pip's quest for the "beginning(s)" of his cry becomes one with his quest for love and fulfillment. Out of the pristine and terrifying loneliness of that initial scene, of reading identity through tombstones, comes a desire to read and be read, to find another to give meaning to the story of self that Pip is trying to create. Pip's erotic journey is, for him, a method of perception, his creation of a self linked to speech and desire. But in this model romantic desire is the primary vehicle for the self coming to consciousness: the young boy "becomes" himself by seeking an object for desire, and by absorbing that object into himself. This romantic consciousness partakes of fulfillment and mastery at the same time; Pip can call himself into being (realize his "expectations") by achieving the object (here, by winning the girl) he has identified as his own.[2] But Pip's expectations are not only of "calling himself Pip" and of winning the girl, but of winning everything associated with her. In pursuing a princess in the tower, one difficult to capture and hard to hold on to, Pip will fulfill his economic expectations as well, running together romantic desire, class anxiety, and the promise of happiness—all conveniently presented in one figure, that of the heroine of the romance, who will become the contested site of "value" in the novel.

Dickens obviously links these worlds of language and desire in the descriptions of how Pip comes to love Estella—or at least in Pip's accounts of them. But I want to trace a different account of identity, one that begins before Pip ever sees Estella: in Pip's attempts to learn to write, his cross-examination of Joe Gargery, and his first trip to Satis House. That story tells a different version of what Pip's "mastery" will mean. It is linked to violence and victimization, and it offers a different kind of home for identity. In that story, if Pip's transformation begins when he learns to read, his real education begins when he learns why Joe cannot.

[2] This process is one best read, I believe, through the dynamics of Freud and Hegel; for a splendid account of these issues, see Jessica Benjamin's *The Bonds of Love: Psychoanalysis, Feminism, and the Problem of Domination.*

Pip's early efforts at reading land him amid a tangle of economies, criminality, and anxiety: he struggles "through the alphabet as if it had been a bramble-bush; getting considerably worried and scratched by every letter"; when he goes on to the numbers, "those thieves, the nine figures," they "seemed every evening to do something new to disguise themselves and baffle recognition." But Pip wants to read only in order to "make" something of himself, and "at last I began, in a purblind groping way, to read, write and cipher, on the very smallest scale." His first literary activity is to write a letter to Joe—for which "there was no indispensable necessity . . . inasmuch as he sat beside me and we were alone" (60). That sense of "alone" and "beside" coexisting is key to this novel, and the aloneness of their togetherness is accentuated when Pip learns Joe cannot read except for the most rudimentary picking out of "J-O." Joe, like Pip, looks in texts only for what he can find of himself.

But Joe's account of his inability to read connects literary knowledge with sexual domination. When Pip asks Joe why he cannot read, Joe tells a story of his parents: his father, "because he were that good in his hart," "hammered away at my mother," and, whenever Joe and his mother ran away, came with "a most tremenjous crowd" and "took us home and hammered us." "Which . . . were," Joe says, "a drawback on my learning" (61). His story further explains how he met Pip's sister, how he came to love her through her kindness to Pip, and why he must now be careful to learn "on the sly," for "your sister is given to government." While Pip is "startled, for I had some shadowy idea (and I am afraid I must add, hope) that Joe had divorced her in favour of the Lords of the Admiralty, or Treasury," Joe only means "tersay the government of you and myself." And while he feels that Mrs. Joe "would not be over partial to my being a scholar, for fear as I might rise" (63), his explanation of why he doesn't "rise" reinvokes his mother's suffering: "I see so much in my poor mother, of a woman drudging and slaving and breaking her honest hart and never getting no peace in her mortal days, that I'm dead afeerd of going wrong in the way of not doing what's right by a woman, and I'd fur rather of the two go wrong the t'other way, and be a little ill-conwenienced myself" (64). Joe's fear of "not doing what's right by a woman" is constituted in the face of the "hammering" that his father does, a kind of sexual labor that is almost constant in this novel; the novel offers as an explanation, both of Joe's goodness and of his inability to protect Pip, the violence his father did to his mother (and indirectly to him). More ominous in terms of Pip's anxieties about his education, however, is Joe's assertion that it was male sexual violence that has kept (and keeps) him from learning to read: to read, Joe stresses to Pip, is to be "like a sort of rebel."

But Pip's own sense that it is better to suffer than to strike back is only reinforced by Joe's example: Pip's progress into narrative will be through a story he tells himself about "slaving and breaking [his] honest heart," a story that identifies being "ill-conwenienced myself" as the principal way to identity. The novel offers one of its most powerful metaphors of the loneliness of that identity, one linked imagistically to the book's opening on the marshes. Pip goes on:

> Joe made the fire and swept the hearth, and then we went to the door to listen for the chaise-cart. It was a dry cold night, and the wind blew keenly, and the frost was white and hard. A man would die to-night of lying out on the marshes, I thought. And then I looked at the stars, and considered how awful it would be for a man to turn his face up to them as he froze to death, and see no help or pity in all the glittering multitude. (64–65)

Pip's ability to imagine the "awful" fate of this man suggests his willingness to see himself in the same position. It is as if he is choosing his future by choosing his perspective, choosing to live out the role of solitary victim, defined by those things more distant, contemplating his own contemplation of them and his inability to reach them or even read them. At this moment, he is a boy looking for a glittering star; he is looking to freeze to death.

What comes in from the cold in this scene is Mrs. Joe and Uncle Pumblechook, bearing the news of Pip's coming visit to Satis House. When he goes there, Miss Havisham ("so new . . . so strange, and so fine—and melancholy") sends him to the door to call Estella, where he finds only more coldness and more strangeness: "To stand in the dark in a mysterious passage of an unknown house, bawling Estella to a scornful young lady neither visible nor responsive, and feeling it a dreadful liberty so to roar out her name, was almost as bad as playing to order. But, she answered at last, and her light came along the long dark passage like a star" (72). Pip plays on the starlight of Estella's name here as if he could make it literal—as Miss Havisham has made literal her broken heart; Magwitch, his desire to "make" a gentleman and revenge his conviction—but Estella's scorn (like that of the distant, uncaring stars) *is* her attraction. For Pip, looking to create the torment he can name and hope to master, Estella's invisible, unresponsive self becomes the light that will guide him both in and out of "a mysterious passage of [the] unknown." Pip's whole identity will circle around that light; he makes her instantly "the embodiment of every graceful fancy that my mind has ever become acquainted with" (335).

This instant instantiation of Estella with meaning is one that persists throughout the novel: late in the book, Pip will tell Estella that she has been a part of "every prospect I have ever seen," and at every moment throughout (as he works at the forge; when he is "rescued" by Jaggers from his apprenticeship; when he learns to be a gentleman) his only question is, will this help me win Estella? But romantic love goes further for Pip, until he cannot tell the difference between himself and Estella, or between Estella and his "fancies" about her. But as he learns perfectly, as Miss Havisham urges, to "love the smiter," it is his own vision that he finally loves—his own narcissistic image, frozen on the marshes, that he turns to. Like any Philip to any Stella, he loves in Estella the image of his own expectations, the image of his own desolation, the image of his own destruction. Pip will go on, near the novel's end, to tell Estella that she "cannot choose but be part of my character": as Freud suggests, "At the height of being in love the boundary between ego and object threatens to melt away. Against all the evidence of his senses, a man who is in love declares that 'I' and 'You' are one, and is prepared to behave as if it were a fact" (*Civilization* 20: 66). For Pip, the "I" and "You" are always the "I": there is no Estella; and yet, there can be a Pip only if he is in love with something he calls Estella.

Pip's story is given unity by his faith in the oneness of their identity and in their eventual union, but the narrative discourse's remarkable tightness of imagery is equally dependent on this imagined union. We get some sense of this in the powerful rush of images when Herbert Pocket suggests that Pip try not to love Estella, that he "detach himself from her": "I turned my head aside, for, with a rush and a sweep, like the old marsh winds coming up from the sea, a feeling like that which had subdued me on the morning when I left the forge, when the mists were solemnly rising, and when I laid my hand upon the village finger-post, smote upon my heart again" (237). Pip can only be "smitten" once more; all the identity he has ever had (mists, village finger-posts, the sea, the forge) is suffused—fused—with Estella; there can be no subjectivity here without his utter subjection to Estella; no (novelistic) language without the images that subdue him again and again. It is his own "embodiment" he creates through his "graceful fancy" of her and his own fancy of loving the smiter.

II

The novel, then, posits a self that realizes itself through violence, through abusive sexuality, by being "smitten" and loving the smiter. Or rather, this is how it seems to posit male subjectivity. The problem of the feminine, or of female subjectivity, is more vexed. In some ways, there can be no freestanding, narrating woman because Pip views himself as the woman in the text: Pip has chosen to identify himself with the feminized; and all subjectivity in the novel, all sentiment, all narration, is female—or rather, the victimized, battered, self-emasculated male. Joe's story offers a clear choice, and Pip, like Joe, chooses to be a mother, not a father; a wife, not a husband; a girl, not a boy. He will "play" a hero's part, but he feels himself to be the passionate, abused heroine; it is for that reason, perhaps, that he has so much trouble telling the difference between Estella and himself.

But these differences exist, and they are registered along linguistic, psychological axes: what they point to is a different relationship of power and of volition in the novel. What Pip cannot see is that to the extent that he is forcing Estella to abuse him, he is in turn an abuser. His identification of her with "the smiter" is as much a victimization of her as his (elected) identity as smitten is of him. The difference between them becomes clear in their relation to the violence that marks this novel: where Pip seems to choose pain, out of guilt, out of doubt, Estella seems only to tolerate it—until her marriage, when she seems to embrace it. When Pip asks if she has chosen to "fling [her]self away upon a brute," she answers, "On whom should I fling myself away? . . . Should I fling myself away upon the man who would the soonest feel (if people do feel such things) that I took nothing to him? . . . I am tired of the life I have led, which has very few charms for me, and I am willing enough to change it" (334–35). Estella's "fling" is into a world of violence: as Pip recognizes "in despair," Drummle is "such a mean brute, such a stupid brute." But she replies, "Don't be afraid of my being a blessing to him" (335). Lost, like Pip, in a world of "mother[s] by adoption" (284), Estella has no self that is a "blessing": her self, like Pip's, seems made ("formed" or "forged," in the novel's terms) to be thrown away. What Estella's "fling[ing]" herself away does in other ways, though, is to subvert the exchange value thinking in the novel, the ways in which all emotional relationships take place in the world of what Dickens's contemporary Thomas Carlyle called the "cash-nexus," a world in which people have value only insofar as they can be exchanged, or bring profit. In that view, Estella is herself a commodity, an attraction, someone who "uses" others—as Miss Havisham begs her to do—only to find herself "used" in turn. To throw oneself away is to no longer have any price: it is a costly gambit, but it is one way to regain value for one's self.

A psychoanalytic reading might argue that if Pip's victimization suggests male narcissism, Estella's reflects in part what Freud and subsequent feminist theorists have argued of female narcissism. Mary Jacobus has referred to the world of narcissistic women as "a lost paradise of narcissistic completeness, [which] leaves the [woman's] lover forever unsatisfied": applying her language to Estella, we might claim that what Estella has kept is the "self-sufficiency" of loving only herself (105). As Freud argues, while love for men has the effect of "an impoverishment of the ego as regards libido in favor of the love-object," narcissistic women can love only themselves "with an intensity comparable to that of the man's love for them," and in fact they have "the greatest fascination for men not only for aesthetic reasons . . . but because . . . another person's narcissism has a great attraction for those who have renounced part of their own narcissism and are in search of object-love" ("Narcissism" 14: 88–89). This essence of woman, as Sarah Kofman theorizes it, represents to men the lost "part" of their own narcissism, their fascination with their own double; but to do so it must involve a woman who is not defined in terms of loss, a woman who does not "need" men. Like Freud, Dickens seems at moments to fear, to "run from," the narcissistic woman; but, like Freud again, Dickens also raises the question of what the woman who is a projection for a man has for herself. We can know what the attraction is for the man; what can we know of the woman who possesses fully (only) her own status as enigma?

In this novel, questions of self are always questions of (self-) possession and the material world, and Estella, a child who is abandoned and bought, a jewel who is brought up to display the jewels of others, is the savviest economist in the novel. In her early scene with the Pocket family, as they gather around the funereal birthday table and Camilla recounts how she, valuing the "credit of the family," forced Matthew to buy funeral weeds, it is Estella who asks the important question: "'*He* paid for them, did he not?' " "'It's not a question, my dear child, who paid for them,' returned Camilla, '*I* bought them'" (92), but Estella learns early the difference between buying and paying. The emotional language of the novel is similarly rewritten as economic exchange: in the same scene, Estella slaps Pip's face and asks, "Why don't you cry again, you little wretch," to which he replies, "'Because I'll never cry for you again,' . . . Which was, I suppose, as false a declaration as ever was made; for I was inwardly crying for her then, and I know what I know of *the pain she cost me afterwards*" (92; emphasis added). But Pip's knowledge of "costs" is retrospective, whereas Estella's of "payment" is immediate: one might argue that Pip will learn what things cost in part at Estella's expense. At the end of this scene, Estella beckons to Pip, saying, "Come here! You may kiss me if you like!" When he does, he explains, "I felt that the kiss was given to the coarse common boy as a piece of money might have been, and that it was worth nothing" (101). To ask what it was "worth," again, is not to ask what it "costs" Estella to give; "the Estella" (290), as he calls her later, was created to "give" kisses, but not, as Estella will remind Miss Havisham, to feel love. She is a kind of instructive prostitute here, giving a sentimental education—breaking Pip's heart and forming it, precisely because she is unable to feel herself anything but "worth nothing." She is Pip's prize, but she possesses nothing of value, only the value accorded her by others.

To argue for Estella's value apart from Pip's valuation of her, to argue against his casting of Estella as the bewitching princess who batters and wounds him, is to argue against his vision of his story—and that of most critics. Her value, like that of the narcissistic woman Freud imagines, has always existed only in Pip's idealization (and our potential denigration) of her. To imagine valuing her differently might seem a deliberate perversity, an anachronistic reading possible only from the perspective of contemporary feminism, rather than one the novel suggests. Within the novel itself, however, it is Estella who most often critiques Pip's vision, who points out to him the folly of his obsession and the unnecessary heartbreak he has written for himself. When she asks Pip if he wants her to deceive and entrap him, and Pip responds by asking if she deceives and entraps Bentley Drummle, she answers, "Yes, and many others—all of them but you" (291). Earlier, "seem[ing] to pity me," she asks,

"Pip, Pip. . . . will you never take warning?"
"Of what?"
"Of me."
"Warning not to be attracted by you, do you mean, Estella?"
"Do I mean! If you don't know what I mean, you are blind."
(281)

Pip imagines a range of conventional responses ("I should have replied that Love was commonly reputed blind"), but he does not make them, he claims, because he thinks her unable to answer, "pressed" by Miss Havisham's orders; but certainly, he is as much pressed by his vision of himself as a lover. He is, as Estella calls him, a "visionary boy" (335). Imagined from Estella's perspective—precisely what this scene encourages us to imagine—their "courtship" looks very different. Miss Havisham hired her, as a child, to break hearts; the one person she could hope would know better, around whom she could be something other than "the Estella," refuses to free her from that role.

Pip himself seems to see her function in economic terms—and what he resents most is the reminder that he is economically, as much as erotically, bound to her. While her value is always in both her cost and the value she carries with her, what he fears is the economic reading of his "enslavement," which might otherwise look merely like ambition. His most detailed denunciation of her suggests that he both knows—and resents—any analysis of who "pays":

> I suffered every kind and degree of torture that Estella could cause me. The nature of my relations with her, which placed me on terms of familiarity without placing me on terms of favour, conduced to my distraction. *She made use of me* to tease other admirers, and she turned the very familiarity between herself and me, *to the account of putting a constant slight on my devotion to her.* If I had been her secretary, steward, half-brother, poor relation—if I had been a younger brother of her appointed husband—I could not have seemed to myself, further from my hopes when I was nearest to her. (280–81; emphasis added)

Pip is exactly those things he fears being: a secretary, a steward, half-brother, poor relation. And when he goes on to describe how "maddening" she is, one can read again how maddening *he* is. In her "slighting" of his devotion, we hear her voice, saying to him as directly as she does before marrying Bentley, "Pip, don't be foolish": it is only in Pip's mind that she is leading him into the flame; only in his mind that he has any "hopes"; only in his mind that what he calls "my trials" exist.

These are, of course, the trials of romantic love, and Pip's most moving statements encourage us to read Estella as his visionary mistress, his star, his expectation. Pip's authorship is so strong as to make Estella's story almost disappear, to make Estella almost disappear. When Pip says, "You are part of my existence, part of myself," he takes her away from herself, swallows her up, makes her into his story. As he himself says to her, "Estella, to the last hour of my life, you cannot choose but remain part of my character, part of the little good in me, part of the evil" (335). Where in this equation, with its careful partitioning, is Estella's character?—and where is her choice?

To read Estella's character back into the novel, to separate her story from Pip's subsuming of it, takes us in two directions: into a discussion of plot and into a discussion of metaphor. On the level of plot, Estella's story is one with a pattern of disruptive plotting, disruptive to Pip and his expectations, throughout the novel. It is remarkable, here and elsewhere in the novel, how many of Pip's mistakes are connected to confusion about female plotting, both the plots that women are spinning and the stories that women are made a part of. He assumes, consistently, that Estella intends to flirt with him; he assumes, almost fatally, that Miss Havisham intends him for Estella; and he assumes, pathetically, almost to the novel's end, that Biddy will wait for him to choose her. Other men, more powerful readers of female plots, similarly build expectations on them: Jaggers, after all, "made" his career on Molly's trial, the trial that brought him to Miss Havisham's attention and that prompted her to ask him to bring her a child; more movingly, it was the love of his lost daughter, Estella, that caused Magwitch to respond so powerfully to the orphan boy Pip and to vow to make him a gentleman. Women and the violence directed against them seem behind much of the plotting, overt and covert, in the novel; but female plots have unexpected kicks and quirks in them, and they tend here, as elsewhere in Dickens, to turn against the men who think they read women so well.

But the second way in which we might revise the novel beyond Pip's misreading of Estella is through a reading of novelistic language itself and the relationship of imagery to desire. At the heart of this view of romantic love (and I think it is Dickens's critique of Pip that speaks here) is the violence of Pip's metaphorical subsuming of Estella. This might seem to contradict Pip's earlier self-presentation, in which he is the masochistic victim of the cold, distant woman, but it suggests the deeper pleasure Pip received from the story that he has told of himself as victim, the pleasure he takes in what is essentially a fantasy of control in which he gets to have it both ways, to be both smiter and smitten, narrator and character. Within his story, Pip never sees himself as violent, pushing most of his aggression onto the more plausible figure of Orlick, but where Estella is concerned, he maneuvers his violence onto Bentley Drummle—whom he sees, not incidentally, near the village, and who "reminded me of Orlick" (329). Orlick avenges Pip by beating Mrs. Joe; it is Bentley who will accomplish Pip's metaphorical ravishing of Estella, marrying the woman who doesn't truly love him, then literally beating her into submission and (until the novel's end) silencing her voice.

When Pip dines with Mr. Jaggers just after Estella's wedding, Jaggers announces that Drummle ("our friend the Spider") has "won the pool." As I have suggested, it is impossible to discuss women in this novel without economic metaphors; there are no women who are not to be paid for, except those who can be "won" from others.

> "He is a promising fellow—in his way—but he may not have it all his own way. The stronger will win in the end, but the stronger has to be found out first. If he should turn to, and beat her——"
>
> "Surely," I interrupted, with a burning face and heart, "you do not seriously think that he is scoundrel enough for that, Mr. Jaggers?"
>
> "I didn't say so, Pip. I am putting a case. If he should turn to and beat her, he may possibly get the strength on his side; if it should be a question of intellect, he certainly will not. . . . A fellow like our friend the Spider . . . either beats, or cringes. He may cringe and growl, or cringe and not growl; but he either beats or cringes." (357)

Pip is "burning" (always a significant word in this novel) because this is a "painful" subject for him, but there is a weird excitement here—in Jaggers's telling of the story, in Pip's listening, in the certainty of the ostensibly vague "putting a case." The reader might ask, what, then, is Pip's "case"? And will Pip, in turn, "beat or cringe"?

The novel has certainly heretofore been more concerned with beating than cringing, and the violence seems only to escalate after this conversation. The scene is followed by Pip's recognition of Estella's face and hands in those of Molly, Jaggers's murderous, tamed housekeeper; it takes place in a nexus of violent sexuality that surfaces constantly in the novel. In Orlick's threat to rape Biddy, in the incestuous violence of Clara's "gruffandgrim" father, in Miss Havisham's pounding of her own heart ("broken"), we, like Pip, are constantly initiated into scenes of dark passion, "secret" loves, and (de)formed bodies. The end of the novel is a series of visions of violated women: Magwitch tells both the story of Arthur Havisham's death, haunted by the apparition of Miss Havisham, and the story of Compeyson's wife, Sally, "which Compeyson kicked mostly." Pip envisions Miss Havisham "hanging to the beam," and then (in a dangerously sexual scene) he smothers her in blankets "like a prisoner" while she burns. Herbert tells Pip the story of Molly strangling another woman, then swearing she has strangled her own child. The novel in both versions ends, almost comforted, with the story that Estella *has* been beaten by Drummle, who "used her with great cruelty, and who had become quite renowned as a compound of pride, avarice, brutality and meanness." "Suffering," Estella says in the second ending, "has been stronger than all other teaching, and has taught me to understand what your heart used to be. I have been bent and broken, but—I hope—into a better shape" (439). The beatings that Drummle has given her, in short, have transformed her into a woman who can love Pip.

But this is Pip's view of Estella: once again, as readers, we play out the differences between the Estella whom Pip sees and the one who moves free of his vision. Moreover, we focus on the fiercely transformative power of his vision: if she is his "fancy," he can remake her as he pleases. His doing so, however, depends on her silence, her passivity, her fixity as object. His doing so, then, on one hand echoes accounts of violence against women in the period (ranging from rape trials, in which women were refused the right to testify, to cases of wife abuse, in which women had no legal status from which to bring charges).[3] On the other hand, it is linked to the work Dickens is doing in the novel, the work of metaphorization: Estella "is like"; she never "is." The novel is pointing to something cannibalistic in its own acts of metaphorizing, something Dickens plays with constantly in highlighting the *constructedness* of the metaphors that hold the novel together so tightly.

This attention to metaphor is crucial to the novel's story of identity: in the speech in which he links Estella to "every prospect I have ever seen," Pip both gives a story of origin for his own imagination and reveals that imagination as a self-conscious construct. Estella has been "in every line I have ever read" (and, one imagines, in every line he has ever written, a key revelation for the autobiographer); she has also been "in every prospect I have ever seen since—on the river, on the sails of the ships, on the marshes, in the clouds, in the light, in the darkness, in the wind, in the woods, in the sea, in the streets." At this moment, she becomes not only a part of writing and of vision, but also—and again, this is Pip's version, but it points to the process of

---

[3]For a compelling discussion of such violence, see Anna Clark, *Women's Silence, Men's Violence: Sexual Assault in England 1770–1845*.

metaphor-creation in the novel—"the embodiment of every graceful fancy that my mind has ever become acquainted with." As he says, she could move "the stones of which the strongest London buildings are made" as easily as she could displace her presence and influence on him (335). Estella both *is* embodied solely in metaphor and *represents* the embodiment of metaphor for Pip. How could she, indeed, escape this process, inevitable and random, powerful and fanciful, as it seems?

Virtually every metaphor in the novel works in this way, playing up its own literalness *and* its arbitrariness. It is all simply too obvious: Miss Havisham, like any hysteric, has turned her body into its own sign; she is the symbol of her own grief, and it hardly surprises us when she turns up in someone else's dream with that metaphor made literal: when her brother sees her, there is blood on her chest, "where . . . *you* [Compeyson] broke it" (322) exactly as she prophesied when she first told Pip that her heart is "Broken!" (72). It is her metaphor, and it is only right that others "see" it. Moreover, we "see" her symbolic structures being repaired: in the scene after Estella and Miss Havisham fight, and Estella takes her only extended leap into metaphor in her speech about the sun, we, with Pip, watch Estella on her knees, sewing the tatters on Miss Havisham's dress. And Estella is literally fixing the tatters, not the dress—the dress must remain in a permanent state of collapse; it must always be repaired to stay in disrepair, so that the spectacle Miss Havisham presents, one Pip originally compared to "wax-works" and to a "skeleton in the ashes of a rich dress" (71), can continue. The metaphor is at once natural and created: like Pip's allegorizing fantasy of Estella, it can both be seen and be seen through, for it constantly gives itself away.

To argue that rape and metaphor share a common structure in this novel and that both depend primarily on a male narcissistic fantasy of female fixity is also to return us to the terrifyingly unfixed world with which the novel begins. Pip, when turned upside down by the convict, prefers to see (believe) the church standing on its steeple; Miss Havisham, abandoned on her birthday by her bridegroom, prefers (needs) to see that abandonment as the birth of a new, creative (if monstrous) self. If it is the fabulist self that these characters create, it is still a divided self that these fables reflect. These are fantasies of necessity. Like Pip's story of "the Estella," they give the unstable self an object toward which to move, but like Pip's story of Estella, they also enforce silence on the other.

But as the self smites others, so it is smitten itself. If Pip's anger has been acted out by a series of violent surrogates, its excesses have stayed with him: in his own hysterical dreams, he "confounded impossible existences with my own identity; [dreamed] that I was a brick in the house wall, and yet entreating to be released from the giddy place where the builders had set me; that I was a steel beam of a vast engine, clashing and whirling over a gulf, and yet that I implored in my own person to have the engine stopped, and my part in it hammered off" (420). Pip has divided himself nearly fatally here, "implor[ing] in my own person to have . . . my part . . . hammered off," and yet the end of the novel recreates the utopian (narcissistic) dream of seeing "the shadow of no parting," reunifying the self through union with Estella. No wonder, then, that he, too, hopes Estella has been bent and broken into a "better shape."

III

The end of this novel, however, does not easily unite these "parts," but maintains the distance between Pip's and Estella's fictions. To the very end, Estella says one thing and Pip hears another; while he insists he sees "the shadow of no parting," she says they "will continue friends apart" (439). The plotting of sexual violence I have been tracing generates yet another set of "two endings" to perplex us, and it raises questions of Pip's precarious hold on authority. The purpose of this essay is not to argue that Pip's linguistic enclosure of Estella is a form of wife-beating or that his abrogation of her "end" is a literary murder, but rather to point to the consistent violence of language around sexuality, a violence in which Pip participates. Such a reading also suggests that the novel at central moments, and again at its close, separates itself from this pattern of abuse and usurpation, of violent reformation. Even if we read closely the famously ambiguous passages of the "second ending" (the purportedly romantic revision Dickens made of his bleak tale at Bulwer-Lytton's suggestion), that ending does not choose between Pip's and Estella's endings: rather, it points to the difference between them, and it allows that difference to stand.[4]

In part, these characters' versions of "the two endings" reflect the generic differences within the novel. Estella, as always, is the realist: whereas in Dickens's first ending she reads Pip's state erroneously, thinking him married, with child, in the second she is, again, as always,

---

[4]A discussion of this "doubling" of the ending which parallels and nicely balances mine is D. A. Miller's in *Narrative and Its Discontents;* Miller is the only other critic I know of to have noticed that Pip and Estella do not share an ending.

painfully attentive, curious, responsive, but decisive. Pip's novel, however, remains a mistier romance: he is still entranced by her beauty; more, he maintains, eleven years later, "you have always held your place in *my* heart" (439), still reproaching her, subtly, for not always having accorded him a parallel place. The fairy princess and now successfully embourgeoised pauper still seem to be in different books; he is still trying to get her to agree to his "fancies."

The second ending is almost always read as Dickens's attempt to satisfy his "romantic" readers—and perhaps his secret, romantic self—at the expense of the grim realism this novel had, uncharacteristically for Dickens, aspired to; it has, in short, been read as trying to unwrite itself. But the second ending, unlike the first, might merely allow Pip to believe once again in his own expectations. Despite its misty ambiguities, Pip reads this ending as allowing for no partings—something that a trail of scholarship suggests we might have more difficulty doing. The second ending actually accomplishes something else: it gives Estella back her voice. The line that had previously ended the novel was Pip's, as he searches her face for certainty: "I was very glad afterwards to have had the interview; for in her face, and in her voice, and in her touch, she gave me the assurance that suffering had been stronger than Miss Havisham's teaching, and had given her a heart to understand what my heart used to be." In the first ending, Estella has said nothing except "I am greatly changed"; her face, voice, and touch are what "assure" Pip, and the distance of his reference to "what my heart used to be" gives us a false assurance that Pip's education is complete (440). But in the second ending, when Estella *says* suffering has been stronger than all other teaching, has taught her to understand what his heart used to be, and that she has been bent and broken, she concludes by saying, "Be as considerate and good to me as you were, and tell me we are friends." At this moment she is asking for what Pip has always been incapable of—the friendship that would give her a separate existence, a "parting," an existence in which she is not a "shadow." This novel is haunted by shadowy women, half-women, victimized women, women whom Pip cannot see clearly, women who hide from the light. Estella seems to step out from the mists here into the "broad expanse of tranquil light" (439), the "expanse" suggesting the "expense" she has escaped, a way out of the cash-nexus, out of violence and self-abuse, into a self she never quite owned, a self who wants only "to continue friends apart."

The most effective shading of the slippery second ending and of Pip's unspoken response ("*I* saw the shadow of no parting") is the question with which we are left: Has Pip escaped the realm of romance and fantasy, satisfied with "a sufficient" living, or is he still drawn on, a moth to the flame? Has he really left the "old place," or is he still the "visionary boy," still "abroad," still visiting the ruins "for her sake," lost in the "poor dream," lost in his own "expectations," unable to see even (with another emphasis) the "*shadow* of no parting from her"? The second ending turns the question on us: on our desire to see those dreams continue, at the same time that we want to be "satisfied" at last, to see the novel truly end, with nothing else to want.

What the conclusion does make clear—and it is what is most frightening and most moving about this novelist who knows the secret ways to get at a boy's heart—is that the novel, to *be* a novel, must share Pip's expectations. My own reading of the novel is that it delib-erately leaves us without a guide, without a monitor, without a star to follow, that that ambiguity is its final lesson. But however critical of its own tradition it may be at moments, and wherever its misty ending leaves us, like Pip, *Great Expectations* could not "be" without the prospect of Estella. It is the desire for "vision" that creates this novel; it is its creation of its own countervision that gives it the depth that at once challenges and rewards other expectations.

WORKS CITED

Benjamin, Jessica. *The Bonds of Love: Psychoanalysis, Feminism, and the Problem of Domination*. New York: Pantheon, 1988.

Brooks, Peter. "Repetition, Repression, and Return: The Plotting of *Great Expectations*," in *Reading for the Plot: Design and Intention in Narrative*. New York: Knopf, 1984.

Clark, Anna. *Women's Silence, Men's Violence: Sexual Assault in England 1770–1845*. London: Pandora, 1987.

Freud, Sigmund. *Civilization and Its Discontents. The Standard Edition of the Complete Psychological Works of Sigmund Freud*. Ed. James Strachey, 24 vols. London: Hogarth. 1953–74.

———. "On Narcissism: An Introduction." *Standard Edition*.

Jacobus, Mary. "Is There a Woman in This Text?" *Reading Women: Essays in Feminist Criticism*. New York: Columbia UP, 1986. 83–109.

Kofman, Sarah. *The Enigma of Woman: Women in Freud's Writings*. Trans. Catherine Porter. Ithaca: Cornell UP, 1985.

Miller, D. A. *Narrative and Its Discontents: Problems of Closure in the Traditional Novel*. Princeton: Princeton UP, 1981.

Gender Criticism
and
Great Expectations

WHAT IS GENDER CRITICISM?

Feminist criticism was accorded academic legitimacy in American universities "around 1981," Jane Gallop claims in her book *Around 1981: Academic Feminist Literary Theory*. With Gallop's title and approximation in mind, Naomi Schor has since estimated that, "around 1985, feminism began to give way to what has come to be called gender studies." She chose that date, she explains, "in part because it marks the publication of *Between Men*" (275–76). Although many would quarrel with Schor's notion that feminist criticism has been giving way to gender studies, they might agree that the publication of Eve Kosofsky Sedgwick's book, whose full title is *Between Men: English Literature and Male Homosocial Desire*, marked the beginnings of a new and important development in literary studies.

What to call this development, how to define it, what to include in or to exclude from its purview, however, are much more difficult questions to answer. Even more than feminism, gender studies raises issues that are endlessly contested and perhaps necessarily problematic. Because gender criticism has become to some extent allied with or even identified with gay and lesbian criticism, there is a danger that the term *gender studies* may simply seem to be a way of referring to *gay and lesbian criticism* without having to use that highly charged phrase.

For the purposes of this introduction, however, gay and lesbian criticism is construed as a particular kind of gender studies, although not all gay and lesbian critics would categorize their work in this way, and not all gender critics are lesbian or gay critics. In offering an encompassing rather than restrictive categorization of its subject, this introduction attempts to set out the major debates that structure a wide variety of interests in and conceptions of gender.

As Naomi Schor's account suggests, *Between Men* is a good place to start because in it Sedgwick brings a feminist perspective to her interest in the ways in which men relate to each other. In effect, she analyzes the relations not only between men but also between gender and sexuality. One of the principal achievements of gender studies—arguably, its principal achievement—has been to stress the importance of differentiating sex, gender, and sexuality from each other, while, at the same time, recognizing their relationships to each other. As Teresa de Lauretis points out in *Technologies of Gender* (1987), feminists of the 1970s tended to equate gender with sex, gender difference with sexual difference. After positing that "we need a notion of gender that is not so bound up with sexual difference," de Lauretis provides such a distinction by arguing that "gender is not a property of bodies or something originally existent in human beings"; rather, it is "the product of various social technologies, such as cinema" (2). Gender is, in other words, a construct, an effect of language, culture, and its institutions.

This insight, central to the work of many feminists, has been taken several steps further by a number of gender theorists. In *Epistemology of the Closet*, the book that followed *Between Men,* Sedgwick explains that sex—"chromosomal sex," the physical differences between men and women—should, of course, be differentiated from the cultural system of gender, but gender must also be differentiated from sexuality, a range of acts and inclinations and pleasures that may have little to do with either gender or chromosomal sex, dependent as upon them as an understanding of sexuality may be (27–29). Judith Butler, a theorist trained in philosophy, has complicated these issues even further in *Gender Trouble* by questioning the validity of the distinction between sex and gender. Butler argues that "'sex' is as culturally constructed as gender": since an understanding of gender depends upon a notion of a precultural sex, that notion is not the "natural" opposite of gender; it is, rather, created as an effect of the cultural construction of gender (6–7).

As these arguments suggest, although gender studies takes some of

its impetus from feminist theory, it has developed in problematic relation to feminist perspectives. For instance, gender critics have taken
issue with those French feminists who have spoken of a feminine language and writing and who have grounded differences of language
and writing in the female body. For much the same reason, they have
disagreed with those French-influenced Anglo-American critics who,
like Toril Moi and Nancy K. Miller, have posited an essential relationship between sexuality and textuality. An early gender critic like Peggy
Kamuf posits a relationship only between *gender* and textuality, between what most men and women *become* after they are born and the
way in which they write. She is therefore less interested in the author's
sexual "signature," — that is, in whether the author was a woman writing, than in whether the author was "Writing Like a Woman." Feminists like Miller have suggested that no man could write the "female
anger, desire, and selfhood" that Emily Brontë, for instance, inscribed
in her poetry and in *Wuthering Heights* (72). In the view of gender
critics, however, it is and has been possible for a man to write like a
woman, a woman to write like a man, or for women to read as men,
men as women.

   Another distinction between feminist and gender criticism is based
on the *essentialist* views of many feminist critics and the *constructionist*
views of many gender critics (both those who would call themselves
feminists and those who would not). Stated simply, the word *essentialist* refers to the view that women are essentially different from men.
Constructionist, by contrast, refers to the view that most of those differences are characteristics not of the male and female sex (nature) but,
rather, of the masculine and feminine genders (nurture). On one
hand, some "extreme constructionists" or "postfeminists" argue that
nature itself is a cultural construct or, as Schor puts it, "there is nothing outside or before culture, no nature that is not always and already
enculturated" (278). On the other hand, the most essentialist feminists write as if no amount of inculturation could alter female nature,
female difference. Because of its essentialist tendencies, "radical feminism," according to Sedgwick, "tends to deny that the meaning of
gender or sexuality has ever significantly changed; and more damag-
ingly, it can make future change appear impossible" (*Between Men* 13).

   Most obviously essentialist would be those feminists who emphasize the female body, its difference, and the manifold implications of
that difference. The equation made by some avant-garde French feminists between the female body and the *maternal* body has proved especially troubling to some gender critics, who worry that it may para-

doxically play into the hands of extreme conservatives and fundamentalists seeking to reestablish patriarchal family values. In her book *The Reproduction of Mothering* (1978), Nancy Chodorow, a sociologist of gender, admits that what we call "mothering"—not having or nursing babies but mothering more broadly conceived—is commonly associated not just with the feminine gender but also with the female sex, often considered nurturing by nature. But she critically interrogates this common assumption that it is in women's nature or biological destiny to "mother" in this broader sense, arguing that the separation of home and workplace brought about by the development of capitalism and the ensuing industrial revolution made mothering *appear* to be essentially a woman's job in modern Western society.

Whether critiques of gender such as Chodorow's should be categorized as the work of feminist analysis or that of gender studies is open to debate. Eve Kosofsky Sedgwick attempts to deal with the issues raised by such a question when she explains that gender criticism, unlike feminist criticism, is "not criticism *through* the categories of gender" but a "criticism *of* them." In effect, then, gender critics "explore what resists" explanation through categories of gender ("Gender" 273). According to Sedgwick, it is sexuality that most obviously and insistently resists such analysis. Gender criticism, therefore, has explored the issues raised by a variety of sexualities: homo-, hetero-, trans-, bi-, and—to use the term now applied defiantly and proudly to forms of sexuality that are not in the service of reproductive heterosexuality—queer. (In different contexts, as Judith Butler points out, the term *queer* may be a "discursive rallying point for younger lesbians and gays . . . and for bisexuals and straights for whom the term expresses an affiliation with anti-homophobic politics" [*Bodies* 230].) In gender studies, then, it is often, but not exclusively, the variety of possible sexual identifications and affiliations that allows the critic or theorist to interrogate gender as we commonly conceive of it, to expose its insufficiency and inadequacy as a category. In practice, however, other kinds of gender criticism—some forms of feminism, some forms of gay and lesbian criticism—are invested in exploring issues other than sexuality, although that issue may certainly be seen as the one that gave impetus to what is now a wide-ranging and significant movement in literary studies.

In singling out a catalyst of gender studies, many historians of criticism have pointed to Michel Foucault. In his *History of Sexuality* (1976, tr. 1978), Foucault distinguished sexuality from sex, calling the former a "technology of sex." De Lauretis, who has deliberately developed her theory of gender "along the lines of . . . Foucault's theory of sexuality," explains his use of "technology" this way: "sexuality, commonly thought to be a natural as well as a private matter, is in fact completely constructed in culture according to the political aims of the society's dominant class" (*Technologies* 2, 12).

Foucault suggests that homosexuality as we now think of it was to a great extent an invention of the nineteenth century. In earlier periods there had been "acts of sodomy" and individuals who committed them, but the "sodomite" was, according to Foucault, "a temporary aberration," not the "species" he became with the advent of the modern concept of homosexuality (42–43). According to Foucault, in other words, sodomitic acts did not define people so markedly as the word *homosexual* tags and marks people now. Sodomitic *acts* have been replaced by homosexual *persons,* and in the process the range of acceptable relationships between individuals of the same gender has been restrictively altered. As Sedgwick writes, "to specify someone's sexuality [today] is not to locate her or him on a map teeming with zoophiles, gynecomasts, sexoesthetic inverts, and so forth. . . . In the late twentieth century, if I ask you what your sexual orientation or sexual preference is, you will understand me to be asking precisely one thing: whether you are homosexual or heterosexual" ("Gender" 282).

By historicizing sexuality, Foucault made it possible for his successors to consider the possibility that all the categories and assumptions that currently come to mind when we think about sex, sexual difference, gender, and sexuality are social artifacts, the products of cultural discourses. Following Foucault's lead, some gay and lesbian critics have argued that the heterosexual/homosexual distinction is as much a cultural construct as is the masculine/feminine dichotomy.

Arguing that sexuality is a continuum, not a fixed and static set of binary oppositions, a number of gay and lesbian critics have critiqued heterosexuality, arguing that it has been an enforced corollary and consequence of what Gayle Rubin has referred to as the "sex/gender system" ("Traffic"). According to this system, persons of the male sex are assumed to be masculine, masculine men are assumed to be attracted to women, and therefore it is supposedly natural for men to be attracted to women and unnatural for them to be attracted to men. Lesbian critics have also taken issue with some feminists on the grounds that they proceed from fundamentally heterosexual and even heterosexist assumptions. Particularly offensive to lesbians have been those feminists who, following Doris Lessing, have implied that to affirm a lesbian identity is to act out feminist hostility against men. According to poet-critic Adrienne Rich,

> The fact is that women in every culture throughout history have undertaken the task of independent, nonheterosexual, women-centered existence, to the extent made possible by their context, often in the belief that they were the "only ones" ever to have done so. They have undertaken it even though few women have been in an economic position to resist marriage altogether; and even though attacks against [them] have ranged from aspersions and mockery to deliberate gynocide. . . .

Rich goes on to suggest, in her essay entitled "Compulsory Heterosexuality," that "heterosexuality [is] a beachhead of male dominance," and that, "like motherhood, [it] needs to be recognized and studied as a political institution" (141, 143, 145).

If there is such a thing as reading like a woman and such a thing as reading like a man, how then do lesbians read? Are there gay and lesbian ways of reading? Many would say that there are. Rich, by reading Emily Dickinson's poetry as a lesbian—by not assuming that "heterosexual romance is the career to a woman's life and work"—has introduced us to a poet quite different from the one heterosexual critics have made familiar (*Lies* 158). As for gay reading, Wayne Koestenbaum has defined "the (male twentieth-century first world) gay reader" as one who "reads resistantly for inscriptions of his condition, for texts that will confirm a social and private identity founded on a desire for other men. . . . Reading becomes a hunt for histories that deliberately foreknow or unwittingly trace a desire felt not by author but by reader, who is most acute when searching for signs of himself" (Boone and Cadden 176–77).

Lesbian critics have produced a number of compelling reinterpretations of works by authors as diverse as Virginia Woolf and Toni Morrison. As a result of these provocative readings, significant disagreements have arisen between straight and lesbian critics and among lesbian critics as well. Perhaps the most famous and interesting example of this kind of interpretive controversy involves the claim by Barbara Smith and Adrienne Rich that Morrison's novel *Sula* can be read as a lesbian text—and author Toni Morrison's counterclaim that it cannot. Smith argues that *Sula* "works as a lesbian novel not only because of the passionate friendship between Sula and Nel but because of Morrison's consistently critical stance toward . . . heterosexual institutions" such as marriage and the family (175). To such a claim,

Morrison responds emphatically, "There is no homosexuality in *Sula*" (Tate 118).

Gay male critics have produced a body of readings no less revisionist and controversial, focusing on such canonical writers as Henry James and Wallace Stevens. Melville's *Billy Budd* has been "a centerpiece for gay, gay-affirmative, or gay-related reading of American culture, and for readings by gay critics" (Sedgwick, *Epistemology* 92) even before the term *gay* was used in this way. Robert K. Martin, in a provocative book on Melville entitled *Hero, Captain, and Stranger* (1986), provides such a reading of *Billy Budd* as a representation of a triangulation of homosexual desire. Martin argues that *Moby-Dick* presents an analogous triangle. The hero must choose between a captain who represents "the imposition of the male on the female" and a "Dark Stranger" (Queequeg) who "offers the possibility of an alternate sexuality, one that is less dependent upon performance and conquest" (5). Other gender critics focusing on masculinity have analyzed "the anthropology of boyhood," a phrase coined by Mark Seltzer in an article in which he comparatively reads, among other things, Stephen Crane's *Red Badge of Courage*, Jack London's *White Fang*, and the first *Boy Scouts of America* handbook (Boone and Cadden 150). Still others have examined the fear men have that artistry is unmasculine, a guilty worry that surfaces perhaps most obviously in "The Custom-House," Hawthorne's lengthy preface to *The Scarlet Letter*. Similarly, critics have studied the representation in literature of subtly erotic disciple-patron relationships, relationships like the ones between Nick Carraway and Jay Gatsby, Marlow and Lord Jim, Doctor Watson and Sherlock Holmes, and any number of characters in Henry James's stories.

Recently the issues raised by such earlier readings have been complicated and enriched by the emergence of queer theory, sustained and rigorous inquiries into gender and sexuality from antihomophobic and antiheterosexist perspectives. Although D. A. Miller might not categorize his work in this way, he certainly gave impetus to it in his study of nineteenth-century fiction, *The Novel and the Police*. In his chapter on *David Copperfield*, Miller refers to, but refuses to specify, his own "personal" response as a boy named David reading a book about another David. He uses this experience, however, as the impetus for a sophisticated meditation on the "impersonal" relation between secrecy and subjectivity and their relation to the genre of the novel (200). Eve Kosofsky Sedgwick specifically acknowledges the importance of this chapter of *The Novel and the Police* to her writing of *Epistemology of the*

Closet, in which she interrogates the distinction between hetero- and homosexuality. Because, as she argues, questions of sexuality have had such a privileged role in the construction of identities since the end of the nineteenth century, the analysis of this distinction is central to "an understanding of virtually any aspect of modern Western culture" (1). Judith Butler—to offer one final example among many possible instances—in "Critically Queer," the important final chapter of *Bodies That Matter*, moves from a consideration of the term *queer* to a challenging account of how identities are formed through the "gender performativity" of discourse (230). As these examples suggest, perhaps the importance of queer theory will be to demonstrate the centrality of a perspective that many might still be tempted to dismiss as marginal. As historians of sexuality point out, the term *heterosexual* developed only some time after the use of the term *homosexual* (Sedgwick, *Epistemology* 2); and queer theory, in many of its elaborations, explores the ways in which an understanding of heterosexuality, like the word itself, depends upon a conception of queerness.

Necessary as it is, in an introduction such as this one, to define the differences between feminist criticism on one hand and gender criticism on the other, it is equally necessary to conclude by unmaking that distinction, at least partially. The alliance I have been creating between gender criticism and constructionist assumptions is complicated greatly by the fact that not all gay and lesbian critics are constructionists. Indeed, a number of them (Robert K. Martin included) share with many feminists the essentialist point of view; they believe homosexuals and heterosexuals to be essentially different, different by nature, just as a number of feminists believe men and women to be different. What identifies the work of such gay men and lesbians as gender criticism is their conception of sexuality as the issue that "troubles," to use Judith Butler's term, conventional notions of gender.

The critique of gender as a category of analysis continues to make its distinctive contributions in increasingly varied and expanding areas of inquiry. Performance theory has engaged gender studies with the renewed interest in Joan Riviere's "Womanliness as a Masquerade" (1929), in which the author argues that there is no femininity that is *not* masquerade. Marjorie Garber, a cultural critic, has analyzed the constructed nature of gender by focusing on people who have apparently achieved gender identity through transvestism, transsexualism, and other forms of "cross-dressing" evident in cultural productions ranging from Shakespeare to Elvis, from "Little Red Riding Hood" to

La Cage aux Folles. Because film has played a primary role in gender construction during our lifetimes, gender critics have analyzed films from *Rebel without a Cause* to *Tootsie* to last year's Best Picture. *Tendencies,* Eve Kosofsky Sedgwick's most recent book, begins with commentary on subjects as diverse—and connected—as the suicide rate among gay teenagers, the American way of Christmas, AIDS, queer reading, and contemporary journalism. If the category of gender criticism remains productively fluid and encompassing, its future in the increasingly interdisciplinary context of academic inquiry seems secure. Establishing the significance of gender, however defined, in its various representations—not only in poems and novels, but also in video and on television and in everyday life—is already the indisputable achievement of gender studies.

Ross C Murfin

GENDER CRITICISM:
A SELECTED BIBLIOGRAPHY

Studies of Gender and Sexuality

Boone, Joseph A., and Michael Cadden, eds. *Engendering Men: The Question of Male Feminist Criticism.* New York: Routledge, 1990.

Butler, Judith. *Gender Trouble: Feminism and the Subversion of Identity.* New York: Routledge, 1990.

Chodorow, Nancy. *The Reproduction of Mothering: Psychoanalysis and the Sociology of Gender.* Berkeley: U of California P, 1978.

Claridge, Laura, and Elizabeth Langland, eds. *Out of Bounds: Male Writing and Gender(ed) Criticism.* Amherst: U of Massachusetts P, 1990.

de Lauretis, Teresa. *Technologies of Gender: Essays on Theory, Film, and Fiction.* Bloomington: Indiana UP, 1987.

Doane, Mary Ann. "Masquerade Reconsidered: Further Thoughts on the Female Spectator." *Discourse* 11 (1988–89): 42–54.

Flynn, Elizabeth A., and Patrocinio P. Schweickart, eds. *Gender and Reading: Essays on Readers, Texts, and Contexts.* Baltimore: Johns Hopkins UP, 1986.

Foucault, Michel. *The History of Sexuality.* Vol. 1. Trans. Robert Hurley. New York: Random, 1978.

Kamuf, Peggy. "Writing Like a Woman." *Women and Language in Literature and Society.* New York: Praeger, 1980. 284–99.

Laqueur, Thomas. *Making Sex: Body and Gender from the Greeks to Freud.* Cambridge: Harvard UP, 1990.

Riviere, Joan. "Womanliness as a Masquerade." 1929. Rpt. in *Formations of Fantasy*. Ed. Victor Burgin, James Donald, and Cora Kaplan. London: Methuen, 1986. 35–44.

Rubin, Gayle. "Thinking Sex: Notes for a Radical Theory of the Politics of Sexuality." *The Lesbian and Gay Studies Reader*. Abelove et al. New York: Routledge, 1993. 3–44.

———. "The Traffic in Women: Notes on the 'Political Economy' of Sex." *Toward an Anthropology of Women*. Ed. Rayna R. Reiter. New York: Monthly Review, 1975. 157–210.

Schor, Naomi. "Feminist and Gender Studies." *Introduction to Scholarship in Modern Languages and Literatures*. Ed. Joseph Gibaldi. New York: MLA, 1992. 262–87.

Sedgwick, Eve Kosofsky. *Between Men: English Literature and Male Homosocial Desire*. New York: Columbia UP, 1988.

———. "Gender Criticism." *Redrawing the Boundaries: The Transformation of English and American Literary Studies*. Ed. Stephen Greenblatt and Giles Gunn. New York: MLA, 1992. 271–302.

Lesbian and Gay Criticism

Abelove, Henry, Michèle Aina Barale, and David Halperin, eds. *The Lesbian and Gay Studies Reader*. New York: Routledge, 1993.

Butters, Ronald, John M. Clum, and Michael Moon, eds. *Displacing Homophobia: Gay Male Perspectives in Literature and Culture*. Durham: Duke UP, 1989.

Craft, Christopher. *Another Kind of Love: Male Homosexual Desire in English Discourse, 1850–1920*. Berkeley: U of California P, 1994.

de Lauretis, Teresa. *The Practice of Love: Lesbian Sexuality and Perverse Desire*. Bloomington: Indiana UP, 1994.

Dollimore, Jonathan. *Sexual Dissidence: Augustine to Wilde, Freud to Foucault*. Oxford: Clarendon, 1991.

Fuss, Diana, ed. *Inside/Out: Lesbian Theories, Gay Theories*. New York: Routledge, 1991.

Garber, Marjorie. *Vested Interests: Cross-Dressing and Cultural Anxiety*. New York: Routledge, 1992.

Halperin, David M. *One Hundred Years of Homosexuality and Other Essays on Greek Love*. New York: Routledge, 1990.

The Lesbian Issue. Special issue, *Signs* 9 (1984).

Martin, Robert K. *Hero, Captain, and Stranger: Male Friendship, Social Critique, and Literary Form in the Sea Novels of Herman Melville*. Chapel Hill: U of North Carolina P, 1986.

Munt, Sally, ed. *New Lesbian Criticism: Literary and Cultural Readings*. New York: Harvester Wheatsheaf, 1992.

Rich, Adrienne. "Compulsory Heterosexuality and Lesbian Existence." *The "Signs" Reader: Women, Gender, and Scholarship*. Ed. Elizabeth Abel and Emily K. Abel. Chicago: U of Chicago P, 1983. 139–68.

Smith, Barbara. "Toward a Black Feminist Criticism." *The New Feminist Criticism*. Ed. Elaine Showalter. New York: Pantheon, 1985. 168–85.

Stimpson, Catherine R. "Zero Degree Deviancy: The Lesbian Novel in English." *Critical Inquiry* 8 (1981): 363–79.

Weeks, Jeffrey. *Sexuality and Its Discontents: Meanings, Myths, and Modern Sexualities*. London: Routledge, 1985.

Wittig, Monique. "The Mark of Gender." *The Poetics of Gender*. Ed. Nancy K. Miller. New York: Columbia UP, 1986. 63–73.

———. "One Is Not Born a Woman." *Feminist Issues* 1.2 (1981): 47–54.

———. *The Straight Mind and Other Essays*. Boston: Beacon, 1992.

Queer Theory

Butler, Judith. *Bodies That Matter: On the Discursive Limits of "Sex."* New York: Routledge, 1993.

Cohen, Ed. *Talk on the Wilde Side: Towards a Genealogy of Discourse on Male Sexualities*. New York: Routledge, 1993.

de Lauretis, Teresa, ed. Issue on Queer Theory, *differences* 3.2 (1991).

Sedgwick, Eve Kosofsky. *Epistemology of the Closet*. Berkeley: U of California P, 1991.

———. *Tendencies*. Durham: Duke UP, 1993.

Sinfield, Alan. *Cultural Politics—Queer Reading*. Philadelphia: U of Pennsylvania P, 1994.

———. *The Wilde Century: Effeminacy, Oscar Wilde, and the Queer Moment*. New York: Columbia UP, 1994.

Other Works Referred to in "What Is Gender Criticism?"

Gallop, Jane. *Around 1981: Academic Feminist Literary Theory*. New York: Routledge, 1992.

Miller, D. A. *The Novel and the Police*. Berkeley: U of California P, 1988.

Miller, Nancy K. *Subject to Change: Reading Feminist Writing*. New York: Columbia UP, 1988.

Rich, Adrienne. *On Lies, Secrets, and Silence: Selected Prose, 1966–1979*. New York: Norton, 1979.

Tate, Claudia. *Black Women Writers at Work*. New York: Continuum, 1983.

Gender Criticism of *Great Expectations*

Brown, Carolyn. "'Great Expectations': Masculinity and Modernity." *English and Cultural Studies*. Ed. Michael Green. London: Murray, 1987. 60–74.

Siegel, Carol. "Postmodern Women Novelists Review Victorian Male Masochism." *Genders* 11 (1991): 1–16.

A PERSPECTIVE ON GENDER AND SEXUALITY

Introduction

As Ross Murfin has suggested in his introduction to this section, *gender* is an omnibus term that might be applied to the subjects studied by a wide range of analysts—feminists, scholars of women's studies or men's studies, gay and lesbian critics, and practitioners of queer theory. Yet, as he also points out, it is important to recognize that the use of such an all-encompassing term invites and even requires careful distinctions. According to at least one theorist, Gayle S. Rubin, gender is the subject of feminist inquiry, and sexuality is the subject of a quite different kind of study, which is often now called "gender studies." As Rubin sets out this distinction in her groundbreaking essay "Thinking Sex" (1984), gender is a culturally constructed category of difference, upon which the oppressions of patriarchal societies depend; sexuality—and here she quotes Michel Foucault in *The History of Sexuality*—involves "the sensations of the body, the quality of pleasures, and the nature of impressions" (qtd. 33; Foucault 106).

As the plural nouns in Foucault's definition suggest, sexuality might be more properly discussed as sexuali*ties*, a range and variety of responses felt by and enacted upon bodies but understood only through the terms made available at a particular time by a particular culture. Both sex and sexualities, no less than genders, are historically

and culturally constructed; again as Gayle Rubin puts it, "we never encounter the body unmediated by the meanings that cultures give to
it." As counterintuitive as it might seem, sexuality is not "primarily a
biological phenomenon or an aspect of individual psychology" (Rubin
10), although it is often experienced as such. It is precisely this emphasis on sexualities as a range of culturally incited and culturally controlled phenomena that distinguishes the brand of gender criticism
that William A. Cohen practices in his essay on *Great Expectations.*

"Manual Conduct" begins and ends by positing the analogical
relation between masturbation—or the "onanistic vice," as it was
called—and the imaginative self-stimulation of reading novels, a com-
parably solitary mode of arousal and satisfaction. But this focus on one
form of sexual activity is simply the beginning of Cohen's encompassing account of Victorian sexual ideology as it pertains not only to masturbation but also to homoeroticism, pedophilia, women's sexuality,
and heterosexuality.

To "read sexuality" in *Great Expectations,* Cohen analyzes the
novel's representations of hands as both "the site of sexual signification and a dangerous sexual implement." As he quite pertinently
notes, for the almost completely clothed and covered Victorians, the
hands were a part of the body through which one could effectively
"read sexuality," and he cites Victorian medical and physiological authorities to show how often such readings occurred. The Dickens who
emerges from this analysis is an author deeply fascinated by men's
bodies and by men's possible relations to their own and to others'
bodies. Through its representations of hands, *Great Expectations* presents a "sexual taxonomy," an almost scientific and certainly comprehensive classification of sexualities, without, however, directly mentioning the subject. As Foucault puts it in *The History of Sexuality,* a
repressive society is necessarily obsessed by what it purports to sup-
press; and it paradoxically, therefore, "speaks verbosely of its own silences [and] takes great pains to relate in detail the things it does not
say" (8). By analyzing "the hands doing the touching" in *Great Expectations,* Cohen reveals the ways in which the novel "speaks verbosely"
of the places that they silently touch.

To a remarkable extent, Cohen argues, *Great Expectations* negates
and flees from the sexualities that it represents. Masturbation arouses
"manual shame," a "sexualization of refusal." Instances of men touching men, in handshakes or fistfights, prompt rebuke or resistance.
Women are presented as either incapable of sexual response or utterly
tamed if they have such capacities. Even though "the novel attempts

to school . . . men's bodies in normative heterosexual touching," heterosexuality is also presented as a contradictory negation of the sexual energy it purportedly is able to put to good use. The ban on all kinds of sexuality throughout the novel seems to be so efficient and so complete that it erases even the one form of sexuality that the prohibition on other forms is meant to enhance. What Dickens offers his readers at the end of the novel is the pleasure sought and experienced by "the solitary imagination," by Pip writing his own story and by his reader reading it, and it is the kind of pleasure, like sexual pleasure, that is, as Cohen argues, sustained only as long as it does not attain its object.

Cohen's essay is challenging particularly because it requires its readers to contemplate what the text says without saying it. Analyzing such paradoxes and contradictions is central to what he accomplishes here: he finds in *Great Expectations* "at the very heart of the Victorian literary canon a deeply saturated perversity." Although *Great Expectations* is a novel that has traditionally been taken to be "about romance" and only much more recently "about gender," there is no better way to introduce William Cohen's work than to say, as Gayle Rubin did in the first sentence of her seminal theoretical essay, "The time has come to think about sex" (3).

Janice Carlisle

Works Cited

Foucault, Michel. *The History of Sexuality.* Vol. 1. Trans. Robert Hurley. New York: Vintage, 1980.

Rubin, Gayle S. "Thinking Sex: Notes for a Radical Theory of the Politics of Sexuality." *The Lesbian and Gay Studies Reader.* Ed. Henry Abelove, Michèle Aina Barale, and David M. Halperin. New York: Routledge, 1993. 3–44.

WILLIAM A. COHEN
Manual Conduct in *Great Expectations*[1]

If one were writing the masturbator's guide to the English novel, certain correspondences would soon become evident. Like the novel, the discourse that constitutes masturbation (as a medical condition, a moral sin, a personal identity, a psychological stage) first arose early in the eighteenth century; like the novel, too, it achieved full cultural currency by the Victorian period and began its decline early in the present century. By the middle of the nineteenth century, both masturbatory practice and novel-reading were firmly installed in popular imagination and culture. With the cultural designation of these practices as significant, anxieties about an unregulated, excessively productive imagination arose, impelling both anti-onanist doctrine and anti-novel invective. Through famously repressive techniques, medical authorities sought to control the onanistic vice, while the novel, so perilously implicated in encouraging kindred forms of imaginative self-abuse, had to find ways of managing the erotic reveries it was accused of arousing in its readers.

Having been stigmatized for its association with fantasy, the novel eventually internalized and accommodated that charge. By the mid-nineteenth century, fictional narratives were seeking to exonerate themselves from incrimination in readers' imaginations. Even as the novel strove to redirect its readers *away* from masturbatory vice, however, this now-dominant form of imaginative literature could hardly cease its sexual provocations. The novel increasingly learned how to perform this simultaneously regulatory and arousing function while having ever *less* to say about sex overtly. Through specifiable narrative techniques, the Victorian novel at once encrypted representations of sexuality and demonstrated a frantic need for managing and redeeming sexual practices.

In the masturbator's guide to the English novel, at least under the heading "men's bodies," Charles Dickens would doubtless merit a good deal of attention. Charley Bates, a character in *Oliver Twist* (1837–39), first alerts us to the valence of the term in Dickens's corpus. When, as sometimes happens, he is called "Master Bates," we are assured of not being able to lose sight of the pun; yet when, more usu-

---

[1]A substantially longer version of this essay was published in *ELH* 60 (Spring 1993), 217–59, copyright 1993 by The Johns Hopkins University Press, and it is reproduced here by permission. Please see the full version for bibliographical references.

ally, he is referred to as "Master Charles Bates," we are guaranteed to continue imagining it—like the onanist, always fantasizing about what is not at hand in order to keep aroused what is. The volatility of Charley's name might in itself make us suspicious, for in the mouth of the narrator it constantly shifts toward and away from the little joke. When he first appears, for instance, he is described as "a very sprightly young friend . . . who was now formally introduced to [Oliver] as Charley Bates." Farther down on the page, he is referred to as "Mr. Charles Bates." Finally, he delivers the gear for cleaning up whatever mess his name might imply: "'Wipes,' replied Master Bates; at the same time producing four pocket-handkerchiefs" (109).

Dickens's linguistic attention to the male body and male eroticism compels all his *Bildungsromane* to trace not only their heroes' social, emotional, and intellectual development, but their sexual maturation as well. While *Oliver Twist* confines its fantasies about boys' budding bodies to closeted puns, *Great Expectations* (1860–61) refers those same sexual feelings back onto the bodies of its characters. In so doing, however, the later novel relegates sexual sensations to parts of the body different from those in which they are usually imagined to originate; *Great Expectations*, on this reading, manages to anatomize whole species of erotic dispositions without ever mentioning sex.

Let us look, for example, at a scene in *Great Expectations* in which Dickens raises the issue of masturbation by referring to it in such a way as to announce the impossibility of articulating it as such. The scene that probably constitutes Dickens's most vivid account of the pleasures and anxieties of autoeroticism occurs just when one would expect it in the maturation of the novel's prepubescent hero. Soon after his encounter with Magwitch in the graveyard, still stunned by the fear of it, and a long way from knowing what it means, Pip lifts a slice of bread-and-butter from his sister's table and hides it for later delivery to the convict. In describing the action, Pip's language evades denotation: "Conscience is a dreadful thing," he states, "when it accuses man or boy; but when, in the case of a boy, that secret burden co-operates with another secret burden down the leg of his trousers, it is (as I can testify) a great punishment" (32). Pip carefully avoids a definition of that "secret burden," and his ambiguity allows the bread-and-butter to function as an alibi for the arousal that he is—as anyone familiar with the perturbations of male adolescence can attest—at such pains to conceal.

Having secreted the morsel down his pants leg, Pip continues to be harassed by his "wicked secret" (41) through the novel's early scenes. When he undertakes the chore of stirring the Christmas pudding, he finds himself altogether discomfited: "I tried it with the load upon my leg (and that made me think afresh of the man with the load on *his* leg), and found the tendency of exercise to bring the bread-and-butter out at my ankle, quite unmanageable. Happily, I slipped away, and deposited that part of my conscience in my garret bedroom" (32). Stealing the meager repast does not merely coincide ("co-operate") with the primary arousal ("another secret burden down the leg of his trousers"): it literalizes the economic metaphor, by which masturbation is classically imagined, of counterproductive labor. Likewise, while the load of which Pip relieves himself surreptitiously in his bedroom signals the irresistible culmination of such titillation, it also completes the analogy between masturbation and theft through a common charge of wastefulness.

If the discovery of this suspiciously buttery emission in Pip's bedroom suggests an excessively lubricious reading strategy, disavowal of this discovery would itself partake of the very paranoia that structures Pip's response. Victorian proscriptions of self-abuse and the concomitant vigilance in preventing their infringement notoriously inspired among habituated onanists the kind of guilt to which Pip attests. Not least in an effort to resist the continuing allure of the prohibitions against a practice otherwise made thoroughly banal today, this reading will insist that *Great Expectations* is imbued with lessons about the erotic dispositions of bodies. Rather than recapitulate the protagonist's phobic recoiling against sexual possibilities, I will, in what follows, propose to locate at the very heart of the Victorian literary canon a deeply saturated perversity. One of the nineteenth-century novel's principal accomplishments is to formulate a literary language that expresses eroticism even as it designates sexuality the supremely unmentionable subject. While the regulatory, often punitive dimension of these articulations cannot be overestimated, there is a comparable danger in recognizing nothing other than their prohibitive aspect, thereby merely relocating the critical institutions that have traditionally prevented readers from identifying erotic pleasures—call them perversions—within so respectable a text as *Great Expectations*. The novel both arouses and coerces its readers' desires; tracing the productive interplay of pleasure and power allows not only a reconception of this classic work but a charting of Victorian sexual ideology's formidable operations.

Thanks to the Victorian novel's renowned loquaciousness, the subjects it cannot utter generate particularly nagging silences. How can we make these silences speak? Precisely through attention to the rhetoric of unspeakability, to the signifying practices that fill in these enforced absences. The novel encrypts sexuality not in its plot or in its announced intentions, but in its margins, at the seemingly incidental moments of its figurative language, where, paradoxically, it is so starkly obvious as to be invisible. The novel offers a model for such reading in, for instance, young Pip's assumption that "the shape of the letters" (23) on the tombstones conveys the physical appearance of his parents, or in the silenced Mrs. Joe's ideogram for Orlick—the hammer—which everyone misreads *as* a letter (128). If the very letters that constitute its matter bear meanings beyond the literal, then by analogy we can detect other sorts of hidden information in aspects of the novel's surface usually considered so conspicuous as to be undeserving of comment. The register of the unnoticeable (or what it comes down to, the unnoteworthy) shelters what can hardly be thought, much less articulated, in the novel.

The placement of hand on genitals remains a secret in the Victorian novel, but like all secrets it wants to be told. The scene with which we have been concerned, of masturbation's near exposure, is only the most explicit instance of a pattern that runs throughout *Great Expectations,* a pattern that metonymically figures the sexual caress not in the genitals being handled but in the hands doing the touching. From this early point, at which the boy's bulge virtually speaks its own name, the narrative quickly relegates such unutterable instances of provocation and arousal to the commonplace, benign, and unblushing representation of characters' hands.

Why hands? An account of their place in Victorian culture would consider the wealth of its tracts on chirology, palmistry, and graphology. The fact is not simply that the hand was paid a great deal of attention, but that—given the extent of Victorian self-regulation, both literary and sartorial—it was one of the few anatomical parts regularly available *for* attention: the usual costume of middle-class English adults in the nineteenth century covered all of the body but the head and the hands. Much has been made of the former body part, the head, both in literary representation and in those famous Victorian pseudosciences, phrenology and physiognomy. But critics have had little to say about the other part of the body that could be examined—the hand. Nineteenth-century observers felt the hand to be fully saturated with information about its possessor's character; a book entitled *The Hand Phrenologically Considered: Being a Glimpse at the Relation of the Mind with the Organisation of the Body* (1848) exemplifies the

Victorian investment in readings of the hand, the technicist discourse of the work enabling it to sidestep the dubiousness of palmistry:

> The hand not only affords us characters by which the age and sex may be determined, it is likewise an index of the general habit of body, of the kind of temperament, and of the mental tendency and disposition. . . . A soft, thick hand, loaded with fat, denotes little energy of character, and a soft, yielding, inactive disposition; while, on the contrary, a thin, bony, or muscular hand indicates a rough, active, energetic nature. (56–58)

Whether through its physiology, the lines that mark it, or the writing with which it is synonymous, the hand is so freighted with significance as to reveal all the vital information about the body and mind behind it.

For the Victorian reader, the hand would immediately be available both as a site of sexual signification and as a dangerous sexual implement. Hands are particularly important to any rendering of masturbation, as the putative etymology of the word suggests: *manus* (hand) + *stuprare* (to defile). Preferring a Greek derivation, the Victorian urologist William Acton suggests "chiromania" as a synonym for onanism, which, he writes, "can be properly applied, in the case of males, only to emission or ejaculation induced by titillation and friction of the virile member with the hand" (38). I cite Victorian manual and medical authorities not to establish any specific resonance with *Great Expectations* but instead to demonstrate the kinds of attention that the hand received in the period. We need not show that Dickens was familiar with these works to prove Pip a masturbator; we hardly want to, in fact, for the novel nowhere delivers the reified identity of "the onanist." The history of masturbation is both institutional *and* private (however oblique our access to the latter), and its story is one of both proscription and excitation.

When hands take on a specifically sexual meaning, I have suggested, they speak of masturbation; but their sexual qualities are also *generalizable*. The metonymic association of hands with autoeroticism functions as a conduit between representation and sexuality, but it does not restrict manual signification to a solitary sexual act. *Great Expectations* constructs its sexual taxonomy through its representation of hands, and while its master trope is therefore masturbation, the novel oversees a remarkably wide range of what will come to be known as sexualities. I will consider the links between the overt representation of the manual, on the one hand, and the mystification of sexuality, on the other, first through the novel's thematics of male masturbation. I will then proceed to broaden the affiliation of the manual and the erotic by examining the hand's capacity to signify non-solitary sexuality, specifically through its potential for both inciting and regulating male homoeroticism. Finally, I will assess the novel's efforts at representing and managing women's sexuality through increasingly phantasmatic conjurations of the female hand.

Like many avid masturbators, Pip is deeply ashamed, and, just short of growing hair on his palms, he transfers his generalized sense of guilt onto the hands themselves. Pip is sorely touched by Estella's disdainful remark upon their first meeting: "'And what coarse hands he has.'" He responds, "I had never thought of being ashamed of my hands before; but I began to consider them a very indifferent pair. Her contempt for me was so strong, that it became infectious, and I caught it" (73). Pip's hands focus and localize the virulent shame that, articulated here in the register of social class, bears with it all the marks of a sexual embarrassment. What he learns from Estella, that is to say, is that embodied signs of labor are distasteful; the way in which he learns it, though, is through the shaming of a physical exposure, having his vulgar, vulnerable members seen by a girl. The disgrace that attaches to the hand would, to Dickens and his audience, as surely be coded for that other subject routinely repressed—work—as it would be for sex. Humiliation over the laboring (productive) hand converges on shame over the autoerotic (wasteful) one.

Pip's rough appendages perennially trouble him, and the novel meticulously traces the coalescence between the laboring hand and the masturbatory one under the sign of embarrassment. When he tells his family tall tales of his first visit to Satis House—his initial step out of the working class—he strikes the pose of the guilt-ridden onanist: "They both stared at me, and I, with an obtrusive show of artlessness on my countenance, stared at them, and plaited the right leg of my trousers with my right hand" (80–81). Once he comes into his expectations, Pip's newfound riches—or is it his newly bulging body?—plague him with another kind of awkwardness: "I went circuitously to Miss Havisham's by all the back ways, and rang at the bell constrainedly, on account of the stiff long fingers of my gloves" (157). This manual erection coincides with Pip's rising expectations, as overt anxiety about class again takes the narrative form of a sexualized humiliation. The process of Pip's *Bildung* is an aggressive repudiation of the labor inscribed on his body: it tells the story of his refusal to *be* a hand. Consequently, he takes the rowing master's compliment that he has "the arm of a blacksmith" (189) as the worst kind of insult.

When masturbation and labor are supplemented with a third sense of the hand—writing itself—the manual shame embedded in the narrative discloses its profound effects. Unlike most first-person novels, *Great Expectations* lacks an explicit scene of writing—that scene before the beginning and after the end in which readers are offered an account of the text's genesis. Like the worker, the writer is ashamed of his hand; he insists upon effacing the signs of his own manual labor at bringing the novel into being. Although we never witness the inscription of the novel itself, the narrative obsessively renders the exertions of the writing hand: from Pip's early problems learning to cipher ("getting considerably worried and scratched by every letter" [59]) down to his final scrivening labor for the firm whose name merely embellishes that of his occupation—"I was clerk to Clarriker and Co." (436)—the hero writes throughout the story. We would expect the writer's hand, like the productive one of the laborer, to exhibit the telltale marks of its toil (calluses, ink stains, cramps), but the narrator never displays his laboring hand. Only when he lives as a gentleman does Pip have the leisure to read, and he then does little else; writing is thus as much a mark of the protagonist's class descent (the economic necessity of writing) as of his rise (the intellectual ability to do so). We are prohibited from seeing Pip write this fiction for reasons both economic and sexual: on one side, the writing of his life is itself the signal of a fall in class terms, which must be occluded; on the other, any exposure of himself in the act of imagining his life would violate the autoerotic scene with which the solitary reverie, accompanied by manual manipulation, has already been aligned. Writing, like masturbation, cannot be narrated outright—yet it also *need not* be, for it has already left its mark (spilled its ink) everywhere; it too is made shameful, so chastened by that interiorized conduct manual, the conscience, that it is evident only in its traces. Whether it covers work, writing, or sex, the coy hand thus seems to signal displacement itself.

For Pip, hands take over the expression of emotions such as shame, self-assurance, arousal, or dejection more usually affiliated with sexuality. If Pip's hands thus encode certain features of autoeroticism, we might inquire how they became so accomplished. The narrative offers an initial explanation: from the first, Pip avers that his sister "had established a great reputation with herself and the neighbours because she had brought me up 'by hand,'" and that he knows "her to have a hard and heavy hand, and to be much in the habit of laying it upon her husband as well as upon me" (28). Here is one source, then, for so total a valuation of the hand: it is both the punished and the punisher, the organ that sins and the one that disciplines. By taking literally the euphemism "being brought up 'by hand'" (conventionally used in reference to a child who is not breast-fed), Pip's joke suggests how, in substituting for the maternal breast, the hand comes to be sexually charged. While Pip's hands designate him a masturbator, Mrs. Joe's thus serve unambiguously to phallicize her (particularly through their tool, Tickler)—at least until her penchant for dealing blows is dealt a stronger one and she is silenced "by some unknown hand" (125), which unsurprisingly turns out to be Orlick's "murderous hand" (390).

To the muscular femininity of his surrogate mother's "bad cop," Pip's father figure correspondingly exhibits the sentimental masculinity of a "good" one: "Joe laid his hand upon my shoulder with the touch of a woman. . . . O dear good Joe, whom I was so ready to leave and so unthankful to, I see you again, with your muscular blacksmith's arm before your eyes, and your broad chest heaving, and your voice dying away" (143–44). The portrayal of Joe is in keeping with the usual representation of male sentimentality; the class signification of bodily attributes provides that the "muscular blacksmith's arm," which could so humiliate Pip on the Thames crew team, functions in the forge from which it derives as the sign of an unimpeachably wholesome and regenerate masculinity. The antithesis of his wife's hand, the "woman's touch" that characterizes Joe's paradoxically serves to fortify, not to destabilize, the edifice of his virility, even as it threatens Pip, the precarious arriviste, whose feminized masculinity has an entirely different class valence. Where Mrs. Joe's hand trains Pip's through violence and terror, Joe's works more subtly, as a nostalgic— but for all that, no less thoroughly repudiated—negative exemplar. The child is always in danger of being slapped by "mother" for touching himself; the gentleman is always in danger of becoming as manly as "father," and thus losing his class standing, or seeming as womanly as he, and thus losing his manhood.

It might be imagined that Pip's early assimilation to a masturbatory erotics functions in keeping with a developmental narrative, so that his discovery of an interest in Estella can sweep over the adolescent vice and mature heterosexuality install itself. But the presence of at least one adult character in the novel who is equally, although in different ways, coded for autoeroticism, challenges this model. The characteristics most associated with the body of Pip's guardian, Jaggers, are those of touching himself—his trademark "biting the side of his great forefinger"—and otherwise drawing attention to his unaccountably large hands. Even if we overlooked the finger he keeps in his mouth, we could hardly avoid noticing the one stashed in his pocket, for Pip's is not the only pants leg found bulging with secret burdens: Jaggers "pushed Miss Havisham in her chair before him, with one of his large hands, and put the other in his trousers-pocket as if the pocket were full of secrets" (229). The secrets in Jaggers's pockets connote the other reason for keeping one's hands there—to lay hold of money—and his secretive skills make him adept at getting money (even if not spending) in his pockets. Through Jaggers, the novel lends vivid materiality to the usual Victorian analogy between male sexuality and a money economy. According to this formulation—condensed in the theory of "spermatic economy"—a man must jealously conserve his fixed capital of bodily energy, not squander it in unproductive forms of sexual release.

If Jaggers's version of autoeroticism functions in one sense as that which is sublimated by his acquisitiveness and in another as, say, the bodily inscription of his propensity for taking charge of others' secrets, in a third sense it registers the consistent pattern of his solipsistic withdrawal from scenes of potential erotic arousal. His taste for Drummle, for instance—and, in particular, for his arm—is "quite inexplicable" (206). For Jaggers, autoeroticism functions as a mode of resisting engagement with others, and his finger-biting and pocketed secrets textually code the sexualization of refusal. While Pip's autoerotic practice is guilty, excessive, and uncontrolled—a sexual strategy for repudiating the manual labor he abhors—Jaggers's is manipulative, parsimonious, and recoiling, a performance and extension of his economic motivations.

The solitary hands we have observed thus far in *Great Expectations* are marked, via a metonymic connection, for male masturbation: when hand and genital organ touch, the former (speakable) can connote the latter (unspeakable). The novel's erotic investment in hands is so general, however, as to allow for metaphoric links as well, so that sexual practices less directly managed by the hand may nonetheless be imagined as manual. We now shift our attention from singular hands to redoubled ones in order to read sexuality: the moments at which two men's hands are engaged arise first, in the most highly socialized form of male hand-holding, the handshake, and then, in the other shape they principally assume in the novel, pugilism.

Handshaking is the one social ritual by which men, most especially those who are strangers, routinely touch each other, and in the world of this novel it has a curiously negative valence. In general, it functions to draw people together by holding them apart, interposing hands between other body parts as a safe form of contact. Yet despite the largeness of his endowment, Jaggers is all but unwilling to extend his hand: he is, as Pip says, "a remarkably short shaker" (268). This ritual is thoroughly castigated in the form of Pumblechook's unctuous insistence on it, with his notorious "'May I— *may* I—?'" (154). At the moment that the novel raises the possibility that in the most familiar code of manual conduct—the handshake—something might supervene upon the literal, the narrative can be nothing but derisive, as if to confirm that hands are evocative only where they are not (in the novel's conscious terms) meant to be so. At the point where connotations of the manual seem most likely to multiply, the mode of parodic excess preempts all meanings but the most repugnant hypocrisy.

While the handshake routinizes and defuses manual contact among characters, the other context in which hands regularly meet—fisticuffs—tends in a rather different direction. Unlike the ostentatious signification with which the text loads handshaking (meanings so manifest that they are paradoxically emptied out), the novel's most fully embodied moments of physical violence are either so curiously undermotivated or so thoroughly overdetermined as to proliferate the meanings available to a manual semiotics. Although in the logic of the novel's plot, fights interpose at junctures of fierce romantic rivalry, the *narration* of the battles consistently provides the occasion for the playing out of erotic contact between combatants.

At Pip's first encounter with Herbert Pocket, for instance, the relationship is one of immediate and unmediated physical aggression: "'Come and fight,' said the pale young gentleman." As Herbert's provocation appears wholly unmotivated, he soon supplies the incitement it is felt to require: "'I ought to give you a reason for fighting, too. There it is!' In a most irritating manner he instantly slapped his hands against one another, daintily flung one of his legs up behind him, pulled my hair, slapped his hands again, dipped his head, and butted it into my stomach" (100). To such ungentlemanly conduct the gentleman's reaction—that is, the bellicosity Herbert desires—itself must be reconfigured, albeit in hindsight, as a form of chivalrous combat for feminine affections. Thus, Pip's payoff for sparring with Herbert is the opportunity to kiss Estella, the scene's unseen observer. Yet even if this putative erotic aim were capable of sustaining a state of arousal, it would nonetheless function only retrospectively and defensively as the alibi for the more provoking touches elaborated in the battle with Herbert. In fact, Pip feels as a result that he has prostituted himself, "that the kiss was given to the coarse common boy as a piece of money might have been, and that it was worth nothing" (101). In compensation for the tussle's lack of motivation, then, the text supplies a series of rationales—ranging from insult to romance to monetary recompense—whose insufficiency is demonstrated by the very rapidity of their deployment.

However persuasive the pretext for pugnacity in the novel may be (in this case, hardly at all), it thus functions primarily as the occasion for physical contact between adversaries. The relationship most thoroughly structured around hand-to-hand combat is not finally Pip's friendship with Herbert but his enmity with Orlick. The novel consistently evokes, while still refusing to denote, linguistic terms for male sexuality around Orlick, in combination with his physical violence. "He pretended that his christian name was Dolge—a clear impossibility—but he was a fellow of that obstinate disposition that I believe him to have been the prey of no delusion in this particular, but wilfully to have imposed that name upon the village as an affront to its understanding" (118). With no other objection than this—that in its inscrutability the name simply *feels* obscene—Pip implies that a lack of definition itself signifies a transgression against propriety. Pip's assertion of this name's "impossibility" aims to bolster the straightness and clarity of his own narrative, yet the proximate impossibility of his own name belies this effort, as the novel's opening words attest. The case for the perversity of connotation becomes unequivocal when Pip cites "the penalty of being jiggered, [which] was a favourite supposititious case of [Orlick's]. He attached no definite meaning to the word that I am aware of, but used it, like his own pretended christian name, to affront mankind, and convey an idea of something savagely damaging. When I was younger, I had had a general belief that if he had jiggered me personally, he would have done it with a sharp and twisted hook" (135). Here the insistent nonmeaning of the word redounds upon the victimized body with a sexual signification that cannot otherwise be uttered. The denotative refusal entailed in the "supposititious case" functions as a place-holder for sexual meanings, not simply by obliterating some other, straightforward language (as in this example, by eliding the term "buggered"), but by producing those meanings *as* inarticulable.

Orlick's pugnacity toward Pip issues in the inevitable corporal confrontation between them, at the sluice-house by the limekiln. In returning to characters' bodies, the scene naturally refers us, through its usual synecdochal route, to their hands. Throughout the final chapters Pip is sorely disabled by the burns his arms received at Satis House, and Orlick's attack is so effective in part because it exacerbates that condition. If the hand of Pip's that touches his own body is regularly subject to rebuke, the one that feels (and is felt by) other men is even more thoroughly penalized. Yet here the brutal ferocity of "a strong man's hand" and its arousing caress are absolutely coterminous. Fearsomely violent as this assault is, its erotic sensations are manifest: the "strong man's breast" set against Pip's mouth, and, in return, the attacker's own "hot breath" against him, serve to literalize the "kiss" implicit in Orlick's name (to "lick" the "or" [Latin *os, ora,* "mouth"]; 386). As if to draw on Pip's youthful training matches with Herbert and Bentley—as if to dramatize the tantalizing prospect of being "jiggered"—this serious adult business with Orlick enacts all the erotic potential of murderous male combat. The particular correspondence that the novel has established between the manual and the genital only barely prepares us for the scene's concatenation of terror and tenderness, of the one hand that savors to inflict pain and the other that anguishes to endure it.

At this point we can identify what might be termed the novel's homophobia. On the one hand, it denies the handshake any of the erotic valence we might well expect to attend this ritual: either because of others' refusal (Jaggers's) or because of Pip's own repulsion (at Pumblechook), this manual contact is insufficient to bring men together. On the other hand, Pip's pugilistics with Herbert, Drummle, and Orlick represent increasingly savage forms of violence. If the cost of men touching men is that one of them be pummeled, we must recognize a certain ideological resistance in the text to such an erotics. To this apparent dead end, however, the novel proposes several alternate routes, thanks largely to the fluidity with which *Great Expectations* structures the thematic of hands.

For instance, let us, in pursuing our investigation of pugilism, witness the novel's strenuous effort to redeem it for normative heterosexuality. Wemmick, Jaggers's second, finds he must overcome the resistance of his fiancée, Miss Skiffins, to yield to his hands. Upon meeting her, Pip "might have pronounced her gown a little too decidedly orange, and her gloves a little too intensely green"; he notes further that

"Miss Skiffins . . . retained her green gloves during the evening as an outward and visible sign that there was company" (276). Miss Skiffins knows full well the hand's capability to signify. These gloves ensure her genteel incapacity for domestic labor as much as they conceal her dishpan hands: she "washed up the tea-things, in a trifling lady-like amateur manner that compromised none of us. Then, she put on her gloves again" (278). But while the gloves afford Miss Skiffins an "outward and visible sign" of *class* propriety, their verdancy promises a *sexual* steaminess as surely as her unwillingness to remove them withholds it.

The elaborate charade by which Wemmick makes a pass at his inamorata confirms this dynamic; it is his hands now that her gloves must peel off (278). By contrast with the performances of sexual excitation we have previously observed, this one can afford to be frankly erotic. Yet even as this pantomime of heterosexual courtship struggles to establish a relation to the normative, it repeatedly collapses into the realm of proscribed sexuality. Even—perhaps especially—when the flavor of eroticism is most vanilla (heterosexual, monogamous, genital), its pungency does not diminish against the palate; through the very nearness of its *exposure* in the narration, the representation of sexuality here continues to sting the readerly tongue. The "slow and gradual elongation of Mr. Wemmick's mouth" and the collateral distention of his arm, for example, only barely keep under wraps the other turgidity to which they give rise. The "mechanical" procedure of Miss Skiffins's resistance itself is metaphorised as *déshabillement* (she "unwound his arm again as if it were an article of dress, and . . . took off that girdle"), as though to confirm that so hot a refusal functions as an enticement to arousal. Furthermore, however superficially normative this passage's sexual thematics may be, the *mise en scène* returns us to a spectacle of sexual impropriety: in a manner unusual in the novel, Pip is here positioned as observer of others' erotic play, and his "interval of suspense . . . that was quite enthralling and almost painful" bespeaks a more-than-passive relation to the scene (279). Indeed, the pas de deux between Wemmick's arm and Miss Skiffins's gloves titillates Pip into a state of voyeuristic autoeroticism no different from that which novels themselves were accused of arousing.

Finally, the contest between "his hand" and her "green glove" drifts irresistibly toward an allegory of fisticuffs: "I saw his hand appear on the other side of Miss Skiffins. Instantly, Miss Skiffins stopped it with the neatness of a placid boxer, took off that girdle or cestus as before, and laid it on the table" (279). The narrative alignment of the modest maiden to "a placid boxer" installs the scene among those of pugilism between men; at its most explicit moment of heterosexual pursuit, then, the novel's erotic language modulates into the definitionally male and homosocial. For all that Miss Skiffins boxes with kid gloves on, it seems to say, she throws her punches with determination. Yet if in one sense the current of fistic homoeroticism unsettles the characters most preoccupied with bourgeois propriety, the Wemmick-Skiffins match also works in the other direction toward the reform and sanitization of boxing and its attendant sexual connotations.

Indeed, the novel works arduously to redirect the erotic meanderings set loose here. Lest the state of premarital arousal prove unsustainable, Miss Skiffins eventually removes her green gloves (still fully cognizant of their utility as signifiers) as a means of marking a new order of conjugally sanctioned eroticism. Arriving at church with Wemmick, Pip observes: "That discreet damsel was attired as usual, except that she was now engaged in substituting for her green kid gloves, a pair of white" (412). Refusal having been abandoned as an erotic mode, domesticity triumphs in the Castle at Walworth: "It was pleasant to observe that Mrs. Wemmick no longer unwound Wemmick's arm when it adapted itself to her figure, but sat in a high-backed chair against the wall, like a violoncello in its case, and submitted to be embraced as that melodious instrument might have done" (413). The spur to desire is now so fully normalized by the institution of marriage that it loses its edge: although Wemmick evinces no sign of disappointment, one need only set an ungirdled boxer beside an encased 'cello to determine which woman—Miss Skiffins or Mrs. Wemmick—is the more enticing. In the miniature, mechanical, businesslike form that the Wemmicks lend it, the marriage plot's usual propensity for damage is made starkly evident: characters' bodies are disciplined into conformity, domesticity cancels eros, married life instantly obliterates memories of the prior excitation requisite for having brought it about. Here proven in its punishing aspect is a cardinal rule of the novel as a genre: that nuptials represent the end, not the beginning of things.

The fights we have examined illustrate different modes of repression, in varying degrees of punitiveness, for managing and disciplining the play of hands. In each instance, the sexual possibilities generated by hands are expunged from the plot—from the register of articulated representation—by means of violence, only to resurface in the contours of the narrative voice, where they can pass by virtue of going unheard inside the novel. Male homosocial desire is expressed as brutal-

ity, while premarital sex is narratable only insofar as it fuels the hegemony of matrimony. But in addition to these transformations of errant
manual desire accomplished through battle, the novel manages other,
less violently chastening ones. As against the compulsions of the handshake and the fistfight, we will want now to consider the *consensual*
modality of male manual regulation in the novel.

Herbert's youthful belligerence, as I have suggested, is rehabili-
tated as properly sublimated, adult male homosociality. For Magwitch,
the other figure given to excessive handling of Pip, socialization requires a more radical reconfiguring of eros. From the first, Magwitch
embodies a certain pedophilia: the novel's opening, showing his
combined aggression and affection for Pip, suggests a species of man-
boy love, and it is primarily through his manhandling of Pip that we
come to register such pederastic impulses. The recognition scene between patron and protégé later in the novel stages the climax of the
touching initiated there, in the form of an erotic ballet performed by
the hands, and its narration has a perilously overt sexual charge: one
need hardly cite the bended knee, the kissing of hands, the prostration
on the couch, the insistent caresses, to locate the courtship conventions of which it partakes (294–95). Pip's gag reflex serves to bolster,
not to diminish, the eroticism of the episode, for it demonstrates his
revulsion to be as highly charged as the convict's attraction. The narrative attention to Magwitch's manipulation, in its root sense, empowers
his cataclysmic revelation even as it threatens to run out of control
through a homoeroticism we are made to feel and, through Pip, to
feel repulsed by. But like his former partner, Molly, this "terrible
beast" (298) must be tamed as well.

How does the novel recuperate Magwitch's erotic palpation and
Pip's corresponding palpitation? For Pip, the immediate antidote to the
fearsome caress of the grizzled convict's "large brown veinous hands"
(294) arrives in the form of his companion's reassuring embrace: "Herbert received me with open arms . . . got up, and linked his arm in mine"
(317). Through the developments of the plot, moreover, Pip is capable
of turning Magwitch's lecherous pawing back upon him, lending it a
normalized, moralized signification. In the scene at Magwitch's
deathbed (417–19), Pip is at last able to translate his benefactor's uncomfortable stroking into heterosexual terms by giving that touch a
proper meaning *in* the plot: he transposes it onto the heterosexual economy by lending it the valence of the "consent of a beloved's father to a
suitor's entreaty." Those earlier, less fully accountable hand-squeezings

are now available to him because they have been reworked retrospectively as the beneficence of a future father-in-law.

Both Magwitch and Herbert thus partake of a homoerotic handling of Pip and both must be retrofitted in order to discipline those desires. Whether through visceral repugnance or progressive socialization, the novel attempts to school the men's bodies in normative heterosexual touching. It is not only through other men that Pip learns these lessons, however, for the women in his story must also undergo dramatic transformations to rectify the manual problems they present. The two modes of regulating sexuality that we have identified for the men—the violently coercive and the consensual—also structure female eroticism. While Biddy submits to her training for respectable femininity, Molly resists domestication to the utmost; Estella, meanwhile, never has the option of choosing because she never properly has any desires that require management. The novel, moreover, makes a distinction between male and female sexuality broadly conceived, through its phantasmatic construction of the latter, which functions largely in the service of a solitary male dream of its own sexual capacity. In situating erotic subject and object in the same body, autoeroticism, as we have seen, alienates the onanist from himself, thereby paradoxically constituting him *as* a subject. Rarely more than fantasy objects, the female characters buttress the narrative's masturbatory mode, for the novel's sexual architectonics bars them from sustaining a position as desiring subjects.

Biddy and Pip start out as perfect counterparts, their as-yet ungendered identities equally oriented around the manual. "She was an orphan like myself," says Pip; "like me, too, had been brought up by hand" (59). Also like Pip, Biddy exhibits a hand replete with the dirtying signs of both manual labor and onanistic indulgence: "her hands always wanted washing" (59), Pip notes early on; and at one point, to reassure him, "she put her hand, which was a comfortable hand though roughened by work, upon my hands, one after another" (133). For all their youthful likeness, however, the specter that Biddy presents of female masturbation and of an affirmative female desire is more than Pip can abide. The novel manages the anxiety Biddy inspires by ascribing to her all the dreariness of provincial working-class life, the ignominy of which is routed specifically through the femininity of her touch. The uncleanliness of her hands distresses Pip vividly at the point he repudiates her: while they converse, Biddy is shown "plucking a black currant leaf," "looking closely at the leaf in her hand," and "having rubbed the leaf to pieces between her hands—and the smell of a black currant bush has ever since recalled to me that evening in the little garden by the side of the lane" (150). Like Jaggers's hands, Biddy's generate a characteristic aroma; but where "scented soap" indicates an anxious fastidiousness, the provocative image of Biddy's "black currant bush" bespeaks an *odor di femina* that sends Pip running. If in Pip's imagination Biddy represents a distressing (all too available, all too appropriate) sexual possibility, whatever desires she herself can be said to express finally appear thoroughly managed and manageable. Ultimately the new Mrs. Joe exhibits a hand fully accommodated to matrimonial-maternal orthodoxy: "Biddy looked down at her child, and put its little hand to her lips, and then put the good matronly hand with which she had touched it, into mine. There was something in the action and in the light pressure of Biddy's wedding-ring, that had a very pretty eloquence in it" (437). Light though it may be, the wedding ring exerts sufficient pressure to remind Pip of the female trajectory parallel to, but divergent from, his own.

Unlike Miss Skiffins, who requires combat—however figurative— to bring about the bliss of connubial sterility, Biddy accedes willingly to marital hegemony. Molly, by contrast with both, perpetrates the story's only bout between women, and she is consequently subject to an even more violent form of correction. The punishment she suffers for her manual conduct is a life sentence of "taming" at Jaggers's hands, but more is at stake in her representation than a wholesale denial of female eroticism: she exemplifies the way in which repression functions as a vigilant and perpetual *management* of eros. Jaggers exhibits a sadistic pleasure in displaying and exercising the "wild beast tamed" (195) to the young men he gathers for dinner: "'If you talk of strength,' said Mr. Jaggers, '*I*'ll show you a wrist. Molly, let them see your wrist. . . . Very few men have the power of wrist that this woman has. It's remarkable what mere force of grip there is in these hands. I have had occasion to notice many hands; but I never saw stronger in that respect, man's or woman's, than these'" (206). The sheer power of Molly's hands requires the sheer coercion of Jaggers's discipline; his delight at showing her off derives not from admiration of her strength but from pride in having controlled it.

While Molly is perpetually and actively tamed, her daughter, Estella, is so almost by definition. Her irascible demeanor and the sexual frigidity that accompanies it have less to do with serving her own desires than with her fashioning as a suitably impossible object for the male characters captivated by her looks. To the extent that Estella appears as a desiring subject, she does so as the "mere puppet" (253) of her guardian, Miss Havisham; and as if to ensure that the willfulness evident in her aggressive passivity will be utterly disarmed, she receives a decisive pummeling at the hands of her husband, Drummle (437). Unlike those of the other female characters we have considered, Estella's hands are virtually maintenance-free; there is little of interest to say about them, except that little is said of them. Since she signals the overt representation of the subject's desire, Estella's appearances in the narrative obviate the necessity for sex appeal to reside wholly in the linguistic timbre. As if to amplify the silence of her own desire, Estella is shown simply to have a "white hand" (227); and although Pip can fondle it, hers is possibly the least erogenous hand in the book. Estella succeeds as Pip's proper erotic object by the very thoroughness of her deeroticization in the narrative. She does not simply represent the refusal ordinarily requisite to provoke desire; she is constituted as phantasmatic. Although we are meant to register Pip's arousal at the alluring sight of her, the narrative voice—otherwise so rich in provocative periphrasis—becomes reticent around her "beauty," relying on such tropes as "indescribable majesty and . . . indescribable charm" (438). While the novel elsewhere registers eroticism in a combination of denotative refusal and connotative titillation, at the points of Pip's greatest official erotic interest, these strategies are reversed: in asserting fortissimo Pip's desire for Estella, the narrative need no longer marshal its battery of sotto voce techniques. At the moment desire's tale can be told, the narrative modulates into abstract diction, abandoning all of its prior engagement with corporeality: "She was so much changed, was so much more beautiful, so much more womanly, in all things winning admiration had made such wonderful advance, that I seemed to have made none" (224).

For those who take the singular voicing *in* the plot of Pip's feelings for Estella to indicate the text's only genuine eroticism, the novel reads as a conventional romance. Such readers, however, are obliged to account for the fact that, even in its famously revised ending, *Great Expectations* resists bringing about the usual novelistic resolution in matrimony. As though to clear the space necessary for sanctioned, sanctified heterosexual romance, male homoeroticism is finally repudiated and female subjectivity thoroughly thwarted. Yet we are left wondering why, despite these preparations, the romance plot is not more emphatically accomplished. One might, of course, point to the final

version of the novel's ending, where Pip records the sensation of
"what [he] had never felt before . . . the friendly touch of the once insensible hand" (438). If the novel does conclude in happy domesticity,
then its last sentence—"I took her hand in mine, and we went out of
the ruined place . . . " (439)—would provide a coherent resolution
for its manual thematics. Yet the suspended animation entailed not
only by the preservation of the original ending but also by the ambiguity of the final version itself ("I saw no shadow of another parting from
her") makes so smug a termination precarious. Despite critics' attesta-
tions to the plot's "perfection," the fact that the story is waylaid *before*
the threshold has left readers notoriously unsettled about its ultimate
outcome.

Why should a novel with such copious erotic investments finally
fail to resolve the basic romance plot? One answer is that its strategies
for regulating the vagaries of sexual desire simply prove *too* effective:
they discipline all sexuality, even the most orthodox, quite out of existence. Although the novel entertains a range of sexual designations,
exchanges, developments, and diffusions, the sexual hegemony in
which it issues becomes so powerful as finally to suspend not only that
order's own ideal—institutionalized heterosexual monogamy—but
anything that exceeds the fantasy of the solitary subject.

Yet despite the apparent elimination of all erotic possibilities, this
sole remainder—the solitary imagination—suggests that bodily self-
regulation may generate its own rewards. For even as the novel incul-
cates lessons about sexual continence in its audience, it agitates and incorporates the erotogenic pleasures of solitary reading. Indeed, the
very irresolution of the ending offers an alternative to erotic renunciation, one that animates the oscillation between the coerciveness of the
marriage plot and the violence of its refusal. Rather than resolving all
the previous travails of hands through the story, the novel's ultimate
ambivalence may instead reinscribe the mode of sexual deferral by
which it has operated from the first: in the manner of an imaginary object held perpetually at bay by autoerotic reverie, its eroticism can persist precisely by being suspended as undecidable. Just as Estella can
never be more to Pip than a "poor dream" (377)—the object of solitary sexual fantasy—so the residuum of the novel's ending finally
demonstrates the sustainability, rather than the complete evacuation,
of the masturbatory thematic that has mobilized its eroticism throughout. The ambiguity of the ending thus accomplishes a shift in the location of the novel's erotics that I have already suggested: in its finality it
extinguishes the evocative narration through which sexuality has been

connoted; but in the irresolution of its plot—its denotative practice—
it now preserves those concerns as strictly undecidable. Even as it
draws to an end, the novel resituates masturbation—sustains it, that is
to say, by refusing closure. The originary sexuality that enables the
novel's flood of erotic potentials, masturbation also serves as the remainder left behind when all other possibilities have been forsworn.

WORKS CITED

Acton, William. *The Functions and Disorders of the Reproductive Or-
    gans.* 1857. 6th ed. London: Churchill, 1875.

Dickens, Charles. *Oliver Twist.* London: Penguin, 1966.

*The Hand Phrenologically Considered: Being a Glimpse at the Relation
    of the Mind with the Organisation of the Body.* London: Chapman
    and Hall, 1848.

Cultural Criticism
and
Great Expectations

WHAT IS CULTURAL CRITICISM?

What do you think of when you think of culture? The opera or ballet? A performance of a Mozart symphony at Lincoln Center, or a Rembrandt show at the Metropolitan Museum of Art? Does the phrase "cultural event" conjure up images of young people in jeans and T-shirts or of people in their sixties dressed formally? Most people hear "culture" and think "High Culture." Consequently, most people, when they first hear of cultural criticism, assume it would be more formal than, well, say, formalism. They suspect it would be "highbrow," in both subject and style.

Nothing could be further from the truth. In fact, one of the goals of cultural criticism is to oppose Culture with a capital C, in other words, that *view* of culture which always and only equates it with what we sometimes call "high culture." Cultural critics want to make the term *culture* refer to *popular* culture as well as to that culture we associate with the so-called classics. Cultural critics are as likely to write about *Star Trek* as they are to analyze James Joyce's *Ulysses*. They want to break down the boundary between high and low, and to dismantle the hierarchy that the distinction implies. They also want to discover the (often political) reasons *why* a certain kind of aesthetic product is more valued than others.

A cultural critic writing on a revered classic might concentrate on a movie or even comic strip version. Or she might see it in light of some more common form of reading material (a novel by Jane Austen might be viewed in light of Gothic romances or ladies' conduct manuals), as the reflection of some common cultural myths or concerns (*Huckleberry Finn* might be shown to reflect and shape American myths about race, concerns about juvenile delinquency), or as an example of how texts move back and forth across the alleged boundary between "low" and "high" culture. A history play by Shakespeare, as one group of cultural critics has pointed out, may have started off as a popular work enjoyed by working people, later become a "highbrow" play enjoyed only by the privileged and educated, and, still later, due to a film version produced during World War II, become popular again—this time because it has been produced and viewed as a patriotic statement about England's greatness during wartime (Humm 6–7). More recently, cultural critics have analyzed the "cultural work" being done cooperatively by Mel Gibson and Shakespeare in Franco Zeffirelli's movie *Hamlet.*

In combating old definitions of what constitutes culture, of course, cultural critics sometimes end up combating old definitions of what constitutes the literary canon, that is, the once-agreed-upon honor roll of Great Books. They tend to do so, however, neither by adding books (and movies and television sitcoms) *to* the old list of texts that every "culturally literate" person should supposedly know, nor by substituting for it some kind of Counterculture Canon. Rather, they tend to combat the canon by critiquing the very *idea* of canon. Cultural critics want to get us away from thinking about certain works as the "best" ones produced by a given culture (and therefore as the novels that best represent a given culture). They seek to be more descriptive and less evaluative, more interested in relating than rating cultural products and events.

It is not surprising, then, that in an article on "The Need for Cultural Studies," four groundbreaking cultural critics have written that "Cultural Studies should . . . abandon the goal of giving students access to that which represents a culture." Instead, these critics go on to argue, it should show works in reference to other works, economic contexts, or broad social discourses (about childbirth, women's education, rural decay, etc.) within whose contexts the work makes sense. Perhaps most important, critics doing cultural studies should counter the prevalent notion that culture is some wholeness that has already been formed. Culture, rather, is really a set of interactive *cultures,* alive and growing and changing, and cultural critics should be present- and even future-oriented. Cultural critics should be "resisting intellectuals," and cultural studies should be "an emancipatory project" (Giroux 478–80).

The paragraphs above are peppered with words like *oppose, counter, deny, resist, combat, abandon,* and *emancipatory.* What such words suggest—and quite accurately—is that a number of cultural critics view themselves in political, even oppositional, terms. Not only are cultural critics likely to take on the literary canon while offering political readings of popular films, but they are also likely to take on the institution of the university, for that is where the old definitions of culture as High Culture (and as something formed and finished and canonized) have been most vigorously preserved, defended, and reinforced.

Cultural critics have been especially critical of the departmental structure of universities, for that structure, perhaps more than anything else, has kept the study of the "arts" more or less distinct from the study of history, not to mention from the study of such things as television, film, advertising, journalism, popular photography, folklore, current affairs, shoptalk, and gossip. By doing so, the departmental structure of universities has reasserted the high/low culture distinction, implying that all the latter subjects are best left to historians, sociologists, anthropologists, linguists, and communication theorists. But such a suggestion, cultural critics would argue, keeps us from seeing the aesthetics of an advertisement as well as the propagandistic elements of a work of literature. For these reasons, cultural critics have mixed and matched the most revealing analytical procedures developed in a variety of disciplines, unabashedly jettisoning the rest. For these reasons, too, they have formed—and encouraged other scholars to form—networks other than and outside of those enforced departmentally.

Some initially loose interdisciplinary networks have, over time, solidified to become Cultural Studies programs and majors, complete with courses on comics and surveys of soaps. As this has happened, a significant if subtle danger has arisen. Cultural critics, Richard Johnson has warned, must strive diligently to keep cultural studies from becoming a discipline unto itself—one in which students encounter cartoons as a canon and belief in the importance of such popular forms as an "orthodoxy" (39). The only principles that critics doing cultural studies can doctrinally espouse, Johnson suggests, are the two that have thus far been introduced: namely, the principle that "culture" has been an "inegalitarian" concept, a "tool" of "condescension," and the belief that a new, "interdisciplinary (and sometimes antidisciplinary)" approach to *true* culture (that is, to the forms in which culture actually lives now) is required now that history and art and media are so complex and interrelated (42).

Johnson, ironically, played a major part in the institutionalization of cultural studies. Together with Stuart Hall and Richard Hoggart, he developed the Centre for Contemporary Cultural Studies, founded by Hoggart and Hall at Birmingham University, in England, in 1964. The fact that the Centre was founded in the mid-1960s is hardly surprising; cultural criticism, based as it is on a critique of elitist definitions of culture, spoke powerfully to and gained great energy and support from a decade of student unrest and revolt. The fact that the first center for cultural studies was founded in England, in Europe, is equally unsurprising. Although the United States has probably contributed more than any other nation to the *media* through which culture currently lives, critics in Europe, drawing upon the ideas of both Marxist and non-Marxist theorists, first articulated the need for something like what we now call cultural criticism or cultural studies. Indeed, to this day, European critics are more involved than Americans, not only in the analysis of popular cultural forms and products but also in the analysis of human subjectivity or consciousness *as* a form or product of culture. ("Subjectivities," Johnson argues, are "produced, not given, and are . . . objects of inquiry" inevitably related to "social practices," whether those involve factory rules, supermarket behavior patterns, reading habits, advertisements watched, myths perpetrated, or languages and other signs to which people are exposed [44–45].)

Among the early continental critics now seen as forerunners of present-day cultural critics were those belonging to the *Annales* school, so-called because of the name of the journal that Marc Bloch and Lucien Febvre launched, in France, in 1929: *Annales: Economies, Sociétés, Civilisations.* The *Annales* school critics greatly influenced later thinkers like Michel Foucault, who, in turn, influenced other *Annales* thinkers such as Roger Chartier, Jacques Ravel, François Furet, and Robert Darnton. Both first- and second-generation *Annales* school critics warn against the development of "topics" of study by cultural critics—unless those same critics are bent on "developing . . . [a] sense of cohesion or interaction between topics" (Hunt 9). At the same time, interested as they are in cohesion, *Annales* school critics have warned against seeing the "rituals and other forms of symbolic action" as "express[ing] a central, coherent, communal meaning."

They have reminded us that texts affect different readers "in varying and individual ways" (Hunt 13–14).

Michel Foucault is another strong, continental influence on present-day cultural criticism—and perhaps *the* strongest influence on American cultural criticism and the so-called new historicism, an interdisciplinary form of historical criticism whose evolution has often paralleled that of cultural criticism. Influenced by early *Annales* critics and contemporary Marxists (but neither an *Annales* critic nor a Marxist himself), Foucault sought to study cultures in terms of power relationships. Unlike Marxists and some *Annales* school critics, he refused to see power as something exercised by a dominant over a subservient class. Indeed, he emphasized that power is not just *repressive* power: a tool of conspiracy by one individual or institution against another. Power, rather, is a whole complex of forces; it is that which produces what happens.

Thus even a tyrannical aristocrat does not simply wield power, for he is empowered by "discourses"—accepted ways of thinking, writing, and speaking—and practices that amount to power. Foucault tried to view all things, from punishment to sexuality, in terms of the widest possible variety of discourses. As a result, he traced the "genealogy" of topics he studied through texts that more traditional historians and literary critics would have overlooked, looking at (in Lynn Hunt's words) "memoirs of deviants, diaries, political treatises, architectural blueprints, court records, doctors' reports—appl[ying] consistent principles of analysis in search of moments of reversal in discourse, in search of events as loci of the conflict where social practices were transformed" (Hunt 39). Foucault tended not only to build interdisciplinary bridges but also, in the process, to bring into the study of culture the "histories of women, homosexuals, and minorities"—groups seldom studied by those interested in culture with a capital C (Hunt 45).

Of the British influences on cultural studies and criticism as it is today, several have already been mentioned. Of those who have not, two early forerunners stand out. One of these, the Marxist critic E. P. Thompson, revolutionized study of the industrial revolution by writing about its impact on human attitudes, even consciousness. He showed how a shared cultural view, specifically that of what constitutes a fair or just price, influenced crowd behavior and caused such things as the food riots and rick burnings of the nineteenth century. The other, even greater, early British influence on contemporary cultural criticism and cultural studies was the late Raymond Williams. In works like *The Long Revolution* and *Culture and Society, 1780–1950,* Williams demonstrated that culture is not a fixed and finished but, rather, a living and changing thing. One of the changes he called for was the development of a common socialist culture.

Like Marxists, with whom he often both argued and sympathized, Williams viewed culture in relation to ideologies, what he termed the "residual," "dominant," or "emerging" ways of viewing the world held by classes or individuals holding power in a given social group. But unlike Thompson and Richard Hoggart, he avoided emphasizing *social* classes and class *conflict* in discussing those forces most powerfully shaping and changing culture. And, unlike certain continental Marxists, he could never see the cultural "superstructure" as being a more or less simple "reflection" of the economic "base." Williams's tendency was to focus on people as people, on how they experience conditions they find themselves in and creatively respond to those conditions in their social practices. A believer in the resiliency of the individual, he produced a body of criticism notable for what Hall has called its "humanism" (63).

As is clear from the paragraphs above, the emergence and evolution of cultural studies or criticism are difficult to separate entirely from the development of Marxist thought. Marxism is, in a sense, the background to the background of most cultural criticism, and some contemporary cultural critics consider themselves Marxist critics as well. Thus, some mention of Marxist ideas—and of the critics who developed them—is necessary here. Of particular importance to the evolution of cultural criticism are the works of Walter Benjamin, Antonio Gramsci, Louis Althusser, and Mikhail Bakhtin.

Bakhtin was a Russian, later a Soviet, critic so original in his thinking and wide-ranging in his influence that some would say he was never a Marxist at all. He viewed language—especially literary texts—in terms of discourses and dialogues *between* discourses. Within a novel written in a society in flux, for instance, the narrative may include an official, legitimate discourse, plus another infiltrated by challenging comments and even retorts. In a 1929 book on Dostoyevsky and a 1940 study *Rabelais and His World,* Bakhtin examined what he calls "polyphonic" novels, each characterized by a multiplicity of voices or discourses. In Dostoyevsky the independent status of a given character is marked by the difference of his or her language from that of the narrator. (The narrator's voice, too, can in fact be a dialogue.) In works by Rabelais, Bakhtin finds that the (profane) language of the carnival and of other popular festivities play against and parody the more official discourses, that is, of the magistrates or the Church. Bakhtin influenced modern cultural criticism by showing, in a sense, that the conflict between "high" and "low" culture takes place not only between classic and popular texts but also between the "dialogic" voices that exist within all great books.

Walter Benjamin was a German Marxist who, during roughly the same period, attacked certain conventional and traditional literary forms that he felt conveyed a stultifying "aura" of culture. He took this position in part because so many previous Marxist critics and, in his own day, Georg Lukács, had seemed to be stuck on appreciating nineteenth-century realistic novels—and opposed to the modernist works of their own time. Benjamin not only praised modernist movements, such as Dadaism, but also saw as hopeful the development of new art forms utilizing mechanical production and reproduction. These forms, including radio and films, offered the promise of a new definition of culture via a broader, less exclusive domain of the arts.

Antonio Gramsci, an Italian Marxist best known for his *Prison Notebooks* (first published as *Lettere dal carcere* in 1947), critiqued the very concept of literature and, beyond that, of culture in the old sense, stressing not only the importance of culture more broadly defined but the need for nurturing and developing proletarian, or working-class, culture. He suggested the need to view intellectuals politically—and the need for what he called "radical organic" intellectuals. Today's cultural critics calling for colleagues to "legitimate the notion of writing reviews and books for the general public," to "become involved in the political reading of popular culture," and, in general, to "repoliticize . . . scholarship" have often cited Gramsci as an early advocate of their views (Giroux 482).

Finally, and most importantly, Gramsci related literature to the ideologies of the culture that produced it and developed the concept of "hegemony," a term he used to describe the pervasive, weblike system of meanings and values—ideologies—that shapes the way things look, what they mean and, therefore, what reality *is* for the majority of people within a culture. Gramsci did not see people, even poor people, as the helpless victims of hegemony, as ideology's idiotic robots. Rather, he believed that people have the freedom and power to struggle against ideology, to alter hegemony. As Patrick Brantlinger has suggested in *Crusoe's Footprints: Cultural Studies in Britain and America* (1990), Gramsci's thought is unspoiled by the "intellectual arrogance that views the vast majority of people as deluded zombies, the victims or creatures of ideology" (100).

Of those Marxists who, after Gramsci, explored the complex relationship between literature and ideology, the French Marxist Louis Althusser also had a significant impact on cultural criticism. Unlike Gramsci, Althusser tended to see ideology in control of people, and not vice versa. He argued that the main function of ideology is to reproduce the society's existing relations of production, and that that function is even carried out in most literary texts, although literature is relatively autonomous from other "social formations." Dave Laing has explained Althusser's position by saying that the "ensemble of habits, moralities, [and] opinions" that can be found in any work of literature tend to "ensure that the work-force (and those responsible for reproducing them in the family, school, etc.) are maintained in their position of subordination to the dominant class" (91).

In many ways, though, Althusser is as good an example of where Marxism and cultural criticism part ways as he is of where cultural criticism is indebted to Marxists and their ideas. For although Althusser did argue that literature is relatively autonomous—more independent of ideology than, say, Church, press, or State—*he* meant by literature not just literature in the narrow sense but something even narrower. He meant Good Literature, certainly not the popular forms that present-day cultural critics would want to set beside Tolstoy and Joyce, Eliot and Brecht. Those popular fictions, Althusser assumed, were mere packhorses designed (however unconsciously) to carry the baggage of a culture's ideology, mere brood mares destined to reproduce it.

Thus, while cultural critics have embraced *both* Althusser's notion that works of literature reflect certain ideological formations *and* his notion that, at the same time, literary works may be relatively distant from or even resistant to ideology, they have rejected the narrow limits within which Althusser and other Marxists have defined literature. In "Marxism and Popular Fiction" (1986), Tony Bennett uses *Monty Python's Flying Circus* and another British television show, *Not the 9 o'clock News,* to argue that the Althusserian notion that all forms of popular culture are to be included "among [all those] many material forms which ideology takes . . . under capitalism" is "simply not true." The "entire field" of "popular fiction"—which Bennett takes to include films and television shows as well as books—is said to be "replete with instances" of works that do what Bennett calls the "work" of "distancing." That is, they have the effect of separating the audience from, not rebinding the audience to, prevailing ideologies (249).

Although there are Marxist cultural critics (Bennett himself is one, carrying on through his writings what may be described as a lover's quarrel with Marxism), most cultural critics are not Marxists in any strict sense. Anne Beezer, in writing about such things as advertisements and women's magazines, contests the "Althusserian view of ideology as the construction of the subject" (qtd. in Punter 103). That is to say, she gives both the media she is concerned with and their audiences more credit than Althusserian Marxists presumably would. Whereas they might argue that such media make people what they are, she points out that the same magazines that may, admittedly, tell women how to please their men may, at the same time, offer liberating advice to women about how to preserve their independence by not getting too serious romantically. And, she suggests, many advertisements advertise their status as ads, just as many people who view or read them see advertising as advertising and interpret it accordingly.

The complex and subtle sort of analysis that Beezer has brought to bear on women's magazines and advertisements has been focused on paperback romance novels by Tania Modleski and Janice Radway, in *Loving with a Vengeance* (1982) and *Reading the Romance* (1984), respectively. Radway, a feminist cultural critic who uses but finally exceeds Marxist critical discourse, points out that many women who read romances do so in order to carve out a time and space that is wholly their own, not to be intruded upon by their husbands or children. Also, Radway argues, such novels may end in marriage, but the marriage is usually between a feisty and independent heroine and a powerful man she has "tamed," that is, made sensitive and caring. And why do so many such stories involve such heroines and end as they do? Because, Radway demonstrates through painstaking research into publishing houses, bookstores, and reading communities, their consumers *want* them to be that way. They don't buy—or if they buy, they don't recommend—romances in which, for example, a heroine is raped: thus, in time, fewer and fewer such plots find their way onto the racks by the supermarket checkout.

Radway's reading is typical of feminist cultural criticism in that it is *political*—but not exclusively about oppression. The subjectivities of women may be "produced" by romances—that is, their thinking is governed by what they read—but the same women also govern, to some extent, what gets written or produced, thus doing "cultural work" of their own. Rather than seeing all forms of popular culture as manifestations of ideology, soon to be remanifested in the minds of victimized audiences, non-Marxist cultural critics tend to see a sometimes disheartening but always dynamic synergy between cultural forms and the culture's consumers.

Mary Poovey does this in *The Proper Lady and the Woman Writer* (1984), a book in which she traces the evolution of female "propriety." Poovey closely connects the proprieties taught by eighteenth-century women who wrote conduct manuals, ladies' magazines, and even novels with patriarchal notions of women and men's *property*. (Since property was inherited, an unfaithful woman could threaten the disposition of a man's inheritance by giving birth to children who were not his. Therefore, writings by women that reinforced proprieties also shored up the proprietary status quo.) Finally, though, Poovey also shows that some of the women writers who reinforced proprieties and were seen as "textbook Proper Ladies" in fact "crossed the borders of that limited domain" (40). They may have written stories showing the audacity, for women, of trying to lead an imaginative, let alone audacious, life beyond the bounds of domestic propriety. But they did so imaginatively and audaciously.

Ross C Murfin

CULTURAL CRITICISM:
A SELECTED BIBLIOGRAPHY

General Introductions to
Cultural Criticism, Cultural Studies

Brantlinger, Patrick. *Crusoe's Footprints: Cultural Studies in Britain and America*. New York: Routledge, 1990.

Desan, Philippe, Priscilla Parkhurst Ferguson, and Wendy Griswold. "Editors' Introduction: Mirrors, Frames, and Demons: Reflections on the Sociology of Literature." *Literature and Social Practice*. Ed. Desan, Ferguson, and Griswold. Chicago: U of Chicago P, 1989. 1–10.

Eagleton, Terry. "Two Approaches in the Sociology of Literature." *Critical Inquiry* 14 (1988): 469–76.

Giroux, Henry, David Shumway, Paul Smith, and James Sosnoski. "The Need for Cultural Studies: Resisting Intellectuals and Oppositional Public Spheres." *Dalhousie Review* 64.2 (1984): 472–86.

Graff, Gerald, and Bruce Robbins, "Cultural Criticism." *Redrawing the Boundaries.* Ed. Stephen Greenblatt and Giles Gunn. New York: MLA, 1992.

Gunn, Giles. *The Culture of Criticism and the Criticism of Culture.* New York: Oxford UP, 1987.

Hall, Stuart. "Cultural Studies: Two Paradigms." *Media, Culture and Society* 2 (1980): 57–72.

Humm, Peter, Paul Stigant, and Peter Widdowson, eds. *Popular Fictions: Essays in Literature and History.* New York: Methuen, 1986.

Hunt, Lynn, ed. *The New Cultural History: Essays.* Berkeley: U of California P, 1989.

Johnson, Richard. "What Is Cultural Studies Anyway?" *Social Text: Theory/Culture/Ideology* 16 (1986–87): 38–80.

Pfister, Joel. "The Americanization of Cultural Studies." *Yale Journal of Criticism* 4 (1991): 199–229.

Punter, David, ed. *Introduction to Contemporary Critical Studies.* New York: Longman, 1986. See especially Punter's "Introduction: Culture and Change" 1–18, Tony Dunn's "The Evolution of Cultural Studies" 71–91, and the essay "Methods for Cultural Studies Students" by Anne Beezer, Jean Grimshaw, and Martin Barker 95–118.

Cultural Studies:
Some Early British Examples

Hoggart, Richard. *Speaking to Each Other.* 2 vols. London: Chatto, 1970.

————. *The Uses of Literacy: Changing Patterns in English Mass Culture.* Boston: Beacon, 1961.

Thompson, E. P. *The Making of the English Working Class.* New York: Pantheon, 1977.

————. *William Morris: Romantic to Revolutionary.* New York: Pantheon, 1977.

Williams, Raymond. *Culture and Society, 1780–1950.* New York: Harper, 1958.

————. *The Long Revolution.* New York: Columbia UP, 1961.

Cultural Studies:
Continental and Marxist Influences

Althusser, Louis, *For Marx.* Trans. Ben Brewster. New York: Pantheon, 1969.

Althusser, Louis, and Etienne Balibar. *Reading Capital.* Trans. Ben Brewster. New York: Pantheon, 1971.

Bakhtin, Mikhail. *The Dialogic Imagination: Four Essays.* Ed. Michael Holquist. Trans. Caryl Emerson. Austin: U of Texas P, 1981.

———. *Rabelais and His World.* Cambridge: MIT P, 1968.

Benjamin, Walter. *Illuminations.* Ed. with intro. by Hannah Arendt. Trans. H. Zohn. New York: Harcourt, 1968.

Bennett, Tony. "Marxism and Popular Fiction." *Popular Fiction: Essays in Literature and History.* Ed. Humm, Stigant, and Widdowson. New York: Methuen, 1986.

Foucault, Michel. *Discipline and Punish: The Birth of the Prison.* Trans. Alan Sheridan. New York: Pantheon, 1978.

———. *The History of Sexuality.* Vol. 1. Trans. Robert Hurley. New York: Random, 1990.

Gramsci, Antonio. *Selections from the Prison Notebooks.* Ed. Quintin Hoare and Geoffrey Nowell Smith. New York: International, 1971.

Laing, Dave. *The Marxist Theory of Art: An Introductory Survey.* Boulder, CO: Westview P, 1986.

Modern Cultural Studies: Selected British and American Examples

Colls, Robert, and Philip Dodd, eds. *Englishness: Politics and Culture, 1880–1920.* London: Croom Helm, 1986.

Modleski, Tania. *Loving with a Vengeance: Mass-Produced Fantasies for Women.* Hamden: Archon, 1982.

Poovey, Mary. *The Proper Lady and the Woman Writer: Ideology as Style in the Works of Mary Wollstonecraft, Mary Shelley, and Jane Austen.* Chicago: U of Chicago P, 1984.

———. *Uneven Developments: The Ideological Work of Gender in Mid-Victorian England.* Chicago: U of Chicago P, 1988.

Radway, Janice. *Reading the Romance: Women, Patriarchy, and Popular Literature.* Chapel Hill: U of North Carolina P, 1984.

Cultural Criticism of *Great Expectations*

Cottom, Daniel. "Paranomasia, Culture, and the Power of Meaning." *Text and Culture: The Politics of Interpretation.* Vol. 62 of *Theory and History of Literature*. Minneapolis: U of Minnesota P, 1989. 103–53.

Marlow, James E. "English Cannibalism: Dickens after 1859." *SEL* 23 (1983): 647–66.

Morris, Pam. "*Great Expectations:* A Bought Self." *Dickens's Class Consciousness: A Marginal View*. New York: St. Martin's, 1991. 103–19.

Tambling, Jeremy. "Prison-bound: Dickens and Foucault." *Essays in Criticism* 37 (1986): 11–30.

A CULTURAL PERSPECTIVE

Introduction

Like many, but certainly not all, essays in cultural studies, Jay Clayton's work on *Great Expectations* is concerned with contemporary American culture. In answering the question "Is Pip Postmodern?" Clayton traces the ways in which Dickens's work currently survives through an afterlife of allusions and references in arenas as diverse as high art and shopping malls. As his title points out, Clayton proposes a specific understanding of contemporary experience: *postmodern* is the term that he uses to describe what it means to live in the last years of this century. Like the term *culture*, *postmodernism* encompasses, as it defines, vast areas of experience. When, for instance, Jean-François Lyotard first used the word prominently in 1979, he called contemporary culture, in the title of his book, *The Postmodern Condition* to suggest the extent and inescapability of postmodernism's reach.

Although Jay Clayton's definition of the postmodern emerges in the course of his essay, some preliminary formulations may be helpful. For Lyotard, the postmodern condition is most significantly characterized by a disbelief or "incredulity toward" what he calls "metanarratives" (xxiv), the grand, traditional stories that offer totalizing explanations of experience and history. One of the most powerful of metanarratives is the nineteenth-century story of progress that is so prominent in *Great Expectations:* societies and individuals will, this narrative asserts, necessarily improve, although often only through the hard lessons of experience. While such stories survive in bits and pieces, as *Great Expectations* itself does, they cannot satisfy the longings for order and meaning as fully as they once supposedly did.

In socioeconomic terms, *postmodernism* refers to the culture of a postindustrial, multinational, late capitalist era—a society less devoted to making things than to consuming them. But it also refers to a specific understanding of what things are being consumed—images, ideas, services, more prominently than even food, clothes, and automobiles. Another theorist of the postmodern, Jean Baudrillard, defines it as a world of simulacra: the real (if there ever was such a condition) has disappeared to be replaced by parades of confusing, incommensurate images. There is no distinction between appearance and reality, copy and original. Everything is equally a simulation. Everywhere jumbles of unordered and heterogeneous images compete for the consumer's attention. For that reason, Baudrillard announces that Disneyland, with its "play of illusions and phantasms," where nothing is not a copy, is the epitome of postmodern life. Because it is so aggressively and unmistakably a simulacrum, Disneyland allows the viewer the illusion that the rest of America is "real" (204).

One of the complaints often made about culture at the end of the twentieth century is that it lacks a sense not only of the real but of the real in time, of history: an understanding of ordered events unfolding in a meaningful fashion has, like metanarrative, been lost. As Fredric Jameson explains, postmodernism is a "symptom" of the "waning of our historicity, of our lived possibility of experiencing history in some active way" (200). Clayton raises this issue, then uses the example of *Great Expectations* to offer telling, if brief, accounts of major social and economic trends from the middle of the nineteenth century to the end of the twentieth. Postmodernism's reputed ahistoricity becomes, for Clayton, an opportunity to record the history that can be read through the various survivals of *Great Expectations* into later eras and to specify the historical implications of postmodernism itself. To achieve this goal, Clayton's essay breaks down the traditional distinctions that are put in question by cultural studies. High and popular art, visual and verbal media, business and aesthetics, academic disciplines such as literature and history—all come together to provide evidence for Clayton's argument.

Finally, this essay begins with a particularly postmodern form of imitation, pastiche. Fredric Jameson has analyzed the "well-nigh universal practice today" of pastiche as a symptom of the "disappearance of the individual subject." He explains that unlike modernist forms of imitation, which "deviate from a norm which then reasserts itself" or earlier forms of satire, pastiche is imitation that does not attempt to point a lesson or provide a meaning. It is, rather, "the imitation of dead styles, speech through all the masks and voices stored up in the imaginary museum of a now global culture" (197). The global reach of the material covered in Clayton's essay certainly fits that definition, but, more important, so does the form of its first paragraph. There Clayton adopts the "dead language" characteristic of Dickens's journalistic essays in his magazines *Household Words* and *All the Year Round*—elaborate evocations of contemporary social scenes from the London slums to the central post office, all embellished with the statistics and details that Victorians so relished. Central to Dickens's journalistic writings was the stance of the observer, the individual who, in seeing such scenes, gives them significance and coherence. Although the fiction of such an observer may no longer be tenable—was Clayton's "observer" really at that train station in Nashville?—his essay delineates the ways in which Dickens's fiction, in its multitudinous afterlives, continues to do its cultural work now as effectively as it has in the past.

Janice Carlisle

Works Cited

Baudrillard, Jean. *Simulations.* Trans. Paul Foss, Paul Patton, and Philip Beitchman. New York: Semiotext(e). 1983. Rpt. in Easthope and McGowan, 202–05.

Easthope, Anthony, and Kate McGowan, eds. *A Critical and Cultural Theory Reader.* Toronto: U of Toronto P, 1992.

Jameson, Fredric. *Postmodernism or, The Cultural Logic of Late Capitalism.* 1984. Durham: Duke UP, 1991. Rpt. in Easthope and McGowan, 196–201.

Lyotard, Jean-François. *The Postmodern Condition: A Report on Knowledge.* Trans. Geoff Bennington and Brian Massumi. 1979. Manchester: Manchester UP; Minneapolis: U of Minnesota P, 1984.

JAY CLAYTON

Is Pip Postmodern? Or, Dickens at the End of the Twentieth Century

One overcast day in February, under the failing light of a late-afternoon sun, several curiously dressed couples were seen hurrying down the platform of the Riverfront Depot in Nashville, Tennessee. Most days of the week a gang of teenagers might rollerblade from one end of the platform to the other without endangering human life. But this evening the depot was astir: the powerful locomotive—a renovated 1952 model E8A, weighing 318,000 pounds and developing 2,250 horsepower—hissed and vibrated, pulsing with anticipation; porters beckoned anxiously to late-arriving passengers, while men in white sequined suits, with bushy sideburns and hair swept forward over their brows, escorted ladies in tight-skirted red dresses toward the elegant dining cars. One couple in particular drew the observer's attention, as they paused before a poster of the Roy Acuff movie *Night Train to Memphis*. This couple, although dressed as creatively as the other passengers, appeared more shy than most, as though this were their first date, and perhaps a blind one at that. Hoping to discover what had occasioned the unwonted bustle at the depot, the observer moved closer; and, happily, the gentleman's first words dispelled the entire mystery. Tonight, the Elvis Love Train was offering another of its "Great Expectations Specials."

Every Thursday during the month of February 1994, Great Expectations Services for Singles, the nationwide video dating company, offered its members free tickets on the two-and-a-half hour dinner excursion on the rails, a $42.95 value. An Elvis Menu of his personal favorite foods—hamburger steak, mashed potatoes, and corn bread—was available for dinner. Alas, this attractive package no longer exists. Shortly after the Elvis Love Train began running, the company received notice from Graceland that their use of Elvis's name represented an unauthorized infringement of trademark. But, for a few brief weeks, inquisitive observers had the chance to view firsthand what few perhaps had ever imagined: the marriage of Elvis and Estella.

This union brings together some of the most marketable cultural commodities from two different centuries. It nicely evokes the emotional appeal, the sentimentality, the promotional genius, the commercial crassness, and the legal maneuvering that surrounded both Dickens and Elvis in their respective eras. That it should all take place at trainside, a principal symbol of nineteenth-century technological progress, adds the finishing touch. My purpose in recording this ephemeral conjunction, however, is not to compare these very different figures but to register one instance of Dickens's continuing presence in contemporary popular culture. Like it or not, this sort of phenomenon is a way in which Dickens lives on at the end of the twentieth century. A grotesque, misshapen afterlife, one might say, as unsettling as the manias that animate some of Dickens's own creations: Miss Havisham in her decaying bridal dress, or Pip fantasizing about his great expectations.

There is a logic in this afterlife, however, a logic not entirely alien to the patterns in Dickens's own stories, as my last comparison is meant to suggest. Another way of putting this point is to say that Dickens anticipates some of the characteristic features of postmodern life. The term *postmodern* means different things to different people, but in the current context, it is as good a word as any to name the dominant cultural practices of today's consumer society. It encompasses, in ways that I will outline, a whole range of contemporary phenomena, including "high" cultural forms such as art, literature, music, and architecture; popular forms such as film, television, comics, and advertising; social developments such as consumer practices and lifestyle choices; and even belief patterns, such as the subcultural belief that Elvis is alive.[1] If Dickens did anticipate some of these phenomena, then tracing the misshapen forms of his survival in today's world will tell readers something about themselves—and about Dickens too.

Let me begin by mentioning a few other examples of Dickens's afterlife.[2] Once one starts to look for him, this author pops up at every turn. Through 1992, at least sixty-three movies have been made from his works, five from *Great Expectations* alone (DeBona 78). In the course of my inquiries, I have been told of or have seen television episodes of *The Donna Reed Show*, *Cheers*, *Wings*, *Quantum Leap*, and

[1] For a more extended account of the various ways in which this term is used in cultural studies, see Clayton.

[2] As is only fitting in a paper about postmodernism, I have made use in my research of the electronic bulletin board VICTORIA (listserv@iubvm.ucs.indiana.edu). In response to my query about references to Dickens in popular culture, I received wonderful, quirky, occasionally inspired suggestions. Some items I had already thought of myself, of course, but others were completely new to me. In the next five paragraphs, I incorporate many of the references that turned up in that forum. In addition to the postings cited individually in the text, let me acknowledge the suggestions made by Steve Bernstein, Andrea Broomfield, James Bucanek, Dennis Denisoff, Sandy Donaldson, Brad Gadberry, Sheldon Goldfarb, Libby Gruner, Kathy Holliday, Emily Jenkins, Devoney Looser, James McKeown, Deborah McMillion, Theresa Muir, Christina Rieger, Meri-Jane Rochelson, Linda Schulze, Dave Smith, Herbert Tucker, Timothy Watson, and Alan Winston. Alison McKee and Andrea Kalas responded individually to my request for assistance in locating archives of television serials. In addition, I am grateful to Janice Carlisle for encouraging me to undertake this project; to Louise Graham of Tulane University for her intelligent questions and assistance; to Jamie Adams of Vanderbilt's Learning Resource Center for help with preparing slides; and to my colleagues Julie Fesmire, Greg Hecimovich, and Mark Schoenfield for their comments on a draft of this essay.

The Simpsons that presented takeoffs of Dickens novels. *The Paper Chase* and *Happy Days* each have segments titled "Great Expectations," and *The Twilight Zone* called one show "In Praise of Pip." On Saturday morning cartoons, Disney's *Scrooge McDuck* remains a perennial favorite. And the very week in which I began writing this piece, *L.A. Law* featured a case involving a stereotypical "Victorian" librarian and a young man who dropped his lawsuit against her because of a conversion experience brought on by reading *Bleak House.*

An equal number of examples can be drawn from other spheres of contemporary culture. Many readers will remember a singer named Tiny Tim, who made a name for himself with "Tiptoe through the Tulips." In the 1970s there was a rock band called Uriah Heep (and, by the by, a Macintosh programming tool with the same name). The Eagles' 1976 hit "New Kid in Town" tells of a boy's "great expectations," which lead even his old friends to treat him like he's something new. More recently, Tasmin Archer called her 1993 debut album *Great Expectations.* Journalism provides even better hunting grounds. A search of a magazine database turned up fifty-nine articles published in 1993 that used the phrase "great expectations" in their titles, and although some of these pieces do not explicitly allude to Dickens, many do—such as the article on President Clinton's first one hundred days titled "Great Expectations Meet Bleak House."

The nostalgic character of Dickens's presence in today's world is especially visible around Christmas time, when productions of *A Christmas Carol* vie with *It's a Wonderful Life* and *Miracle on 34th Street* for airtime on television. Such nostalgia for a simpler life is by no means incompatible with commercial exploitation, as the novelist himself well knew. Scrooge is a familiar figure in magazine and television commercials, such as the Canadian Tire jingle that runs "Spend like Santa, Save like Scrooge." In gift shops around the country, the beloved Dickens Christmas Village is a best-seller; this "collectible" shows how Dickens's creations can literally be transformed into what Wemmick calls "portable property," as Christina Rieger remarked on the electronic bulletin board VICTORIA. At the Mt. Hope Victorian Estate and Winery, near Hershey, Pennsylvania, the great novelist himself annually hosts a party of nineteenth-century notables in what is billed as a "Charles Dickens Victorian Christmas"; advance reservations may be purchased over the phone with a major credit card. But Christmas is not the only holiday season when Dickens may turn up. The Rex parade of the 1993 Mardi Gras carnival in New Orleans featured *Great Expectations* prominently. The theme that year was "Royal British Scribes," and the lead float depicted Miss Havisham enthroned between two bridal cakes and surrounded by members of an all-male secret society, wearing masks and bridal costumes themselves.[3]

The economic impact of Dickens is even greater in education circles, where the dissemination of his works is a matter not only of devotion but also of professional obligation. This sector is a multimillion-dollar industry, which encompasses secondary school teachers, college professors, editors, publishers, book distributors, bookstore owners, librarians, and more. To speak only of the academic end of the spectrum, one observes that the professional interest in nineteenth-century British literature has spawned an international network of critical journals, academic book publishers, scholarly societies, conferences, foundation grants, graduate fellowships, and salaried positions in colleges and universities.

More visible traces of the economic potential of the Dickens icon can be found on street corners and in malls all across the continent. Who has not run across antique stores called The Olde Curiosity Shoppe? Philadelphia offers a pub called the Dickens Inn, and right around the corner is another one called The Artful Dodger (this latter name turns up in Saskatoon, Saskatchewan, too). Dallas is home to one of a nationwide chain of maternity stores called Great Expectations. In the Richmond area, there is a candle shop called Great Waxpectations; in Winnipeg, a dessert restaurant called Baked Expectations; in Brooklyn, a beauty salon called Great Hair-Spectations; in Manhattan, a wine tasting called Grape Expectations. To complete the roll call of bad puns, I once saw a *Saturday Night Live* skit called "Great Expectorations," and more recently, a sports feature about the hockey star Wayne Gretzky called "Gretz Expectations."

Now, if you are like me, you are about to shriek at the incongruity of naming maternity shops, hair salons, and dessert restaurants after a phrase that denominates the inevitability of disappointment, of broken hearts, of false hopes and punctured dreams. This incongruity, however, is echoed and redoubled by other ironies, equally apparent but

---

[3]For a reading of the political dynamics behind the 1993 New Orleans Carnival, see Vennman. Barbara Vennman generously sent me photographs she had taken of the "Charles Dickens" float. Her article also notes that one of the "oldest, private, white men's clubs" in New Orleans is the Pickwick Club (13).

worth underscoring, such as the mixture of sentimentality and commercialism in the Dickens Christmas, or the combination in academia of idealism and love of literature with an institutional apparatus requiring professional credentialing, publication for tenure, and the ranking of universities. This kind of irony, I am arguing, characterizes Dickens's presence in contemporary culture. Incongruity, contradiction, the juxtaposition of mismatched signifiers and ill-assorted values—these are the tokens by which Dickens travels today. And for this reason, if for no other, Dickens is perhaps the most postmodern nineteenth-century writer.

Dickens was aware that his vision went well with the commercial spirit. Many Victorian writers worked hard to make money from their fiction, but Dickens was extraordinarily fertile in devising new ways to capitalize on his imagination. Perhaps his greatest coup was his invention of a new genre, the Christmas tales, which were increasingly successful as specially printed seasonal books and which later were carefully orchestrated to prop up circulation of the magazines he ran. These works did so much to transform the nature of the holiday that the novelist's most recent biographer has remarked that "Dickens can be said to have almost single-handedly created the modern idea of Christmas" (Ackroyd 34). Many aspects of contemporary society might surprise Dickens, but the commercialization of Christmas—and his part in it—would not be one of them.

Dickens was prescient in recognizing the economic shift that was occurring in his lifetime. In the middle of the nineteenth century, England underwent a transition from an industrial economy, driven by the production of coal, iron, heavy machinery, and railroads, to a consumer economy, with its investment in advertising, marketing strategies, and household goods. As historians and cultural critics such as Martin J. Wiener, Jennifer Wicke, and Thomas Richards have demonstrated, in the decades after the Great Exhibition of 1851 a "new commodity culture dominated by advertising drew on and ultimately supplanted any alternatives to it" (Richards 1). This change helped foster a booming secondary market for Dickens's creations. In his own lifetime, Dickens saw the Little Nell Cigar, Pickwick Snuff, Gamp Umbrellas, and a host of other products bearing his characters' names; he went out of his way to visit a tavern named after his novel *Our Mutual Friend* (Dickens, *Speeches* 349). Although there was no provision for licensing such spin-offs, he understood the publicity value that came from their wide diffusion. From *Pickwick* onward, the green monthly numbers that serialized his novels carried advertisements for consumer goods ranging from foundation garments to washing machines and self-rising flour; the novelist eventually came to exercise control over what ads appeared, how they were arranged, and even what their copy should be (Wicke 50). He also led the way in advertising his own works. His later novels were announced by placards on the sides of buses, billboards in steamboats and railway stations, and posters wrapped around lampposts (Ackroyd 947). Moreover, his public readings had dramatic effects on the sales of his work, which were available in the lobby after each performance. The fit was perfect: Dickens both exploited and was exploited by a burgeoning consumer economy. But consumer capitalism was only in its infancy during the novelist's lifetime. Today, one sees the full effects of this one-hundred-year-long transformation.

The most successful contemporary venture to capitalize on Dickens's *Great Expectations* is the one with which this essay began, the video dating service, Great Expectations Services for Singles. With some forty offices in cities across the country and more than one hundred and twenty-five thousand members, it claims to produce "almost two weddings a day" (Winokur 239). The enterprise is a nice model of the kind of cultural pastiche that characterizes the postmodern era. It fuses information technology with that nostalgically Dickensian name, and it charges hefty fees (often approaching $2,000) for performing a richly ambiguous personal service: supplying partners for marriage and/or casual sex. Its founder and president, Jeffrey Ullman, who conceived the idea for this multimillion-dollar corporation while living in a Berkeley commune during the counterculture years (Kravitz 277), conflates venerable political rhetoric about self-determination with contemporary jargon about lifestyles and the single person. Similarly, the company's brochure jumbles together incompatible values deriving from several different cultural epochs. Note the clash between the claims to technocratic efficiency, leisured dignity, workaholic time pressures, and a hip ability to size up strangers in this passage from a promotional letter addressed to "Dear Single": Great Expectations "is a wonderfully efficient—and dignified—way to find the kind of person you prefer to socialize with, before you agree to meet with them. So you don't waste your precious time on blind dates or with losers." In a telephone interview on 29 June 1994, Ullman confirmed that the inspiration for his company's name came from Dickens, although it was the brainchild of his father, a pediatrician born in an earlier age.

After suggesting the name, Ullman's father remarked that the title came into his head because he was old enough "to have gone to school with Boz"; his son, having never heard of Dickens's pen name, thought his father must be referring to Boz Scaggs. The cultural markers that adorn this dating service are scarcely less disparate than these: fledgling Victorian novelist meets blues guitarist.

Dickens's presence in the popular culture of this century has not always been characterized by incongruity. At an earlier moment, during and just after World War II, when the great "modern" values of democratic nations had been under severe challenge, Dickens's image was more serious and coherent, an instrument of cultural consolidation, not consumerist expansion. I can bring out the difference by contrasting two carefully marketed images of the author, the Classics Illustrated comic book versions of *Great Expectations*. The first version of this story was published in 1947, whereas the second, entirely new version came out in 1990.[4] The first version rapidly became a collector's item—today, a copy in mint condition sells for over $800. Although this issue is number 43 in the series, it is the most valuable Classics Illustrated ever published because it was never reissued once it became the target of an attack in a best-selling book about comics by Dr. Fredric Wertham, *Seduction of the Innocent* (1954). Here are a few lines from Dr. Wertham's attack:

> There is a comic book which has on its cover two struggling men, one manacled with chains locked around hands and feet, the other with upraised fist and a reddened, bloody bandage around his head; onlookers: a man with a heavy iron mallet on one side and a man with a rifle and a bayonet on the other. The first eight pictures of this comic book show an evil-looking man with a big knife held like a dagger threatening a child who says: "Oh, don't cut my throat, sir!" Am I correct in classifying this as a crime comic? Or should I accept it as what it pretends to be—Dickens's *Great Expectations*? (311)

A glance at the cover reveals that Dr. Wertham described the scene

[4] I want to thank Joseph Witek for guidance and insight into the world of Classics Illustrated comic books and to the work of Rick Geary. His excellent *Comic Books as History* provided me with my first orientation to the criticism of this genre. Assistance with locating copies of the 1947 Classics Illustrated *Great Expectations* was provided by Dan Malan, editor of *Classics Collector Magazine;* Hollis Lawrence O'Neal of Nashville, Tennessee; and Rich Rostel of Louisville, Kentucky.

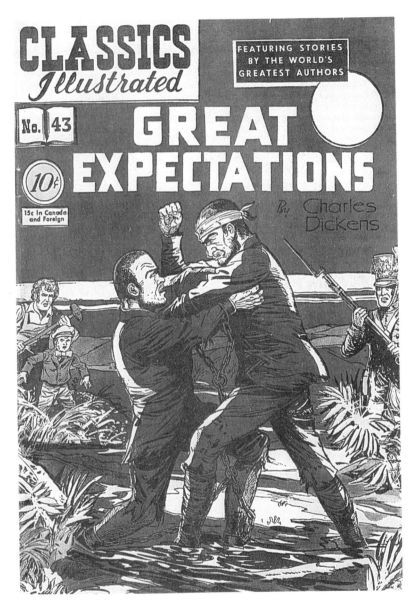

Figure 1. *Classics Illustrated*, 1947.

fairly well, as far as he went (Figure 1). His description of the succeeding pictures was equally accurate. My point, however, has nothing to do with violence in comic books, a topic that today seems almost quaint. Rather, I want to draw attention to the cultural markers embedded in this scene, markers of masculinity, power, legal authority, and ultimately, national identity. An honest, square-jawed blacksmith, a well-equipped soldier, and a boy dressed in his best Christmas suit witness a struggle between determined adversaries, the free and gallantly bandaged Magwitch beginning to rise above the treacherous, deservedly manacled Compeyson—a struggle between good and evil, clearly enough, with the values of a nation's men at stake.

When one turns to the 1990 version of the same story, the first thing one notices is the very different scene the artist has chosen as the centerpiece of his interpretation (Figure 2). The cover of a comic book is meant to grab the attention of the potential buyer, and these covers employ very different strategies for that end. Both covers dramatize formative moments in a child's life, and both emphasize the impressible young boy's status as an observer. In each, he is outside the scene, watching with rapt attention. But one is an action scene, full of violence, and involving only males; the other is a scene of stasis—indeed, it symbolizes the deathly stasis of Miss Havisham—and features two female characters. The visual dynamics of watching are present in both covers, but the later version introduces a self-reflexive dimension that is missing from the earlier. The picture is an optical illusion, in which Pip appears to be looking at a painting or a tapestry, framed by the border of the carpet and by what may be a doorjamb to his left. Moreover, the spectatorial act is even more prominent, since the reader, who is positioned behind Pip's head, sees what Pip is seeing and thus shares what film theorists call his "gaze."

Lest one think I am reading notions of gender and self-reflexivity into a work entirely innocent of such pretensions, let me provide a bit of background on Rick Geary, the creator of the 1990 comic. Geary first gained notice as a cartoonist for the *National Lampoon*, where his strips were praised for their droll, deadpan humor and their interest in the oddity of everyday life. Prior to working on *Great Expectations*, he had published several collections of cartoons, two of which were *A Treasury of Victorian Murder* and *Rick Geary's Oddities*. After finishing the Dickens story, he produced two original comic books titled *Blanche Goes to New York* (1992) and *Blanche Goes to Hollywood* (1993), both set in the early years of this century. The choice of a female heroine and a historical setting for these quirky mysteries indicate

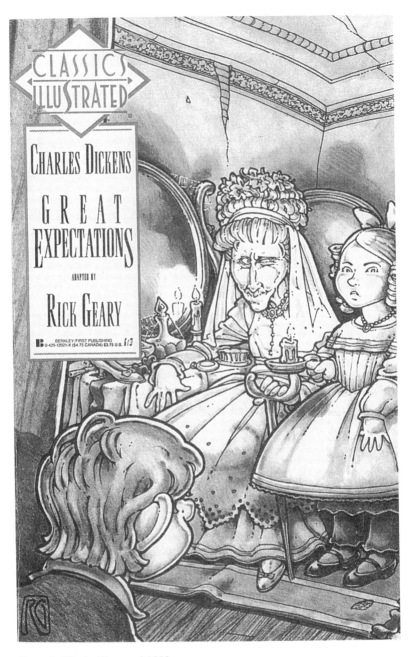

Figure 2. *Classics Illustrated*, 1990.

something of his interest in the topics of gender and history. Although both comics display his fascination with what film theorists call "the gaze," the second Blanche story makes this concern explicit by having the heroine come under the patronage of the movie director D. W. Griffith. (This director, it is worth mentioning, was said by Eisenstein to have learned the technique of montage from reading Dickens.) Finally, Geary's story also highlights the artist's political concerns, for it sympathetically recounts the struggle of the Wobblies to unionize the film industry.

What should one make of the differences between the two comics, of the shift from a male scene of power and authority to a female domestic scene of stasis, of the heightened self-reflexivity about the dynamics of spectators and the gaze? Clearly, the masculine scenario owes much to the prevailing conventions of World War II army comics. The two muscular figures struggling on the cover evoke Sergeant Rock or Sergeant Fury more than half-starved escapees from a nineteenth-century prison ship. An even more direct influence may have been David Lean's movie of *Great Expectations*, which came out the preceding year. The comic's plot follows the movie in several places more closely than the book—particularly in the decision to leave out the character of Orlick entirely, a choice generally regarded as a major flaw in the movie (see Moynahan; MacKay; Giddings; Tharaud). Geary had no such immediate visual precursor. Perhaps, too, Geary was aware of the controversy over violence that engulfed the earlier version. Still, the 1990 comic, with its camp awareness of its own cultural positioning, is mocking at the very points where its predecessor was earnest. The original Classics Illustrated were marketed as being "better" than ordinary comics, more serious, more educational. That was why Dr. Wertham's critique could have such a devastating effect. Although the publisher of the contemporary Classics Illustrated gestures toward this same educational mission in his prefatory note, he spends more time touting the "distinctive, fresh and innovative" styles of his contemporary adapters. The publisher is well aware that the largest market for these $3.75 books consists not of thrill-seeking children, nor even of students looking for a crib, but of adolescent and adult comic collectors, who value this art form for its own sake. In the best postmodern fashion, Geary dispels any sense that Dickens should be treated as an object of veneration and focuses instead on the quirky and bizarre. This comic might just as well have been called, in homage to Geary's other works, *A Treasury of Dickensian Oddities*. But perhaps to a postmodern sensibility such a title would have seemed redundant.

To conclude this contrast, let me return to David Lean's 1946 movie. This classic film has received ample attention, but one question relevant to this discussion has never been addressed: Why was this director, who was to become the preeminent cinematic poet of colonialism in works such as *The Bridge on the River Kwai* (1957), *Lawrence of Arabia* (1962), and *A Passage to India* (1984), attracted to Charles Dickens? Is there a link between Lean's vision of *Great Expectations* and his later fascination with the fate of the British empire? The connection is to be found in his depiction of Magwitch after the convict's return to England from his transportation to the colonies. The deathbed scene between Magwitch and Pip is the true climax of the movie, far more important, in Lean's rendering, than Pip's reconciliation with Joe, or even the extravagant happy ending with Estella that so many viewers have deplored. The bond between these two men generates the most intensely felt emotion in the picture, an emotion that enables the two figures to overcome all the divisions of class, education, and age. In the presence of this emotional bond, one is reminded of the other intense relationships in Lean's oeuvre between males from remote cultures: Lawrence with the Arab boys, Faraj and Daud; Colonel Nicholson with his Japanese counterpart, Colonel Saito; Fitzgerald with the Indian, Aziz. This last pairing is responsible for Lean's greatest liberty with E. M. Forster's novel, the Indian and the Englishman clasping hands in friendship at the film's end. Anita Desai, Rustom Bharucha, and Millicent Bell have rightly denounced this bit of colonial nostalgia, but the motif is clearly crucial to Lean's vision, and it was there, in embryo, in the love between Magwitch and Pip. The fantasy is that a certain kind of bond between men of honor can overcome the violence, the horrors, the injustices of this world. The genesis of Lean's fantasy came just after World War II, when Britain's hold over its colonial others had been lost. Dickens served the ends of this fantasy, providing a symbol of those qualities in the national character that might still secure the hegemony of British civilization, even if the nation's place in the new world order was permanently diminished.

In the aftermath of the war, Lean's vision was not as outrageous as it may seem today. George Orwell, writing a few years earlier in 1940, identified the same fantasy as the core of Dickens's appeal: "His whole 'message' is one that at first glance looks like an enormous platitude: If men would behave decently the world would be decent" (Orwell

417). To a postmodern novelist, however, born in one of Britain's former colonies, the message seems little less than appalling. Salman Rushdie, writing in 1984 about both Orwell and the Lean of *A Passage to India*, finds this fantasy to be at the core of the "zombie-like revival of the defunct Empire" (101). Rushdie calls his essay "Outside the Whale," signaling his rejection of the stance Orwell took in the title piece of his collection, *Inside the Whale* (1940). As it happens, this slender volume is where Orwell's essay on Dickens appears, a Dickensian (or postmodern?) coincidence that helps locate each judgment in its respective historical moment.

Rushdie is pertinent to this discussion for another reason. He is one of several postmodern novelists who have responded to Dickens in their fiction (others include Kathy Acker and Graham Swift). In *The Satanic Verses* (1989), Rushdie invokes a different Dickens text, his last completed novel, *Our Mutual Friend*. A climactic moment in the narrative takes place at a party on the set of a movie version of a musical based on Dickens's work, now retitled *Friend!* The set is a "huge re-creation of Dickensian London" (421), which condenses the nineteenth-century city so that the landmarks of Dickens's imagination lie shoulder to shoulder in hallucinatory proximity. "Real" celebrities mingle with "counterfeit" guests, hired for the occasion to wear period costumes. One of the extras, a buxom maid with a map of London drawn in red magic marker on her right breast, tries to seduce Saladin Chamcha in a mock Curiosity Shop. This drunken encounter combines familiar postmodern playfulness about the indistinguishability of imitations and originals with more disturbing motifs: nationalism, xenophobia, misogyny, and racism. As she unfastens her blouse, this "cartographically bosomed stranger" (425) sings a parody of one of the musical's solos, mocking the accents of foreigners in a "Rex-Harrisonian" patter and praising London as the "World's Metropolis." Chamcha stands horrified, transfixed by the sight of her breast. "The metropolis summons him"—but which one?—until, "giving an entirely Dickensian cry, [he] pushes his way out of the Curiosity Shop into the madness of the street" (424).

In postmodern terms, Rushdie's movie set is a simulacrum; but, then, Dickens's London has always been a simulacrum, an image more real than reality, one that attracted its first tourists during his own lifetime and that continues to draw them by the busload today. Such perplexities are a far cry from the "message" of Dickens in the 1940s. Rather than serving to consolidate a coherent national identity, this author has come to symbolize, for Rushdie, a form of madness characteristic of contemporary existence. The madness of the street stems from the fact that, in a postcolonial world, "There is no consensus about reality," to quote again from Rushdie's essay on Orwell and Lean (100). One character in *Satanic Verses* remarks, "The modern city is the locus classicus of incompatible realities,"[5] and this comment applies as much to the London outside the movie set as to the Dickensian simulacrum within. But if Chamcha now experiences the streets of London as a form of madness, it is only, Rushdie seems to say, because of a logic already visible in the "roaring streets" Dickens wrote about in the last line of *Little Dorrit*.

Let me draw some conclusions about contemporary culture from what I have said so far. It has become commonplace to assert that a consumer society has no historical sense, that advanced capitalism depends upon a single-minded focus on novelty. At the same time, shoppers cruise through a landscape saturated by nostalgic references to the past, hair salons and candle stores labeled with bad historical puns. These allusions are so bizarrely out of context, so laughably inappropriate, that one scarcely notices them. For most people, they have certainly lost any literal reference to the past. They exist only as a kind of cultural malapropism, good for a brief smile, if that. Consequently, the experience of cultural dissonance has become a routine part of daily life. But one can learn many things from it. I will mention three: First, the experience of cultural dissonance one encounters on television and at the mall represents a distinctive form of historical sensibility, as common in "high" as in "popular" cultural expressions. Postmodern literature, art, and architecture refer to history through devices so excessive that they have become signs of the time. These devices include allusion, parody, and hyperbole, all of which are used to place isolated cultural details in incongruous juxtapositions. By taking features of past cultures out of their contexts, the postmodern work promotes a particular form of historical sensibility: ironic, self-reflexive, textualized, eclectic, and discontinuous. One can see this sensibility on display not only in Salman Rushdie's fiction but also in the promotional brochures of Great Expectations Services for Singles. Second, this mode of historical experience, which critics often regard as a defining feature of postmodernism, was not unknown to the nineteenth century. It was, in fact, one of the principal ways in which Dickens encountered the cultural (as opposed to his personal) past, and that is

[5]My thanks to Timothy Watson, who drew attention to this passage from *Satanic Verses* in his thoughtful posting on VICTORIA.

why the Dickensian city seems so appropriate a symbol for the "incompatible realities" of contemporary society. One should not be surprised at the grotesque afterlife of Dickens in today's world. It reflects a logic at work in his own texts. Third, this logic means something different in 1994 from what it meant to David Lean and the makers of Classics Illustrated in 1946 and 1947—or to Dickens and his contemporaries in 1861. A genuinely historical inquiry requires one to specify these differences, even if one insists on the lines of continuity as well.

Great Expectations—and at last I refer to the novel by Charles Dickens—mixes cultural signs from different periods as pervasively and as incongruously as any postmodern text. Joe, the simple blacksmith, for example, represents a nostalgic portrait of a figure from an earlier era, a phase of capitalism fast disappearing in 1861, when the novel was published, although not as uncommon in rural areas in the 1820s, when the novel was set. The values associated with Joe—integrity, unswerving loyalty, pride in one's craft—accrue to this residual economic order, thus serving as an implicit critique of the more highly developed dominant economy of London. Staging the contrast as one between country and city helps to reduce the sense of incongruity for readers. Still, the incompatibility of this ideal with modern existence is dramatized at the end of the novel. The only way Pip can find to be true to the lessons he has learned from Joe is to spend eleven years away from the forge in his company's colonial branch in Cairo. Pip's summary of those eleven years represents the most "Victorian" moment in the book. His only consolation, the thing that enables him to hold up his head when he thinks of how badly he has behaved, is that now he "lived frugally, and paid my debts." If the reader had any doubts about the middle-class positioning of this Victorian ethic, Pip clears them up without delay: "I must not leave it to be supposed that we were ever a great House, or that we made mints of money. We were not in a grand way of business, but we had a good name, and worked for our profits" (436).

If Joe is a holdover from a rural, pre-Victorian mode of early capitalism and Pip matures into a thoroughly up-to-date middle-class Victorian, then is there anyone in the novel who might be said to foreshadow postmodernism? I am happy to say that there is. That person is not Pip, so the answer to the question in my title must be: No, Pip is not postmodern. The character who has the best claim to that role is a minor figure, although a favorite with readers down through the years: Wemmick.

Mr. Jaggers's clerk conflates enough incongruous cultural signs in his humble person to become a veritable icon of the Dickens icon. A model of businesslike decorum at the office, with his post-office mouth and his invariable advice to look after "portable property," he is an entirely different man at home, where he indulges his Aged P, shyly courts Miss Skiffins, and lovingly tends to his house and garden. The split between these two incarnations is so profound that Pip speculates that there must be "twin Wemmicks" (356). A division of this kind, between the self in its "private and personal capacity," to use Wemmick's words (273), and the public, professional self is seen often enough today but is hardly restricted to postmodernism. This kind of alienation was, in fact, one of the hallmarks of the "modern" self, a condition that Marx famously identified as a consequence of urban capitalism.

If a divided self were Wemmick's only distinctive characteristic, then he would be an unusually pure representative of a single historical type, "modern man." But Wemmick's interest hardly stops there. His home at Walworth is his other claim to fame. It is a little wooden cottage, which Wemmick has transformed into a miniature Gothic castle, perfect in every detail, including mock fortifications, a moat with its own drawbridge, a flag, and a cannon, which is discharged punctually at nine o'clock every evening. He lives in a simulacrum of another era, a theme park version of feudal England. And like today's theme parks, he takes pride in bringing to life a cliché. Wemmick has turned his house into a literal incarnation of the saying "A man's home is his castle." His mode of existence—inside this simulacrum—reproduces the economic conditions of a "freehold" (200), as far as is possible in a suburb of nineteenth-century London. As Wemmick proudly explains, "I am my own engineer, and my own carpenter, and my own plumber, and my own gardener, and my own Jack of all Trades" (200).

Inside the castle is Wemmick's prized "collection of curiosities." His treasures "were mostly of a felonious character," including a forger's pen and "a distinguished razor or two" (201). The collection is a treasury of Victorian murder, as odd as Rick Geary's postmodern comic book of that name. The Aged P is so proud of his son's accomplishment that he thinks "it ought to be kept together by the Nation, after my son's time, for the people's enjoyment" (200). After visiting some of the houses preserved by the British National Trust, with their mismatched architectural styles and their (far more expensive) collections of curiosities, I sometimes wonder if they did. In short, Wemmick's home is a postmodern pastiche, a simulacrum, as misshapen— and comical—as "Great Hair-Spectations" at the local mall.

With Wemmick as a guide, one begins to notice that *Great Expec-*

tations itself is a palimpsest of different cultural periods. Raymond Williams has pointed out that no era is ever characterized by a single ideology, and he has proposed dividing cultural beliefs along temporal lines into the "residual, dominant, and emergent." In Dickens's novel, one can identify traces of at least five different epochs, each competing with the others for cultural space: (1) the "feudal" freehold of Wemmick's castle; (2) the preindustrial capitalism of Joe's forge; (3) the "Victorian" middle-class values of Pip's mature years, with their clear connections to the fortunes of empire; (4) the "modern" alienation that splits Wemmick into twin selves; and (5) the "postmodern" world of simulacra and pastiche. The discontinuity among these layers contributes to many of the novel's most enduring effects: the comedy of Wemmick, the tenderness toward Joe, the ethical growth of Pip, and the social commentary on modern urban alienation. Yet few readers before today have ever read them as signs that there is "no consensus about reality." The more usual procedure has been to single out one strand and elevate it as the master discourse of the text. Where Dickens's contemporaries saw the novel as a return to the comic types and affectionate portraits of his youthful fiction, modernist critics perceived a new, "dark" phase of social criticism, and David Lean and the Classics Illustrated of the 1940s discerned images of masculinity and national identity that could symbolically replace the loss of empire. Only at the end of the twentieth century have people begun to focus on discontinuity itself, seeing in Dickens a foreshadowing of the "incompatible realities" of postmodernism. When Elvis comes calling for Estella, can any marriage be too far-fetched?

WORKS CITED

Acker, Kathy. *Great Expectations.* New York: Grove, 1982.

Ackroyd, Peter. *Dickens.* New York: HarperCollins, 1990.

Bell, Millicent. "What Happened in the Cave?" *Partisan Review* 53 (1986): 103–10.

Bharucha, Rustom. "The 'Boom' of David Lean's *A Passage to India.*" *Before His Eyes: Essays in Honor of Stanley Kauffmann.* Ed. Bert Cardullo. Lanham, MD: UP of America, 1986.

Clayton, Jay. "Dickens and the Genealogy of Postmodernism." *Nineteenth-Century Literature* 46 (1991): 181–95.

DeBona, Guerric. "Doing Time; Undoing Time: Plot Mutations in David Lean's *Great Expectations.*" *Literature/Film Quarterly* 20 (1992): 77–100.

Desai, Anita. "The Rage for the Raj." *The New Republic* (25 Nov. 1985): 46–50.

Dickens, Charles. *The Speeches of Charles Dickens*. Ed. K. J. Fielding. Oxford: Clarendon, 1960.

Eisenstein, Sergei. "Dickens, Griffith, and the Film Today." *Film Form: Essays in Film Theory*. Ed. Jan Leyda. New York: Harcourt, 1949.

Giddings, Robert. "Great Misrepresentations: Dickens and Film." *Critical Survey* 3 (1991): 305–12.

Kravitz, Lee. "Finding the Ideal Matchmaker." *Cosmopolitan*. 205.4 (Oct. 1988): 274–77.

MacKay, Carol Hanbery. "A Novel's Journey into Film: The Case of *Great Expectations*." *Literature/Film Quarterly* 13 (1985): 127–34.

Moynahan, Julian. "Seeing the Book, Reading the Movie." *The English Novel and the Movies*. Ed. Michael Klein and Gillian Parker. New York: Ungar, 1981.

Orwell, George. "Charles Dickens." *Inside the Whale* (1940). Rpt. in *An Age Like This, 1920–1940*. Vol. 1 of *The Collected Essays, Journalism and Letters of George Orwell*. 3 vols. Ed. Sonia Orwell and Ian Angus. New York: Harcourt, 1968.

Richards, Thomas. *The Commodity Culture of Victorian England: Advertising and Spectacle, 1851–1914*. Stanford: Stanford UP, 1990.

Rushdie, Salman. "Outside the Whale." In *Imaginary Homelands: Essays and Criticism 1981–1991*. London: Granta, 1991. 87–101.

———. *The Satanic Verses*. New York: Viking, 1989.

Tharaud, Barry. "*Great Expectations* as Literature and Film." *The Dickensian* 87 (1991): 102–10.

Vennman, Barbara. "New Orleans 1993 Carnival: Tradition at Play in *Papier-Mache* and Stone." *Theatre Insight* 10 (1993): 5–14.

Wertham, Fredric, M.D. *Seduction of the Innocent*. New York: Rinehart, 1954.

Wicke, Jennifer. *Advertising Fictions: Literature, Advertisement, and Social Reading*. New York: Columbia UP, 1988.

Wiener, Martin J. *English Culture and the Decline of the Industrial Spirit, 1850–1980*. Cambridge: Cambridge UP, 1981.

Winokur, Scott. "Matchmakers of the Nineties—From Yentas to Computers." *Cosmopolitan* 210.6 (June 1991): 236–39.

Witek, Joseph. *Comic Books as History: The Narrative Art of Jack Jackson, Art Spiegelman, and Harvey Pekar*. Jackson: UP of Mississippi, 1989.

Glossary of Critical
and Theoretical Terms

Most terms have been glossed parenthetically where they first appear in the text. Mainly, the glossary lists terms that are too complex to define in a phrase or a sentence or two. A few of the terms listed are discussed at greater length elsewhere (feminist criticism, for instance); these terms are defined succinctly and a page reference to the longer discussion is provided.

AFFECTIVE FALLACY First used by William K. Wimsatt and Monroe C. Beardsley to refer to what they regarded as the erroneous practice of interpreting texts according to the psychological responses of readers. "The Affective Fallacy," they wrote in a 1946 essay later republished in *The Verbal Icon* (1954), "is a confusion between the poem and its *results* (what it *is* and what it *does*). . . . It begins by trying to derive the standards of criticism from the psychological effects of a poem and ends in impressionism and relativism." The affective fallacy, like the intentional fallacy (confusing the meaning of a work with the author's expressly intended meaning), was one of the main tenets of the New Criticism, or formalism. The affective fallacy has recently been contested by reader-response critics, who have deliberately dedicated their efforts to describing the way individual readers and "interpretive communities" go about "making sense" of texts.

See also: Authorial Intention, Formalism, Reader-Response Criticism.

AUTHORIAL INTENTION Defined narrowly, an author's intention in writing a work, as expressed in letters, diaries, interviews, and conversations. Defined more broadly, "intentionality" involves unexpressed motivations, designs, and purposes, some of which may have remained unconscious.

The debate over whether critics should try to discern an author's intentions (conscious or otherwise) is an old one. William K. Wimsatt and Monroe C. Beardsley, in an essay first published in the 1940s, coined the term "intentional fallacy" to refer to the practice of basing interpretations on the expressed or implied intentions of authors, a practice they judged to be erroneous. As proponents of the New Criticism, or formalism, they argued that a work of literature is an object in itself and should be studied as such. They believed that it is sometimes helpful to learn what an author intended, but the critic's real purpose is to show what is actually in the text, not what an author intended to put there.

See also: Affective Fallacy, Formalism.

BASE *See* Marxist Criticism.

BINARY OPPOSITIONS *See* Oppositions.

BLANKS *See* Gaps.

CANON Since the fourth century, used to refer to those books of the Bible that the Christian church accepts as being Holy Scripture. The term has come to be applied more generally to those literary works given special status, or "privileged," by a culture. Works we tend to think of as "classics" or the "Great Books" produced by Western culture—texts that are found in every anthology of American, British, and world literature—would be among those that constitute the canon.

Recently, Marxist, feminist, minority, and postcolonial critics have argued that, for political reasons, many excellent works never enter the canon. Canonized works, they claim, are those that reflect—and respect—the culture's dominant ideology and/or perform some socially acceptable or even necessary form of "cultural work." Attempts have been made to broaden or redefine the canon by discovering valuable texts, or versions of texts, that were repressed or ignored for political reasons. These have been published both in traditional and in nontraditional anthologies. The most outspoken critics of the canon, especially radical critics practicing cultural criticism, have called into question the whole concept of canon or "canonicity." Privileging no form of artistic expression that reflects and revises the culture, these critics treat cartoons, comics, and soap operas with the same cogency and respect they accord novels, poems, and plays.

See also: Cultural Criticism, Feminist Criticism, Ideology, Marxist Criticism.

CONFLICTS, CONTRADICTIONS *See* Gaps.

CULTURAL CRITICISM A critical approach that is sometimes referred to as "cultural studies" or "cultural critique." Practitioners of cultural criticism oppose "high" definitions of culture and take seriously popular cultural forms. Grounded in a variety of continental European influences, cultural criticism nonetheless gained institutional force in England, in 1964, with the founding of the Centre for Contemporary Cultural Studies at Birmingham University. Broadly interdisciplinary in its scope and approach, cultural criticism views the text as the locus and catalyst of a complex network of political and economic discourses. Cultural critics share with Marxist critics an interest in the ideological contexts of cultural forms. See "What Is Cultural Criticism?" pp. 592–601.

DECONSTRUCTION A poststructuralist approach to literature that is strongly influenced by the writings of the French philosopher Jacques Derrida. Deconstruction, partly in response to structuralism and formalism, posits the undecidability of meaning for all texts. In fact, as the deconstructionist critic J. Hillis Miller points out, "deconstruction is not a dismantling of the structure of a text but a demonstration that it has already dismantled itself." See "What Is Deconstruction?" pp. 502–09.

DIALECTIC Originally developed by Greek philosophers, mainly Socrates and Plato, as a form and method of logical argumentation; the term later came to denote a philosophical notion of evolution. The German philosopher G. W. F. Hegel described dialectic as a process whereby a thesis, when countered by an antithesis, leads to the synthesis of a new idea. Karl Marx and Friedrich Engels, adapting Hegel's idealist theory, used the phrase "dialectical materialism" to discuss the way in which a revolutionary class war might lead to the synthesis of a new social economic order. The American Marxist critic Fredric Jameson has coined the phrase "dialectical criticism" to refer to a Marxist critical approach that synthesizes structuralist and poststructuralist methodologies.

See also: Marxist Criticism, Poststructuralism, Structuralism.

DIALOGIC *See* Discourse.

DISCOURSE Used specifically, can refer to (1) spoken or written discussion of a subject or area of knowledge; (2) the words in, or text of, a narrative as opposed to its story line; or (3) a "strand" within a given narrative that argues a certain point or defends a given value system.

More generally, "discourse" refers to the language in which a subject or area of knowledge is discussed or a certain kind of business is transacted. Human knowledge is collected and structured in discourses. Theology and medicine are defined by their discourses, as are politics, sexuality, and literary criticism.

A society is generally made up of a number of different discourses or "discourse communities," one or more of which may be dominant or serve the dominant ideology. Each discourse has its own vocabulary, concepts, and rules, knowledge of which constitutes power. The psychoanalyst and psychoanalytic critic Jacques Lacan has treated the unconscious as a form of discourse, the patterns of which are repeated in literature. Cultural critics, following Mikhail Bakhtin, use the word "dialogic" to discuss the dialogue *between* discourses that takes place within language or, more specifically, a literary text.

See also: Cultural Criticism, Ideology, Narrative, Psychoanalytic Criticism.

FEMINIST CRITICISM An aspect of the feminist movement whose primary goals include critiquing masculine-dominated language and literature by showing how they reflect a masculine ideology; writing the history of unknown or undervalued women writers, thereby earning them their rightful place in the literary canon; and helping create a climate in which women's creativity may be fully realized and appreciated. See "What Is Feminist Criticism?" pp. 527–34.

FIGURE *See* Metaphor, Metonymy, Symbol.

FORMALISM Also referred to as the New Criticism, formalism reached its height during the 1940s and 1950s, but it is still practiced today.

Formalists treat a work of literary art as if it were a self-contained, self-referential object. Rather than basing their interpretations of a text on the reader's response, the author's stated intentions, or parallels between the text and historical contexts (such as the author's life), formalists concentrate on the relationships *within* the text that give it its own distinctive character or form. Special attention is paid to repetition, particularly of images or symbols, but also of sound effects and rhythms in poetry.

Because of the importance placed on close analysis and the stress on the text as a carefully crafted, orderly object containing observable formal patterns, formalism has often been seen as an attack on Romanticism and impressionism, particularly impressionistic criticism. It has sometimes even been called an "objective" approach to literature. Formalists are more likely than certain other critics to believe and say that the meaning of a text can be known objectively. For instance, reader-response critics see meaning as a function either of each reader's experience or of the norms that govern a particular "interpretive community," and deconstructors argue that texts mean opposite things at the same time.

Formalism was originally based on essays written during the 1920s and 1930s by T. S. Eliot, I. A. Richards, and William Empson. It was significantly developed later by a group of American poets and critics, including R. P. Blackmur, Cleanth Brooks, John Crowe Ransom, Allen Tate, Robert Penn Warren, and William K. Wimsatt. Although we associate formalism with certain principles and terms (such as the "Affective Fallacy" and the "Intentional Fallacy" as defined by Wimsatt and Monroe C. Beardsley), formalists were trying to make a cultural statement rather than establish a critical dogma. Generally southern, religious, and culturally conservative, they advocated the inherent value of literary works (particularly of literary works regarded as beautiful art objects) because they were sick of the growing ugliness of modern life and contemporary events. Some recent theorists even suggest that the rising popularity of formalism after World War II was a feature of American isolationism, the formalist tendency to isolate literature from biography and history being a manifestation of the American fatigue with wider involvements.

See also: Affective Fallacy, Authorial Intention, Deconstruction, Reader-Response Criticism, Symbol.

GAPS   When used by reader-response critics familiar with the theories of Wolfgang Iser, refers to "blanks" in texts that must be filled in by readers. A gap may be said to exist whenever and wherever a reader perceives something to be missing between words, sentences, paragraphs, stanzas, or chapters. Readers respond to gaps actively and creatively, explaining apparent inconsistencies in point of view, accounting for jumps in chronology, speculatively supplying information missing from plots, and resolving problems or issues left ambiguous or "indeterminate" in the text.

Reader-response critics sometimes speak as if a gap actually exists in a text; a gap is, of course, to some extent a product of readers' perceptions. Different readers may find gaps in different texts, and different gaps in the same text. Furthermore, they may fill these gaps in different ways, which is why a reader-response critic might argue, works are interpreted in different ways.

Although the concept of the gap has been used mainly by reader-response critics, it has also been used by critics taking other theoretical approaches.

Practitioners of deconstruction might use "gap" when speaking of the radical contradictoriness of a text. Marxists have used the term to speak of everything from the gap that opens up between economic base and cultural superstructure to the two kinds of conflicts or contradictions to be found in literary texts. The first of these, they would argue, results from the fact that texts reflect ideology, within which certain subjects cannot be covered, things that cannot be said, contradictory views that cannot be recognized as contradictory. The second kind of conflict, contradiction, or gap within a text results from the fact that works don't just reflect ideology: they are also fictions that, consciously or unconsciously, distance themselves from the same ideology.

See also: Deconstruction, Ideology, Marxist Criticism, Reader-Response Criticism.

GENDER CRITICISM   Developing out of feminist criticism in the mid-1980s, this fluid and inclusive movement by its nature defies neat definition. Its practitioners include, but are not limited to, self-identified feminists, gay and lesbian critics, queer and performance theorists, and poststructuralists interested in deconstructing oppositions such as masculine/feminine, heterosexual/homosexual. This diverse group of critics shares an interest in interrogating categories of gender and sexuality and exploring the relationships between them, though it does not necessarily share any central assumptions about the nature of these categories. For example, some gender critics insist that all gender identities are cultural constructions, but others have maintained a belief in essential gender identity. Often gender critics are more interested in examining gender issues through a literary text than a literary text through gender issues. See "What Is Gender Criticism?" pp. 558–66.

GENRE   A French word referring to a kind or type of literature. Individual works within a genre may exhibit a distinctive form, be governed by certain conventions, and/or represent characteristic subjects. Tragedy, epic, and romance are all genres.

Perhaps inevitably, the term "genre" is used loosely. Lyric poetry is a genre, but so are characteristic *types* of the lyric, such as the sonnet, the ode, and the elegy. Fiction is a genre, as are detective fiction and science fiction. The list of genres grows constantly as critics establish new lines of connection between individual works and discern new categories of works with common characteristics. Moreover, some writers form hybrid genres by combining the characteristics of several in a single work.

Knowledge of genres helps critics to understand and explain what is conventional and unconventional, borrowed and original, in a work.

HEGEMONY   Given intellectual currency by the Italian communist Antonio Gramsci, the word (a translation of *egemonia*) refers to the pervasive system of assumptions, meanings, and values—the web of ideologies, in other words—that shapes the way things look, what they mean, and therefore what reality *is* for the majority of people within a given culture.

See also: Ideology, Marxist Criticism.

IDEOLOGY   A set of beliefs underlying the customs, habits, and/or practices common to a given social group. To members of that group, the beliefs seem obviously true, natural, and even universally applicable. They may seem just as obviously arbitrary, idiosyncratic, and even false to outsiders or members of another group who adhere to another ideology. Within a society, several ideologies may coexist, or one or more may be dominant.

Ideologies may be forcefully imposed or willingly subscribed to. Their component beliefs may be held consciously or unconsciously. In either case, they come to form what Johanna M. Smith has called "the unexamined ground of our experience." Ideology governs our perceptions, judgments, and prejudices—our sense of what is acceptable, normal, and deviant. Ideology may cause a revolution; it may also allow discrimination and even exploitation.

Ideologies are of special interest to sociologically oriented critics of literature because of the way in which authors reflect or resist prevailing views in their texts. Some Marxist critics have argued that literary texts reflect and reproduce the ideologies that produced them; most, however, have shown how ideologies are riven with contradictions that works of literature manage to expose and widen. Still other Marxists have focused on the way in which texts themselves are characterized by gaps, conflicts, and contradictions between their ideological and anti-ideological functions.

Feminist critics have addressed the question of ideology by seeking to expose (and thereby call into question) the patriarchal ideology mirrored or inscribed in works written by men—even men who have sought to counter sexism and break down sexual stereotypes. New historicists have been interested in demonstrating the ideological underpinnings not only of literary representations but also of our interpretations of them. Fredric Jameson, an American Marxist critic, argues that all thought is ideological, but that ideological thought that knows itself as such stands the chance of seeing through and transcending ideology.

See also: Cultural Criticism, Feminist Criticism, Marxist Criticism, New Historicism.

IMAGINARY ORDER One of the three essential orders of the psychoanalytic field (see Real and Symbolic Order), it is most closely associated with the senses (sight, sound, touch, taste, and smell). The infant, who by comparison to other animals is born premature and thus is wholly dependent on others for a prolonged period, enters the Imaginary order when it begins to experience a unity of body parts and motor control that is empowering. This usually occurs between six and eighteen months, and is called by Lacan the "mirror stage" or "mirror phase," in which the child anticipates mastery of its body. It does so by identifying with the *image* of wholeness (that is, seeing its own image in the mirror, experiencing its mother as a whole body, and so on). This sense of oneness, and also difference from others (especially the mother or primary caretaker), is established through an image or a vision of harmony that is both a mirroring and a "mirage of maturation" or false sense of individuality and independence. The Imaginary is a metaphor for unity, is related to the visual order, and is always part of human subjectivity. Because the subject is fundamentally separate from others and also internally divided (conscious/unconscious), the apparent coherence of the Imaginary, its fullness and grandiosity, is always false, a *mis*recognition that the ego (or "me") tries to deny by imagining itself as coherent and empowered. The Imaginary operates in conjunction with the Real and Symbolic and is not a "stage" of development equivalent to Freud's "pre-oedipal stage," nor is it prelinguistic.

See also: Psychoanalytic Criticism, Real, Symbolic Order.

IMPLIED READER A phrase used by some reader-response critics in place of the phrase "the reader." Whereas "the reader" could refer to any idiosyncratic individual who happens to have read or to be reading the text, "the implied reader" is *the* reader intended, even created, by the text. Other reader-response critics seeking to describe this more generally conceived reader have spoken of the "informed reader" or the "narratee," who is "the necessary counterpart of a given narrator."

See Reader-Response Criticism.

INTENTIONAL FALLACY *See* Authorial Intention.

INTENTIONALITY *See* Authorial Intention.

INTERTEXTUALITY The condition of interconnectedness among texts. Every author has been influenced by others, and every work contains explicit and implicit references to other works. Writers may consciously or unconsciously echo a predecessor or precursor; they may also consciously or unconsciously disguise their indebtedness, making intertextual relationships difficult for the critic to trace.

Reacting against the formalist tendency to view each work as a freestanding object, some poststructuralist critics suggested that the meaning of a work emerges only intertextually, that is, within the context provided by other works. But there has been a reaction, too, against this type of intertextual criticism. Some new historicist critics suggest that literary history is itself too narrow a context and that works should be interpreted in light of a larger set of cultural contexts.

There is, however, a broader definition of intertextuality, one that refers to the relationship between works of literature and a wide range of narratives and discourses that we don't usually consider literary. Thus defined, intertextuality could be used by a new historicist to refer to the significant interconnectedness between a literary text and nonliterary discussions of or discourses about contemporary culture. Or it could be used by a poststructuralist to suggest that a work can only be recognized and read within a vast field of signs and tropes that is *like* a text and that makes any single text self-contradictory and "undecidable."

See also: Discourse, Formalism, Narrative, New Historicism, Poststructuralism, Trope.

MARXIST CRITICISM An approach that treats literary texts as material products, describing them in broadly historical terms. In Marxist criticism, the text is viewed in terms of its production and consumption, as a product *of* work that does identifiable cultural work of its own. Following Karl Marx, the founder of communism, Marxist critics have used the terms "base" to refer to economic reality and "superstructure" to refer to the corresponding or "homologous" infrastructure consisting of politics, law, philosophy, religion, and the arts. Also following Marx, they have used the word "ideology" to refer to that set of cultural beliefs that literary works at once reproduce, resist, and revise.

METAPHOR The representation of one thing by another related or similar thing. The image (or activity or concept) used to represent or "figure" something else is known as the "vehicle" of the metaphor; the thing represented is called the "tenor." In other words, the vehicle is what we substitute for the tenor. The relationship between vehicle and tenor can provide much additional meaning. Thus, instead of saying, "Last night I read a book," we might say, "Last night I plowed through a book." "Plowed through" (or the activity of plowing) is the vehicle of our metaphor; "read" (or the act of reading) is the tenor, the thing being figured. The increment in meaning through metaphor is fairly obvious. Our audience knows not only *that* we read but also *how* we read, because to read a book in the way that a plow rips through earth is surely to read in a relentless, unreflective way. Note that in the sentence above, a new metaphor—"rips through"—has been used to explain an old one. This serves (which is a metaphor) as an example of just how thick (another metaphor) language is with metaphors!

Metaphor is a kind of "trope" (literally, a "turning," that is, a figure of speech that alters or "turns" the meaning of a word or phrase). Other tropes include allegory, conceit, metonymy, personification, simile, symbol, and synecdoche. Traditionally, metaphor and symbol have been viewed as the principal tropes; minor tropes have been categorized as *types* of these two major ones. Similes, for instance, are usually defined as simple metaphors that usually employ "like" or "as" and state the tenor outright, as in "My love is like a red, red rose." Synecdoche involves a vehicle that is a *part* of the tenor, as in "I see a sail" meaning "I see a boat." Metonymy is viewed as a metaphor involving two terms commonly if arbitrarily associated with (but not fundamentally or intrinsically related to) each other. Recently, however, deconstructors such as Paul de Man and J. Hillis Miller have questioned the "privilege" granted to metaphor and the metaphor/metonymy distinction or "opposition." They have suggested that all metaphors are really metonyms and that all figuration is arbitrary.

See also: Deconstruction, Metonymy, Oppositions, Symbol.

METONYMY   The representation of one thing by another that is commonly and often physically associated with it. To refer to a writer's handwriting as his or her "hand" is to use a metonymic "figure" or "trope." The image or thing used to represent something else is known as the "vehicle" of the metonym; the thing represented is called the "tenor."

Like other tropes (such as metaphor), metonymy involves the replacement of one word or phrase by another. Liquor may be referred to as "the bottle," a monarch as "the crown." Narrowly defined, the vehicle of a metonym is arbitrarily, not intrinsically, associated with the tenor. In other words, the bottle just happens to be what liquor is stored in and poured from in our culture. The hand may be involved in the production of handwriting, but so are the brain and the pen. There is no special, intrinsic likeness between a crown and a monarch; it's just that crowns traditionally sit on monarchs' heads and not on the heads of university professors. More broadly, "metonym" and "metonymy" have been used by recent critics to refer to a wide range of figures and tropes. Deconstructors have questioned the distinction between metaphor and metonymy.

See also: Deconstruction, Metaphor, Trope.

NARRATIVE   A story or a telling of a story, or an account of a situation or of events. A novel and a biography of a novelist are both narratives, as are Freud's case histories.

Some critics use the word "narrative" even more generally; Brook Thomas, a new historicist, has critiqued "narratives of human history that neglect the role human labor has played."

NEW CRITICISM *See* Formalism.

NEW HISTORICISM First practiced and articulated in the late 1970s and early 1980s in the work of critics such as Stephen Greenblatt—who named this movement in contemporary critical theory—and Louis Montrose, its practitioners share certain convictions, primarily that literary critics need to develop a high degree of historical consciousness and that literature should not be viewed apart from other human creations, artistic or otherwise. They share a belief in referentiality—a belief that literature refers to and is referred to by things outside itself—that is fainter in the works of formalist, poststructuralist, and even reader-response critics. Discarding old distinctions between literature, history, and the social sciences, new historicists agree with Greenblatt that the "central concerns" of criticism "should prevent it from permanently sealing off one type of discourse from another, or decisively separating works of art from the minds and lives of their creators and their audiences."

See also: Authorial Intention, Deconstruction, Formalism, Ideology, Poststructuralism, Psychoanalytic Criticism.

OPPOSITIONS A concept highly relevant to linguistics, since linguists maintain that words (such as "black" and "death") have meaning not in themselves but in relation to other words ("white" and "life"). Jacques Derrida, a poststructuralist philosopher of language, has suggested that in the West we think in terms of these "binary oppositions" or dichotomies, which on examination turn out to be evaluative hierarchies. In other words, each opposition—beginning/end, presence/absence, or consciousness/unconsciousness—contains one term that our culture views as superior and one term that we view as negative or inferior.

Derrida has "deconstructed" a number of these binary oppositions, including two—speech/writing and signifier/signified—that he believes to be central to linguistics in particular and Western culture in general. He has concurrently critiqued the "law" of noncontradiction, which is fundamental to Western logic. He and other deconstructors have argued that a text can contain opposed strands of discourse and, therefore, mean opposite things: reason *and* passion, life *and* death, hope *and* despair, black *and* white. Traditionally, criticism has involved choosing between opposed or contradictory meanings and arguing that one is present in the text and the other absent.

French feminists have adopted the ideas of Derrida and other deconstructors, showing not only that we think in terms of such binary oppositions as male/female, reason/emotion, and active/passive, but that we also associate reason and activity with masculinity and emotion and passivity with femininity. Because of this, they have concluded that language is "phallocentric," or masculine-dominated.

See also: Deconstruction, Discourse, Feminist Criticism, Poststructuralism.

PHALLUS The symbolic value of the penis that organizes libidinal development and which Freud saw as a stage in the process of human subjectivity. Lacan viewed the Phallus as the representative of a fraudulent power (male over female) whose "law" is a principle of psychic division (conscious/unconscious) and sexual difference (masculine/feminine). The Symbolic order (*see* Symbolic Order) is ruled by the Phallus, which of itself has no inherent meaning *apart from* the power and meaning given to it by individual cultures and societies, and represented by the name of the father as lawgiver and namer.

POSTSTRUCTURALISM   The general attempt to contest and subvert structuralism initiated by deconstructors and certain other critics associated with psychoanalytic, Marxist, and feminist theory. Structuralists, using linguistics as a model and employing semiotic (sign) theory, posit the possibility of knowing a text systematically and revealing the "grammar" behind its form and meaning. Poststructuralists argue against the possibility of such knowledge and description. They counter that texts can be shown to contradict not only structuralist accounts of them but also themselves. In making their adversarial claims, they rely on close readings of texts and on the work of theorists such as Jacques Derrida and Jacques Lacan.

Poststructuralists have suggested that structuralism rests on distinctions between "signifier" and "signified" (signs and the things they point toward), "self" and "language" (or "text"), texts and other texts, and text and world that are overly simplistic, if not patently inaccurate. Poststructuralists have shown how all signifieds are also signifiers, and they have treated texts as "intertexts." They have viewed the world as if it *were* a text (we desire a certain car because it *symbolizes* achievement) and the self as the subject, as well as the user, of language; for example, we may shape and speak through language, but it also shapes and speaks through us.

See also: Deconstruction, Feminist Criticism, Intertextuality, Psychoanalytic Criticism, Semiotics, Structuralism.

PSYCHOANALYTIC CRITICISM   Grounded in the psychoanalytic theories of Sigmund Freud, it is one of the oldest critical methodologies still in use. Freud's view that works of literature, like dreams, express secret, unconscious desires led to criticism and interpreted literary works as manifestations of the authors' neuroses. More recently, psychoanalytic critics have come to see literary works as skillfully crafted artifacts that may appeal to *our* neuroses by tapping into our repressed wishes and fantasies. Other forms of psychological criticism that diverge from Freud, although they ultimately derive from his insights, include those based on the theories of Carl Jung and Jacques Lacan. See "What Is Psychoanalytic Criticism?" pp. 463–73.

READER-RESPONSE CRITICISM   An approach to literature that, as its name implies, considers the way readers respond to texts, as they read. Stanley Fish describes the method by saying that it substitutes for one question, "What does this sentence mean?" a more operational question, "What does this sentence do?" Reader-response criticism shares with deconstruction a strong textual orientation and a reluctance to define a single meaning for a work. Along with psychoanalytic criticism, it shares an interest in the dynamics of mental response to textual cues.

REAL   One of the three orders of subjectivity (*see* Imaginary Order and Symbolic Order), the Real is the intractable and substantial world that resists and exceeds interpretation. The Real cannot be imagined, symbolized, or known directly. It constantly eludes our efforts to name it (death, gravity, the physicality of objects are examples of the Real), and thus challenges both the

Imaginary and the Symbolic orders. The Real is fundamentally "Other," the mark of the divide between conscious and unconscious, and is signaled in language by gaps, slips, speechlessness, and the sense of the uncanny. The Real is not what we call "reality." It is the stumbling block of the Imaginary (which thinks it can "imagine" anything, including the Real) and of the Symbolic, which tries to bring the Real under its laws (the Real exposes the "phallacy" of the Law of the Phallus). The Real is frightening; we try to tame it with laws and language and call it "reality."

See also: Imaginary Order, Psychoanalytic Criticism, Symbolic Order.

SEMIOLOGY, SEMIOTIC   *See* Semiotics.

SEMIOTICS   The study of signs and sign systems and the way meaning is derived from them. Structuralist anthropologists, psychoanalysts, and literary critics developed semiotics during the decades following 1950, but much of the pioneering work had been done at the turn of the century by the founder of modern linguistics, Ferdinand de Saussure, and the American philosopher Charles Sanders Peirce.

Semiotics is based on several important distinctions, including the distinction between "signifier" and "signified" (the sign and what it points toward) and the distinction between "langue" and "parole." *Langue* (French for "tongue," as in "native tongue," meaning language) refers to the entire system within which individual utterances or usages of language have meaning; *parole* (French for "word") refers to the particular utterances or usages. A principal tenet of semiotics is that signs, like words, are not significant in themselves, but instead have meaning only in relation to other signs and the entire system of signs, or langue.

The affinity between semiotics and structuralist literary criticism derives from this emphasis placed on langue, or system. Structuralist critics, after all, were reacting against formalists and their procedure of focusing on individual words as if meanings didn't depend on anything external to the text.

Poststructuralists have used semiotics but questioned some of its underlying assumptions, including the opposition between signifier and signified. The feminist poststructuralist Julia Kristeva, for instance, has used the word "semiotic" to describe feminine language, a highly figurative, fluid form of discourse that she sets in opposition to rigid, symbolic masculine language.

See also: Deconstruction, Feminist Criticism, Formalism, Poststructuralism, Oppositions, Structuralism, Symbol.

SIMILE   *See* Metaphor.

SOCIOHISTORICAL CRITICISM   *See* New Historicism.

STRUCTURALISM   A science of humankind whose proponents attempted to show that all elements of human culture, including literature, may be understood as parts of a system of signs. Structuralism, according to Robert Scholes, was a reaction to "'modernist' alienation and despair."

Using Ferdinand de Saussure's linguistic theory, European structuralists such as Roman Jakobson, Claude Lévi-Strauss, and Roland Barthes (before his shift toward poststructuralism) attempted to develop a "semiology" or "semiotics" (science of signs). Barthes, among others, sought to recover literature and even language from the isolation in which they had been studied and to show that the laws that govern them govern all signs, from road signs to articles of clothing.

Particularly useful to structuralists were two of Saussure's concepts: the idea of "phoneme" in language and the idea that phonemes exist in two kinds of relationships: "synchronic" and "diachronic." A phoneme is the smallest consistently significant unit in language; thus, both "a" and "an" are phonemes, but "n" is not. A diachronic relationship is that which a phoneme has with those that have preceded it in time and those that will follow it. These "horizontal" relationships produce what we might call discourse or narrative and what Saussure called "parole." The synchronic relationship is the "vertical" one that a word has in a given instant with the entire system of language ("langue") in which it may generate meaning. "An" means what it means in English because those of us who speak the language are using it in the same way at a given time.

Following Saussure, Lévi-Strauss studied hundreds of myths, breaking them into their smallest meaningful units, which he called "mythemes." Removing each from its diachronic relations with other mythemes in a single myth (such as the myth of Oedipus and his mother), he vertically aligned those mythemes that he found to be homologous (structurally correspondent). He then studied the relationships within as well as between vertically aligned columns, in an attempt to understand scientifically, through ratios and proportions, those thoughts and processes that humankind has shared, both at one particular time and across time. One could say, then, that structuralists followed Saussure in preferring to think about the overriding langue or language of myth, in which each mytheme and mytheme-constituted myth fits meaningfully, rather than about isolated individual paroles or narratives. Structuralists followed Saussure's lead in believing what the poststructuralist Jacques Derrida later decided he could not subscribe to—that sign systems must be understood in terms of binary oppositions. In analyzing myths and texts to find basic structures, structuralists tended to find that opposite terms modulate until they are finally resolved or reconciled by some intermediary third term. Thus, a structuralist reading of *Paradise Lost* would show that the war between God and the bad angels becomes a rift between God and sinful, fallen man, the rift then being healed by the Son of God, the mediating third term.

See also: Deconstruction, Discourse, Narrative, Poststructuralism, Semiotics.

SUPERSTRUCTURE   *See* Marxist Criticism.

SYMBOL   A thing, image, or action that, although it is of interest in its own right, stands for or suggests something larger and more complex—often an idea or a range of interrelated ideas, attitudes, and practices.

Within a given culture, some things are understood to be symbols: the flag of the United States is an obvious example. More subtle cultural symbols might be the river as a symbol of time and the journey as a symbol of life and its manifold experiences.

Instead of appropriating symbols generally used and understood within their culture, writers often create symbols by setting up, in their works, a complex but identifiable web of associations. As a result, one object, image, or action suggests others, and often, ultimately, a range of ideas.

A symbol may thus be defined as a metaphor in which the "vehicle," the thing, image, or action used to represent something else, represents many related things (or "tenors") or is broadly suggestive. The urn in Keats's "Ode on a Grecian Urn" suggests many interrelated concepts, including art, truth, beauty, and timelessness.

Symbols have been of particular interest to formalists, who study how meanings emerge from the complex, patterned relationships between images in a work, and psychoanalytic critics, who are interested in how individual authors and the larger culture both disguise and reveal unconscious fears and desires through symbols. Recently, French feminists have also focused on the symbolic. They have suggested that, as wide-ranging as it seems, symbolic language is ultimately rigid and restrictive. They favor semiotic language and writing, which, they contend, is at once more rhythmic, unifying, and feminine.

See also: Feminist Criticism, Metaphor, Psychoanalytic Criticism, Trope.

SYMBOLIC ORDER One of the three orders of subjectivity (see Imaginary Order and Real), it is the realm of law, language, and society; it is the repository of generally held cultural beliefs. Its symbolic system is language, whose agent is the father or lawgiver, the one who has the power of naming. The human subject is commanded into this preestablished order by language (a process that begins long before a child can speak) and must submit to its orders of communication (grammar, syntax, and so on). Entrance into the Symbolic order determines subjectivity according to a primary law of referentiality that takes the male sign (phallus, see Phallus) as its ordering principle. Lacan states that both sexes submit to the Law of the Phallus (the law of order, language, and differentiation) but their individual relation to the law determines whether they see themselves as—and are seen by others to be—either "masculine" or "feminine." The Symbolic institutes repression (of the Imaginary), thus creating the unconscious, which itself is structured like the language of the symbolic. The unconscious, a timeless realm, cannot be known directly, but it can be understood by a kind of translation that takes place in language—psychoanalysis is the "talking cure." The Symbolic is not a "stage" of development (as is Freud's "oedipal stage") nor is it set in place once and for all in human life. We constantly negotiate its threshold (in sleep, in drunkenness) and can "fall out" of it altogether in psychosis.

See also: Imaginary Order, Psychoanalytic Criticism, Real.

SYNECDOCHE *See* Metaphor, Metonymy.

TENOR *See* Metaphor, Metonymy, Symbol.

TROPE A figure, as in "figure of speech." Literally a "turning," that is, a turning or twisting of a word or phrase to make it mean something else. Principal tropes include metaphor, metonymy, personification, simile, and synecdoche.

See also: Metaphor, Metonymy.

VEHICLE *See* Metaphor, Metonymy, Symbol.

About the Contributors

THE VOLUME EDITOR

Janice Carlisle is professor of English at Tulane University. Her most recent publications include *John Stuart Mill and the Writing of Character* (1991) and a co-edited collection of essays, *Narrative and Culture* (1994).

THE CRITICS

Peter Brooks is the Chester T. Tripp Professor of Humanities at Yale University. His most recent books include *Body Work: Objects of Desire in Modern Narrative* (1993) and *Psychoanalysis and Storytelling* (1994).

Jay Clayton is professor of English at Vanderbilt University. His most recent book is *The Pleasures of Babel: Contemporary American Literature and Theory* (1993).

William A. Cohen is assistant professor of English at the University of Maryland. Forthcoming from Duke University Press is his book on sex scandals and the novel in the Victorian period.

Edward W. Said is University Professor at Columbia University. His most recent books include *Culture and Imperialism* (1993), *Representations of the Intellectual* (1994), and *The Politics of Dispossession: The Struggle for Palestinian Self-Determination, 1969–1994* (1994).

Hilary M. Schor is associate professor of English at the University of Southern California. She is the author of *Scheherezade in the Marketplace: Elizabeth Gaskell and the Victorian Novel* (1992), and she is completing a book on Dickens and the female narrative.

THE SERIES EDITOR

Ross C Murfin, general editor of *Case Studies in Contemporary Criticism,* is dean of the College of Arts and Sciences and professor of English at the University of Miami. He has taught at Yale University and the University of Virginia and has published scholarly studies of Joseph Conrad, Thomas Hardy, Nathaniel Hawthorne, and D. H. Lawrence.

Largely Literary Charles Dickens Coffee Mug. © 1992 Steven Cragg. Used by permission from *Largely* Literary® Designs, a Division of Antioch Publishing, manufacturer and distributor of Largely Literary products.

"Repetition, Repression, and Return: The Plotting of *Great Expectations*" by Peter Brooks. From *Reading for the Plot* by Peter Brooks. New York: Knopf, 1984. Copyright © 1984 by Peter Brooks. Reprinted by permission of Alfred A. Knopf, Inc.

"Manual Conduct in *Great Expectations*" by William A. Cohen. Copyright 1993 by The Johns Hopkins University Press. Reprinted by permission.

"Two Commentaries on *Great Expectations*" by Edward W. Said. "Dickens and Derrida" from *The World, the Text, and the Critic* by Edward W. Said. Cambridge, MA: Harvard University Press, 1983. Copyright © 1983 by Edward W. Said. Reprinted by permission of the author and the publisher. "Dickens and Australia" from *Culture and Imperialism* by Edward W. Said. New York: Knopf, 1993. Copyright © 1993 by Edward W. Said. Reprinted by permission of Alfred A. Knopf, Inc. and Chatto & Windus, Ltd.

Classics Illustrated covers of *Great Expectations* (1945 and 1990). Copyright © 1991, 1994 Classics International Entertainment, Inc. All rights reserved. Classics Illustrated® is a registered trademark of Frawley Corporation. Classics International Entertainment™ is a trademark of Classics International Entertainment, Inc., 919 North Michigan Avenue, 34th Floor, Chicago, IL 60611.